Buddenbrooks

Thomas Mann

BUDDENBROOKS

Translated from the German by

H. T. LOWE–PORTER

VINTAGE BOOKS

A Division of Random House

NEW YORK

VINTAGE BOOKS EDITION,
May 1984

Originally published in German under the same title
Copyright 1901 by S. Fischer Verlag, Berlin

ISBN: 394-72637-5

MANUFACTURED IN THE UNITED STATES OF AMERICA
456789

TRANSLATOR'S NOTE

Buddenbrooks was written before the turn of the century; it was first published in 1902, and became a German classic. It is one of those novels — we possess many of them in English — which are at once a work of art and the unique record of a period and a district. *Buddenbrooks* is great in its psychology, great as the monument of a vanished cultural tradition, and ultimately great by the perfection of its art: the classic purity and beautiful austerity of its style.

The translation of a book which is a triumph of style in its own language, is always a piece of effrontery. *Buddenbrooks* is so leisurely, so chiselled: the great gulf of the war divides its literary method from that of our time. Besides, the author has recorded much dialect. This difficulty is insuperable. Dialect cannot be transferred.

So the present translation is offered with humility. It was necessary to recognize that the difficulties were great. Yet it was necessary to set oneself the bold task of transferring the spirit first and the letter so far as might be; and above all, to make certain that the work of art, coming as it does to the ear, in German, like music out of the past, should, in English, at least *not* come like a translation — which is, " God bless us, a thing of naught."

H. T. Lowe-Porter

Buddenbrooks

PART ONE

CHAPTER I

" AND — and — what comes next? "

"Oh, yes, yes, what the dickens does come next? *C'est la question, ma très chère demoiselle!* "

Frau Consul Buddenbrook shot a glance at her husband and came to the rescue of her little daughter. She sat with her mother-in-law on a straight white-enamelled sofa with yellow cushions and a gilded lion's head at the top. The Consul was in his easy-chair beside her, and the child perched on her grandfather's knee in the window.

" Tony," prompted the Frau Consul, " ' I believe that God ' — "

Dainty little eight-year-old Antonie, in her light shot-silk frock, turned her head away from her grandfather and stared aimlessly about the room with her blue-grey eyes, trying hard to remember. Once more she repeated "What comes next? " and went on slowly: " ' I believe that God ' — " and then, her face brightening, briskly finished the sentence: " ' created me, together with all living creatures.' " She was in smooth waters now, and rattled away, beaming with joy, through the whole Article, reproducing it word for word from the Catechism just promulgated, with the approval of an omniscient Senate, in that very year of grace 1835. When you were once fairly started, she thought, it was very like going down " Mount Jerusalem " with your brothers on the little sled: you had no time to think, and you couldn't stop even if you wanted to.

" ' And clothes and shoes,' " she said, " ' meat and drink, hearth and home, wife and child, acre and cow . . .' " But old Johann Buddenbrook could hold in no longer. He burst out laughing, in a high, half-smothered titter, in his glee at being able to make fun of the Catechism. He had probably put the child through this little examination with no other end in view. He inquired after Tony's acre and cow, asked how much she wanted for a sack of wheat, and tried to drive a bargain with her.

His round, rosy, benevolent face, which never would look cross no matter how hard he tried, was set in a frame of snow-white powdered hair, and the suggestion of a pigtail fell over the broad collar of his mouse-coloured coat. His double chin rested comfortably on a white lace frill. He still, in his seventies, adhered to the fashions of his youth: only the lace frogs and the big pockets were missing. And never in all his life had be worn a pair of trousers.

They had all joined in his laughter, but largely as a mark of respect for the head of the family. Madame Antoinette Buddenbrook, born Duchamps, tittered in precisely the same way as her husband. She was a stout lady, with thick white curls over her ears, dressed in a plain gown of striped black and grey stuff which betrayed the native quiet simplicity of her character. Her hands were still white and lovely, and she held a little velvet work-bag on her lap. It was strange to see how she had grown, in time, to look like her husband. Only her dark eyes, by their shape and their liveliness, suggested her half-Latin origin. On her grandfather's side Madame Buddenbrook was of French-Swiss stock, though born in Hamburg.

Her daughter-in-law, Frau Consul Elizabeth Buddenbrook, born Kröger, laughed the sputtering Kröger laugh and tucked in her chin as the Krögers did. She could not be called a beauty, but, like all the Krögers, she looked distinguished; she moved with graceful deliberation and had a clear, well-modulated voice. People liked her and felt confidence in her. Her reddish hair curled over her ears and was piled in a crown on top of her head; and she had the brilliant white complexion that goes with such hair, set off with a tiny freckle here and there. Her nose was rather too long, her mouth somewhat small; her most striking facial peculiarity was the shape of her lower lip, which ran straight into the chin without a curve. She had on a short bodice with high puffed sleeves, that left exposed a flawlessly modelled neck adorned with a spray of diamonds on a satin ribbon.

The Consul was leaning forward in his easy-chair, rather fidgety. He wore a cinnamon-coloured coat with wide lapels and leg-of-mutton sleeves close-fitting at the wrists, and white linen trousers with black stripes up the outside seams. His chin nestled in a stiff choker collar, around which was folded a silk cravat that flowed down amply over his flowered waistcoat.

He had his father's deep-set blue observant eyes, though their expression was perhaps more dreamy; but his features were clearer-cut and more serious, his nose was prominent and aquiline, and his cheeks, half-covered with a fair curling beard, were not so plump as the old man's.

Madame Buddenbrook put her hand on her daughter-in-law's

arm and looked down at her lap with a giggle. " Oh, *mon vieux* —
he's always the same, isn't he, Betsy? "

The Consul's wife only made a motion with her delicate hand,
so that her gold bangles tinkled slightly. Then, with a gesture
habitual to her, she drew her finger across her face from the corner
of her mouth to her forehead, as if she were smoothing back a
stray hair.

But the Consul said, half-smiling, yet with mild reproach:
" There you go again, Father, making fun of sacred things."

They were sitting in the " landscape-room " on the first floor
of the rambling old house in Meng Street, which the firm of
Johann Buddenbrook had acquired some time since, though the
family had not lived in it long. The room was hung with heavy
resilient tapestries put up in such a way that they stood well out
from the walls. They were woven in soft tones to harmonize with
the carpet, and they depicted idyllic landscapes in the style of the
eighteenth century, with merry vine-dressers, busy husbandmen,
and gaily beribboned shepherdesses who sat beside crystal streams
with spotless lambs in their laps or exchanged kisses with amorous
shepherds. These scenes were usually lighted by a pale yellow
sunset to match the yellow coverings on the white enamelled furniture and the yellow silk curtains at the two windows.

For the size of the room, the furniture was rather scant. A
round table, its slender legs decorated with fine lines of gilding,
stood, not in front of the sofa, but by the wall opposite the little
harmonium, on which lay a flute-case; some stiff arm-chairs were
ranged in a row round the walls; there was a sewing-table by the
window, and a flimsy ornamental writing-desk laden with knick-
.knacks.

On the other side of the room from the windows was a glass
door, through which one looked into the semi-darkness of a pillared hall; and on the left were the lofty white folding doors that
led to the dining-room. A semi-circular niche in the remaining
wall was occupied by the stove, which crackled away behind a
polished wrought-iron screen.

For cold weather had set in early. The leaves of the little lime-
trees around the churchyard of St. Mary's, across the way,
had turned yellow, though it was but mid-October. The wind
whistled around the corners of the massive Gothic pile, and a cold,
thin rain was falling. On Madame Buddenbrook's account, the
double windows had already been put in.

It was Thursday, the day on which all the members of the family living in town assembled every second week, by established

custom. To-day, however, a few intimate friends as well had been
bidden to a family dinner; and now, towards four o'clock in the
afternoon, the Buddenbrooks sat in the gathering twilight and
awaited their guests.

Little Antonie had not let her grandfather interfere with her
toboggan-ride. She merely pouted, sticking out her already prominent upper lip still further over the lower one. She was at the
bottom of her Mount Jerusalem, but not knowing how to stop
herself, she shot over the mark. "Amen," she said. "I know
something, Grandfather."

"*Tiens!*" cried the old gentleman. "She knows something!"
He made as if he were itching all over with curiosity. "Did you
hear, Mamma? She knows something. Can any one tell me — ?"

"If the lightning," uttered Tony, nodding her head with every
word, "sets something on fire, then it's the lightning that strikes.
If it doesn't, why, then it's the thunder!" She folded her arms
and looked around her like one sure of applause. But old Buddenbrook was annoyed by this display of wisdom. He demanded to
know who had taught her such nonsense. It turned out that the
culprit was the nursery governess, Ida Jungmann, who had lately
been engaged from Marienwerder. The Consul had to come to
her defence.

"You are too strict, Papa. Why shouldn't the child have her
own little ideas about such things, at her age?"

"*Excusez, mon cher! . . . Mais c'est une folie!* You know I
don't like the children's heads muddled with such things. 'The
thunder strikes,' does it? Oh, very well, let it strike, and get along
with your Prussian woman!"

The truth was, the old gentleman hadn't a good word to say
for Ida Jungmann. Not that he was narrow-minded. He had
seen something of the world, having travelled by coach to Southern
Germany in 1813 to buy up wheat for the Prussian army; he had
been to Amsterdam and Paris, and was too enlightened to condemn everything that lay beyond the gabled roofs of his native
town. But in social intercourse he was more apt than his son to
draw the line rigidly and give the cold shoulder to strangers. So
when this young girl — she was then only twenty — had come
back with his children from a visit to Western Prussia, as a sort of
charity-child, the old man had made his son a scene for the act
of piety, in which he spoke hardly anything but French and low
German. Ida was the daughter of an inn-keeper who had died
just before the Buddenbrooks' arrival in Marienwerder. She had
proved to be capable in the household and with the children, and

her rigid honesty and Prussian notions of caste made her perfectly suited to her position in the family. She was a person of aristocratic principles, drawing hair-line distinctions between class and class, and very proud of her position as servant of the higher orders. She objected to Tony's making friends with any schoolmate whom she reckoned as belonging only to the respectable middle class.

And now the Prussian woman herself came from the pillared hall through the glass door — a fairly tall, big-boned girl in a black frock, with smooth hair and an honest face. She held by the hand an extraordinarily thin small child, dressed in a flowered print frock, with lustreless ash-coloured hair and the manner of a little old maid. This was Clothilde, the daughter of a nephew of old Buddenbrook who belonged to a penniless branch of the family and was in business at Rostock as an estates agent. Clothilde was being brought up with Antonie, being about the same age and a docile little creature.

"Everything is ready," Mamsell Jungmann said. She had had a hard time learning to pronounce her *r's*, so now she rolled them tremendously in her throat. "Clothilde helped very well in the kitchen, so there was not much for cook to do."

Monsieur Buddenbrook sneered behind his lace frill at Ida's accent. The Consul patted his little niece's cheek and said: "That's right, Tilda. Work and pray. Tony ought to take a pattern from you; she's far too likely to be saucy and idle."

Tony dropped her head and looked at her grandfather from under her eyebrows. She knew he would defend her — he always did.

"No, no," he said, "hold your head up, Tony. Don't let them frighten you. We can't all be alike. Each according to his lights. Tilda is a good girl — but we're not so bad, either. Hey, Betsy?"

He turned to his daughter-in-law, who generally deferred to his views. Madame Antoinette, probably more from shrewdness than conviction, sided with the Consul; and thus the older and the younger generation crossed hands in the dance of life.

"You are very kind, Papa," the Consul's wife said. "Tony will try her best to grow up a clever and industrious woman. . . . Have the boys come home from school?" she asked Ida.

Tony, who from her perch on her grandfather's knee was looking out the window, called out in the same breath: "Tom and Christian are coming up Johannes Street . . . and Herr Hoffstede . . . and Uncle Doctor. . . ."

The bells of St. Mary's began to chime, ding-dong, ding-dong —

rather out of time, so that one could hardly tell what they were playing; still, it was very impressive. The big and the little bell announced, the one in lively, the other in dignified tones, that it was four o'clock; and at the same time a shrill peal from the bell over the vestibule door went ringing through the entry, and Tom and Christian entered, together with the first guests, Jean Jacques coloured. But he was thinner and more active than his old friend, Hoffstede, the poet, and Doctor Grabow, the family physician.

CHAPTER II

HERR JEAN JACQUES HOFFSTEDE was the town poet. He undoubtedly had a few verses in his pocket for the present occasion. He
was nearly as old as Johann Buddenbrook, and dressed in much
the same style except that his coat was green instead of mouse-
coloured. But he was thinner and more active than his old friend,
with bright little greenish eyes and a long pointed nose.

"Many thanks," he said, shaking hands with the gentlemen and
bowing before the ladies — especially the Frau Consul, for whom
he entertained a deep regard. Such bows as his it was not given
to the younger generation to perform; and he accompanied them
with his pleasant quiet smile. "Many thanks for your kind invitation, my dear good people. We met these two young ones, the
Doctor and I " — he pointed to Tom and Christian, in their blue
tunics and leather belts — "in King Street, coming home from
school. Fine lads, eh, Frau Consul? Tom is a very solid chap.
He'll have to go into the business, no doubt of that. But Christian
is a devil of a fellow — a young *incroyable*, hey? I will not conceal
my *engouement*. He must study, I think — he is witty and brilliant."

Old Buddenbrook used his gold snuff-box. "He's a young
monkey, that's what he is. Why not say at once that he is to be a
poet, Hoffstede? "

Mamsell Jungmann drew the curtains, and soon the room was
bathed in mellow flickering light from the candles in the crystal
chandelier and the sconces on the writing-desk. It lighted up
golden gleams in the Frau Consul's hair.

"Well, Christian," she said, "what did you learn to-day? " It
appeared that Christian had had writing, arithmetic, and singing
lessons. He was a boy of seven, who already resembled his father
to an almost comic extent. He had the same rather small round
deep-set eyes and the same prominent aquiline nose; the lines of his
face below the cheek-bones showed that it would not always re-
tain its present child-like fulness.

"We've been laughing dreadfully," he began to prattle, his eyes darting from one to another of the circle. "What do you think Herr Stengel said to Siegmund Kostermann?" He bent his back, shook his head, and declaimed impressively: "'Outwardly, outwardly, my dear child, you are sleek and smooth; but inwardly, my dear child, you are black and foul.' . . ." He mimicked with indiscribably funny effect not only the master's odd pronunciation but the look of disgust on his face at the "outward sleekness" he described. The whole company burst out laughing.

"Young monkey!" repeated old Buddenbrook. But Herr Hoffstede was in ecstasies. "*Charmant!*" he cried. "If you know Marcellus Stengel — that's he, to the life. Oh, that's too good!"

Thomas, to whom the gift of mimicry had been denied, stood near his younger brother and laughed heartily, without a trace of envy. His teeth were not very good, being small and yellowish. His nose was finely chiselled, and he strikingly resembled his grandfather in the eyes and the shape of the face.

The company had for the most part seated themselves on the chairs and the sofa. They talked with the children or discussed the unseasonable cold and the new house. Herr Hoffstede admired a beautiful Sèvres inkstand, in the shape of a black and white hunting dog, that stood on the escritoire. Doctor Grabow, a man of about the Consul's age, with a long mild face between thin whiskers, was looking at the table, set out with cakes and currant bread and salt-cellars in different shapes. This was the "bread and salt" that had been sent by friends for the house warming; but the "bread" consisted of rich, heavy pastries, and the salt came in dishes of massive gold, that the senders might not seem to be mean in their gifts.

"There will be work for me here," said the Doctor, pointing to the sweetmeats and threatening the children with his glance. Shaking his head, he picked up a heavy salt and pepper stand from the table.

"From Lebrecht Kröger," said old Buddenbrook, with a grimace. "Our dear kinsman is always open-handed. I did not spend as much on him when he built his summer house outside the Castle Gate. But he has always been like that — very lordly, very free with his money, a real cavalier à-la-mode. . . ."

The bell had rung several times. Pastor Wunderlich was announced; a stout old gentleman in a long black coat and powdered hair. He had twinkling grey eyes set in a face that was jovial if rather pale. He had been a widower for many years, and considered himself a bachelor of the old school, like Herr Gratjens, the broker, who entered with him. Herr Gratjens was a tall man who

went around with one of his thin hands up to his eye like a telescope, as if he were examining a painting. He was a well-known
art connoisseur.

Among the other guests were Senator Doctor Langhals and his
wife, both friends of many years' standing; and Köppen the wine-
merchant, with his great crimson face between enormous padded
sleeves. His wife, who came with him, was nearly as stout as he.

It was after half past four when the Krögers put in an appearance — the elders together with their children; the Consul Krögers
with their sons Jacob and Jürgen, who were about the age of Tom
and Christian. On their heels came the parents of Frau Consul
Kröger, the lumber-dealer Överdieck and his wife, a fond old
pair who still addressed each other in public with nicknames from
the days of their early love.

"Fine people come late," said Consul Buddenbrook, and kissed
his mother-in-law's hand.

"But look at them when they do come!" and Johann Buddenbrook included the whole Kröger connection with a sweeping
gesture, and shook the elder Kröger by the hand. Lebrecht
Kröger, the cavalier à-la-mode, was a tall, distinguished figure.
He wore his hair slightly powdered, but dressed in the height of
fashion, with a double row of jewelled buttons on his velvet waistcoat. His son Justus, with his turned-up moustache and small
beard, was very like the father in figure and manner, even to the
graceful easy motions of the hands.

The guests did not sit down, but stood about awaiting the principle event of the evening and passing the time in casual talk. At
length, Johann Buddenbrook the older offered his arm to Madame
Köppen and said in an elevated voice, "Well, *mesdames et messieurs*, if you are hungry . . ."

Mamsell Jungmann and the servant had opened the folding-
doors into the dining-room; and the company made its way with
studied ease to table. One could be sure of a good square meal at
the Buddenbrooks'.

CHAPTER III

As the party began to move toward the dining-room, Consul Buddenbrook's hand went to his left breast-pocket and fingered a
paper that was inside. The polite smile had left his face, giving
place to a strained and care-worn look, and the muscles stood out
on his temples as he clenched his teeth. For appearance's sake he
made a few steps toward the dining-room, but stopped and sought
his mother's eye as she was leaving the room on Pastor Wunderlich's arm, among the last of her guests.

"Pardon me, dear Herr Pastor . . . just a word with you,
Mamma." The Pastor nodded gaily, and the Consul drew his
Mother over to the window of the landscape-room.

"Here is a letter from Gotthold," he said in low, rapid tones.
He took out the sealed and folded paper and looked into her dark
eyes. "That is his writing. It is the third one, and Papa answered
only the first. What shall I do? It came at two o'clock, and I ought
to have given it to him already, but I do not like to upset him to-
day. What do you think? I could call him out here. . . ."

"No, you are right, Jean; it is better to wait," said Madame
Buddenbrook. She grasped her son's arm with a quick, habitual
movement. "What do you suppose is in it?" she added uneasily.
"The boy won't give in. He's taken it into his head he must be
compensated for his share in the house. . . . No, no, Jean. Not
now. To-night, perhaps, before we go to bed."

"What am I to do?" repeated the Consul, shaking his bent head.
"I have often wanted to ask Papa to give in. I don't like it to look
as if I had schemed against Gotthold and worked myself into a
snug place. I don't want Father to look at it like that, either. But,
to be honest . . . I am a partner, after all. And Betsy and I pay a
fair rent for the second storey. It is all arranged with my sister in
Frankfort: her husband gets compensation already, in Papa's lifetime — a quarter of the purchase price of the house. That is good
business: Papa arranged it very cleverly, and it is very satisfactory
from the point of view of the firm. And if Papa acts so unfriendly
to Gotthold — "

"Nonsense, Jean. Your position in the matter is quite clear. But it is painful for me to have Gotthold think that his step-mother looks out after her own children and deliberately makes bad blood between him and his father!"

"But it is his own fault," the Consul almost shouted, and then, with a glance at the dining-room door, lowered his voice. "It is his fault, the whole wretched thing. You can judge for yourself. Why couldn't he be reasonable? Why did he have to go and marry that Stüwing girl and . . . the shop. . . ." The Consul gave an angry, embarrassed laugh at the last word. "It's a weakness of Father's, that prejudice against the shop; but Gotthold ought to have respected it. . . ."

"Oh, Jean, it would be best if Papa would give in."

"But ought I to advise him to?" whispered the Consul excitedly, clapping his hand to his forehead. "I am an interested party, so I ought to say, Pay it. But I am also a partner. And if Papa thinks he is under no obligation to a disobedient and rebellious son to draw the money out of the working capital of the firm . . . It is a matter of eleven thousand thaler, a good bit of money. No, no, I cannot advise him either for or against. I'd rather wash my hands of the whole affair. But the scene with Papa is so *désagréable* —"

"Late this evening, Jean. Come now; they are waiting."

The Consul put the paper back into his breast-pocket, offered his arm to his mother, and led her over the threshold into the brightly lighted dining-room, where the company had already taken their places at the long table.

The tapestries in this room had a sky-blue background, against which, between slender columns, white figures of gods and goddesses stood out with plastic effect. The heavy red damask window-curtains were drawn; stiff, massive sofas in red damask stood ranged against the walls; and in each corner stood a tall gilt candelabrum with eight flaming candles, besides those in silver sconces on the table. Above the heavy sideboard, on the wall opposite the landscape room, hung a large painting of an Italian bay, the misty blue atmosphere of which was most effective in the candle-light.

Every trace of care or disquiet had vanished from Madame Buddenbrook's face. She sat down between Pastor Wunderlich and the elder Kröger, who presided on the window side.

"*Bon appétit!*" she said, with her short, quick, hearty nod, flashing a glance down the whole length of the table till it reached the children at the bottom.

CHAPTER IV

" OUR best respects to you, Buddenbrook — I repeat, our best respects! " Herr Köppen's powerful voice drowned the general
conversation as the maid-servant, in her heavy striped petticoat,
her fat arms bare and a little white cap on the back of her head,
passed the *potage aux fines herbes* and toast, assisted by Mamsell
Jungmann and the Frau Consul's maid from upstairs. The guests
began to use their soup-spoons.

" Such plenty, such elegance! I must say, you know how to
do things! — I must say — " Herr Köppen had never visited the
house in its former owner's time. He did not come of a patrician
family, and had only lately become a man of means. He could
never quite get rid of certain vulgar tricks of speech — like the
repetition of " I must say "; and he said " respecks " for " respects."

" It didn't cost anything, either," remarked Herr Gratjens drily
— he certainly ought to have known — and studied the wall-paint-
ing through the hollow of his hand.

As far as possible, ladies and gentlemen had been paired off, and
members of the family placed between friends of the house. But
the arrangement could not be carried out in every case; the two
Överdiecks were sitting, as usual, nearly on each other's laps,
nodding affectionately at one another. The elder Kröger was bolt
upright, enthroned between Madame Antoinette and Frau Senator Langhals, dividing his pet jokes and his flourishes between the
two ladies.

" When was the house built? " asked Herr Hoffstede diagonally
across the table of old Buddenbrook, who was talking in a gay
chaffing tone with Madame Köppen.

" Anno . . . let me see . . . about 1680, if I am not mistaken.
My son is better at dates than I am."

" Eighty-two," said the Consul, leaning forward. He was sitting
at the foot of the table, without a partner, next to Senator Langhals. " It was finished in the winter of 1682. Ratenkamp and
Company were just getting to the top of their form. . . . Sad,
how the firm broke down in the last twenty years! "

A general pause in the conversation ensued, lasting for half a minute, while the company looked down at their plates and pondered on the fortunes of the brilliant family who had built and lived in the house and then, broken and impoverished, had left it.

"Yes," said Broker Gratjens, "it's sad, when you think of the madness that led to their ruin. If Dietrich Ratenkamp had not taken that fellow Geelmaack for a partner! I flung up my hands, I know, when he came into the management. I have it on the best authority, gentlemen, that he speculated disgracefully behind Ratenkamp's back, and gave notes and acceptances right and left in the firm's name. . . . Finally the game was up. The banks got suspicious, the firm couldn't give security. . . . You haven't the least idea . . . who looked after the warehouse, even? Geelmaack, perhaps? It was a perfect rats' nest there, year in, year out. But Ratenkamp never troubled himself about it."

"He was like a man paralysed," the Consul said. A gloomy, taciturn look came on his face. He leaned over and stirred his soup, now and then giving a quick glance, with his little round deep-set eyes, at the upper end of the table.

"He went about like a man with a load on his mind; I think one can understand his burden. What made him take Geelmaack into the business — a man who brought painfully little capital, and had not the best of reputations? He must have felt the need of sharing his heavy responsibility with some one, not much matter who, because he realized that the end was inevitable. The firm was ruined, the old family *passée*. Geelmaack only gave it the last push over the edge."

Pastor Wunderlich filled his own and his neighbour's wineglass. "So you think my dear Consul," he said with a discreet smile, "that even without Geelmaack, things would have turned out just as they did?"

"Oh, probably not," the Consul said thoughtfully, addressing nobody in particular. "But I do think that Dietrich Ratenkamp was driven by fate when he took Geelmaack into partnership. That was the way his destiny was to be fulfilled. . . . He acted under the pressure of inexorable necessity. I think he knew more or less what his partner was doing, and what the state of affairs was at the warehouse. But he was paralysed."

"*Assez*, Jean," interposed old Buddenbrook, laying down his spoon. "That's one of your *idées*. . . ."

The Consul rather absently lifted his glass to his father. Lebrecht Kröger broke in: "Let's stick by the jolly present!" He took up a bottle of white wine that had a little silver stag on the stopper; and with one of his fastidious, elegant motions he held it on its side and examined the label. " C. F. Köppen," he read, and nodded to the wine-merchant. " Ah, yes, where should we be without you? "

Madame Antoinette kept a sharp eye on the servants while they changed the gilt-edged Meissen plates; Mamsell Jungmann called orders through the speaking-tube into the kitchen, and the fish was brought in. Pastor Wunderlich remarked, as he helped himself:

" This ' jolly present ' isn't such a matter of course as it seems, either. The young folk here can hardly realize, I suppose, that things could ever have been different from what they are now. But I think I may fairly claim to have had a personal share, more than once, in the fortunes of the Buddenbrook family. Whenever I see one of these, for instance — " he picked up one of the heavy silver spoons and turned to Madame Antoinette — " I can't help wondering whether they belong to the set that our friend the philosopher Lenoir, Sergeant under his Majesty the Emperor Napoleon, had in his hands in the year 1806 — and I think of our meeting in Alf Street, Madame."

Madame Buddenbrook looked down at her plate with a smile half of memory, half of embarrassment. Tom and Tony, at the bottom of the table, cried out almost with one voice, "Oh, yes, tell about it, Grandmama! " They did not want the fish, and they had been listening attentively to the conversation of their elders. But the Pastor knew that she would not care to speak herself of an incident that had been rather painful to her. He came to her rescue and launched out once more upon the old story. It was new, perhaps, to one or two of the present company. As for the children, they could have listened to it a hundred times.

" Well, imagine a November afternoon, cold and rainy, a wretched day; and me coming back down Alf Street from some parochial duty. I was thinking of the hard times we were having. Prince Blücher had gone, and the French were in the town. There was little outward sign of the excitement that reigned everywhere: the streets were quiet, and people stopped close in their houses. Prahl the master-butcher had been shot through the head, just for standing at the door of his shop with his hands in his pockets and making a menacing remark about its being hard to bear. Well, thought I to myself, I'll just have a look in at the Buddenbrooks'. Herr Buddenbrook is down with erysipelas, and Madame has a great deal to do, on account of the billeting.

" At that very moment, whom should I see coming towards me but our honoured Madame Buddenbrook herself? What a state she was in! Hurrying through the rain hatless, stumbling rather than walking, with a shawl flung over her shoulders, and her hair falling down — yes, Madame, it is quite true, it *was* falling down!

" 'This is a pleasant surprise,' I said. She never saw me, and I made bold to lay my hand on her sleeve, for my mind misgave me about the state of things. 'Where are you off to in such a hurry, my dear?' She realized who I was, looked at me, and burst out: 'Farewell, farewell! All is over — I'm going into the river!'

" 'God forbid,' cried I — I could feel that I went white. 'That is no place for you, my dear.' And I held her as tightly as decorum permitted. 'What has happened?' 'What has happened!' she cried, all trembling. 'They've got at the silver, Wunderlich! That's what has happened! And Jean lies there with erysipelas and can't do anything — he couldn't even if he were up. They are stealing my spoons, Wunderlich, and I am going into the river!'

" Well, I kept holding her, and I said what one would in such cases: 'Courage, dear lady. It will be all right. Control yourself, I beg of you. We will go and speak with them. Let us go.' And I got her to go back up the street to her house. The soldiery were up in the dining-room, where Madame had left them, some twenty of them, at the great silver-chest.

" 'Gentlemen,' I say politely, 'with which one of you may I have the pleasure of a little conversation?' They begin to laugh, and they say: 'With all of us, Papa.' But one of them steps out and presents himself, a fellow as tall as a tree, with a black waxed moustache and big red hands sticking out of his braided cuffs. 'Lenoir,' he said, and saluted with his left hand, for he had five or six spoons in his right. 'Sergeant Lenoir. What can I do for you?'

" 'Herr Officer,' I say, appealing to his sense of honour, 'after your magnificent charge, how can you stoop to this sort of thing? The town has not closed its gates to the Emperor.'

" 'What do you expect?' he answered. 'War is war. The people need these things. . . .'

" 'But you ought to be careful,' I interrupted him, for an idea had come into my head. 'This lady,' I said — one will say anything at a time like that — 'the lady of the house, she isn't a German. She is almost a compatriot of yours — she is a Frenchwoman. . . .' 'Oh, a Frenchwoman,' he repeated. And then what do you suppose he said, this big swashbuckler? 'Oh, an *émigrée?* Then she is an enemy of philosophy!'

" I was quite taken aback, but I managed not to laugh. 'You are a man of intellect, I see,' said I. 'I repeat that I consider your conduct unworthy.' He was silent for a moment. Then he got red, tossed his half-dozen spoons back into the chest, and exclaimed, 'Who told you I was going to do anything with these things but look at them? It's fine silver. If one or two of my men take a piece as a souvenir . . .'

"Well, in the end, they took plenty of souvenirs, of course. No use appealing to justice, either human or divine. I suppose they knew no other god than that terrible little Corsican. . . ."

CHAPTER V

"Did you ever see him, Herr Pastor?"

The plates were being changed again. An enormous brick-red boiled ham appeared, strewn with crumbs and served with a sour brown onion sauce, and so many vegetables that the company could have satisfied their appetites from that one vegetable-dish. Lebrecht Kröger undertook the carving, and skilfully cut the succulent slices, with his elbows slightly elevated and his two long forefingers laid out along the back of the knife and fork. With the ham went the Frau Consul's celebrated "Russian jam," a pungent fruit conserve flavoured with spirits.

No, Pastor Wunderlich regretted to say that he had never set eyes on Bonaparte. Old Buddenbrook and Jean Jacques Hoffstede had both seen him face to face, one in Paris just before the Russian campaign, reviewing the troops at the Tuileries; the other in Dantzig.

"I must say, he wasn't a very cheerful person to look at," said the poet, raising his brows, as he disposed of a forkful of ham, potato, and sprouts. "But they say he was in a lively mood, at Dantzig. There was a story they used to tell, about how he would gamble all day with the Germans, and make them pay up too, and then spend the evening playing with his generals. Once he swept a handful of gold off the table, and said: ' *Les Allemands aiment beaucoup ces petits Napoléons, n'est-ce pas*, Rapp? ' ' *Oui, Sire, plus que le Grand!* ' Rapp answered."

There was general laughter — Hoffstede had told the story very prettily, even mimicking the Emperor's manner. Old Buddenbrook said: " Well, joking aside, one can't help having respect for his personal greatness. . . . What a nature! "

The Consul shook his head gravely.

"No, no — we of the younger generation do not see why we should revere the man who murdered the Duc d'Engien, and butchered eight hundred prisoners in Egypt. . . ."

"All that is probably exaggerated and overdrawn," said Pastor Wunderlich. " The Duke was very likely a feather-brained and

seditious person, and as for the prisoners, their execution was probably the deliberate and necessary policy of a council of war." And
he went on to speak of a book at which he had been looking, by
one of the Emperor's secretaries, which had appeared some years
before and was well worth reading.

"All the same," persisted the Consul, snuffing a flickering candle
in the sconce in front of him, "I cannot understand it — I cannot
understand the admiration people have for this monster. As a
Christian, as a religious man, I can find no room in my heart for
such a feeling."

He had, as he spoke, the slightly inclined head and the rapt look
of a man in a vision. His father and Pastor Wunderlich could be
seen to exchange the smallest of smiles.

"Well, anyhow," grinned the old man, "the little napoleons
aren't so bad, eh? My son has more enthusiasm for Louis Philippe,"
he said to the company in general.

"Enthusiasm?" repeated Jean Jacques Hoffstede, rather sar-
castically. . . . That is a curious juxtaposition, Philippe Égalité
and enthusiasm. . . ."

"God knows, I feel we have much to learn from the July Monarchy," the Consul said, with serious zeal. "The friendly and
helpful attitude of French constitutionalism toward the new, practical ideals and interests of our time . . . is something we should
be deeply thankful for. . . ."

"Practical ideals — well, ye-s — " The elder Buddenbrook gave
his jaws a moment's rest and played with his gold snuff-box.
"Practical ideals — well — h'm — they don't appeal to me in the
least." He dropped into dialect, out of sheer vexation. "We have
trade schools and technical schools and commercial schools springing up on every corner; the high schools and the classical education suddenly turn out to be all foolishness, and the whole world
thinks of nothing but mines and factories and making money.
. . . That's all very fine, of course. But in the long run, pretty
stupid, isn't it? . . . I don't know why, but it irritates me like the
deuce. . . . I don't mean, Jean, that the July Monarchy is not an
admirable régime. . . ."

Senator Langhals, as well as Gratjens and Köppen, stood by the
Consul. . . . They felt that high praise was due to the French
government, and to similar efforts that were being made in Germany. It was worthy of all respect — Herr Köppen called it "re-
speck." He had grown more and more crimson from eating, and
puffed audibly as he spoke. Pastor Wunderlich had not changed

colour; he looked as pale, refined, and alert as ever, while drinking down glass after glass of wine.

The candles burned down slowly in their sockets. Now and then they flickered in a draught and dispersed a faint smell of wax over the table.

There they all sat, on heavy, high-backed chairs, consuming good heavy food from good heavy silver plate, drinking full-bodied wines and expressing their views freely on all subjects. When they began to talk shop, they slipped unconsciously more and more into dialect, and used the clumsy but comfortable idioms that seemed to embody to them the business efficiency and the easy well-being of their community. Sometimes they even used an over-drawn pronunciation by way of making fun of themselves and each other, and relished their clipped phrases and exaggerated vowels with the same heartiness as they did their food.

The ladies had not long followed the discussion. Madame Kröger gave them the cue by setting forth a tempting method of boiling carp in red wine. " You cut it into nice pieces, my dear, and put it in the saucepan, add some cloves, and onions, and a few rusks, a little sugar, and a spoonful of butter, and set it on the fire. . . . But don't wash it, on any account. All the blood must remain in it."

The elder Kröger was telling the most delightful stories; and his son Justus, who sat with Dr. Grabow down at the bottom of the table, near the children, was chaffing Mamsell Jungmann. She screwed up her brown eyes and stood her knife and fork upright on the table and moved them back and forth. Even the Överdiecks were very lively. Old Frau Överdieck had a new pet name for her husband: " You good old bell-wether," she said, and laughed so hard that her cap bobbed up and down.

But all the various conversations around the table flowed together in one stream when Jean Jacques Hoffstede embarked upon his favourite theme, and began to describe the Italian journey which he had taken fifteen years before with a rich Hamburg relative. He told of Venice, Rome, and Vesuvius, of the Villa Borghese, where Goethe had written part of his Faust; he waxed enthusiastic over the beautiful Renaissance fountains that wafted coolness upon the warm Italian air, and the formal gardens through the avenues of which it was so enchanting to stroll. Some one mentioned the big wilderness of a garden outside the Castle Gate, that belonged to the Buddenbrooks.

" Upon my word," the old man said, " I still feel angry with myself that I have never put it into some kind of order. I was out there the other day — and it is really a disgrace, a perfect primeval forest. It would be a pretty bit of property, if the grass were cut and the trees trimmed into formal shapes."

The Consul protested strenuously. "Oh, no, Papa! I love to go out there in the summer and walk in the undergrowth; it would quite spoil the place to trim and prune its free natural beauty."

"But, deuce take it, the free natural beauty belongs to me — haven't I the right to put it in order if I like?"

"Ah, Father, when I go out there and lie in the long grass among the undergrowth, I have a feeling that I belong to nature and not she to me. . . ."

"Krishan, don't eat too much," the old man suddenly called out, in dialect. "Never mind about Tilda — it doesn't hurt her. She can put it away like a dozen harvest hands, that child!"

And truly it was amazing, the prowess of this scraggy child with the long, old-maidish face. Asked if she wanted more soup, she answered in a meek drawling voice: "Ye-es, ple-ase." She had two large helpings both of fish and ham, with piles of vegetables; and she bent short-sightedly over her plate, completely absorbed in the food, which she chewed ruminantly, in large mouthfuls. "Oh, Un-cle," she replied, with amiable simplicity, to the old man's gibe, which did not in the least disconcert her. She ate: whether it tasted good or not, whether they teased her or not, she smiled and kept on, heaping her plate with good things, with the instinctive, insensitive voracity of a poor relation — patient, persevering, hungry, and lean.

CHAPTER VI

AND now came, in two great cut-glass dishes, the " Plettenpudding." It was made of layers of macaroons, raspberries, lady-
fingers, and custard. At the same time, at the other end of the
table, appeared the blazing plum-pudding which was the children's
favourite sweet.

" Thomas, my son, come here a minute," said Johann Buddenbrook, taking his great bunch of keys from his trousers pocket.
" In the second cellar to the right, the second bin, behind the red
Bordeaux, two bottles — you understand? " Thomas, to whom
such orders were familiar, ran off and soon came back with the
two bottles, covered with dust and cobwebs; and the little dessert-
glasses were filled with sweet, golden-yellow malmsey from these
unsightly receptacles. Now the moment came when Pastor Wunderlich rose, glass in hand, to propose a toast; and the company
fell silent to listen. He spoke in the pleasant, conversational tone
which he liked to use in the pulpit; his head a little on one side,
a subtle, humorous smile on his pale face, gesturing easily with
his free hand. " Come, my honest friends, let us honour ourselves
by drinking a glass of this excellent liquor to the health of our host
and hostess in their beautiful new home. Come, then — to the
health of the Buddenbrook family, present and absent! May they
live long and prosper! "

" Absent? " thought the Consul to himself, bowing as the company lifted their glasses. " Is he referring to the Frankfort Buddenbrooks, or perhaps the Duchamps in Hamburg — or did old
Wunderlich really mean something by that? " He stood up and
clinked glasses with his father, looking him affectionately in the
eye.

Broker Gratjens got up next, and his speech was rather long-
winded; he ended by proposing in his high-pitched voice a health
to the firm of Johann Buddenbrook, that it might continue to
grow and prosper and do honour to the town.

Johann Buddenbrook thanked them all for their kindness, first
as head of the family and then as senior partner of the firm — and

sent Thomas for another bottle of Malmsey. It had been a mistake
to suppose that two would be enough.

Lebrecht Kröger spoke too. He took the liberty of remaining
seated, because it looked less formal, and gestured with his head
and hands most charmingly as he proposed a toast to the two ladies
of the family, Madame Antoinette and the Frau Consul. As he
finished, the Plettenpudding was nearly consumed, and the Malmsey nearing its end; and then, to a universal, long-drawn " Ah-h! "
Jean Jacques Hoffstede rose up slowly, clearing his throat. The
children clapped their hands with delight.

" *Excusez!* I really couldn't help it," he began. He put his finger to his long sharp nose and drew a paper from his coat pocket.
. . . A profound silence reigned throughout the room.

His paper was gaily parti-coloured. On the outside of it was
written, in an oval border surrounded by red flowers and a pro-
fusion of gilt flourishes:

" *On the occasion of my friendly participation in a delightful house-
warming party given by the Buddenbrook family. October 1835.*"

He read this aloud first; then turning the paper over, he began,
in a voice that was already somewhat tremulous:

> Honoured friends, my modest lay
> Hastes to greet you in these walls:
> May kind Heaven grant to-day
> Blessing on their spacious halls.
>
> Thee, my friend with silver hair,
> And thy faithful, loving spouse,
> And your children young and fair —
> I salute you, and your house.
>
> Industry and beauty chaste
> See we linked in marriage band:
> Venus Anadyomene
> And cunning Vulcan's busy hand.
>
> May no future storms dismay
> With unkind blast the joyful hour;
> May each new returning day
> Blessings on your pathway shower.
>
> Ceaselessly shall I rejoice
> O'er the fortune that is yours:
> As to-day I lift my voice,
> May I still, while life endures.

> In your splendid walls live well,
> And cherish with affection true
> Him who in his humble cell
> Penned to-day these lines for you.

He bowed to a unanimous outburst of applause.

"Charming, Hoffstede," cried old Buddenbrook. "It was too charming for words. I drink your health."

But when the Frau Consul touched glasses with the poet, a delicate blush mantled her cheek; for she had seen the courtly bow he made in her direction when he came to the part about the Venus Anadyomene.

CHAPTER VII

THE GENERAL merriment had now reached its height. Herr Köppen felt a great need to unfasten a few buttons of his waistcoat;
but it obviously wouldn't do, for not even the elderly gentlemen
were permitting themselves the liberty. Lebrecht Kröger sat up
as straight as he did at the beginning; Pastor Wunderlich's face was
as pale as ever, his manner as correct. The elder Buddenbrook had
indeed sat back a little in his chair, but he maintained perfect decorum. There was only Justus Kröger — he was plainly a little
overtaken.

But where was Dr. Grabow? The butter, cheese and fruit had
just been handed round; and the Frau Consul rose from her chair
and unobtrusively followed the waitress from the room; for the
Doctor, Mamsell Jungmann, and Christian were no longer in their
places, and a smothered wail was proceeding from the hall. There
in the dim light, little Christian was half lying, half crouching on
the round settee that encircled the central pillar. He was uttering
heart-breaking groans. Ida and the Doctor stood beside him.

" Oh dear, oh dear," said she, " the poor child is very bad! "

" I'm ill, Mamma, damned ill," whimpered Christian, his little
deep-set eyes darting back and forth, and his big nose looking bigger than ever. The " damned " came out in a tone of utter despair;
but the Frau Consul said: " If we use such words, God will punish
us by making us suffer still more! "

Doctor Grabow felt the lad's pulse. His kindly face grew
longer and gentler.

" It's nothing much, Frau Consul," he reassured her. " A touch
of indigestion." He prescribed in his best bed-side manner: " Better put him to bed and give him a Dover powder — perhaps a cup
of camomile tea, to bring out the perspiration. . . . And a rigorous diet, you know, Frau Consul. A little pigeon, a little French
bread . . ."

" I don't want any pigeon," bellowed Christian angrily. " I
don't want to eat anything, ever any more. I'm ill, I tell you,
damned ill! " The fervour with which he uttered the bad word
seemed to bring him relief.

Doctor Grabow smiled to himself — a thoughtful, almost a melancholy smile. He would soon eat again, this young man. He would do as the rest of the world did — his father, and all their relatives and friends: he would lead a sedentary life and eat four good, rich, satisfying meals a day. Well, God bless us all! He, Friedrich Grabow, was not the man to upset the habits of these prosperous, comfortable tradesmen and their families. He would come when he was sent for, prescribe a few days' diet — a little pigeon, a slice of French bread — yes, yes, and assure the family that it was nothing serious this time. Young as he was, he had held the head of many an honest burgher who had eaten his last joint of smoked meat, his last stuffed turkey, and, whether overtaken unaware in his counting-house or after a brief illness in his solid old four-poster, had commended his soul to God. Then it was called paralysis, a " stroke," a sudden death. And he, Friedrich Grabow, could have predicted it, on all of these occasions when it was " nothing serious this time " — or perhaps at the times when he had not even been summoned, when there had only been a slight giddiness after luncheon. Well, God bless us all! He, Friedrich Grabow, was not the man to despise a roast turkey himself. That ham with onion sauce had been delicious, hang it! And the Plettenpudding, when they were already stuffed full — macaroons, raspberries, custard . . . " A rigorous diet, Frau Consul, as I say. A little pigeon, a little French bread . . ."

CHAPTER VIII

THEY were rising from table.

"Well, ladies and gentlemen, *gesegnete Mahlzeit!* Cigars and coffee in the next room, and a liqueur if Madame feels generous. . . . Billiards for whoever chooses. Jean, you will show them the way back to the billiard-room? Madame Köppen, may I have the honour?"

Full of well-being, laughing and chattering, the company trooped back through the folding doors into the landscape-room. The Consul remained behind, and collected about him the gentlemen who wanted to play billiards.

"You won't try a game, Father?"

No, Lebrecht Kröger would stop with the ladies, but Justus might go if he liked. . . . Senator Langhals, Köppen, Gratjens, and Doctor Grabow went with the Consul, and Jean Jacques Hoffstede said he would join them later. "Johann Buddenbrook is going to play the flute," he said. "I must stop for that. *Au revoir, messieurs.*"

As the gentlemen passed through the hall, they could hear from the landscape-room the first notes of the flute, accompanied by the Frau Consul on the harmonium: an airy, charming little melody that floated sweetly through the lofty rooms. The Consul listened as long as he could. He would have liked to stop behind in an easy-chair in the landscape-room and indulge the reveries that the music conjured up; but his duties as host . . .

"Bring some coffee and cigars into the billiard-room," he said to the maid whom he met in the entry.

"Yes, Line, coffee!" Herr Köppen echoed, in a rich, well-fed voice, trying to pinch the girl's red arm. The *c* came from far back in his throat, as if he were already swallowing the coffee.

"I'm sure Madame Köppen saw you through the glass," Consul Kröger remarked.

"So you live up there, Buddenbrook?" asked Senator Langhals. To the right a broad white staircase with a carved baluster led up to the sleeping-chambers of the Consul's family in the second

storey; to the left came another row of rooms. The party descended the stairs, smoking, and the Consul halted at the landing.

"The entresol has three rooms," he explained, "the breakfast-room, my parents' sleeping-chamber, and a third room which is seldom used. A corridor runs along all three. . . . This way, please. The wagons drive through the entry; they can go all the way out to Bakers' Alley at the back."

The broad echoing passageway below was paved with great square flagstones. At either end of it were several offices. The odour of the onion sauce still floated out from the kitchen, which, with the entrance to the cellars, lay on the left of the steps. On the right, at the height of a storey above the passageway, a scaffolding of ungainly but neatly varnished rafters thrust out from the wall, supporting the servants' quarters above. A sort of ladder which led up to them from the passage was their only means of ingress or egress. Below the scaffolding were some enormous old cupboards and a carved chest.

Two low, worn steps led through a glass door out to the court-yard and the small wash-house. From here you could look into the pretty little garden, which was well laid out, though just now brown and sodden with the autumn rains, its beds protected with straw mats against the cold. At the other end of the garden rose the "portal," the rococo façade of the summer house. From the courtyard, however, the party took the path to the left, leading between two walls through another courtyard to the annexe.

They entered by slippery steps into a cellar-like vault with an earthen floor, which was used as a granary and provided with a rope for hauling up the sacks. A pair of stairs led up to the first storey, where the Consul opened a white door and admitted his guests to the billiard-room.

It was a bare, severe-looking room, with stiff chairs ranged round the sides. Herr Köppen flung himself exhausted into one of them. "I'll look on for a while," said he, brushing the wet from his coat. "It's the devil of a Sabbath day's journey through your house, Buddenbrook!"

Here too the stove was burning merrily, behind a brass lattice. Through the three high, narrow windows one looked out over red roofs gleaming with the wet, grey gables and courtyards.

The Consul took the cues out of the rack. "Shall we play a *carambolage*, Senator?" he asked. He went around and closed the pockets on both tables. "Who is playing with us? Gratjens? The Doctor? All right. Then will you take the other table, Gratjens and Justus? Köppen, you'll have to play."

The wine-merchant stood up and listened, with his mouth full of smoke. A violent gust of wind whistled between the houses, lashed the window-panes with rain, and howled down the chimney.

" Good Lord! " he said, blowing out the smoke. " Do you think the *Wullenwewer* will get into port, Buddenbrook? What abominable weather! "

Yes, and the news from Travemünde was not of the best, Consul Kröger agreed, chalking his cue. Storms everywhere on the coast. Nearly as bad as in 1824, the year of the great flood in St. Petersburg. Well, here was the coffee.

They poured it out and drank a little and began their game. The talk turned upon the Customs Union, and Consul Buddenbrook waxed enthusiastic.

" An inspiration, gentlemen," he said. He finished a shot and turned to the other table, where the topic had begun. " We ought to join at the earliest opportunity."

Herr Köppen disagreed. He fairly snorted in opposition. " How about our independence? " he asked incensed, supporting himself belligerently on his cue. " How about our self-determination? Would Hamburg consent to be a party to this Prussian scheme? We might as well be annexed at once! Heaven save us, what do we want of a customs union? Aren't we well enough as we are? "

" Yes, you and your red wine, Köppen. And the Russian products are all right. But there is little or nothing else imported. As for exports, well, we send a little corn to Holland and England, it is true. But I think we are far from being well enough as we are. In days gone by a very different business went on. Now, with the Customs Union, the Mecklenburgs and Schleswig-Holstein would be opened up — and private business would increase beyond all reckoning. . . ."

" But look here, Buddenbrook," Gratjens broke in, leaning far over the table and shifting his cue in his bony hand as he took careful aim, " I don't get the idea. Certainly our own system is perfectly simple and practical. Clearing on the security of a civic oath — "

" A fine old institution," the Consul admitted.

" Do you call it fine, Herr Consul? " Senator Langhals spoke with some heat. " I am not a merchant; but to speak frankly — well, I think this civic oath business has become little short of a farce: everybody makes light of it, and the State pockets the loss. One hears things that are simply scandalous. I am convinced that our entry into the Customs Union, so far as the Senate is concerned — "

Herr Köppen flung down his cue. " Then there will be a conflick," he said heatedly, forgetting to be careful with his pronunciation. " I know what I'm sayin' — God help you, but you don't know what you're talkin' about, beggin' your pardon."

Well, thank goodness! thought the rest of the company, as Jean Jacques entered at this point. He and Pastor Wunderlich came together, arm in arm, two cheerful, unaffected old men from another and less troubled age.

" Here, my friends," he began. " I have something for you: a little rhymed epigram from the French."

He sat down comfortably opposite the billiard-players, who leaned upon their cues across the tables. Drawing a paper from his pocket and laying his long finger with the signet ring to the side of his pointed nose, he read aloud, with a mock-heroic intonation:

> " When the Maréchal Saxe and the proud Pompadour
> Were driving out gaily in gilt coach and four,
> Frelon spied the pair: ' Oh, see them,' he cried:
> ' The sword of our king — and his sheath, side by side.' "

Herr Köppen looked disconcerted for a minute. Then he dropped the " conflick " where it was and joined in the hearty laughter that echoed to the ceiling of the billiard-room. Pastor Wunderlich withdrew to the window, but the movement of his shoulders betrayed that he was chuckling to himself.

Herr Hoffstede had more ammunition of the same sort in his pocket, and the gentlemen remained for some time in the billiard-room. Herr Köppen unbuttoned his waistcoat all the way down, and felt much more at ease here than in the dining-room. He gave vent to droll low-German expressions at every turn, and at frequent intervals began reciting to himself with enormous relish:

> " When the Maréchal Saxe . . ."

It sounded quite different in his harsh bass.

CHAPTER IX

It was rather late, nearly eleven, when the party began to break up. They had reassembled in the landscape-room, and they all made their adieux at the same time. The Frau Consul, as soon as her hand had been kissed in farewell, went upstairs to see how Christian was doing. To Mamsell Jungmann was left the supervision of the maids as they set things to rights and put away the silver. Madame Antoinette retired to the entresol. But the Consul accompanied his guests downstairs, across the entry, and outside the house.

A high wind was driving the rain slantwise through the streets as the old Krögers, wrapped in heavy fur mantles, slipped as fast as they could into their carriage. It had been waiting for hours before the door. The street was lighted by the flickering yellow rays from oil lamps hanging on posts before the houses or suspended on heavy chains across the streets. The projecting fronts of some of the houses jutted out into the roadway; others had porticos or raised benches added on. The street ran steeply down to the River Trave; it was badly paved, and sodden grass sprang up between the cracks. The church of St. Mary's was entirely shrouded in rain and darkness.

"*Merci*," said Lebrecht Kröger, shaking the Consul's hand as he stood by the carriage door. "*Merci*, Jean; it was too charming!" The door slammed, and the carriage drove off. Pastor Wunderlich and Broker Gratjens expressed their thanks and went their way. Herr Köppen, in a mantle with a five-fold cape and a broad grey hat, took his plump wife on his arm and said in his gruff bass: "G'night, Buddenbrook. Go in, go in; don't catch cold. Best thanks for everything — don't know when I've fed so well! So you like my red wine at four marks? Well, g'night, again."

The Köppens went in the same direction as the Krögers, down toward the river; Senator Langhals, Doctor Grabow, and Jean Jacques Hoffstede turned the other way. Consul Buddenbrook stood with his hands in his trousers pockets and listened to their footsteps as they died away down the empty, damp, dimly-lighted street. He shivered a little in his light clothes as he stood there a few paces from his own house, and turned to look up at its grey gabled façade. His eyes lingered upon the motto carved in the stone over the entrance, in antique lettering: *Dominus providebit* — " The Lord will provide." He bowed his head a little and went in, bolting the door carefully behind him. Then he locked the vestibule door and walked slowly across the echoing floor of the great entry. The cook was coming down the stairs with a tray of glasses in her hands, and he asked her, " Where's the master, Trina? "

" In the dining-room, Herr Consul," said she, and her face went as red as her arms, for she came from the country and was very bashful.

As he passed through the dark hall, he felt in his pocket for the letter. Then he went quickly into the dining-room, where a few small candle-ends in one of the candelabra cast a dim light over the empty table. The sour smell of the onion sauce still hung on the air.

Over by the windows Johann Buddenbrook was pacing comfortably up and down, with his hands behind his back.

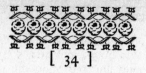

CHAPTER X

"Well, Johann, my son, where are you going? " He stood still and put his hand out to his son — his white Buddenbrook hand, a little too short, though finely modelled. His active figure showed indistinctly against the dark red curtains, the only gleams of white being from his powdered hair and the lace frill at his throat.

"Aren't you sleepy? I've been here listening to the wind; the weather is something fearful. Captain Kloht is on his way from Riga. . . ."

"Oh, Father, with God's help all will be well."

"Well, do you think I can depend on that? I know you are on intimate terms with the Almighty — "

The Consul felt his courage rise at this display of good humour.

"Well, to get to the point," he began, "I came in here not to bid you good night, but to — you won't be angry, will you, Papa? . . . I didn't want to disturb you with this letter on such a festive occasion . . . it came this afternoon. . . ."

"*Monsieur Gotthold, voilà!* " The old man affected to be quite unmoved as he took the sealed blue paper. "Herr Johann Buddenbrook, Senior. Personal. A careful man, your step-brother, Jean! Have I answered his second letter, that came the other day? And so now he writes me a third." The old man's rosy face grew sterner as he opened the seal with one finger, unfolded the thin paper, and gave it a smart rap with the back of his hand as he turned about to catch the light from the candles. The very hand-writing of this letter seemed to express revolt and disloyalty. All the Buddenbrooks wrote a fine, flowing hand; but these tall straight letters were full of heavy strokes, and many of the words were hastily underlined.

The Consul had drawn back a little to where the row of chairs stood against the wall; he did not sit down, as his father did not; but he grasped one of the high chair-backs nervously and watched the old man while he read, his lips moving rapidly, his brows drawn together, and his head on one side.

FATHER,

I am probably mistaken in entertaining any further hope of your sense of justice or any appreciation of my feelings at receiving no reply from my second pressing letter concerning the matter in question. I do not comment again on the character of the reply I received to my first one. I feel compelled to say, however, that the way in which you, by your lamentable obstinacy, are widening the rift between us, is a sin for which you will one day have to answer grievously before the judgment seat of God. It is sad enough that when I followed the dictates of my heart and married against your wishes, and further wounded your insensate pride by taking over a shop, you should have repulsed me so cruelly and remorselessly; but the way in which you now treat me cries out to Heaven, and you are utterly mistaken if you imagine that I intend to accept your silence without a struggle. The purchase price of your newly acquired house in the Mengstrasse was a hundred thousand marks; and I am aware that Johann, your business partner and your son by your second marriage, is living with you as your tenant, and after your death will become the sole proprietor of both house and business. With my step-sister in Frankfort, you have entered into agreements which are no concern of mine. But what does concern me, your eldest son, is that you carry your un-Christian spirit so far as to refuse me a penny of compensation for my share in the house. When you gave me a hundred thousand marks on my marriage and to set me up in business, and told me that a similar sum and no more should be bequeathed me by will, I said nothing, for I was not at the time sufficiently informed as to the amount of your fortune. Now I know more: and not regarding myself as disinherited in principle, I claim as my right the sum of thirty-three thousand and three hundred and thirty-three marks current, or a third of the purchase price. I make no comment on the damnable influences which are responsible for the treatment I have received. But I protest against them with my whole sense of justice as a Christian and a business man. Let me tell you for the last time that, if you cannot bring yourself to recognize the justice of my claims, I shall no longer be able to respect you as a Christian, a parent, or a man of business.

GOTTHOLD BUDDENBROOK.

"You will excuse me for saying that I don't get much pleasure out of reading that rigmarole all over again. — *Voilà!*" And Johann Buddenbrook tossed the letter to his son, with a contemptuous gesture. The Consul picked it up as it fluttered to his feet, and looked at his father with troubled eyes, while the old man took the long candle-snuffers from their place by the window and with angry strides crossed the room to the candelabrum in the corner.

"*Assez*, I say. *N'en parlons plus!* To bed with you — *en avant!*" He quenched one flame after another under the little metal cap. There were only two candles left when the elder turned again to his son, whom he could hardlly see at the far end of the room.

"*Eh bien* — what are you standing there for? Why don't you say something?"

"What shall I say, Father? I am thoroughly taken aback."

"You are pretty easily taken aback, then," Johann Buddenbrook rapped out irritably, though he knew that the reproach was far from being a just one. His son was in fact often his superior when it came to a quick decision upon the advantageous course.

"'Damnable influences,'" the Consul quoted. "That is the first line I can make out. Do you know how it makes me feel, Father? And he reproaches us with 'unchristian behaviour!'"

"You'll let yourself be bluffed by this miserable scribble, will you?" Johann Buddenbrook strode across to his son, dragging the extinguisher on its long stick behind him. "'Unchristian behaviour!' Ha! He shows good taste, doesn't he, this canting money-grabber? I don't know what to make of you young people! Your heads are full of fantastic religious humbug — practical idealism, the July Monarchy, and what not: and we old folk are supposed to be wretched cynics. And then you abuse your poor old Father in the coarsest way rather than give up a few thousand thaler. . . . So he deigns to look down upon me as a business man, does he? Well, as a business man, I know what *faux-frais* are! — *Faux-frais*," he repeated, rolling the *r* in his throat. "I shan't make this high-falutin scamp of a son any fonder of me by giving him what he asks for, it seems to me."

"What can I say, Father? I don't care to feel that he has any justification when he talks of 'influences.' As an interested party I don't like to tell you to stick out, but — It seems to me I'm as good a Christian as Gotthold . . . but still . . ."

"'Still' — that is exactly it, Jean, you are right to say 'still.' What is the real state of the case? He got infatuated with his Mademoiselle Stüwing and wouldn't listen to reason; he made scene after scene, and finally he married her, after I had absolutely refused to give my consent. Then I wrote to him: '*Mon très cher fils:* you are marrying your shop — very well, that's an end of it. We cease to be on friendly terms from now on. I won't cut you off, or do anything melodramatic. I am sending you a hundred thousand marks as a wedding present, and I'll leave you another hundred thousand in my will. But that is absolutely all you'll get, not another shilling!' That shut his mouth. — What have our arrangements got to do with him? Suppose you and your sister do get a bit more, and the house has been bought out of your share?"

"Father, surely you can understand how painful my position is! I ought to advise you in the interest of family harmony — but . . ." The Consul sighed. Johann Buddenbrook peered at him, in the dim light, to see what his expression was. One of the two candles had gone out of itself; the other was flickering. Every now and then a tall, smiling white figure seemed to step momentarily out of the tapestry and then back again.

"Father," said the Consul softly. "This affair with Gotthold depresses me."

"What's all this sentimentality, Jean? How does it depress you?"

"We were all so happy here to-day, Father; we had a glorious celebration, and we felt proud and glad of what we have accomplished, and of having raised the family and firm to a position of honour and respect. . . . But this bitter feud with my own brother, with your eldest son, is like a hidden crack in the building we have erected. A family should be united, Father. It must keep together. 'A house divided against itself will fall.'"

"There you are with your milk-and-water stuff, Jean! All I say is, he's an insolent young puppy."

A pause ensued. The last candle burned lower and lower.

"What are you doing, Jean?" asked Johann Buddenbrook. "I can't see you."

The Consul said shortly, "I'm calculating." He was standing erect, and the expression in his eyes had changed. They had looked dreamy all the evening; but now they stared into the candle-flame with a cold sharp gaze. "Either you give thirty-three thousand, three hundred and thirty-three marks to Gotthold, and fifteen thousand to the family in Frankfort — that makes forty-eight thousand, three hundred and thirty-five in all — or, you give nothing to Gotthold, and twenty-five thousand to the family in Frankfort. That means a gain of twenty-three thousand, three hundred and thirty-five for the firm. But there is more to it than that. If you give Gotthold a compensation for the house, you've started the ball rolling. He is likely to demand equal shares with my sister and me after your death, which would mean a loss of hundreds of thousands to the firm. The firm could not face it, and I, as sole head, could not face it either." He made a vigorous gesture and drew himself more erect than before. "No, Papa," he said, and his tone bespoke finality, "I must advise you not to give in."

"Bravo!" cried the old man. "There 's an end of it! *N'en parlons plus! En avant!* Let's get to bed."

And he extinguished the last candle. They groped through the pitch-dark hall, and at the foot of the stairs they stopped and shook hands.

"Good night, Jean. And cheer up. These little worries aren't anything. See you at breakfast!"

The Consul went up to his rooms, and the old man felt his way along the baluster and down to the entresol. Soon the rambling old house lay wrapped in darkness and silence. Hopes, fears, and ambitions all slumbered, while the rain fell and the autumn wind whistled around gables and street corners.

PART TWO

CHAPTER I

It was mid-April, two and a half years later. The spring was more advanced than usual, and with the spring had come to the Buddenbrook family a joy that made old Johann sing about the house and moved his son to the depths of his heart.

The Consul sat at the big roll-top writing-desk in the window of the breakfast-room, at nine o'clock one Sunday morning. He had before him a stout leather portfolio stuffed with papers, from among which he had drawn a gilt-edged notebook with an embossed cover, and was busily writing in it in his small, thin, flowing script. His hand hurried over the paper, never pausing except to dip his quill in the ink.

Both the windows were open, and the spring breeze wafted delicate odours into the room, lifting the curtains gently. The garden was full of young buds and bathed in tender sunshine; a pair of birds called and answered each other pertly. The sunshine was strong, too, on the white linen of the breakfast-table and the gilt borders of the old china.

The folding doors into the bed-room were open, and the voice of old Johann could be heard inside, singly softly to a quaint and ancient tune:

> A kind papa, a worthy man,
> He rocks the baby in the cradle,
> He feeds the children sugar-plums
> And stirs the porridge with a ladle.

He sat beside the little green-curtained cradle, close to the Frau Consul's lofty bed, and rocked it softly with one hand. Madame Antoinette, in a white lace cap and an apron over her striped frock, was busy with flannel and linen at the table. The old couple had given up their bedroom to the Frau Consul for the time being, to make things easier for the servants, and were sleeping in the unused room in the entresol.

Consul Buddenbrook gave scarcely a glance at the adjoining room, so absorbed was he in his work. His face wore an expression of earnest, almost suffering piety, his mouth slightly open, the chin a little dropped; his eyes filled from time to time. He wrote:

"Today, April 14, 1838, at six o'clock in the morning, my dear wife, Elizabeth Buddenbrook, born Kröger, was, by God's gracious help, happily delivered of a daughter, who will receive the name of Clara in Holy Baptism. Yea, the Lord hath holpen mightily; for according to Doctor Grabow, the birth was somewhat premature, and her condition not of the best. She suffered great pain. Oh, Lord God of Sabaoth, where is there any other God save Thee? who helpest us in all our times of need and danger, and teachest us to know Thy will aright, that we may fear Thee and obey Thy commandments! O Lord, lead us and guide us all, so long as we live upon this earth. . . ." The pen hurried glibly over the paper, with here and there a commercial flourish, talking with God in every line. Two pages further on: "I have taken out," it said, "an insurance policy for my youngest daughter, of one hundred and fifty thaler current! Lead her, O Lord, in Thy ways, give her a pure heart, O God, that she may one day enter into the mansions of eternal peace. For inasmuch as our weak human hearts are prone to forget Thy priceless gift of the sweet, blessed Jesus . . ." And so on for three pages. Then he wrote "Amen." But still the faint scratching sound of the pen went on, over several more pages. It wrote of the precious spring that refreshes the tired wanderer, of the Saviour's holy wounds gushing blood, of the broad way and the narrow way, and the glory of the Eternal God. It is true that after a while the Consul began to feel that he had written enough; that he might let well enough alone, and go in to see his wife, or out to the counting-house. Oh, fie, fie! Did one so soon weary of communion with his Lord and Saviour? Was it not robbing his God to scant Him of this service? No, he would go on, as a chastisement for these unholy impulses. He cited whole pages of Scripture, he prayed for his parents, his wife, his children, and himself, he prayed even for his brother Gotthold. And then, with a last quotation and three final "Amens," he strewed sand on the paper and leaned back with a sigh of relief.

He crossed one leg over the other and slowly turned the pages of the notebook, reading dates and entries here and there, written in his own hand, and thanking the Lord afresh as he saw how in every time of need and danger He had stretched out His hand to aid. Once he had lain so ill of small-pox that his life had been despaired of — yet it had been saved. And once, when he was a boy, a beer-vat had fallen on him. A large quantity of beer was being brewed for a wedding, in the old days when the brewing was done at home; and a vat had fallen over, pinning the boy beneath it. It had taken six people to lift it up again, and his head had been crushed so that the blood ran down in streams. He was carried into a shop, and, as he still breathed, the doctor and the surgeon were sent for. They told the father to prepare for the worst and to bow to the will of God. But the Almighty had blessed the work of healing, and the boy was saved and restored to health. The Consul dwelt a while upon this account, re-living the accident in his mind. Then he took his pen again and wrote after his last "Amen": "Yea, O God, I will eternally praise Thee!"

Another time, his life had been saved from danger by water, when he had gone to Bergen, as a young man. The account read:

"At high water, when the freight boats of the Northern Line are in, we have great difficulty getting through the press to our landing. I was standing on the edge of the scow, with my feet on the thole-pins, leaning my back against the sailboat, trying to get the scow nearer in, when, as luck would have it, the oak thole-pins broke, and I went head over heels into the water. The first time I came up, nobody was near enough to get hold of me; the second time, the scow went over my head. There were plenty of people there anxious to save me, but they had to keep the sailboat and the scow off, so that I should not come up under them; and all their shoving would probably have been in vain if a rope had not suddenly broken on one of the sailboats belonging to the Line, so that she swung further out; and this, by the grace of God, gave me room enough to come up in free water. It was only the top of my head, with the hair, that they saw; but it was enough, for they were all lying on their stomachs with their heads sticking out over the scow, and the man at the bow grabbed me by the hair, and I got hold of his arm. He was in an unsafe position himself and could not hold me, but he gave a yell, and they all took hold of him around the waist and pulled. I hung on, though he bit me to make me let go. So they got me in at last." There followed a long prayer of thanksgiving, which the Consul re-read with tear-wet eyes.

On another page he had said: "I could write much more, were I minded to reveal the passions of my youth. . . ." The Consul passed over this, and began to read here and there from the period of his marriage and the birth of his first child. The union, to be frank, could hardly be called a love-match. His father had tapped him on the shoulder and pointed out to him the daughter of the wealthy Kröger, who could bring the firm a splendid marriage portion. He had accepted the situation with alacrity; and from the first moment had honoured his wife as the mate entrusted to him by God.

After all, his father's second marriage had been of much the same kind.

"'A kind Papa, a worthy man.'"

He could still hear old Johann softly humming in the bedroom. What a pity he had so little taste for those old records! He stood with both feet firmly planted in the present, and concerned himself seldom with the past of his family. Yet in times gone by he too had made a few entries in the gilt-edged book. The Consul turned to those pages, written in a florid hand on rather coarse paper that was already yellowing with age. They were chiefly about his first marriage. Ah, Johann Buddenbrook must have adored his first wife, the daughter of a Bremen merchant! The one brief year it had been granted him to live with her was the happiest of his life — " *l'année la plus heureuse de ma vie*," he had written there. The words were underlined with a wavy line, for all the world, even Madame Antoinette, to see.

Then Gotthold had come, and Josephine had died. And here some strange things had been written on the rough paper. Johann Buddenbrook must have openly and bitterly hated his child, even when, while still in the womb, it had caused its mother to faint and agonize under the lusty burden. It was born strong and active, while Josephine buried her bloodless face deeper in the pillows and passed away. Johann never forgave the ruthless intruder. He grew up vigorous and pushing, and Johann thought of him as his mother's murderer. This was, to the Consul's mind, incomprehensible. She had died, he thought, fulfilling the holy duty of a woman: "the love I bore to her would have passed over in all its tenderness to her child," he said to himself. It had not been so. Later the father married again, his bride being Antoinette Duchamps, the daughter of a rich and much-esteemed Hamburg family, and the two had dwelt together with mutual respect and deference.

The Consul went on turning over the pages. There at the end were written the small histories of his own children: how Tom had had the measles, and Antonie jaundice, and Christian chickenpox. There were accounts of various journeys he had taken with his wife, to Paris, Switzerland, Marienbad. Then the Consul turned back to the front of the book, to some pages written in bluish ink, in a hand full of flourishes, on paper that was like parchment, but tattered and spotted with age. Here his grandfather

Johann had set down the genealogy of the main branch of the Buddenbrooks. At the end of the sixteenth century, the first Buddenbrook of whom they had knowledge lived in Parchim, and his son had been a Senator of Grabau. Another Buddenbrook, a tailor by trade, and " very well-to-do " (this was underlined) had married in Rostock and begotten an extraordinary number of children, who lived or died, as the case might be. And again, another, this time a Johann, had lived in Rostock as a merchant, from whom the Consul's grandfather had descended, who had left Rostock to settle himself in this very town, and was the founder of the present grain business. There was much about him set down in detail: when he had had the purples, and when genuine small-pox; when he had fallen out of the malt-kiln and been miraculously saved, when he might have fallen against the beams and been crushed; how he had had fever and been delirious — all these events were meticulously described. He had also written down wise admonitions for the benefit of his descendants, like the following, which was carefully painted and framed, in a tall Gothic script set off with a border: " My son, attend with zeal to thy business by day; but do none that hinders thee from thy sleep by night." He had also stated that his old Wittenberg Bible was to descend to his eldest son, and thence from first-born to first-born in each generation.

Consul Buddenbrook reached for the old leather portfolio and took out the remaining documents. There were letters, on torn and yellow paper, written by anxious mothers to their sons abroad — which the sons had docketed: " Received and contents duly noted." There were citizens' papers, with the seal and crest of the free Hansa town; insurance policies; letters inviting this or that Buddenbrook to become god-father for a colleague's child; congratulatory epistles and occasional poems. Sons travelling for the firm to Stockholm or Amsterdam had written back, to the parent or partner at home, letters in which business was touchingly mingled with inquiries after wife and child. There was a separate diary of the Consul's journey through England and Brabant; the cover had an engraving of Edinburgh Castle and the Grass-market. Lastly, there were Gotthold's late angry letters to his father — painful documents, to offset which was the poem written by Jean Jacques Hoffstede to celebrate the house-warming.

A faint, rapid chime came from above the secretary, where there hung a dull-looking painting of an old market-square, with a church-tower that possessed a real clock of its own. It was now striking the hour, in authentic if tiny tones. The Consul closed the portfolio and stowed it away carefully in a drawer at the back of the desk. Then he went into the bed-chamber.

Here the walls and the high old bed were hung with dark flow-ered chintz, and there was in the air a feeling of repose, of con-valescence — of calm after an anxious and painful ordeal. A min-gled odour of cologne and drugs hung in the mild, dim-lighted atmosphere. The old pair bent over the cradle side by side and watched the slumbering child; and the Consul's wife lay pale and happy, in an exquisite lace jacket, her hair carefully dressed. As she put out her hand to her husband, her gold bracelets tinkled slightly. She had a characteristic way of stretching out her hand with the palm upward, in a sweeping gesture that gave it added gracious-ness.

" Well, Betsy, how are you? "

" Splendid, splendid, my dear Jean."

He still held her hand as he bent over and looked at the child, whose rapid little breaths were distinctly audible. For a moment he inhaled the tender warmth and the indescribable odour of well-being and cherishing care that came up from the cradle. Then he kissed the little creature on the brow and said softly: " God bless you! " He noticed how like to a bird's claws were the tiny yellow, crumpled fingers.

" She eats splendidly," Madame Antoinette said. " See how she has gained."

" I believe, on my soul, she looks like Netta," old Johann said, beaming with pride and pleasure. " See what coal-black eyes she has! "

The old lady waved him away. " How can anybody tell who she looks like yet? " she said. " Are you going to church, Jean? "

" Yes, it is ten o'clock now, and high time. I am only waiting for the children."

The children were already making an unseemly noise on the stairs, and Clothilde could be heard telling them to hush. They came in in their fur tippets — for it would still be wintry in St. Mary's — trying to be soft and gentle in the sick-room. They wanted to see the little sister, and then go to church. Their faces were rosy with excitement. This was a wonderful red-letter day, for the stork had brought not only the baby sister, but all sorts of presents as well. How tremendously strong the stork must be, to carry all that! There was a new seal-skin school-bag for Tom, a big doll for Antonie, that had real hair — imagine that! — for Chris-tian a complete toy theatre, with the Sultan, Death, and the Devil; and a book with pictures for demure Clothilde, who accepted it with thanks, but was more interested in the bag of sweeties that fell to her lot as well.

They kissed their mother, and were allowed a peep under the green curtains of the baby's bed. Then off they went with their father, who had put on his fur coat and taken the hymn book. They were followed by the piercing cry of the new member of the family, who had just waked up.

CHAPTER II

EARLY in the summer, sometimes as early as May or June, Tony Buddenbrook always went on a visit to her grandparents, who lived outside the Castle Gate. This was a great pleasure.

For life was delightful out there in the country, in the luxurious villa with its many outbuildings, servants' quarters and stables, and its great parterres, orchards, and kitchen-gardens, which ran steeply down to the river Trave. The Krögers lived in the grand style; there was a difference between their brilliant establishment and the solid, somewhat heavy comfort of the paternal home, which was obvious at a glance, and which impressed very much the young Demoiselle Buddenbrook.

Here there was no thought of duties in house or kitchen. In the Mengstrasse, though her Mother and Grandfather did not seem to think it important, her Father and her Grandmother were always telling her to remember her dusting, and holding up Clothilde as an example. The old feudal feeling of her Mother's side of the family came out strongly in the little maid: one could see how she issued her orders to the footman or the abigail — and to her Grandmother's servants and her Grandfather's coachman as well.

Say what you will, it is pleasant to awake every morning in a large, gaily tapestried bed-chamber, and with one's first movements to feel the soft satin of the coverlet under one's hand; to take early breakfast in the balcony room, with the sweet fresh air coming up from the garden through the open glass door; to drink, instead of coffee, a cup of chocolate handed one on a tray — yes, proper birthday chocolate, with a thick slice of fresh cup-cake! True, she had to eat her breakfast alone, except on Sundays, for her grandparents never came down until long after she had gone to school. When she had munched her cake and drunk her chocolate, she would snatch up her satchel and trip down the terrace and through the well-kept front garden.

She was very dainty, this little Tony Buddenbrook. Under her straw hat curled a wealth of blond hair, slowly darkening with the years. Lively grey-blue eyes and a pouting upper lip gave her

fresh face a roguish look, borne out by the poise of her graceful
little figure; even the slender legs, in their immaculate white stockings, trotted along over the ground with an unmistakable air of
ease and assurance. People knew and greeted the young daughter
of Consul Buddenbrook as she came out of the garden gate and up
the chestnut-bordered avenue. Perhaps an old market-woman,
driving her little cart in from the village, would nod her head in
its big flat straw hat with its light green ribbons, and call out
" Mornin', little missy! " Or Matthiesen the porter, in his wide
knee-breeches, white hose, and buckled shoes, would respectfully
take off his hat as she passed.

Tony always waited for her neighbour, little Julie Hagenström; the two children went to school together. Julie was a high-
shouldered child, with large, staring black eyes, who lived close
by in a vine-covered house. Her people had not been long in the
neighbourhood. The father, Herr Hagenström, had married a
wife from Hamburg, with thick, heavy black hair and larger diamonds in her ears than any one had ever seen before. Her name
was Semlinger. Hagenström was partner in the export firm of
Strunck and Hagenström. He showed great zeal and ambition in
municipal affairs, and was always acting on boards and committees and administrative bodies. But he was not very popular. His
marriage had rather affronted the rigid traditions of the older
families, like the Möllendorpfs, Langhals, and Buddenbrooks; and,
for another thing, he seemed to enjoy thwarting their ideas at
every turn — he would go to work in an underhand way to oppose
their interests, in order to show his own superior foresight and
energy. " Hinrich Hagenström makes trouble the whole time,"
the Consul would say. " He seems to take a personal pleasure in
thwarting me. To-day he made a scene at the sitting of the Central
Paupers' Deputation; and a few days ago in the Finance Department. . . ." " The old skunk! " Johann Buddenbrook interjected. Another time, father and son sat down to table angry and
depressed. What was the matter? Oh, nothing. They had lost a
big consignment of rye for Holland: Strunck and Hagenström
had snapped it up under their noses. He was a fox, Hinrich Hagenström.

Tony had often heard such remarks, and she was not too well
disposed toward Julie Hagenström; the two children walked together because they were neighbours, but usually they quarrelled.

" My Father owns a thousand thalers," said Julchen. She
thought she was uttering the most terrible falsehood. " How much
does yours? "

Tony was speechless with envy and humiliation. Then she said, with a quiet, off-hand manner: " My chocolate tasted delicious this morning. What do you have for breakfast, Julie? "

" Before I forget it," Julie would rejoin, " would you like one of my apples? Well, I won't give you any! " She pursed up her lips, and her black eyes watered with satisfaction.

Sometimes Julie's brother Hermann went to school at the same time with the two girls. There was another brother too, named Moritz, but he was sickly and did his lessons at home. Hermann was fair-haired and snub-nosed. He breathed through his mouth and was always smacking his lips.

" Stuff and nonsense! " he would say. " Papa has a lot more than a thousand thaler." He interested Tony because of the luncheon he took to school: not bread, but a soft sort of lemon bun with currants in it, and sausage or smoked goose between. It seemed to be his favourite luncheon. Tony had never seen anything like it before. Lemon bun, with smoked goose — it must be wonderful! He let her look into his box, and she asked if she might have some. Hermann said: " Not to-day, Tony, because I can't spare any. But to-morrow I'll bring another piece for you, if you'll give me something."

Next morning, Tony came out into the avenue, but there was no Julie. She waited five minutes, but there was no sign. Another minute — there came Hermann alone, swinging his lunch-box by the strap and smacking his lips.

" Now," he said, " here's a bun, with some goose between — all lean; there's not a bit of fat to it. What will you give me for it? "

" A shilling? " suggested Tony. They were standing in the middle of the avenue.

" A shilling? " repeated Hermann. Then he gave a gulp and said, " No, I want something else."

" What? " demanded Tony; for she was prepared to pay a good price for the dainty.

" A kiss! " shouted Hermann Hagenström. He flung his arms around Tony, and began kissing at random, never once touching her face, for she flung her head back with surprising agility, pushed him back with her left hand — it was holding her satchel — against his breast, while with her right hand she dealt him three or four blows in the face with all her strength. He stumbled backward; but at that moment sister Julie appeared from behind a tree, like a little black demon, and, falling upon Tony, tore off her hat and scratched her cheeks unmercifully. After this affair, naturally, the friendship was about at an end.

It was hardly out of shyness that Tony had refused the kiss. She was on the whole a forward damsel, and had given the Consul no little disquiet with her tomboy ways. She had a good little head, and did as well in the school as one could desire; but her conduct in other ways was far from satisfactory. Things even went so far that one day the schoolmistress, a certain Fräulein Agathe Vermehren, felt obliged to call upon the Frau Consul, and, flushed with embarrassment, to suggest with all due politeness that the child should receive a paternal admonition. It seemed that Tony, despite frequent correction, had been guilty, not for the first time, of creating a disturbance in the street!

There was, of course, no harm in the fact that the child knew everybody in town. The Consul quite approved of this, and argued that it displayed love of one's neighbour, a sense of human fellowship, and a lack of snobbishness. So Tony, on her way through the streets, chattered with all and sundry. She and Tom would clamber about in the granaries on the water-side, among the piles of oats and wheat, prattling to the labourers and the clerks in the dark little ground-floor offices; they would even help haul up the sacks of grain. She knew the butchers with their trays and aprons, when she met them in Broad Street; she accosted the dairy women when they came in from the country, and made them take her a little way in their carts. She knew the grey-bearded craftsmen who sat in the narrow goldsmiths' shops built into the arcades in the market square; and she knew the fish-wives, the fruit- and vegetable-women, and the porters that stood on the street corners chewing their tobacco.

So far, this was very well. But it was not all.

There was a pale, beardless man, of no particular age, who was often seen wandering up and down Broad Street with a wistful smile on his face. This man was so nervous that he jumped every time he heard a sudden noise behind him; and Tony delighted in making him jump every time she set eyes on him. Then there was an odd, tiny little woman with a large head, who put up a huge tattered umbrella at every sign of a storm. Tony would harass this poor soul with cries of "Mushroom!" whenever she had the chance. Moreover, she and two or three more of her ilk would go to the door of a tiny house in an alley off John Street, where there lived an old woman who did a tiny trade in worsted dolls; they would ring the bell and, when the old dame appeared, inquire with deceptive courtesy, if Herr and Frau Spittoon were at home — and then run away screaming with laughter. All these ragamuffinly tricks Tony Buddenbrook was guilty of — indeed, she seemed to perform them with the best conscience in the world. If one of her victims threatened her, she would step back a pace or two, toss her pretty head, pout with her pretty lip, and say "Pooh!" in a half mocking, half angry tone which meant: "Try it if you like. I am Consul Buddenbrook's daughter, if you don't know!"

Thus she went about in the town like a little queen; and like a queen, she was kind or cruel to her subjects, as the whim seized her.

CHAPTER III

JEAN JACQUES HOFFSTEDE's verdict on the two sons of Consul Buddenbrook undoubtedly hit the mark.

Thomas had been marked from the cradle as a merchant and future member of the firm. He was on the modern side of the old school which the boys attended; an able, quick-witted, intelligent lad, always ready to laugh when his brother Christian mimicked the masters, which he did with uncanny facility. Christian, on the classical side, was not less gifted than Tom, but he was less serious. His special and particular joy in life was the imitation, in speech and manner, of a certain worthy Marcellus Stengel, who taught drawing, singing, and some other of the lighter branches.

This Herr Marcellus Stengel always had a round half-dozen beautifully sharpened pencils sticking out of his pocket. He wore a red wig and a light brown coat that reached nearly down to his ankles; also a choker collar that came up almost to his temples. He was quite a wit, and loved to play with verbal distinctions, as: " You were to make a line, my child, and what have you made? You have made a dash! " In singing-class, his favourite lesson was " The Forest Green." When they sang this, some of the pupils would go outside in the corridor; and then, when the chorus rose inside: " We ramble so gaily through field and wood," those outside would repeat the last word very softly, as an echo. Once Christian Buddenbrook, his cousin Jürgen Kröger, and his chum Andreas Gieseke, the son of the Fire Commissioner, were deputed as echo; but when the moment came, they threw the coal-scuttle downstairs instead, and were kept in after school by Herr Stengel in consequence. But alas, by that time Herr Stengel had forgotten their crime. He bade his housekeeper give them each a cup of coffee, and then dismissed them.

In truth, they were all admirable scholars, the masters who taught in the cloisters of the old school — once a monastic foundation — under the guidance of a kindly, snuff-taking old head. They were, to a man, well-meaning and sweet-humoured; and they were one in the belief that knowledge and good cheer are not mutually exclusive. The Latin classes in the middle forms were heard by a former preacher, one Pastor Shepherd, a tall man with brown whiskers and a twinkling eye, who joyed extremely in the happy coincidence of his name and calling, and missed no chance of having the boys translate the word *pastor*. His favourite expression was "boundlessly limited"; but it was never quite clear whether this was actually meant for a joke or not! When he wanted to dumbfound his pupils altogether, he would draw in his lips and blow them quickly out again, with a noise like the popping of a champagne cork. He would go up and down with long strides in his class-room, prophesying to one boy or another, with great vividness, the course which his life would take. He did this avowedly with the purpose of stimulating their imaginations; and then he would set to work seriously on the business in hand, which was to repeat certain verses on the rules of gender and difficult constructions. He had composed these verses himself, with no little skill, and took much pride in declaiming them, with great attention to rhyme and rhythm.

Thus passed Tom's and Christian's boyhood, with no great events to mark its course. There was sunshine in the Buddenbrook family, and in the office everything went famously. Only now and again there would be a sudden storm, a trifling mishap, like the following:

Herr Stuht the tailor had made a new suit for each of the Buddenbrook lads. Herr Stuht lived in Bell-Founders' Street. He was a master tailor, and his wife bought and sold old clothes, and thus moved in the best circles of society. Herr Stuht himself had an enormous belly, which hung down over his legs, wrapped in a flannel shirt. The suits he made for the young Masters Buddenbrook were at the combined cost of seventy marks; but at the boys' request he had consented to put them down in the bill at eighty marks and to hand them the difference. It was just a little arrangement among themselves — not very honourable, indeed, but then, not very uncommon either. However, fate was unkind, and the bargain came to light. Herr Stuht was sent for to the Consul's office, whither he came, with a black coat over his woollen shirt, and stood there while the Consul subjected Tom and Christian to a severe cross-examination. His head was bowed and his legs far apart, his manner vastly respectful. He tried to smooth things over as much as he could for the young gentlemen, and said that what was done was done, and he would be satisfied with the seventy marks. But the Consul was greatly incensed by the trick. He gave it long and serious consideration; yet finally ended by increasing the lads' pocket-money — for was it not written: "Lead us not into temptation?"

It seemed probable that more might be expected from Thomas Buddenbrook than from his brother Christian. He was even-tempered, and his high spirits never crossed the bounds of discretion. Christian, on the other hand, was inclined to be moody: guilty at times of the most extravagant silliness, at others he would be seized by a whim which could terrify the rest of them in the most astonishing way.

The family are at table eating dessert and conversing pleasantly the while. Suddenly Christian turns pale and puts back on his plate the peach into which he has just bitten. His round, deep-set eyes, above the too-large nose, have opened wider.

"I will never eat another peach," he says.

"Why not, Christian? What nonsense! What's the matter?"

"Suppose I accidentally — suppose I swallowed the stone, and it stuck in my throat, so I couldn't breathe, and I jumped up, strangling horribly — and all of you jump up — Ugh . . . !" and he suddenly gives a short groan, full of horror and affright, starts up in his chair, and acts as if he were trying to escape.

The Frau Consul and Ida Jungmann actually do jump up.

"Heavens, Christian! — you haven't swallowed it, have you?" For his whole appearance suggests that he has.

"No," says Christian slowly. "No" — he is gradually quieting down — "I only mean, suppose I actually *had* swallowed it!"

The Consul has been pale with fright, but he recovers and begins to scold. Old Johann bangs his fist on the table and forbids any more of these idiotic practical jokes. But Christian, for a long, long time, eats no more peaches.

CHAPTER IV

IT was not simply the weakness of age that made Madame Antoinette Buddenbrook take to her lofty bed in the bed-chamber
of the entresol, one cold January day after they had dwelt some
six years in Meng Street. The old lady had remained hale and
active, and carried her head, with its clustering white side-curls,
proudly erect to the very last. She had gone with her husband
and children to most of the large dinners given in the town, and
presided no whit less elegantly than her daughter-in-law when the
Buddenbrooks themselves entertained. But one day an indefinable
malady had suddenly made itself felt — at first in the form of a
slight intestinal catarrh, for which Dr. Grabow prescribed a mild
diet of pigeon and French bread. This had been followed by colic
and vomiting, which reduced her strength so rapidly as to bring
about an alarming decline.

Dr. Grabow held hurried speech with the Consul, outside on
the landing, and another doctor was called in consultation — a
stout, black-bearded, gloomy-looking man who began going in
and out with Dr. Grabow. And now the whole atmosphere of the
house changed. They went about on their tip-toes and spoke in
whispers. The wagons were no longer allowed to roll through the
great entry-way below. The family looked in each other's eyes
and saw there something strange. It was the idea of death that had
entered, and was holding silent sway in the spacious rooms.

But there was no idle watching, for visitors came: old Senator
Duchamps, the dying woman's brother, from Hamburg, with his
daughter; and a few days later, the Consul's sister from Frankfort
and her husband, who was a banker. The illness lasted fourteen
or fifteen days, during which the guests lived in the house, and
Ida Jungmann had her hands full attending to the bedrooms and
providing heavy breakfasts, with shrimps and port wine. Much
roasting and baking went on in the kitchen.

Upstairs, Johann Buddenbrook sat by the sick-bed, his old
Netta's limp hand in his, and stared into space with his brows
knitted and his lower lip hanging. A clock hung on the wall and

ticked dully, with long pauses between; not so long, however, as the pauses between the dying woman's fluttering breaths. A black-robed sister of mercy busied herself about the beef-tea which they still sought to make the patient take. Now and then some member of the family would appear at the door and disappear again.

Perhaps the old man was thinking how he had sat at the death-bed of his first wife, forty-six years before. Perhaps he recalled his frenzy of despair and contrasted it with the gentle melancholy which he felt now, as an old man, gazing into the face of his old wife — a face so changed, so listless, so void of expression. She had never given him either a great joy or a great sorrow; but she had decorously played her part beside him for many a long year — and now her life was ebbing away.

He was not thinking a great deal. He was only looking with fixed gaze back into his own past life and at life in general. It all seemed to him now quite strange and far away, and he shook his head a little. That empty noise and bustle, in the midst of which he had once stood, had flowed away imperceptibly and left him standing there, listening in wonder to sounds that died upon his ear. " Strange, strange," he murmured.

Madame Buddenbrook breathed her last brief, effortless sigh; and they prayed by her side in the dining-room, where the service was held; and the bearers lifted the flower-covered coffin to carry it away. But old Johann did not weep. He only gave the same gentle, bewildered head-shake, and said, with the same half-smiling look: " Strange, strange! " It became his most frequent expression. Plainly, the time for old Johann too was near at hand.

He would sit silent and absent in the family circle; sometimes with little Clara on his knee, to whom he would sing one of his droll catches, like

" The omnibus drives through the town "

or perhaps

" Look at the blue-fly a-buzzin' on the wall."

But he might suddenly stop in the middle, like one aroused out of a train of thought, put the child down on the floor, and move away, with his little head-shake and murmur: " Strange, strange! " One day he said: " Jean — it's about time, eh? "

It was soon afterward that neatly printed notices signed by father and son were sent about through the town, in which Johann Buddenbrook senior respectfully begged leave to announce that his increasing years obliged him to give up his former business

activities, and that in consequence the firm of Johann Buddenbrook, founded by his late father anno 1768, would as from that
day be transferred, with its assets and liabilities, to his son and
former partner Johann Buddenbrook as sole proprietor; for whom
he solicited a continuance of the confidence so widely bestowed
upon him. Signed, with deep respect, Johann Buddenbrook —
who would from now on cease to append his signature to business papers.

These announcements were no sooner sent out than the old
man refused to set foot in the office; and his apathy so increased
that it took only the most trifling cold to send him to bed, one
March day two months after the death of his wife. One night
more — then came the hour when the family gathered round his
bed and he spoke to them: first to the Consul: " Good luck, Jean,
and keep your courage up! " And then to Thomas: " Be a help
to your Father, Tom! " And to Christian: " Be something worth
while! " Then he was silent, gazing at them all; and finally, with
a last murmured " Strange! " he turned his face to the wall. . . .

To the very end, he did not speak of Gotthold, and the latter
encountered with silence the Consul's written summons to his
father's death-bed. But early the next morning, before the announcements were sent out, as the Consul was about to go into
the office to attend to some necessary business, Gotthold Buddenbrook, proprietor of the linen firm of Siegmund Stüwing and
Company, came with rapid steps through the entry. He was
forty-six years old, broad and stocky, and had thick ash-blond
whiskers streaked with grey. His short legs were cased in baggy
trousers of rough checked material. On the steps he met the Consul, and his eyebrows went up under the brim of his grey hat.

He did not put out his hand. " Johann," he said, in a high-
pitched, rather agreeable voice, " how is he? "

" He passed away last night," the Consul said, with deep emotion, grasping his brother's hand, which held an umbrella. " The
best of fathers! "

Gotthold drew down his brows now, so low that the lids nearly
closed. After a silence, he said pointedly: " Nothing was changed
up to the end? "

The Consul let his hand drop and stepped back. His round,
deep-set blue eyes flashed as he answered, " Nothing."

Gotthold's eyebrows went up again under his hat, and his eyes
fixed themselves on his brother with an expression of suspense.

" And what have I to expect from your sense of justice? " he
asked in a lower voice.

It was the Consul's turn to look away. Then, without lifting his eyes, he made that downward gesture with his hand that always betokened decision; and in a quiet voice, but firmly, he answered:

"In this sad and solemn moment I have offered you my brotherly hand. But if it is your intention to speak of business matters, then I can only reply in my capacity as head of the honourable firm whose sole proprietor I have to-day become. You can expect from me nothing that runs counter to the duties I have to-day assumed; all other feelings must be silent."

Gotthold went away. But he came to the funeral, among the host of relatives, friends, business associates, deputies, clerks, porters, and labourers that filled the house, the stairs, and the corridors to overflowing and assembled all the hired coaches in town in a long row all the way down the Mengstrasse. Gotthold came, to the sincere joy of the Consul. He even brought his wife, born Stüwing, and his three grown daughters: Friederike and Henriette, who were too tall and thin, and Pfiffi, who was eighteen, and too short and fat.

Pastor Kölling of St. Mary's, a heavy man with a bullet head and a rough manner of speaking, held the service at the grave, in the Buddenbrook family burying-ground, outside the Castle Gate, at the edge of the cemetery grove. He extolled the godly, temperate life of the deceased and compared it with that of " gluttons, drunkards, and profligates " — over which strong language some of the congregation shook their heads, thinking of the tact and moderation of their old Pastor Wunderlich, who had lately died. When the service and the burial were over, and the seventy or eighty hired coaches began to roll back to town, Gotthold Buddenbrook asked the Consul's permission to go with him, that they might speak together in private. He sat with his brother on the back seat of the high, ungainly old coach, one short leg crossed over the other — and, wonderful to relate, he was gentle and conciliatory. He realized more and more, he said, that the Consul was bound to act as he was doing; and he was determined to cherish no bitter memories of his father. He renounced the claims he had put forward, the more readily that he had decided to retire from business and live upon his inheritance and what capital he had left; for he had no joy of the linen business, and it was going so indifferently that he could not bring himself to put any more money into it. . . . " His spite against our Father brought him no blessing," the Consul thought piously. Probably Gotthold thought so too.

When they got back, he went with his brother up to the breakfast-room; and as both gentlemen felt rather chilly, after standing so long in their dress-coats in the early spring air, they drank a glass of old cognac together. Then Gotthold exchanged a few courteous words with his sister-in-law, stroked the children's heads, and went away. But he appeared at the next "children's day," which took place at the Krögers', outside the Castle Gate. And he began to wind up his business at once.

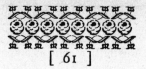

CHAPTER V

It grieved the Consul sorely that the grandfather had not lived to see the entry of his grandson into the business — an event which took place at Easter-time of the same year.

Thomas had left school at sixteen. He was grown strong and sturdy, and his manly clothes made him look still older. He had been confirmed, and Pastor Kölling, in stentorian tones, had enjoined upon him to practise the virtues of moderation. A gold chain, bequeathed him by his grandfather, now hung about his neck, with the family arms on a medallion at the end — a rather dismal design, showing on an irregularly hatched surface a flat stretch of marshy country with one solitary, leafless willow tree. The old seal ring with the green stone, once worn, in all probability, by the well-to-do tailor in Rostock, had descended to the Consul, together with the great Bible.

Thomas's likeness to his grandfather was as strong as Christian's to his father. The firm round chin was the old man's, and the straight, well-chiselled nose. Thomas wore his hair parted on one side, and it receded in two bays from his narrow veined temples. His eyelashes were colourless by contrast, and so were the eyebrows, one of which he had a habit of lifting expressively. His speech, his movements, even his laugh, which showed his rather defective teeth, were all quiet and adequate. He already looked forward seriously and eagerly to his career.

It was indeed a solemn moment when, after early breakfast, the Consul led him down into the office and introduced him to Herr Marcus the confidential clerk, Herr Havermann the cashier, and the rest of the staff, with all of whom, naturally, he had long been on the best of terms. For the first time he sat at his desk, in his own revolving chair, absorbed in copying, stamping, and arranging papers. In the afternoon his father took him through the magazines on the Trave, each one of which had a special name, like the " Linden," the " Oak," the " Lion," the " Whale." Tom was thoroughly at home in every one of them, of course, but now for the first time he entered them to be formally introduced as a fellow worker.

He entered upon his tasks with devotion, imitating the quiet, tenacious industry of his father, who was working with his jaws set, and writing down many a prayer for help in his private diary. For the Consul had set himself the task of making good the sums paid out by the firm on the occasion of his father's death. It was a conception . . . an ideal. . . . He explained the position quite fully to his wife late one evening in the landscape-room.

It was half-past eleven, and Mamsell Jungmann and the children were already asleep in the corridor rooms. No one slept in the second story now — it was empty save for an occasional guest. The Frau Consul sat on the yellow sofa beside her husband, and he, cigar in mouth, was reading the financial columns of the local paper. She bent over her embroidery, moving her lips as she counted a row of stitches with her needle. Six candles burned in a candelabrum on the slender sewing-table beside her, and the chandelier was unlighted.

Johann Buddenbrook was nearing the middle forties, and had visibly altered in the last years. His little round eyes seemed to have sunk deeper in his head, his cheek-bones and his large aquiline nose stood out more prominently than ever, and the ash-blond hair seemed to have been just touched with a powder-puff where it parted on the temples. The Frau Consul was at the end of her thirties, but, while never beautiful, was as brilliant as ever; her dead-white skin, with a single freckle here and there, had lost none of its splendour, and the candle-light shone on the rich red-blond hair that was as wonderfully dressed as ever. Giving her husband a sidelong glance with her clear blue eyes, she said:

"Jean, I wanted to ask you to consider something: if it would not perhaps be advisable to engage a man-servant. I have just been coming to that conclusion. When I think of my parents — "

The Consul let his paper drop on his knee and took his cigar out of his mouth. A shrewd look came into his eyes: here was a question of money to be paid out.

"My dear Betsy," he said — and he spoke as deliberately as possible, to gain time to muster his excuses — "do you think we need a man-servant? Since my parents' death we have kept on all three maids, not counting Mamsell Jungmann. It seems to me — "

"Oh, but the house is so big, Jean. We can hardly get along as it is. I say to Line, 'Line it's a fearfully long time since the rooms in the annexe were dusted'; but I don't like to drive the girls too hard; they have their work cut out to keep everything clean and tidy here in the front. And a man-servant would be so useful for errands and so on. We could find some honest man from the country, who wouldn't expect much. . . . Oh, before I forget it — Louise Möllendorpf is letting her Anton go. I've seen him serve nicely at table."

" To tell you the truth," said the Consul, and shuffled about a little uneasily, " it is a new idea to me. We aren't either entertaining or going out just now — "

" No, but we have visitors very often — for which I am not responsible, Jean, as you know, though of course I am always glad to see them. You have a business friend from somewhere, and you invite him to dinner. Then he has not taken a room at a hotel, so we ask him to stop the night. A missionary comes, and stops the week with us. Week after next, Pastor Mathias is coming from Kannstadt. And the wages amount to so little — "

" But they mount up, Betsy! We have four people here in the house — and think of the pay-roll the firm has! "

" So we really can't afford a man-servant? " the Frau Consul asked. She smiled as she spoke, and looked at her husband with her head on one side. " When I think of all the servants my Father and Mother had — "

" My dear Betsy! Your parents — I really must ask you if you understand our financial position? "

" No, Jean, I must admit I do not. I'm afraid I have only a vague idea — "

" Well, I can tell you in a few words," the Consul said. He sat up straight on the sofa, with one knee crossed over the other, puffed at his cigar, knit his brows a little, and marshalled his figures with wonderful fluency.

" To put it briefly, my Father had, before my sister's marriage, a round sum of nine hundred thousand marks net, not counting, of course, real estate, and the stock and good will of the firm. Eighty thousand went to Frankfort as dowry, and a hundred thousand to set Gotthold up in business. That leaves seven hundred and twenty thousand. The price of this house, reckoning off what we got for the little one in Alf Street, and counting all the improvements and new furnishings, came to a good hundred thousand. That brings it down to six hundred and twenty thousand. Twenty-five thousand to Frankfort, as compensation on the house, leaves five hundred and ninety-five thousand — which is what we should have had at Father's death if we hadn't partly made up for all these expenses through years, by a profit of some two hundred thousand marks current. The entire capital amounted to seven hundred and ninety-five thousand marks, of which another hundred thousand went to Gotthold, and a few thousand marks for the minor legacies that Father left to the Holy Ghost Hospital, the Fund for Tradesmen's Widows, and so on. That brings us down to around four hundred and twenty thousand, or another hundred thousand with your own dowry. There is the position, in round figures, aside from small fluctuations in the capital. You see, my dear Betsy, we are not rich. And while the capital has grown smaller, the running expenses have not; for the whole business is established on a certain scale, which it costs about so much to maintain. Have you followed me? "

The Consul's wife, her needle-work in her lap, nodded with some hesitation. " Quite so, my dear Jean," she said, though she was far from having understood everything, least of all what these big figures had to do with her engaging a man-servant.

The Consul puffed at his cigar till it glowed, threw back his head and blew out the smoke, and then went on:

" You are thinking, of course, that when God calls your dear parents unto Himself, we shall have a considerable sum to look forward to — and so we shall. But we must not reckon too blindly on it. Your Father has had some heavy losses, due, we all know, to your brother Justus. Justus is certainly a charming personality, but business is not his strong point, and he has had bad luck too. According to all accounts he has had to pay up pretty heavily, and transactions with bankers make dear money. Your Father has come to the rescue several times, to prevent a smash. That sort of thing may happen again — to speak frankly, I am afraid it will. You will forgive me, Betsy, for my plain speaking, but you know that the style of living which is so proper and pleasing in your Father is not at all suitable for a business man. Your Father has nothing to do with business any more; but Justus — you know what I mean — he isn't very careful, is he? His ideas are too large, he is too impulsive. And your parents aren't saving anything. They live a lordly life — as their circumstances permit them to."

The Frau Consul smiled forbearingly. She well knew her husband's opinion of the luxurious Kröger tastes.

" That's all," he said, and put his cigar into the ash-receiver. " As far as I'm concerned, I live in the hope that God will preserve my powers unimpaired, and that by His gracious help I may succeed in reëstablishing the firm on its old basis. . . . I hope you see the thing more clearly now, Betsy? "

" Quite, quite, my dear Jean," the Frau Consul hastened to re-

ply; for she had given up the man-servant, for the evening. "Shall
we go to bed? It is very late — "

A few days later, when the Consul came in to dinner in an unusually good mood, they decided at the table to engage the Möllendorpfs' Anton.

CHAPTER VI

"We shall put Tony into Fräulein Weichbrodt's boarding-school," said the Consul. He said it with such decision that so it was.

Thomas was applying himself with talent to the business; Clara was a thriving, lively child; and the appetite of the good Clothilde must have pleased any heart alive. But Tony and Christian were hardly so satisfactory. It was not only that Christian had to stop nearly every afternoon for coffee with Herr Stengel — though even this became at length too much for the Frau Consul, and she sent a dainty missive to the master, summoning him to conference in Meng Street. Herr Stengel appeared in his Sunday wig and his tallest choker, bristling with lead-pencils like lance-heads, and they sat on the sofa in the landscape-room, while Christian hid in the dining-room and listened. The excellent man set out his views, with eloquence if some embarrassment: spoke of the difference between "line" and "dash," told the tale of "The Forest Green" and the scuttle of coals, and made use in every other sentence of the phrase "in consequence." It probably seemed to him a circumlocution suitable to the elegant surroundings in which he found himself. After a while the Consul came and drove Christian away. He expressed to Herr Stengel his lively regret that a son of his should give cause for dissatisfaction. "Oh, Herr Consul, God forbid! Buddenbrook minor has a wide-awake mind, he is a lively chap, and in consequence — Just a little *too* lively, if I might say so; and in consequence —" The Consul politely went with him through the hall to the entry, and Herr Stengel took his leave. . . . Ah, no, this was far from being the worst!

The worst, when it became known, was as follows: Young Christian Buddenbrook had leave one evening to go to the theatre in company with a friend. The performance was Schiller's Wilhelm Tell; and the rôle of Tell's son Walter was played by a young lady, a certain Mademoiselle Meyer-de-la-Grange. Christian's worst, then, had to do with this young person. She wore when on the stage, whether it suited her part or not, a dia-

mond brooch, which was notoriously genuine; for, as everybody knew, it was the gift of young Consul Döhlmann — Peter
Döhlmann, son of the deceased wholesale dealer in Wall Street outside Holsten Gate. Consul Peter, like Justus Kröger, belonged to
the group of young men whom the town called " fast." His way of
life, that is to say, was rather loose! He had married, and had one
child, a little daughter; but he had long ago quarrelled with his
wife, and he led the life of a bachelor. His father had left him a
considerable inheritance, and he carried on the business, after a
fashion; but people said he was already living on his capital. He
lived mostly at the Club or the Rathskeller, was often to be met
somewhere in the street at four o'clock in the morning; and made
frequent business trips to Hamburg. Above all, he was a zealous
patron of the drama, and took a strong personal interest in the
caste. Mademoiselle Meyer-de-la-Grange was the latest of a line
of young ladies whom he had, in the past, distinguished by a gift
of diamonds.

Well, to arrive at the point, this young lady looked so charming
as Walter Tell, wore her brooch and spoke her lines with such effect, that Christian felt his heart swell with enthusiasm, and tears
rose to his eyes. He was moved by his transports to a course that
only the very violence of emotion could pursue. He ran during the
entr'acte to a flower-shop opposite, where, for the sum of one mark
eight and a half shillings, he got at a bargain a bunch of flowers;
and then this fourteen-year-old sprat, with his big nose and his
deep-lying eyes, took his way to the green-room, since nobody
stopped him, and came upon Fräulein Meyer-de-la-Grange, talking with Consul Peter Döhlmann at her dressing-room door. Peter
Döhlmann nearly fell over with laughing when he saw Christian
with the bouquet. But the new wooer, with a solemn face, bowed
in his best manner before Walter Tell, handed her the bouquet,
and, nodding his head, said in a voice of well-nigh tearful conviction: " Ah, Fräulein, how *beautifully* you act! "

" Well, hang me if it ain't Krishan Buddenbrook! " Consul Döhlmann cried out, in his broadest accent. Fräulein Meyer-de-la-
Grange lifted her pretty brows and asked: " The son of Consul
Buddenbrook? " And she stroked the cheek of her young admirer
with all the favour in the world.

Such was the story that Consul Peter Döhlmann told at the
Club that night; it flew about the town like lightning, and reached
the ears of the head master, who asked for an audience with Consul
Buddenbrook. And how did the Father take this affair? He was,
in truth, less angry than overwhelmed. He sat almost like a

broken man, after telling the Frau Consul the story in the landscape-room.

"And this is our son," he said. "So is he growing up — "

"But Jean! Good heavens, your Father would have laughed at
it. Tell it to my Father and Mother on Thursday — you will
see how Papa will enjoy it — "

But here the Consul rose up in anger. "Ah, yes, yes! I am sure
he will enjoy it, Betsy. He will be glad to know that his light blood
and impious desires live on, not only in a rake like Justus, his own
son, but also in a grandson of his as well! Good God, you drive
me to say these things! — He goes to this — person; he spends his
pocket-money on flowers for this — *lorette!* I don't say he knows
what he is doing — yet. But the inclination shows itself — it shows
itself, Betsy! "

Ah, yes, this was all very painful indeed. The Consul was perhaps the more beside himself for the added reason that Tony's behaviour, too, had not been of the best. She had given up, it is true,
shouting at the nervous stranger to make him dance; and she no
longer rang the doorbell of the tiny old woman who sold worsted
dolls. But she threw back her head more pertly than ever, and
showed, especially after the summer visits with her grandparents,
a very strong tendency to vanity and arrogance of spirit.

One day the Consul surprised her and Mamsell Jungmann reading together. The book was Clauren's "Mimili"; the Consul
turned over some of the leaves, and then silently closed it — and it
was opened no more. Soon afterward it came to light that Tony —
Antonie Buddenbrook, no less a person — had been seen walking
outside the City wall with a young student, a friend of her brother.
Frau Stuht, she who moved in the best circles, had seen the pair,
and had remarked at the Möllendorpfs', whither she had gone to
buy some cast-off clothing, that really Mademoiselle Buddenbrook
was getting to the age where — And Frau Senator Möllendorpf
had lightly repeated the story to the Consul. The pleasant strolls
came to an end. Later it came out that Fräulein Antonie had made
a post-office of the old hollow tree that stood near the Castle Gate,
and not only posted therein letters addressed to the same student,
but received letters from him as well by that means. When these
facts came to light, they seemed to indicate the need of a more
watchful oversight over the young lady, now fifteen years old; and
she was accordingly, as we have already said, sent to boarding-
school at Fräulein Weichbrodt's, Number seven, Millbank.

CHAPTER VII

THERESE WEICHBRODT was humpbacked. So humpbacked that she was not much higher than a table. She was forty-one years old. But as she had never put her faith in outward seeming, she dressed like an old lady of sixty or seventy. Upon her padded grey locks rested a cap the green ribbons of which fell down over shoulders narrow as a child's. Nothing like an ornament ever graced her shabby black frock — only the large oval brooch with her mother's miniature in it.

Little Miss Weichbrodt had shrewd, sharp brown eyes, a slightly hooked nose, and thin lips which she could compress with extraordinary firmness. In her whole insignificant figure, in her every movement, there indwelt a force which was, to be sure, somewhat comic, yet exacted respect. And her mode of speech helped to heighten the effect. She spoke with brisk, jerky motions of the lower jaw and quick, emphatic nods. She used no dialect, but enunciated clearly and with precision, stressing the consonants. Vowel-sounds, however, she exaggerated so much that she said, for instance, " botter " instead of " butter " — or even " batter! " Her little dog that was forever yelping she called Babby instead of Bobby. She would say to a pupil: " Don-n't be so stu-upid, child," and give two quick knocks on the table with her knuckle. It was very impressive — no doubt whatever about that! And when Mlle. Popinet, the Frenchwoman, took too much sugar to her coffee, Miss Weichbrodt had a way of gazing at the ceiling and drumming on the cloth with one hand while she said: " Why not take the who-ole sugar-basin? I would! " It always made Mlle. Popinet redden furiously.

As a child — heavens, what a tiny child she must have been! — Therese Weichbrodt had given herself the nickname of Sesemi, and she still kept it, even letting the best and most favoured of the day- as well as of the boarding-pupils use it. " Call me Sesemi, child," she said on the first day to Tony Buddenbrook, kissing her briefly, with a sound as of a small explosion, on the forehead. " I like it." Her elder sister, however, Madame Kethelsen, was called Nelly.

Madame Kethelsen was about forty-eight years old. She had been left penniless when her husband died, and now lived in a little upstairs bedroom in her sister's house. She dressed like Sesemi, but by contrast was very tall. She wore woollen wristlets on her thin wrists. She was not a mistress, and knew nothing of discipline. A sort of inoffensive and placid cheerfulness was all her being. When one of the pupils played a prank, she would laugh so heartily that she nearly cried, and then Sesemi would rap on the table and call out " Nelly! " very sharply — it sounded like " Nally " — and Madame Kethelsen would shrink into herself and be mute.

Madame Kethelsen obeyed her younger sister, who scolded her as if she were a child. Sesemi, in fact, despised her warmly. Therese Weichbrodt was a well-read, almost a literary woman. She struggled endlessly to keep her childhood faith, her religious assurance that somewhere in the beyond she was to be recompensed for the hard, dull present. But Madame Kethelsen, innocent, uninstructed, was all simplicity of nature. " Dear, good Nelly, what a child she is! She never doubts or struggles, she is always happy." In such remarks there was always as much contempt as envy. Contempt was a weakness of Sesemi's — perhaps a pardonable one.

The small red-brick suburban house was surrounded by a neatly kept garden. Its lofty ground floor was entirely taken up by schoolrooms and dining-room; the bedrooms were in the upper story and the attic. Miss Weichbrodt did not have a large number of pupils. As boarders she received only older girls, while the day-school consisted of but three classes, the lowest ones. Sesemi took care to have only the daughters of irreproachably refined families in her house. Tony Buddenbrook, as we have seen, she welcomed most tenderly. She even made " bishop " for supper — a sort of sweet red punch to be taken cold, in the making of which she was a past mistress. " A little more beeshop," she urged with a hearty nod. It sounded so tempting; nobody could resist!

Fräulein Weichbrodt sat on two sofa-cushions at the top of the table and presided over the meal with tact and discretion. She held her stunted figure stiffly erect, tapped vigilantly on the table, cried " Nally " or " Babby," and subdued Mlle. Popinet with a glance whenever the latter seemed about to take unto herself all the cold veal jelly. Tony had been allotted a place between two other boarders, Armgard von Schilling, the strapping blond daughter of a Mecklenburg landowner, and Gerda Arnoldsen, whose home was in Amsterdam — an unusual, elegant figure, with dark red hair, brown eyes close together, and a lovely, pale, haughty face. Opposite her sat a chattering French girl who looked like a negress, with huge gold earrings. The lean English Miss Brown, with her sourish smile, sat at the bottom of the table. She was a boarder too.

It was not hard, with the help of Sesemi's bishop, to get acquainted. Mlle. Popinet had had nightmares again last night — *ah, quel horreur!* She usually screamed " Help, thieves; help, thieves! " until everybody jumped out of bed. Next, it appeared that Gerda Arnoldsen did not take piano like the rest of them, but the violin, and that Papa — her Mother was dead — had promised her a real Stradivarius. Tony was not musical — hardly any of the Buddenbrooks and none of the Krögers were. She could not even recognize the chorals they played at St. Mary's. — Oh, the organ in the new Church at Amsterdam had a *vox humana* — a human voice — that was just wonderful. Armgard von Schilling talked about the cows at home.

It was Armgard who from the earliest moment had made a great impression on Tony. She was the first person from a noble family whom Tony had ever known. What luck, to be called *von* Schilling! Her own parents had the most beautiful old house in the town, and her grandparents belonged to the best families; still, they were called plain Buddenbrook and Kröger — which was a pity, to be sure. The granddaughter of the proud Lebrecht Kröger glowed with reverence for Armgard's noble birth. Privately, she sometimes thought that the splendid " von " went with her better than it did with Armgard; for Armgard did not appreciate her good luck, dear, no! She had a thick pigtail, good-natured blue eyes, and a broad Mecklenburg accent, and went about thinking just nothing at all on the subject. She made absolutely no pretensions to being aristocratic; in fact, she did not know what it was. But the word " aristocratic " stuck in Tony's small head; and she emphatically applied it to Gerda Arnoldsen.

Gerda was rather exclusive, and had something foreign and queer about her. She liked to do up her splendid red hair in striking ways, despite Sesemi's protests. Some of the girls thought it was " silly " of her to play the violin instead of the piano — and, be it known, " silly " was a term of very severe condemnation. Still, the girls mostly agreed with Tony that Gerda was artistocratic — in her figure, well-developed for her years; in her ways, her small possessions, everything. There was the ivory toilet set from Paris, for instance; that Tony could appreciate, for her own parents and grandparents also had treasures which had been brought from Paris.

The three girls soon made friends. They were in the same class

and slept together in the same large room at the top of the house.
What delightful, cosy times they had going to bed! They gossiped
while they undressed — in undertones, however, for it was ten
o'clock and next door Mlle. Popinet had gone to bed to dream of
burglars. Eva Ewers slept with her. Eva was a little Hamburger,
whose father, an amateur painter and collector, had settled in
Munich.

The striped brown blinds were down, the low, red-shaded lamp
burned on the table, there was a faint smell of violets and fresh
wash, and a delicious atmosphere of laziness and dreams.

" Heavens," said Armgard, half undressed, sitting on her bed,
" how Dr. Newmann can talk! He comes into the class and stands
by the table and tells about Racine — "

" He has a lovely high forehead," remarked Gerda, standing before the mirror between the windows and combing her hair by the
light of two candles.

" Oh, yes, hasn't he? " Armgard said eagerly.

" And you are taking the course just on his account, Armgard;
you gaze at him all the time with your blue eyes, as if — "

" Are you in love with him? " asked Tony. " I can't undo my
shoe-lace; please, Gerda. Thanks. Why don't you marry him?
He is a good match — he will get to be a High School Professor."

" I think you are both horrid. I'm not in love with him, and I
would not marry a teacher, anyhow. I shall marry a country
gentleman."

" A nobleman? " Tony dropped her stocking and looked
thoughtfully into Armgard's face.

" I don't know, yet. But he must have a large estate. Oh, girls,
I just love that sort of thing! I shall get up at five o'clock every
morning, and attend to everything. . . ." She pulled up the bed-
covers and stared dreamily at the ceiling.

" Five hundred cows are before your mind's eye," said Gerda,
looking at her in the mirror.

Tony was not ready yet; but she let her head fall on the pillow,
tucked her hands behind her neck, and gazed dreamily at the ceiling in her turn.

" Of course," she said, " I shall marry a business man. He must
have a lot of money, so we can furnish elegantly. I owe that to my
family and the firm," she added earnestly. " Yes, you'll see, that's
what I shall do."

Gerda had finished her hair for the night and was brushing her
big white teeth, using the ivory-backed hand-mirror to see them
better.

" I shall *probably* not marry at all," she said, speaking with some difficulty on account of the tooth-powder. " I don't see why I should. I am not anxious. I'll go back to Amsterdam and play duets with Daddy and afterwards live with my married sister."

" What a pity," Tony said briskly. " What a pity! You ought to marry here and stay here for always. Listen: you could marry one of my brothers — "

" The one with the big nose? " asked Gerda, and gave a dainty little yawn, holding the hand-mirror before her face.

" Or the other; it doesn't matter. You could furnish beautifully. Jacobs could do it — the upholsterer in Fish Street. He has lovely taste. I'd come to see you every day — "

But then there came the voice of Mlle. Popinet. It said: " Oh, mesdemoiselles! Please go to bed. It is too late to get married any more this evening! "

Sundays and holidays Tony spent in Meng Street or outside the town with her grandparents. How lovely, when it was fine on Easter Sunday, hunting for eggs and marzipan hares in the enormous Kröger garden! Then there were the summer holidays at the seashore; they lived in the Kurhouse, ate at the table-d'hôte, bathed, and went donkey-riding. Some seasons when the Consul had business, there were long journeys. But Christmases were best of all. There were three present-givings: at home, at the grandparents', and at Sesemi's, where bishop flowed in streams. The one at home was the grandest, for the Consul believed in keeping the holy feast with pomp and ceremony. They gathered in the landscape-room with due solemnity. The servants and the crowd of poor people thronged into the pillared hall, where the Consul went about shaking their purple hands. Then outside rose the voices of the choir-boys from St. Mary's in a quartette, and one's heart beat loudly with awe and expectation. The smell of the Christmas tree was already coming through the crack in the great white folding doors; and the Frau Consul took the old family Bible with the funny big letters, and slowly read aloud the Christmas chapter; and after the choir-boys had sung another carol, everybody joined in " O Tannenbaum " and went in solemn procession through the hall into the great salon, hung with tapestries that had statuary woven into them. There the tree rose to the ceiling, decorated with white lilies, twinkling and sparkling and pouring out light and fragrance; and the table with the presents on it stretched from the windows to the door. Outside, the Italians with the barrel-organ were making music in the frozen, snowy streets, and a great hubbub came over from the Christmas market in Market

Square. All the children except little Clara stopped up to late supper in the salon, and there were mountains of carp and stuffed
turkey.

In these years Tony Buddenbrook visited two Mecklenburg
estates. She stopped for two weeks one summer with her friend
Armgard, on Herr von Schilling's property, which lay on the coast
across the bay from Travemünde. And another time she went
with Cousin Tilda to a place where Bernard Buddenbrook was
inspector. This estate was called " Thankless," because it did not
bring in a penny's income; but for a summer holiday it was not to
be despised.

Thus the years went on. It was, take it all in all, a happy youth
for Tony.

PART THREE

CHAPTER I

On a June afternoon, not long after five o'clock, the family were sitting before the " portal " in the garden, where they had drunk coffee. They had pulled the rustic furniture outside, for it was too close in the white-washed garden house, with its tall mirror decorated with painted birds and its varnished folding doors, which were really not folding doors at all and had only painted latches.

The Consul, his wife, Tony, Tom, and Clothilde sat in a half-circle around the table, which was laid with its usual shining service. Christian, sitting a little to one side, conned the second oration of Cicero against Catiline. He looked unhappy. The Consul smoked his cigar and read the *Advertiser*. His wife had let her embroidery fall into her lap and sat smiling at little Clara; the child, with Ida Jungmann, was looking for violets in the grass-plot. Tony, her head propped on both hands, was deep in Hoffman's " Serapion Brethren," while Tom tickled her in the back of the neck with a grass-blade, an attention which she very wisely ignored. And Clothilde, looking thin and old-maidish in her flowered cotton frock, was reading a story called " Blind, Deaf, Dumb, and Still Happy." As she read, she scraped up the biscuit-crumbs carefully with all five fingers from the cloth and ate them.

A few white clouds stood motionless in the slowly paling sky. The small town garden, with its carefully laid-out paths and beds, looked gay and tidy in the afternoon sun. The scent of the mignonette borders floated up now and then.

" Well, Tom," said the Consul expansively, and took the cigar out of his mouth, " we are arranging that rye sale I told you about, with van Henkdom and Company."

" What is he giving? " Tom asked with interest, ceasing to tickle Tony.

" Sixty thaler for a thousand kilo — not bad, eh? "

" That's very good." Tom knew this was excellent business.

" Tony, your position is not *comme il faut*," remarked the Frau Consul. Whereat Tony, without raising her eyes from her book, took one elbow off the table.

" Never mind," Tom said. " She can sit how she likes, she will always be Tony Buddenbrook. Tilda and she are certainly the beauties of the family."

Clothilde was astonished almost to death. "Good gracious, Tom," she said. It was inconceivable how she could drawl out the syllables. Tony bore the jeer in silence. It was never any use, Tom was more than a match for her. He could always get the last word and have the laugh on his side. Her nostrils dilated a little, and she shrugged her shoulders. But when the Consul's wife began to talk of the coming dance at the house of Consul Huneus, and let fall something about new patent leather shoes, Tony took the other elbow off the table and displayed a lively interest.

"You keep talking and talking," complained Christian fretfully, "and I'm having such a hard time. I wish I were a business man."

"Yes, you're always wanting something different," said Tom. Anton came across the garden with a card on his tray. They all looked at him expectantly.

"Grünlich, Agent," read the Consul. "He is from Hamburg —an agreeable man, and well recommended, the son of a clergyman. I have business dealings with him. There is a piece of business now. — Is it all right, Betsy, if I ask him to come out here? "

A middle-sized man, his head thrust a little forward of his body, carrying his hat and stick in one hand, came across the garden. He was some two-and-thirty years old; he wore a fuzzy greenish-yellow suit with a long-skirted coat, and grey worsted gloves. His face, beneath the sparse light hair, was rosy and smiling; but there was an undeniable wart on one side of his nose. His chin and upper lip were smooth-shaven; he wore long, drooping side-whiskers, in the English fashion, and these adornments were conspicuously golden-yellow in colour. Even at a distance, he began making obsequious gestures with his broad-brimmed grey hat, and as he drew near he took one last very long step, and arrived describing a half-circle with the upper part of his body, by this means bowing to them all at once.

"I am afraid I am disturbing the family circle," he said in a soft voice, with the utmost delicacy of manner. "You are conversing, you are indulging in literary pursuits — I must really beg your pardon for my intrusion."

"By no means, my dear Herr Grünlich," said the Consul. He and his sons got up and shook hands with the stranger. "You are very welcome. I am delighted to see you outside the office and in my family circle. Herr Grünlich, Betsy — a friend of mine and a keen man of business. This is my daughter Antonie, and my niece

Clothilde. Thomas you know already, and this is my second son,
Christian, in High School." Herr Grünlich responded to each
name with an inclination of the body.

"I must repeat," he said, "that I have no desire to intrude. I
came on business. If the Herr Consul would be so good as to take
a walk with me round the gardens —" The Consul's wife answered: "It will give us pleasure to have you sit down with us for
a little before you begin to talk business with my husband. Do
sit down."

"A thousand thanks," said Herr Grünlich, apparently quite
flattered. He sat down on the edge of the chair which Tom
brought, laid his hat and stick on his knees, and settled himself,
running his hand over his long beard with a little hemming and
hawing, as if to say, "Well, now we've got past the introduction
— what next?"

The Frau Consul began the conversation. "You live in Hamburg?" she asked, inclining her head and letting her work fall
into her lap.

"Yes, Frau Consul," responded Herr Grünlich with a fresh
bow. "At least, my house is in Hamburg, but I am on the road a
good deal. My business is very flourishing — ahem — if I may be
permitted to say so."

The Frau Consul lifted her eyebrows and made respectful motions with her mouth, as if she were saying "Ah — indeed?"

"Ceaseless activity is a condition of my being," added he, half
turning to the Consul. He coughed again as he noticed that
Fräulein Antonie's glance rested upon him. She gave him, in fact,
the cold, calculating stare with which a maiden measures a strange
young man — a stare which seems always on the point of passing
over into actual contempt.

"We have relatives in Hamburg," said she, in order to be saying something.

"The Duchamps," explained the Consul. "The family of my
late Mother."

"Oh, yes," Herr Grünlich hastened to say. "I have the honour
of a slight acquaintance with the family. They are very fine people, in mind and heart. Ahem! This would be a better world if
there were more families like them in it. They have religion,
benevolence, and genuine piety; in short, they are my ideal of the
true Christlike spirit. And in them it is united to a rare degree
with a brilliant cosmopolitanism, an elegance, an aristocratic bearing, which I find most attractive, Frau Consul."

Tony thought: "How can he know my Father and Mother so

well? He is saying exactly what they like best to hear." The Consul responded approvingly, "The combination is one that is becoming in everybody." And the Frau Consul could not resist stretching out her hand to their guest with her sweeping gesture, palm upward, while the bracelets gave a little jingle. "You speak as though you read my inmost thoughts, dear Herr Grünlich," she said.

Upon which, Herr Grünlich made another deep bow, settled himself again, stroked his beard, and coughed as if to say: "Well, let us get on."

The Frau Consul mentioned the disastrous fire which had swept Hamburg in May of the year 1842. "Yes, indeed," said Herr Grünlich, "truly a fearful misfortune. A distressing visitation. The loss amounted to one hundred and thirty-five millions, at a rough estimate. I am grateful to Providence that I came off without any loss whatever. The fire raged chiefly in the parishes of St. Peter and St. Nicholas. — What a charming garden!" he interrupted himself, taking the cigar which the Consul offered. "It is so large for a town garden, and the beds of colour are magnificent. I confess my weakness for flowers, and for nature in general. Those climbing roses over there trim up the garden uncommonly well." He went on, praising the refinement of the location, praising the town itself, praising the Consul's cigar. He had a pleasant word for each member of the circle.

"May I venture to inquire what you are reading, Fräulein Antonie?" he said smiling.

Tony drew her brows together sharply at this, for some reason, and answered without looking at him, "Hoffmann's 'Serapion Brethren.'"

"Really! He is a wonderful writer, is he not? Ah, pardon me — I forgot the name of your younger son, Frau Consul?"

"Christian."

"A beautiful name. If I may so express myself" — here he turned again to the Consul — "I like best the names which show that the bearer is a Christian. The name of Johann, I know, is hereditary in your family — a name which always recalls the beloved disciple. My own name — if I may be permitted to mention it," he continued, waxing eloquent, "is that of most of my forefathers — Bendix. It can only be regarded as a shortened form of Benedict. And you, Herr Buddenbrook, are reading — ? ah, Cicero. The works of this great Roman orator make pretty difficult reading, eh? 'Quousque tandem — Catilina' . . . ahem. Oh, I have not forgotten quite all my Latin."

" I disagree with my late Father on this point," the Consul said.
" I have always objected to the perpetual occupation of young
heads with Greek and Latin. When there are so many other important subjects, necessary as a preparation for the practical affairs
of life — "

" You take the words out of my mouth," Herr Grünlich hastened to say. " It is hard reading, and not by any means always
unexceptionable — I forgot to mention that point. Everything else
aside, I can recall passages that were positively offensive — "

There came a pause, and Tony thought " Now it's my turn."
Herr Grünlich had turned his gaze upon her. And, sure enough:
he suddenly started in his chair, made a spasmodic but always
highly elegant gesture toward the Frau Consul and whispered
ardently, " Pray look, Frau Consul, I beg of you. — Fräulein, I
implore you," he interrupted himself aloud, just as if Tony could
not hear the rest of what he said, " to keep in that same position
for just a moment. Do you see," he began whispering again, " how
the sunshine is playing in your daughter's hair? Never," he said
solemnly, as if transported, speaking to nobody in particular,
" have I seen more beautiful hair." It was as if he were addressing
his remarks to God or to his own soul.

The Consul's wife smiled, well pleased. The Consul said,
" Don't be putting notions into the girl's head." And again Tony
drew her brows together without speaking. After a short pause,
Herr Grünlich got up.

" But I won't disturb you any longer now — no, Frau Consul,
I refuse to disturb you any longer," he repeated. " I only came
on business, but I could not resist — indeed, who could resist you?
Now duty calls. May I ask the Consul — "

" I hope I do not need to assure you that it would give us
pleasure if you would let us put you up while you are here," said
the Frau Consul. Herr Grünlich appeared for the moment struck
dumb with gratitude. " From my soul I am grateful, Frau Consul,"
he said, and his look was indeed eloquent with emotion. " But I
must not abuse your kindness. I have a couple of rooms at the
City of Hamburg — "

" A *couple* of rooms," thought the Frau Consul — which was
just what Herr Grünlich meant her to think.

" And, in any case," he said, as she offered her hand cordially,
" I hope we have not seen each other for the last time." He kissed
her hand, waited a moment for Antonie to extend hers — which
she did not do — described another half-circle with his upper torso,
made a long step backward and another bow, threw back his head

and put his hat on with a flourish, then walked away in company
with the Consul.

"A pleasant man," the Father said later, when he came back and
took his place again.

"I think he's silly," Tony permitted herself to remark with
some emphasis.

"Tony! Heavens and earth, what an idea!" said the Consul's
wife, displeased. "Such a Christian young man!"

"So well brought up, and so cosmopolitan," went on the Consul.
"You don't know what you are talking about." He and his wife
had a way of taking each other's side like this, out of sheer politeness. It made them the more likely to agree.

Christian wrinkled up his long nose and said, "He was so important. 'You are conversing'—when we weren't at all. And the
roses over there 'trim things up uncommonly.' He acted some of
the time as if he were talking to himself. 'I am disturbing you'—
'I beg pardon'—'I have never seen more beautiful hair.'" Christian mocked Herr Grünlich so cleverly that they all had to laugh,
even the Consul.

"Yes, he gave himself too many airs," Tony went on. "He
talked the whole time about himself—*his* business is good, and *he*
is fond of nature, and *he* likes such-and-such names, and *his* name
is Bendix—what is all that to us, I'd like to know? Everything he
said was just to spread himself." Her voice was growing louder
all the time with vexation. "He said all the very things you like
to hear, Mamma and Papa, and he said them just to make a fine
impression on you both."

"That is no reproach, Tony," the Consul said sternly. "Everybody puts his best foot foremost before strangers. We all take
care to say what will be pleasant to hear. That is a commonplace."

"I think he is a good man," Clothilde pronounced with drawling serenity—she was the only person in the circle about whom
Herr Grünlich had not troubled himself at all. Thomas refrained
from giving an opinion.

"Enough," concluded the Consul. "He is a capable, cultured,
and energetic Christian man, and you, Tony, should try to bridle
your tongue—a great girl of eighteen or nineteen years old, like
you! And after he was so polite and gallant to you, too. We are
all weak creatures; and you, let me say, are one of the last to have
a right to throw stones. Tom, we'll get to work."

Pert little Tony muttered to herself "A golden goat's beard!"
and scowled as before.

CHAPTER II

TONY, coming back from a walk some days later, met Herr Grünlich at the corner of Meng Street. "I was most grieved to have missed you, Fräulein," he said. "I took the liberty of paying my respects to your Mother the other day, and I regretted your absence more than I can say. How delightful that I should meet you like this!"

Fräulein Buddenbrook had paused as he began to speak; but her half-shut eyes looked no further up than the height of Herr Grünlich's chest. On her lips rested the mocking, merciless smile with which a young girl measures and rejects a man. Her lips moved — what should she say? It must be something that would demolish this Herr Bendix Grünlich once and for all — simply annihilate him. It must be clever, witty, and effective, must at one and the same time wound him to the quick and impress him tremendously.

"The pleasure is not mutual, Herr Grünlich," said she, keeping her gaze meanwhile levelled at his chest. And after she had shot this poisoned arrow, she left him standing there and went home, her head in the air, her face red with pride in her own powers of repartee — to learn that Herr Grünlich had been invited to dinner next Sunday.

And he came. He came in a not quite new-fashioned, rather wrinkled, but still handsome bell-shaped frock coat which gave him a solid, respectable look. He was rosy and smiling, his scant hair carefully parted, his whiskers curled and scented. He ate a ragout of shell-fish, julienne soup, fried soles, roast veal with creamed potatoes and cauliflower, maraschino pudding, and pumpernickel with roquefort; and he found a fresh and delicate compliment for each fresh course. Over the sweet he lifted his dessert-spoon, gazed at one of the tapestry statues, and spoke aloud to himself, thus: "God forgive me, I have eaten far too well already. But this pudding — ! It is *too* wonderful! I must beg my good hostess for another slice." And he looked roguishly at the Consul's wife. With the Consul he talked business and politics, and spoke soundly and weightily. He discussed the theatre and

the fashions with the Frau Consul, and he had a good word for
Tom and Christian and Clothilde, and even for little Clara and
Ida Jungmann. Tony sat in silence, and she did not undertake to
engage her; only gazing at her now and then, with his head a little
tilted, his face looking dejected and encouraged by turns.

When Herr Grünlich took his leave that evening, he had only
strengthened the impressions left by his first visit. "A thoroughly
well-bred man," said the Frau Consul. "An estimable Christian
gentleman," was the Consul's opinion. Christian imitated his
speech and actions even better than before; and Tony said her
good nights to them all with a frowning brow, for something told
her that she had not yet seen the last of this gentleman who had
won the hearts of her parents with such astonishing ease and
rapidity.

And, sure enough, coming back one afternoon from a visit with
some girl friends, she found Herr Grünlich cosily established in
the landscape-room, reading aloud to the Frau Consul out of Sir
Walter Scott's "Waverley." His pronunciation was perfect, for,
as he explained, his business trips had taken him to England. Tony
sat down apart with another book, and Herr Grünlich softly
questioned: "Our book is not to your taste, Fräulein?" To which
she replied, with her head in the air, something in a sarcastic vein,
like "Not in the very least."

But he was not taken aback. He began to talk about his long-
dead parents and communicated the fact that his father had been a
clergyman, a Christian, and at the same time a highly cosmopolitan
gentleman. — After this visit, he departed for Hamburg. Tony
was not there when he called to take leave. "Ida," she said to
Mamsell Jungmann, "Ida, the man has gone." But Mamsell Jungmann only replied, "You'll see, child."

And eight days later, in fact, came that scene in the breakfast
room. Tony came down at nine o'clock and found her father and
mother still at table. She let her forehead be kissed and sat down,
fresh and hungry, her eyes still red with sleep, and helped herself
to sugar, butter, and herb cheese.

"How nice to find you still here, for once, Papa," she said as
she held her egg in her napkin and opened it with her spoon.

"But to-day I have been waiting for our slug-a-bed," said the
Consul. He was smoking and tapping on the table with his folded
newspaper. His wife finished her breakfast with her slow, graceful motions, and leaned back in the sofa.

"Tilda is already busy in the kitchen," went on the Consul,
" and I should have been long since at work myself, if your Mother

and I had not been speaking seriously about a matter that concerns our little daughter."

Tony, her mouth full of bread and butter, looked first at her father and then her mother, with a mixture of fear and curiosity. "Eat your breakfast, my child," said the Frau Consul. But Tony laid down her knife and cried, "Out with it quickly, Papa — please." Her father only answered: "Eat your breakfast first."

So Tony drank her coffee and ate her egg and bread and cheese silently, her appetite quite gone. She began to guess. The fresh morning bloom disappeared from her cheek, and she even grew a little pale. She said "Thank you" for the honey, and soon after announced in a subdued voice that she had finished.

"My dear child," said the Consul, "the matter we desire to talk over with you is contained in this letter." He was tapping the table now with a big blue envelope instead of the newspaper. "To be brief: Bendix Grünlich, whom we have learned, during his short stay here, to regard as a good and a charming man, writes to me that he has conceived a strong inclination for our daughter, and he here makes a request in form for her hand. What does my child say?"

Tony was leaning back in her seat, her head bent, her right hand slowly twirling the silver napkin-ring round and round. But suddenly she looked up, and her eyes had grown quite dark with tears. She said, her voice full of distress: "What does this man want of me? What have I done to him?" And she burst into weeping.

The Consul shot a glance at his wife and then regarded his empty cup, embarrassed.

"Tony dear," said the Frau Consul gently, "why this — *échauffement?* You know quite well your parents can only desire your good. And they cannot counsel you to reject forthwith the position offered you. I know you feel so far no particular inclination for Herr Grünlich, but that will come; I assure you it comes, with time. Such a young thing as you is never sure what she wants. The mind is as confused as the heart. One must just give the heart time — and keep the mind open to the advice of experienced people who think and plan only for our good."

"I don't know him the least little bit," Tony said in a dejected tone, wiping her eyes on the little white batiste serviette, stained with egg. "All I know is, he has a yellow beard, like a goat's, and a flourishing business — " Her upper lip, trembling on the verge of tears, had an expression that was indescribably touching.

With a movement of sudden tenderness the Consul jerked his chair nearer hers and stroked her hair, smiling.

"My little Tony, what should you like to know of him? You are still a very young girl, you know. You would know him no better if he had been here for fifty-two weeks instead of four. You are a child, with no eyes yet for the world, and you must trust other people who mean well by you."

"I don't understand — I don't understand," Tony sobbed help-lessly, and put down her head as a kitten does beneath the hand that strokes it. "He comes here and says something pleasant to everybody, and then goes away again; and then he writes to you that he — that I — I don't understand. What made him? What have I done to him?"

The Consul smiled again. "You said that once before, Tony; and it illustrates so well your childish way of reasoning. My little daughter must not feel that people mean to urge or torment her. We can consider it all very quietly; in fact, we must consider it all very quietly and calmly, for it is a very serious matter. Mean-while I will write an answer to Herr Grünlich's letter, without either consenting or refusing. There is much to be thought of. — Well, is that agreed? What do you say? — And now Papa can go back to his work, can't he? — Adieu, Betsy."

"Au revoir, dear Jean."

"Do take a little more honey, Tony," said the Frau Consul to her daughter, who sat in her place motionless, with her head bent. "One must eat."

Tony's tears gradually dried. Her head felt hot and heavy with her thoughts. Good gracious, what a business! She had always known, of course, that she should one day marry, and be the wife of a business man, and embark upon a solid and advantageous mar-ried life, commensurate with the position of the family and the firm. But suddenly, for the first time in her life, somebody, some actual person, in serious earnest, wanted to marry her. How did people act? To her, her, Tony Buddenbrook, were now applica-ble all those tremendous words and phrases which she had hitherto met with only in books: her "hand," her "consent," "as long as life shall last!" Goodness gracious, what a step to take, all at once!

"And you, Mamma? Do you too advise me to — to — to yield my consent?" She hesitated a little before the "yield my con-sent." It sounded high-flown and awkward. But then, this was the first occasion in her life that was worthy of fine language. She began to blush for her earlier lack of self-control. It seemed to her now not less unreasonable than it had ten minutes ago that she should marry Herr Grünlich; but the dignity of her situation began to fill her with a sense of importance which was satisfying indeed.

"*I* advise you to accept, my child? Has Papa advised you to do so? He has only not advised you not to, that is all. It would be very irresponsible of either of us to do that. The connection offered you is a very good one, my dear Tony. You would go to Hamburg on an excellent footing and live there in great style."

Tony sat motionless. She was having a sort of vision of silk portières, like those in grandfather's salon. And, as Madame Grünlich, should she drink morning chocolate? She thought it would not be seemly to ask.

"As your Father says, you have time to consider," the Frau Consul continued. "But we are obliged to tell you that such an offer does not come every day, that it would make your fortune, and that it is exactly the marriage which duty and vocation prescribe. This, my child, it is my business to tell you. You know yourself that the path which opens before you to-day is the prescribed one which your life ought to follow."

"Yes," Tony said thoughtfully. She was well aware of her responsibilities toward the family and the firm, and she was proud of them. She was saturated with her family history — she, Tony Buddenbrook, who, as the daughter of Consul Buddenbrook, went about the town like a little queen, before whom Matthiesen the porter took off his hat and made a low bow! The Rostock tailor had been very well off, to begin with; but since his time, the family fortunes had advanced by leaps and bounds. It was her vocation to enhance the brilliance of family and firm in her allotted way, by making a rich and aristocratic marriage. To the same end, Tom worked in the office. Yes, the marriage was undoubtedly precisely the right one. But — but — She saw him before her, saw his gold-yellow whiskers, his rosy, smiling face, the wart on his nose, his mincing walk. She could feel his woolly suit, hear his soft voice. . . .

"I felt sure," the Consul's wife said, "that we were accessible to quiet reason. Have we perhaps already made up our mind? "

"Oh, goodness, *no!* " cried Tony, suddenly. She uttered the "Oh" with an outburst of irritation. "What nonsense! Why should I marry him? I have always made fun of him. I never did anything else. I can't understand how he can possibly endure me. The man must have some sort of pride in his bones! " She began to drip honey upon a slice of bread.

CHAPTER III

THIS year the Buddenbrooks took no holiday during Christian's and Clara's vacation. The Consul said he was too busy; but it was Tony's unsettled affair as well, that kept them lingering in Mengstrasse. A very diplomatic letter, written by the Consul himself, had been dispatched to Herr Grünlich; but the progress of the wooing was hindered by Tony's obstinacy. She expressed herself in the most childish way. "Heaven forbid, Mamma," she would say. "I simply can't en*dure* him!" with tremendous emphasis on the second syllable. Or she would explain solemnly, "Father" (Tony never otherwise said anything but "Papa"), "I can never yield him my consent."

And at this point the matter would assuredly have stuck, had it not been for events that occurred some ten days after the talk in the breakfast-room — in other words, about the middle of July.

It was afternoon — a hot blue afternoon. The Frau Consul was out, and Tony sat with a book alone at the window of the landscape room, when Anton brought her a card. Before she had time to read the name, a young man in a bell-skirted coat and pea-green pantaloons entered the room. It was, of course, Herr Grünlich, with an expression of imploring tenderness upon his face.

Tony started up indignantly and made a movement to flee into the next room. How could one possibly talk to a man who had proposed for one's hand? Her heart was in her throat and she had gone very pale. While he had been at a safe distance she had hugely enjoyed the solemn conferences with her Father and Mother and the suddenly enhanced importance of her own person and destiny. But now, here he was — he stood before her. What was going to happen? And again she felt that she was going to weep.

At a rapid stride, his head tipped on one side, his arms outstretched, with the air of a man who says: "Here I am, kill me if you will!" he approached. "What a providence!" he cried. "I find you here, Antonie — " (He said "Antonie"!)

Tony stood erect, her novel in her right hand. She stuck out her lips and gave her head a series of little jerks upward, relieving her irritation by stressing, in that manner, each word as she spoke it. She got out: "What is the matter with you?"—But the tears were already rising. And Herr Grünlich's own excitement was too great for him to realize the check.

"How could I wait longer? Was I not driven to return?" he said in impassioned tones. "A week ago I had your Father's letter, which filled me with hope. I could bear it no longer. Could I thus linger on in half-certainty? I threw myself into a carriage, I hastened hither, I have taken a couple of rooms at the City of Hamburg—and here I am, Antonie, to hear from your lips the final word which will make me happier than I can express."

Tony was stunned. Her tears retreated abashed. This, then, was the effect of her Father's careful letter, which had indefinitely postponed the decision. Two or three times she stammered: "You are mistaken—you are mistaken."

Herr Grünlich had drawn an arm-chair close to her seat in the window. He sat down, he obliged her to sit as well, and, bowing over her hand, which, limp with indecision, she resigned to him, he went on in a trembling voice: "Fräulein Antonie, since first I saw you, that afternoon,—do you remember that afternoon, when I saw you, a vision of loveliness, in your own family circle?—Since then, your name has been indelibly written on my heart." He went back, corrected himself, and said "graven": "Since that day, Fräulein Antonie, it has been my only, my most ardent wish, to win your beautiful hand. What your Father's letter permitted me only to hope, that I implore you to confirm to me now in all certainty. I may feel sure of your consent—I may be assured of it?" He took her other hand in his and looked deep into her wide-open, frightened eyes. He had left off his worsted gloves to-day, and his hands were long and white, marked with blue veins. Tony stared at his pink face, at his wart, at his eyes, which were as blue as a goose's.

"Oh, no, no," she broke out, rapidly, in terror. And then she added, "No, I will never yield my consent." She took great pains to speak firmly, but she was already in tears.

"How have I deserved this doubt and hesitation?" he asked in a lower, well-nigh reproachful tone. "I know you are a maiden cherished and sheltered by the most loving care. But I swear to you, I pledge you my word of honour as a man, that I would carry you in my arms, that as my wife you would lack nothing, that you would live in Hamburg a life altogether worthy of you—"

Tony sprang up. She freed her hand and, with the tears rolling down her cheeks, cried out in desperation, "No, no! I said *no!* I am refusing you—for heaven's sake, can't you understand?" Then Herr Grünlich rose up too. He took one backward step and stretched out his arms toward her, palms up. Seriously, like a man of honour and resolution, he spoke.

"Mademoiselle Buddenbrook, you understand that I cannot permit myself to be insulted?"

"But I am not insulting you, Herr Grünlich," said Tony, repenting her brusqueness. Oh, dear, oh dear, *why* did all this have to happen to her? Such a wooing as this she had never imagined. She had supposed that one only had to say: "Your offer does me great honour, but I cannot accept it," and that would be an end of the matter. "Your offer does me great honour," she said, as calmly as she could, "but I cannot accept it. And now I must go; please excuse me—I am busy—" But Herr Grünlich stood in front of her.

"You reject me?" he said gloomily.

"Yes," Tony said; adding with tact, "unfortunately."

Herr Grünlich gave a gusty sigh. He took two big steps backward, bent his torso to one side, pointed with his forefinger to the carpet and said in an awful voice: "Antonie!" Thus for the space of a moment they stood, he in a posture of commanding rage, Tony pale, weepy, and trembling, her damp handkerchief to her mouth. Then he turned from her and, with his hands on his back, measured the room twice through, as if he were at home. He paused at the window and looked out into the early dusk. Tony moved cautiously toward the glass doors, but she got only as far as the middle of the room when he stood beside her again.

"Tony!" he murmured, and gently took her hand. Then he sank, yes, he sank slowly upon his knees beside her! His two gold whiskers lay across her hand!

"Tony!" he repeated. "You behold me here—you see to what you have brought me. Have you a heart to feel what I endure? Listen. You behold a man condemned to death, devoted to destruction, a man who—who will certainly die of grief," he interrupted himself, "if you scorn his love. Here I lie. Can you find it in your heart to say: 'I despise you'?"

"No, no," Tony said quickly in a consoling tone. Her tears were conquered, pity stirred. Heavens, how he must adore her, to go on like that, while she herself felt completely indifferent! Was it to her, Tony Buddenbrook, that all this was happening? One read of it in the novels. But here in real life was a man in a frock-coat, on his knees in front of her, weeping, imploring. The idea of marrying him was simply idiotic, because she had found him silly; but just at this moment he did not seem silly; heavens, no! Honourable, upright, desperate entreaty were in his voice and face.

"No, no," she repeated, bending over him quite touched. "I don't despise you, Herr Grünlich. How can you say such a thing? Do get up — please do! "

"Then you will not kill me? " he asked again; and she answered, in a consoling, almost motherly tone, "No, no."

"That is a promise! " he cried, springing to his feet. But when he saw Tony's frightened face he got down again and went on in a wheedling tone: "Good, good, say no more, Antonie. Enough, for this time. We shall speak of this again. No more now — farewell. I will return — farewell! " He had got quickly to his feet. He took his broad grey hat from the table, kissed her hand, and was out through the glass doors in a twinkling.

Tony saw him take his stick from the hall and disappear down the corridor. She stood, bewildered and worn out, in the middle of the room, with the damp handkerchief in one of her limp hands.

CHAPTER IV

CONSUL BUDDENBROOK said to his wife: "If I thought Tony had a motive in refusing this match — But she is a child, Betsy. She enjoys going to balls and being courted by the young fellows; she is quite aware that she is pretty and from a good family. Of course, it is possible that she is consciously or unconsciously seeking a mate herself — but I know the child, and I feel sure she has never yet found her heart, as the saying goes. If you asked her, she would turn this way and that way, and consider — but she would find nobody. She is a child, a little bird, a hoyden. Directly she once says yes, she will find her place. She will have *carte blanche* to set herself up, and she will love her husband, after a few days. He is no beau, God knows. But he is perfectly presentable. One mustn't ask for five legs on a sheep, as we say in business. If she waits for somebody to come along who is an Adonis and a good match to boot — well, God bless us, Tony Buddenbrook could always find a husband, but it's a risk, after all. Every day is fishing-day, but not every day catching-day, to use another homely phrase —. Yesterday I had a long talk with Grünlich. He is a most constant wooer. He showed me all his books. They are good enough to frame. I told him I was completely satisfied. The business is young, but in fine condition — assets must be somewhere about a hundred and twenty thousand thaler, and that is obviously only the situation at the moment, for he makes a good slice every year. I asked the Duchamps. What they said doesn't sound at all bad. They don't know his connections, but he lives like a gentleman, mingles in society, and his business is known to be expanding. And some other people in Hamburg have told me things — a banker named Kesselmeyer, for instance — that I feel pleased with. In short, as you know, Betsy, I can only wish for the consummation of this match, which would be highly advantageous for the family and the firm. I am heartily sorry the child feels so pressed. She hardly speaks at all, and acts as if she were in a state of siege. But I can't bring myself to refuse him out and out. You know, Betsy, there is another thing I can't emphasize often enough: in these last years we haven't been doing any too brilliantly. Not that there's anything to complain of. Oh, no. Faithful work always finds its reward. Business goes quietly on — but a bit *too* quietly for me. And it only does that because I am eternally vigilant. We haven't perceptibly advanced since Father was taken away. The times aren't good for merchants. No, our prospects are not too bright. Our daughter is in a position to make a marriage that would undoubtedly be honourable and advantageous; she is of an age to marry, and she ought to do it. Delay isn't advisable — it isn't advisable, Betsy. Speak to her again. I said all I could, this afternoon."

Tony was besieged, as the Consul said. She no longer said no — but she could not bring herself to say yes. She could not wring a "yes" out of herself — God knew why; she did not.

Meanwhile, first her Father would draw her aside and speak seriously, and then her Mother would take up the tale, both pressing for a decision. Uncle Gotthold and family were not brought into the affair; their attitude toward the Mengstrasse was not exactly sympathetic. But Sesemi Weichbrodt got wind of it and came to give good advice, with correct enunciation. Even Mademoiselle Jungmann said, "Tony, my little one, why should you worry? You will always be in the best society." And Tony could not pay a visit to the admired silken salon outside the Castle Gate without getting a dose from old Madame Kröger: "A propos, little one, I hear there is an affair! I hope you are going to listen to reason, child."

One Sunday, as she sat in St. Mary's with her parents and brothers, Pastor Kölling began preaching from the text about the wife leaving father and mother and cleaving only to her husband. His language was so violent that she began listening with a jump, staring up to see if he were looking at her. No, thank goodness, his head was turned in the other direction, and he seemed to be preaching in general to all the faithful. Still, it was plain that this was a new attack upon her, — every word struck home. A young, a still childish girl, he said, could have as yet no will and no wisdom; and if she set herself up against the loving advice of her parents she was as deserving of punishment as the guilty are; she was one of those whom the Lord spews out of his mouth. With this phrase, which was the kind Pastor Kölling adored, she encountered a piercing glance from his eyes, as he made a threatening gesture with his right arm. Tony saw how her Father, sitting next to her, raised his hand, as though he would say, "Not so hard." But it was perfectly plain that either he or her Mother had let the

Pastor into the secret. Tony crouched in her place with her face like fire, and felt the eyes of all the world upon her. Next Sunday she flatly refused to go to church.

She moved dumbly about the house, she laughed no more, she lost her appetite. Sometimes she gave such heart-breaking sighs as would move a stone to pity. She was growing thinner too, and would soon lose her freshness. It would not do. At length the Consul said:

"This cannot go on, Betsy. We must not ill-use the child. She must get away a bit, to rest and be able to think quietly. You'll see she will listen to reason then. I can't leave, and the holidays are almost over. But there is no need for us to go. Yesterday old Schwarzkopf from Travemünde was here, and I spoke to him. He said he would be glad to take the child for a while. I'd give them something for it. She would have a good home, where she could bathe and be in the fresh air and get clear in her mind. Tom can take her — so it's all arranged. Better to-morrow than day after."

Tony was much pleased with this idea. True, she hardly ever saw Herr Grünlich, but she knew he was in town, in touch with her parents. Any day he might appear before her and begin shrieking and importuning. She would feel safer at Travemünde, in a strange house. So she packed her trunk with alacrity, and on one of the last days in July she mounted with Tom into the majestic Kröger equipage. She said good-bye in the best of spirits; and breathed more freely as they drove out of the Castle Gate.

CHAPTER V

THE ROAD to Travemünde first crosses the ferry and then goes
straight ahead. The grey high-road glided away under the hoofs
of Lebrecht Kröger's fat brown Mecklenburgs. The sound of
their trotting was hollow and rhythmical, the sun burned hot, and
dust concealed the meagre view. The family had eaten at one
o'clock, an hour earlier than usual, and the brother and sister set
out punctually at two. They would arrive shortly after four; for
what a hired carriage could do in three hours, the Kröger pair were
mettlesome enough to make in two.

Tony sat half asleep, nodding under her broad straw hat and
her lace-trimmed parasol, which she held tipped back against the
hood of the chaise. The parasol was twine-grey with cream-
coloured lace, and matched her neat, simply cut frock. She re-
clined in the luxurious ease proper to the equipage, with her feet,
in their white stockings and strap shoes, daintily crossed before
her.

Tom was already twenty years old. He wore an extremely
well cut blue suit, and sat smoking Russian cigarettes, with his hat
on the back of his head. He was not very tall; but already he
boasted a considerable moustache, darker in tone than his brows
and eyelashes. He had one eyebrow lifted a trifle — a habit with
him — and sat looking at the dust and the trees that fled away behind them as the carriage rolled on.

Tony said: " I was never so glad to come to Travemünde before
— for various reasons. You needn't laugh, Tom. I wish I could
leave a certain pair of yellow mutton-chops even further behind!
And then, it will be an entirely different Travemünde at the
Schwarzkopfs', on the sea front. I shan't be bothered with the
Kurhouse society, I can tell you that much. I am not in the mood
for it. Besides, that — that man could come there too as well as not.
He has nerve enough — it wouldn't trouble him at all. Some day
he'd be bobbing up in front of me and putting on all his airs and
graces."

Tom threw away the stub of his cigarette and took a fresh one
out of the box, a pretty little affair with an inlaid picture inside the

lid, of an overturned troika being set upon by wolves. It was a present from a Russian customer of the Consul. The cigarettes, those biting little trifles with the yellow mouthpiece, were Tom's passion. He smoked quantities of them, and had the bad habit of inhaling the smoke, breathing it slowly out again as he talked.

"Yes," he said. "As far as that goes, the garden of the Kurhouse is alive with Hamburgers. Consul Fritsche, who has bought it, is a Hamburger himself. He must be doing a wonderful business now, Papa says. But you'll miss something if you don't take part in it a bit. Peter Döhlmann is there — he never stops in town this time of year. His business goes on at a jog-trot, all by itself, I suppose. Funny! Well — and Uncle Justus comes out for a little on a Sunday, of course, to visit the roulette table. Then there are the Möllendorpfs and the Kistenmakers, I suppose, in full strength, and the Hagenströms — "

"H'm. Yes, of course. They couldn't get on without Sarah Semlinger! "

"Her name is Laura, my child. Let us be accurate."

"And Julchen with her, of course. Julchen ought to get engaged to August Möllendorpf this summer — and she will do it, too. After all, they belong together. Disgusting, isn't it, Tom? This adventurer's family — "

"Yes, but good heavens, they are the firm of Strunck and Hagenström. That is the point."

"Naturally, they make the firm. Of course. And everybody knows *how* they do it. With their *elbows*. Pushing and shoving — entirely without courtesy or elegance. Grandfather said that Hinrich Hagenström could coin money out of paving-stones. Those were his very words."

"Yes, yes, that is exactly it. It is money talks. And this match is perfectly good business. Julchen will be a Möllendorpf, and August will get a snug position — "

"Oh, you just want to make me angry, Tom, that's all. You know how I despise that lot."

Tom began to laugh. "Goodness, one has to get along with them," he replied. "As Papa said the other day, they are the coming people; while the Möllendorpfs, for example — And one can't deny that the Hagenströms are clever. Hermann is already useful in the business, and Moritz is very able. He finished school brilliantly, in spite of his weak chest; and he is going to study law."

"That's all very well, Tom, but all the same I am glad there are families that don't have to knuckle down to them. For instance, we Buddenbrooks — "

" Oh," Tom said, " don't let's begin to boast. Every family has its own skeleton," he went on in a lower voice, with a glance at Jock's broad back. " For instance, God knows what state Uncle Julius' affairs are in. Papa shakes his head when he speaks of him, and Grandfather Kröger has had to come forward once or twice with large sums, I hear. The cousins aren't just the thing, either. Jürgen wants to study, but he still hasn't come up for his finals; and they are not very well satisfied with Jacob, at Dalbeck and Company. He is always in debt, even with a good allowance, and when Uncle Justus refuses to send any more, Aunt Rosalie does — No, I find it doesn't do to throw stones. If you want to balance the scale with the Hagenströms, you'd better marry Grünlich."

" Did we get into this wagon to discuss that subject? — Oh, yes, I suppose you're right. I ought to marry him — but I won't think about it now! I want to forget it. We are going to the Schwarz-kopfs'. I've never seen them to know them: are they nice people? "

" Oh, old Diederich Schwarzkopf — he's not such a bad old chap. Doesn't speak such atrocious dialect, unless he's had more than five glasses of grog. Once he was at the office, and we went together to the Ships' Company. He drank like a tank. His father was born on a Norwegian freighter and grew up to be captain on the very same line. Diederich has had a good education; the pilot command is a responsible office, and pretty well paid. Diederich is an old bear — but very gallant with the ladies. Look out: he'll flirt with you."

" Ah — well, and his wife? "

" I don't know her, myself. She must be nice, I should think. There is a son, too. He was in first or second, in my time at school, and is a student now, I expect. Look, there's the sea. We shall be there inside a quarter of an hour."

They drove for a while along the shore on an avenue bordered with young beech-trees. There was the water, blue and peaceful in the sunshine; the round yellow light-house tower came into view, then the bay and the breakwater, the red roofs of the little town, the harbour with its sails, tackle, and shipping. They drove between the first houses, passed the church, and rolled along the front close to the water and up to a pretty little house, the ve-randah of which was overhung with vines.

Pilot-Captain Schwarzkopf stood before his door and took off his seaman's cap as the calèche drove up. He was a broad, stocky man with a red face, sea-blue eyes, and a bristling grizzled beard that ran fan-shaped from one ear to the other. His mouth turned down at the corners, in one of which he held a wooden pipe. His

smooth-shaven, red upper lip was hard and prominent; he looked
thoroughly solid and respectable, with big bones and well-rounded
paunch; and he wore a coat decorated with gold braid, underneath
which a white piqué waistcoat was visible.

"Servant, Mademoiselle," he said, as he carefully lifted Tony
from the calèche. "We know it's an honour you do us, coming to
stop with us like this. Servant, Herr Buddenbrook. Papa well?
And the honoured Frau Consul? Come in, come in! My wife has
some sort of a bite ready, I suppose. Drive over to Peddersen's
Inn," he said in his broadest dialect to the coachman, who was carrying in the trunk. "You'll find they take good care of the horses
there." Then, turning to Thomas, "you'll stop the night with us,
Herr Buddenbrook? Oh, yes, you must. The horses want a bait
and a rest, and you wouldn't get home until after dark."

"Upon my word, one lives at least as well here as at the Kurhouse," Tony said a quarter of an hour later, as they sat around
the coffee-table in the verandah. "What wonderful air! You can
smell the sea-weed from here. How frightfully glad I am to be in
Travemünde again! "

Between the vine-clad columns of the verandah one could look
out on the broad river-mouths, glittering in the sun; there were the
piers and the boats, and the ferry-house on the "Prival" opposite,
the projecting peninsula of Mecklenburg. — The clumsy, blue-
bordered cups on the table were almost like basins. How different from the delicate old porcelain at home! But there was a
bunch of flowers at Tony's place, the food looked inviting, and the
drive had whetted her appetite.

"Yes, Mademoiselle will see, she will pick up here fast enough,"
the housewife said. "She looks a little poorly, if I might say so.
That is the town air, and the parties."

Frau Schwarzkopf was the daughter of a Schlutup pastor. She
was a head shorter than Tony, rather thin, and looked to be about
fifty. Her hair was still black, and neatly dressed in a large-
meshed net. She wore a dark brown dress with white crocheted
collar and cuffs. She was spotless, gentle, and hospitable, urging
upon her guests the currant bread that lay in a boat-shaped basket
surrounded by cream, butter, sugar, and honeycomb. This basket
had a border of bead-work embroidery, done by little Meta, the
eight-year-old daughter, who now sat next her mother, dressed in
a plaid frock, her flaxen hair in a thick pigtail.

Frau Schwarzkopf made excuses for Tony's room, whither she
had already been to make herself tidy after the journey. It was so
very simple —

"Oh, all the better," Tony said. It had a view of the ocean, which was the main thing. And she dipped her fourth piece of currant bread into her coffee. Tom walked with the pilot-captain about the *Wullenwewer*, now undergoing repairs in the town.

There came suddenly into the verandah a young man of some twenty years. He took off his grey felt hat, blushed, and bowed rather awkwardly.

"Well, my son," said Herr Schwarzkopf, "you are late." He presented him to the guests: "This is my son, studying to be a doctor. He is spending his vacation with us." He had mentioned the young man's name, but Tony failed to understand it.

"Pleased to meet you," said Tony, primly. Tom rose and and shook hands. Young Schwarzkopf bowed again, put down his book, and took his place at the table, blushing afresh. He was of medium height, very slender, and as fair as he could possibly be. His youthful moustaches, colourless as the hair which covered his long head, were scarcely visible; and he had a complexion to match, a tint like translucent porcelain, which grew pink on the slightest provocation. His eyes, slightly darker than his father's, had the same not very animated but good-natured quizzical expression; and his features were regular and rather pleasing. When he began to eat he displayed unusually regular teeth, glistening in close ranks of polished ivory. For the rest, he wore a grey jacket buttoned up, with flaps on the pockets, and an elastic belt at the back.

"Yes, I am sorry I am late," he said. His speech was somewhat slow and grating. "I was reading on the beach, and did not look soon enough at my watch." Then he ate silently, looking up now and then to glance at Tom and Tony.

Later on, Tony being again urged by the housewife to take something, he said, "You can rely on the honey, Fräulein Buddenbrook; it is a pure nature product — one knows what one is eating. You must eat, you know. The air here consumes one — it accelerates the process of metabolism. If you do not eat well, you will get thin." He had a pleasant, naïve, way of now and then bending forward as he spoke and looking at some other person than the one whom he addressed.

His mother listened to him tenderly and watched Tony's face to see the impression he made. But old Schwarzkopf said, "Now, now, Herr Doctor. Don't be blowing off about your metabolism — *we* don't know anything about that sort of talk." Whereupon the young man laughed, blushed again, and looked at Tony's plate.

The pilot-captain mentioned more than once his son's Christian name, but Tony could never quite catch what it was. It sounded like Moor — or Mort; but the Father's broad, flat pronunciation was impossible to understand.

They finished their meal. Herr Diederich sat blinking in the sun, his coat flung wide open over his white waistcoat, and he and his son took out their short pipes. Tom smoked his cigarettes, and the young people began a lively conversation, the subject of which was their old school and all the old school recollections. Tony took part gaily. They quoted Herr Stengel: " What! You were to make a line, and what are you making? A dash! " What a pity Christian was not here! he could imitate him so much better.

Once Tom pointed to the flowers at Tony's place and said to his sister: " That trims things up uncommonly well, as Herr Grün-lich would say! " Whereat Tony, red with anger, gave him a push and darted an embarrassed glance at young Schwarzkopf.

The coffee-hour had been unusually late, and they had prolonged it. It was already half-past six, and twilight was beginning to descend over the Prival, when the captain got up.

" The company will excuse me," he said; " I've some work down at the pilot-house. We'll have supper at eight o'clock, if that suits the young folk. Or even a little later to-night, eh, Meta? And you " (hers he used his son's name again), " don't be lolling about here. Just go and dig up your bones again. Fräulein Buddenbrook will want to unpack. Or perhaps the guests would like to go down on the beach. Only don't get in the way."

" Diederich, for pity's sake, why shouldn't he sit still a bit? " Frau Schwarzkopf said, with mild reproach. " And if our guests like to go down on the beach, why shouldn't he go along? Is he to see nothing at all of our visitors? "

CHAPTER VI

In her neat little room with the flower-covered furniture, Tony
woke next morning with the fresh, happy feeling which one has
at the beginning of a new chapter. She sat up in bed and, with her
hands clasped round her knees and her tousled head flung back,
blinked at the stream of light that poured through the closed shutters into the room. She began to sort out the experiences of the
previous day.

Her thoughts scarcely touched upon the Grünlich affair. The
town, his hateful apparition in the landscape room, the exhorta-
tions of her family and Pastor Kölling — all that lay far behind her.
Here, every morning, there would be a care-free waking. These
Schwarzkopfs were splendid people. Last night there had been
pineapple punch, and they had made part of a happy family circle.
It had been very jolly. Herr Schwarzkopf had told his best sea
tales, and young Schwarzkopf stories about student life at Göttingen. How odd it was, that she still did not know his first name!
And she had strained her ear to hear too, but even at dinner she
did not succeed, and somehow it did not seem proper to ask. She
tried feverishly to think how it sounded — was it Moor — Mord —?
Anyhow, she had liked him pretty well, this young Moor or
Mord. He had such a sly, good-natured laugh when he asked for
the water and called it by letters and numbers, so that his father
got quite furious. But it was only the scientific formula for water
— that is, for ordinary water, for the Travemünde product was a
much more complicated affair, of course. Why, one could find a
jelly-fish in it, any time! The authorities, of course, might have
what notions they chose about fresh water. For this he only got
another scolding from his father, for speaking slightingly of the
authorities. But Frau Schwarzkopf watched Tony all the time,
to see how much she admired the young man — and really, it was
most interesting, he was so learned and so jolly, all at the same
time. He had given her considerable attention. She had complained that her head felt hot, while eating, and that she must have
too much blood. What had he replied? He had given her a careful

scrutiny, and then said, Yes, the arteries in the temples might be
full; but that did not prove that she had too much blood. Perhaps,
instead, it meant she had too little — or rather, that there were too
few red corpuscles in it. In fact, she was perhaps a little anæmic.

The cuckoo sprang out of his carven house on the wall and
cuckooed several times, clear and loud. " Seven, eight, nine,"
counted Tony. " Up with you! " She jumped out of bed and
opened the blinds. The sky was partly overcast, but the sun was
visible. She looked out over the Leuchtenfeld with its tower, to
the ruffled sea beyond. On the right it was bounded by the curve
of the Mecklenburg coast; but before her it stretched on and on
till its blue and green streaks mingled with the misty horizon. " I'll
bathe afterwards," she thought, " but first I'll eat a big breakfast,
so as not to be consumed by my metabolism." She washed and
dressed with quick, eager movements.

It was shortly after half-past nine when she left her room. The
door of the chamber in which Tom had slept stood open; he had
risen early and driven back to town. Even up here in the upper
story, it smelled of coffee — that seemed to be the characteristic
odour of the little house, for it grew stronger as she descended
the simple staircase with its plain board baluster and went down
the corridor, where lay the living-room, which was also the dining-
room and the office of the pilot-captain. She went out into the verandah, looking, in her white piqué frock, perfectly fresh, and in
the gayest of tempers. Frau Schwarzkopf sat with her son at the
table. It was already partly cleared away, and the housewife wore
a blue checked kitchen apron over her brown frock. A key-basket
stood beside her.

" A thousand pardons for not waiting," she said, as she stood up.
" We simple folk rise early. There is so much to be done!
Schwarzkopf is in his office. I hope you don't take it ill? "

Tony excused herself in her turn. " You must not think I always sleep so late as this," she said. " I feel very guilty. But the
punch last night — "

The young man began to laugh. He stood behind the table with
his short pipe in his hand and a newspaper before him.

" Good morning," Tony said. " Yes, it is your fault. You kept
urging me. Now I deserve only cold coffee. I ought to have had
breakfast and a bathe as well, by this time."

" Oh, no, that would be rather too early, for a young lady. At
seven o'clock the water was rather cold — eleven degrees. That's
pretty sharp, after a warm bed."

" How do you know I wanted a warm bath, monsieur? " and

Tony sat down beside Frau Schwarzkopf. "Oh, you have kept the coffee hot for me, Frau Schwarzkopf! But I will pour it out myself, thank you so much."

The housewife looked on as her guest began to eat. "Fräulein slept well, the first night? The mattress, dear knows, is only stuffed with sea-weed — we are simple folk! And now, good appetite, and a good morning. You will surely find many friends on the beach. If you like, my son shall bear you company. Pardon me for not sitting longer, but I must look after the dinner. The joint is in the oven. We will feed you as well as we can."

"I shall stick to the honeycomb," Tony said when the two were alone. "You know what you are getting."

Young Schwarzkopf laid his pipe on the verandah rail.

"But please smoke. I don't mind it at all. At home, when I come down to breakfast, Papa's cigar-smoke is already in the room. Tell me," she said suddenly. "Is it true that an egg is as good as a quarter of a pound of meat?"

He grew red all over. "Are you making fun of me?" he asked, partly laughing but partly vexed. "I got another wigging from my Father last night for what he calls my silly professional airs."

"No, really, I was asking because I wanted to know." Tony stopped eating in consternation. "How could anybody call them airs? I should be so glad to learn something. I'm such a goose, you see. At Sesemi Weichbrodt's I was always one of the very laziest. I'm sure you know a great deal." Inwardly her thoughts ran: "Everybody puts his best foot foremost, before strangers. We all take care to say what will be pleasant to hear — that is a commonplace. . . ."

"Well, you see they are the same thing, in a way. The chemical constituents of food-stuffs — " And so on, while Tony breakfasted. Next they talked about Tony's boarding-school days, and Sesemi Weichbrodt, and Gerda Arnoldsen, who had gone back to Amsterdam, and Armgard von Schilling, whose home, a large white house, could be seen from the beach here, at least in clear weather. Tony finished eating, wiped her mouth, and asked, pointing to the paper, "Is there any news?" Young Schwarzkopf shook his head and laughed cynically.

"Oh, no. What would there be? You know these little provincial news-sheets are wretched affairs."

"Oh, are they? Papa and Mamma always take it in."

He reddened again. "Oh, well, you see I always read it, too. Because I can't get anything else. But it is not very thrilling to hear that So-and-So, the merchant prince, is about to celebrate his silver

wedding. Yes, you laugh. But you ought to read other papers —
the *Königsberg Gazette*, for instance, or the *Rhenish Gazette*.
You'd find a different story there, entirely. There it's what the
King of Prussia says."

"What does he say? "

" Well — er — I really couldn't repeat it to a lady." He got red
again. " He expressed himself rather strongly on the subject of this
same press," he went on with another cynical laugh, which, for a
moment, made a painful impression on Tony. " The press, you
know, doesn't feel any too friendly toward the government or the
nobility or the parsons and junkers. It knows pretty well how to
lead the censor by the nose."

" Well, and you? Aren't you any too friendly with the nobility,
either? "

" I? " he asked, and looked very embarrassed. Tony rose.

" Shall we talk about this again another time? " she suggested.
" Suppose I go down to the beach now. Look, the sky is blue
nearly all over. It won't rain any more. I am simply longing to
jump into the water. Will you go down with me? "

CHAPTER VII

SHE had put on her big straw hat, and she raised her sunshade; for it was very hot, though there was a little sea-breeze. Young Schwarzkopf, in his grey felt, book in hand, walked beside her and sometimes gave her a shy side-glance. They went along the front and walked through the garden of the Kurhouse, which lay there in the sun shadeless and still, with its rose-bushes and pebbly paths. The music pavilion, hidden among pine trees, stood opposite the Kurhouse, the pastry-cook's, and the two Swiss cottages, which were connected by a long gallery. It was about half-past eleven, and the hotel guests were probably down on the beach.

They crossed the playground, where there were many benches and a large swing, passed close to the building where one took the hot baths, and strolled slowly across the Leuchtenfeld. The sun brooded over the grass, and there rose up a spicy smell from the warm weeds and clover; blue-bottle flies buzzed and droned about. A dull, booming roar came up from the ocean, whose waters now and then lifted a crested head of spray in the distance.

"What is that you are reading?" Tony asked. The young man took the book in both hands and ran it quickly through, from cover to cover.

"Oh, that is nothing for you, Fräulein Buddenbrook. Nothing but blood and entrails and such awful things. This part treats of nodes in the lungs. What we call pulmonary catarrh. The lungs get filled up with a watery fluid. It is a very dangerous condition, and occurs in inflammation of the lungs. In bad cases, the patient simply chokes to death. And that is all described with perfect coolness, from a scientific point of view."

"Oh, horrors! But if one wants to be a doctor — I will see that you become our family physician, when old Grabow retires. You'll see!"

"Ha, ha! And what are you reading, if I may ask, Fräulein Buddenbrook?"

"Do you know Hoffmann?" Tony asked.

"About the choir-master, and the gold pot? Yes, that's very

pretty. But it is more for ladies. Men want something different, you know."

"I must ask you one thing," Tony said, taking a sudden resolution, after they had gone a few steps. "And that is, do, I beg of you, tell me your first name. I haven't been able to understand it a single time I've heard it, and it is making me dreadfully nervous. I've simply been racking my brains — I have, quite."

"You have been racking your brains?"

"Now don't make it worse — I'm sure it couldn't have been proper for me to ask, only I'm naturally curious. There's really no reason whatever why I should know."

"Why, my name is Morten," said he, and became redder than ever.

"Morten? That is a nice name."

"Oh — *nice!* "

"Yes, indeed. At least, it's prettier than to be called something like Hinz, or Kunz. It is unusual; it sounds foreign."

"You are romantic, Fräulein Buddenbrook. You have read too much Hoffmann. My grandfather was half Norwegian, and I was named after him. That is all there is to it."

Tony picked her way through the rushes on the edge of the beach. In front of them was a row of round-topped wooden pavilions, and beyond they could see the basket-chairs at the water's edge and people camped by families on the warm sand — ladies with blue sun-spectacles and books out of the loan-library; gentlemen in light suits idly drawing pictures in the sand with their walking-sticks; sun-burnt children in enormous straw hats, tumbling about, shovelling sand, digging for water, baking with wooden moulds, paddling bare-legged in the shallow pools, floating little ships. To the right, the wooden bathing-pavilion ran out into the water.

"We are going straight across to Möllendorpf's pier," said Tony. "Let's turn off."

"Certainly; but don't you want to meet your friends? I can sit down yonder on those boulders."

"Well, I suppose I ought to just greet them. But I don't want to, you know. I came here to be in peace and quiet."

"Peace? From what?"

"Why — from — from —"

"Listen, Fräulein Buddenbrook. I must ask you something. No, I'll wait till another day — till we have more time. Now I will say au revoir and go and sit down there on the rocks."

" Don't you want me to introduce you, then? " Tony asked, importantly.

" Oh, no," Morten said, hastily. " Thanks, but I don't fit very well with those people, you see. I'll just sit down over there on the rocks."

It was a rather large company which Tony was approaching while Morten Schwarzkopf betook himself to the great heap of boulders on the right, near to the bathing-house and washed by the waves. The party was encamped before the Möllendorpfs' pier, and was composed of the Möllendorpf, Hagenström, Kistenmaker, and Fritsche families. Except for Herr Fritsche, the owner, from Hamburg, and Peter Döhlmann, the idler, the group consisted of women, for it was a week-day, and most of the men were in their offices. Consul Fritsche, an elderly, smooth-shaven gentleman with a distinguished face, was up on the open pier, busy with a telescope, which he trained upon a sailboat visible in the distance. Peter Döhlmann, with a broad-brimmed straw hat and a beard with a nautical cut, stood chatting with the ladies perched on camp-stools or stretched out on rugs on the sand. There were Frau Senator Möllendorpf, born Langhals, with her long-handled lor- gnon and untidy grey hair; Frau Hagenström, with Julchen, who had not grown much, but already wore diamonds in her ears, like her mother; Frau Consul Kistenmaker and her daughters; and Frau Consul Fritsche, a wrinkled little lady in a cap, who performed the duties of hospitality at the bath and went about perpetually hot and tired, thinking only about balls and routs and raffles, chil- dren's parties and sailboat excursions. At a little distance sat her paid companion.

Kistenmaker and Son was the new firm of wine-merchants which had, in the last few years, managed to put C. F. Köppen rather in the shade. The two sons, Edouard and Stephan, worked in their father's office. Consul Döhlmann possessed none of those graces of manner upon which Justus Kröger laid such stress. He was an idler pure and simple, whose special characteristic was a sort of rough good humour. He could and did take a good many lib- erties in society, being quite aware that his loud, brusque voice and bluff ways caused the ladies to set him down as an original. Once at a dinner at the Buddenbrooks', when a course failed to come in promptly and the guests grew dull and the hostess flustered, he came to the rescue and put them into a good humour by bellowing in his big voice the whole length of the table: " Please don't wait for me, Frau Consul! " Just now, in this same reverberating voice, he was relating questionable anecdotes seasoned with low-German idioms. Frau Senator Möllendorpf, in paroxysms of laughter, was crying out over and over again: " Stop, Herr Döhlmann, stop! for heaven's sake, don't tell any more."

They greeted Tony — the Hagenströms coldly, the others with great cordiality. Consul Fritsche even came down the steps of the pier, for he hoped that the Buddenbrooks would return next year to swell the population of the baths.

" Yours to command, Fräulein Buddenbrook," said Consul Döhlmann, with his very best pronunciation; for he was aware that Mademoiselle did not especially care for his manners.

" Mademoiselle Buddenbrook! "

" You here? "

" How lovely! "

" When did you come? "

" What a sweet frock! "

" Where are you stopping? "

" At the Schwarzkopfs'? "

" With the pilot-captain? How original! "

" How *frightfully* original."

" You are stopping in the town? " asked Consul Fritsche, the owner of the baths. He did not betray that he felt the blow.

" Will you come to our next assembly? " his wife asked.

" Oh, you are only here for a short time? " — this from another lady.

" Don't you think, darling, the Buddenbrooks rather give themselves airs? " Frau Hagenström whispered to Frau Senator Möllendorpf.

" Have you been in yet? " somebody asked. " Which of the rest of you hasn't bathed yet, young ladies? Marie? Julie, Louise? Your friends will go bathing with you, of course, Fräulein Antonie." Some of the young girls rose, and Peter Döhlmann insisted on accompanying them up the beach.

" Do you remember how we used to go back and forth to school together? " Tony asked Julie Hagenström.

" Yes, and you were always the one that got into mischief," Julie said, joining in her laugh. They went across the beach on a foot-bridge made of a few boards, and reached the bathhouse. As they passed the boulders where Morten Schwarzkopf sat, Tony nodded to him from a distance, and somebody asked, " who is that you are bowing to, Tony? "

" That was young Schwarzkopf," Tony answered. " He walked down here with me."

"The son of the pilot-captain?" Julchen asked, and peered across at Morten with her staring black eyes. He on his side watched the gay troop with rather a melancholy air. Tony said in a loud voice: "What a pity August is not here. It must be stupid on the beach."

CHAPTER VIII

AND now began for Tony Buddenbrook a stretch of beautiful summer weeks, briefer, lovelier, than any she had ever spent in Travemünde. She bloomed as she felt her burden no longer upon her; her gay, pert, careless manner had come back. The Consul looked at her with satisfaction when he came on Sundays with Tom and Christian. On those days they ate at the table-d'hôte, sat under the awnings at the pastry-cook's, drinking coffee and listening to the band, and peeped into the roulette-room at the gay folk there, like Justus Kröger and Peter Döhlmann. The Consul himself never played. Tony sunned herself, took baths, ate sausages with ginger-nut sauce, and took long walks with Morten. They went out on the high-road to the next village, or along the beach to the "ocean temple" on its height, whence a wide view was to be had over land and sea; or to the woods behind the Kurhouse, where was a great bell used to call the guests to the table-d'hôte. Sometimes they rowed across the Trave to the Prival, to look for amber.

Morten made an entertaining companion, though his opinions were often dogmatic, not to say heated. He had a severe and righteous judgment for everything, and he expressed it with finality, blushing all the time. It saddened Tony to hear him call the nobility idiots and wretches and to see the contemptuous if awkward gesture that accompanied the words. She scolded him, but she was proud to have him express so freely in her presence the views and opinions which she knew he concealed from his parents. Once he confided in her: "I'll tell you something: I've a skeleton in my room at Göttingen — a whole set of bones, you know, held together by wire. I've put an old policeman's uniform on it. Ha, ha! Isn't that great? But don't say anything to my Father about it."

Tony was naturally often in the society of her town friends, or drawn into some assembly or boating party. Then Morten "sat on the rocks." And after their first day this phrase became a convenient one. To "sit on the rocks" meant to feel bored and lonely.

When a rainy day came and a grey mist covered the sea far and wide till it was one with the deep sky; when the beach was drenched and the roads streaming with wet, Tony would say: "To-day we shall both have to sit on the rocks — that is, in the verandah or sitting-room. There is nothing left to do but for you to play me some of your student songs, Morten — even if they do bore me horribly."

"Yes," Morten said, "come and sit down. But you know that when you are here, there are no rocks!" He never said such things when his father was present. His mother he did not mind.

"Well, what now?" asked the pilot-captain, as Tony and Morten both rose from table and were about to take their leave. "Where are the young folk off to?"

"I was going to take a little walk with Fräulein Antonie, as far as the temple."

"Oh, is that it? Well, my son Filius, what do you say to going up to your room and conning over your nerves? You'll lose everything out of your head before you get back to Göttingen."

But Frau Schwarzkopf would intervene: "Now, Diederich, aren't these his holidays? Why shouldn't he take a walk? Is he to have nothing of our visitor?" So Morten went.

They paced along the beach close to the water, on the smooth, hard sand that made walking easy. It was strewn with common tiny white mussel-shells, and others too, pale opalescent and longish in shape; yellow-green wet seaweed with hollow round fruit that snapped when you squeezed it; and pale, translucent, reddish-yellow jelly-fish, which were poisonous and burned your leg when you touched one bathing.

"I used to be frightfully stupid, you know," Tony said. "I wanted the bright star out of the jelly-fish, so I brought a lot home in my pocket-handkerchief and put them on the balcony, to dry in the sunshine. When I looked at them again, of course there was just a big wet spot that smelled of sea-weed."

The waves whispered rhythmically beside them as they walked, and the salt wind blew full in their faces, streaming over and about them, closing their ears to other sounds and causing a pleasant slight giddiness. They walked in this hushed, whispering peacefulness by the sea, whose every faint murmur, near or far, seemed to have a deep significance.

To their left was a precipitous cliff of lime and boulders, with jutting corners that came into view as they rounded the bay. When the beach was too stony to go on, they began to climb, and continued upward through the wood until they reached the temple. It was a round pavilion, built of rough timbers and boards, the inside of which was covered with scribbled inscriptions and poetry, carved hearts and initials. Tony and Morten seated themselves in one of the little rooms facing the sea; it smelled of wood, like the cabins at the bathhouse. It was very quiet, even solemn, up here at this hour of the afternoon. A pair of birds chattered, and the faint rustling of the leaves mingled with the sound of the sea spread out below them. In the distance they could see the rigging of a ship. Sheltered now from the wind that had been thrumming at their ears, they suddenly experienced a quiet, almost pensive mood.

Tony said, " Is it coming or going? "

" What? " asked Morten, his subdued voice sounding as if he were coming back from a far distance. " Oh – going – That is the *Bürgermeister Steenbock*, for Russia." He added after a pause: " I shouldn't like to be going with it. It must be worse there than here."

" Now," Tony said, " you are going to begin again on the nobility. I see it in your face. And it's not at all nice of you. Tell me, did you ever know a single one of them? "

" No! " Morten shouted, quite insulted. " Thank God, no."

" Well, there, then, I have – Armgard von Schilling over there, that I told you about. She was much better-natured than either of us; she hardly knew she was a *von* – she ate sausage-meat and talked about her cows."

" Oh, of course. There are naturally exceptions. Listen, Fräulein Tony. You are a woman, you see, so you take everything personally. You happen to know a single member of the nobility, and you say she is a good creature – certainly! But one does not need to know any of them to be able to judge them all. It is a question of the principle, you understand – of – the organization of the state. You can't answer that, can you? They need only to be born to be the pick of everything, and look down on all the rest of us. While we, however hard we strive, cannot climb to their level." Morten spoke with a naïve, honest irritation. He tried to fit his speech with gestures, then perceived that they were awkward, and gave it up. But he was in the vein to talk, and he went on, sitting bent forward, with his thumb between the buttons of his jacket, a defiant expression in his usually good-natured eyes. " We, the bourgeoisie – the Third Estate, as we have been called – we recognize only that nobility which consists of merit; we refuse to admit any longer the rights of the indolent aristocracy, we repudiate the class distinctions of the present day, we desire that all men should be free and equal, that no person shall be subject to another, but all subject to the law. There shall be no more privilege and arbitrary rule. All shall be sovereign children of the state; and as no middlemen exist any longer between the people and almighty God, so shall the citizen stand in direct relation to the State. We will have freedom of the press, of trade and industry, so that all men, without distinction, shall be able to strive together and receive their reward according to their merit. We are enslaved, muzzled! — What was it I wanted to say? Oh, yes! Four years ago they renewed the laws of the Confederation touching the universities and the press. Fine laws they are! No truth may be written or taught which might not agree with the established order of things. Do you understand? The truth is suppressed — forbidden to be spoken. Why? For the sake of an obsolete, idiotic, decadent class which everybody knows will be destroyed some day, anyhow. I do not think you can comprehend such meanness. It is the stupid, brutal application of force, the immediate physical strength of the police, without the slightest understanding of new, spiritual forces. And apart from all that, there is the final fact of the great wrong the King of Prussia has done us. In 1813, when the French were in the country, he called us together and promised us a Constitution. We came to the rescue, we freed Germany from the invader — "

Tony, chin in hand, stole a look at him and wondered for a moment if he could have actually helped to drive out Napoleon.

" — but do you think he kept his promise? Oh, no! The present king is a fine orator, a dreamer; a romantic, like you, Fräulein Tony. But I'll tell you something: take any general principle or conception of life. It always happens that, directly it has been found wanting and discarded by the poets and philosophers, there comes along a King to whom it is a perfectly new idea, and who makes it a guiding principle. That is what kings are like. It is not only that kings are men — they are even very distinctly average men; they are always a good way in the rear. Oh, yes, Germany is just like a students' society; it had its brave and spirited youth at the time of the great revolution, but now it is just a lot of fretful Philistines."

"Ye — es," Tony said. "But let me ask you this: Why are you so interested in Prussia? You aren't a Prussian."

"Oh, it is all the same thing, Fräulein Buddenbrook. Yes, I said Fräulein Buddenbrook on purpose, I ought even to have said Demoiselle Buddenbrook, and given you your entire title. Are the men here freer, more brotherly, more equal than in Prussia? Con-

ventions, classes, aristocracy, here as there. You have sympathy
for the nobility. Shall I tell you why? Because you belong to it
yourself. Yes, yes, didn't you know it? Your father is a great
gentleman, and you are a princess. There is a gulf between you
and us, because we do not belong to your circle of ruling families.
You can walk on the beach with one of us for the sake of your
health, but when you get back into your own class, then the rest of
us can go and sit on the rocks." His voice had grown quite
strangely excited.

"Morten," said Tony, sadly. "You have been angry all the
time, then, when you were sitting on the rocks! And I always
begged you to come and be introduced."

"Now you are taking the affair personally again, like a young
lady, Fräulein Tony, I'm only speaking of the principle. I say that
there is no more fellowship of humanity with us than in Prussia. —
And even if I were speaking personally," he went on, after a little
pause, with a softer tone, out of which, however, the strange excitement had not disappeared, "I shouldn't be speaking of the
present, but rather, perhaps, of the future. When you as Madame
So-and-So finally vanish into your proper sphere, one is left to sit
on the rocks all the rest of one's life."

He was silent, and Tony too. She did not look at him, but in
the other direction, at the wooden partition. There was an uneasy
stillness for some time.

"Do you remember," Morten began again, "I once said to you
that there was a question I wanted to ask you? Yes, I have wanted
to know, since the first afternoon you came. Don't guess. You
couldn't guess what I mean. I am going to ask you another time;
there is no hurry; it has really nothing to do with me; it is only
curiosity. No, to-day I will only show you one thing. Look."
He drew out of the pocket of his jacket the end of a narrow gaily-
striped ribbon, and looked with a mixture of expectation and triumph into Tony's eyes.

"How pretty," she said uncomprehendingly. "What is it? "

Morten spoke solemnly: "That means that I belong to a students' fraternity in Göttingen. — Now you know. I have a cap in
the same colours, but my skeleton in the policeman's uniform is
wearing it for the holidays. I couldn't be seen with it here, you
understand. I can count on your saying nothing, can't I? Because
it would be very unfortunate if my father were to hear of it."

"Not a word, Morten. You can rely on me. But I don't understand — have you all taken a vow against the nobility? What is it
you want? "

" We want freedom," Morten said.

" Freedom? " she asked.

" Yes, freedom, you know — *Freedom!* " he repeated; and he made a vague, awkward, fervent gesture outward and downward, not toward the side where the coast of Mecklenburg narrowed the bay, but in the direction of the open sea, whose rippling blue, green, yellow, and grey stripes rolled as far as eye could see out to the misty horizon.

Tony followed his gesture with her eye; they sat, their hands lying close together on the bench, and looked into the distance. Thus they remained in silence a long time, while the sea sent up to them its soft enchanting whispers. . . . Tony suddenly felt herself one with Morten in a great, vague yearning comprehension of this portentous something which he called " Freedom."

CHAPTER IX

"It is wonderful how one doesn't get bored, here at the seashore, Morten. Imagine lying anywhere else for hours at a time, flat on your back, doing nothing, not even thinking — "

"Yes. But I must confess that I used to be bored sometimes — only not in the last few weeks."

Autumn was at hand. The first strong wind had risen. Thin, tattered grey clouds raced across the sky. The dreary, tossing sea was covered far and wide with foam. Great, powerful waves rolled silently in, relentless, awesome; towered majestically, in a metallic dark-green curve, then crashed thundering on the sand.

The season was quite at an end. On that part of the beach usually occupied by the throng of bathers, the pavilions were already partly dismantled, and it lay as quiet as the grave, with only a very few basket-chairs. But Tony and Morten spent the afternoon in a distant spot, at the edge of the yellow loam, where the waves hurled their spray as far up as Sea-gull Rock. Morten had made her a solid sand fortress, and she leaned against it with her back, her feet in their strap shoes and white stockings crossed in front of her. Morten lay turned toward her, his chin in his hands. Now and then a sea-gull flew past them, shrieking. They looked at the green wall of wave, streaked with sea-weed, that came threateningly on and on and then broke against the opposing boulders, with the eternal, confused tumult that deafens and silences and destroys all sense of time.

Finally Morten made a movement as though rousing himself from deep thought, and said, "Well, you will soon be leaving us, Fräulein Tony."

"No; why?" Tony said absently.

"Well, it is the tenth of September. My holidays are nearly at an end, anyhow. How much longer can it last? Shall you be glad to get back to the society of your own kind? Tell me — I suppose the gentlemen you dance with are very agreeable? — No, no, that was not what I wanted to say. Now you must answer me," he said, with a sudden resolution, shifting his chin in his hands and looking

at her. "Here is the question I have been waiting so long to ask.
Now: who is Herr Grünlich?"

Tony sat up, looking at him quickly, her eyes shifting back and
forth like those of a person recollecting himself on coming out of
a dream. She was feeling again the sense of increased personal
importance first experienced when Herr Grünlich proposed for
her hand.

"Oh, is that what you want to know, Morten?" she said
weightily. "Well, I will tell you. It was really very painful for
me to have Thomas mention his name like that, the first afternoon; but since you have already heard of him — well, Herr Grünlich, Bendix Grünlich, is a business friend of my father, a well-to-
do Hamburg merchant, who has asked for my hand. No, no," she
replied quickly to a movement of Morten's, "I have refused him;
I have never been able to make up my mind to yield him my consent for life."

"And why not? — if I may ask," said Morten awkwardly.

"Why? Oh, good heavens, because I couldn't endure him,"
she cried out in a passion. "You ought to have seen him, how
he looked and how he acted. Among other things, he had yellow
whiskers — dreadfully unnatural. I'm sure he curled them and put
on gold powder, like the stuff we use for the Christmas nuts. And
he was underhanded. He fawned on my Father and Mother and
chimed in with them in the most shameful way — "

Morten interrupted her. "But what does this mean: 'That
trims it up uncommonly'?"

Tony broke into a nervous giggle.

"Well, he talked like that, Morten. He wouldn't say 'That
looks very well' or 'It goes very well with the room.' He
was frightfully silly, I tell you. And very persistent; he simply
wouldn't be put off, although I never gave him anything but sar-
casm. Once he made such a scene — he nearly wept — imagine a
man weeping!"

"He must have worshipped you," Morten said softly.

"Well, what affair was that of mine?" she cried out, astonished, turning around on her sand-heap.

"You are cruel, Fräulein Tony. Are you always cruel? Tell
me: You didn't like this Herr Grünlich. But is there any one
to whom you have been more gracious? Sometimes I think: Has
she a cold heart? Let me tell you something: a man is not idiotic
simply because he weeps when you won't look at him. I swear it.
I am not sure, not at all, that I wouldn't do the same thing. You
see, you are such a dainty, spoilt thing. Do you always make fun

of people that lie at your feet? Have you really a cold heart? "

After the first giggle, Tony's lip began to quiver. She turned on him a pair of great distressed eyes, which slowly filled with tears as she said softly: " No, Morten, you should not think that of me — you must not think that of me."

" I don't; indeed I don't," he cried, with a laugh of mingled emotion and hardly suppressed exultation. He turned fully about, so that he lay supporting himself on his elbows, took her hands in both his, and looked straight into hers with his kind steel-blue eyes, which were excited and dreamy and exalted all at once.

" Then you — you won't mock at me if I tell you — ? "

" I know, Morten," she answered gently, looking away from him at the fine white sand sifting through the fingers of her free hand.

" You know — and you — oh, Fräulein Tony! "

" Yes, Morten. I care a great deal for you. More than for any one else I know."

He started up, making awkward gestures with his arms, like a man bewildered. Then he got to his feet, only to throw himself down again by her side and cry in a voice that stammered, wavered, died away and rose again, out of sheer joy: " Oh, thank you, thank you! I am so happy! more than I ever was in all my life! " And he fell to kissing her hands. After a moment he said more quietly: " You will be going back to town soon, Tony, and my holidays will be over in two weeks; then I must return to Göttingen. But will you promise me that you will never forget this afternoon here on the beach — till I come back again with my degree, and can ask your Father — however hard that's going to be? And you won't listen to any Herr Grünlich meantime? Oh, it won't be so long — I will work like a — like anything! it will be so easy! "

" Yes, Morten," she said dreamily, looking at his eyes, his mouth, his hands holding hers.

He drew her hand close to his breast and asked very softly and imploringly: " And won't you — may I — seal the promise? "

She did not answer, she did not look at him, but moved nearer to him on the sand-heap, and Morten kissed her slowly and solemnly on the mouth. Then they stared in different directions across the sand, and both felt furiously embarrassed.

CHAPTER X

Dearest Mademoiselle Buddenbrook,

For how long must the undersigned exist without a glimpse of his enchantress? These few lines will tell you that the vision has never ceased to hover before his spiritual eye; that never has he during these interminably anxious months ceased to think of the precious afternoon in your parental salon, when you let fall a blushing promise which filled me with bliss unspeakable! Since then long weeks have flown, during which you have retired from the world for the sake of calm and self-examination. May I now hope that the period of probation is past? The undersigned permits himself, dearest Mademoiselle, to send the enclosed ring as an earnest of his undying tenderness. With the most tender compliments, and devotedly kissing your hand, I remain,

Your obedient servant,
Grünlich.

Dear Papa,

How angry I've been! I had the enclosed letter and ring just now from Grünlich, and my head aches fearfully from excitement. I don't know what else to do but send them both to you. He simply will not understand me, and what he so poetically writes about the promise isn't in the least true, and I beg you emphatically to make it immediately perfectly clear to him that I am a thousand times less able to say yes to him than I was before, and that he must leave me in peace. He makes himself ridiculous. To you, my dearest Father, I can say that I have bound myself elsewhere, to one who adores me and whom I love more than I can say. Oh, Papa! I could write pages to you! I mean Herr Morten Schwarzkopf, who is studying to be a physician, and who as soon as that happens will ask for my hand. I know that it is the rule of the family to marry a business man, but Morten belongs to the other section of respectable men, the scholars. He is not rich, which I know is important to you and Mamma: but I must tell you that, young as I

am, I have learned that riches do not make every one happy. With
a thousand kisses,

Your obedient daughter,
ANTONIE.

P.S. I find the ring very poor gold, and too narrow.

MY DEAR TONY,

Your letter duly received. As regards its contents, I must tell
you that I did not fail to communicate them to Herr Grünlich:
the result was of such a nature as to shock me very much. You are
a grown girl, and at a serious time of life, so I need not scruple to
tell you the consequences that a frivolous step of yours may draw
after it. Herr Grünlich, then, burst into despair at my announcement, declaring that he loved you so dearly, and could so little
console himself for your loss, that he would be in a state to take
his own life if you remain firm in your resolve. As I cannot take
seriously what you write me of another attachment, I must beg
you to master your excitement over the ring, and consider everything again very carefully. It is my Christian conviction, my dear
daughter, that one must have regard for the feelings of others. We
do not know that you may not be made responsible by the most
high Judge if a man whose feelings you have coldly and obstinately
scorned should trespass against his own life. But the thing I have
so often told you by word of mouth, I must recall again to your
remembrance, and I am glad to have the occasion to repeat it in
writing; for though speech is more vivid and has the more immediate effect, the written word has the advantage that it can be
chosen with pains and fixed in a form well-weighed and calculated by the writer, to be read over and over again, with propor-
tionate effect. — My child, we are not born for that which, with
our short-sighted vision, we reckon to be our own small personal
happiness. We are not free, separate, and independent entities, but
like links in a chain, and we could not by any means be what we are
without those who went before us and showed us the way, by following the straight and narrow path, not looking to right or left.
Your path, it seems to me, has lain all these weeks sharply marked
out for you, and you would not be my daughter, nor the granddaughter of your Grandfather who rests in God, nor a worthy
member of our own family, if you really have it in your heart,
alone, wilfully, and light-headedly to choose your own unregulated path. Your Mother, Thomas, Christian, and I beg you, my

dear Antonie, to weigh all this in your heart. Mlle. Jungmann and Clara greet you affectionately, likewise Clothilde, who has been the last several weeks with her father at Thankless. We all rejoice at the thought of embracing you once more.

With unfailing affection,

YOUR LOVING FATHER.

CHAPTER XI

IT rained in streams. Heaven, earth, and sea were in flood, while the driving wind took the rain and flung it against the panes as though not drops but brooks were flowing down and making them impossible to see through. Complaining and despairing voices sounded in the chimney.

When Morten Schwarzkopf went out into the verandah with his pipe shortly after dinner to look at the sky, he found there a gentleman with a long, narrow yellow-checked ulster and a grey hat. A closed carriage, its top glistening with wet, its wheels clogged with mud, was before the door. Morten stared irresolutely into the rosy face of the gentleman. He had mutton-chop whiskers that looked as though they had been dressed with gold paint.

The gentleman in the ulster looked at Morten as one looks at a servant, blinking gently without seeing him, and said in a soft voice: " Is Herr Pilot-Captain Schwarzkopf at home? "

" Yes," stammered Morten, " I think my Father — "

Hereupon the gentleman fixed his eyes upon him; they were as blue as a goose's.

" Are you Herr Morten Schwarzkopf? " he asked.

" Yes, sir," answered Morten, trying to keep his face straight.

" Ah — indeed! " remarked the gentleman in the ulster, and went on, " Have the goodness to announce me to your Father, young man. My name is Grünlich."

Morten led the gentleman through the verandah, opened for him the right-hand door that led into the office, and went back into the sitting-room to tell his Father. Then the youth sat down at the round table, resting his elbow on it, and seemed, without noticing his Mother, who was sitting at the dark window mending stockings, to busy himself with the " wretched news-sheet " which had nothing in it except the announcements of the silver wedding of Consul So-and-So. Tony was resting in her room.

The pilot-captain entered his office with the air of a man satisfied with his meal. His uniform-coat stood open over the usual white waistcoat. His face was red, and his ice-grey beard coldly set off against it; his tongue travelled about agreeably among his teeth, making his good mouth take the most extraordinary shapes. He bowed shortly, jerkily, with the air of one conforming to the conventions as he understood them.

" Good afternoon," he said. " At your service."

Herr Grünlich, on his side, bowed with deliberation, although one corner of his mouth seemed to go down. He said softly: " Ahem! "

The office was rather a small room, the walls of which had wainscoting for a few feet and then simple plaster. Curtains, yellow with smoke, hung before the window, on whose panes the rain beat unceasingly. On the right of the door was a rough table covered with papers, above it a large map of Europe, and a smaller one of the Baltic Sea fastened to the wall. From the middle of the ceiling hung the well-cut model of a ship under full sail.

The Captain made his guest take the sloping sofa, covered with cracked oil-cloth, that stood opposite the door, and made himself comfortable in a wooden arm-chair, folding his hands across his stomach; while Herr Grünlich, his ulster tightly buttoned up, his hat on his knees, sat bolt upright on the edge of the sofa.

" My name is, I repeat, Grünlich," he said; " from Hamburg. I may say by way of introduction that I am a close business friend of Herr Buddenbrook."

" Servant, Herr Grünlich; pleased to make your acquaintance. Won't you make yourself comfortable? Have a glass of grog after your journey? I'll send right into the kitchen."

" I must permit myself to remark that my time is limited, my carriage is waiting, and I am really obliged to ask for the favour of a few words with you."

" At your service," repeated Herr Schwarzkopf, taken aback. There was a pause.

" Herr Captain," began Herr Grünlich, wagging his head with determination and throwing himself back on his seat. After this he was silent again; and by way of enhancing the effect of his address he shut his mouth tight, like a purse drawn together with strings.

" Herr Captain," he repeated, and went on without further pause, " The matter about which I have come to you directly concerns the young lady who has been for some weeks stopping in your house."

" Mademoiselle Buddenbrook? " asked the Consul.

" Precisely," assented Herr Grünlich. He looked down at the

floor, and spoke in a voice devoid of expression. Hard lines came out at the corners of his mouth.

"I am obliged to inform you," he went on in a sing-song tone, his sharp eyes jumping from one point in the room to another and then to the window, "that some time ago I proposed for the hand of Mademoiselle Buddenbrook. I am in possession of the fullest confidence of both parents, and the young lady herself has unmistakably given me a claim to her hand, though no betrothal has taken place in form."

"You don't say — God keep us!" said Herr Schwarzkopf, in a sprightly tone. "I never heard that before! Congratulations, Herr — er — Grünlich. She's a good girl — genuine good stuff."

"Thank you for the compliment," said Herr Grünlich, coldly. He went on in his high sing-song: "What brings me to you on this occasion, my good Herr Captain, is the circumstance that certain difficulties have just arisen — and these difficulties — appear to have their source in your house — ?" He spoke the last words in a questioning tone, as if to say, "Can this disgraceful state of things be true, or have my ears deceived me?"

Herr Schwarzkopf answered only by lifting his eyebrows as high as they would go, and clutching the arms of his chair with his brown, blond-felled fisherman's hands.

"Yes. This is the fact. So I am informed," Herr Grünlich said, with dreary certitude. "I hear that your son — *studiosus medicinae*, I am led to understand — has allowed himself — of course unconsciously — to encroach upon my rights. I hear that he has taken advantage of the present visit of the young lady to extract certain promises from her."

"What?" shouted the pilot-captain, gripping the arms of his chair and springing up. "That we shall soon — we can soon see — !" With two steps he was at the door, tore it open, and shouted down the corridor in a voice that would have outroared the wildest seas: "Meta, Morten! Come in here, both of you."

"I shall regret it exceedingly if the assertion of my prior rights runs counter to your fatherly hopes, Herr Captain."

Diederich Schwarzkopf turned and stared, with his sharp blue eyes in their wrinkled setting, straight into the stranger's face, as though he strove in vain to comprehend his words.

"Sir!" he said. Then, with a voice that sounded as though he had just burnt his throat with hot grog, "I'm a simple sort of a man, and don't know much about landlubber's tricks and skin games; but if you mean, maybe, that — well, sir, you can just set it down right away that you've got on the wrong tack, and are making a pretty bad miscalculation about my fatherly hopes. I know who my son is, and I know who Mademoiselle Buddenbrook is, and there's too much respect and too much pride in my carcase to be making any plans of the sort you've mentioned. — And now," he roared, jerking his head toward the door, " it's your turn to talk, boy. You tell me what this affair is; what is this I hear — hey? "

Frau Schwarzkopf and her son stood in the doorway, she innocently arranging her apron, he with the air of a hardened sinner. Herr Grünlich did not rise at their entrance. He waited, erect and composed, on the edge of the sofa, buttoned up tight in his ulster.

" So you've been behaving like a silly fool? " bellowed the captain to Morten.

The young man had his thumb stuck between the buttons of his jacket. He scowled and puffed out his cheeks defiantly.

" Yes, Father," he said, " Fräulein Buddenbrook and I — "

" Well, then, I'll just tell you you're a perfect Tom-fool, a young ninny, and you'll be packed off to-morrow for Göttingen — to-morrow, understand? It's all damned childish nonsense, and rascality into the bargain."

" Good heavens, Diederich," said Frau Schwarzkopf, folding her hands, " you can't just say that, you know. Who knows — ? " She stopped, she said no more; but it was plain from her face that a mother's beautiful dream had been shattered in that moment.

" Would the gentleman like to see the young lady? " Schwarzkopf turned to Herr Grünlich and spoke in a harsh voice.

" She is upstairs in her room asleep," Frau Schwarzkopf said with feeling.

" I regret," said Herr Grünlich, and he got up, obviously relieved. " But I repeat that my time is limited, and the carriage waits. I permit myself," he went on, describing with his hat a motion in the direction of Herr Schwarzkopf, " to acknowledge to you, Herr Captain, my entire recognition of your manly and high-principled bearing. I salute you. Good-bye."

Diederich Schwarzkopf did not offer to shake hands with him. He merely gave a jerky bow with the upper part of his heavy figure, that had an air of saying: " This is the proper thing, I suppose."

Herr Grünlich, with measured tread, passed between Morten and his mother and went out the door.

CHAPTER XII

THOMAS appeared with the Kröger calèche. The day was at hand.

The young man arrived at ten o'clock in the forenoon and took a bite with the family in the living-room. They sat together as on the first day, except that now summer was over; it was too cold and windy to sit in the verandah; and — Morten was not there. He was in Göttingen. Tony and he had not even been able to say good-bye. The Captain had stood there and said, " Well, so that's the end of that, eh! "

At eleven the brother and sister mounted into the wagon, where Tony's trunk was already fastened at the back. She was pale and shivered in her soft autumn coat — from cold, weariness, excitement, and a grief that now and then rose up suddenly and filled her breast with a painful oppression. She kissed little Meta, pressed the house-wife's hand, and nodded to Herr Schwarzkopf when he said, " Well, you won't forget us, little Miss, will you? And no bad feeling, eh? And a safe journey and best greetings to your honoured Father and the Frau Consul." Then the coach door slammed, the fat brown horses pulled at their traces, and the three Schwarzkopfs waved their handkerchiefs.

Tony crooked her neck in the corner of the coach, in order to peer out of the window. The sky was covered with white cloud-flakes; the Trave broke into little waves that hurried before the wind. Now and then drops of rain pattered against the glass. At the end of the front people sat in the doors of their cottages and mended nets; barefoot children came running to look curiously at the carriage. *They* did not have to go away!

As they left the last houses behind, Tony bent forward to look at the lighthouse; then she leaned back and closed her tired and burning eyes. She had hardly slept for excitement. She had risen early to finish her packing, and discovered no desire for breakfast. There was a dull taste in her mouth, and she felt so weak that she made no effort to dry the slow, hot tears that kept rising every minute.

But directly her eyes were shut, she found herself again in Travemünde, on the verandah. She saw Morten in the flesh before her; he seemed to speak and to lean toward her as he always did, and then look good-naturedly and searchingly at the next person, unconsciously showing his beautiful teeth as he smiled. Slowly her mind grew calm and peaceful again. She recalled everything that she had heard and learned from him in many a talk, and it solaced her to promise herself that she would preserve all this as a secret holy and inviolate and cherish it in her heart. That the King of Prussia had committed a great wrong against his people; that the local newspaper was a lamentable sheet; yes, that the laws of the League concerning universities had been renewed four years ago — all these were from now on consoling and edifying truths, a hidden treasure which she might store up within herself and contemplate whenever she chose. On the street, in the family circle, at the table she would think of them. Who knew? Perhaps she might even go on in the path prescribed for her and marry Herr Grünlich — that was a detail, after all — but when he spoke to her she could always say to herself, " I know something you don't: the nobility is in principle despicable."

She smiled to herself and was assuaged. But suddenly, in the noise of the wheels, she heard Morten's voice with miraculous clearness. She distinguished every nuance of his kindly, dragging speech as he said: " To-day we must both ' sit on the rocks,' Fräulein Tony," and this little memory overpowered her. Her breast contracted with her grief, and she let the tears flow down unopposed. Bowed in her corner, she held her handkerchief before her face and wept bitterly.

Thomas, his cigarette in his mouth, looked somewhat blankly at the high-road. " Poor Tony," he said at last, stroking her jacket. " I feel so sorry — I understand so well, you know. But what can you do? One has to bear these things. Believe me, I do understand what you feel."

" Oh, you don't understand at all, Tom," sobbed Tony.

" Don't say that. Did you know it is decided that I am to go to Amsterdam at the beginning of next year? Papa has obtained a place for me with van der Kellen and Company. That means I must say good-bye for a long, long time."

" Oh, Tom! Saying good-bye to your father and mother and sisters and brothers — that isn't anything."

" Ye-es," he said, slowly. He sighed, as if he did not wish to say more, and was silent. He let the cigarette rove from one corner of his mouth to the other, lifted one eyebrow, and turned his head away.

"Well, it doesn't last for ever," he began again after a while. "Naturally one forgets."

"But I don't want to forget," Tony cried out in desperation. "Forgetting — is that any consolation?"

CHAPTER XIII

THEN came the ferry, and Israelsdorf Avenue, Jerusalem Hill, the Castle Field. The wagon passed the Castle Gate, with the walls of the prison rising on the right, and rolled along Castle Street and over the Koberg. Tony looked at the grey gables, the oil lamps hung across the streets, Holy Ghost Hospital with the already almost bare lindens in front of it. Oh, how everything was exactly as it had been! It had been standing here, in immovable dignity, while she had thought of it as a dream worthy only to be forgotten. These grey gables were the old, the accustomed, the traditional, to which she was returning, in the midst of which she must live. She wept no more. She looked about curiously. The pain of parting was almost dulled at the sight of these well-known streets and faces. At that moment—the wagon was rolling through Broad Street—the porter Matthiesen passed and took off his stove-pipe hat so obsequiously that it seemed he must be thinking, "Bow, you dog of a porter—you can't bow low enough."

The equipage turned into the Mengstrasse, and the fat brown horses stood snorting and stamping before the Buddenbrook door. Tom was very attentive in helping his sister out, while Anton and Line hastened up to unfasten the trunk. But they had to wait before they could enter the house. Three great lorries were being driven through, one close behind another, piled high with full corn sacks, with the firm name written on them in big black letters. They jolted along over the great boards and down the shallow steps to the cart-yard with a heavy rumbling noise. Part of the corn was evidently to be unloaded at the back of the house and the rest taken to the "Walrus," the "Lion," or the "Oak."

The Consul came out of the office with his pen behind his ear as the brother and sister reached the entry, and stretched out his arms to his daughter.

"Welcome home, my dear Tony!"

She kissed him, looking a little shame-faced, her eyes still red with weeping. But he was very tactful; he made no allusions; he only said: "It is late, but we waited with the second breakfast."

The Frau Consul, Christian, Clothilde, Clara, and Ida Jungmann stood above on the landing to greet her.

Tony slept soundly and well the first night in Mengstrasse. She rose the next morning, the twenty-second of September, refreshed and calmed, and went down into the breakfast-room. It was still quite early, hardly seven o'clock. Only Mamsell Jungmann was there, making the morning coffee.

"Well, well, Tony, my little child," she said, looking round with her small, blinking brown eyes. " Up so early? "

Tony sat down at the open desk, clasped her hands behind her head, and looked for a while at the pavement of the court, gleaming black with wet, and at the damp, yellow garden. Then she began to rummage curiously among the visiting-cards and letters on the desk. Close by the inkstand lay the well-known large copy-book with the stamped cover, gilt edges, and leaves of various qualities and colours. It must have been used the evening before, and it was strange that Papa had not put it back in its leather port-folio and laid it in its special drawer.

She took it and turned over the pages, began to read, and became absorbed. What she read were mostly simple facts well known to her; but each successive writer had followed his predecessor in a stately but simple chronicle style which was no bad mirror of the family attitude, its modest but honourable self-respect, and its reverence for tradition and history. The book was not new to Tony; she had sometimes been allowed to read in it. But its con-tents had never made the impression upon her that they made this morning. She was thrilled by the reverent particularity with which the simplest facts pertinent to the family were here treated. She propped herself on her elbows and read with growing ab-sorption, seriousness and pride.

No point in her own tiny past was lacking. Her birth, her childish illnesses, her first school, her boarding-school days at Mademoiselle Weichbrodt's, her confirmation — everything was carefully entered, with an almost reverent observation of facts, in the Consul's small, flowing business hand; for was not the least of them the will and work of God, who wonderfully guided the destinies of the family? What, she mused, would there be entered here in the future after her name, which she had received from her grandmother Antoinette? All that was yet to be written there would be conned by later members of the family with a piety equal to her own.

She leaned back sighing; her heart beat solemnly. She was filled with reverence for herself: the familiar feeling of personal importance possessed her, heightened by all she had been reading. She felt thrilled and shuddery. "Like a link in a chain," Papa had written. Yes, yes. She was important precisely as a link in this chain. Such was her significance and her responsibility, such her task: to share by deed and word in the history of her family.

She turned back to the end of the great volume, where on a rough folio page was entered the genealogy of the whole Buddenbrook family, with parentheses and rubrics, indicated in the Consul's hand, and all the dates set down: from the marriage of the earliest scion of the family with Brigitta Schuren, the pastor's daughter, down to the wedding of Consul Johann Buddenbrook with Elizabeth Kröger in 1825. From this marriage, it said, four children had resulted: whereupon these were all entered, with the days and years of their birth, and their baptismal names, one after another. Under that of the eldest son it was recorded that he had entered as apprentice in his father's business in the Easter of 1842.

Tony looked a long time at her name and at the blank space next it. Then, suddenly, with a jerk, with a nervous, feverish accompaniment of sobbing breaths and quick-moving lips — she clutched the pen, plunged it rather than dipped it into the ink, and wrote, with her forefinger crooked, her hot head bent far over on her shoulder, in her awkward handwriting that climbed up the page from left to right: "Betrothed, on Sept. 22, 1845, to Herr Bendix Grünlich, Merchant, of Hamburg."

CHAPTER XIV

"I ENTIRELY agree with you, my good friend. This important matter must be settled. In short, then: the usual dowry of a young girl of our family is seventy thousand marks."

Herr Grünlich cast at his future father-in-law a shrewd, calculating glance — the glance of the genuine man of business.

"As a matter of fact," he said — and this "matter of fact" was of precisely the same length as his left-hand whisker, which he was drawing reflectively through his fingers; he let go of the end just as "of fact" was finished.

"You know, my honoured father," he began again, "the deep respect I have for traditions and principles. Only — in the present case is not this consideration for the tradition a little exaggerated? A business increases — a family prospers — in short, conditions change and improve."

"My good friend," said the Consul, "you see in me a fair-dealing merchant. You have not let me finish, or you would have heard that I am ready and willing to meet you in the circumstances, and add ten thousand marks to the seventy thousand without more ado."

"Eighty thousand, then," said Herr Grünlich, making motions with his mouth, as though to say: "Not *too* much; but it will do."

Thus they came to an affectionate settlement; the Consul jingled his keys like a man satisfied as he got up. And, in fact, his satisfaction was justified; for it was only with the eighty thousand marks that they had arrived at the dowry traditional in the family.

Herr Grünlich now said good-bye and departed for Hamburg. Tony as yet realized but little of her new estate. She still went to dances at the Möllendorpfs', Kistenmakers', and Langhals', and in her own home; she skated on the Burgfield and the meadows of the Trave, and permitted the attentions of the young gentlemen of the town. In the middle of October she went to the betrothal feast at the Möllendorpfs' for the oldest son of the house and Juliet Hagenström. "Tom," she said, "I won't go. It is disgusting." But she went, and enjoyed herself hugely. And, as for the rest, by the entry with the pen in the family history-book, she had won the privilege of going, with the Frau Consul or alone, into all the shops in town and making purchases in a grand style for her trousseau. It was to be a brilliant trousseau. Two seamstresses sat all day in the breakfast-room window, sewing, embroidering monograms, and eating quantities of house-bread and green cheese.

"Is the linen come from Lentföhr, Mamma?"

"No, but here are two dozen tea-serviettes."

"That is nice. But he promised it by this afternoon. My goodness, the sheets still have to be hemmed."

"Mamsell Bitterlich wants to know about the lace for the pillow-cases, Ida."

"It is in the right-hand cupboard in the entry, Tony, my child."

"Line — ! "

"You could go yourself, my dear."

"Oh, if I'm marrying for the privilege of running up and down stairs — ! "

"Have you made up your mind yet about the material for the wedding-dress, Tony?"

"Moiré antique, Mamma — I won't marry without moiré antique! "

So passed October and November. At Christmas time Herr Grünlich appeared, to spend Christmas in the Buddenbrook family circle and also to take part in the celebration at the Krögers'. His conduct toward his bride showed all the delicacy one would have expected from him. No unnecessary formality, no importunity, no tactless tenderness. A light, discreet kiss upon the forehead, in the presence of the parents, sealed the betrothal. Tony sometimes puzzled over this, the least in the world. Why, she wondered, did his present happiness seem not quite commensurate with the despair into which her refusal had thrown him? He regarded her with the air of a satisfied possessor. Now and then, indeed, if they happened to be alone, a jesting and teasing mood seemed to overcome him; once he attempted to fall on his knees and approach his whiskers to her face, while he asked in a voice apparently trembling with joy, "Have I indeed captured you? Have I won you for my own?" To which Tony answered, "You are forgetting yourself," and got away with all possible speed.

Soon after the holidays Herr Grünlich went back to Hamburg, for his flourishing business demanded his personal attention; and the Buddenbrooks agreed with him that Tony had had time enough before the betrothal to make his acquaintance.

The question of a house was quickly arranged. Tony, who

looked forward extravagantly to life in a large city, had expressed
the wish to settle in Hamburg itself, and indeed in the Spitalstrasse,
where Herr Grünlich's office was. But the bridegroom, by manly
persistence, won her over to the purchase of a villa outside the
city, near Eimsbüttel, a romantic and retired spot, an ideal nest
for a newly-wedded pair — "*procul negotiis.*" — Ah, he had not
yet forgotten quite all his Latin!

Thus December passed, and at the beginning of the year '46 the
wedding was celebrated. There was a splendid wedding feast, to
which half the town was bidden. Tony's friends — among them
Armgard von Schilling, who arrived in a towering coach —
danced with Tom's and Christian's friends, among them Andreas
Gieseke, son of the Fire Commissioner and now *studiosus juris;*
also Stephan and Edouard Kistenmaker, of Kistenmaker and Son.
They danced in the dining-room and the hall, which had been
strewn with talc for the occasion. Among the liveliest of the lively
was Consul Peter Döhlmann; he got hold of all the earthenware
crocks he could find and broke them on the flags of the big passage.

Frau Stuht from Bell-Founders' Street had another opportunity
to mingle in the society of the great; for it was she who helped
Mamsell Jungmann and the two seamstresses to adjust Tony's
toilette on the great day. She had, as God was her judge, never
seen a more beautiful bride. Fat as she was, she went on her knees;
and, with her eyes rolled up in admiration, fastened the myrtle
twigs on the white moiré antique. This was in the breakfast-room.
Herr Grünlich, in his long-skirted frock-coat and silk waistcoat,
waited at the door. His rosy face had a correct and serious expression, his wart was powdered, and his gold-yellow whiskers carefully curled.

Above in the hall, where the marriage was to take place, the
family gathered — a stately assemblage. There sat the old Krögers,
a little ailing both of them, but distinguished figures always. There
was Consul Kröger with his sons Jürgen and Jacob, the latter having come from Hamburg, like the Duchamps. There were Gotthold Buddenbrook and his wife, born Stüwing, with their three
offspring, Friederike, Henriette, and Pfiffi, none of whom was,
unfortunately, likely to marry. There was the Mecklenburg
branch, represented by Clothilde's father, Herr Bernhard Buddenbrook, who had come in from Thankless and looked with large
eyes at the seignorial house of his rich relations. The relatives
from Frankfort had contented themselves with sending presents;
the journey was too arduous. In their place were the only guests
not members of the family. Dr. Grabow, the family physician,

and Mlle. Weichbrodt, Tony's motherly friend — Sesemi Weichbrodt, with fresh ribbons on her cap over the side curls, and a little
black dress. "Be happy, you *good* child," she said, when Tony
appeared at Herr Grünlich's side in the hall. She reached up and
kissed her with a little explosion on the forehead. The family was
satisfied with the bride: Tony looked pretty, gay, and at her ease,
if a little pale from excitement and tension.

The hall had been decorated with flowers and an altar arranged
on the right side. Pastor Kölling of St. Mary's performed the
service, and laid special stress upon moderation. Everything went
according to custom and arrangement, Tony brought out a hearty
yes, and Herr Grünlich gave his little ahem, beforehand, to clear
his throat. Afterward, everybody ate long and well.

While the guests continued to eat in the salon, with the pastor
in their midst, the Consul and his wife accompanied the young
pair, who had dressed for their journey, out into the snowy, misty
air, where the great travelling coach stood before the door, packed
with boxes and bags.

After Tony had expressed many times her conviction that she
should soon be back again on a visit, and that they too would not
delay long to come to Hamburg to see her, she climbed in good
spirits into the coach and let herself be carefully wrapped up by
the Consul in the warm fur rug. Her husband took his place by
her side.

"And, Grünlich," said the Consul, "the new laces are in the
small satchel, on top. You take a little in under your overcoat,
don't you? This excise — one has to get around it the best one can.
Farewell, farewell! Farewell, dear Tony. God bless you."

"You will find good accommodation in Arensburg, won't
you?" asked the Frau Consul. "Already reserved, my dear
Mamma," answered Herr Grünlich.

Anton, Line, Trine, and Sophie took leave of Ma'am Grünlich.
The coach door was about to be slammed, when Tony was overtaken by a sudden impulse. Despite all the trouble it took, she
unwound herself again from her wrappings, climbed ruthlessly
over Herr Grünlich, who began to grumble, and embraced her
Father with passion. "Adieu, Papa, adieu, my good Papa." And
then she whispered softly: "Are you satisfied with me?"

The Consul pressed her without words to his heart, then put her
from him and shook her hands with deep feeling.

Now everything was ready. The coach door slammed, the
coachman cracked his whip, the horses dashed away so that the
coach windows rattled; the Frau Consul let fly her little white

handkerchief; and the carriage, rolling down the street, disappeared in the mist.

The Consul stood thoughtfully next to his wife, who drew her cloak about her shoulders with a graceful movement.

" There she goes, Betsy."

" Yes, Jean, the first to leave us. Do you think she is happy with him? "

" Oh, Betsy, she is satisfied with herself, which is better; it is the most solid happiness we can have on this earth."

They went back to their guests.

CHAPTER XV

THOMAS BUDDENBROOK went down Meng Street as far as the " Five
Houses." He avoided Broad Street so as not to be accosted by
acquaintances and obliged to greet them. With his hands deep in
the big pockets of his warm dark grey overcoat, he walked, sunk
in thought, over the hard, sparkling snow, which crunched under
his boots. He went his own way, and whither it led no one knew
but himself. The sky was pale blue and clear, the air biting and
crisp — a still, severe, clear weather, with five degrees of frost; in
short, a matchless February day.

Thomas walked down the " Five Houses," crossed Bakers' Alley,
and went along a narrow cross-street into Fishers' Lane. He followed this street, which led down to the Trave parallel to Meng
Street, for a few steps, and paused before a small house, a modest
flower-shop, with a narrow door and dingy show-window, where
a few pots of bulbs stood on a pane of green glass.

He went in, whereupon the bell above the door began to give
tongue, like a little watch-dog. Within, before the counter, talking to the young saleswoman, was a little fat elderly lady in a
Turkey shawl. She was choosing a pot of flowers, examining,
smelling, criticizing, chattering, and constantly obliged to wipe her
mouth with her handkerchief. Thomas Buddenbrook greeted her
politely and stepped to one side. She was a poor relation of the
Langhals', a good-natured garrulous old maid who bore the name
of one of the best families without herself belonging to their set:
that is, she was not asked to the large dinners, but to the small
coffee circles. She was known to almost all the world as Aunt
Lottchen. She turned toward the door, with her pot of flowers,
wrapped up in tissue paper, under her arm; and Thomas, after
greeting her again, said in an elevated voice to the shop girl, " Give
me a couple of roses, please. Never mind the kind — well, La
France."

Then, after Aunt Lottchen had shut the door behind her and
gone away, he said in a lower voice, " Put them away again, Anna.
How are you, little Anna? Here I am — and I've come with a
heavy heart."

Anna wore a white apron over her simple black frock. She was wonderfully pretty. Delicately built as a fawn, she had an almost mongol type of face, somewhat prominent cheek-bones, narrow black eyes full of a soft gleam, and a pale yellow skin the like of which is rare anywhere. Her hands, of the same tint, were narrow, and more beautiful than a shop girl's are wont to be.

She went behind the counter at the right end, so that she could not be seen through the shop-window. Thomas followed on the outside of the counter and, bending over, kissed her on the lips and the eyes.

" You are quite frozen, poor boy," she said.

" Five degrees," said Tom. " I didn't notice it, I've felt so sad coming over."

He sat down on the table, keeping her hand in his, and went on: " Listen, Anna; we'll be sensible to-day, won't we? The time has come."

" Oh, dear," she said miserably, and lifted her apron to her eyes.

" It had to happen some time, Anna. No, don't weep. We were going to be reasonable, weren't we? What else is there to do? One has to bear such things."

" When? " asked Anna, sobbing.

" Day after to-morrow."

" Oh, God, no! Why to-morrow? A week longer — five days! Please, oh, please! "

" Impossible, dear Anna. Everything is arranged and in order. They are expecting me in Amsterdam. I couldn't make it a day longer, no matter how much I wanted."

" And that is so far away — so far away! "

" Amsterdam? Nonsense, that isn't far. We can always think of each other, can't we? And I'll write to you. You'll see, I'll write directly I've got there."

" Do you remember," she said, " a year and a half ago, at the Rifle-club fair? "

He interrupted her ardently. " Do I remember? Yes, a year and a half ago! I took you for an Italian. I bought a pink and put it in my button-hole. — I still have it — I am taking it with me to Amsterdam. — What a heat: how hot and dusty it was on the meadow! "

" Yes, you bought me a glass of lemonade from the next booth. I remember it like yesterday. Everything smelled of fatty-cakes and people."

" But it was fine! We knew right away how we felt — about each other! "

"You wanted to take me on the carrousel, but I couldn't go; I had to be in the shop. The old woman would have scolded."

"No, I know it wouldn't have done, Anna."

She said softly and clearly, "But that is the only thing I've refused you."

He kissed her again, on the lips and the eyes. "Adieu, darling little Anna. We must begin to say good-bye."

"Oh, you will come back to-morrow?"

"Yes, of course, and day after to-morrow early, if I can get away. — But there is one thing I want to say to you, Anna. I am going, after all, rather far away. Amsterdam *is* a long way off — and you are staying here. But — don't throw yourself away, I tell you."

She wept into her apron, holding it up with her free hand to her face. "And you — and you?"

"God knows, Anna, what will happen. One isn't young for ever — you are a sensible girl, you have never said anything about marriage and that sort of thing — "

"God forbid — that I should ask such a thing of you!"

"One is carried along — you see. If I live, I shall take over the business, and make a good match — you see, I am open with you at parting, Anna. I wish you every happiness, darling, darling little Anna. But don't throw yourself away, do you hear? For you haven't done that — with me — I swear it."

It was warm in the shop. A moist scent of earth and flowers was in the air. Outside, the winter sun was hurrying to its repose, and a pure delicate sunset, like one painted on porcelain, beautified the sky across the river. People hurried past the window, their chins tucked into their turned-up collars; no one gave a glance into the corner of the little flower-shop, at the two who stood there saying their last farewells.

PART FOUR

CHAPTER I

April 30, 1846

My dear Mamma,

A thousand thanks for your letter, in which you tell me of Armgard von Schilling's betrothal to Herr von Maiboom of Pöppenrade. Armgard herself sent me an invitation (very fine, with a gilt edge), and also a letter in which she expresses herself as enchanted with her bridegroom. He sounds like a very handsome and refined man. How happy she must be! Everybody is getting married. I have had a card from Munich too, from Eva Ewers. I hear she's getting a director of a brewery.

Now I must ask you something, dearest Mamma: Why do I hear nothing of a visit from the Buddenbrooks? Are you waiting for an official invitation from Grünlich? If so, it isn't necessary; and besides, when I remind him to ask you, he says, "Yes, yes, child, your Father has something else to do." Or do you think you would be disturbing me? Oh, dear me, no; quite the contrary! Perhaps you think you would make me homesick again? But don't you know I am a reasonable woman, already middle-aged and experienced?

I've just been to coffee at Madame Käselau's, a neighbour of mine. They are pleasant people, and our left-hand neighbours, the Gussmanns (but there is a good deal of space between the houses) are sociable people too. We have two friends who are at the house a good deal, both of whom live out here: Doctor Klaasen, of whom I must tell you more later, and Kesselmeyer, the banker, Grünlich's intimate friend. You don't know what a funny old man he is. He has a stubbly white beard and thin black and white hair on his head, that looks like down and waves in the breeze. He makes funny motions with his head, like a bird, and talks all the time, so I call him the magpie, but Grünlich has forbidden me to say that, because magpies steal, and Herr Kesselmeyer is an honourable man. He stoops when he walks, and rows along with his arms. His fuzz only reaches half-way down his head in the back, and from there on his neck is all red and seamy. There is something so awfully sprightly about him! Sometimes he pats me on the cheek and says, "You good little wifey! what a blessing for Grünlich that he has got you." Then he takes out his eye-glasses (he always wears three of them, on long cords, that are forever getting tangled up in his white waistcoat) and sticks them on his nose, which he wrinkles up to make them stop on, and looks at me with his mouth open, until I have to laugh, right in his face. But he takes no offence at that.

Grünlich is very busy; he drives into town in the morning in our little yellow wagon and often does not come back till late. Sometimes he sits down with me and reads the paper.

When we go into society — for example, to Kesselmeyer's, or to Consul Goudstikker on the Alster Dam, or Senator Bock's in City Hall Street — we have to take a hired coach. I have begged Grünlich again and again to get a coupé, for it is really a necessity out here. He has half promised, but, strange to say, he does not like to go into society with me and is evidently displeased when I visit people in the town. Do you suppose he is jealous?

Our villa, which I've already described to you in detail, dear Mamma, is really very pretty, and is much prettier by reason of the new furnishings. You could not find a flaw in the upstairs sitting-room — all in brown silk. The dining-room next is prettily wainscoted. The chairs cost twenty-five marks apiece. I sit in the "pensée-room," which we use as a sitting-room. There is also a little room for smoking and playing cards. The salon, which takes up the whole other half of the parterre, has new yellow blinds now and looks very well. Above are the bed, bath, and dressing-rooms and the servants' quarters. We have a little groom for the yellow wagon. I am fairly well satisfied with the two maid-servants. I am not sure they are quite honest, but thank God I don't have to look after every kreuzer. In short, everything is really worthy of the family and the firm.

And now, dear Mamma, comes the most important part of my letter, which I have kept till the last. A while ago I was feeling rather queer — not exactly ill and yet not quite well. I told Dr. Klaasen about it when I had the chance. He is a little bit of a man with a big head and a still bigger hat. He carries a cane with a flat round handle made of a piece of bone, and walks with it pressed against his whiskers, which are almost light-green from being dyed so many years. Well, you should have seen him! he did not answer my questions at all, but jerked his eye-glasses, twinkled his little eyes, wrinkled his nose at me — it looks like a potato — snickered, giggled, and stared so impertinently that I did not know what to do. Then he examined me, and said everything was going on well, only I must drink mineral water, because I am perhaps a little anaemic. Oh, Mamma, do tell Papa about it, so he can put it in the family book. I will write you again as soon as possible, you may be sure.

Give my love to Papa, Christian, Clara, Clothilde and Ida Jung-mann. I wrote to Thomas just lately.

Your dutiful daughter,
ANTONIE.

August 2, 1846

MY DEAR THOMAS,

I have read with pleasure the news of your meeting with Christian in Amsterdam. It must have been a happy few days for both of you. I have no word as yet of your brother's further journey to England via Ostende, but I hope that with God's mercy it has been safely accomplished. It may not be too late, since Christian has decided to give up a professional career, for him to learn much that is valuable from his chief, Mr. Richardson; may he prosper and find blessing in the mercantile line! Mr. Richardson, Thread-needle Street, is, as you know, a close business friend of our house; I consider myself lucky to have placed both my sons with such friendly-disposed firms. You are now experiencing the good result of such a policy; and I feel profound satisfaction that Herr van der Kellen has already raised your salary in the quarter of a year you have been with him, and that he will continue to give you advancement. I am convinced that you have shown and will continue to show yourself, by your industry and good behaviour, worthy of these favours.

I regret to hear that your health is not so good as it should be. What you write me of nervousness reminds me of my own youth, when I was working in Antwerp and had to go to Ems to take a cure. If anything of the sort seems best for you, my son, I am ready to encourage you with advice and assistance, although I am avoiding such expense for the rest of us in these times of political unrest.

However, your Mother and I took a trip to Hamburg in the middle of June to visit your sister Tony. Her husband had not invited us, but he received us with the greatest cordiality and devoted himself to us so entirely during the two days of our visit, that he neglected his business and hardly left me time for a visit to Duchamps in the town. Antonie is in her fifth month, and her physician assures her that everything is going on in a normal and satisfactory way.

I have still to mention a letter from Herr van der Kellen, from which I was pleased to learn that you are a favoured guest in his family circle. You are now, my son, at an age to begin to harvest the fruits of the upbringing your parents gave you. It may be helpful to you if I tell you that at your age, both in Antwerp and Bergen, I formed a habit of making myself useful and agreeable to my principals; and this was of the greatest service to me. Aside from the honour of association with the family of the head of the firm, one acquires an advocate in the person of the principal's wife; and she may prove invaluable in the undesirable contingency of an oversight at the office or the dissatisfaction of your chief for some slight cause or other.

As regards your business plans for the future, my son, I rejoice in the lively interest they indicate, without being able entirely to agree with them. You start with the idea that the market for our native products — for instance, grain, rape-seed, hides and skins, wool, oil, oil-cake, bones, etc. — is our chief concern; and you think it would be of advantage for you to turn yourself to the commission branch of the business. I once occupied myself with these ideas, at a time when the competition was small (it has since distinctly increased), and I made some experiments in them. My journey to England had for its chief purpose to look out connections there for my undertakings. To this end I went as far as Scotland, and made many valuable acquaintances; but I soon recognized the precarious nature of an export trade hither, and decided to discourage further expansion in that direction. Thus I kept in mind the warning of our forefather, the founder of the firm, which he bequeathed to us, his descendants: "My son, attend with zeal to thy business by day, but do none that hinders thee from thy sleep at night."

This principle I intend to keep sacred, now as in the past, though one is sometimes forced to entertain a doubt, on contemplating the operations of people who seem to get on better without it. I am thinking of Strunck and Hagenström, who have made such notable progress while our own business seems almost at a stand-still. You know that the house has not enlarged its business since the set-back consequent upon the death of your grandfather; and I pray to God that I shall be able to turn over the business to you in its present state. I have an experienced and cautious adviser in our head clerk Marcus. If only your Mother's family would hang on to their groschen a little better! The inheritance is a matter of real importance for us.

I am unusually full of business and civic work. I have been made alderman of the Board of the Bergen Line; also city deputy for the Finance Department, the Chamber of Commerce, the Auditing Commission, and the Almshouse of St. Anne, one after the other.

Your Mother, Clara and Clothilde send greetings. Also several gentlemen — Senator Möllendorpf, Doctor Överdieck, Consul Kistenmaker, Gosch the broker, C. F. Köppen, and Herr Marcus in the office, have asked to be remembered. God's blessing on you, my dear son. Work, pray, and save.

With affectionate regards,
YOUR FATHER.

October 8, 1846

DEAR AND HONOURED PARENTS,

The undersigned is overjoyed to be able to advise you of the happy *accouchement*, half an hour ago, of your daughter, my beloved wife Antonie. It is, by God's will, a daughter; I can find no words to express my joyful emotion. The health of the dear patient, as well as of the infant, is unexceptionable. Dr. Klaasen is entirely satisfied with the way things have gone; and Frau Grossgeorgis, the midwife, says it was simply nothing at all. Excitement obliges me to lay down my pen. I commend myself to my worthy parents with the most respectful affection.

B. GRÜNLICH.

If it had been a boy, I had a very pretty name. As it is, I wanted to name her Meta, but Grünlich is for Erica.

CHAPTER II

"WHAT is the matter, Betsy?" said the Consul, as he came to the table and lifted up the plate with which his soup was covered. "Aren't you well? You don't look just right to me."

The round table in the great dining-room was grown very small. Around it there gathered in these days, besides the parents, only little Clara, now ten years old, Mamsell Jungmann, and Clothilde, as humble, lean, and hungry as ever. The Consul looked about him: every face was long and gloomy. What had happened? He himself was troubled and anxious; for the Bourse was unsteady, owing to this complicated Schleswig-Holstein affair. And still another source of disquiet was in the air; when Anton had gone to fetch in the meat course, the Consul heard what had happened. Trina, the cook, who had never before been anything but loyal and dutiful to her mistress, had suddenly shown clear signs of revolt. To the Frau Consul's great vexation, she had been maintaining relations — a sort of spiritual affinity, it seemed — with the butcher's apprentice; and that man of blood must have influenced her political views in a most regrettable way. The Consul's wife had addressed some reproach to her in the matter of an unsuccessful sauce, and she had put her naked arms akimbo and delivered herself as follows: "You jus' wait, Frau Consul; 'tain' goin' t' be much longer — there'll come another order inter the world. 'N' then *I'll* be sittin' on the sofa in a silk gownd, an' you'll be servin' me." Naturally, she received summary notice.

The Consul shook his head. He himself had had similar troubles. The old porters and labourers were of course respectful enough, and had no notions in their heads; but several here and there among the young ones had shown by their bearing that the new spirit of revolt had entered into them. In the spring there had been a street riot, although a constitution corresponding to the demands of the new time had already been drafted; which, a little later, despite the opposition of Lebrecht Kröger and other stubborn old gentlemen, became law by a decree of the Senate. The citizens met together and representatives of the people were elected. But there was no rest. The world was upside down. Every one wanted to revise the constitution and the franchise, and the citizens grumbled. "Voting by estates," said some — Consul Johann Buddenbrook among them. "Universal franchise," said the others; Hinrich Hagenström was one of these. Still others cried: "Universal voting by estates" — and dear knew what they meant by that! All sorts of ideas were in the air; for instance, the abolition of disabilities and the general extension of the rights of citizenship — even to non-Christians! No wonder Buddenbrook's Trina had imbibed such ideas about sofas and silk gowns! Oh, there was worse to come! Things threatened to take a fearful turn.

It was an early October day of the year 1848. The sky was blue, with a few light floating clouds in it, silvered by the rays of the sun, the strength of which was indeed not so great but that the stove was already going, behind the polished screen in the landscape-room. Little Clara, whose hair had grown darker and whose eyes had a rather severe expression, sat with some embroidery before the sewing-table, while Clothilde, busy likewise with her needlework, had the sofa-place near the Frau Consul. Although Clothilde Buddenbrook was not much older than her married cousin — that is to say, only twenty-one years — her long face already showed pronounced lines; and with her smooth hair, which had never been blond, but always a dull greyish colour, she presented an ideal portrait of a typical old maid. But she was content; she did nothing to alter her condition. Perhaps she thought it best to grow old early and thus to make a quick end of all doubts and hopes. As she did not own a single sou, she knew that she would find nobody in all the wide world to marry her, and she looked with humility into her future, which would surely consist of consuming a tiny income in some tiny room which her influential uncle would procure for her out of the funds of some charitable establishment for maidens of good family.

The Consul's wife was busy reading two letters. Tony related the good progress of the little Erica, and Christian wrote eagerly of his life and doings in London. He did not give any details of his industry with Mr. Richardson of Threadneedle Street. The Frau Consul, who was approaching the middle forties, complained bitterly of the tendency of blond women to grow old too soon. The delicate tint which corresponded to her reddish hair had grown dulled despite all cosmetics; and the hair itself began relentlessly to grey, or would have done so but for a Parisian tincture of which the Frau Consul had the receipt. She was determined never to grow white. When the dye would no longer perform its

office, she would wear a blond wig. On top of her still artistic
coiffure was a silk scarf bordered with white lace, the beginning,
the first adumbration of a cap. Her silk frock was wide and flowing, its bell-shaped sleeves lined with the softest mull. A pair of
gold circlets tinkled as usual on her wrist.

It was three o'clock in the afternoon. Suddenly there was a
noise of running and shouting: a sort of insolent hooting and cat-
calling, the stamping of feet on the pavement, a hubbub that grew
louder and came nearer.

" What is that noise, Mamma? " said Clara, looking out of the
window and into the gossip's glass. " Look at the people! What
is the matter with them? What are they so pleased about? "

" My God! " shouted the Frau Consul, throwing down her letters and springing to the window. " Is it — ? My God, it is the
Revolution! It is the people! "

The truth was that the town had been the whole day in a state
of unrest. In the morning the windows of Benthien the draper's
shop in Broad Street had been broken by stones — although God
knew what the owner had to do with politics!

" Anton," the Consul's wife called with a trembling voice into
the dining-room, where the servants were bustling about with the
silver. " Anton! Go below! Shut the outside doors. Make everything fast. It is a mob."

" Oh, Frau Consul," said Anton. " Is it safe for me to do that?
I am a servant. If they see my livery — "

" What wicked people," Clothilde drawled without putting
down her work. Just then the Consul crossed the entrance hall
and came in through the glass door. He carried his coat over his
arm and his hat in his hand.

" You are going out, Jean? " asked the Frau Consul in great excitement and trepidation.

" Yes, my dear, I must go to the meeting."

" But the mob, Jean, the Revolution — "

" Oh, dear me, Betsy, it isn't so serious as that! We are in God's
hand. They have gone past the house already. I'll go down the
back way."

" Jean, if you love me — do you want to expose yourself to this
danger? Will you leave us here unprotected? I am afraid, I tell
you — I am afraid."

" My dear, I beg of you, don't work yourself up like this. They
will only make a bit of a row in front of the Town Hall or in the
market. It may cost the government a few window-panes — but
that's all."

" Where are you going, Jean? "

" To the Assembly. I am late already. I was detained by business. It would be a shame not to be there to-day. Do you think your Father is stopping away, old as he is? "

" Then go, in God's name, Jean. But be careful, I beg of you. And keep an eye on my Father. If anything hit him — "

" Certainly, my dear."

" When will you be back? " the Frau Consul called after him.

" Well, about half past four or five o'clock. Depends. There is a good deal of importance on the agenda, so I can't exactly tell."

" Oh, I'm frightened, I'm frightened," repeated the Frau Consul, walking restlessly up and down.

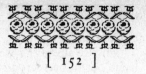

CHAPTER III

CONSUL BUDDENBROOK crossed his spacious ground floor in haste. Coming out into Bakers' Alley, he heard steps behind him and saw Gosch the broker, a picturesque figure in his long cloak and Jesuit hat, also climbing the narrow street to the meeting. He lifted his hat with one thin long hand, and with the other made a deferential gesture, as he said, " Well, Herr Consul — how are you? " His voice sounded sinister.

This broker, Siegismund Gosch, a bachelor of some forty years, was, despite his demeanour, the best and most honest soul in the world; but he was a wit and an oddity. His smooth-shaven face was distinguished by a Roman nose, a protruding pointed chin, sharp features, and a wide mouth drooping at the corners, whose narrow lips he was in the habit of pressing together in the most taciturn and forbidding manner. His grey hair fell thick and sombre over his brow, and he actually regretted not being hump-backed. It was his whim to assume the rôle of a wild, witty, and reckless intrigant — a cross between Mephistopheles and Napoleon, something very malevolent and yet fascinating too; and he was not entirely unsuccessful in his pose. He was a strange yet attractive figure among the citizens of the old city; still, he belonged among them, for he carried on a small brokerage business in the most modest, respectable sort of way. In his narrow, dark little office, however, he had a large book-case filled with poetry in every language, and there was a story that he had been engaged since his twentieth year on a translation of Lope de Vega's collected dramas. Once he had played the rôle of Domingo in an amateur performance of Schiller's " Don Carlos " — this was the culmination of his career. A common word never crossed his lips; and the most ordinary business expressions he would hiss between his clenched teeth, as if he were saying " Curses on you, villain," instead of some commonplace about stocks and commissions. He was, in many ways, the heir and successor to Jean Jacques Hoff-stede of blessed memory, except that his character had certain elements of the sombre and pathetic, with none of the playful liveliness of that old 18th-century friend of Johann Buddenbrook.

One day he lost at a single blow, on the Bourse, six and a half thaler on two or three papers which he had bought as a speculation. This was enough. He sank upon a bench; he struck an attitude which looked as though he had lost the Battle of Waterloo; he struck his clenched fist against his forehead and repeated several times, with a blasphemous roll of the eyes: "Ha, accursed, accursed!" He must have been, at bottom, cruelly bored by the small, safe business he did and the petty transfer of this or that bit of property; for this loss, this tragic blow with which Heaven had stricken him down — him, the schemer Gosch — delighted his inmost soul. He fed on it for weeks. Some one would say, "So you've had a loss, Herr Gosch, I'm sorry to hear." To which he would answer: "Oh, my good friend, '*uomo non educato dal dolore riman sempre bambino*'!" Probably nobody understood that. Was it, possibly, Lope de Vega? Anyhow, there was no doubt that this Siegismund Gosch was a remarkable and learned man.

"What times we live in," he said, limping up the street with the Consul, supported by his stick. "Times of storm and unrest."

"You are right," replied the Consul. "The times are unquiet. This morning's sitting will be exciting. The principle of the estates — "

"Well, now," Herr Gosch went on, "I have been about all day in the streets, and I have been looking at the mob. There are some fine fellows in it, their eyes flaming with excitement and hatred — "

Johann Buddenbrook began to laugh. "You like that, don't you? But you have the right end of it after all, let me tell you. It is all childishness! What do these men want? A lot of uneducated rowdies who see a chance for a bit of a scrimmage."

"Of course. Though I can't deny — I was in the crowd when Berkemeyer, the journeyman butcher, smashed Herr Benthien's window. He was like a panther." Herr Gosch spoke the last word with his teeth particularly close together, and went on: "Oh, the thing has its fine side, that's certain. It is a change, at least, you know; something that doesn't happen every day. Storm, stress, violence — the tempest! Oh, the people are ignorant, I know — still, my heart, this heart of mine — it beats with theirs!" They were already before the simple yellow-painted house on the ground floor of which the sittings of the Assembly took place.

The room belonged to the beer-hall and dance-establishment of a widow named Suerkringel; but on certain days it was at the service of the gentlemen burgesses. The entrance was through a narrow whitewashed corridor opening into the restaurant on the right side, where it smelled of beer and cooking, and thence through a handleless, lockless green door so small and narrow that no one could have supposed such a large room lay behind it. The room was empty, cold, and barnlike, with a whitewashed roof in which the beams showed, and whitewashed walls. The three rather high windows had green-painted bars, but no curtains. Opposite them were the benches, rising in rows like an amphitheatre, with a table at the bottom for the chairman, the recording clerk, and the Committee of the Senate. It was covered with a green cloth and had a clock, documents, and writing-materials on it. On the wall opposite the door were several tall hat-racks with hats and coats.

The sound of voices met the Consul and his companion as they entered through the narrow door. They were the last to come. The room was filled with burgesses, hands in their trousers pockets, on their hips, or in the air, as they stood together in groups and discussed. Of the hundred and thirty members of the body at least a hundred were present. A number of delegates from the country districts had been obliged by circumstances to stop at home.

Near the entrance stood a group composed of two or three small business men, a high-school teacher, the orphan asylum " father," Herr Mindermann, and Herr Wenzel, the popular barber. Herr Wenzel, a powerful little man with a black moustache, an intelligent face, and red hands, had shaved the Consul that very morning; here, however, he stood on an equality with him. He shaved only in the best circles; he shaved almost exclusively the Möllendorpfs, Langhals, Buddenbrooks, and Överdiecks, and he owed his vote in the Assembly to his omniscience in city affairs, his sociability and ease, and his remarkable power of decision at a division.

" Have you heard the latest, Herr Consul? " he asked with round-eyed eagerness as his patron came up.

" What is there to hear, my dear Wenzel? "

" Nobody knew it this morning. Well, permit me to tell you, Herr Consul, the latest is that the crowd are not going to collect before the Town Hall, or in the market — they are coming here to threaten the burgesses. Editor Rübsam has stirred them up."

" Is it possible? " said the Consul. He pressed through the various groups to the middle of the room, where he saw his father-in-law with Senators Dr. Langhals and James Möllendorpf. " Is it true, gentlemen? " he asked, shaking hands with them.

But there was no need to answer. The whole assemblage was full of it: the peace-breakers were coming; they could be heard already in the distance.

" *Canaille!* " said Lebrecht Kröger with cold scorn. He had driven hither in his carriage. On an ordinary day the tall, distin-

guished figure of the once famous cavalier showed the burden of
his eighty years; but to-day he stood quite erect with his eyes half
closed, the corners of his mouth contemptuously drawn down, and
the points of his white moustaches sticking straight up. Two rows
of jewelled buttons sparkled on his black velvet waistcoat.

Not far from this group was Hinrich Hagenström, a square-
built, fleshy man with a reddish beard sprinkled with grey, a heavy
watch-chain across his blue-checked waistcoat, and his coat open
over it. He was standing with his partner Herr Strunck, and did
not greet the Consul.

Herr Benthien, the draper, a prosperous looking man, had a
large group of gentlemen around him, to whom he was circum-
stantially describing what had happened to his show-window. " A
brick, gentlemen, a brick, or at least half a brick — *crack!* through
it went and landed on a roll of green rep. The rascally mob! Oh,
the Government will have to take it up! It's their affair! "

And in every corner of the room unceasingly resounded the
voice of Herr Stuht from Bell-Founders' Street. He had on a black
coat over his woollen shirt; and he so deeply sympathized with
the narrative of Herr Benthien that he never stopped saying, in
outraged accents, " Infamous, un-heard-of! "

Johann Buddenbrook found and greeted his old friend G. F.
Köppen, and then Köppen's rival, Consul Kistenmaker. He moved
about in the crowd, pressed Dr. Grabow's hand, and exchanged a
few words with Herr Gieseke the Fire Commissioner, Contractor
Voigt, Dr. Langhals, the Chairman, brother of the Senator, and
several merchants, lawyers, and teachers.

The sitting was not yet opened, but debate was already lively.
Everybody was cursing that pestilential scribbler, Editor Rübsam;
everybody knew he had stirred up the crowd — and what for?
The business in hand was to decide whether they were to go on
with the method of selecting representatives by estates, or whether
there was to be universal and equal franchise. The Senate had already proposed the latter. But what did the people want? They
wanted these gentlemen by the throats — no more and no less. It
was the worst hole they had ever found themselves in, devil take it!
The Senatorial Committee was surrounded, its members' opinion
eagerly sought. They approached Consul Buddenbrook, as one
who should know the attitude of Burgomaster Överdieck; for
since Senator Doctor Överdieck, Consul Justus Kröger's brother-
in-law, had been made President last year, the Buddenbrooks were
related to the Burgomaster; which had distinctly enhanced the regard in which they were held.

All of a sudden the tumult began outside. Revolution had arrived under the windows of the Sitting. The excited exchange of opinions inside ceased simultaneously. Every man, dumb with the shock, folded his hands upon his stomach and looked at his fellows or at the windows, where fists were being shaken in the air and the crowd was giving vent to deafening and frantic yelling. But then, most astonishingly, as though the offenders themselves had suddenly grown aghast at their own behaviour, it became just as still outside as in the hall; and in that deep hush, one word from the neighbourhood of the lowest benches, where Lebrecht Kröger was sitting, was distinctly audible. It rang through the hall, cold, emphatic, and deliberate — the word "Canaille!" And, like an echo, came the word "Infamous," in a fat, outraged voice from the other corner of the hall. Then the hurried, trembling, whispering utterance of the draper Benthien: "Gentlemen, gentlemen! Listen! I know the house. There is a trap door on to the roof from the attic. I used to shoot cats through it when I was a lad. We can climb on to the next roof and get down safely."

"Cowardice," hissed Gosch the broker between his teeth. He leaned against the table with his arms folded and head bent, directing a blood-curdling glance through the window.

"Cowardice, do you say? How cowardice? In God's name, sir, aren't they throwing bricks? I've had enough of that."

The noise outside had begun again, but without reaching its former stormy height. It sounded quieter and more continuous, a prolonged, patient, almost comfortable hum, rising and falling; now and then one heard whistles, and sometimes single words like "principle" and "rights of citizens." The assembly listened respectfully.

After a while the chairman, Herr Dr. Langhals, spoke in a subdued tone: "Gentlemen, I think we could come to some agreement if we opened the meeting."

But this humble suggestion did not meet with the slightest support from anybody.

"No good in that," somebody said, with a simple decisiveness that permitted no appeal. It was a peasant sort of man, named Pfahl, from the Ritzerau district, deputy for the village of Little Schretstaken. Nobody remembered ever to have heard his voice raised before in a meeting, but its very simplicity made it weighty at the present crisis. Unafraid and with sure political insight, Herr Pfahl had voiced the feeling of the entire assemblage.

"God keep us," Herr Benthien said despondently. "If we sit

on the benches we can be seen from outside. They're throwing
stones — I've had enough of that."

"And the cursed door is so narrow," burst out Köppen the
wine-merchant, in despair. "If we start to go out, we'll probably
get crushed."

"Infamous, un-heard-of," Herr Stuht intoned.

"Gentlemen," began the Chairman urgently once more. "I
have to put before the Burgomaster in the next three days a draft of
to-day's protocol, and the town expects its publication through the
press. I should at least like to get a vote on that subject, if the
sitting would come to order — "

But with the exception of a few citizens who supported the
chairman, nobody seemed ready to come to the consideration of
the agenda. A vote would have been useless anyhow — they must
not irritate the people. Nobody knew what they wanted, so it was
no good to offend them by a vote, in whatever direction. They
must wait and control themselves. The clock of St. Mary's struck
half past four.

They confirmed themselves and each other in this resolve of
patient waiting. They began to get used to the noise that rose
and fell outside, to feel quieter; to make themselves more comfortable, to sit down on the lower benches and chairs. The natural instinct toward industry, common to all these good burghers, began to assert itself: they ventured to bargain a little,
to pick up a little business here and there. The brokers sat down
by the wholesale dealers. These beleaguered gentlemen talked
together like people shut in by a sudden storm, who speak of
other things, and now and then pause to listen with respectful
faces to the thunder. It was five o'clock — half-past five. It was
getting dark. Now and then somebody sighed and said that the
wife would be waiting with the coffee — and then Herr Benthien
would venture to mention the trap-door. But most of them were
like Herr Stuht, who said fatalistically, shaking his head, "I'm too
fat."

Mindful of his wife's request Johann Buddenbrook had kept
an eye on his father-in-law. He said to him: "This little adventure
isn't disturbing you, is it, Father?"

Lebrecht Kröger's forehead showed two swollen blue veins under his white wig. He looked ill. One aristocratic old hand played
with the opalescent buttons on his waistcoat; the other, with its
great diamond ring, trembled on his knee.

"Fiddlesticks, Buddenbrook," he said; but his voice showed extreme fatigue. "I am sick of it, that's all." Then he betrayed himself by suddenly hissing out: "Parbleu, Jean, this infamous rabble ought to be taught some respect with a little powder and shot. *Canaille!* Scum!"

The Consul hummed assent. "Yes, yes, you are right; it is a pretty undignified affair. But what can we do? We must keep our tempers. It's getting late. They'll go away after a bit."

"Where is my carriage? I desire my carriage," said the old man in a tone of command, suddenly quite beside himself. His anger exploded; he trembled all over. "I ordered it for five o'clock: where is it? This sitting will never be held. Why should I stop any longer? I don't care about being made a fool of. My carriage! What are they doing to my coachman? Go see after it, Buddenbrook."

"My dear Father-in-Law, for heaven's sake be calm. You are getting excited. It will be bad for you. Of course I will go and see after the carriage. I think myself we have had enough of this. I will speak to the people and tell them to go home."

Close by the little green door he was accosted by Siegismund Gosch, who grasped his arm with a bony hand and asked in a gruesome whisper: "Whither away, Herr Consul?"

The broker's face was furrowed with a thousand lines. His pointed chin rose almost up to his nose, his face expressed the most desperate resolution; his grey hair streamed distractedly over brow and temples; his head was so drawn in between his shoulders that he really almost achieved his ambition of looking like a dwarf — and he rapped out: "You behold me resolved to speak to the people."

The Consul said: "No, let me do it, Gosch. I really know more of them than you do."

"Be it so," answered the broker tonelessly. "You are a bigger man than I." And, lifting his voice, he went on: "But I will accompany you, I will stand at your side, Consul Buddenbrook. Let the wrath of the outraged people tear me in pieces — "

"What a day, what a night!" he said as they went out. There is no doubt he had never felt so happy before in his life. "Ha, Herr Consul! Here are the people."

They had gone down the corridor and outside the outer door, where they stood at the top of three little steps that went down to the pavement. The street was indeed a strange sight. It was as still as the grave. At the open and lighted windows of the houses round, stood the curious, looking down upon the black mass of the insurgents before the Burgesses' House. The crowd was not much bigger than that inside the hall. It consisted of young labourers from the harbour and granaries, servants, school pupils, sailors from the merchant ships, and other people from the little streets, alleys, courts, and rabbit-hutches round about. There were even two or three women — who had probably promised themselves the same millennium as the Buddenbrooks' cook. A few of the insurrectionists, weary of standing, had sat down with their feet in the gutter and were eating sandwiches.

It was nearly six o'clock. Though twilight was well advanced, the oil lamps hung unlighted above the street. This fact, this open and unheard-of interruption of the regular order, was the first thing that really made Consul Buddenbrook's temper rise, and was responsible for his beginning to speak in a rather short and angry tone and the broadest of pronunciations:

"Now then, all of you, what is the meaning of this foolishness? "

The picnickers sprang up from the sidewalk. Those in the back ranks, beyond the foot-pavement, stood on their tiptoes. Some navvies, in the service of the Consul, took off their caps. They stood at attention, nudged each other, and muttered in low tones, "'Tis Consul Buddenbrook. He be goin' to talk. Hold yer jaw, there, Chrishan; he can jaw like the devil himself! Ther's Broker Gosch — look! What a monkey he is! Isn't he gettin' o'erwrought! "

"Carl Smolt! " began the Consul again, picking out and fastening his small, deep-set eyes upon a bow-legged young labourer of about two-and-twenty, with his cap in his hand and his mouth full of bread, standing in front of the steps. "Here, speak up, Carl Smolt! Now's the time! I've been here the whole afternoon — "

"Yes, Herr Consul," brought out Carl Smolt, chewing violently. "The thing is — ower — it's a soart o' — we're makin' a rivolution."

"What kind of nonsense is that, then? "

"Lord, Herr Consul, ye knaw what that is. We're not satisfied wi' things as they be. We demand another order o' things; tain't any more'n that — that's what it is."

"Now, listen, Carl Smolt and the rest of you. Whoever's got any sense will go home and not bother himself over any revolutions, disturbing the regular order of things — "

"The sacred order," interrupted Herr Gosch dramatically.

"The regular order, I say," finished the Consul. "Why, even the lamps aren't lighted. That's going too far with the revolution."

Carl Smolt had swallowed his mouthful by now, and, with the people at his back, stood his ground and made some objections.

"Well, Herr Consul, ye may say that. But we're only agin the principle of the voate — "

"God in heaven, you ninny," shouted the Consul, forgetting, in his excitement, to speak dialect. "You're talking the sheerest nonsense — "

"Lord, Herr Consul," said Carl Smolt, somewhat abashed, "thet's oall as it is. Rivolution it has to be. Ther's rivolution ivery-wheer, in Berlin, in Paris — "

"But, Smolt, what do you want? Just tell me that, if you can."

"Lord, Herr Consul, I say we wants a republic; that's wat I be sayin'."

"But, you fool, you've got one already."

"Well, Herr Consul, then we wants another."

Some of the bystanders, who understood the matter better, began to laugh rudely and heartily; and although few even heard Carl's answer, the laughter spread until the whole crowd of republicans stood shaking good-naturedly. Some of the gentlemen from inside the hall appeared at the window with curious faces and beer-mugs in their hands. The only person disappointed and painted by this turn of affairs was Siegismund Gosch.

"Now, people," shouted Consul Buddenbrook finally, "I think the best thing for you all to do is to go home."

Carl Smolt, quite crestfallen over the result he had brought about, answered: "That's right, Herr Consul. Then things'll be quieted down. And Herr Consul doesn't take it ill of me, do'e, now? Good-bye, Herr Consul!"

The crowd began to disperse, in the best of humours.

"Wait a minute, Smolt," shouted the Consul. "Have you seen the Kröger carriage? the calèche from outside the Castle Gate?"

"Yes, sir, Herr Consul. He's here; he be driven up in some court somewhere."

"Then run quick and say he's to come at once; his master wants to go home."

"Servant, Herr Consul," and, throwing his cap on his head and pulling the leather visor well down over his brows, Carl Smolt ran with great swinging strides down the street.

CHAPTER IV

WHEN the Consul and Siegismund Gosch returned to the hall, the
scene was a more comfortable one than it had been a quarter of
an hour before. It was lighted by two large oil lamps standing on
the Committee table, in whose yellow light the gentlemen sat or
stood together, pouring out beer into shining tankards, touching
glasses and talking loudly, in the gayest of humours. Frau Suerkringel, the widow, had consoled them. She had loyally taken on
her enforced guests and given them good advice, recommending
that they fortify themselves for the siege, which might endure
some while yet. And thus she had profitably employed the time
by selling a considerable quantity of her light yet exhilarating beer.
As the others entered, the house-boy, in shirt-sleeves and good-
natured grin, was just bringing in a fresh supply of bottles. While
it was certainly late, too late to consider further the revision of the
Constitution, nobody seemed inclined to interrupt the meeting and
go home. It was too late for coffee, in any case.

After the Consul had received congratulatory handshakes on his
success, he went up to his father-in-law. Lebrecht Kröger was
the only man in the room whose mood had not improved. He sat
in his place, cold, remote, and lofty, and answered the information
that the carriage would be around at once by saying scornfully, in
a voice that trembled more with bitterness than age: " Then the
mob permits me to go home? "

With stiff movements that no longer had in them anything of
the charm that had been his, he had his fur mantle put about his
shoulders, and laid his arm, with a careless " *Merci,*" on that of the
Consul, who offered to accompany him home. The majestic coach,
with two large lanterns on the box, stood in the street, where, to
the Consul's great satisfaction, the lamps were now being lighted.
They both got in. Silent and stiffly erect, with his eyes half-closed,
Lebrecht Kröger sat with the rug over his knees, the Consul at his
right hand, while the carriage rolled through the streets. Beneath
the points of the old man's white moustaches two lines ran down
perpendicularly from the corners of his mouth to his chin. He was

gnawed by chagrin at the insult that had been offered him, and he stared, weary and chilled, at the cushions opposite.

There was more gaiety in the streets than on a Sunday evening. Obviously a holiday temper reigned. The people, delighted at the successful outcome of the revolution, were out in the gayest mood. There was singing. Here and there youngsters shouted "Hurrah!" as the carriage drove past, and threw their caps into the air.

"I really think, Father, you let the matter affect you too much," the Consul said. "When one thinks of it, what a tom-fool business the whole thing was — simply a farce." In order to get some reply from the old man he went on to talk about the revolution in lively tones. "When the propertyless class begin to realize how little they serve their own ends — why, good heavens, it's the same everywhere. I was talking this afternoon with Gosch the broker, a wonderful man, looking at everything with the eyes of a poet and writer. You see, Father, this revolution was made at the æsthetic tea-tables of Berlin. Then the people take their own skin to market — for, of course, they will be the ones to pay for it!"

"It would be a good thing if you would open the window on your side," said Herr Kröger.

Johann Buddenbrook gave him a quick glance and let the glass down hastily.

"Aren't you feeling well, dear Father?" he asked anxiously.

"Not at all," answered Lebrecht Kröger severely.

"You need food and rest," the Consul said; and in order to be doing something he drew up the fur rug closer about his father-in-law's knees.

Suddenly — the carriage was rolling through Castle Street — a wretched thing happened. Fifteen paces from the Castle Gate, in the half-dark, they passed a group of noisy and happy street urchins, and a stone flew through the open window. It was a harmless little stone, the size of a hen's egg, flung by the hand of some Chris Snut or Heine Voss to celebrate the revolution; certainly not with any bad intent, and probably not directed toward the carriage at all. It came noiselessly through the window and struck Lebrecht Kröger in his chest, which was covered with the thick fur rug. Then it rolled down over the cover and fell upon the floor of the coach.

"Clumsy fools!" said the Consul angrily. "Is everybody out of their senses this evening? It didn't hurt you, did it?"

Old Kröger was silent — alarmingly silent. It was too dark in the carriage to see his expression. He sat straighter, higher, stiffer than ever, without touching the cushions. Then, from deep within him, slowly, coldly, dully, came the single word: "Canaille."

For fear of angering him further, the Consul made no answer. The carriage clattered through the gate, and three minutes later was in the broad avenue before the gilt-tipped railings that bounded the Kröger domain. A drive bordered with chestnut trees went from the garden gate up to the terrace; and on either side of the gate a gilt-topped lantern was burning brightly. The Consul saw his father-in-law's face by this light — it was yellow and wrinkled; the firm, contemptuous set of the mouth had given way: it had changed to the lax, silly, distorted expression of a very old man. The carriage stopped before the terrace.

"Help me out," said Lebrecht Kröger; but the Consul was already out, had thrown back the rug, and offered his arm and shoulder as a support. He led the old man slowly for a few paces across the gravel to the white stone steps that went up to the dining-room. At the foot of these, the old man bent at the knee-joints. His head fell so heavily on his breast that the lower jaw clashed against the upper. His eyes rolled — grew dim; Lebrecht Kröger, the gallant, the cavalier à-la-mode, had joined his fathers.

CHAPTER V

A YEAR and two months later, on a misty, snowy morning in January of the year 1850, Herr and Madame Grünlich sat at breakfast with their little three-year-old daughter, in the brown wainscoted dining-room, on chairs that cost twenty-five marks apiece.

The panes of both windows were opaque with mist; behind them one had vague glimpses of bare trees and bushes. A red glow and a gentle, scented warmth came from the low, green-tiled stove standing in a corner. Through the open door next it one could see the foliage-plants in the " pensée-room." On the other wall, half-drawn green stuff portières gave a view of the brown satin salon and of a lofty glass door leading on to a little terrace beyond. The cracks in this door were carefully stopped with cotton-wool, and there was nothing to be seen through its panes but the whitish-grey mist beyond.

The snow-white cloth of woven damask on the round table had an embroidered green runner across it, laid with gold-bordered porcelain so translucent that it gleamed like mother-of-pearl. The tea-kettle was humming. There was a finely worked silver bread-basket in the shape of a curling leaf, with slices and rolls of fine bread; under one crystal bell were little balls of butter, under another different sorts of cheese, white, yellow, and green. There was even a bottle of wine standing before the master of the house; for Herr Grünlich had a full breakfast every morning.

His whiskers were freshly curled, and at this early hour his rosy face was rosier than ever. He sat with his back to the salon, already arrayed in a black coat and light trousers with a pattern of large checks, eating a grilled chop, in the English manner. His wife thought this very elegant, but also very disgusting — she had never brought herself to take it instead of her usual breakfast of bread and butter and an egg.

Tony was in her dressing-gown. She adored dressing-gowns. Nothing seemed more elegant to her than a handsome negligée, and as she had not been allowed to indulge this passion in the parental house she was the more given to it as a wife. She had three of these dainty clinging garments, to the fashioning of which can go so much more taste and fantasy than to a ball-gown. To-day she wore her dark red one. Its colour toned beautifully with the paper above the wainscoting, and its large-flowered stuff, of a beautiful soft texture, was embroidered all over with sprays of tiny glass beads of the same colour, while row after row of red velvet ribbons ran from neck to hem.

Her thick ash-blond hair, with its dark red velvet band, curled about her brows. She had now, as she was herself well aware, reached the highest point of her physical bloom; yet her pretty, pouting upper lip retained just the naïve, provocative expression of her childhood. The lids of her grey-blue eyes were reddened with cold water. Her hands, the white Buddenbrook hands, finely shaped if a little stumpy, their delicate wrists caressed by the velvet cuffs of her dressing-gown, handled her knife and fork and tea-cup with motions that were to-day, for some reason or other, rather jerky and abrupt. Her little daughter Erica sat near her in a high chair. She was a plump child with short blond hair, in a funny shapeless, knitted frock of pale blue wool. She held a large cup in both tiny hands, entirely concealing her face, and drank her milk with little sighs of satisfaction.

Frau Grünlich rang, and Tinka, the housemaid, came from the entry to take the child from her high chair and carry her upstairs into the play-room. "You may take her walking outside for a half-hour, Tinka," said Tony. "But not longer; and put on her thick jacket. It is very damp and foggy." She remained alone with her husband.

"You only make yourself seem absurd," she said then, after a silence, obviously continuing an interrupted conversation. "What are your objections? Give me some reason. I can't be always attending to the child."

"You are not fond of children, Antonie."

"Fond of children, indeed! I have no time. I am taken up with the housekeeping. I wake up with twenty things that must be done, and I go to bed with forty that have not been done."

"There are two servants. A young woman like you — "

"Two servants. Good. Tinka has to wash up, to clean, to serve. The cook is busy all the time. You have chops early in the morning. Think it over, Grünlich. Sooner or later, Erica must have a *bonne*, a governess."

"But to get a governess for her so soon is not suited to our means."

" Our means! Goodness, you *are* absurd! Are we beggars? Are we forced to live within the smallest limits we can? I think I brought you in eighty thousand marks — "

" Oh, you and your eighty thousand marks — ! "

" Yes, I know you like to make light of them. They were of no importance to you because you married me for love! Good. But do you still love me? You deliberately disregard my wishes. The child is not to have a governess. And I don't even speak any more of the coupé, which we need quite as much as we need food and drink. And why do you insist on our living out here in the country, if it isn't in accordance with our means to keep a carriage so that we can go into society respectably? Why do you never like it when I go in to town? You would always rather just have me bury myself out here, so I should never see a living soul. I think you are very ill-tempered."

Herr Grünlich poured some wine into his glass, lifted up one of the crystal bells, and began on the cheese. He made no reply.

" Don't you love me any more? " repeated Tony. " Your silence is so insulting, it drives me to remind you of a certain day when you entered our landscape-room. You made a fine figure of yourself! But from the very first day after our marriage you have sat with me only in the evening, and that only to read the paper. Just at first you showed some little regard for my wishes. But that's been over with for a long while now. You neglect me."

" And you? You are ruining me."

" I? I am ruining you? "

" Yes, you are ruining me with your indolence, your extravagance, and love of luxury."

" Oh, pray don't reproach me with my good upbringing! In my parents' house I never had to lift a finger. Now I have hard work to get accustomed to the housekeeping; but I have at least a right to demand that you do not refuse me the ordinary assistance. Father is a rich man; he would never dream that I could lack for service."

" Then wait for this third servant until we get hold of some of those riches."

" Oh, you are wishing for my Father's death. But I mean that we are well-to-do people in our own right. I did not come to you with empty hands."

Herr Grünlich smiled an embarrassed and dejected smile, although he was in the act of chewing his breakfast. He made no other reply, and his silence bewildered Tony.

"Grünlich," she said more quietly, "why do you smile and talk about our 'means'? Am I mistaken? Has business been bad? Have you — ? "

Just then somebody drummed on the corridor door, and Herr Kesselmeyer walked in.

CHAPTER VI

HERR KESSELMEYER entered unannounced, as a friend of the house, without hat or coat. He paused, however, near the door. His looks corresponded exactly to the description Tony had given to her Mother. He was slightly thick-set as to figure, but neither fat nor lean. He wore a black, already somewhat shiny coat, short tight trousers of the same material, and a white waistcoat, over which went a long thin watch-chain and two or three eye-glass cords. His clipped white beard was in sharp contrast with his red face. It covered his cheeks and left his chin and lips free. His mouth was small and mobile, with two yellowish pointed teeth in the otherwise vacant gum of his lower jaw, and he was pressing these into his upper lip, as he stood absently by the door with his hands in his trousers pockets and the black and white down on his head waving slightly, although there was not the least perceptible draught.

Finally he drew his hands out of his pockets, bowed, released his lip, and with difficulty freed one of the eye-glass cords from the confusion on his waistcoat. He lifted his pince-nez and put it with a single gesture astride his nose. Then he made the most astonishing grimaces, looked at the husband and wife, and remarked: "Ah, ha! "

He used this expression with extraordinary frequency and a surprising variety of inflections. He might say it with his head thrown back, his nose wrinkled up, mouth wide open, hands swishing about in the air, with a long-drawn-out, nasal, metallic sound, like a Chinese gong; or he might, with still funnier effect, toss it out, gently, *en passant;* or with any one of a thousand different shades of tone and meaning. His *a* was very clouded and nasal. To-day it was a hurried, lively " Ah ha! " accompanied with a jerk of the head, that seemed to arise from an unusually pleasant mood, and yet might not be trusted to be so; for the fact was, Banker Kesselmeyer never behaved more gaily than when he was dangerous. When he jumped about emitting a thousand " Ah ha's," lifting his glasses to his nose and letting them fall again, waving his

arms, chattering, plainly quite beside himself with light-headed-
ness, then you might be sure that evil was gnawing at his inwards.
Herr Grünlich looked at him blinking, with unconcealed mistrust.

"Already — so early?" he asked.

"Ah, ha!" answered Herr Kesselmeyer, and waved one of his
small, red, wrinkled hands in the air, as if to say: "Patience, there
is a surprise coming." "I must speak with you, without any delay;
I must speak with you."

The words sounded irresistibly comic as he rolled each one about
before giving it out, with exaggerated movements of his little
toothless, mobile mouth. He rolled his *r*'s as if his palate were
greased. Herr Grünlich blinked more and more suspiciously.

"Come and sit down, Herr Kesselmeyer," said Tony. "I'm
glad you've come. Listen. You can decide between us. Grünlich
and I have been disagreeing. Now tell me: ought a three-year-old
child to have a governess or not?"

But Herr Kesselmeyer seemed not to be attending. He had
seated himself and was rubbing his stubbly beard with his forefinger, making a rasping sound, his mouth as wide open as possible,
nose as wrinkled, while he stared over his glasses with an indescribably sprightly air at the elegantly appointed breakfast-table, the
silver bread-basket, the label on the wine-bottle.

"Grünlich says I am ruining him," Tony continued.

Herr Kesselmeyer looked at her; then he looked at Herr Grünlich; then he burst out into an astonishing fit of laughter. "You
are ruining him? — you? *You* are ruining him — that's it, is it?
Oh good gracious, heavens and earth, you don't say! That *is* a
joke. That is a tre-men-dous, tre-men-dous joke." He let out a
stream of ha ha's all run in together.

Herr Grünlich was plainly nervous. He squirmed on his seat.
He ran his long finger down between his collar and his neck and
let his golden whiskers glide through his hand.

"Kesselmeyer," he said. "Control yourself, man. Are you out
of your head? Stop laughing! Will you have some wine? Or a
cigar? What are you laughing at?"

"What am I laughing at? Yes, yes, give me a glass of wine, give
me a cigar. Why am I laughing? So you think your wife is ruining you?"

"She is very luxuriously inclined," Herr Grünlich said irritably.

Tony did not contradict him. She leaned calmly back, her hands
in her lap on the velvet ribbons of her frock and her pert upper lip
in evidence: "Yes, I am, I know. I have it from Mamma. All the
Krögers are fond of luxury."

She would have admitted in the same calm way that she was
frivolous, revengeful, or quick-tempered. Her strongly developed
family sense was instinctively hostile to conceptions of free will
and self-development; it inclined her rather to recognize and accept her own characteristics wholesale, with fatalistic indifference
and toleration. She had, unconsciously, the feeling that any trait
of hers, no matter of what kind, was a family tradition and therefore worthy of respect.

Herr Grünlich had finished breakfast, and the fragrance of the
two cigars mingled with the warm air from the stove. "Will you
take another, Kesselmeyer?" said the host. "I'll pour you out another glass of wine. — You want to see me? Anything pressing? Is
it important? — Too warm here, is it? We'll drive into town together afterward. It is cooler in the smoking-room." To all this
Herr Kesselmeyer simply shook his hand in the air, as if to say:
"This won't get us anywhere, my dear friend."

At length they got up; and, while Tony remained in the dining-
room to see that the servant-maid cleared away, Herr Grünlich led
his colleague through the "pensée-room," with his head bent,
drawing his long beard reflectively through his fingers. Herr
Kesselmeyer rowed into the room with his arms and disappeared
behind his host.

Ten minutes passed. Tony had gone into the salon to give the
polished nut-wood escritoire and the curved table-legs her personal attention with the aid of a gay little feather duster. Then she
moved slowly through the dining-room into the living-room with
dignity and marked self-respect. The Demoiselle Buddenbrook
had plainly not grown less important in her own eyes since becoming Madame Grünlich. She held herself very erect, chin in, and
looked down at the world from above. She carried in one hand her
little lacquered key-basket; the other was in the pocket of her
gown, whose soft folds played about her. The naïve expression of
her mouth betrayed that the whole of her dignity and importance
were a part of a beautiful, childlike, innocent game which she was
constantly playing with herself.

In the "pensée-room" she busied herself with a little brass
sprinkler, watering the black earth around her plants. She loved
her palms, they gave so much elegance to the room. She touched
carefully a young shoot on one of the thick round stems, examined
the majestically unfolded fans, and cut away a yellow tip here and
there with the scissors. Suddenly she stopped. The conversation
in the next room, which had for several minutes been assuming a

livelier tone, became so loud that she could hear every word, though the door and the portières were both heavy.

"Don't shriek like that — control yourself, for God's sake! " she heard Herr Grünlich say. His weak voice could not stand the strain, and went off in a squeak. "Take another cigar," he went on, with desperate mildness.

"Yes, thanks, with the greatest pleasure," answered the banker, and there was a pause while he presumably helped himself. Then he said: "In short, will you or won't you: one or the other? "

"Kesselmeyer, give me an extension."

"Ah, ha! No, no, my friend. There is no question of an extension. That's not the point now."

"Why not? What is stirring you up to this? Be reasonable, for heaven's sake. You've waited this long."

"Not a day longer, my friend. Yes, we'll say eight days, but not an hour longer. But can't we rely any longer on — ? "

"No names, Kesselmeyer."

"No names. Good. But doesn't some one rely any longer on his estimable Herr Pa— "

"No hints, either. My God, don't be a fool."

"Very good; no hints, either. But have we no claim any longer on the well-known firm with whom our credit stands and falls, my friend? How much did it lose by the Bremen failure? Fifty thousand? Seventy thousand? A hundred thousand? More? The sparrows on the housetops know that it was involved, heavily involved. Yesterday — well, no names. Yesterday the well-known firm was good, and it was unconsciously protecting you against pressure. To-day its stock is flat — and B. Grünlich's stock is the flattest of the flat. Is that clear? Do you grasp it? You are the first man to notice a thing like that. How are people treating you? How do they look at you? Beck and Goudstikker are perfectly agreeable, give you the same terms as usual? And the bank? "

"They will extend."

"You aren't lying, are you? Oh, no! I know they gave you a jolt yesterday — a very, very stimulating jolt, eh? You see? Oh, don't be embarrassed. It is to your interest, of course, to pull the wool over my eyes, so that the others will be quiet. Hey, my dear friend? Well, you'd better write to the Consul. I'll wait a week."

"A part payment, Kesselmeyer! "

"Part payment, rubbish! One accepts part payment to convince oneself for the time of a debtor's ability to pay. Do I need to make experiments of that kind on you? I am perfectly well-informed about your ability to pay. Ah, ha, ah, ha! Part payment! That's a very good joke."

"Moderate your voice, Kesselmeyer. Don't laugh all the time in that cursed way. My position is so serious — yes, I admit, it is serious. But I have such-and-such business in hand — everything may still come out all right. Listen, wait a minute: Give me an extension and I'll sign it for twenty per cent."

"Nothing in it, nothing in it, my friend. Very funny, very amusing. Oh, yes, I'm in favour of selling at the right time. You promised me eight per cent, and I extended. You promised me twelve and sixteen per cent, and I extended, every time. Now, you might offer me forty per cent, and I wouldn't consider it — not for a moment. Since Brother Westfall in Bremen fell on his nose, everybody is for the moment freeing himself from the well-known firm and getting on a sound basis. As I say, I'm for selling at the right time. I've held your signatures as long as Johann Buddenbrook was good — in the meantime I could write up the interest on the capital and increase the per cent. But one only keeps a thing so long as it is rising or at least keeping steady. When it begins to fall, one sells — which is the same as saying I want my capital."

"Kesselmeyer, you are shameless."

"Ah, ha, a-ha! Shameless, am I? That's very charming, very funny. What do you want? You must apply to your father-in-law. The Credit Bank is raging — and you know you are not exactly spotless."

"No, Kesselmeyer. I adjure you to hear me quietly. I'll be perfectly frank. I confess that my situation is serious. You and the Credit Bank are not the only ones — there are notes of hand — everything seems to have gone to pieces at once!"

"Of course — naturally. It is certainly a clean-up — a liquidation."

"No, Kesselmeyer; hear me out. Do take another cigar."

"This one is not half finished. Leave me alone with your cigars. Pay up."

"Kesselmeyer, don't let me smash! — You are a friend of mine — you have eaten at my table."

"And maybe you haven't eaten at mine?"

"Yes, yes — but don't refuse me credit now, Kesselmeyer!"

"Credit? It's credit, now, is it? Are you in your senses? A new loan?"

"Yes, Kesselmeyer, I swear to you — A little — a trifle. I only need to make a few payments and advances here and there to get on my feet again and restore confidence. Help me and you will be doing a big business. As I said, I have a number of affairs on hand. They may still all come out right. You know how shrewd and re-sourceful I am."

" I know what a numbskull you are! A dolt, a nincompoop, my dear friend! Will you have the goodness to tell me what your resourcefulness can accomplish at this stage? Perhaps there is a bank somewhere in the wide world that will lend you a shilling? Or another father-in-law? Ah, no; you have already played your best card. You can't play it twice. — With all due respect, my dear fellow, and my highest regards."

" Speak lower, devil take you! "

" You are a fool. Shrewd and resourceful, are you? Yes, to the other chap's advantage. You're not scrupulous, I'll say that for you, but much good it's done you! You have played tricks, and wormed capital out of people by hook or crook, just to pay me my twelve or sixteen per cent. You threw your honour overboard without getting any return. You have a conscience like a butcher's dog, and yet you are nothing but a ninny, a scapegoat. There are always such people — they are too funny for words. Why is it you are so afraid to apply to the person we mean with the whole story? Isn't it because there was crooked work four years ago? Perhaps it wasn't all quite straight — what? Are you afraid that certain things — ? "

" Very well, Kesselmeyer; I will write. But suppose he refuses? Suppose he lets me down? "

" Oh — ah, ha! Then we will just have a bankruptcy, a highly amusing little bankruptcy. That doesn't bother me at all. So far as I am concerned, I have about covered my expenses with the interest you have scratched together, and I have the priority with the assets. Oh, you wait; I shan't come short. I know everything pretty well, my good friend; I have an inventory already in my pocket. Ah, ha! We shall see that no dressing-gown and no silver bread-basket gets away."

" Kesselmeyer, you have sat at my table — "

" Oh, be quiet with your table! In eight days I'll be back for the answer. I shall walk in to town — the fresh air will do me good. Good morning, my friend, good morning! "

And Herr Kesselmeyer seemed to depart — yes, he went. She heard his odd, shuffling walk in the corridor, and imagined him rowing along with his arms. . . .

Herr Grünlich entered the " pensée-room " and saw Tony standing there with the little watering-can in her hand. She looked him in the face.

"What are you looking at? Why are you staring like that?" he said to her. He showed his teeth, and made vague movements in the air with his hands, and wiggled his body from side to side. His rosy face could not become actually pale; but it was spotted red and white like a scarlet-fever patient's.

CHAPTER VII

CONSUL JOHANN BUDDENBROOK arrived at the villa at two o'clock
in the afternoon. He entered the Grünlich salon in a grey
travelling-cloak and embraced his daughter with painful intensity.
He was pale and seemed older. His small eyes were deep in their
sockets, his large pointed nose stuck out between the fallen cheeks,
his lips seemed to have grown thinner, and the beard under his
chin and jaws half covered by his stiff choker and high neck-band
— he had lately ceased to wear the two locks running from the
temples half-way down the cheeks — was as grey as the hair on his
head.

The Consul had hard, nerve-racking days behind him. Thomas
had had a haemorrhage; the Father had learned of the misfortune
in a letter from Herr van der Kellen. He had left his business in
the careful hands of his clerk and hurried off to Amsterdam. He
found nothing immediately dangerous about his son's illness, but
an open-air cure was necessary, in the South, in Southern France;
and as it fortunately happened that a journey of convalescence had
been prescribed for the young son of the head of the firm, the
two young men had left for Pau as soon as Thomas was able to
travel.

The Consul had scarcely reached home again when he was attacked by a fresh misfortune, which had for the moment shaken
his firm to its foundations and by which it had lost eighty thousand
marks at one blow. How? Discounted cheques drawn on Westfall
Brothers had come back to the firm, liquidation having begun.
He had not failed to cover them. The firm had at once showed
what it could do, without hesitation or embarrassment. But that
could not prevent the Consul from experiencing all the sudden
coldness, the reserve, the mistrust at the banks, with "friends,"
and among firms abroad, which such an event, such a weakening
of working capital, was sure to bring in its train.

Well, he had pulled himself together, and had reviewed the
whole situation; had reassured, reinforced, made head. And then,
in the midst of the struggle, among telegrams, letters, and calculations, this last blow broke upon him as well: B. Grünlich, his

daughter's husband, was insolvent. In a long, whining, confused letter he had implored, begged, and prayed for an assistance of a hundred to a hundred and twenty thousand marks. The Consul replied curtly and non-committally that he would come to Hamburg to met Herr Grünlich and Kesselmeyer the banker, made a brief, soothing explanation to his wife, and started off.

Tony received him in the salon. She was fond of receiving visits in her brown silk salon, and she made no exception now; particularly as she had a very profound impression of the importance of the present occasion, without comprehending in the least what it was about. She looked blooming and yet becomingly serious, in her pale grey frock with its laces at breast and wrists, its bell-shaped sleeves and long train, and little diamond clasp at the throat. "How are you, Papa? At last you have come to see us again. How is Mamma? Is there good news from Tom? Take off your things, Father dear. Will you dress? The guest-room is ready for you. Grünlich is dressing."

"Don't call him, my child. I will wait for him here. You know I have come for a talk with your husband — a very, very serious talk, my dear Tony. Is Herr Kesselmeyer here?"

"Yes, he is in the pensée-room looking at the album."

"Where is Erica?"

"Up in the nursery with Tinka. She is very well. She is bathing her doll — of course, not in real water; I mean — she is a waxdoll, she only —"

"Of course." The Consul drew a deep breath and went on: "Evidently you have not been informed as to — to the state of affairs with your husband."

He had sat down in an arm-chair near the large table, and Tony placed herself at his feet on a little seat made of three cushions on top of one another. The finger of her right hand toyed gently with the diamond at her throat.

"No, Papa," answered Tony. "I must confess I know nothing. Heavens, I am a goose! — I have no understanding at all. I heard Kesselmeyer talking lately to Grünlich — at the end it seemed to me he was just joking again — he always talks so drolly. I heard your name once or twice —"

"You heard my name? In what connection?"

"Oh, I know nothing of the connection, Papa. Grünlich has been insufferably sulky ever since that day, I must say. Until yesterday — yesterday he was in a good mood, and asked me a dozen times if I loved him, and if I would put in a good word for him with you if he had something to ask you."

" Oh! "

" Yes, he told me he had written you and that you were coming here. It is good you have come. Everything is so queer. Grünlich had the card-table put in here. There are a lot of paper and pencils on it — for you to sit at, and hold a council together."

" Listen, my dear child," said the Consul, stroking her hair. " I want to ask you something very serious. Tell me: you love your husband with your whole heart, don't you? "

" Of course, Papa," said Tony with a face of child-like hypocrisy — precisely the face of the child Tony when she was asked: " You won't tease the old doll-woman again, Tony? " The Consul was silent a minute.

" You love him so much," he asked again, " that you could not live without him, under any circumstances, even if by God's will your situation should alter so that he could no longer surround you with all these things? " And his hand described a quick movement over the furniture and portières, over the gilt clock on the étagère, and finally over her own frock.

" Certainly, Papa," repeated Tony, in the soothing tone she nearly always used when any one spoke seriously to her. She looked past her father out of the window, where a heavy veil of rain was silently descending. Her face had the expression children wear when some one tells them a fairy story and then tactlessly introduces a generalization about conduct and duty — a mixture of embarrassment and impatience, piety and boredom.

The Consul looked at her without speaking for a minute. Was he satisfied with her response? He had weighed everything thoroughly, at home and during the journey.

It is comprehensible that Johann Buddenbrook's first impulse was to refuse his son-in-law any considerable payment. But when he remembered how pressing — to use a mild word — he had been about this marriage; when he looked back into the past, and recalled the words: " Are you satisfied with me? " with which his child had taken leave of him after the wedding, he gave way to a burdensome sense of guilt against her and said to himself that the thing must be decided according to her feelings. He knew perfectly that she had not made the marriage out of love, but he was obliged to reckon with the possibility that these four years of life together and the birth of the child had changed matters; that Tony now felt bound body and soul to her husband and would be driven by considerations both spiritual and worldly to shrink from a separation. In such a case, the Consul argued, he must accommodate himself to the surrender of whatever sum was necessary.

Christian duty and wifely feeling did indeed demand that Tony should follow her husband into misfortune; and if she actually took this resolve, he did not feel justified in letting her be deprived of all the ease and comfort to which she had been accustomed since childhood. He would feel himself obliged to avert the catastrophe, and to support B. Grünlich at any price. Yet the final result of his considerations was the desire to take his daughter and her child home with him and let Grünlich go his own way. God forbid that the worst should happen!

In any case, the Consul invoked the pronouncement of the law that a continued inability to provide for wife and children justified a separation. But, before everything, he must find out his daughter's real feelings.

"I see," he said, "my dear child, that you are actuated by good and praiseworthy motives. But — I cannot believe that you are seeing the thing as, unhappily, it really is — namely, as actual fact. I have not asked what you would do in this or that case, but what you to-day, now, will do. I do not know how much of the situation you know or suspect. It is my painful duty to tell you that your husband is obliged to call his creditors together; that he cannot carry on his business any longer. I hope you understand me."

"Grünlich is bankrupt?" Tony asked under her breath, half rising from the cushions and seizing the Consul's hand quickly.

"Yes, my child," he said seriously. "You did not know it?"

"My suspicions were not definite," she stammered. "Then Kesselmeyer was not joking?" she went on, staring before her at the brown carpet. "Oh, my God!" she suddenly uttered, and sank back on her seat.

In that minute all that was involved in the word "bankrupt" rose clearly before her: all the vague and fearful hints which she had heard as a child. "Bankrupt" — that was more dreadful than death, that was catastrophe, ruin, shame, disgrace, misery, despair. "He is bankrupt," she repeated. She was so cast down and shaken by the fatal word that the idea of escape, of assistance from her father, never occurred to her. He looked at her with raised eyebrows, out of his small deep-set eyes, which were tired and sad and full of an unusual suspense. "I am asking you," he said gently, "my dear Tony, if you are ready to follow your husband into misery?" He realized at once that he had used the hard word instinctively to frighten her, and he added: "He can work himself up again, of course."

"Certainly, Papa," answered she. But it did not prevent her from bursting into tears. She sobbed into her batiste handkerchief, trimmed with lace and with the monogram A. G. She still wept just like a child; quite unaffectedly and without embarrassment. Her upper lip had the most touching expression.

Her father continued to probe her with his eyes. " That is your serious feeling, my child? " he asked. He was as simple as she.

" I must, mustn't I? " she sobbed. " Don't I have to — ? "

" Certainly not," he said. But with a guilty feeling he added: " I would not force you to it, my dear Tony. If it should be the case that your feelings did not bind you indissolubly to your husband — "

She looked at him with uncomprehending, tear-streaming eyes. " How, Papa? "

The Consul twisted and turned, and found a compromise. " My dear child, you can understand how painful it would be for me to have to tell you all the hardships and suffering that would come about through the misfortune of your husband, the breaking-up of the business and of your household. I desire to spare you these first unpleasantnesses by taking you and little Erica home with me. You would be glad of that, I think? "

Tony was silent a moment, drying her tears. She carefully breathed on her handkerchief and pressed it against her eyes to heal their inflammation. Then she asked in a firm tone, without lifting her voice: " Papa, is Grünlich to blame? Is it his folly and lack of uprightness that has brought him to this? "

" Very probably," said the Consul. " That is — no, I don't know, my child. The explanation with him and the banker has not taken place yet."

She seemed not to be listening. She sat crouched on her three silk cushions, her elbow on her knee, her chin in her hand, and with her head bowed looked dreamily into the room.

" Ah, Papa," she said softly, almost without moving her lips, " wouldn't it have been better — ? "

The Consul could not see her face — but it had the expression it often wore those summer evenings at Travemünde, as she leaned at the window of her little room. One arm rested on her Father's knee, the hand hanging down limply. This very hand was expressive of a sad and tender abandonment, a sweet, pensive longing, travelling back into the past.

" Better? " asked Consul Buddenbrook. " If what, my child? "

He was thoroughly prepared for the confession that it would have been better had this marriage not taken place; but Tony only answered with a sigh: " Oh, nothing."

She seemed rapt by her thoughts, which had borne her so far

away that she had almost forgotten the "bankrupt." The Consul felt himself obliged to utter what he would rather only have confirmed.

"I think I guess your thoughts, Tony," he said, "and I don't on my side hesitate to confess that in this hour I regret the step that seemed to me four years ago so wise and advisable. I believe, before God, I am not responsible. I think I did my duty in trying to give you an existence suitable to your station. Heaven has willed otherwise. You will not believe that your Father played lightly and unreflectingly with your happiness in those days! Grünlich came to us with the best recommendations, a minister's son, a Christian and a cosmopolitan man. Later I made business inquiries, and it all sounded as favourable as possible. I examined the connections. All that is still very dark; and the explanation is yet to come. But you don't blame me — ? "

"No, Papa — how can you say such a thing? Come, don't take it to heart, poor Papa! You look pale. Shall I give you a little cordial? " She put her arm around his neck and kissed his cheek.

"Thank you, no," he said. "There, there! It is all right. Yes, I have bad days behind me. I have had much to try me. These are all trials sent from God. But that does not help my feeling a little guilty toward you, my child. Everything depends on the question I have already asked you. Speak openly, Tony. Have you learned to love your husband in these years of marriage? "

Tony wept afresh; and covering her eyes with both hands, in which she held the batiste handkerchief, she sobbed out: "Oh, what are you asking me, Papa? I have never loved him — he has always been repulsive to me. You know that."

It would be hard to say what went on in Johann Buddenbrook. His eyes looked shocked and sad; but he bit his lips hard together, and great wrinkles came in his cheeks, as they did when he had brought a piece of business to a successful conclusion. He said softly: "Four years — "

Tony's tears ceased suddenly. With her damp handkerchief in her hand, she sat up straight on her seat and said angrily: "Four years! Yes! Sometimes, in those four years, he sat with me in the evening and read the paper."

"God gave you a child," said the Father, moved.

"Yes, Papa. And I love Erica very much, although Grünlich says I am not fond of children. I would not be parted from her, that is certain. But Grünlich — no! Grünlich, no. And now he is bankrupt. Ah, Papa, if you will take Erica and me home — oh, gladly."

The Consul compressed his lips again. He was extremely well satisfied. But the main point had yet to be touched upon; though, by the decision Tony showed, he did not risk much by asking.

" You seem not to have thought it might be possible to do something, to get help. I have already said to you that I do not feel myself altogether innocent of the situation, and — in case you should expect — hope — I might intervene, to prevent the failure and cover your husband's debts, the best I could, and float his business — "

He watched her keenly, and her bearing filled him with satisfaction. It expressed disappointment.

" How much is it? " she asked.

" What is that to the point, my child? A very large sum." And Consul Buddenbrook nodded several times, as though the weight of the very thought of such a sum swung his head back and forth. " I should not conceal from you," he went on, " that the firm has suffered losses already quite apart from this affair, and that the surrender of a sum like this would be a blow from which it would recover with difficulty. I do not in any way say this to — "

He did not finish. Tony had sprung up, had even taken a few steps backward, and with the wet handkerchief still in her hand she cried: "Good! Enough! Never! " She looked almost heroic. The words " the firm " had struck home. It is highly probable that they had more effect than even her dislike of Herr Grünlich. " You shall not do that, Papa," she went on, quite beside herself. " Do you want to be bankrupt too? Never, never! "

At this moment the hall door opened a little uncertainly and Herr Grünlich entered.

Johann Buddenbrook rose, with a movement that meant: " That's settled."

CHAPTER VIII

HERR GRÜNLICH's face was all mottled with red; but he had dressed carefully in a respectable-looking black coat and pea-green trousers like those in which he had made his first visits in Meng Street. He stood still, with his head down, looking very limp, and said in a weak exhausted sort of voice: " Father? "

The Consul bowed, not too cordially, and straightened his neck-cloth with an energetic movement.

" Thank you for coming," said Herr Grünlich.

" It was my duty, my friend," replied the Consul. " But I am afraid it will be about all I can do for you."

Herr Grünlich threw him a quick look and seemed to grow still more limp.

" I hear," the Consul went on, " that your banker, Herr Kesselmeyer, is awaiting us — where shall the conference be held? I am at your service."

" If you will be so good as to follow me," Herr Grünlich murmured. Consul Buddenbrook kissed his daughter on the forehead and said, " Go up to your child, Antonie."

Then he went, with Herr Grünlich fluttering in front of and behind him to open the portières, through the dining-room into the living-room.

Herr Kesselmeyer stood at the window, the black and white down softly rising and falling upon his cranium.

" Herr Kesselmeyer, Herr Consul Buddenbrook, my father-in-law," said Herr Grünlich, meekly. The Consul's face was impassive. Herr Kesselmeyer bowed with his arms hanging down, both yellow teeth against his upper lip, and said: " Pleasure to meet you, Herr Consul."

" Please excuse us for keeping you waiting, Kesselmeyer," said Herr Grünlich. He was not more polite to one than to the other. " Pray sit down."

As they went into the smoking-room, Herr Kesselmeyer said vivaciously: " Have you had a pleasant journey? Ah, rain? Yes, it is a bad time of year, a dirty time. If we had a little frost, or snow, now — but rain, filth — very, very unpleasant."

"What a queer creature!" thought the Consul.

In the centre of the little room with its dark-flowered wall-paper stood a sizable square table covered with green baize. It rained harder and harder; it was so dark that the first thing Herr Grünlich did was to light the three candles on the table. Business letters on blue paper, stamped with the names of various firms, torn and soiled papers with dates and signatures, lay on the green cloth. There were a thick ledger and a metal inkstand and sand-holder, full of well-sharpened pencils and goose-quills.

Herr Grünlich did the honours with the subdued and tactful mien of a man greeting guests at a funeral. "Dear Father, do take the easy chair," he said. "Herr Kesselmeyer, will you be so kind as to sit here?"

At last they were settled. The banker sat opposite the host, the Consul presided on the long side of the table. The back of his chair was against the hall door.

Herr Kesselmeyer bent over, released his upper lip, disentangled a glass from his waistcoat and stuck it on his nose, which he wrinkled for the purpose, and opened his mouth wide. Then he scratched his stubbly beard with an ugly rasping noise, put his hands on his knees, and remarked in a sprightly tone, jerking his head toward the piles of papers: "Well, there we have the whole boiling."

"May I look into matters a little more closely?" asked the Consul, taking up the ledger. But Herr Grünlich suddenly stretched out his hands over the table — long, trembling hands marked with high blue veins — and cried out in a voice that trembled too: "A moment, Father. Just a moment. Let me make just a few explanations. Yes, you will get an insight into everything — nothing will escape your glance; but, believe me, you will get an insight into the situation of an unfortunate, not a guilty man. You see in me a man who fought unwearied against fate, but was finally struck down. I am innocent of all — "

"We shall see, my friend, we shall see," said the Consul, with obvious impatience; and Herr Grünlich took his hands away and resigned himself to his fate.

Then there were long dreadful minutes of silence. The three gentlemen sat close together in the flickering candlelight, shut in by the four dark walls. There was not a sound but the rustling of the Consul's papers and the falling rain outside.

Herr Kesselmeyer stuck his thumbs in the arm-holes of his

waistcoat and played piano on his shoulders with his fingers, looking with indescribable jocosity from one to the other. Herr Grünlich sat upright in his chair, hands on the table, staring gloomily
before him, and now and then stealing an anxious glance at his
father-in-law out of the tail of his eye. The Consul examined the
ledger, followed columns of figures with his finger, compared
dates, and did indecipherable little sums in lead-pencil on a scrap
of paper. His worn features expressed astonishment and dismay at
the conditions into which he now " gained an insight." Finally he
laid his left arm on Herr Grünlich's and said with evident emotion:
" You poor man! "

" Father," Herr Grünlich broke out. Two great tears rolled
down his cheeks and ran into the golden whiskers. Herr Kesselmeyer followed their course with the greatest interest. He even
raised himself a little, bent over, and looked his vis-à-vis in the
face, with his mouth open. Consul Buddenbrook was moved.
Softened by his own recent misfortunes, he felt himself carried
away by sympathy; but he controlled his feelings.

" How is it possible? " he said, with a sad head-shake. " In so
few years — "

" Oh, that's simple," answered Herr Kesselmeyer, good-tem-
peredly. " One can easily ruin oneself in four years. When we
remember that it took an even shorter time for Westfal Brothers
in Bremen to go smash — " The Consul stared at him, but without
either seeing or hearing him. He himself had not expressed his
own actual thoughts, his real misgivings. Why, he asked himself
with puzzled suspicion, why was this happening now? It was as
clear as daylight that, just where he stood to-day, B. Grünlich
had stood two years, three years before. But his credit had been
inexhaustible, he had had capital from the banks, and for his undertakings continual endorsement from sound houses like Senator
Bock and Consul Goudstikker. His paper had passed as current as
banknotes. Why now, precisely now — and the head of the firm
of Johann Buddenbrook knew well what he meant by this " now "
— had there come this crash on all sides, this complete withdrawal
of credit as if by common consent, this unanimous descent upon
B. Grünlich, this disregard of all consideration, all ordinary business courtesy? The Consul would have been naïve indeed had he
not realized that the good standing of his own firm was to the
advantage of his son-in-law. But had the son-in-law's credit so
entirely, so strikingly, so exclusively depended upon his own?
Had Grünlich himself been nothing at all? And the information
the Consul had had, the books he had examined — ? Well, how-

ever the thing stood, his resolution was firmer than ever not to lift a finger. They had reckoned without their host.

Apparently B. Grünlich had known how to make it appear that he was connected with the firm of Buddenbrook — well, this widely-circulated error should be set right once for all. And this Kesselmeyer — he was going to get a shock too. The clown! Had he no conscience whatever? It was very plain how shamelessly he had speculated on the probability that he, Johann Buddenbrook, would not let his daughter's husband be ruined; how he had continued to finance Grünlich long after he was unsound, and exacted from him an ever crueller rate of interest.

"Now," he said shortly, "let us get to the point. If I am asked as a merchant to say frankly what I think, I am obliged to say that if the situation is that of an unfortunate man, it is also in a great degree that of a guilty one."

"Father!" stammered Herr Grünlich.

"The name does not come well to my ears," said the Consul, quickly and harshly. "Your demands on Herr Grünlich amount, sir" — turning for a moment to the banker — "to sixty thousand marks, I believe?"

"With the back interest they come to sixty-eight thousand seven hundred and fifty-five marks and fifteen shillings," answered Herr Kesselmeyer pleasantly.

"Very good. And you would not be inclined under any circumstances to be patient for a longer time?"

Herr Kesselmeyer simply began to laugh. He laughed with his mouth open, in spasms, without a trace of scorn, even good-naturedly, looking at the Consul as though he were inviting him to join in the fun.

Johann Buddenbrook's little deep eyes clouded over and began to show red rims around them that ran down to the cheek-bones. He had only asked for form's sake, being aware that a postponement on the part of one creditor would not materially alter the situation. But the manner of this man's refusal was mortifying indeed. With a motion of the hand he pushed away everything from in front of him, laid the pencil down with a jerk on the table, and said, "Then I must express myself as unwilling to concern myself any further with this affair."

"Ah, ha!" cried Herr Kesselmeyer, shaking his hands in the air. "That's the way to talk. The Herr Consul will settle everything out of hand — we shan't have any long speeches. Without more ado." Johann Buddenbrook did not even look at him.

"I cannot help you, my friend." He turned calmly to Herr

Grünlich. "Things must go on as they have begun. Pull yourself
together, and God will give you strength and consolation. I must
consider our interview at an end."

Herr Kesselmeyer's face took on a serious expression which was
vastly becoming to it. But then he nodded encouragingly to Herr
Grünlich. The latter sat motionless at the table, only wringing
his hands so hard that the fingers cracked.

"Father — Herr Consul," he said, with a trembling voice. "You
will not — you cannot desire my ruin. Listen. It is a matter of a
hundred and twenty thousand marks in all — you can save me!
You are a rich man. Regard it as you like — as a final arrangement,
as your daughter's inheritance, as a loan subject to interest. I will
work — you know I am keen and resourceful — "

"I have spoken my last word," said the Consul.

"Permit me — may I ask whether you could if you would?"
asked Herr Kesselmeyer, looking at him through his glasses, with
his nose wrinkled up. "I suggest to the Consul that this would be
a most advantageous time to display the strength of the firm of
Buddenbrook."

"You would do well, sir, to leave the good name of my house
to me. I do not need to throw my money in the nearest ditch in
order to show how good my credit is."

"Dear me, no, of course not — ditch, ah, ha! — Ditch is very
funny. But doesn't the gentleman think the failure of his son-in-
law places his own credit in a bad light — er — ah — ?"

"I can only recommend you again to remember that my credit
in the business world is entirely my own affair," said the Consul.

Herr Grünlich looked at his banker helplessly and began afresh:
"Father! I implore you again: think what you are doing. Is it a
question of me alone? I — oh, I myself might be allowed to perish.
But your daughter, my wife, whom I love, whom I won after such
a struggle — and our child — both innocent children — are they to
be brought low as well? No, Father, I will not bear it; I will kill
myself. Yes, I would kill myself with this hand. Believe me —
and may heaven pardon you if it will."

Johann Buddenbrook leaned back in his arm-chair quite white,
with a fast-beating heart. For the second time the emotions of this
man played upon him, and their expression had the stamp of truth;
again he heard, as when he told Herr Grünlich the contents of his
daughter's letter from Travemünde, the same terrible threat, and
again there shuddered through him all the fanatical reverence of
his generation for human feelings, which yet had always been in
conflict with his own hard practical sense. But the attack lasted

no longer than a moment. "A hundred thousand marks," he repeated to himself; and then he said quietly and decisively: "Antonie is my daughter. I shall know how to protect her from unmerited suffering."

"What do you mean by that?" asked Herr Grünlich, slowly stiffening.

"That you will see," answered the Consul. "For the present I have nothing to add." And he got up, pushed back his chair, and turned toward the door.

Herr Grünlich sat silent, stiff, irresolute; his mouth opened and closed without a word coming out. But the sprightliness of Herr Kesselmeyer returned at this conclusive action of the Consul. Yes, it got the upper hand entirely, it passed all bounds, it became frightful. The glasses fell from his nose, which went skyward, while his little mouth, with the two triangular yellow teeth, looked as though it were splitting. He rowed with his little red hands in the air, the fuzz on his head waved up and down, his whole face, with its bristly white beard distorted and grotesque with uncontrolled hilarity, had grown the colour of cinnamon.

"Ah, ha, ha, ah, ha!" he yelled, his voice cracking. "I find that in the last — degree — funny! You ought to consider, Consul Buddenbrook, before you consign to the grave such a valuable — such a supreme specimen of a son-in-law. Anything so shrewd, so resourceful as he is, won't be born upon God's wide earth a second time. Aha! Four years ago — when the knife was at our throat, the rope around our neck — suddenly we made a match with Fräulein Buddenbrook, and spread the news on 'Change, even before it had actually come off! Congratulations, my dear friend; my best respects!"

"Kesselmeyer," groaned Herr Grünlich, making spasmodic motions with his hands, as though waving off an evil spirit. He rushed into one corner of the room, where he sat down and buried his face in his hands. The ends of his whiskers lay on his shanks, and he rocked his knees up and down in his emotion.

"How did we do that?" went on Herr Kesselmeyer. "How did we actually manage to catch the little daughter and the eighty thousand marks? O-ho, ah, ha! That is easy. Even if one has no more shrewdness and resourcefulness than a tallow candle, it is easy! You show the saviour Papa nice, pretty, clean books, in which everything is put in the right way — only that they don't quite correspond with the plain fact — for the plain fact is that three-quarters of the dowry is already debts."

The Consul stood at the door deathly pale, the handle in his hand. Shivers ran up and down his back. He seemed to be standing in this little room lighted by the flickering candles, between a swindler and an ape gone mad with spite.

"I despise your words, sir," he brought out with uncertain emphasis. "I despise your wild utterances the more that they concern me as well. I did not hand my daughter over light-headedly to misfortune; I informed myself as to my son-in-law's prospects. The rest was God's will."

He turned — he would not hear any more — he opened the door. But Herr Kesselmeyer shrieked after him: "Aha, inquiries? Where? Of Bock? Of Goudstikker? Of Petersen? Of Massmann and Timm? They were all in it. They were all in it up to their necks. They were all uncommonly pleased to be secured by the wedding —" The Consul slammed the door behind him.

CHAPTER IX

Dora the cook, about whose honesty Tony had had her doubts, was busy in the dining-room.

"Ask Madame Grünlich to come down," ordered the Consul. "Get yourself ready, my child," he said as Tony appeared. He went with her into the salon. "Get ready as soon as possible, and get Erica ready too. We are going to the city. We shall sleep to-night in a hotel and travel home to-morrow."

"Yes, Papa," Tony said. Her face was red; she was distracted and bewildered. She made unnecessary and hurried motions about her waist, as if not knowing where to begin and not grasping the actuality of the occasion.

"What shall I take, Papa?" she asked distractedly. "Everything? All our clothes? One trunk or two? Is Grünlich really bankrupt? Oh, my God! But can I take my jewelry, then? Papa, the servants must leave — I cannot pay them. Grünlich was to have given me housekeeping money to-day or to-morrow."

"Never mind, my child; things will all be arranged here. Just take what is necessary in a small trunk. They can send your own things after you. Hurry, do you hear?"

Just then the portières were parted and Herr Grünlich came into the salon. With quick steps, his arms outstretched, his head on one side, with the bearing of a man who says: "Here I am; kill me if you will," he hurried to his wife and sank down on his knees right in front of her. His appearance was pitiable. His golden whiskers were dishevelled, his coat crumpled, his neck-cloth askew, his collar open; little drops stood upon his forehead.

"Antonie!" he said. "Have you a heart that can feel? Hear me. You see before you a man who will be utterly ruined, if — yes, who will die of grief, if you deny him your love. Here I lie; can you find it in your heart to say to me: 'I despise you — I am leaving you'?"

Tony wept. It was just the same as that time in the landscape room. Once more she saw his anguished face, his imploring eyes directed upon her; again she saw, and was moved to see, that this pleading, this anguish, were real and unfeigned.

" Get up, Grünlich," she said, sobbing. " Please, please get up."
She tried to raise his shoulders. " I do not despise you. How can
you say such a thing? " Without knowing what else she should
say, she turned helplessly to her father. The Consul took her hand,
bowed to his son-in-law, and moved with her toward the hall
door.

" You are going? " cried Herr Grünlich, springing to his feet.

" I have told you already," said the Consul, " that I cannot be
responsible for leaving my innocent child in misfortune — and I
might add that you cannot, either. No, sir, you have misprized the
possession of my daughter. You may thank your Creator that the
child's heart is so pure and unsuspicious that she parts from you
without repulsion. Farewell."

But here Herr Grünlich lost his head. He could have borne to
hear of a brief parting — of a return and a new life and perhaps
the saving of the inheritance. But this was too much for his powers
of self-command, his shrewdness and resource. He might have
taken the large bronze plaque that stood on the étagère, but he
seized instead a thin painted vase with flowers that stood next it,
and threw it on the ground so that it smashed into a thousand bits.

" Ha, good, good! " he screamed. " Get along with you! Did
you think I'd whine after you, you goose? You are very much
mistaken, my darling. I only married you for your money; and it
was not nearly enough, so you may as well go home. I'm through
with you — through — through — through! "

Johann Buddenbrook ushered his daughter silently out. Then
he turned, went up to Herr Grünlich, who was standing in the
window with his hands behind his back staring out at the rain,
touched him softly on the shoulder, and spoke with soft admonish-
ment. " Pull yourself together. *Pray!* "

CHAPTER X

A CHASTENED mood reigned for some time at the old house in Meng Street after Madame Grünlich and her little daughter returned thither to take up their abode. The family went about rather subdued and did not speak much about " it," with the exception of the chief actor in the affair, who, on the contrary, talked about " it " inexhaustibly, and was entirely in her element.

Tony had moved with Erica into the rooms in the second storey which her parents had occupied in the time of the elder Buddenbrooks. She was a little disappointed to find that it did not occur to her Papa to engage a servant for her, and she had rather a pensive half-hour when he gently explained that it would be fitting for her to live a retired life and give up the society of the town: for though, he said, according to human judgments she was an innocent victim of the fate which God had sent to try her, still her position as a divorced wife made a very quiet life advisable, particularly at first. But Tony possessed the gift of adaptability. She could adjust herself with ease and cheerfulness to any situation. She soon grew charmed with her rôle of the injured wife returned to the house of her fathers; wore dark frocks, dressed her ash-blond hair primly like a young girl's, and felt richly repaid for her lack of society by the weight she had acquired in the household, the seriousness and dignity of her new position, and above all by the immense pleasure of being able to talk about Herr Grünlich and her marriage and to make general observations about life and destiny, which she did with the utmost gusto.

Not everybody gave her this opportunity, it is true. The Frau Consul was convinced that her husband had acted correctly and out of a sense of duty; but when Tony began to talk, she would put up her lovely white hand and say: " *Assez*, my child; I do not like to hear about it."

Clara, now twelve years old, understood nothing, and Cousin Clothilde was just as stupid. " Oh, Tony! " — that was all she could say, with drawling astonishment. But the young wife found an attentive listener in Mamsell Jungmann, who was now thirty-five years old and could boast of having grown grey in the service of the best society. "You don't need to worry, Tony, my child," she would say. "You are young; you will marry again." And she devoted herself to the upbringing of little Erica, telling her the same stories, the same memories of her youth, to which the Consul's children had listened fifteen years before; and, in particular, of that uncle who died of hiccoughs at Marienwerder "because his heart was broken."

But it was with her father that Tony talked most and longest. She liked to catch him after the noonday meal or in the morning at early breakfast. Their relations had grown closer and warmer; for her feeling had been heretofore one of awe and respect rather than affection, on account of his high position in the town, his piety, his solid, stern ability and industry. During that talk in her own salon he had come humanly near to her, and it had filled her with pride and emotion to be found worthy of that serious and confidential consultation. He, the infallible parent, had put the decision into her hands: he had confessed, almost humbly, to a sense of guilt. Such an idea would never have entered Tony's head of itself; but since he said it, she believed it, and her feeling for him had thereby grown warmer and tenderer. As for the Consul, he believed himself bound to make up to his daughter for her misfortune by redoubled love and care.

Johann Buddenbrook had himself taken no steps against his untrustworthy son-in-law. Tony and her Mother did hear from him, in the course of conversation, what dishonourable means Grünlich had used to get hold of the eighty thousand marks; but the Consul was careful to give the matter no publicity. He did not even consider going to the courts with it. He felt wounded in his pride as a merchant, and he wrestled silently with the disgrace of having been so thoroughly taken in.

But he pressed the divorce suit energetically as soon as the failure of Grünlich came out, which it soon did, thereby causing no inconsiderable losses to certain Hamburg firms.

It was this suit, and the thought that she herself was a principal in it, that gave Tony her most delicious and indescribable feelings of importance.

"Father," she said — for in these conversations she never called him "Papa" — "Father, how is our affair going on? Do you think it will be all right? The paragraph is perfectly clear; I have studied it. 'Incapacity of the husband to provide for his family': surely they will say that is quite plain. If there were a son, Grünlich would keep him — "

Another time she said: " I have thought a great deal about the four years of my marriage, Father. That was certainly the reason the man never wanted us to live in the town, which I was so anxious to do. That was the reason he never liked me even to be in the town or go into society. The danger was much greater there than in Eimsbüttel, of my hearing somehow or other how things stood. What a scoundrel! "

" We must not judge, my child," answered the Consul.

Or, when the divorce was finally pronounced: " Have you entered it in the family papers, Father? No? Then I'd better do it. Please give me the key to the escritoire." With bustling pride she wrote, beneath the lines she had set there four years ago under her name: " This marriage was dissolved by law in February, 1850." Then she put away the pen and reflected a minute.

" Father," she said, " I understand very well that this affair is a blot on our family history. I have thought about it a great deal. It is exactly as if there were a spot of ink in the book here. But never mind. That is my affair. I will erase it. I am still young. Don't you think I am still quite pretty? Though Frau Stuht, when she saw me again, said to me: ' Oh, Heavens, Mme. Grünlich, how old you've grown! ' Well, I certainly couldn't remain all my life the goose I was four years ago! Life takes one along with it. Anyhow, I shall marry again. You will see, everything can be put right by a good marriage."

" That is in God's hand, my child. It is most unfitting to speak of such things."

Tony began at this time to use very frequently the expression " Such is life "; and with the word " life " she would open her eyes wide with a charming serious look, indicating the deep insight she had acquired into human affairs and human destinies.

Thomas returned from Pau in August of that year. The dining-table was opened out again, and Tony had a fresh audience for her tale. She loved and looked up to her brother, who had felt for her pain in that departure from Travemünde, and she respected him as the future head of the firm and the family.

" Yes, yes," he said; " we've both of us gone through things, Tony."

The corner of his eyebrow went up, and his cigarette moved from one corner of his mouth to the other: his thoughts were probably with the little flower-girl with the Malay face, who had lately married the son of her employer and now herself carried on the shop in Fishers' Lane.

Thomas Buddenbrook, though still a little pale, was strikingly elegant. The last few years had entirely completed his education. His hair was brushed so that it stood out in two clumps above his ears, and his moustache was trimmed in the French mode, with sharp points that were stiffened with the tongs and stuck straight out. His stocky broad-shouldered figure had an almost military air.

His constitution was not of the best; the blue veins showed too plainly at the narrow temples, and he had a slight tendency to chills, which good Dr. Grabow struggled with in vain. In the details of his physical appearance — the chin, the nose, and especially the hands, which were wonderfully true to the Buddenbrook type — his likeness to his grandfather was more pronounced than ever.

He spoke French with a distinctly Spanish accent, and astonished everybody by his enthusiasm for certain modern writers of a satiric and polemic character. Broker Gosch was the only person in town who sympathized with his tastes. His father strongly reprehended them.

But the Father's pride and joy in his eldest son were plain to be seen; they shone in the Consul's eyes. He welcomed him joyfully home as his colleague in the firm, and himself began to work with increased satisfaction in his office — especially after the death of old Madame Kröger, which took place at the end of the year.

The old lady's loss was one to be borne with resignation. She had grown very old, and lived quite alone at the end. She went to God, and the firm of Buddenbrooks received a large sum of money, a round hundred thousand thaler, which strengthened the working capital of the business in a highly desirable way.

The Consul's brother-in-law Justus, weary of continual business disappointments, as soon as he had his hands on his inheritance settled his business and retired. The gay son of the cavalier à-la-mode was not a happy man. He had been too careless, too generous to attain a solid position in the mercantile world. But he had already spent a considerable part of his inheritance; and now Jacob, his eldest son, was the source of fresh cares to him.

The young man had become addicted to light, not to say disreputable, society in the great city of Hamburg. He had cost his father a huge sum in the course of years, and when Consul Kröger refused to give him more, the mother, a weak, sickly woman, sent money secretly to the son, and wretched clouds had sprung up between husband and wife.

The final blow came at the very time when B. Grünlich was making his failure: something happened at Dalbeck and Company in Hamburg, where Jacob Kröger worked. There had been some kind of dishonesty. It was not talked about; no questions were asked of Justus Kröger; but it got about that Jacob had a position as travelling man in New York and was about to sail. He was seen once in the town before his boat left, a foppishly dressed, unwholesome-looking youth. He had probably come hither to get more money out of his mother, besides the passage money his father sent him.

It finally came about that Justus spoke exclusively of "my son," as though he had none but the one heir, his second son, Jürgen, who would certainly never be guilty of a false step, but who seemed on the other hand to be mentally limited. He had had difficulty getting through the High School; after which he spent some time in Jena, studying law — evidently without either pleasure or profit.

Johann Buddenbrook felt keenly the cloud on his wife's family and looked with the more anxiety to the future of his own children. He was justified in placing the utmost confidence in the ability and earnestness of his older son. As for Christian, Mr. Richardson had written that he showed an unusual gift for acquiring English, but no genuine interest in the business. He had a great weakness for the theatre and for other distractions of the great city. Christian himself wrote that he had a longing to travel and see the world. He begged eagerly to be allowed to take a position " over there " — which meant in South America, perhaps in Chile. " That's simply love of adventure," the Consul said, and told him to remain with Mr. Richardson for another year and acquire mercantile experience. There followed an exchange of letters on the subject, with the result that in the summer of 1851 Christian Buddenbrook sailed for Valparaiso, where he had hunted up a position. He travelled direct from England, without coming home.

So much for his two sons. As for Tony, the Consul was gratified to see with what self-possession she defended her position in the town as a Buddenbrook born; for as a divorced wife she had naturally to overcome all sorts of prejudice on the part of the other families.

" Oh! " she said, coming back with flushed cheeks from a walk and throwing her hat on the sofa in the landscape-room. " This Juliet Möllendorpf, or Hagenström — or Semmlinger — whatever she is, the creature! — Imagine, Mamma! She doesn't speak. She doesn't say ' How do you do? ' She waits for me to speak first. What do you say to that? I passed her in Broad Street with my head up and looked straight at her."

"You go too far, Tony. There is a limit to everything. Why shouldn't you speak first? You are the same age, and she is a married woman, just as you were."

"Never, Mamma! Never under the shining sun! Such rag-tag and bob-tail! "

"*Assez,* my love. Such vulgar expressions — "

"Oh, it makes me feel perfectly beside myself! "

Her hatred of the upstart family was fed by the mere thought that the Hagenströms might now feel justified in looking down on her — especially considering the present good fortune of the clan. Old Hinrich had died at the beginning of 1851, and his son Hermann — he of the lemon buns and the boxes on the ear — was doing a very brilliant business with Herr Strunck as partner. He had married, less than a year later, the daughter of Consul Huneus, the richest man in town, who had made enough out of his business to leave each of his three children two million marks. Hermann's brother Moritz, despite his lung trouble, had a brilliant career as student, and had now settled down in the town to practise law. He had a reputation for being able, witty, and literary, and soon acquired a considerable business. He did not look like the Semmlingers, having a yellow face and pointed teeth with wide spaces between.

Even in the family Tony had to take care to hold her head up. Uncle Gotthold's temper toward his fortunate step-brother had grown more mild and resigned now that he had given up business and spent his time care-free in his modest house, munching lozenges out of a tin box — he loved sweets. Still, considering his three unmarried daughters, he could not have failed to feel a quiet satisfaction over Tony's unfortunate venture; and his wife, born Stüwing, and his three daughters, twenty-six, twenty-seven, and twenty-eight years old, showed an exaggerated interest in their cousin's misfortune and the divorce proceedings; more, in fact, than they had in her betrothal and wedding. When the "children's Thursdays" began again in Meng Street after old Madame Kröger's death, Tony found it no easy work to defend herself.

"Oh, heavens, you poor thing! " said Pfiffi, the youngest, who was little and plump, with a droll way of shaking herself at every word. A drop of water always came in the corner of her mouth when she spoke. "Has the decree been pronounced? Are you exactly as you were before? "

"Oh, on the contrary," said Henriette, who, like her elder sister, was extraordinarily tall and withered-looking. "You are much worse off than if you had never married at all."

"Yes," Friederike chimed in. "Then it is ever so much better never to have married at all."

"Oh, no, dear Friederike," said Tony, erecting her head, while she bethought herself of a telling and clever retort. "You make a mistake there. Marriage teaches one to know life, you see. One is no longer a silly goose. And then I have more prospect of marrying again than those who have never married at all!"

"Oh!" cried the others with one voice. They said it with a long hissing intake of breath which made it sound very sceptical indeed.

Sesemi Weichbrodt was too good and tactful even to mention the subject. Tony sometimes visited her former teacher in the little red house at Millbrink No. 7. It was still occupied by a troop of girls, though the boarding-school was slowly falling out of fashion. The lively old maid was also invited to Meng Street on occasion to partake of a haunch of venison or a stuffed goose. She always raised herself on tiptoe to kiss Tony on the forehead, with a little exploding noise. Madame Kethelsen, her simple sister, had grown rapidly deaf and had understood almost nothing of Tony's affair. She still laughed her painfully hearty laugh on the most unsuitable occasions, and Sesemi still felt it necessary to rap on the table and cry "Nally!"

The years went on. Gradually people forgot their feelings over Tony's affair. She herself would only think now and then of her married life, when she saw on Erica's healthy, hearty little face some expression that reminded her of Bendix Grünlich. She dressed again in colours, wore her hair in the old way, and made the same old visits into society.

Still, she was always glad that she had the chance to be away from the town for some time in the summer. The Consul's health made it necessary for him to visit various cures.

"Oh, what it is to grow old!" he said. "If I get a spot of coffee on my trousers and put a drop of cold water on it, I have rheumatism. When one is young, one can do anything." He suffered at times also from spells of dizziness.

They went to Obersalzbrunn, to Ems and Baden-Baden, to Kissingen, whence they made a delightful and edifying journey to Nuremberg and Munich and the Salzburg neighbourhood, to Ischl and Vienna, Prague, Dresden, Berlin, and home again. Madame Grünlich had been suffering from a nervous affection of the digestion, and was obliged to take a strenuous cure at the baths; but nevertheless she found the journey a highly desirable change, for she did not conceal her opinion that it was a little slow at home.

"Heavens, yes — you know how it is, Father," she would say, regarding the ceiling with a thoughtful air. "Of course, I have learned what life is like — but just for that reason it is rather a dull prospect for me to be always sitting here at home like a stupid goose. I hope you don't think I mean I do not like to be with you, Papa. I ought to be whipped if I did, it would be so ungrateful. But I only mean life is like that, you know."

The hardest thing she had to bear was the increasing piety of her parents' home. The Consul's religious fervour grew upon him in proportion as he himself felt the weight of years and infirmity; and his wife too, as she got older, began to find the spiritual side to her taste. Prayers had always been customary in the Buddenbrook house, but now for some time the family and the servants had assembled mornings and evenings in the breakfast-room to hear the Master read the Bible. And the visits of ministers and missionaries increased more and more from year to year. The godly patrician house in Meng Street, where, by the way, such good dinners were to be had, had been known for years as a spiritual haven to the Lutheran and reformed clergy and to both foreign and home missions. From all quarters of the Fatherland came long-haired, black-coated gentlemen, to enjoy the pious intercourse and the nourishing meals, and to be furnished with the sinews of their spiritual warfare. The ministers of the town went in and out as friends of the house.

Tom was much too discreet and prudent even to let any one see him smile; but Tony mocked quite openly. She even, sad to say, made fun of these pious worthies whenever she had a chance.

Sometimes when the Frau Consul had a headache, it was Tony's turn to play the housekeeper and order the dinner. One day, when a strange clergyman whose appetite was the subject of general hilarity, was a guest, Tony mischievously ordered "bacon broth," the famous local dish: a bouillon made with sour cabbage, in which was served the entire meal — ham, potatoes, beet-root, cauliflower, peas, beans, pears, sour plums, and goodness knows what, juice and all — a dish which nobody except those born to it could possibly eat.

"I do hope you are enjoying the soup, Herr Pastor," she said several times. "No? Oh, dear, who would have thought it?" And she made a very roguish face, and ran her tongue over her lips, a trick she had when she thought of some prank or other.

The fat man laid down his spoon resignedly and said mildly: "I will wait till the next course."

"Yes," the Frau Consul said hastily, "there is a little something afterwards." But a "next course" was unthinkable, after this mighty dish; and despite the French toast and apple jelly which finished the meal, the reverend guest had to rise hungry from table, while Tony tittered, and Tom, with fine self-control, lifted one eyebrow.

Another time Tony stood with Stina, the cook, in domestic discourse in the entry, when Pastor Mathias from Kannstadt, who was stopping a few days in the house, came back from a walk and rang at the outer door. Stina ran to open, with her peasant waddle, and the Pastor, with the view of saying an edifying word and testing her a little, asked in a friendly tone: "Do you love the Master?"

Perhaps he had the idea of giving her a tip if she professed herself on the side of the Saviour.

"Lord, Herr Pastor," said Stina, trembling and blushing, with wide eyes. "Which one do Herr Pastor mean? T' old un or t' young un?" Madame Grünlich did not fail to tell the story at the table, so that even the Frau Consul burst out into her sputtering Kröger laugh. The Consul, however, looked down in displeasure at his plate.

"A misunderstanding," said Herr Mathias, highly embarrassed.

CHAPTER XI

WHAT follows happened in the late summer of 1855, on a Sunday afternoon. The Buddenbrooks were sitting in the landscape-room waiting for the Consul, who was below dressing himself. They had arranged to take a holiday walk to a pleasure garden outside the City Gate, where, all except Clara and Clothilde, they were to drink coffee and, if the weather permitted, go for a row on the river. Clara and Clothilde went always on Sunday evenings to the house of a friend, where they knitted stockings for little negro children.

"Papa is ridiculous," Tony said, using her habitual strong language. "Can he never be ready on time? He sits and sits and sits at his desk: something or other *must* be finished — good heavens, perhaps it is something really necessary, I don't know. But I don't believe we should actually become bankrupt if he put down his pen a quarter of an hour sooner. Well, when it is already ten minutes too late, he remembers his appointment and comes upstairs, always two steps at a time, although he knows he will get palpitation at the top. And it is like that at every company, before every expedition. Isn't it possible for him to leave himself time enough? And stop soon enough? It's so irresponsible of him; you ought to talk to him about it, Mamma." She sat on the sofa beside her Mother, dressed in the changeable silk that was fashionable that summer; while the Frau Consul wore a heavy grey ribbed silk trimmed with black lace, and a cap of lace and stiffened tulle, tied under her chin with a satin bow. The lappets of her cap fell down on her breast. Her smooth hair was still inexorably reddish-blond in colour, and she held a work-bag in both her white delicately veined hands. Tom was lounging in an easy-chair beside her smoking his cigarette, while Clara and Clothilde sat opposite each other at the window. It was a mystery how much good and nourishing food that poor Clothilde could absorb daily without any result whatever! She grew thinner and thinner, and her shapeless black frock did not conceal the fact. Her face was as long, straight, and expressionless as ever, her hair as smooth and ash-coloured, her nose as straight, but full of large pores and getting thick at the end.

"Don't you think it will rain?" said Clara. The young girl had the habit of not elevating her voice at the end of a question and of looking everybody straight in the face with a pronounced and rather forbidding look. Her brown frock was relieved only by a little stiff turn-over collar and cuffs. She sat straight up, her hands in her lap. The servants had more respect for her than for any one else in the family; it was she who held the services morning and evening now, for the Consul could not read aloud without getting a feeling of oppression in the head.

"Shall you take your new Baschlik?" she asked again. "The rain will spoil it. It would be a pity. I think it would be better to put off the party."

"No," said Tom. "The Kistenmakers are coming. It doesn't matter. The barometer went down so suddenly — . There will be a storm — it will pour, but not last long. Papa is not ready yet; so we can wait till it is over."

The Frau Consul raised a protesting hand. "You think there will be a severe storm, Tom? You know I am afraid of them."

"No," Tom answered. "I was down at the harbour this morning talking to Captain Kloot. He is infallible. There will be a heavy rain, but no wind."

The second week in September had brought belated hot weather with it. There was a south-west wind, and the city suffered more than in July. A strange-looking dark blue sky hung above the roof-tops, pale on the skyline as it is in the desert. After sunset a sultry breath, like a hot blast from an oven, streamed out of the small houses and up from the pavement of the narrow streets. To-day the wind had gone round to the west, and at the same time the barometer had fallen sharply. A large part of the sky was still blue, but it was slowly being overcast by heavy grey-blue clouds that looked like feather pillows.

Tom added: "It would be a good thing if it did rain, I think. We should collapse if we had to walk in this atmosphere. It is an unnatural heat. Hotter than it ever was in Pau."

Ida Jungmann, with little Erica's hand in hers, came into the room. The child looked a droll little figure in her stiffly starched cotton frock; she smelled of starch and soap. She had Herr Grünlich's eyes and his rosy skin, but the upper lip was Tony's.

The good Ida was already quite grey, almost white, although not out of the forties. It was a trait of her family: the uncle that died had had white hair at thirty. But her little brown eyes looked as shrewd and faithful as ever. She had been now for twenty

years with the Buddenbrooks, and she realized with pride that she
was indispensable. She oversaw kitchen, larders, linen and china
cupboards, she made the most important purchases, she read to little Erica, made clothes for her dolls, and fetched her from school,
with a slice of French bread, to take her walking on the Mill-wall.
Every lady said to Frau Consul or her daughter: "What a treasure
your Mamsell is, my dear! Goodness, she is worth her weight in
gold! Twenty years — and she will be useful at sixty and more;
these wiry people are. What faithful eyes she has! I envy you,
my love." But Ida Jungmann was very reserved. She knew her
own position, and when some ordinary nurse-girl came and sat
down with her charge on the same bench and tried to enter into
conversation, Ida Jungmann would say: "There is a draught here,
Erica," and get up and go.

Tony drew her little daughter to her and kissed the rosy cheeks,
and the Frau Consul stretched out her hand with rather an absent
smile; for she was looking anxiously at the sky, which grew darker
and darker. Her left hand fingered the sofa pillows nervously, and
her light eyes wandered restlessly to the window.

Erica was allowed to sit next her Grandmother, and Ida sat up
straight on a chair and began to knit. Thus all waited silently for
the Consul. The air was heavy. The last bit of blue had disappeared; the dark grey sky lowered heavy and swollen over them.
The colours in the room changed, the yellow of furniture and
hangings and the tones of the landscapes on the walls were all
quenched, like the gay shades in Tony's frock and the brightness
of their eyes. Even the west wind, which had been playing in the
churchyard of St. Mary's and whirling the dust around in the
darkening street, was suddenly quiet.

This breathless moment of absolute calm came without warning,
like some unexpected, soundless, awful event. The sultriness grew
heavier, the atmosphere seemed to increase its weight in a second;
it oppressed the brain, it rested on the heart, it prevented the
breathing. A swallow flew so low over the pavement that its wings
touched. And this pressure that one could not lift, this tension,
this growing weight on the whole organism, would have become
unbearable had it lasted even the smallest part of a second longer,
if at its height there had not come a relief, a release — a little break
somewhere, soundless, yet perceptible; and at the same moment,
without any premonitory drops, the rain fell down in sheets, filling
the gutters and overflowing the pavements.

Thomas, whose illness had taught him to pay attention to his
nerves, bent over in this second, made a motion toward his head,

and flung away his cigarette. He looked around the circle to see
if the others had felt anything. He thought his Mother had, perhaps; the others did not seem to be aware. The Frau Consul was
looking out now into the thick-streaming rain, which quite hid
the church from view; she sighed " Thank God."

" There," said Tony, " that will cool the air in two minutes.
But the drops will be hanging on the trees outside — we can drink
coffee in the verandah. Open the window, Tilda."

The noise of the rain grew louder. It almost roared. Everything
pattered, streamed, rushed, foamed. The wind came up and blew
the thick veils of water, tore them apart, and flung them about. It
grew cooler every minute.

Lina, the maid-servant, came running through the hall and burst
so suddenly into the room that Ida Jungmann called out sharply:
" I say, what do you mean — ? " Lina's expressionless blue eyes
were wide open, her jaws worked without making a sound —

" Oh, Frau Consul," she got out, at last. " Come, come quick!
oh, what a scare — "

" Yes," Tony said, " she's probably broken something again.
Very likely the good porcelain. Oh, these servants of yours,
Mamma! "

But the girl burst out: " Oh, no, Ma'am Grünlich — if that's all
it was! — It's the Master — I were bringing him his boots, and there
he sits and can't speak, on his chair, and I says to myself, there's
something wrong there; the Herr Consul — "

" Get Grabow," cried Thomas and ran out of the room.

" My God — oh, my God! " cried the Frau Consul, putting her
hands to her face and hurrying out.

" Quick, get a wagon and fetch Grabow," Tony repeated
breathlessly.

Everybody flew downstairs and through the breakfast-room
into the bedroom.

But Johann Buddenbrook was already dead.

PART FIVE

CHAPTER I

"Good evening, Justus," said the Frau Consul. "How are you? Sit down."

Consul Kröger embraced her tenderly and shook hands with his elder niece, who was also present in the dining-room. He was now about fifty-five years old, and wore a heavy round whisker as well as his moustache, leaving his chin free. It was quite grey. His scanty hair was carefully combed over the broad pink expanse of his skull. The sleeve of his elegant frock-coat had a broad mourning band.

"Do you know the latest, Betsy?" he asked. "Yes, Tony, this will particularly interest you. To put it briefly, our property outside the Castle Gate is sold — guess to whom? Not to one man, but to two: for the house is to be pulled down, and a hedge run through diagonally, and Benthien will build himself a dog-kennel on the right side, and Sorenson one on the left. God bless us!"

"Whoever heard the like?" said Frau Grünlich, folding her hands in her lap and gazing up at the ceiling. "Grandfather's property! Well, now the estate is all haggled up. Its great charm was its extent: there was really too much of it, but that was what made it elegant. The large garden, all the way down to the Trave, the house set far back with the drive, and the chestnut avenue. So it is to be divided. Benthien will stand in front of one door and Sorenson in front of the other. I say, 'God bless us,' too, Uncle Justus! I suppose there is nobody grand enough these days to occupy the whole thing. It is good that Grandpapa is not here to see it."

The sense of mourning still lay too heavily on the air for Tony to give expression to her outraged feelings in livelier or stronger terms. It was the day on which the will had been read, two weeks after the death of the Consul, at half-past five in the afternoon. Frau Consul Buddenbrook had invited her brother to Meng Street, in order that he might talk over the provisions made by the deceased with Thomas and with Herr Marcus the confidential clerk. Tony had announced her intention to be present at the settlements. This attention, she said, she owed to the firm as well as to the fam-

ily, and she took pains to give the meeting the character of a family
council. She had closed the curtains, and despite the two oil lamps
on the green-covered dining-table, drawn out to its full extent, she
had lighted all the candles in the great gilded candelabrum as well.
And, though there was no particular need of them, she had put on
the table a quantity of writing paper and sharpened pencils.

Tony's black frock gave her figure a maidenly slimness. She,
of them all, was perhaps most deeply moved by the death of the
Consul, to whom she had drawn so close in the last months that
even to-day the thought of him made her burst out twice in bitter
weeping; yet the prospect of this family council, this solemn little
conference in which she could bear a worthy part, had power to
flush her pretty cheek, brighten her glance, and give her motions
dignity and even joy. The Frau Consul, on the other hand, worn
with anxiety and grief and the thousand formalities of the funeral
and the mourning, looked ailing. Her face, framed in the black
lace of her cap-strings, seemed paler, and her light blue eyes were
tired and dull. But there was not a single white hair to be seen in
her smooth red-blond coiffure. Was this still the Parisian tonic,
or was it the wig? Mamsell Jungmann alone knew, and she would
not have betrayed the secret even to the other ladies of the family.

They sat at the end of the table and waited for Herr Marcus and
Thomas to come out of the office. The painted statues seemed to
stand out white and proud on their pedestals against the sky-blue
background.

The Frau Consul said: " The thing is — I bade you come, my
dear Justus — in short, it is about Clara, the child. My beloved
husband left to me the choice of a guardian for her — she will need
one for three years. I know you do not want to be overburdened
with responsibilities. You have duties to your wife and sons — "

" My son, Betsy."

" Yes, yes, we must be Christlike and merciful, Justus. As we
forgive our debtors, it says. Think of our gracious Father in
Heaven."

Her brother looked at her, a little aggrieved. Such turns of
phrase had come in the past only from the mouth of the Consul.

" Enough," she went on. " There are as good as no obligations
connected with this service of love. I should like to ask you to accept it."

" Gladly, Betsy; of course, I'll do it with pleasure. May I not
see my ward? A little too serious, isn't she, the good child — ? "
Clara was called. She slowly appeared, all black and pallid, her
movements melancholy and full of restraint. She had spent the

time since her father's death in her room praying almost without ceasing. Her dark eyes were immobile; she seemed frozen with grief and awe.

Uncle Justus the gallant stepped up to her, bowed as he pressed her hand, and murmured something appropriate. She went out, after receiving the Frau Consul's kiss on her stiff lips.

" How is Jürgen? " began the Frau Consul again. Does it agree with him in Wismar? "

" Very well," answered Justus Kröger, sitting down again with a shrug of the shoulders. " I think he has found his place now. He is a good lad, Betsy, a lad of principle, but — after he had failed twice in the examination, it seemed best — He did not like the law himself, and the position in the post-office at Wismar is quite suitable. Tell me — I hear Christian is coming? "

" Yes, Justus, he is coming. May God watch over him on the seas! I wrote to him the next day after Jean's death, but he hasn't even had the letter yet, and then he will take about two months with the sailing-vessel after that. But he must come, Justus; I must see him. Tom says Jean would never have been willing for Christian to give up his position in Valparaiso; but I ask you — nearly eight years since I have seen him! And then, under the circumstances! No, I must have them all about me in this painful time — that is a natural feeling for a mother."

" Surely, surely," said Consul Kröger; for she had begun to weep.

" Thomas agrees with me now, too," she went on; " for where will Christian be better off than in his own father's business, in Tom's business? He can stay here, work here. I have been in constant fear that the climate over there might be bad for him — "

Thomas Buddenbrook, accompanied by Herr Marcus, came into the room. Friederich Wilhelm Marcus, for years the dead Consul's confidential clerk, was a tall man in a brown-skirted coat with a mourning band. He spoke softly, hesitatingly stammering a little and considering each word before he uttered it. He had a habit of slowly and cautiously stroking the red-brown moustache that grew over his mouth with the extended middle and index fingers of his left hand; or he would rub his hands together and let his round brown eyes wander so aimlessly about that he gave the impression of complete confusion and absent-mindedness, though he was always most watchfully bent on the matter in hand.

Thomas Buddenbrook, now the youthful head of the great house, displayed real dignity in manner and bearing. But he was pale. His hands in particular, on one of which shone the Consul's

signet ring with the green stone, were as white as the cuffs beneath
his black sleeves — a frozen whiteness which showed that they
were quite dry and cold. He had extraordinarily sensitive hands,
with beautifully cared-for oval bluish fingernails. Sometimes, in
a difficult situation, they would take positions or make little nervous movements that were indescribably expressive of shrinking
sensibility and painful reserve. This was an individual trait strange
heretofore to the rather broad, though finely articulated Buddenbrook hand.

Tom's first care was to open the folding doors into the landscape-room in order to get the benfit of the warmth from the stove
burning there behind the wrought-iron lattice. Then he shook
hands with Consul Kröger and sat down at the table with Herr
Marcus opposite him. He looked at his sister Tony, and his eyebrow went up in surprise. But she flung her head back and tucked
in her chin in a way that warned him to suppress any comment on
her presence.

"Well, and one may not say Herr Consul?" asked Justus
Kröger. "The Netherlands hope in vain that you should represent
them, Tom, my dear chap?"

"Yes, Uncle Justus, I thought it was better. You see, I could
have taken over the Consulate along with so many other responsibilities, but in the first place I am a little too young — and then I
spoke to Uncle Gotthold, and he was very pleased to accept it."

"Very sensible, my lad; very politic. And very gentlemanly."

"Herr Marcus," said the Frau Consul, "my dear Herr Marcus!"
And with her usual sweeping gesture she reached out her hand,
which he took slowly, with a respectful side-glance: "I have asked
you to come up — you know what the affair is; and I know that
you are agreed with us. My beloved husband expressed in his final
arrangements the wish that after his death you would put your
loyal and well-tried powers at the service of the firm, not as an out-
sider but as partner."

"Certainly, Frau Consul," said Herr Marcus, "I must protest
that I know how to value the honour your offer does me, being
aware, as I am, that the resources I can bring to the firm are but
small. In God's name, I know nothing better to do than thank-
fully to accept the offer you and your son make me."

"Yes, Marcus. And I thank you in my turn, most warmly, for
your willingness to share with me the great responsibilities which
would perhaps be too heavy for me alone." Thomas Buddenbrook
spoke quickly and whole-heartedly, reaching his hand across the

table to his partner; for they were already long since agreed on the subject, and this was only the formal expression.

"Company is trumpery — you will spoil our chat, between you," said Consul Kröger. "And now, shall we run through the provisions, my children? All I have to look out for is the dowry of my ward. The rest is not my affair. Have you a copy of the will here, Betsy? And have you made a rough calculation, Tom?"

"I have it in my head," said Thomas; and he began, leaning back, looking into the landscape-room, and moving his gold pencil back and forth on the table, to explain how matters stood. The truth was that the Consul's estate was more considerable than any one had supposed. The dowry of his oldest daughter, indeed, was gone, and the losses which the firm had suffered in the Bremen failure in 1851 had been a heavy blow. And the year '48, as well as the present year '55, with their unrest and interval of war, had brought losses. But the Buddenbrook share of the Kröger estate of four hundred thousand current marks had been full three hundred thousand, for Justus had already had much of his beforehand. Johann Buddenbrook had continually complained, as a merchant will; but the losses of the firm had been made good by the accrued profits of some fifteen years, amounting to thirty thousand thaler, and thus the property, aside from real estate, amounted in round figures, to seven hundred thousand marks.

Thomas himself, with all his knowledge of the business, had been left in ignorance by his father of this total. The Frau Consul took the announcement with discreet calm; Tony put on an adorable expression of pride and ignorance, and then could not repress an anxious mental query: Is that a lot? Are we very rich now? Herr Marcus slowly rubbed his hands, apparently in absence of mind, and Consul Kröger was obviously bored. But the sum filled Tom himself, as he stated it, with such a rush of excited pride that the effort at self-control made him seem dejected. "We must have already passed the million," he said. He controlled his voice, but his hands trembled. "Grandfather could command nine hundred thousand marks in his best time; and we've made great efforts since then, and had successes, and made fine *coups* here and there. And Mamma's dowry, and Mamma's inheritance! There was the constant breaking up — well, good heavens, that lay in the nature of things! Please forgive me if I speak just now in the sense of the firm and not of the family. These dowries and payments to Uncle Gotthold and to Frankfort, these hundreds of thousands which had to be drawn out of the business — and then there were only two heirs beside the head of the firm. Good; we have our work cut out for us, Marcus." The thirst for action, for power and success, the longing to force fortune to her knees, sprang up quick and passionate in his eyes. He felt all the world looking at him expectantly, questioning if he would know how to command prestige for the firm and the family and protect its name. On exchange he had been meeting measuring side-looks out of jovial, mocking old eyes, that seemed to be saying " So you're taking it on, my son! " " I *am!* " he thought.

Friederich Wilhelm Marcus rubbed his hands circumspectly, and Justus Kröger said: " Quietly, quietly, my dear chap. Times aren't what they were when your grandfather was a Prussian army contractor."

There began now a detailed conversation upon the provisions of the will, in which they all joined, and Consul Kröger took a lighter tone, referring to Thomas as " his Highness the reigning Prince " and saying, " The warehouses will go with the crown, according to tradition." In general, of course, it was decided that as far as possible everything should be left together, that Frau Elizabeth Buddenbrook should be considered the sole heir, and that the entire property should remain in the business. Herr Marcus announced that as partner he should be able to strengthen the working capital by a hundred and twenty thousand marks current. A sum of fifty thousand marks was set aside as a private fortune for Thomas, and the same for Christian, in case he wished to establish himself separately. Justus Kröger paid close attention to the passage that ran: " The fixing of the dowry of my beloved daughter Clara I leave to the discretion of my dear wife." " Shall we say a hundred thousand? " he suggested, leaning back, one leg crossed over the other, and turning up his short grey moustache with both hands. He was affability itself. But the sum was fixed at eighty thousand. " In case of a second marriage of my dearly loved older daughter Antonie, in view of the fact that eighty thousand marks have already been applied to her first marriage, the sum of seventeen thousand thaler current must not be exceeded." Frau Antonie waved her arm with a graceful but excited gesture which tossed back her flowing sleeve; she looked at the ceiling and said loudly: " Grünlich, indeed! " It sounded like a challenge, like a little trumpet-call. " You know, Herr Marcus," she said, " about that man. We are sitting, one fine afternoon, perfectly innocent, in the garden, in front of the door — you know the portal, Herr Marcus. Well! Who appears? a person with gold-coloured whiskers — the scoundrel! "

" Yes," Thomas said. " We will talk about Herr Grünlich afterward."

" Very well; but you are a clever creature, and you will admit, Tom, that in this life things don't always happen fairly and squarely. That's been my experience, though a short time ago I was too simple to realize it."

" Yes," Tom said. They went into detail, noting the Consul's instructions about the great family Bible, about his diamond buttons, and many, many other matters.

Justus Kröger and Herr Marcus stopped for supper.

CHAPTER II

In the beginning of February, 1856, after eight years' absence, Christian Buddenbrook returned to the home of his fathers. He arrived in the post-coach from Hamburg, wearing a yellow suit with a pattern of large checks, that had a distinctly exotic look. He brought the bill of a swordfish and a great sugar-cane, and received the embraces of his mother with a half-embarrassed, half-absent air.

He wore the same air when, on the next afternoon after his arrival, the family went to the cemetery outside the Castle Gate to lay a wreath on the grave. They stood together on the snowy path in front of the large tablet on which were the names of those resting there, surrounding the family arms cut in the stone. Before them was the upright marble cross that stood at the edge of the bare little churchyard grove. They were all there except Clothilde, who was at Thankless, nursing her ailing father.

Tony laid the wreath on the tablet, where her father's name stood on the stone in fresh gold letters: then, despite the snow, she knelt down by the grave to pray. Her black veil played about her, and her full skirt lay spread out in picturesque folds. God alone knew how much grief and religious emotion — and, on the other hand, how much of a pretty woman's self-conscious pleasure — there was in the bowed attitude. Thomas was not in the mood to think about it. But Christian looked sidewise at his sister with a mixture of mockery and misgiving, as if to say: " Can you really carry that off? Shan't you feel silly when you get up? How uncomfortable! " Tony caught this look as she rose, but she was not in the least put out. She tossed her head back, arranged her veil and skirt, and turned with dignified assurance to go; whereupon Christian was obviously relieved.

The deceased Consul's fanatical love of God and of the Saviour had been an emotion foreign to his forebears, who never cherished other than the normal, every-day sentiments proper to good citizens. The two living Buddenbrooks had in their turn their own idiosyncrasies. One of these appeared to be a nervous distaste for

the expression of feeling. Thomas had certainly felt the death of
his father with painful acuteness, much as his grandfather had felt
the loss of his. But he could not sink on his knees by his grave.
He had never, like his sister Tony, flung himself across the table
sobbing like a child; and he shrank from hearing the heart-broken
words in which Madame Grünlich, from roast to dessert, loved to
celebrate the character and person of her dead father. Such out-
bursts he met with composed silence or a reserved nod. And yet,
when nobody had mentioned or was thinking of the dead, it would
be just then that his eyes would fill with slow tears, although his
facial expression remained unchanged.

It was different with Christian. He unfortunately did not succeed in preserving his composure at the naïve and childish outpourings of his sister. He bent over his plate, turned his head
away, and looked as though he wanted to sink through the floor;
and several times he interrupted her with a low, tormented " Good
God, Tony! " his large nose screwed into countless tiny wrinkles.

In fact, he showed disquiet and embarrassment whenever the
conversation turned to the dead. It seemed as though he feared
and avoided not only the indelicate expression of deep and solemn
feeling, but even the feeling itself.

No one had seen him shed a tear over the death of his father;
and his long absence alone hardly explained this fact. A more remarkable thing, however, was that he took his sister Tony aside
again and again to hear in vivid detail the events of that fatal afternoon; for Madame Grünlich had a gift of lively narration.

" He looked yellow? " he asked for the fifth time. " What was
it the girl shrieked when she came running in to you? He looked
quite yellow, and died without saying another word? What did
the girl say? What sort of sound was it he made? " Then he
would be silent — silent a long time — while his small deep-set eyes
travelled round the room in thought.

" Horrible," he said suddenly, and a visible shudder ran over him
as he got up. He would walk up and down with the same unquiet
and brooding eyes. Madame Grünlich felt astonished to see that
who for some unknown reason was so embarrassed when she bewailed her father aloud, liked to reproduce with a sort of dreadful
relish the dying efforts to speak which he had inquired about in detail of Line the maid-servant.

Christian had certainly not grown better looking. He was lean
and pallid. The skin was stretched over his skull very tightly; his
large nose, with a distinct hump, stuck out fleshless and sharp between his cheek-bones, and his hair was already noticeably scantier.

His neck was too thin and long and his lean legs decidedly bowed. His London period seemed to have made a lasting impression upon him. In Valparaiso, too, he had mostly associated with Englishmen; and his whole appearance had something English about it which somehow seemed rather appropriate. It was partly the comfortable cut and durable wool material of his clothing, the broad, solid elegance of his boots, his crotchety expression, and the way in which his red-blond moustache drooped over his mouth. Even his hands had an English look: they were a dull porous white from the hot climate, with round, clean, short-trimmed nails.

" Tell me," he said, abruptly, " do you know that feeling — it is hard to describe — when you swallow something hard, the wrong way, and it hurts all the way down your spine? " His whole nose wrinkled as he spoke.

" Yes," said Tony; " that is quite common. You take a drink of water — "

" Oh," he said in a dissatisfied tone. " No, I don't think we mean the same thing." And a restless look floated across his face.

He was the first one in the house to shake off his mourning and re-assume a natural attitude. He had not lost the art of imitating the deceased Marcellus Stengel, and he often spoke for hours in his voice. At the table he asked about the theatre — if there were a good company and what they were giving.

" I don't know," said Tom, with a tone that was exaggeratedly indifferent, in order not to seem irritated. " I haven't noticed lately."

But Christian missed this altogether and went on to talk about the theatre. " I am too happy for words in the theatre. Even the *word* ' theatre ' makes me feel happy. I don't know whether any of you have that feeling. I could sit for hours and just look at the curtain. I feel as I used to when I was a child and we went in to the Christmas party here. Even the sound of the orchestra beforehand! I would go if only to hear that and nothing more. I like the love scenes best. Some of the heroines have such a fetching way of taking their lovers' heads between their hands. But the actors — in London and Valparaiso I have known a lot of actors. At first I was very proud to get to know them in ordinary life. In the theatre I watched their every movement. It is fascinating. One of them says his last speech and turns around quietly and goes deliberately, without the least embarrassment, to the door, although he knows that the eyes of the whole audience are on his back. How can he do that? I used to be continually thinking about going be-

hind the scenes. But now I am pretty much at home there, I must say. Imagine: once, in an operetta — it was in London — the curtain went up one evening when I was on the stage! I was talking with Miss Waterhouse, a very pretty girl. Well, suddenly there was the whole audience! Good Lord, I don't know how I got off the stage."

Madame Grünlich was the only one who laughed, to speak of, in the circle round the table. But Christian went on, his eyes wandering back and forth. He talked about English *café-chantant* singers; about an actress who came on in powdered wig, and knocked with a long cane on the ground and sang a song called: "That's Maria." "Maria, you know — Maria is the most scandalous of the lot. When somebody does something perfectly shocking, why — 'that's Maria' — the bad lot, you know — utterly depraved!" He said this last with a frightful expression and raised his right hand with the fingers formed into a ring.

"*Assez*, Christian," said the Frau Consul. "That does not interest us in the least."

But Christian's gaze flickered absently over her head; he would probably have stopped without her suggestion, for he seemed to be sunk in a profound, disquieting dream of Maria and her depravity, while his little round deep eyes wandered back and forth.

Suddenly he said: "Strange — sometimes I can't swallow. Oh, it's no joke. I find it very serious. It enters my head that perhaps I can't swallow, and then all of a sudden I can't. The food is already swallowed, but the muscles — right here — they simply refuse. It isn't a question of will-power. Or rather, the thing is, I don't dare really will it."

Tony cried out, quite beside herself: "Christian! Good Lord, what nonsense! You don't dare to make up your mind to swallow! What are you talking about? You are absurd!"

Thomas was silent. But the Frau Consul said: "That is nerves, Christian. Yes, it was high time you came home; the climate over there would have killed you in the end."

After the meal Christian sat down at the little harmonium that stood in the dining-room and imitated a piano virtuoso. He pretended to toss back his hair, rubbed his hands, and looked around the room; then, without a sound, without touching the bellows — for he could not play in the least, and was entirely unmusical, like all the Buddenbrooks — he bent quite over and began to belabour the bass, played unbelievable passages, threw himself back, looked in ecstasy at the ceiling, and banged the key-board in a triumphant finale. Even Clara burst out laughing. The illusion was convincing; full of assurance and charlatanry and irresistible comicality of the burlesque, eccentric English-American kind; so certain of its own effect that the result was not in the least unpleasant.

"I have gone a great deal to concerts," he said. "I like to watch how the people behave with their instruments. It is really beautiful to be an artist."

Then he began to play again, but broke off suddenly and became serious, as though a mask had fallen over his features. He got up, ran his hand through his scanty hair, moved away, and stood silent, obviously fallen into a bad mood, with unquiet eyes and an expression as though he were listening to some kind of uncanny noise.

"Sometimes I find Christian a little strange," said Madame Grünlich to her brother Thomas, one evening, when they were alone. "He talks so, somehow. He goes so unnaturally into detail, seems to me — or what shall I say? He looks at things in such a strange way; don't you think so?"

"Yes," said Tom, "I understand what you mean very well, Tony. Christian is very incautious — undignified — it is difficult to express what I mean. Something is lacking in him — what people call equilibrium, mental poise. On the one hand, he does not know how to keep his countenance when other people make naïve or tactless remarks — he does not understand how to cover it up, and he just loses his self-possession altogether. But the same thing happens when he begins to be garrulous himself, in the unpleasant way he has, and tells his most intimate thoughts. It gives one such an uncanny feeling — it is just the way people speak in a fever, isn't it? Self-control and personal reserve are both lacking in the same way. Oh, the thing is quite simple: Christian busies himself too much with himself, with what goes on in his own insides. Sometimes he has a regular mania for bringing out the deepest and the pettiest of these experiences — things a reasonable man does not trouble himself about or even want to know about, for the simple reason that he would not like to tell them to any one else. There is such a lack of modesty in so much communicativeness. You see, Tony, anybody, except Christian, may say that he loves the theatre. But he would say it in a different tone, more *en passant*, more modestly, in short. Christian says it in a tone that says: ' Is not my passion for the stage something very marvellous and interesting? ' He struggles, he behaves as if he were really wrestling to express something supremely delicate and difficult.

"I'll tell you," he went on after a pause, throwing his cigarette through the wrought-iron lattice into the stove: " I have thought a great deal about this curious and useless self-preoccupation, because I had once an inclination to it myself. But I observed that it made me unsteady, hare-brained, and incapable — and control, equilibrium, is, at least for me, the important thing. There will always be men who are justified in this interest in themselves, this detailed observation of their own emotions; poets who can express with clarity and beauty their privileged inner life, and thereby enrich the emotional world of other people. But the likes of us are simple merchants, my child; our self-observations are decidedly inconsiderable. We can sometimes go so far as to say that the sound of orchestra instruments gives us unspeakable pleasure, and that we sometimes do not dare try to swallow — but it would be much better, deuce take it, if we sat down and accomplished something, as our fathers did before us."

"Yes, Tom, you express my views exactly. When I think of the airs those Hagenströms put on — oh, Heavens, what truck! Mother doesn't like the words I use, but I find they are the only right ones. Do you suppose they think they are the only good family in town? I have to laugh, you know; I really do."

CHAPTER III

THE HEAD of the firm of Johann Buddenbrook had measured his brother on his arrival with a long, scrutinizing gaze. He had given him passing and unobtrusive observation during several days; and then, though he did not allow any sign of his opinion to appear upon his calm and discreet face, his curiosity was satisfied, his mind made up. He talked with him in the family circle in a casual tone on casual subjects and enjoyed himself like the others when Christian gave a performance. A week later he said to him: "Well, shall we work together, young man? So far as I know, you consent to Mamma's wish, do you not? As you know, Marcus has become my partner, in proportion to the quota he has paid in. I should think that, as my brother, you could ostensibly take the place he had — that of confidential clerk. What your work would be — I do not know how much mercantile experience you have really had. You have been loafing a bit, so far — am I right? Well, in any case, the English correspondence will suit you. But I must beg one thing of you, my dear chap. In your position as brother of the head of the house, you will actually have a superior position to the others; but I do not need to tell you that you will impress them far more by behaving like their equal and doing your duty, than you will by making use of privileges and taking liberties. Are you willing to keep office hours and observe appearances? "

And then he made a proposal in respect of salary, which Christian accepted without consideration, with an embarrassed and inattentive face that betrayed very little love of gain and a great zeal to settle the matter quickly. Next day Thomas led him into the office; and Christian's labours for the old firm began.

The business had taken its uninterrupted and solid course after the Consul's death. But soon after Thomas Buddenbrook seized the reins, a fresher and more enterprising spirit began to be noticeable in the management. Risks were taken now and then. The credit of the house, formerly a conception, a theory, a luxury, was consciously strained and utilized. The gentlemen on 'Change nodded at each other. "Buddenbrook wants to make money with

both hands," they said. They thought it was a good thing that
Thomas had to carry the upright Friederich Wilhelm Marcus
along with him, like a ball and chain on his foot. Herr Marcus'
influence was the conservative force in the business. He stroked
his moustache with his two fingers, punctiliously arranged his writing materials and glass of water on his desk, looked at everything
on both sides and top and bottom; and, five or six times in the day,
would go out through the courtyard into the wash-kitchen and
hold his head under the tap to refresh himself.

"They complement each other," said the heads of the great
houses to each other; Consul Heneus said it to Consul Kistenmaker.
The small families echoed them; and the dockyard and warehouse
hands repeated the same opinion. The whole town was interested
in the way young Buddenbrook would "take hold." Herr Stuht
in Bell Founders' Street would say to his wife, who knew the best
families: "They balance each other, you see."

But the personality of the business was plainly the younger
partner. He knew how to handle the personnel, the ship-captains,
the heads in the warehouse offices, the drivers and the yard hands.
He could speak their language with ease and yet keep a distance
between himself and them. But when Herr Marcus spoke in dialect to some faithful servant it sounded so outlandish that his
partner would simply begin to laugh, and the whole office would
dissolve in merriment.

Thomas Buddenbrook's desire to protect and increase the prestige of the old firm made him love to be present in the daily struggle for success. He well knew that his assured and elegant bearing, his tact and winning manners were responsible for a great
deal of good trade.

"A business man cannot be a bureaucrat," he said to Stephen
Kistenmaker, of Kistenmaker and Sons, his former school-fellow.
He had remained the oracle of this old playmate, who listened to
his every word in order to give it out later as his own. "It takes
personality — that is my view. I don't think any great success is to
be had from the office alone — at least, I shouldn't care for it. I
always want to direct the course of things on the spot, with a look,
a word, a gesture — to govern it with the immediate influence of
my will and my talent — my luck, as you call it. But, unfortunately,
personal contact is going out of fashion. The times move on, but
it seems to me they leave the best behind. Relations are easier and
easier; the connections better and better; the risk gets smaller —
but the profits do too. Yes, the old people were better off. My
grandfather, for example — he drove in a four-horse coach to

Southern Germany, as commissary to the Prussian army — an old
man in pumps, with his head powdered. And there he played his
charms and his talents and made an astonishing amount of money,
Kistenmaker. Oh, I'm afraid the merchant's life will get duller
and duller as time goes on."

It was feelings like these that made him relish most the trade he
came by through his own personal efforts. Sometimes, entirely by
accident, perhaps on a walk with the family, he would go into a
mill for a chat with the miller, who would feel himself much honoured by the visit; and quite *en passant*, in the best of moods, he
would conclude a good bargain. His partner was incapable of that
sort of thing.

As for Christian, he seemed at first to devote himself to his task
with real zest and enjoyment, and to feel exceptionally well and
contented. For several days he ate with appetite, smoked his short
pipe, and squared his shoulders in the English jacket, giving expression to his sense of ease and well-being. In the morning he went to
the office at about the same time as Thomas, and sat opposite his
brother and Herr Marcus in a revolving arm-chair like theirs. First
he read the paper, while he comfortably smoked his morning cigarette. Then he would fetch out an old cognac from his bottom
desk drawer, stretch out his arms in order to feel himself free to
move, say "Well!" and go to work good-naturedly, his tongue
roving about among his teeth. His English letters were extraordinarily able and effective, for he wrote English as he spoke it, simply and fluently, without effort.

He gave expression to his mood in his own way in the family
circle.

"Business is really a fine, gratifying calling," he said. "Respectable, satisfying, industrious, comfortable. I was really born to it —
fact! And as a member of the house! — well, I've never felt so
good before. You come fresh into the office in the morning, and
look through the paper, smoke, think about this and that, take
some cognac, and then go to work. Comes midday; you eat with
your family, take a rest, then to work again. You write, on smooth,
good business paper, with a good pen, rule, paper-knife, stamp —
everything first-class and all in order. You keep at it, get things
done one after the other, and finish up. To-morrow is another day.
When you go home to supper, you feel thoroughly satisfied — satisfied in every limb. Even your hands — "

"Heavens, Christian," cried Tony. "What rubbish! How can
your hands feel satisfied? "

"Why, yes, of course — can't you understand that? I mean — "

He made a painstaking effort to express and explain. " You can shut your fist, you see. You don't make a violent effort, of course, because you are tired from your work. But it isn't flabby; it doesn't make you feel irritable. You have a sense of satisfaction in it; you feel easy and comfortable — you can sit quite still without feeling bored."

Every one was silent. Then Thomas said in a casual tone, so as not to show that he disagreed: " It seems to me that one doesn't work for the sake of — " He broke off and did not continue. " At least, I have different reasons," he added after a minute. But Christian did not hear. His eyes roamed about, sunk in thought; and he soon began to tell a story of Valparaiso, a tale of assault and murder of which he had personal knowledge. " Then the fellow ripped out his knife — " For some reason Thomas never applauded these tales. Christian was full of them, and Madame Grünlich found them vastly entertaining. The Frau Consul, Clara, and Clothilde sat aghast, and Mamsell Jungmann and Erica listened with their mouths open. Thomas used to make cool sarcastic comments and act as if he thought Christian was exaggerating or hoaxing — which was certainly not the case. He narrated with colour and vividness. Perhaps Thomas found unpleasant the reflection that his younger brother had been about and seen more of the world than he! Or were his feelings of repulsion due to the glorification of disorder, the exotic violence of these knife- and revolver-tales? Christian certainly did not trouble himself over his brother's failure to appreciate his stories. He was always too much absorbed in his narrative to notice its success or lack of success with his audience, and when he had finished he would look pensively or absently about the room.

But if in time the relations between the two brothers came to be not of the best, Christian was not the one who thought of showing or feeling any animosity against his brother. He silently took for granted the pre-eminence of his elder, his superior capacity, earnestness, and respectability. But precisely this casual, indiscriminate acknowledgment irritated Thomas, for it had the appearance of setting no value upon superior capacity, earnestness, or respectability.

Christian appeared not to notice the growing dislike of the head of the firm. Thomas's feelings were indeed quite justifiable; for unfortunately Christian's zeal for business visibly decreased, even after the first week, though more after the second. His little preparations for work, which, in the beginning, wore the air of a prolonged and refined anticipation: the reading of the paper, the af-

ter-breakfast cigarette, the cognac, began to take more and more
time, and finally used up the whole morning. It gradually came
about that Christian freed himself largely from the constraint of
office hours. He appeared later and later with his breakfast cigarette to begin his preparations for work; he went at midday to eat
at the Club, and came back late or not at all.

This Club, to which mostly unmarried business men belonged,
occupied comfortable rooms in the first story of a restaurant,
where one could eat and meet in unrestrained and sometimes not
altogether harmless conversation — for there was a roulette table.
Even some of the more light-minded fathers of families, like Justus
Kröger and, of course, Peter Döhlmann, were members, and police
senator Crema was here " the first man at the hose." That was the
expression of Dr. Gieseke — Andreas Gieseke, the son of the Fire
Commissioner and Christian's old schoolmate. He had settled as a
lawyer in the town, and Christian renewed the friendship with
him, though he ranked as rather a wild fellow. Christian — or, as
he was called everywhere, Chris — had known them all more or
less in the old days, for nearly all of them had been pupils of Marcellus Stengel. They received him into the Club with open arms;
for, while neither business men nor scholars found him a genius,
they recognized his amusing social gifts. It was here that he gave
his best performances and told his best stories. He did the virtuoso
at the club piano and imitated English and transatlantic actors and
opera singers. But the best things he did were stories of his affairs
with women, related in the most harmless and entertaining way
imaginable — adventures that had befallen him on shipboard, on
trains, in St. Paul's, in Whitechapel, in the virgin forest. There was
no doubt that Christian's weakness was for women. He narrated
with a fluency and power that entranced his listeners, in an ex-
haustless stream, with his somewhat plaintive, drawling voice, burlesque and innocent, like an English humourist. He told a story
about a dog that had been sent in a satchel from Valparaiso to San
Francisco and was mangy to boot. Goodness knew what was the
point of the anecdote — in his mouth it was indescribably comic.
And while everybody about him writhed with laughter, unable to
leave off, he himself sat there cross-legged, a strange, uneasy seriousness in his face with its great hooked nose, his thin, long neck,
his sparse light-red hair and little round deep-set eyes. It almost
seemed as if the laugh were at his expense, as if they were laughing
at him. But that never occurred to him.

At home his favourite tales were about his office in Valparaiso.
He told of the extreme heat there, and about a young Londoner,

named Johnny Thunderstorm, a ne'er-do-well, an extraordinary chap, whom he had " never seen do a stroke of work, God damn me," and who yet was a remarkable business man.

" Good God, the heat! " he said. " Well, the chief came into the office — there we all lay, eight of us, like flies, and smoked ciga-rettes to keep the mosquitoes away. Good God! Well, the chief said: ' You are not working, gentlemen? ' ' No, sir,' says Johnny Thunderstorm, ' as you see, sir! ' And we all blew our cigarette-smoke in his face. Good God! "

" Why do you keep saying ' good God '? " asked Thomas ir-ritably. But his irritation was at bottom because he felt that Chris-tian told this story with particular relish just because it gave him a chance to sneer at honest work.

The Mother would discreetly change the subject. There were many hateful things in the world, thought the Frau Consul, born Kröger. Brothers could despise and dislike each other, dreadful as it sounded; but one didn't mention such things. They had to be covered up and ignored.

CHAPTER IV

IN May it happened that Uncle Gotthold — Consul Gotthold Buddenbrook, now sixty years old — was seized with a heart attack one night and died in the arms of his wife, born Stüwing.

The son of poor Madame Josephine had had the worst of it in life, compared with the younger and stronger brother and sister born of Madame Antoinette. But he had long since resigned himself to his fortunes; and in his later years, especially after his nephew turned over to him the Consulate of the Netherlands, he ate his lozenges out of his tin box and harboured the friendliest feelings. It was his ladies who kept up the feud now: not so much his good-natured wife as the three elderly damsels, who could not look at Frau Consul, or Antonie, or Thomas, without a spark in their eyes.

On the traditional " children's day," at four o'clock, they all gathered in the big house in Meng Street, to eat dinner and spend the evening. Sometimes Consul Kröger or Sesemi Weichbrodt came too, with her simple sister. On these occasions the three Miss Buddenbrooks from Broad Street loved to turn the conversation to Tony's former marriage and to dart sharp glances at each other while they egged Madame Grünlich on to use strong language. Or they would make general remarks on the subject of the undignified vanity of dyeing one's hair. Or they would enquire particularly after Jacob Kröger, the Frau Consul's nephew. They made jokes at the expense of poor, innocent, Clothilde — jokes not so harmless as those which the charity girl received in good part every day from Tom and Tony. They made fun of Clara's austerity and bigotry. They were quick to find out that Tom and Christian were not on the best of terms; also, that they did not need to pay much attention to Christian anyhow, for he was a sort of Tomfool. As for Thomas himself, who had no weak point for them to ferret out, and who always met them with a good-humoured indulgence, that signified " I understand what you mean, and I am very sorry " — him they treated with respect tinctured with bitterness. Next came the turn of little Erica. Rosy and plump as she was, they found her alarmingly backward in her growth. And

Pfiffi in a series of little shakes drew attention several times to the child's shocking resemblance to the deceiver Grünlich.

But now they stood with their mother about their Father's death-bed, weeping; and a message was sent to Meng Street, though the feeling was not entirely wanting that their rich relations were somehow or other to blame for this misfortune too.

In the middle of the night the great bell downstairs rang; and as Christian had come home very late and was not feeling up to much, Tom set out alone in the spring rain.

He came just in time to see the last convulsive motions of the old gentleman. Then he stood a long time in the death-chamber and looked at the short figure under the covers, at the dead face with the mild features and white whiskers. "You haven't had a very good time, Uncle Gotthold," he thought. "You learned too late to make concessions and show consideration. But that is what one has to do. If I had been like you, I should have married a shop girl years ago. But for the sake of appearances — ! I wonder if you really wanted anything different? You were proud, and probably felt that your pride was something idealistic; but your spirit had little power to rise. To cherish the vision of an abstract good; to carry in your heart, like a hidden love, only far sweeter, the dream of preserving an ancient name, an old family, an old business, of carrying it on, and adding to it more and more honour and lustre — ah, that takes imagination, Uncle Gotthold, and imagination you didn't have. The sense of poetry escaped you, though you were brave enough to love and marry against the will of your father. And you had no ambition, Uncle Gotthold. The old name is only a burgher name, it is true, and one cherishes it by making the grain business flourish, and oneself beloved and powerful in a little corner of the earth. Did you think: 'I will marry her whom I love, and pay no attention to practical considerations, for they are petty and provincial?' Oh, we are travelled and educated enough to realize that the limits set to our ambition are small and petty enough, looked at from outside and above. But everything in this world is comparative, Uncle Gotthold. Did you know one can be a great man, even in a small place; a Cæsar even in a little commercial town on the Baltic? But that takes imagination and idealism — and you didn't have it, whatever you may have thought yourself."

Thomas Buddenbrook turned away. He went to the window and looked out at the dim grey gothic façade of the Town Hall opposite, shrouded in rain. He had his hands behind his back and a smile on his intelligent face.

The office and title of the Royal Consulate of the Netherlands, which Thomas Buddenbrook might have taken after his father's death, went back to him now, to the boundless satisfaction of Tony Grünlich; and the curving shield with the lions, the arms, and the crown was once more to be seen on the gabled front of the house in Meng Street, under the " Dominus providebit."

Soon after this was accomplished, in June of the same year, the young Consul set out to Amsterdam on a business journey the duration of which he did not know.

CHAPTER V

DEATHS in the family usually induce a religious mood. It was not surprising, after the decease of the Consul, to hear from the mouth of his widow expressions which she had not been accustomed to use.

But it was soon apparent that this was no passing phase. Even in the last years of the Consul's life, his wife had more and more sympathized with his spiritual cravings; and it now became plain that she was determined to honour the memory of her dead by adopting as her own all his pious conceptions.

She strove to fill the great house with the spirit of the deceased — that mild and Christlike spirit which yet had not excluded a certain dignified and hearty good cheer. The morning and evening prayers were continued and lengthened. The family gathered in the dining-room, and the servants in the hall, to hear the Frau Consul or Clara read a chapter out of the great family Bible with the big letters. They also sang a few verses out of the hymn-book, accompanied by the Frau Consul on the little organ. Or, often, in place of the chapter from the Bible, they had a reading from one of those edifying or devotional books with the black binding and gilt edges — those Little Treasuries, Jewel-Caskets, Holy Hours, Morning Chimes, Pilgrims' Staffs, and the like, whose common trait was a sickly and languishing tenderness for the little Jesus, and of which there were all too many in the house.

Christian did not often appear at these devotions. Thomas once chose a favourable moment to disparage the practice, half-jestingly; but his objection met with a gentle rebuff. As for Madame Grünlich, she did not, unfortunately, always conduct herself correctly at the exercises. One morning when there was a strange clergyman stopping with the Buddenbrooks, they were invited to sing to a solemn and devout melody the following words: —

> I am a reprobate,
> A warped and hardened sinner;
> I gobble evil down
> Just like the joint for dinner.

> Lord, fling thy cur a bone
> Of righteousness to chew
> And take my carcass home
> To Heaven and to you.

Whereat Frau Grünlich threw down her book and left the room, bursting with suppressed giggles.

But the Frau Consul made more demands upon herself than upon her children. She instituted a Sunday School, and on Sunday afternoon only little board-school pupils rang at the door of the house in Meng Street. Stine Voss, who lived by the city wall, and Mike Stuht from Bell-Founders' Street, and Fike Snut from the river-bank or Groping Alley, their straw-coloured locks smoothed back with a wet comb, crossed the entry into the garden-room, which for a long time now had not been used as an office, and in which rows of benches had been arranged and Frau Consul Buddenbrook, born Kröger, in a gown of heavy black satin, with her white re-fined face and still whiter lace cap, sat opposite to them at a little table with a glass of sugar-water and catechized them for an hour.

Also, she founded the " Jerusalem evenings," which not only Clara and Clothilde but also Tony were obliged to attend, willy-nilly. Once a week they sat at the extension table in the dining-room by the light of lamps and candles. Some twenty ladies, all of an age when it is profitable to begin to look after a good place in heaven, drank tea or bishop, ate delicate sandwiches and pud-dings, read hymns and sermons aloud to each other, and did em-broidery, which at the end of the year was sold at a bazaar and the proceeds sent to the mission in Jerusalem.

This pious society was formed in the main from ladies of the Frau Consul's own social rank: Frau Senator Langhals, Frau Con-sul Möllendorpf, and old Frau Consul Kistenmaker belonged; but other, more worldly and profane old ladies, like Mme. Köppen, made fun of their friend Betsy. The wives of the clergy-men of the town were all members, likewise the widowed Frau Consul Buddenbrook, born Stüwing, and Sesemi Weichbrodt and her simple sister. There is, however, no rank and no discrimina-tion before Jesus; and so certain humble oddities were also guests at the Jerusalem evenings — for example, a little wrinkled creature, rich in the grace of God and knitting-patterns, who lived in the Holy Ghost Hospital and was named Himmelsburger. She was the last of her name — " the last Himmelsburger," she called herself humbly, and ran her knitting-needle under her cap to scratch her head.

But far more remarkable were two other extraordinary old

creatures, twins, who went about hand in hand through the town doing good deeds, in shepherdess hats out of the eighteenth century and faded clothes out of the long, long ago. They were named Gerhardt, and asserted that they descended in a direct line from Paul Gerhardt. People said they were by no means poor; but they lived wretchedly and gave away all they had. "My dears," remarked the Frau Consul, who was sometimes rather ashamed of them, "God sees the heart, I know; but your clothes are really a little — one must take some thought for oneself." But she could not prevent them kissing their elegant friend on the brow with the forbearing, yearning, pitying superiority of the poor in heart over the worldly great who seek salvation. They were not at all stupid. In their homely shrivelled heads — for all the world like ancient parrots — they had bright soft brown eyes and they looked out at the world with a wonderful expression of gentleness and understanding. Their hearts were full of amazing wisdom. They knew that in the last day all our beloved gone before us to God will come with song and salvation to fetch us home. They spoke the words "the Lord" with the fluent authority of early Christians, as if they had heard out of the Master's own mouth the words, "Yet a little while and ye shall see me." They possessed the most remarkable theories concerning inner light and intuition and the transmission of thought. One of them, named Lea, was deaf, and yet she nearly always knew what was being talked about!

It was usually the deaf Gerhardt who read aloud at the Jerusalem evenings, and the ladies found that she read beautifully and very affectingly. She took out of her bag an old book of a very disproportionate shape, much taller than it was broad, with an inhumanly chubby presentment of her ancestor in the front. She held it in both hands and read in a tremendous voice, in order to catch a little herself of what she read. It sounded as if the wind were imprisoned in the chimney:

"If Satan me would swallow."

"Goodness!" thought Tony Grünlich, "how could Satan want to swallow her?" But she said nothing and devoted herself to the pudding, wondering if she herself would ever become as ugly as the two Miss Gerhardts.

She was not happy. She felt bored and out of patience with all the pastors and missionaries, whose visits had increased ever since the death of the Consul. According to Tony they had too much to say in the house and received entirely too much money. But this last was Tom's affair, and he said nothing, while his sister now and

then murmured something about people who consumed widows'
homes and made long prayers.

She hated these black gentlemen bitterly. As a mature woman
who knew life and was no longer a silly innocent, she found herself
unable to believe in their irreproachable sanctity. " Mother," she
said, " oh dear, I know I must not speak evil of my neighbours.
But one thing I must say, and I should be surprised if life had not
taught you that too, and that is that not all those who wear a long
coat and say 'Lord, Lord' are always entirely without blemish."

History does not say what Tom thought of his sister's opinion
on this point. Christian had no opinion at all. He confined himself to watching the gentlemen with his nose wrinkled up, in
order to imitate them afterward at the club or in the family circle.

But it is true that Tony was the chief sufferer from the pious
visitants. One day it actually happened that a missionary named
Jonathan, who had been in Arabia and Syria — a man with great,
reproachful eyes and baggy cheeks — was stopping in the house,
and challenged her to assert that the curls she wore on her forehead
were consistent with true Christian humility. He had not reckoned with Tony Grünlich's skill at repartee. She was silent a moment, while her mind worked rapidly; and then out it came. " May
I ask you, Herr Pastor, to concern yourself with your own curls? "
With that she rustled out, shoulders up, head back, and chin well
tucked in. Pastor Jonathan had very few curls on his head — it
would be nearer truth to say that he was quite bald.

And once she had an even greater triumph. There was a certain Pastor Trieschke from Berlin. His nickname was Teary
Trieschke, because every Sunday he began to weep at an appropriate place in his sermon. Teary Trieschke had a pale face, red
eyes, and cheek-bones like a horse's. He had been stopping for
eight or ten days with the Buddenbrooks, conducting devotions
and holding eating contests with poor Clothilde, turn about. He
happened to fall in love with Tony — not with her immortal soul,
oh no, but with her upper lip, her thick hair, her pretty eyes and
charming figure. And the man of God, who had a wife and numerous children in Berlin, was not ashamed to have Anton leave a letter in Madame Grünlich's bedroom in the upper storey, wherein
Bible texts and a kind of fawning sentimentality were surpass-
ingly mingled. She found it when she went to bed, read it, and
went with a firm step downstairs into the Frau Consul's bedroom,
where by the candle-light she read aloud the words of the soul-
saver to her Mother, quite unembarrassed and in a loud voice; so
that Teary Trieschke became impossible in Meng Street.

" They are all alike," said Madame Grünlich; " ah, they are all alike. Oh, heavens, what a goose I was once! But life has destroyed my faith in men. Most of them are scoundrels — alas, it is the truth. Grünlich — " The name was, as always, like a summons to battle. She uttered it with her shoulders lifted and her eyes rolled up.

CHAPTER VI

SIEVERT TIBURTIUS was a small, narrow man with a large head and a thin, long, blond beard parted in the middle, so that he sometimes put the ends back over his shoulders. A quantity of little woolly ringlets covered his round head. His ears were large and outstanding, very much curled up at the edges and pointed at the tips like the ears of a fox. His nose sat like a tiny flat button in his face, his cheek-bones stood out, and his grey eyes, usually drawn close together and blinking about rather stupidly, could at certain moments widen quite extraordinarily, and get larger and larger, protruding more and more until they almost sprang out of their sockets.

This Pastor Tiburtius, who came from Riga, had preached for some years in central Germany, and now touched at the town on his way back home, where a living had been offered to him. Armed with the recommendation of a brother of the cloth who had eaten at least once in Meng Street of mock-turtle soup and ham with onion sauce, he waited upon the Frau Consul and was invited to be her guest for a few days. He occupied the spacious guest-chamber off the corridor in the first storey. But he stopped longer than he had expected. Eight days passed, and still there was this or that to be seen: the dance of death and the apostle-clock in St. Mary's, the Town Hall, the ancient Ships' Company, the Cathedral clock with the movable eyes. Ten days passed, and he spoke repeatedly of his departure, but at the first word of demur from anybody would postpone anew.

He was a better man than Herr Jonathan or Teary Trieschke. He thought not at all about Frau Antonie's curls and wrote her no letters. Strange to say, he paid his attentions to Clara, her younger and more serious sister. In her presence, when she spoke, entered or left the room, his eyes would grow surprisingly larger and larger and open out until they nearly jumped out of his head. He would spend almost the entire day in her company, in spiritual or worldly converse or reading aloud to her in his high voice and with the droll, jerky pronunciation of his Baltic home.

Even on the first day he said: " Permit me to say, Frau Consul, what a treasure and blessing from God you have in your daughter Clara. She is certainly a wonderful child."

" You are right," replied the Frau Consul. But he repeated his opinion so often that she began looking him over with her pale blue eyes, and led him on to speak of his home, his connections, and his prospects. She learned that he came of a mercantile family, that his mother was with God, that he had no brothers and sisters, and that his old father had retired and lived on his income in Riga — an income which would some time fall to him, Pastor Tiburtius. He also had a sufficient living from his calling.

Clara Buddenbrook was now in her nineteenth year. She had grown to be a young lady of an austere and peculiar beauty, with a tall, slender figure, dark, smooth hair, and stern yet dreamy eyes. Her nose was slightly hooked, her mouth a little too firmly closed. In the household she was most intimate with her poor and pious cousin Clothilde, whose father had lately died, and whose idea it was to " establish herself " soon — which meant to go into a pension somewhere with the money and furniture which she had inherited. Clara had nothing of Clothilde's meek and hungry submissiveness. On the contrary, with the servants and even with her brothers and sister and mother, a commanding tone was usual with her. Her low voice, which seemed only to drop with decision and never to rise with a question, had an imperious sound and could often take on a short, hard, impatient, haughty quality — on days, for example, when Clara had a headache.

Before the father's death had shrouded the family in mourning, she had taken part with irreproachable dignity in the society of her parents' house and other houses of like rank. But when the Frau Consul looked at her, she could not deny that, despite the stately dowry and Clara's domestic prowess, it would not be easy to marry her off. None of the godless, jovial, claret-drinking merchants of their circle would answer in the least; a clergyman would be the only suitable partner for this earnest and God-fearing maiden. After the Frau Consul had conceived this joyful idea, she responded with friendliness to the delicate advances of Pastor Tiburtius.

And truly the affair developed with precision. On a warm, cloudless July afternoon the family took a walk: the Frau Consul, Antonie, Christian, Clara, Clothilde, Erica Grünlich, and Mamsell Jungmann, with Pastor Tiburtius in their midst, went out far beyond the Castle Gate to eat strawberries and clotted milk or porridge at a wooden table laid out-of-doors, going after the meal into the large nut-garden which ran down to the river, in the shade of all sorts of fruit-trees, between currant and gooseberry bushes, asparagus and potato patches.

Sievert Tiburtius and Clara Buddenbrook stopped a little behind the others. He, much the smaller of the two, with his beard parted back over his shoulders, had taken off his broad-brimmed black hat from his big head; and he wiped his brow now and then with his handkerchief. His eyes were larger than usual and he carried on with her a long and gentle conversation, in the course of which they both stood still, and Clara, with a serious, calm voice said her "Yes."

After they returned, the Frau Consul, a little tired and over-heated, was sitting alone in the landscape-room, when Pastor Tiburtius came and sat beside her. Outside there reigned the pensive calm of the Sabbath afternoon; and they sat inside and held, in the brightness of the summer evening, a long, low conversation, at the end of which the Frau Consul said: "Enough, my dear Herr Pastor. Your offer coincides with my motherly plans for my daughter; and you on your side have not chosen badly — that I can assure you. Who would have thought that your coming and your stay here in our house would be so wonderfully blest! I will not speak my final word to-day, for I must write first to my son, the Consul, who is at present, as you know, away. You will travel to-morrow, if you live and have your health, to Riga, to take up your work; and we expect to go for some weeks to the seashore. You will receive word from me soon, and God grant that we shall have a happy meeting."

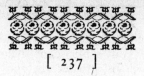

CHAPTER VII

AMSTERDAM, July 30th, 1856
HOTEL HET HASSJE

MY DEAR MOTHER,

I have just received your important letter, and hasten to thank you for the consideration you show me in asking for my consent in the affair under discussion. I send you, of course, not only my hearty agreement, but add my warmest good-wishes, being thoroughly convinced that you and Clara have made a good choice. The fine name Tiburtius is known to me, and I feel sure that Papa had business relations with the father. Clara comes into pleasant connections, in any case, and the position as pastor's wife will be very suited to her temperament.

And Tiburtius has gone back to Riga, and will visit his bride again in August? Well, it will be a gay time then with us in Meng Street — gayer than you realize, for you do not know the reason why I was so joyfully surprised by Mademoiselle Clara's betrothal, nor what a charming company it is likely to be. Yes, my dear good Mother: I am complying with the request to send my solemn consent to Clara's betrothal from the Amstel to the Baltic. But I do so on condition that you send me a similar consent by return of post! I would give three solid gulden to see your face, and even more that of our honest Tony, when you read these lines. But I will come to the point.

My clean little hotel is in the centre of the town with a pretty view of the canal. It is not far from the Bourse; and the business on which I came here — a question of a new and valuable connection, which you know I prefer to look after in person — has gone successfully from the first day. I have still considerable acquaintance here from the days of my apprenticeship; so, although many families are at the shore now, I have been invited out a good deal. I have been at small evening companies at the Van Henkdoms and the Moelens, and on the third day after my arrival I had to put on my dress clothes to go to a dinner at the house of my former chief, van der Kellen, which he had arranged out of season in my honour. Whom did I take in to dinner? Should you like to guess? Fräulein Arnoldsen, Tony's old school-fellow. Her father, the great merchant and almost greater violin artist, and his married daughter and her husband were also of the party.

I well remember that Gerda — if I may call her so — from the beginning, even when she was a young girl at school at Fräulein Weichbrodt's on the Millbrink, made a strong impression on me, never quite obliterated. But now I saw her again, taller, more developed, lovelier, more animated. Please spare me a description, which might so easily sound overdrawn — and you will soon see each other face to face.

You can imagine we had much to talk about at the table, but we had left the old memories behind by the end of the soup, and went on to more serious and fascinating matters. In music I could not hold my own with her, for we poor Buddenbrooks know all too little of that, but in the art of the Netherlands I was more at home, and in literature we were fully agreed.

Truly the time flew. After dinner I had myself presented to old Herr Arnoldsen, who received me with especial cordiality. Later, in the salon, he played several concert pieces, and Gerda also performed. She looked wonderful as she played, and although I have no notion of violin playing, I know that she knew how to sing upon her instrument (a real Stradivarius) so that the tears nearly came into my eyes. Next day I went to call on the Arnoldsens. I was received at first by an elderly companion, with whom I spoke French, but then Gerda came, and we talked as on the day before for perhaps an hour, only that this time we drew nearer together and made still more effort to understand and know each other. The talk was of you, Mamma, of Tony, of our good old town, and of my work.

And on that day I had already taken the firm resolve: this one or no one, now or never! I met her again by chance at a garden party at my friend van Svindren's, and I was invited to a musical evening at the Arnoldsens', in the course of which I sounded the young lady by a half-declaration, which was received encouragingly. Five days ago I went to Herr Arnoldsen to ask for permission to win his daughter's hand. He received me in his private office. "My dear Consul," he said, "you are very welcome, hard as it will be for an old widower to part from his daughter. But what does she say? She has already held firmly to her resolve never to marry. Have you a chance?" He was extremely surprised when I told him that Fräulein Gerda had actually given me ground for hope.

He left her some time for reflection, and I imagine that out of pure selfishness he dissuaded her. But it was useless. She had chosen me — since yesterday evening the betrothal is an accomplished fact.

No, my dear Mother, I am not asking a written answer to this letter, for I am leaving to-morrow. But I am bringing with me the Arnoldsens' promise that father, daughter, and married sister will visit us in August, and then you will be obliged to confess that she is the very wife for me. I hope you see no objection in the fact that Gerda is only three years younger than I? I am sure you never thought I would marry a chit out of the Möllendorpf-Langhals, Kistenmaker-Hagenström circle.

And now for the dowry. I am almost frightened to think how Stephan Kistenmaker and Hermann Hagenström and Peter Döhlmann and Uncle Justus and the whole town will blink at me when they hear of the dowry. For my future father-in-law is a millionaire. Heavens, what is there to say? We are such complex, contradictory creatures! I deeply love and respect Gerda Arnoldsen; and I simply will not delve deep down enough in myself to find out how much the thought of the dowry, which was whispered into my ear that first evening, contributed to my feeling. I love her: but it crowns my happiness and pride to think that when she becomes mine, our firm will at the same time gain a very considerable increase of capital.

I must close this letter, dear Mother; considering that in a few days, we shall be talking over my good fortune together, it is already too long. I wish you a pleasant and beneficial stay at the baths, and beg you to greet all the family most heartily for me. Your loving and obedient son,

                                                            T.

CHAPTER VIII

THAT year there was indeed a merry midsummer holiday in the Buddenbrook home. At the end of July Thomas returned to Meng Street and visited his family at the shore several times, like the other business men in the town. Christian had allotted full holidays unto himself, as he complained of an indefinite ache in his left leg. Dr. Grabow did not seem to treat it successfully, and Christian thought of it so much the more.

" It is not a pain — one can't call it a pain," he expatiated, rubbing his hand up and down his leg, wrinkling his big nose, and letting his eyes roam about. " It is a sort of ache, a continuous, slight, uneasy ache in the whole leg and on the left side, the side where the heart is. Strange. I find it strange — what do you think about it, Tom? "

" Well, well," said Tom, " you can have a rest and the sea-baths."

So Christian went down to the shore to tell stories to his fellow-guests, and the beach resounded with their laughter. Or he played roulette with Peter Döhlmann, Uncle Justus, Dr. Gieseke, and other Hamburg high-fliers.

Consul Buddenbrook went with Tony, as always when they were in Travemünde, to see the old Schwarzkopfs on the front. " Good-day, Ma'am Grünlich," said the pilot-captain, and spoke low German out of pure good feeling.

" Well, well, what a long time ago that was! And Morten, he's a doctor in Breslau and has all the practice in the town, the rascal." Frau Schwarzkopf ran off and made coffee, and they supped in the green verandah as they used to — only all of them were a good ten years older, and Morten and little Meta were not there, she having married the magistrate of Haffkrug. And the captain, already white-haired and rather deaf, had retired from his office — and Madame Grünlich was not a goose any more! Which did not prevent her from eating a great many slices of bread and honey, for, as she said: " Honey is a pure nature product — one knows what one is getting."

At the beginning of August the Buddenbrooks, like most of the other families, returned to town; and then came the great moment when, almost at the same time, Pastor Tiburtius from Prussia and the Arnoldsens from Holland arrived for a long visit in Meng Street.

It was a very pretty scene when the Consul led his bride for the first time into the landscape-room and took her to his mother, who received her with outstretched arms. Gerda had grown tall and splendid. She walked with a free and gracious bearing; with her heavy dark-red hair, her close-set brown eyes with the blue shadows round them, her large, gleaming teeth which showed when she smiled, her straight strong nose and nobly formed mouth, this maiden of seven-and-twenty years had a strange, aristocratic, haunting beauty. Her face was white and a little haughty, but she bowed her head as the Frau Consul with gentle feeling took it between her hands and kissed the pure, snowy forehead. "Yes, you are welcome to our house and to our family, you dear, beautiful, blessed creature," she said. "You will make him happy. Do I not see already how happy you make him?" And she drew Thomas forward with her other arm, to kiss him also.

Never, except perhaps in Grandfather's time, was there more gay society in the great house, which accommodated its guests with ease. Pastor Tiburtius had modestly chosen a bed-chamber in the back building next the billiard-room. But the rest divided the unoccupied space on the ground floor next the hall and in the first storey: Gerda; Herr Arnoldsen, a quick, clever man at the end of the fifties, with a pointed grey beard and a pleasant impetuosity in every motion; his oldest daughter, an ailing-looking woman; and his son-in-law, an elegant man of the world, who was turned over to Christian for entertainment in the town and at the club.

Antonie was overjoyed that Sievert Tiburtius was the only parson in the house. The betrothal of her adored brother rejoiced her heart. Aside from Gerda's being her friend, the parti was a brilliant one, gilding the family name and the firm with such new glory! And the three-hundred-thousand-mark dowry and the thought of what the town and particularly the Hagenströms would say to it, put her in a state of prolonged and delightful enchantment. Three times daily, at least, she passionately embraced her future sister-in-law.

"Oh, Gerda," she cried, "I love you — you know I always did love you. I know you can't stand me — you used to hate me; but —"

"Why, Tony!" said Fräulein Arnoldsen. "How could I have

hated you? Did you ever do anything to me? " For some reason,
however — probably out of mere wantonness and love of talking
— Tony asserted stoutly that Gerda had always hated her, while
she on her side had always returned the hate with love. She took
Thomas aside and told him: " You have done very well, Tom. Oh,
heavens, how well you have done! If Father could only see this —
it is just dreadful that he cannot! Yes, this wipes out a lot of things
— not least the affair with that person whose name I do not even
like to speak."

Which put it into her head to take Gerda into an empty room
and tell her with awful detail the story of her married life with
Bendix Grünlich. Then they talked for hours about boarding-
school days and the bed-time gossip; of Armgard von Schilling in
Mecklenburg and Eva Ewers in Munich. Tony paid little or no
attention to Sievert Tiburtius and his bethrothed — which troubled
them not at all. The lovers sat quietly together hand in hand, and
spoke gently and earnestly of the beautiful future before them.

As the year of mourning was not quite over, the two betrothals
were celebrated only in the family. But Gerda quickly became a
celebrity in the town. Her person formed the chief subject of conversation on the Bourse, at the club, at the theatre, and in society.
" Tip-top," said the gallants, and clucked their tongues, for that
was the latest Hamburg slang for a superior article, whether a
brand of claret, a cigar, or a " deal." But among the solid, respectable citizens there was much head-shaking. " Something queer
about her," they said. " Her hair, her face, the way she dresses —
a little too unusual." Sorenson expressed it: " She has a certain
something about her! " He made a face as if he were on the Bourse
and somebody had made him a doubtful proposition. But it was
all just like Consul Buddenbrook: a little pretentious, not like his
forebears. Everybody knew — not least Benthien the draper —
that he ordered his clothes from Hamburg: not only the fine new-
fashioned materials for his suits — and he had a great many of them,
cloaks, coats, waistcoats, and trousers — but his hats and cravats
and linen as well. He changed his shirt every day, sometimes twice
a day, and perfumed his handkerchief and his moustache, which he
wore cut like Napoleon III. All this was not for the sake of the
firm, of course — the house of Johann Buddenbrook did not need
that sort of thing — but to gratify his own personal taste for the
superfine and aristocratic — or whatever you might call it. And
then the quotations from Heine and other poets which he dropped
sometimes in the most practical connections, in business or civic
matters! And now, his bride — well, Consul Buddenbrook him-

self had " a certain something " about him! All this, of course, with the greatest respect; for the family was highly esteemed, the firm very, very " good," and the head of it an able and charming man who loved his city and would still serve her well. It was really a devilishly fine match for him; there was talk of a hundred thousand thaler down; but of course . . . Among the ladies there were some who found Gerda " silly "; which, it will be recalled, was a very severe judgment.

But the man who gazed with furious ardour at Thomas Buddenbrook's bride, the first time he saw her on the street, was Gosch the broker. " Ah! " he said in the club or the Ships' Company, lifting his glass and screwing up his face absurdly, " what a woman! Hera and Aphrodite, Brunhilda and Melusina all in one! Oh, how wonderful life is! " he would add. And not one of the citizens who sat about with their beer on the hard wooden benches of the old guild-house, under the models of sailing vessels and big stuffed fish hanging down from the ceiling, had the least idea what the advent of Gerda Arnoldsen meant in the yearning life of Gosch the broker.

The little company in Meng Street, not committed, as we have seen, to large entertainments, had the more leisure for intimacy with each other. Sievert Tiburtius, with Clara's hand in his, talked about his parents, his childhood, and his future plans. The Arnoldsens told of their people, who came from Dresden, only one branch of them having been transplanted to Holland.

Madame Grünlich asked her brother for the key of the secretary in the landscape-room, and brought out the portfolio with the family papers, in which Thomas had already entered the new events. She proudly related the Buddenbrook history, from the Rostock tailor on; and when she read out the old festival verses:

> Industry and beauty chaste
> See we linked in marriage band:
> Venus Anadyomene,
> And cunning Vulcan's busy hand

she looked at Tom and Gerda and let her tongue play over her lips. Regard for historical veracity also caused her to narrate events connected with a certain person whose name she did not like to mention!

On Thursday at four o'clock the usual guests came. Uncle Justus brought his feeble wife, with whom he lived an unhappy existence. The wretched mother continued to scrape together money out of the housekeeping to send to the degenerate and disinherited Jacob in America, while she and her husband subsisted on almost nothing but porridge. The Buddenbrook ladies from Broad Street also came; and their love of truth compelled them to say, as usual, that Erica Grünlich was not growing well and that she looked more than ever like her wretched father. Also that the Consul's bride wore a rather conspicuous coiffure. And Sesemi Weichbrodt came too, and standing on her tip-toes, kissed Gerda with her little explosive kiss on the forehead and said with emotion: "Be happy, my dear child."

At table Herr Arnoldsen gave one of his witty and fanciful toasts in honour of the two bridal pairs. While the rest drank their coffee he played the violin, like a gipsy, passionately, with abandonment—and with what dexterity! . . . Gerda fetched her Stradivarius and accompanied him in his passages with her sweet cantilena. They performed magnificent duets at the little organ in the landscape-room, where once the Consul's grandfather had played his simple melodies on the flute.

"Sublime!" said Tony, lolling back in her easy chair. "Oh, heavens, how sublime that is!" And she rolled up her eyes to the ceiling to express her emotions. "You know how it is in life," she went on, weightily. "Not everybody is given such a gift. Heaven has unfortunately denied it to me, though I used to pray for it at night. I am a goose, a silly creature. You know, Gerda—I am the elder and have learned to know life—let me tell you, you ought to thank your Creator every day on your knees, for being such a gifted creature!"

"Oh, please," said Gerda, with a laugh, showing her beautiful large white teeth.

Later they all ate wine jelly and discussed their plans for the near future. At the end of that month or the beginning of September, it was decided, Sievert Tiburtius and the Arnoldsens would go home. Then, directly after Christmas, Clara's wedding would be celebrated with due solemnity in the great hall. The Frau Consul, health permitting, would attend Tom's wedding in Amsterdam. But it must be put off until the beginning of the next year, that there might be a little pause for rest between. It was no use for Thomas to protest. "Please," said the Frau Consul, and laid her hand on his sleeve. "Sievert should have the precedence, I think."

The Pastor and his bride had decided against a wedding journey. Gerda and Thomas, however, were to take a trip to northern Italy, as far as Florence, and be gone about two months. In the meantime Tony, with the help of the upholsterer Jacobs in Fish Street.

was to make ready the charming little house in Broad Street, the property of a bachelor who had moved to Hamburg. The Consul was already arranging for its purchase. Oh, Tony would furnish it to the Queen's taste. "It will be perfect," she said. They were all sure it would.

Christian looked on while the two bridal pairs held hands, and listened to the talk about weddings and trousseaux and bridal journeys. His nose looked bigger and his legs more crooked than ever. He felt an indefinite sort of pain in the left one, and stared solemnly at them all out of his little round deep-set eyes. Finally, in the accents of Marcellus Stengel, he said to his cousin Clothilde, who sat elderly, dried-up, silent, and hungry, at table among the happy throng: "Well, Tilda, let's *us* get married too — I mean, of course each one for himself."

CHAPTER IX

SOME six months later Consul Buddenbrook returned with his
bride from Italy. The March snows lay in Broad Street as the
carriage drove up at five o'clock before the front door of their
simple painted façade. A few children and grown folk had
stopped to watch the home-coming pair descend. Frau Antonie
Grünlich stood proudly in the doorway, behind her the two
servant-maids, with white caps, bare arms, and thick striped skirts
— she had engaged them beforehand for her sister-in-law. Flushed
with pleasure and industry, she ran impetuously down the steps;
Gerda and Thomas climbed out of the trunk-laden carriage
wrapped in their furs; and she drew them into the house in her
embrace.

"Here you are! You lucky people, to have travelled so far in
the world. ' Knowest thou the house? High-pillared are its walls! '
Gerda, you are more beautiful than ever; here, I must kiss you —
no, so, on the mouth. How are you, Tom, old fellow? — yes, I
must kiss you too. Marcus says everything has gone well here.
Mother is waiting for you at home, but you can first just make
yourselves comfortable. Will you have some tea? Or a bath?
Everything is ready — you won't complain. Jacobs did his best —
and I have done all I could, too."

They went together into the vestibule, and the servants brought
in the luggage with the help of the coachman. Tony said: " The
rooms here in the parterre you will probably not need for the
present. *For the present*," she repeated, running her tongue over
her upper lip. "Look, this is pretty," and she opened a door directly next the vestibule. " Simple oak furniture, ivy at the windows. Over there, the other side of the corridor, is another room,
a larger one. Here on the right are the kitchen and larder. But
let's go up. I will show you everything." They went up the stairs,
which were covered with a dark red runner. Above, behind a
glass partition, was a narrow corridor which led to the dining-
room. This had dark red damask wall-paper, a heavy round table
upon which the samovar was steaming, a massive sideboard, and
chairs of carved nut-wood, with rush seats. Then there was a

comfortable sitting-room upholstered in grey, separated by portières from a small salon with a bay-window and furniture in green
striped rep. A fourth of this whole storey was occupied by a
large hall with three windows.

Then they went into the sleeping-room, on the right of the
corridor. It had flowered hangings and solid mahogany beds.
Tony passed on to a small door with open-work carving in the
opposite wall, and displayed a winding stair leading from the bedroom to the lower floors, the bathroom, and the servants' quarters.

"It is pretty here. I shall stop here," said Gerda, and sank with
a deep breath into the reclining chair beside one of the beds.

The Consul bent over and kissed her forehead. "Tired? I feel
like that too. I should like to tidy up a bit."

"I'll look after the tea," said Tony Grünlich, "and wait for you
in the dining-room."

The tea stood steaming in the Meissenware cups when Thomas
entered. "Here I am," he said. "Gerda would like to rest a little.
She has a headache. Afterward we will go to Meng Street. Well,
how is everything, my dear Tony — all right? Mother, Erica,
Christian? But now," he went on with his most charming manner,
"our warmest thanks — Gerda's too — for all your trouble, you
good soul. How pretty you have made everything! Nothing is
missing. — I only need a few palms for my wife's bay-window; and
I must look about for some suitable oil paintings. But tell me, now,
how are you? What have you been doing all this time?"

He had drawn up a chair for his sister beside himself, and
slowly drank his tea and ate a biscuit as they talked.

"Oh, Tom," she answered. "What should I be doing? My life
is over."

"Nonsense, Tony — you and your life! But it *is* pretty tiresome, is it?"

"Yes, Tom, it is very tiresome. Sometimes I just have to shriek,
out of sheer boredom. It has been nice to be busy with this house,
and you don't know how happy I am at your return. But I am not
happy here — God forgive me, if that is a sin. I am in the thirties
now, but I'm still not quite old enough to make intimate friends
with the last of the Himmelsburgers, or the Miss Gerhardts, or
any of mother's black friends that come and consume widows'
homes. I don't believe in them, Tom; they are wolves in sheep's
clothing — a generation of vipers. We are all weak creatures with
sinful hearts, and when they begin to look down on me for a poor
worldling I laugh in their faces. I've always thought that all men
are the same, and that we don't need any intercessors between us

and God. You know my political beliefs. I think the citizens — "

"Then you feel lonely? " Tom asked, to bring her back to her starting-point. "But you have Erica."

"Yes, Tom, and I love the child with my whole heart — although a certain person did use to declare that I am not fond of children. But you see — I am perfectly frank; I am an honest woman and speak as I think, without making words — "

"Which is splendid of you, Tony."

"Well, in short — it is sad, but the child reminds me too much of Grünlich. The Buddenbrooks in Broad Street think she is very like him too. And then, when I see her before me I always think: 'You are an old woman with a big daughter, and your life is over. Once for a few years you were alive; but now you can grow to be seventy or eighty years old, sitting here and listening to Lea Gerhardt read aloud. That is such an awful thought, Tom, that a lump comes in my throat. Because I still feel so young, and still long to see life again. And besides, I don't feel comfortable — not only in the house, but in the town. You know I haven't been struck blind. I have my eyes in my head and see how things are; I am not a stupid goose any more, I am a divorced woman — and I am made to feel it, that's certain. Believe me, Tom, it lies like a weight on my heart, to know that I have besmirched our name, even if it was not any fault of mine. You can do whatever you will, you can earn money and be the first man in the town — but people will still say: 'Yes, but his sister is a divorced woman.' Julchen Möllendorpf, the Hagenström girl — she doesn't speak to me! Oh, well, she is a goose. It is the same with all families. And yet I can't get rid of the hope that I could make it all good again. I am still young — don't you think I am still rather pretty? Mamma cannot give me very much again, but even what she can give is an acceptable sum of money. Suppose I were to marry again? To confess the truth, Tom, it is my most fervent wish. Then everything would be put right and the stain wiped out. Oh, if I could only make a match worthy of our name, and set myself up again — do you think it is entirely out of the question? "

"Not in the least, Tony. Heaven forbid! I have always thought of it. But it seems to me that in the first place you must get out a little, have a little change, and brighten up a bit."

"Yes, that's it," she cried eagerly. "Now I must tell you a little story."

Thomas was well pleased. He leaned back in his chair and smoked his second cigarette. The twilight was coming on.

"Well, then, while you were away, I almost took a situation —

a position as companion in Liverpool! Would you have thought it
was shocking? Oh, I know it would have been undignified! But
I was so wildly anxious to get away. The plan came to nothing.
I sent my photograph to the lady, and she wrote that she must
decline my services, because I was too pretty — there was a grown
son in the house. 'You are too pretty,' she wrote! I don't know
when I have been so pleased."

They both laughed heartily.

"But now I have something else in mind," went on Tony. "I
have had an invitation, from Eva Ewers, to go to Munich. Her
name is Eva Niederpaur now; her husband is superintendent of a
brewery. Well, she has asked me to visit her, and I think I will take
advantage of the invitation. Of course, Erica could not go with
me. I would put her in Sesemi Weichbrodt's pension. She would
be well taken care of. Have you any objection?"

"Not at all. It is necessary, in any case, that you should make
some new connections."

"Yes, that's it," she said gratefully. "But now, Tom. I have
been talking the whole time about myself; I am a selfish thing.
Now, tell me your affairs. Oh, heavens, how happy you must be!"

"Yes, Tony," he said with emphasis. There was a pause. He
blew out the smoke across the table and continued: "In the first
place, I am very glad to be married and set up an establishment.
You know I should not make a good bachelor. It has a side to it
that suggests loneliness and also laziness — and I am ambitious, as
you know. I don't feel that my career is finished, either in business
or — to speak half jestingly — in politics. And a man gains the confidence of the world better if he is a family man and a father.
Though I came within an ace of not doing it, after all! I am a bit
fastidious. For a long time I thought it would not be possible to
find the right person. But the sight of Gerda decided me. I felt
at once that she was the only one for me: though I know there are
people in town who don't care for my taste. She is a wonderful
creature; there are few like her in the world. She is nothing like
you, Tony, to be sure. You are simpler, and more natural too. My
lady sister is simply more temperamental," he continued, suddenly
taking a lighter tone. "Oh, Gerda has temperament too — her
playing shows that; but she can sometimes be a little cold. In short,
she is not to be measured by the ordinary standards. She is an
artist, an individual, a puzzling, fascinating creature."

"Yes, yes," Tony said. She had given her brother the closest
attention. It was nearly dark, and she had not thought of lighting
the lamps.

The corridor door opened, and there stood before them in the twilight, in a pleated piqué house-frock, white as snow, a slender figure. The heavy dark-red hair framed her white face, and blue shadows lay about her close-set brown eyes. It was Gerda, mother of future Buddenbrooks.

PART SIX

CHAPTER I

THOMAS BUDDENBROOK took a solitary early breakfast in his pretty dining-room. His wife usually left her room late, as she was subject to headaches and vapours in the morning. The Consul went at once to Meng Street, where the offices still were, took his second breakfast with his mother, Christian and Ida Jungmann in the entresol, and met Gerda only at dinner, at four in the afternoon.

The ground floor of the old house still preserved the life and movement of a great business; but the upper storeys were empty and lonely. Little Erica had been received as a boarder by Mademoiselle Weichbrodt, and poor Clothilde had moved with her few sticks of furniture into a cheap pension with the widow of a high school teacher, a Frau Dr. Krauseminz. Even Anton had left the house, and gone over to the young pair, where he was more needed. When Christian was at the club, the Frau Consul and Ida Jungmann sat at four o'clock dinner alone at the round table, in which there was now not a single extra leaf. It looked quite lost in the great spaces of the dining-temple with its images of the gods.

The social life of Meng Street had been extinguished with the death of Consul Johann Buddenbrook. Except for the visits of this or that man of God, the Frau Consul saw no guests but the members of her family, who still came on Thursday afternoons. But the first great dinner had already been given by the young pair in Broad Street. Tables were laid in both dining- and living-room, and there were a hired cook and waiters and Kistenmaker wines. It began at five o'clock, and its sounds and smells were still in the air at eleven. All the business and professional men were present, married pairs and bachelors as well: all the tribe of Langhals, Hagenströms, Huneuses, Kistenmakers, Överdiecks, and Möllendorpfs. It finished off with whist and music. They talked about it in glowing terms on the Bourse for a whole week. The young Frau Consul certainly knew how to entertain! When she and the Consul were alone, in the room lighted by burned-down candles, with the furniture disarranged and the air thick with heavy odours of rich food, wine, cigars, coffee, perfume, and the scent of the

flowers from the ladies' toilettes and the table decorations, he
pressed her hand and said: " Very good, Gerda. We do not need
to be ashamed. This sort of thing is necessary. I have no great
fondness for balls, and having the young people jumping about
here; and, besides, there is not room. But we must entertain the
settled people. A dinner like that costs a bit more — but it is well
spent."

" You are right," she had answered, and arranged the laces
through which her bosom shimmered like marble. " I much prefer
the dinners to the balls myself. A dinner is so soothing. I had been
playing this afternoon, and felt a little queer. My brain feels quite
dead now. If I were to be struck by lightning I should not change
colour."

Next morning at half past eleven the Consul sat down beside his
Mother at the breakfast table, and she read a letter aloud to him:

> MUNICH, April 2, 1857
> MARIENPLATZ 5

MY DEAR MOTHER,

I must beg your pardon — it is a shame that I have not written
before in the eight days I have been here. My time has been so
taken up with all the things there are to see — I'll tell you about
them afterwards. Now I must ask if all the dear ones, you and
Tom and Gerda and Erica and Christian and Tilda and Ida, are
well — that is the most important thing.

Ah, what all I have seen in these days! — the Pinakothek and the
Glyptothek and the Hofbräuhaus and the Court Theatre and the
churches, and quantities of other things! I must tell you of them
when I see you; otherwise I should kill myself writing. We have
also had a drive in the Isar valley, and for to-morrow an excursion
to the Wurmsee is arranged. So it goes on. Eva is very sweet to
me, and her husband, Herr Niederpaur, the brewery superintendent, is an agreeable man. We live in a very pretty square in
the town, with a fountain in the middle, like ours at home in the
market place, and the house is quite near the Town Hall. I have
never seen such a house. It is painted from top to bottom, in all
colours — St. Georges killing dragons, and old Bavarian princes in
full robes and arms. Imagine!

Yes, I like Munich extremely. The air is very strengthening to
the nerves, and for the moment I am quite in order with my stomach trouble. I enjoy drinking the beer — I drink a good deal, the
more so as the water is not very good. But I cannot quite get used
to the food. There are too few vegetables and too much flour,

for instance in the sauces, which are pathetic. They have no idea of a proper joint of veal, for the butchers cut everything very badly. And I miss the fish. It is quite mad to be eating so much cucumber and potato salad with the beer — my tummy rebels audibly.

Yes, one has to get used to a great deal. It is a real foreign country. The strange currency, the difficulty of understanding the common people — I speak too fast to them and they seem to talk gibberish to me — and then the Catholicism. I hate it, as you know; I have no respect for it —

Here the Consul began to laugh, leaning back in the sofa with a piece of bread and herb cheese in his hand.

"Yes, Tom, you are laughing," said his Mother, and tapped with her middle finger on the table. "But it pleases me very much that she holds fast to the faith of her fathers and shuns the unevangelical gim-crackery. I know that you felt a certain sympathy for the papal church, while you were in France and Italy: but that is not religion in you, Tom — it is something else, and I understand what. We must be forbearing; yet in these things a frivolous feeling of fascination is very much to be regretted. I pray God that you and your Gerda — for I well know that she does not belong to those firm in the faith — will in the course of time feel the necessary seriousness. You will forgive your mother her words, I know."

On top of the fountain (she continued reading) there is a Madonna, and sometimes she is crowned with a wreath, and the common people come with rose garlands and kneel down and pray — which looks very pretty, but it is written: "Go into your chamber." You often see monks here in the street; they look very respectable. But — imagine, Mamma! — yesterday in Theatiner Street some high dignitary of the church was driving past me in his coach; perhaps it was an archbishop; anyway, an elderly man — well, this gentleman throws me an ogling look out of the window, like a lieutenant of the Guard! You know, Mother, I've no great opinion of your friends the ministers and missionaries, but Teary Trieschke was certainly nothing compared to this rakish old prince of the Church.

"Horrors!" interjected the Frau Consul, shocked.

"That's Tony, to the life," said the Consul.

"How is that, Tom?"

" Well, perhaps she just invited him a trifle — to try him, you know. I know Tony. And I am sure the ' ogling look ' delighted her hugely, which was probably what the old gentleman wanted."

The Frau Consul did not take this up, but continued to read:

Day before yesterday the Niederpaurs entertained in the evening. It was lovely, though I could not always follow the conversation, and I found the tone sometimes rather questionable. There was a singer there from the Court opera, who sang songs, and a young artist, who asked me to sit for him, which I refused, as I thought it not suitable. I enjoyed myself most with a Herr Permaneder. Would you ever think there could be such a name? He is a hop-dealer, a nice, jolly man, in middle life and a bachelor. I had him at table, and stuck to him, for he was the only Protestant in the party. He is a citizen of Munich, but his family comes from Nuremberg. He assured me that he knew our firm very well by name, and you can imagine how it pleased me, Tom, to hear the respectful tone in which he said that. He asked how many there are of us, and things like that. He asked about Erica and Grünlich too. He comes sometimes to the Niederpaurs', and is probably going to-morrow to Wurmsee with us.

Well, adieu, dear Mamma; I can write no more. If I live and prosper, as you always say, I shall stop here three or four weeks more, and when I come back I will tell you more of Munich, for in a letter it is hard to know where to begin. I like it very much; that I must say — though one would have to train a cook to make decent sauces. You see, I am an old woman, with my life behind me, and I have nothing more to look forward to on earth. But if, for example, Erica should — if she lives and prospers — marry here, I should have nothing against it; that I must say.

Again the Consul was obliged to stop eating and lean back in his chair to laugh.

" She is simply priceless, Mother. And when she tries to dissimulate, she is incomparable. She is a thousand miles away from being able to carry it off."

" Yes, Tom," said the Frau Consul, " she is a good child, and deserves good fortune." And she finished the letter.

CHAPTER II

AT the end of April Frau Grünlich returned home. Another epoch was behind her, and the old existence began again — attending the daily devotions and the Jerusalem evenings and hearing Lea Gerhardt read aloud. Yet she was obviously in a gay and hopeful mood.

Her brother, the Consul, fetched her from the station — she had come from Buchen — and drove her through the Holsten Gate into the town. He could not resist paying her the old compliment — how, next to Clothilde, she was the prettiest one in the family; and she answered: " Oh, Tom, I hate you! To make fun of an old lady like that — "

But he was right, nevertheless: Madame Grünlich kept her good looks remarkably. You looked at the thick ash-blond hair, rolled at the sides, drawn back above the little ears, and fastened on the top of the head with a broad tortoise-shell comb; at the soft expression of her grey-blue eyes, her pretty upper lip, the fine oval and delicate colour of her face — and you thought of three-and-twenty, perhaps; never of thirty. She wore elegant hanging gold earrings, which, in a somewhat different form, her grandmother had worn before her. A loose bodice of soft dark silk, with satin revers and flat lace epaulettes, gave her pretty bosom an enchanting look of softness and fulness.

She was in the best of tempers. On Thursday, when Consul Buddenbrook and the ladies from Broad Street, Consul Kröger, Clothilde, Sesemi Weichbrodt and Erica came to tea, she talked vividly about Munich. The beer, the noodles, the artist who wanted to paint her, and the court coaches had made the greatest impressions. She mentioned Herr Permaneder in passing; and Pfiffi Buddenbrook let fall a word or two to the effect that such a journey might be very agreeable, but did not seem to have any practical results. Frau Grünlich passed this by with dignity, though she put back her head and tucked in her chin. She fell into the habit now, whenever the vestibule bell rang through the entry, of hurrying to the landing to see who had come. What might that

mean? Probably only Ida Jungmann, Tony's governess and year-
long confidante, knew that. Ida would say, "Tony, my child, you
will see: he'll come."

The family was grateful to the returned traveller for her cheering presence; for the atmosphere of the house sadly needed brightening. The relations between the head of the firm and his younger
brother had not improved. Indeed, they had grown sadly worse.
Their Mother, the Frau Consul, followed with anxious misgivings
the course of events and had enough to do to mediate between the
two. Her hints to visit the office more regularly were received in
absent silence by Christian. He met his brother's remonstrances
with a mortified air, making no defence, and for a few days would
apply himself with somewhat more zeal to the English correspondence. But there developed more and more in the elder an irritated
contempt for the younger brother, not decreased by the fact that
Christian received his occasional rebukes without seeming offence,
only looking at him with the usual absent disquiet in his eyes.

Tom's irritable activity and the condition of his nerves would
not let him listen sympathetically or even patiently to Christian's
detailed accounts of his increasing symptoms. To his mother or
sister, he referred to them with disgust as "the silly phenomena
of an obstinate introspection."

The ache, the indefinite ache in Christian's left leg, had yielded
by now to treatment; but the trouble in swallowing came on often
at table, and there was lately a difficulty in breathing, an asthmatic
trouble, which Christian thought for several weeks was consump-
tion. He explained its nature and activity at length to his family,
his nose wrinkled up the while. Dr. Grabow was called in. He said
the heart and lungs were operating soundly, but the occasional
difficulty in breathing was due to muscular sluggishness, and ordered first the use of a fan and secondly that of a green powder
which one burned, inhaling the smoke. Christian used the fan in
the office, and to a remonstrance on the part of the chief answered
that in Valparaiso every man in the office was provided with a
fan on account of the heat: "Johnny Thunderstorm — good
God!" But one day, after he had been wriggling about on his
chair for some time, nervous and restless, he took his powder out
of his pocket and made such a strong and violent-smelling reek in
the room that some of the men began to cough violently, and
Herr Marcus grew quite pale. There was an open explosion, a
scandal, a dreadful talking-to which would have led to a break at
once, but that the Frau Consul once more covered everything all
up, reasoned them out of it, and set things going again.

But this was not all. The life Christian led outside the house, mainly with his old schoolmate Lawyer Gieseke, was observed by the Consul with disgust. He was no prig, no spoil-sport. He knew very well that his native town, this port and trading city, where men walked the streets proud of their irreproachable reputation as business men, was by no means of spotless morality. They made up to themselves for the tedious hours spent in their offices, by dinners with heavy wines and heavy dishes — and by other things. But the broad mantle of civic respectability concealed this side of their life. Thomas Buddenbrook's first law was to preserve " the *dehors*"; wherein he showed himself not so different from his fellow burghers. Lawyer Gieseke was a member of the professional class, whose habits of life were much like those of the merchants. That he was also a " good fellow," anybody could see who looked at him. But, like the other easy men of pleasure in the community, he knew how to avoid trouble by wearing the proper expression and saying the proper thing. And in political and professional matters, he had a reputation of irreproachable respectability. His betrothal to Fräulein Huneus had just been announced; whereby he married a considerable dowry and a place in the best society. He was active in civic affairs, and he had his eye on a seat in the Council — even, ultimately, on the seat of old Burgomaster Överdieck.

But his friend Christian Buddenbrook — the same who could go calmly up to Mlle. Meyer-de-la-Grange, present her his bouquet, and say, " Oh, Fräulein, how beautifully you act! " — Christian had been developed by character and circumstances into a free-liver of the naïve and untrammelled type. In affairs of the heart, as in all others, he was disinclined to govern his feelings or to practise discretion for the sake of preserving his dignity. The whole town had laughed over his affair with an obscure actress at the summer theatre. Frau Stuht in Bell Founders' Street — the same who moved in the best society — told everybody who would listen how Chris had been seen again walking by daylight in the open street with the person from the Tivoli.

Even that did not actually offend people. There was too much candid cynicism in the community to permit a display of serious moral disapproval. Christian Buddenbrook, like Consul Peter Döhlmann — whose declining business put him into somewhat the same artless class — was a popular entertainer and indispensable to gentlemen's companies. But neither was taken seriously. In important matters they simply did not count. It was a significant fact that the whole town, the Bourse, the docks, the club, and the street called them by their first names — Peter and Chris. And enemies, like the Hagenströms, laughed not only at Chris's stories and jokes, but at Chris himself, too.

He thought little or nothing of this. If he noticed it, it passed out of his mind again after a momentary disquiet. But his brother the Consul knew it. Thomas knew that Christian afforded a point of attack to the enemies of the family — and there were already too many such points. The connection with the Överdiecks was distant and would be quite worthless after the Burgomaster's death. The Krögers played no rôle now; they lived retired, after the misfortunes with their son. The marriage of the deceased uncle Gotthold was always unpleasant. The Consul's sister was a divorced wife, even if one did not quite give up hope of her remarrying. And his brother was a laughing-stock in the town, a man with whose clownishness industrious men amused their leisure and then laughed good-naturedly or maliciously. He contracted debts, too, and at the end of the quarter, when he had no more money, would quite openly let Dr. Gieseke pay for him — which was a direct reflection on the firm. Thomas's contemptuous ill will, which Christian bore with quiet indifference, expressed itself in all the trifling situations that come up between members of a family. If the conversation turned upon the Buddenbrook family history, Christian might be in the mood to speak with serious love and admiration of his native town and of his ancestors. It sat rather oddly on him, to be sure, and the Consul could not stand it: he would cut short the conversation with some cold remark. He despised his brother so much that he could not even permit him to love where he did. If Christian had uttered the same sentiments in the dialect of Marcellus Stengel, Tom could have borne it better. He had read a book, a historical work, which had made such a strong impression on him that he spoke about it and praised it in the family. Christian would by himself never have found out the book; but he was impressionable and accessible to every influence; so he also read it, found it wonderful, and described his reactions with all possible detail. That book was spoiled for Thomas for ever. He spoke of it with cold and critical detachment. He pretended hardly to have read it. He completely gave it over to his brother, to admire all by himself.

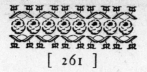

CHAPTER III

CONSUL BUDDENBROOK came from the "Harmony" — a reading-club for men, where he had spent the hour after second breakfast — back into Meng Street. He crossed the yard from behind, entered the side of the garden by the passage which ran between vine-covered walls and connected the back and front courtyards, and called into the kitchen to ask if his brother were at home. They should let him know when he came in. Then he passed through the office (where the men at the desks bent more closely over their work) into the private room; he laid aside his hat and stick, put on his working coat, and sat down in his place by the window, opposite Herr Marcus. Between his pale eyebrows were two deep wrinkles. The yellow end of a Russian cigarette roamed from one corner of his mouth to the other. The movements with which he took up paper and writing materials were so short and jerky that Herr Marcus ran his two fingers up and down his beard and gave his colleague a long, scrutinizing look. The younger men glanced at him with raised eyebrows. The Head was angry.

After half an hour, during which nothing was heard but the scratching of pens and the sound of Herr Marcus discreetly clearing his throat, the Consul looked over the green half-blind and saw Christian coming down the street. He was smoking. He came from the club, where he had eaten and also played a bit. He wore his hat a little awry on his head, and swung his yellow stick, which had come from "over there" and had the bust of a nun for a handle. He was obviously in good health and the best of tempers. He came humming into the office, said "Good morning, gentlemen," although it was a bright spring afternoon, and took his place to "do a bit of work." But the Consul got up and, passing him, said without looking at him, "Oh, may I have a few words with you?" Christian followed him. They walked rather rapidly through the entry. Thomas held his hands behind his back, and Christian involuntarily did the same, turning his big bony hooked nose toward his brother. The red-blond moustache drooped, English fashion, over his mouth. While they went across the court,

Thomas said: " We will walk a few steps up and down the garden, my friend."

" Good," answered Christian. Then there was a long silence again, while they turned to the left and walked, by the outside way, past the rococo " portal " right round the garden, where the buds were beginning to swell. Finally the Consul said in a loud voice, with a long breath, " I have just been very angry, on account of your behaviour."

" My — ? "

" Yes. I heard in the ' Harmony ' about a remark of yours that you dropped in the club last evening. It was so obnoxious, so incredibly tactless, that I can find no words — the stupidity called down a sharp snub on you at once. Do you care to recall what it was? "

" I know now what you mean. Who told you that? "

" What has that to do with it? Döhlmann. — In a voice loud enough so that all the people who did not already know the story could laugh at the joke."

" Well, Tom, I must say I was ashamed of Hagenström."

" You were ashamed — *you* were — ! Listen to me," shouted the Consul, stretching out both hands in front of him and shaking them in excitement. " In a company consisting of business as well as professional men, you make the remark, for everybody to hear, that, when one really considers it, every business man is a swindler — you, a business man yourself, belonging to a firm that strains every nerve and muscle to preserve its perfect integrity and spotless reputation! "

" Good heavens, Thomas, it was a joke! — although, really — " Christian hesitated, wrinkling his nose and stooping a little. In this position he took a few steps.

" A joke! " shouted the Consul. " I think I can understand a joke, but you see how your joke was understood. ' For my part, I have the greatest respect for my calling.' That was what Hermann Hagenström answered you. And there you sat, a good-for-nothing, with no respect for yours — "

" Tom, you don't know what you are talking about. I assure you he spoiled the whole joke. After everybody laughed, as if they agreed with me, there sat this Hagenström and brought out with ridiculous solemnity, ' For my part — ' Stupid fool! I was really ashamed for him. I thought about it a long time in bed last night, and I had a quite remarkable feeling — you know how it feels — "

" Stop chattering, stop chattering, I beg you," interrupted the

Consul. He trembled with disgust in his whole body. "I agree —
I agree with you that his answer was not in the right key, and that
it was tasteless. But that is just the kind of people you pick out to
say such things to! — if it is necessary to say them at all — and so
you lay yourself open to an insolent snub like that. Hagenström
took the opening to — give not only you but us a slap. Do you
understand what 'for my part' meant? It meant: 'You may have
such ideas going about in your brother's office, Herr Buddenbrook.' That's what it meant, you idiot."

"Idiot — ? " said Christian. He looked disturbed and embarrassed.

" And finally, you belong not to yourself alone; I'm supposed to
be indifferent when you make yourself personally ridiculous — and
when don't you make yourself personally ridiculous? " Thomas
cried. He was pale, and the blue veins stood out on his narrow
temples, from which the hair went back in two bays. One of his
light eyebrows was raised; even the long, stiff pointed ends of his
moustache looked angry as he threw his words down at Christian's
feet on the gravel with quick sidewise gestures. " You make yourself a laughing-stock with your love affairs, your harlequinades,
your diseases and your remedies."

Christian shook his head vehemently and put up a warning
finger. "As far as that goes, Tom, you don't understand very
well, you know. The thing is — every one must attend to his own
conscience, so to speak. I don't know if you understand that. —
Grabow has ordered me a salve for the throat muscles. Well — if
I don't use it, if I neglect it, I am quite lost and helpless, I am restless
and uncertain and worried and upset, and I can't swallow. But if
I have been using it, I feel that I have done my duty, I have a good
conscience, I am quiet and calm and can swallow famously. The
salve does not do it, you know, but the thing is that an idea like
that, you understand, can only be destroyed by another idea, an
opposite one. I don't know whether you understand me — "

"Oh, yes — oh, yes! " cried the Consul, holding his head for a
moment with both hands. "Do it, do it, but don't talk about it —
don't gabble about it. Leave other people alone with your horrible
nuances. You make yourself ridiculous with your absurd chatter
from morning to night. I must tell you, and I repeat it, I am not
interested in how much you make a fool of yourself personally.
But I forbid your compromising the firm in the way you did yesterday evening."

Christian did not answer, except to run his hand slowly over his
sparse red-brown locks, while his eyes roamed unsteadily and

absently, and unrest sat upon his face. Undoubtedly he was still busy with the idea which he had just been expressing.

There was a pause. Thomas stalked along with the calmness of despair. "All business men are swindlers, you say," he began afresh. "Good. Are you tired of it? Are you sorry you are a business man? You once got permission from Father — "

"Why, Tom," said Christian reflectively, " I would really rather study. It must be nice to be in the university. One attends when one likes, at one's own free will, sits down and listens, as in the theatre — "

"As in the theatre! Yes, I think your right place is that of a comedian in a café chantant. I am not joking. I am perfectly convinced that is your secret ideal." Christian did not deny it; he merely gazed aimlessly about. "And you have the cheek to make such a remark — when you haven't the slightest notion of work, and spend your days storing up a lot of feelings and sensations and episodes you hear in the theatre and when you are loafing about, God knows where; you take these and pet them and study them and chatter about them shamelessly! "

"Yes, Tom," said Christian. He was a little depressed, and rubbed his hand again over his head. "That is true: you have expressed it quite correctly. That is the difference between us. You enjoy the theatre yourself; and you had your little affairs too, once on a time, between ourselves! And there was a time when you preferred novels and poetry and all that. But you have always known how to reconcile it with regular work and a serious life. I haven't that. I am quite used up with the other; I have nothing left over for the regular life — I don't know whether you understand — "

"Oh, so you see that? " cried Thomas, standing still and folding his arms on his breast. "You humbly admit that, and still you go on the same old way? Are you a dog, Christian? A man has some pride, by God! One doesn't live a life that one may not know how to defend oneself. But so you are. That is your character. If you can only see a thing and understand and describe it — . No, my patience is at an end, Christian." And the Consul took a quick backward step and made a gesture with his arms straight out. "It is at an end, I tell you. — You draw your pay, and stay away from the office. That isn't what irritates me. Go and trifle your life away, as you have been doing, if you choose. But you compromise us, all of us, wherever you are. You are a growth, a fester, on the body of our family. You are a disgrace to us here in this town, and if this house were mine, I'd show you the door! " he screamed, making a wild sweeping gesture over the garden, the court, and the whole property. He had no more control of himself. A long-stored-up well of hatred poured itself out.

" What is the matter with you, Thomas? " said Christian. He was seized with unaccustomed anger, standing there in a position common to bow-legged people, like a questionmark, with head, stomach, and knees all prominent. His little deep eyes were wide open and surrounded by red rims down to the cheek-bones, as his Father's used to be in anger. " How are you speaking to me? What have I done to you? I'll go, without being thrown out. Shame on you! " he added with downright reproach, accompanying the word with a short, snapping motion in front of him, as if he were catching a fly.

Strange to say, Thomas did not meet this outburst by more anger. He bent his head and slowly took his way around the garden. It seemed to quiet him, actually to do him good to have made his brother angry at last — to have pushed him finally to the energy of a protest.

" Believe me," he said quietly, putting his hands behind his back again, " this conversation is truly painful to me. But it had to take place. Such scenes in the family are frightful, but we must speak out once for all. Let us talk the thing over quietly, young one. You do not like your present position, it seems? "

" No, Tom; you are right about that. You see, at first I was very well satisfied. I know I'm better off here than in a stranger's business. But what I want is the independence, I think. I have always envied you when I saw you sit there and work, for it is really no work at all for you. You work not because you must, but as master and head, and let others work for you, and you have the control, make your calculations, and are free. It is quite different."

" Good, Christian. Why couldn't you have said that before? You can make yourself free, or freer, if you like. You know Father left you as well as me an immediate inheritance of fifty thousand marks current; and I am ready at any moment to pay out this sum for a reasonable and sound purpose. In Hamburg, or anywhere else you like, there are plenty of safe but limited firms where they could use an increase of capital, and where you could enter as a partner. Let us think the matter over quietly, each by himself, and also speak to Mother at a good opportunity. I must get to work, and you could for the present go on with the English correspondence." As they crossed the entry, he added, " What do you say, for instance, to H. C. F. Burmeester and Company in Hamburg? Import and export. I know the man. I am certain he would snap at it."

That was in the end of May of the year 1857. At the beginning of June Christian travelled via Buchen to Hamburg — a heavy loss to the club, the theatre, the Tivoli, and the liberal livers of the town. All the " good fellows," among them Dr. Gieseke and Peter Döhlmann, took leave of him at the station, and brought him flowers and cigars, and laughed to split their sides — recalling, no doubt, all the stories Christian had told them. And Lawyer Gieseke, amidst general applause, fastened to Christian's overcoat a great favour made out of gold paper. This favour came from a sort of inn in the neighbourhood of the port, a place of free and easy resort where a red lantern burned above the door at night, and it was always very lively. The favour was awarded to the departing Chris Buddenbrook for his distinguished services.

CHAPTER IV

THE OUTER bell rang, and Frau Grünlich appeared on the landing
to look down into the court — a habit she had lately formed. The
door was hardly opened below when she started, leaned over still
more, and then sprang back with one hand pressing her handkerchief to her mouth and the other holding up her gown. She hurried upstairs.

On the steps to the second storey she met Ida Jungmann, to
whom she whispered in a suffocated voice. Ida gave a joyous
shriek and answered with some Polish gibberish.

The Frau Consul was sitting in the landscape room, crocheting
a shawl or some such article with two large wooden needles. It
was eleven o'clock in the morning.

The servant came through the hall, knocked on the glass door,
and waddled in to bring the Frau Consul a visiting-card. She took
the card, got out her sewing-glasses, and read it. Then she looked
again at the girl's red face; then read again; then looked up again
at the girl. Finally she said calmly but firmly:

"What *is* this, my dear? What does it mean?"

On the card was printed: "X. Noppe and Company." The
"X. Noppe" and the "and" were crossed out with a lead-pencil,
so that only the "Company" was left. "Oh, Frau Consul," said
the maid, "there's a gentleman, but he doesn't speak German, and
he do go on so —"

"Ask the gentleman in," said the Frau Consul; for she understood now that it was the "Company" who desired admittance.
The maid went. Then the glass door was opened again to let in
a stocky figure, who remained in the shadowy background of the
room for a moment and said with a drawling pronunciation something that seemed as if it might have been: "I have the honour —"

"Good morning," said the Frau Consul. "Will you not come
in?" And she supported herself on the sofa-cushion and rose a
little; for she did not know yet whether she ought to rise all the
way or not.

"I take the liberty," replied the gentleman in a pleasant sing-song; while he bowed in the politest manner, and took two steps forward. Then he stood still again and looked around as if searching for something — perhaps for a place to put his hat and stick, for he had brought both — the stick being a horn crutch with the top shaped like a claw and a good foot and a half long — into the room with him.

He was a man of forty years. Short-legged and chubby, he wore a wide-open coat of brown frieze and a light flowered waistcoat which covered the gentle protuberant curve of his stomach and supported a gold watch-chain with a whole bouquet of charms made of horn, bone, silver, and coral. His trousers were of an indefinite grey-green colour and too short. The material must have been extraordinarily stiff, for the edges stood out in a circle around the legs of his short, broad boots. He had a bullet head, untidy hair, and a stubby nose, and the light-blond curly moustache drooping over his mouth made him look like a walrus. By way of contrast, the imperial between his chin and his underlip stood out rather bristly. His cheeks were extremely fat and puffy, crowding his eyes into two narrow light-blue cracks with wrinkles at the corners. The whole face looked swollen and had a funny expression of fierceness, mingled with an almost touching good nature. Directly below his tiny chin a steep line ran into the white neck-cloth: his goiterous neck could not have endured a choker. In fact, the whole lower part of his face and his neck, the back of his head, his cheeks and nose, all ran rather formlessly in together. The whole skin of the face was stretched to an immoderate tightness and showed a roughness at the ear-joinings and the sides of the nose. In one of his short fat white hands the visitor held his stick; in the other his green Tyrolese hat, decorated with a chamois beard.

The Frau Consul had taken off her glasses and was still rising from her sofa-pillow.

"What can I do for you?" she asked politely but pointedly.

The gentleman, with a movement of decision, laid his hat and stick on the lid of the harmonium. He rubbed his free hands with satisfaction and looked at the Frau Consul out of his kindly, light-blue eyes. "I beg the gracious lady's pardon for the card," he said. "I had no other by me. My name is Permaneder — Alois Permaneder, from Munich. Perhaps you might have heard my name from your daughter." He said all this in a puzzling dialect with a rather loud, coarse voice; but there was a confidential gleam from the cracks of his eyes, which seemed to say: "I'm sure we understand each other already."

The Frau Consul had now risen entirely and went forward with her hand outstretched and her head inclined in greeting.

" Herr Permaneder! Is it you? Certainly my daughter has spoken of you. I know how much you contributed to make her visit in Munich pleasant and entertaining. And so some wind has blown you all the way up here? "

" That's it; you're just right there," said Herr Permaneder. He sat down by the Frau Consul in the armchair which she gracefully indicated to him, and began to rub his short round thighs comfortably with both hands.

" I beg your pardon? " asked the Frau Consul. She had not understood a single word of his remark.

" You've guessed it, that's the point," answered Herr Permaneder, as he stopped rubbing his knees.

" How nice! " said the Frau Consul blankly. She leaned back in her chair with feigned satisfaction and folded her hands. Actually, she was quite as much at sea as before, and inly wondering if Antonie were really able to follow the windings of the Bavarian tongue. But Herr Permaneder — though his appearance hardly led one to expect that he possessed acute sensibilities — saw through her at once. He bent forward, making — God knows why — circles in the air with his hand, and, struggling after clarity, enunciated the words: " The gracious lady is surprised? "

" Yes, Herr Permaneder, yes! " she cried, with disproportionate joy, for she had really understood him. Perhaps they could manage after all! But now there came a pause. To fill it out, Herr Permaneder gave a sort of groan, and followed it up by an exclamation in the broadest of dialect: something that shocked the Frau Consul because it sounded so like swearing, though it probably wasn't — at least, she hoped not! Should she ask him to repeat it?

" Ah — what did you say? " she ventured, turning her light eyes a little away, that he might not see the bewilderment they expressed.

Herr Permaneder obliged by repeating, with extraordinary loudness and coarseness. Surely it was something about a crucifix! Horrors!

" How nice! " she stammered again, with desperate finality; and thus this subject also was disposed of. It might be better to talk a little oneself. " May one ask," she went on, " what brings you so far, Herr Permaneder? It is a good long journey from Munich."

" A little business," said Herr Permaneder, as before, and waved his broad hand in the air. It was really touching, the efforts he made. " A little business, my dear lady, with the brewery at Walk-mill."

" Oh, yes — you are hop merchants, of course, my dear Herr Permaneder: Noppe and Company, isn't it? I am sure I have heard good things of your firm from my son," said the Frau Consul cordially. Again she felt as if she were almost upon firm ground. Herr Permaneder waved away the compliment. That was nothing to mention. No, the main thing was, he wanted to pay his respects to the Frau Consul and — see Frau Grünlich again. That was enough to make the journey repay the trouble it cost.

The Frau Consul did not understand it all, but she got the general drift, and was glad. " Oh, thank you," she said, with the utmost heartiness, and again offered him her hand, with the palm outstretched.

" But we must call my daughter," she added, and stood up and went toward the embroidered bell-pull near the glass door.

" Oh, Lord, yes, I'll be glad to see her! " cried the hop merchant, and turned his chair and himself toward the door at one and the same time.

The Frau Consul said to the servant: " Ask Madame Grünlich to come down, my dear."

Then she went back to her sofa, and Herr Permaneder turned himself and his chair around again.

" Lord, yes, I'll be glad! " he repeated, while he stared at the hangings and the furniture and the great Sèvres inkstand on the escritoire. But then he sighed heavily, several times over, rubbed his knees, and gave vent to his favourite outlandish phrase. The Frau Consul thought it more discreet not to inquire again into his meaning; besides, he muttered it under his breath, with a sort of groan, though his mood, otherwise, appeared to be anything but despondent.

And now Frau Grünlich appeared. She had made a little toilette, put on a light blouse, and dressed her hair. Her face looked fresher and prettier than ever, and the tip of her tongue played in the corner of her mouth.

Scarcely had she entered when Herr Permaneder sprang up and went to meet her with tremendous enthusiasm. He vibrated all over. He seized both her hands, shook them and cried: " Well, Frau Grünlich! Well, well, *grüss Gott!* Well, and how's it been going with you? What you been doing up here? Yes, yes! *Grüss Gott!* Lord, I'm just silly glad to see you. Do you think sometimes of little old Munich and what a gay time we had? Oh, my, oh, my! And here we are again. Who would 'a' thought it? "

Tony, on her side, greeted him with great vivacity, drew up a chair, and began to chat with him about her weeks in Munich. Now the conversation went on without hitches, and the Frau Consul followed it, smiling and nodding encouragingly at Herr Permaneder. She would translate this or that expression into her own tongue, and then lean back into the sofa again, well pleased with her own intelligence.

Herr Permaneder had to explain to Frau Antonie in her turn the reason of his appearance. But he laid small stress on the " little business " with the brewery, and it was obviously not the occasion of his visit at all. He asked with interest after the second daughter and the sons of the Frau Consul, and regretted loudly the absence of Clara and Christian, as he had always wanted to get acquainted with the whole family.

He said his stay in the town was of indefinite length, but when the Frau Consul said: " I am expecting my son for second breakfast at any moment, Herr Permaneder. Will you give us the pleasure of your company? " he accepted the invitation almost before she gave it, with such alacrity that it was plain he had expected it.

The Consul came. He had found the breakfast-room empty, and appeared in his office coat, tired and preoccupied, to take a hasty bite. But when he saw the strange guest with the frieze jacket and the fantastic watch-chain, he became all charm. He had heard his name often enough from Frau Antonie, and he threw a quick glance at his sister as he greeted Herr Permaneder in his most fascinating manner. He did not sit down. They went directly down to the entresol, where Mamsell Jungmann had laid the table and set the samovar — a real samovar, a present from Pastor Tiburtius and Clara.

" You've got it good here," said Herr Permaneder, as he let himself down in his chair and looked at the variety of cold meats on the table. His grammar, now and then, was of the most artless and disarming quality.

" It isn't Munich beer, of course, Herr Permaneder, but still it is better than our domestic brew." And the Consul poured him a glass of the brown foaming porter, which he was accustomed to drink himself at midday.

" Thank you kindly, neighbour," said Herr Permaneder, quite unaware of the outraged look Mamsell Jungmann cast at him. But he drank so moderately of the porter that the Frau Consul had a bottle of red wine brought up; whereat he grew visibly gayer and began to talk with Frau Grünlich again. He sat, on account of his prominent stomach, well away from the table, with his legs far apart, and one of his arms, with the plump white hand, hanging down over the chair-back. He put his round head with its walrus moustache on one side and blinked out of the cracks of his eyes naïvely as he listened to Tony's conversation. He looked offensively comfortable. As he had had no experience with sprats, she daintily dismembered them for him, commenting the while on life in general.

"Oh, Heavens, how sad it is, Herr Permaneder, that everything good and lovely in this world is so fleeting," she said, referring to her Munich visit. She laid down her knife and fork a moment and looked earnestly up at the ceiling. She made charming if unsuccessful efforts to speak Bavarian.

During the meal there was a knock at the door, and the office boy brought in a telegram. The Consul read it, letting the long ends of his moustache run through his fingers. He was plainly preoccupied with the contents of the message; but, even as he read it, he asked in the easiest tone: "Well, how is business, Herr Permaneder? — That will do," he said immediately to the apprentice, who disappeared.

"Oh, well, neighbour," answered Herr Permaneder, turning himself about toward the Consul's side with the awkwardness of a man who has a thick, stiff neck, and letting his other arm hang over the chair-back. "There's naught to speak of — it's a fair plague. You see, Munich " — he pronounced the name of his native city in such a way that one could only guess what he meant — " Munich is no commercial town. Everybody wants his peace and quiet and his beer — nobody gets despatches while he's eating; not there. You're a different cut up here — Holy Sacrament! Yes, thank you kindly, I'll take another glass. Tough luck, that's what it is; tough luck. My partner, Noppe, wanted to go to Nuremberg, because they have a Bourse there and are keen on business, but I won't forsake my Munich. Not me! That would be a fine thing to do! You see, there's no competition, and the export trade is just silly. Even in Russia they'll be beginning soon to plant and build for themselves."

Then he suddenly threw the Consul a quick, shrewd look and said: "Oh, well, neighbour, 'tain't so bad as it sounds. Yon's a fair little business. We make money with the joint-stock brewery, that Niederpaur is director of. That was just a small affair, but we've put it on its legs and lent it credit — cash too, four per cent on security — and now we can do business at a profit, and we've collared a blame good trade already." Herr Permaneder declined cigars and cigarettes and asked leave to smoke his pipe. He drew the long horn bowl out of his pocket, enveloped himself in a reek of smoke, and entered upon a business conversation with the Consul, which glided into politics, and Bavaria's relations with Prussia, and King Max, and the Emperor Napoleon. He garnished his views with disjointed sighs and some perfectly unintelligible Munich phrases.

Mamsell Jungmann, out of sheer astonishment, continually forgot to chew, even when she had food in her mouth. She blinked speechlessly at the guest out of her bright brown eyes, standing her knife and fork perpendicularly on the table and swaying them back and forth. This room had never before beheld Herr Permaneder's like. Never had it been filled by such reeking pipe-smoke; such unpleasantly easy manners were foreign to it. The Frau Consul abode in cordial miscomprehension, after she had made inquiries and received information as to the sufferings of the little protestant oasis among the Munich papists. Tony seemed to grow somewhat absent and restive in the course of the meal. But the Consul was highly entertained, asked his mother to order up another bottle of wine, and cordially invited Herr Permaneder to a visit in Broad Street — his wife would be charmed. A good three hours after his arrival the hop dealer began to show signs of leaving — emptied his glass, knocked out his pipe, called something or other " bad luck," and got up.

" I have the honour, madame. Good day, Frau Grünli' and Herr Consul — servant, servant." At this Ida Jungmann actually shivered and changed colour. " Good day, Freilein," he said to her, and he repeated " Good day " at the door.

The Frau Consul and her son exchanged a glance. Herr Permaneder had announced his intention of stopping at the modest inn on the Trave whither he had gone on arrival. The Frau Consul went toward him again. " My daughter's Munich friend," she began, " lives so far away that we shall have no opportunity to repay her hospitality. But if you, my dear sir, would give us the pleasure of your company while you are in town — you would be very welcome." She held her hand out to him; and lo! Herr Permaneder accepted this invitation as blithely as he had the one to dinner. He kissed the hands of both ladies — and a funny sight he was as he did so — fetched his hat and stick from the landscape room, and promised to have his trunk brought at once and to be on the spot at four o'clock, after transacting his business. Then he allowed the Consul to convoy him down the stairs. But even at the vestibule door he turned again and shook hands violently. " No offence, neighbour," he said — " your sister is certainly a great girl — no doubt about it. Good day," and he disappeared, still wagging his head.

The Consul felt an irresistible drawing to go up again and see the ladies. Ida Jungmann had gone to look after the linen for the guest-room. The Frau Consul still sat at the breakfast table, her light eyes fixed on a spot on the ceiling. She was lightly drumming with her white fingers on the cloth. Tony sat at the window, her arms folded, gazing straight ahead of her with a severe air. Silence reigned.

"Well?" said Thomas, standing in the door and taking a cigarette out of the box ornamented with the troika. His shoulders shook with laughter.

"A pleasant man," commented the Frau Consul innocently.

"Quite my opinion." The Consul made a quick, humorous turn toward Tony, as if he were asking her in the most respectful manner for her opinion as well. She was silent, and looked neither to the right nor to the left.

"But I think, Tom, he ought to stop swearing," went on the Frau Consul with mild disapproval. "If I understood him correctly, he kept using the words Sacrament and Cross."

"Oh, that's nothing, Mother — he doesn't mean anything by that."

"And perhaps a little too easy-mannered, Tom?"

"Oh, yes; that is south-German," said the Consul, breathing the smoke slowly out into the room. He smiled at his mother and stole glances at Tony. His mother saw the glances not at all.

"You will come to dinner to-day with Gerda. Please do me the favour, Tom."

"Certainly, Mother, with the greatest of pleasure. To tell the truth, I promise myself much pleasure from this guest, don't you? He is something different from your ministers, in any case."

"Everybody to his taste, Tom."

"Of course. I must go now. — Oh, Tony," he said, the door-handle in his hand, "you have made a great impression on him. No, no joke. Do you know what he called you down there just now? A great girl! Those were his very words."

But here Frau Grünlich turned around and said clearly: "Very good, Tom. You are repeating his words — and I don't know that he would mind; but even so I am not sure it was just the nicest thing to do. But this much I do know: and this much I am going to say: that in this life it does not depend on how things are said and expresed, but on how they are felt and meant in the heart; and if you make fun of Herr Permaneder's language and find him ridiculous — "

or move her eyelids, but shifted the gaze of her light eyes and changed the subject.

She preserved an even, hearty friendliness toward Herr Permaneder — which could hardly be said of her daughter. On the third or fourth day after his arrival the hop dealer let it be known that he had concluded his business with the local brewery. But a week and a half had passed since then, and he had been present for two children's afternoons. On these occasions, Frau Grünlich had sat blushing and watching his every motion, casting quick embarrassed glances at Thomas and the three Buddenbrook cousins. She talked hardly at all, sat for long minutes stiff and speechless, or even got up and left the room.

The green blinds in Frau Grünlich's sleeping-room were gently stirred by the mild air of a June night, for the windows were open. It was a large room, with simple furniture covered in grey linen. On the night table at the side of the high bed several little wicks burned in a glass with oil and water in it, filling the room with faint, even light. Frau Grünlich was in bed. Her pretty head was sunk softly in the lace-edged pillow, and her hands lay folded on the quilted coverlet. But her eyes, too thoughtful to close themselves, slowly followed the movements of a large insect with a long body, which perpetually besieged the glass with a million soundless motions of his wings. Near the bed there was a framed text hanging on the wall, between two old copper-plate views of the town in the Middle Ages. It said: " Commit your ways unto the Lord." But what good is a text like that when you are lying awake at midnight, and you have to decide for your whole life, and other people's too, whether it shall be yes or no?

It was very still. The clock ticked away on the wall, and the only other sound was Mamsell Jungmann's occasional cough. Her room was next to Tony's, divided only by curtains from it. She still had a light. The born-and-bred Prussian was sitting under the hanging lamp at her extension-table, darning stockings for little Erica. The child's deep, peaceful breathing could be heard in the room, for Sesemi's pupils were having summer holidays and Erica was at home again.

Frau Grünlich sighed and sat up a little, propping her head on her hand. " Ida," she called softly, " are you still sitting there mending? "

" Yes, yes, Tony, my child," Ida answered. " Sleep now; you will be getting up early in the morning, and you won't get enough rest."

"All right, Ida. You will wake me at six o'clock?"

"Half past is early enough, child. The carriage is ordered for eight. Go on sleeping, so you will look fresh and pretty."

"Oh, I haven't slept at all yet."

"Now, Tony, that is a bad child. Do you want to look all knocked up for the picnic? Drink seven swallows of water, and then lie down and count a thousand."

"Oh, Ida, do come here a minute. I can't sleep, I tell you, and my head aches for thinking. Feel — I think I have some fever, and there is something the matter with my tummy again. Or is it because I am anæmic? The veins in my temples are all swollen and they beat so that it hurts; but still, there may be too little blood in my head."

A chair was pushed back, and Ida Jungmann's lean, vigorous figure, in her unfashionable brown gown, appeared between the portières.

"Now, now, Tony — fever? Let me feel, my child — I'll make you a compress."

She went with her long firm masculine tread to the chest for a handkerchief, dipped it into the water-basin, and, going back to the bed, laid it on Tony's forehead, stroking her brow a few times with both hands.

"Thank you, Ida; that feels good. — Oh, please sit down a few minutes, good old Ida. Sit down on the edge of the bed. You see, I keep thinking the whole time about to-morrow. What shall I do? My head is going round and round."

Ida sat down beside her, with her needle and the stocking drawn over the darner again in her hand, and bent over them the smooth grey head and the indefatigable bright brown eyes. "Do you think he is going to propose to-morrow?" she asked.

"No doubt of it at all. He won't lose this opportunity. It happened with Clara on just such an expedition. I could avoid it, of course, I could keep with the others all the time and not let him get near me. But then, that would settle it! He is leaving day after to-morrow, he said, and he cannot stay any longer if nothing comes of it to-day. It *must* be decided to-day. — But what shall I say, Ida, when he asks me? You've never been married, so of course you know nothing about life, *really;* but you are a truthful woman, and you have some sense — and you are forty-two years old! Do tell me what you think. — I do so need advice!"

Ida Jungmann let the stocking fall into her lap.

"Yes, yes, Tony child, I have thought a great deal about it. But what I think is, there is nothing to advise about. He can't go away without speaking to you and your Mamma, and if you didn't want him, you should have sent him away before now."

"You are right there, Ida; but I could not do it — I suppose because it *is to be!* But now I keep thinking: 'It isn't too late yet; I can still draw back!' So I am lying here tormenting myself — "

"Do you like him, Tony? Tell me straight out."

"Yes, Ida. It would not be the truth if I should say no. He is not handsome — but that isn't the important thing in this life; and he is as good as gold, and couldn't do anything mean — at least, he seems so to me. When I think about Grünlich — oh, goodness! He was all the time saying how clever and resourceful he was, and all the time hiding his villainy. Permaneder is not in the least like that. You might say he is too easy-going and takes life too comfortably — and that is a fault too; because he will never be a millionaire that way, and he really is too much inclined to let things go and muddle along — as they say down there. They are all like that down there, Ida — that is what I mean. In Munich, where he was among his own kind and everybody spoke and looked as he does, I fairly loved him, he seemed so nice and faithful and comfy. And I noticed it was mutual — but part of that, I dare say, was that he takes me for a rich woman, richer probably than I am; because Mother cannot do much more for me, as you know. But I hardly think that will make much difference to him — a great lot of money would not be to his taste. — But — what was I saying, Ida?"

"That is in Munich, Tony. But here — "

"Oh, here, Ida! You know how it was already: up here he was torn right out of his own element and set against everybody here, and they are all ever so much stiffer, and — more dignified and serious. Here I really often blush for him, though it may be unworthy of me. You know — it even happened several times that he said 'me' instead of 'I.' But they say that down there; even the most cultured people do, and it doesn't hurt anything — it slips out once in a while and nobody minds. But up here — here sits Mother on one side and Tom on the other, looking at him and lifting their eyebrows, and Uncle Justus gives a start and fairly snorts, the way the Krögers do, and Pfiffi Buddenbrook gives her Mother a look, or Friederike or Henriette, and I feel so mortified I want to run out of the room, and it doesn't seem as if I *could* marry him — "

"Oh, childie — it would be Munich that you would live in with him."

"You are right, Ida. But the engagement! — and if I have to

feel the whole time mortified to death before the family and the Kistenmakers and the Möllendorpfs, because they think he is common — Oh, Grünlich was much more refined, though he was certainly black within, as Herr Stengel would have said. — Oh, Ida, my head! do wet the compress again."

"But it must be so, in the end," she went on again, drawing a long breath as the compress went on; "for the main point is and remains that I must get married again, and not stick about here any longer as a divorced woman. Ah, Ida, I think so much about the past these days: about the time when Grünlich first appeared, and the scenes he made me — scandalous, Ida! — and then about Travemünde and the Schwarzkopfs — " She spoke slowly, and her eyes rested for a while dreamily on a darn in Erica's stocking. "And then the betrothal, and Eimsbüttel, and our house. It was quite elegant, Ida. When I think of my morning-gowns — It would not be like that with Permaneder; one gets more modest as life goes on — And Dr. Klaasen and the baby, and Banker Kesselmeyer — and then the end. It was frightful; you can't imagine how frightful it was. And when you have had such dreadful experiences in life — But Permaneder would never go in for anything filthy like that. That is the last thing in the world I should expect of him, and we can rely on him too in a business way, for I really think he makes a good deal with Noppe at the Niederpaur brewery. And when I am his wife, you'll see, Ida, I will take care that he has ambition and gets ahead and makes an effort and is a credit to me and all of us. *That*, at least, he takes upon himself when he marries a Buddenbrook! "

She folded her hands under her head and looked at the ceiling. "Yes, ten years ago and more, I married Grünlich. Ten years! And here I am at the same place again, saying yes to somebody else. You know, Ida, life is very, very serious. Only the difference is that then it was a great affair, and they all pressed me and tormented me, whereas now they are all perfectly quiet and take it for granted that I am going to say yes. Of course you know, Ida, that this engagement to Alois — I say Alois, because of course it is to be — has nothing very gay or festive about it, and it isn't really a question of my happiness at all. I am making this second marriage with my eyes open, to make good the mistake of my first one, as a duty which I owe our name. Mother thinks so, and so does Tom."

"But oh, dear, Tony — if you don't like him, and if he won't make you happy — "

"Ida, I know life, and I am not a little goose any more. I have the use of my senses. I don't say that Mother would actually insist on it — when there is a dispute over anything she usually avoids it and says ' *Assez!* ' But Tom wants it. I know Tom. He thinks: ' Anybody! Anybody who isn't absolutely impossible.' For this time it is not a question of a brilliant match, but just one that will make good the other one. That is what he thinks. As soon as Permaneder appeared, you may be sure that Tom made all the proper inquiries about his business, and found it was all right — and then, as far as he was concerned, the matter was settled. Tom is a politician — he knows what he wants. Who was it threw Christian out? That is strong language, Ida, but that was really the truth of it. And why? Because he was compromising the firm and the family. And in his eyes I do the same thing — not with words or acts, but by my very existence as a divorced woman. He wants that put an end to, and he is right. I love him none the less for that — nor, I hope, does he me. In all these years, I have always longed to be out in the world again; it is so dull here in this house. God punish me if that is a sin: but I am not much more than thirty, and I still feel young. People differ about that. You had grey hair at thirty, like all your family and that uncle that died at Marienwerder."

More and more observations of the same kind followed as the night wore on; and every now and again she would say: " It is to be, after all." But at length she went to sleep, and slept for five hours on end, deeply and peacefully.

CHAPTER VI

A MIST lay over the town. But — or so said Herr Longuet, the livery man in John Street, as he himself drove the covered char-à-banc up to the door of the house in Meng Street: " The sun will be out before an hour is over " — which was most encouraging.

The Frau Consul, Antonie, Herr Permaneder, Erica, and Ida had breakfast together and gathered one after another, ready for the expedition, in the great entry, to wait for Gerda and Tom. Frau Grünlich, in a cream-coloured frock with a satin tie, looked her best, despite the loss of sleep the night before. Her doubts and fears seemed to be laid to rest, and her manner was assured, calm, and almost formal as she talked with their guest and fastened her glove-button. She had regained the tone of the old days. The well-known conviction of her own importance, of the weightiness of her own decisions, the consciousness that once more a day had come when she was to inscribe herself decisively in the family history — all this filled her heart and made it beat higher. She had dreamed of seeing that page in the family papers on which she would write down the fact of her betrothal — the fact that should obliterate and make void the black spot which the page contained. She looked forward to the moment when Tom would appear and she would greet him with a meaning nod.

He came with his wife, somewhat tardily, for the young Frau Consul was not used to make such an early toilet. He looked well and happy in his light-brown checked suit, the broad revers of which showed the white waistcoat beneath; and his eyes had a smile in them as he noted Tony's incomparably dignified mien. Gerda, with her slightly exotic, even morbid beauty, which was always in great contrast to her sister-in-law's healthy prettiness, was not in a holiday mood. Probably she had risen too early. The deep lilac background of her frock suited oddly with her dark-red hair and made her skin look whiter and more even-toned than ever, and the bluish shadows deeper and darker in the corners of her close-set brown eyes. She rather coldly offered her mother-in-law her brow to kiss, gave her hand to Herr Permaneder with

an almost ironical expression on her face, and answered only by
a deprecating smile when Tony clapped her hands and cried out
in her hearty way: " Oh, Gerda, how *lovely* you always look! "

She had a real distaste for expeditions like to-day's, especially in
summer and most especially on Sunday. She lived in the twilight
of her curtained living-rooms, and dreaded the sun, the dust, the
crowds of townsfolk in their holiday clothes, the smell of coffee,
beer, and tobacco; and above everything else in the world she
hated getting hot and upset. When the expedition to Swartau
and the " Giant Bush " was arranged, in order to give the Munich
guest a glimpse of the surroundings of the old town, Gerda said
lightly to her husband: " Dearest, you know how I am made: I
only like peace and quiet. I was not meant for change and excitement. You'll let me off, won't you? "

She would not have married him if she had not felt sure of his
essential agreement with her in these matters.

" Oh, heavens, yes; you are right, of course, Gerda. It is mostly
imagination that one enjoys oneself on such parties. Still, one
goes, because one does not like to seem odd, either to oneself or
to the others. Everybody has that kind of vanity; don't you think
so? People get the idea that you are solitary or else unhappy,
and they have less respect for you. And then, there is something
else, Gerda dear. We all want to pay a little court to Herr
Permaneder. Of course you see what the situation is. Something
is going on; it would be a real pity if it came to nothing."

" I do not see, my dear friend, why my presence — but no
matter. Let it be as you wish. Let us indulge."

They went into the street. And the sun actually began at that
moment to pierce the morning mist. The bells of St. Mary's were
ringing for Sunday, and the twittering of birds filled the air. The
coachman took off his hat, and the Frau Consul greeted him
with the patriarchal kindness which sometimes put Thomas a
little on edge: " Good morning, my friend! — Well, get in now,
my dears. It is just time for early service, but to-day we will
praise God with full hearts in his own free out-of-doors; shall we
not, Herr Permaneder? "

" That's right, Frau Consul."

They climbed one after another up the steps through the narrow
back door of the wagon and made themselves comfortable on
the cushioned seats, which — doubtless in honour of Herr Permaneder — were striped blue and white, the Bavarian colours. The
door slammed, Herr Longuet clucked to the horses and shouted
" Gee " and " Haw," the strong brown beasts tugged at the har-

ness, and the wagon rolled down Meng Street along the Trave and out the Holsten gate and then to the right along the Swartau Road.

Fields, meadows, tree-clumps, farmyards. They stared up into the high, thin blue mist above them for the larks they heard singing there. Thomas, smoking his cigarette, looked about keenly, and when they came to the grain he called Herr Permaneder's attention to its condition. The hop dealer was in a mood of childlike anticipation. He had perched his green hat with the goat's beard on the side of his head, and was balancing his big stick with the horn handle on the palm of his broad white hand and even on his underlip — a feat which, though he never quite succeeded in accomplishing it, was always greeted with applause from little Erica. He repeated over and over remarks like: " 'Twon't be the Zugspitz, but we'll climb a bit and have a little lark — kind of a little old spree, hey, Frau Grünli' ? "

Then he began to relate with much liveliness stories of mountain-climbing with knapsack and alpenstock, the Frau Consul rewarding him with many an admiring " You don't say! " He came by some train of thought or other to Christian, and expressed the most lively regret for his absence — he had heard what a jolly chap he was.

"He varies," the Consul said drily. " On a party like this he is inimitable, it is true. — We shall have crabs to eat, Herr Permaneder," he said in a livelier tone; " crabs and Baltic shrimps! You have had them a few times already at my Mother's, but friend Dieckmann, the owner of the ' Giant Bush,' serves especially fine ones. And ginger-nuts, the famous ginger-nuts of these parts. Has their fame reached even as far as the Isar? Well, you shall try them."

Two or three times Frau Grünlich stopped the wagon to pick poppies and corn-flowers by the roadside, and each time Herr Permaneder testified to his desire to get out and help her, if it were not for his slight nervousness at climbing in and out of the wagon.

Erica rejoiced at every crow she saw; and Ida Jungmann, wearing her mackintosh and carrying her umbrella, as she always did even in the most settled weather, rejoiced with her like a good governess who shares not only outwardly but inwardly in the childish emotions of her charge. She entered heartily into Erica's pleasure, with her rather loud laugh that sounded like a horse neighing. Gerda, who had not seen her growing grey in the family service, looked at her repeatedly with cold surprise.

They were in Oldenberg. The beech groves came in sight.

They drove through the village, across the market square with its well, and out again into the country, over the bridge that spanned the little river Au, and finally drew up in front of the one-story inn, " The Giant Bush." It stood at the side of a flat open space laid out with lawns and sandy paths and country flower-beds; beyond it, the forest rose gradually like an amphitheatre. Each stage was reached by rude steps formed from the natural rocks and tree roots; and on each one white-painted tables, benches, and chairs stood placed among the trees.

The Buddenbrooks were by no means the first guests. A couple of plump maids and a waiter in a greasy dress-coat were hurrying about the square carrying cold meat, lemonades, milk, and beer up to the tables, even the more remote ones, which were already occupied by several families with children.

Herr Dieckmann, the landlord, appeared personally, in shirt-sleeves and a little yellow-embroidered cap, to help the guests dismount, and Longuet drove off to unhitch. The Frau Consul said: " My good man, we will take our walk first, and after an hour or so we should like luncheon served up above — but not too high up; say perhaps at the second landing."

" You must show what you are made of, Herr Dieckmann," added the Consul. " We have a guest who is used to good living."

" Oh, no such thing," Herr Permaneder protested. " A beer and cheese — "

But Herr Dieckmann could not understand him, and began with great fluency: " Everything we have, Herr Consul: crabs, shrimps, all sorts of sausages, all sorts of cheese, smoked eel, smoked salmon, smoked sturgeon — "

" Fine, Dieckmann; give us what you have. And then — six glasses of milk and a glass of beer — if I am not mistaken, Herr Permaneder? "

" One beer, six milks — sweet milk, buttermilk, sour milk, clotted milk, Herr Consul? "

" Half and half, Herr Dieckmann: sweet milk and buttermilk. In an hour, then." They went across the square.

" First, Herr Permaneder, it is our duty to visit the spring," said Thomas. " The spring, that is to say, is the source of the Au; and the Au is the tiny little river on which Swartau lies, and on which, in the grey Middle Ages, our own town was situated — until it burned down. There was probably nothing very permanent about it at that time, and it was rebuilt again, on the Trave. But there are painful recollections connected with the Au. When we were schoolboys we used to pinch each other's arms and say:

'What is the name of the river at Swartau?' Of course, it hurt, and the involuntary answer was the right one. — Look! " he interrupted himself suddenly, ten steps from the ascent, " they've got ahead of us." It was the Möllendorpfs and the Hagenströms.

There, on the third landing of the wooded terrace, sat the principal members of those affiliated families, at two tables shoved close together, eating and talking with the greatest gusto. Old Senator Möllendorpf presided, a pallid gentleman with thin, pointed white mutton-chops; he suffered from diabetes. His wife, born Langhals, wielded her lorgnon; and, as usual, her hair stood up untidily all over her head. Her son Augustus was a blond young man with a prosperous exterior, and there was Julie his wife, born Hagenström, little and lively, with great blank black eyes and diamond earrings that were nearly as large. She sat between her brothers, Hermann and Moritz. Consul Hermann Hagenström had begun to get very stout with good living: people said he began the day with *paté de foie gras*. He wore a full, short reddish-blond beard, and he had his mother's nose, which came down quite flat on the upper lip. Dr. Moritz was narrow-chested and yellow-skinned, and he talked very gaily, showing pointed teeth with gaps between them. Both brothers had their ladies with them — for the lawyer had married, some years since, a Fräulein Puttfarken from Hamburg, a lady with butter-coloured hair and wonderful cold, regular, English features of more than common beauty; Dr. Hagenström had not been able to reconcile with his reputation as connoisseur the idea of taking a plain wife. And, finally, there were the little daughter of Hermann and the little son of Moritz, two white-frocked children, already as good as betrothed to each other, for the Huneus-Hagenström money must be kept together, of course. They all sat there eating ham and scrambled eggs.

Greetings were exchanged when the Buddenbrook party passed at a little distance the company seated at the table. The Frau Consul bowed confusedly; Thomas lifted his hat, his lips moving in a courteous and conventional greeting, and Gerda inclined her head with formal politeness. But Herr Permaneder, stimulated by the climb, swung his green hat unaffectedly and shouted in a loud, bluff voice: " Hearty good morning to all of you! " whereat Frau Senator Möllendorpf made use of her lorgnon. Tony, for her part, flung back her head and tucked in her chin as much as possible, while her shoulders went up ever so slightly, and she greeted the party as if from some remote height — which meant that she stared straight ahead directly over the broad brim of Julie Möllendorpf's elegant hat. Precisely at this moment, her decision of the night before became fixed, unalterable resolve.

"Thanks be to goodness, Tom, we are not going to eat for another hour. I'd hate to have that Julie watching us. Did you see how she spoke? Hardly at all. I only had a glimpse of her hat, but it looked frightfully bad taste."

"Well, as far as that goes, I don't know about the hat — but you were certainly not much more cordial than she was, my love. And don't get irritated — it makes for wrinkles."

"Irritated, Tom? Not at all. If these people think they are the first and foremost, why, one can only laugh at them, that's all. What difference is there between this Julie and me, if it comes to that? She only drew a fool, instead of a knave, for a husband; and if she were in my position now, we should see if she would find another one."

"How can you tell that you will find another one?"

"A fool, Thomas?"

"Very much better than a knave."

"It doesn't have to be either. But it is not a fit subject for discussion."

"Quite right. The others are ahead of us — Herr Permaneder is climbing lustily."

The shady forest road grew level, and it was not long before they reached the "spring," a pretty, romantic spot with a wooden bridge over a little ravine, steep cliffs, and overhanging trees with their roots in the air. The Frau Consul had brought a silver collapsible cup, and they scooped up the water from the little stone basin directly under the source and refreshed themselves with the iron-impregnated spring. And here Herr Permaneder had a slight attack of gallantry, and insisted on Frau Grünlich tasting his cup before presenting it to him. He ran over with friendliness and displayed great tact in chatting with the Frau Consul and Thomas, as well as with Gerda and Tony, and even with little Erica. Gerda, who had up to now been suffering from the heat and a kind of silent and rigid nervousness, began to feel like herself again. They came back to the inn by a shorter way, and sat down at a groaning table on the second of the wooded terraces; and it was Gerda who gave expression in friendly terms to the general regret over Herr Permaneder's early departure, now that they were just becoming a little acquainted and finding less and less difficulty with the language. She was ready to swear that she had heard her friend and sister-in-law, Tony, use several times the most unadulterated Munich dialect!

Herr Permaneder forbore to commit himself on the subject of his departure. Instead, he devoted himself for the time to the dainties that weighted down the table — dainties such as he seldom saw the other side of the Danube.

They sat and consumed the good things at their leisure — what little Erica liked far better than anything else were the serviettes made of tissue paper, much nicer than the big linen ones at home. With the waiter's permission she put a few in her pocket as a souvenir. When they had finished, they still sat; Herr Permaneder smoked several very black cigars with his beer, Thomas smoked cigarettes, and the whole family chatted a long time with their guest. It was noticeable that Herr Permaneder's leaving was not mentioned again; in fact, the future was left shrouded in darkness. Rather, they turned to memories of the past or talked of the political events of recent years. Herr Permaneder shook with laughter over some dozens of stories of the late Herr Consul, which his widow related, and then in his turn told about the Munich Revolution, and about Lola Montez, in whom Frau Grünlich displayed an unbounded interest. The hour after luncheon slowly wore on, and little Erica came back laden with daisies, grasses, and ladies' smocks from an expedition with Ida Jungmann, and recalled the fact that the ginger-nuts were still to be bought. They started on their walk down to the village, not before Frau Consul, who was the hostess of the occasion, had paid the bill with a good-sized gold-piece.

They gave orders at the inn that the wagon should be ready in half an hour, so that there would be time for a rest in town before dinner, and then they rambled slowly down, in the dusty sunshine, to the handful of cottages that formed the village.

After they crossed the bridge they fell naturally into little groups, in which they continued after that to walk: Mamsell Jungmann with her long stride in the van, with little Erica jumping tirelessly alongside, hunting for butterflies; then the Frau Consul, Thomas, and Gerda together; and lastly, at some distance, Frau Grünlich and Herr Permaneder. The first pair made considerable noise, for the child shouted for joy, and Ida joined in with her neighing, good-natured laugh. In the middle, all three were silent; for the dust had driven Gerda into another fit of depression, and the old Frau Consul, and her son as well, were plunged in thought. The couple behind were quiet too, but their quietness was only apparent, for in reality Tony and her Bavarian guest were conversing in subdued and intimate tones. And what was the subject of their discourse? It was Herr Grünlich. . . .

Herr Permaneder had made the pointed remark that little Erica was a dear and pretty child, but that she had not the slightest resemblance to her mother. To which Tony had answered: " She is altogether like her father in looks, and one may say that it is not at all to her disadvantage, for as far as looks go, Grünlich was a gentleman. He had golden-yellow whiskers — very uncommon; I never saw anything like them." When Tony visited the Nieder-paurs in Munich, she had already told Herr Permaneder in considerable detail the story of her first marriage; but now he asked again all the particulars of it, listening with anxiously sympathetic blinks to the details of the bankruptcy.

" He was a bad man, Herr Permaneder, or Father would never have taken me away from him — of that you may be sure. Life has taught me that not everybody in the world has a good heart. I have learned that, young as I am for a person who, as you might say, has been a widow for ten years. He was a bad man, and his banker, Kesselmeyer, was a worse one — and a silly puppy into the bargain. I won't say that I consider myself an angel and perfectly free from all blame — don't misunderstand me. Grünlich neglected me, and even when he was with me he just sat and read the paper; and he deceived me, and kept me in Eimsbüttel, because he was afraid if I went to town I would find out the mess he was in. But I am a weak woman, and I have my faults too, and I've no doubt I did not always go the right way to work. I know I gave him cause to worry and complain over my extravagance and silliness and my new dressing-gowns. But it is only fair to say one thing: I was just a child when I was married, a perfect goose, a silly little thing. Just imagine: only a short time before I was engaged, I didn't even so much as know that the Confederation decrees concerning the universities and the press had been renewed four years before! And fine decrees they were, too! Ah, me, Herr Permaneder! The sad thing is that one lives but once — one can't begin life over again. And one would know so much better the second time! "

She was silent; she looked down at the road — but she was very intent on the reply Herr Permaneder would make, for she had not unskilfully left him an opening, it being only a step to the idea that, even though it was impossible to begin life anew, yet a new and better married life was not out of the question. Herr Permaneder let the chance slip and confined himself to laying the blame on Herr Grünlich, with such violence that his very chin-whiskers bristled.

"Silly ass! If I had the fool here I'd give it to him! What a swine!"

"Fie, Herr Permaneder! No, you really mustn't. We must forgive and forget — 'Vengeance is mine, saith the Lord.' Ask Mother. Heaven forbid — I don't know where Grünlich is, nor what state his affairs are in, but I wish him the best of fortune, even though he doesn't deserve it."

They had reached the village and stood before the little house which was at the same time the bakery. They had stopped walking, almost without knowing it, and were hardly aware that Ida, Erica, the Frau Consul, Thomas, and Gerda had disappeared through the funny, tiny little door, so low that they had to stoop to enter. They were absorbed in their conversation, though it had not got beyond these trifling preliminaries.

They stood by a hedge with a long narrow flower-bed beneath it, in which some mignonette was growing. Frau Grünlich, rather hot, bent her head and poked industriously with her parasol in the black loam. Herr Permaneder stood close to her, now and then assisting her excavations with his walking-stick. His little green hat with the tuft of goat's beard had slid back on his forehead. He was stooping over the bed too, but his small, bulging pale-blue eyes, quite blank and even a little reddish, gazed up at her with a mixture of devotion, distress, and expectancy. It was odd to see how his very moustache, drooping down over his mouth, took the same expression.

"Likely, now," he ventured, "likely, now, ye've taken a silly fright, and are too damned sacred of marriage ever to try it again — hey, Frau Grünlich?"

"How clumsy!" thought she. "Must I say yes to that?" Aloud she answered: "Well, dear Herr Permaneder, I must confess that it would be hard for me to yield to anybody my consent for life; for life has taught me, you see, what a serious step that is. One needs to be sure that the man in question is a thoroughly noble, good, kind soul — "

And now he actually ventured the question whether she could consider him such a man — to which she answered: "Yes, Herr Permaneder, I do." Upon which there followed the few short murmured words which clinched the betrothal and gave Herr Permaneder the assurance that he might speak to Thomas and the Frau Consul when they reached home.

When the other members of the party came forth, laden with bags of ginger-nuts, Thomas let his eye rove discreetly over the heads of the two standing outside, for they were embarrassed to the last degree. Herr Permaneder simply made no effort to conceal the fact, but Tony was hiding her embarrassment under a well-nigh majestic dignity.

They hurried back to the wagon, for the sky had clouded over and some drops began to fall.

Tony was right: her brother had, soon after Herr Permaneder appeared, made proper inquiries as to his situation in life. He learned that X. Noppe and Company did a thoroughly sound if somewhat restricted business, operating with the joint-stock brewery managed by Herr Niederpaur as director. It showed a nice little income, Herr Permaneder's share of which, with the help of Tony's seventeen thousand, would suffice for a comfortable if modest life. The Frau Consul heard the news, and there was a long and particular conversation among her, Herr Permaneder, Antonie, and Thomas, in the landscape-room that very evening, and everything was arranged. It was decided that little Erica should go to Munich too, this being her Mother's wish, to which her betrothed warmly agreed.

Two days later the hop-dealer left for home — " Noppe will be raising the deuce if I don't," he said. But in July Frau Grünlich was again in his native town, accompanied by Tom and Gerda. They were to spend four or five weeks at Bad Kreuth, while the Frau Consul with Erica and Ida were on the Baltic coast. While in Munich, the four had time to see the house in Kaufinger Street which Herr Permaneder was about to buy. It was in the neighborhood of the Niederpaurs' — a perfectly remarkable old house, a large part of which Herr Permaneder thought to let. It had a steep, ladderlike pair of stairs which ran without a turning from the front door straight up to the first floor, where a corridor led on each side back to the front rooms.

Tony went home the middle of August to devote herself to her trousseau. She had considerable left from her earlier equipment, but new purchases were necessary to complete it. One day several things arrived from Hamburg, among them a morning-gown — this time not trimmed with velvet but with bands of cloth instead.

Herr Permaneder returned to Meng Street well on in the autumn. They thought best to delay no longer. As for the wedding festivities, they went off just as Tony expected and de-

sired, no great fuss being made over them. "Let us leave out
the formalities," said the Consul. "You are married again, and it
is simply as if you always had been." Only a few announcements
were sent — Madame Grünlich saw to it that Julie Möllendorpf,
born Hagenström, received one — and there was no wedding
journey. Herr Permaneder objected to making "such a fuss,"
and Tony, just back from the summer trip, found even the
journey to Munich too long. The wedding took place, not in
the hall this time, but in the church of St. Mary's, in the presence
of the family only. Tony wore the orange-blossom, which replaced the myrtle, with great dignity, and Doctor Kölling
preached on moderation, with as strong language as ever, but in
a weaker voice.

Christian came from Hamburg, very elegantly dressed, looking a little ailing but very lively. He said his business with
Burmeister was "tip-top"; thought that he and Tilda would
probably get married "up there" — that is to say, "Each one for
himself, of course"; and came very late to the wedding from the
visit he paid at the club. Uncle Justus was much moved by
the occasion, and with his usual lavishness presented the newly
wedded pair with a beautiful heavy silver epergne. He and his
wife practically starved themselves at home, for the weak woman
was still paying the disinherited and outcast Jacob's debts with
the house-keeping money. Jacob was rumoured to be in Paris at
present. The Buddenbrook ladies from Broad Street made the
remark: "Well, let's hope it will last, this time." The unpleasant
part of this lay in the doubt whether they really hoped it. Sesemi
Weichbrodt stood on her tip-toes, kissed her pupil, now Frau
Permaneder, explosively on the forehead, and said with her most
pronounced vowels: "Be happy, you go-od che-ild!"

CHAPTER VII

IN the morning at eight o'clock Consul Buddenbrook, so soon as
he had left his bed, stolen through the little door and down the
winding stair into the bathroom, taken a bath, and put on his
night-shirt again — Consul Buddenbrook, we say, began to busy
himself with public affairs. For then Herr Wenzel, barber and
member of the Assembly, appeared, with his intelligent face and
his red hands, his razors and other tools, and the basin of warm
water which he had fetched from the kitchen; and the Consul
sat in a reclining-chair and leaned his head back, and Herr Wenzel
began to make a lather; and there ensued almost always a conversation that began with the weather and how you had slept the
night before, went on to politics and the great world, thence to
domestic affairs in the city itself, and closed in an intimate and
familiar key on business and family matters. All this prolonged
very much the process in hand, for every time the Consul said
anything Herr Wenzel had to stop shaving.

"Hope you slept well, Herr Consul? "

"Yes, thanks, Wenzel. Is it fine to-day? "

"Frost and a bit of snow, Herr Consul. In front of St. James's
the boys have made another slide, more than ten yards long — I
nearly sat down, when I came from the Burgomaster's. The young
wretches! "

"Seen the papers? "

"The *Advertiser* and the *Hamburg News* — yes. Nothing in
them but the Orsini bombs. Horrible. It happened on the way
to the opera. Oh, they must be a fine lot over there."

"Oh, it doesn't signify much, I should think. It has nothing
to do with the people, and the only effect will be that the police
will be doubled and there will be twice as much interference with
the press. He is on his guard. Yes, it must be a perpetual strain,
for he has to introduce new projects all the time, to keep himself
in power. But I respect him, all the same. At all events, he can't
be a fool, with his traditions, and I was very much impressed
with the cheap bread affair. There is no doubt he does a great deal
for the people."

"Yes, Herr Kistenmaker says so too."

"Stephan? We were talking about it yesterday."

"It looks bad for Frederick William of Prussia. Things won't last much longer as they are. They say already that the prince will be made Regent in time."

"It will be interesting to see what happens then. He has already shown that he has liberal ideas and does not feel his brother's secret disgust for the Constitution. It is just the chagrin that upsets him, poor man. What is the news from Copenhagen?"

"Nothing new, Herr Consul. They simply won't. The Confederation has declared that a united government for Holstein and Lauenburg is illegal—they won't have it at any price."

"Yes, it is unheard-of, Wenzel. They dare the Bundestag to put it into operation—and if it were a little more lively—oh, these Danes!—Careful with that chapped place, Wenzel.—There's our direct-line Hamburg railway, too. That has cost some diplomatic battles, and will cost more before they get the concession from Copenhagen."

"Yes, Herr Consul. The stupid thing is that the Altona-Kiel Railway Company is against it—and, in fact, all Holstein is. Dr. Överdieck, the Burgomaster, was saying so just now. They are dreadfully afraid of Kiel prospering much."

"Of course, Wenzel. A new connection between the North Sea and the Baltic.—You'll see, the Kiel-Altona line will keep on intriguing. They are in a position to build a rival railway: East Holstein, Neuminster, Neustadt—yes, that is quite on the cards. But we must not let ourselves be bullied, and we must have a direct route to Hamburg."

"Herr Consul must take the matter up himself."

"Certainly, so far as my powers go, and wherever I have any influence. I am interested in the development of our railways—it is a tradition with us from 1851 on. My Father was a director of the Buchen line, which is probably the reason why I was elected so young. I am only thirty-three years old, and my services so far have been very inconsiderable."

"Oh, Herr Consul! How can the Herr Consul say that after his speech in the Assembly—?"

"Yes, that made an impression, and I've certainly shown my good will, at least. I can only be grateful that my Father, Grandfather, and great-Grandfather prepared the way for me, and that I inherited so much of the respect and confidence they received from the town; for without it I could not move as I am now able to. For instance, after '48 and the beginning of this decade, what did my Father not do towards the reform of our postal service? Think how he urged in the Assembly the union of the Hamburg diligences with the postal service; and how in 1850 he forced the Senate by continuous pressure to join the German-Austrian Postal Union! If we have cheap letter postage now, and stamps and book post, and letter-boxes, and telegraphic connection with Hamburg and Travemünde, he is not the last one to be grateful to. Why, if he and a few other people had not kept at the Senate continually, we should most likely still be behind the Danish and the Thurn-and-Taxis postal service! So when I have an opinion nowadays on these subjects, people listen to me."

"The Herr Consul is speaking God's truth. About the Hamburg line, Doctor Överdieck was saying to me only three days ago: 'When we get where we can buy a suitable site for the station in Hamburg, we will send Consul Buddenbrook to help transact the business, for in such dealings he is better than most lawyers.' Those were his very words."

"Well, that is very flattering to me, Wenzel. — Just put a little more lather on my chin, will you? It wants a bit more cleaning up. — Yes, the truth is, we mustn't let the grass grow under our feet. I am saying nothing against Överdieck, but he is getting on. If I were Burgomaster I'd make things move a little faster. I can't tell you how pleased I am that they are installing gas for the street-lighting, and the miserable old oil-lamps are disappearing — I admit I had a little something to do with that change. Oh, how much there is to do! Times are changing, Wenzel, and we have many responsibilities toward the new age. When I think back to my boyhood — you know better than I do what the town looked like then: the streets without sidewalks, grass growing a foot high between the paving-stones, and the houses with porticos and benches sticking out into the streets — and our buildings from the time of the Middle Ages spoilt with clumsy additions, and all tumbling down because, while individuals had money and nobody went hungry, the town had none at all and just muddled along, as my brother-in-law calls it, without ever thinking of repairs. That was a happy and comfortable generation, when my grandfather's crony, the good Jean Jacques Hoffstede, strolled about the town and translated improper little French poems. They had to end, those good old times; they have changed, and they will have to change still more. Then the population was thirty-seven thousand: now it is fifty, you know, and the whole character of the place is altering. There is so much building, and the suburbs are spreading out, and we are able to have good streets and restore the old monuments out of our great period. Yet even all that is merely superficial. The most important matter is still outstanding, my dear Wenzel. I mean, of course, the *ceterum censeo* of my dear Father: the customs union. We must join, Wenzel; there should be no longer any question about it, and you must all help me fight for it. As a business man, believe me, I am better informed than the diplomats, and the fear that we should lose independence and freedom of action is simply laughable in this case. The Mecklenburg and Schleswig-Holstein Inland would take us in, which is the more desirable for the reason that we do not control the northern trade quite to the extent that we once did. — That's enough. Please give me the towel, Wenzel," concluded the Consul.

Then the market price of rye, which stood at fifty-five thaler and showed disquieting signs of falling still further, was talked about, and perhaps there was a mention of some event or other in the town; and then Herr Wenzel vanished by the basement route and emptied the lather out of his shiny basin on to the pavement in the street. And the Consul mounted the winding stair into the bedroom, and found Gerda awake, and kissed her on the forehead. Then he dressed.

These little morning sessions with the lively barber formed the introduction to busy days, full to running over with thinking, talking, writing, reckoning, doing business, going about in the town. Thanks to his travel, his interests, and his knowledge of affairs, Thomas Buddenbrook's mind was the least provincial in the district; and he was certainly the first to realize the limitations of his lot. The lively interest in public affairs which the years of the Revolution had brought in, was suffering throughout the whole country from a period of prostration and arrest, and that field was too sterile to occupy a vigorous talent; but Thomas Buddenbrook possessed the spirit to take to himself that wise old saying that all human achievement is of a merely symbolic value, and thus to devote all that he had of capacity, enthusiasm, energy, and strength of will to the service of the community as well as to the service of his own name and firm. He stood in the front rank of his small society and was seriously ambitious to give his city greatness and power within her sphere — though he had the intellect, too, to smile at himself for the ambition even while he cherished it.

He ate his breakfast, served by Anton, and went to the office in Meng Street, where he remained about an hour, writing two or three pressing letters and telegrams, giving this or that instruction, imparting to the wheels of industry a small push, and then leaving them to revolve under the cautious eye of Herr Marcus.

He went to assemblies and committee meetings, visited the Bourse, which was held under the Gothic arcades in the Market Square, inspected dockyards and warehouses, talked with the captains of the ships he owned, and transacted much and various business all day long until evening, interrupted only by the hasty luncheon with his Mother and dinner with Gerda; after which he took a half-hour's rest on the sofa with his cigarette and the newspaper. Customs, rates, construction, railways, posts, almonry — all this as well as his own business occupied him; and even in matters commonly left to professionals he acquired insight and judgment, especially in finance, where he early showed himself extremely gifted.

He was careful not to neglect the social side. True, he was not always punctual, and usually appeared at the very last minute, when the carriage waited below and his wife sat in full toilette. "I'm sorry, Gerda," he would say; "I was detained"; and he would dash upstairs to don his evening clothes. But when he arrived at a dinner, a ball, or an evening company, he showed lively interest and ranked as a charming *causeur*. And in entertaining he and his wife were not behind the other rich houses. In kitchen and cellar everything was "tip-top," and he himself was considered a most courteous and tactful host, whose toasts were wittier than the common run. His quiet evenings he spent at home with Gerda alone, smoking, listening to her music, or reading with her some book of her selection.

Thus his labours enforced success, his consequence grew in the town, and the firm had excellent years, despite the sums drawn out to settle Christian and to pay Tony's second dowry. And yet there were troubles which had, at times, the power to lame his courage for hours, weaken his elasticity, and depress his mood.

There was Christian in Hamburg. His partner, Herr Burmeester, had died quite suddenly of an apoplectic stroke, in the spring of the year 1858. His heirs drew their money out of the business, and the Consul strongly advised Christian against trying to continue it with his own means, for he knew how difficult it is to carry on a business already established on definite lines if the working capital be suddenly diminished. But Christian insisted upon the continuation of his independence. He took over the assets and the liabilities of H. C. F. Burmeester and Company, and trouble was to be looked for.

Then there was the Consul's sister Clara in Riga. Her marriage with Pastor Tiburtius had remained unblest with children — but then, as Clara Buddenbrook she had never wanted children, and probably had very little talent for motherhood. Now her husband wrote that her health left much to be desired. The severe headaches from which she had suffered even as a girl were now recurring periodically, to an almost unbearable extent.

That was disquieting. And even here at home there was another source of worry — for, as yet, there was no certainty whatever that the family name would live. Gerda treated the subject with sovereign indifference which came very near to being repugnance. Thomas concealed his anxiety. But the old Frau Consul took the matter in hand and consulted Grabow.

"Doctor — just between ourselves — something is bound to happen *sometime*, isn't it? A little mountain air at Kreuth, a little seashore at Glucksberg or Travemünde — but they don't seem to work. What do you advise?" Dr. Grabow's pleasant old prescription: "a nourishing diet, a little pigeon, a slice of French bread," didn't seem strong enough, either, to fit the case. He ordered Pyrmont and Schlangenbad.

Those were three worries. And Tony? Poor Tony!

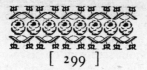

CHAPTER VIII

SHE wrote: ". . . And when I say 'croquettes,' she doesn't understand me, because here they are called 'meaties'; and when she says 'broccoli,' how could any Christian know she means cauliflower? When I say 'baked potatoes,' she screams 'How?' at me, until I remember to say 'roast potatoes,' which is what they call them here. 'How' means 'What did you say?' And she is the second one I've had — I sent away the first one, named Katy, because she was so impertinent — or at least, I thought she was. I'm getting to see now that I may have been mistaken, for I'm never quite sure whether people here mean to be rude or friendly. This one's name is Babette. She has a very pleasing exterior, with something southern, the way some of them have here; black hair and eyes, and teeth that any one might envy. She is willing, too, and I am teaching her how to make some of our home dishes. Yesterday we had sorrel and currants, but I wish I hadn't, for Permaneder objected so much to the sorrel — he picked the currants out with a fork — that he would not speak to me the whole afternoon, but just growled; and I can tell you, Mother, that life is not so easy."

Alas, it was not only the sorrel and the "meaties" that were embittering Tony's life. Before the honeymoon was over she had had a blow so unforeseen, so unexpected, so incomprehensible, that it took away all her joy in life. She could not get over it. And here it was.

Not until after the Permaneder couple had been some weeks in Munich had Consul Buddenbrook liquidated the sum fixed by his Father's will as his sister's second marriage portion. That sum, translated into gulden, had at last safely reached Herr Permaneder's hands, and Herr Permaneder had invested it securely and not unprofitably. But then, what he had said, quite unblushingly and without embarrassment, to his wife, was this: "Tonerl" — he called her "Tonerl" — "Tonerl, that's good enough for me. What do we want of more? I been working my hide off all my days; now I'd like to sit down and have a little peace and quiet, damned if I wouldn't. Let's rent the parterre and the second floor, and still we'll have a good house, where we can sit and eat our bit of pig's meat without screwing ourselves up and putting on so much lug. And in the evening I can go to the Hofbräu house. I'm no swell—I don't care about scraping money together. I want my comfort. I quit to-morrow and go into private life."

"Permaneder!" she had cried; and for the first time she had spoken his name with that peculiar throaty sound which her voice always had when she uttered the name of Grünlich.

"Oh, shut up! Don't take on!" was all he answered. There had followed, thus early in their life together, a quarrel, serious and violent enough to endanger the happiness of any marriage. He came off victorious. Her passionate resistance was shattered upon his urgent longing for "peace and quiet." It ended in Herr Permaneder's withdrawing the capital he had in the hop business, so that now Herr Noppe, in his turn, could strike the "and Company" off his card. After which Tony's husband, like most of the friends whom he met around the table in the Hofbräu House, to play cards and drink his regular three litres of beer, limited his activities to the raising of rents in his capacity of landlord, and to an undisturbed cutting of coupons.

The Frau Consul was notified quite simply of this fact. But Frau Permaneder's distress was evident in the letters which she wrote to her brother. Poor Tony! Her worst fears were more than realized. She had always known that Herr Permaneder possessed none of that "resourcefulness" of which her first husband had had so much; but that he would so entirely confound the expectations she had expressed to Mamsell Jungmann on the eve of her betrothal—that he would so completely fail to recognize the duties he had taken upon himself when he married a Buddenbrook—that she had never dreamed.

But these feelings must be overcome; and her family at home saw from her letters how she resigned herself. She lived on rather monotonously with her husband and Erica, who went to school; she attended to her housekeeping, kept up friendly relations with the people who rented the parterre and the first storey and with the Niederpaur family in Marienplatz; and she wrote now and then of going to the theatre with her friend Eva. Herr Permaneder did not care for the theatre. And it came out that he had grown to more than forty years of age in his beloved Munich without ever having seen the inside of the Pinakothek.

Time passed. But Tony could feel no longer any true happiness in her new life, since the day when Herr Permaneder received her dowry and settled himself down to enjoy his ease.

Hope was no more. She would never be able to write home to announce new ventures and new successes. Just as life was now — free from cares, it was true, but so limited, so lamentably " un-refined," — just so it would remain until the end. It weighed upon her. It was plain from her letters that this very lowness of tone was making it harder for her to adapt herself to the south-German surroundings. In small matters, of course, things grew easier. She learned to make herself understood by the servants and errand-boys, to say " meaties " instead of " croquettes," and to set no more fruit soup before her husband after the one he had called a " sickening mess." But, in general, she remained a stranger in her new home; and she never ceased to taste the bitterness of the knowledge that to be a born Buddenbrook was not to enjoy any particular prestige in her adopted home. She once related in a letter the story of how she met in the street a mason's apprentice, carrying a mug of beer in one hand and holding a large white radish by its tail in the other; who, waving his beer, said jovially: " Neighbour, can ye tell us the time? " She made a joke of it, in the telling; yet even so, a strong undercurrent of irritation be-trayed itself. You might be quite certain that she threw back her head and vouchsafed to the poor man neither answer nor glance in his direction. But it was not alone this lack of formality and absence of distinctions that made her feel strange and unsympa-thetic. She did not live deeply, it is true, into the life or affairs of her new home; but she breathed the Munich air, the air of a great city, full of artists and citizens who habitually did nothing: an air with something about it a little demoralizing, which she some-times found it hard to take good-humouredly.

The days passed. And then it seemed that there was after all a joy in store — in fact, the very one which was longed for in vain in Broad Street and Meng Street. For not long after the New Year of 1859 Tony felt certain that she was again to become a mother.

The joy of it trembled in her letters, which were full of the old childish gaiety and sense of importance. The Frau Consul, who, with the exception of the summer holiday, confined her journey-ings more and more to the Baltic coast, lamented that she could not be with her daughter at this time. Tom and Gerda made plans to go to the christening, and Tony's head was full of giving them an elegant reception. Alas, poor Tony! The visit which took place was sad indeed, and the christening — Tony had cherished visions of a ravishing little feast, with flowers, sweetmeats, and chocolate — never took place at all. The child, a little girl, only entered into life for a tiny quarter of an hour; then, though the doctor did his best to set the pathetic little mechanism going, it faded out of being.

Consul Buddenbrook and his wife arrived in Munich to find Tony herself not out of danger. She was far more ill than before, and a nervous weakness from which she had already suffered prevented her from taking any nourishment at all for several days. Then she began to eat, and on their departure, the Buddenbrooks felt reassured as far as her health was concerned. But in other ways there was much reason for anxiety; for it had been all too plain, especially to the Consul's observant eye, that not even their common loss would suffice to bring husband and wife together again.

There was nothing against Herr Permaneder's good heart. He was truly shaken by the death of the child; big tears rolled down out of his bulging eyes upon his puffy cheeks and on into his frizzled beard. Many times he sighed deeply and gave vent to his favourite expression. But, after all, Tony felt that his " peace and quiet " had not suffered any long interruption. After a few evenings, he sought the Hofbräu House for consolation, and was soon, as he always said, " muddling along " again in his old, good-natured, comfortable, grumbling way, with the easy fatalism natural to him.

But from now on Tony's letters never lost their hopeless, even complaining tone. " Oh, Mother," she wrote, " why do I have to bear everything like this? First Grünlich and the bankruptcy, and then Permaneder going out of business — and then the baby! How have I deserved all these misfortunes? "

When the Consul read these outpourings, he could never quite forego a little smile: for, notwithstanding all the real pain they showed, he heard an undertone of almost comic pride, and he knew that Tony Buddenbrook, as Madame Grünlich or as Madame Permaneder, was and would remain a child. She bore all her mature experiences almost with a child's unbelief in their reality, yet with a child's seriousness, a child's self-importance, and, above all, with a child's power to throw them off at will.

She could not understand how she had deserved her misfortunes; for even while she mocked at her mother's piety, she herself was so full of it that she fervently believed in justice and righteousness on this earth.

Poor Tony! The death of her second child was neither the last nor the hardest blow that fell upon her. As the year 1859 drew to a close, something frightful indeed happened.

CHAPTER IX

IT was a day toward the end of November — a cold autumn day
with a hazy sky. It looked almost as if there would be snow, and
a mist was rising, pierced through every now and then by the
sun. It was one of those days, common in a seaport town, when
a sharp north-east wind whistled round the massive church corners and influenzas were to be had cheap.

Consul Thomas Buddenbrook entered the breakfast-room toward midday, to find his Mother, with her spectacles on her nose,
bent over a paper on the table.

"Tom," she said; and she looked at him, holding the paper
with both hands, as if she hesitated to show it to him. "Don't be
startled. But it is not very good news. I don't understand — It
is from Berlin. Something must have happened."

"Give it to me, please," he said shortly. He lost colour, and
the muscles stood out on his temples as he clenched his teeth. His
gesture as he stretched out his hand was so full of decision that it
was as if he said aloud: "Just tell me quickly. Don't prepare me
for it!"

He read the lines still standing; one of his light eyebrows went
up, and he drew the long ends of his moustache through his fingers. It was a telegram, and it said: "Don't be frightened. Am
coming at once with Erica. All is over. Your unhappy Antonie."

"'At once . . . at once,'" he said, with irritation, looking at
the Frau Consul and giving his head a quick shake. "What does
she mean by 'at once'?"

"That is just a way of putting it, Tom; it doesn't mean anything
particular. She means by the next train, or something like that."

"And from Berlin! What is she doing in Berlin? How did
she get to Berlin?"

"I don't know, Tom; I don't understand it. The dispatch only
came ten minutes ago. But something must have happened, and
we must just wait to see what it is. God in his mercy will turn it
all to good. Sit down, my son, and eat your luncheon."

He took his chair, and mechanically he poured out a glass of
porter.

" 'All is over,' " he repeated. And then " 'Antonie.' How childish! "

He ate and drank in silence.

After a while the Frau Consul ventured to say: " It must be something about Permaneder, don't you think, Tom? "

He shrugged his shoulders without looking up.

As he went away he said, with his hand on the door-knob, " Well, we must wait and see. As she is not likely to burst into the house in the middle of the night, she will probably reach here some time to-morrow. You will let me know, won't you? "

The Frau Consul waited from hour to hour. She had slept very badly, and in the night she rang for Ida Jungmann, who now slept in the back room of the entresol. She had Ida make her some *eau sucrée;* and she sat up in bed for a long time and embroidered. And now the forenoon passed in nervous expectancy. When the Consul came to second breakfast, he said that Tony could not arrive before the three-thirty-three train from Buchen. At that hour the Frau Consul seated herself in the landscape-room and tried to read, out of a book with a black leather cover decorated with a gold palm-leaf.

It was a day like its predecessor: cold, mist, wind. The stove crackled away behind its wrought iron screen. The old lady trembled and looked out of the window whenever she heard a wagon. At four o'clock, when she had stopped watching and almost stopped thinking about her daughter, there was a stir below in the house. She hastily turned toward the window and wiped away the damp with her handkerchief. Yes, a carriage had stopped below, and some one was coming up the steps.

She grasped the arms of her chair with both hands to rise. But then she thought better of it and sank back. She only turned her head as her daughter entered, and her face wore an almost defensive expression. Tony burst impetuously into the room: Erica remained outside at the glass door, with her hand in Ida Jungmann's.

Frau Permaneder wore a fur wrap and a large felt hat with a veil. She looked very pale and ailing, and her upper lip trembled as it used to when the little Tony was about to weep. Her eyes were red. She raised her arms and let them drop, and then she fell on her knees at her Mother's side, burying her face in the folds of her gown and sobbing bitterly. It was as though she had rushed straight hither from Munich all in one breath, and now lay there, having gained the goal of her headlong flight, exhausted but safe. The Frau Consul sat a moment quite still.

" Tony! " she said then, with gentle remonstrance. She drew the long hatpins out of Frau Permaneder's hat and laid it on the window-seat; then she stroked gently and soothingly her daughter's thick ash-blond hair.

" What is it, my child? What has happened? "

But she saw that patience was her only weapon; for it was long before her question drew out any reply.

" Mother! " uttered Frau Permaneder. " Mamma! " But that was all.

The Frau Consul looked toward the glass door and, still embracing her daughter, stretched out her hand to her grandchild, who stood there shyly with her finger to her mouth.

" Come, child; come here and say how do you do. You have grown so big, and you look so strong and well, for which God be thanked. How old are you now, Erica? "

" Thirteen, Grandmamma."

" Good gracious! A young lady! " She kissed the little maiden over Tony's head and told her: " Go up with Ida now — we shall soon have dinner. Just now Mamma and I want to talk."

They were alone.

" Now, my dear Tony? Can you not stop crying? When God sends us a heavy trial, we must bear it with composure. ' Take your cross upon you,' we are told. Would you like to go up first and rest a little and refresh yourself, and then come down to me again? Our good Jungmann has your room ready. Thanks for your telegram — of course, it shocked us a good deal — "

She stopped. For Tony's voice came, all trembling and smothered, out of the folds of her gown: " He is a wicked man — a wicked man! Oh, he is — "

Frau Permaneder seemed not able to get away from this dreadful phrase. It possessed her altogether. She buried her face deeper and deeper in the Frau Consul's lap and clenched her fist beside the Frau Consul's chair.

" Do you mean your husband, my child? " asked the old lady, after a pause. " It ought not to be possible for me to have such a thought in my mind, I know; but you leave me nothing else to think, Tony. Has Herr Permaneder done you an injury? Are you making a complaint of him? "

" Babette," Frau Permaneder brought out. " Babette — "

" Babette? " repeated the Frau Consul, inquiringly. Then she leaned back in her chair, and her pale eyes wandered toward the window. She understood now. There was a pause, broken by Tony's gradually decreasing sobs.

"Tony," said the Frau Consul after a little space, "I see now that there has been an injury done you — that you have cause to complain. But was it necessary to give the sense of injury such violent expression? Was it necessary to travel here from Munich, with Erica, and to make it appear — for other people will not be so sensible as we are — that you have left him permanently; that you will not go back to him?"

"But I won't go back to him — never!" cried Frau Permaneder, and she lifted up her head with a jerk and looked at her Mother wildly with tear-stained eyes, and then buried her face again. The Frau Consul affected not to have heard.

"But now," she went on, in a louder key, slowly nodding her head from one side to the other, "now that you are here, I am glad you are. For you can unburden your heart, and tell me everything, and then we shall see how we can put things right, by taking thought, and by mutual forbearance and affection."

"Never," Tony said again. "Never!" And then she told her story. It was not all intelligible, for she spoke into the folds of her Mother's stuff gown, and broke into her own narrative with explosions of passionate anger. But what had happened was somewhat as follows:

On the night of the twenty-fourth of the month, Madame Permaneder had gone to sleep very late, having been disturbed during the day by the nervous digestive trouble to which she was subject. She had been awakened about midnight, out of a light slumber, by a confused and continuous noise outside on the landing — a half-suppressed, mysterious noise, in which one distinguished the creaking of the stairs, a sort of giggling cough, smothered, protesting words, and, mixed with these, the most singular snarling sounds. But there was no doubt whence they proceeded. Frau Permaneder had hardly, with her sleepy senses, taken them in before she interpreted them as well, in such a way that she felt the blood leave her cheeks and rush to her heart, which contracted and then went on beating with heavy, oppressed pulsations. For a long, dreadful minute she lay among the pillows as if stunned, as if paralysed. Then, as the shameless disturbance did not stop, she had with trembling hands kindled a light, had left her bed, thrilling with horror, repulsion, and despair, had opened the door and hurried out on to the landing in her slippers, the light in her hand — to the top of the "ladder" that went straight

up from the house door to the first storey. And there, on the
upper steps, in all its actuality, was indeed the very scene she had
pictured in her mind's eye as she listened to the compromising
noises. It was an unseemly and indecent scuffle, a sort of wrestling match between Babette the cook and Herr Permaneder.
The girl must have been busied late about the house, for she had
her bunch of keys and her candle in her hand as she swayed back
and forth in the effort to fend her master off. He, with his hat
on the back of his head, held her round the body and kept making
essays, now and then successfully, to press his face, with its great
walrus moustache, against hers. As Antonie appeared, Babette
exclaimed something that sounded like " Jesus, Mary, and
Joseph! " — and " Jesus, Mary, and Joseph! " echoed Herr Permaneder likewise, as he let go. Almost in the same second the
girl vanished, and there was Herr Permaneder left standing before
his wife, with drooping head, drooping arms, drooping moustaches
too; and all he could get out was some idiotic remark like " Holy
Cross, what a mess! " When he ventured to lift his eyes, she was
no longer there. She was in the bed-chamber, half-sitting, half-
lying on the bed, repeating over and over again with frantic sobbing, " Shame, shame! " He leaned rather flabbily in the doorway and jerked his shoulder in her direction — had he been closer,
the gesture would have been a nudge in the ribs. " Hey, Tonerl
— don't be a fool, you know. Say — you know Franz, the Ram-
sau Franz, he had his name-day to-day, and we're all half-seas
over." Strong alcoholic fumes pervaded the room as he spoke;
and they brought Frau Permaneder's excitement to a climax. She
sobbed no more, she was no longer weak and faint. Carried away
by frenzy, incapable of measuring her words, she poured out her
disgust, her abhorrence, her complete and utter contempt and
loathing of him and all his ways. Herr Permaneder did not take it
meekly. His head was hot; for he had treated his friend Franz
not only to many beers, but to " champagne wine " as well. He
answered and answered wildly — the quarrel reached a height
far greater than the one that had signalized Herr Permaneder's
retirement into private life, and it ended in Frau Antonie gathering her clothes together and withdrawing into the living-room
for the night. And at the end he had flung at her a word — a
word which she would not repeat — a word that should never pass
her lips — a word . . .

This was the major content of the confession which Frau Permaneder had sobbed into the folds of her mother's gown. But
the " word," the word that in that fearful night had sunk into her

very depths — no, she would not repeat it; no, she would not, she asseverated, — although her mother had not in the least pressed her to do so, but only nodded her head, slowly, almost imperceptibly, as she looked down on Tony's lovely ash-blond hair.

"Yes, yes," she said; "this is very sad, Tony. And I understand it all, my dear little one, because I am not only your Mamma, but I am a woman like you as well. I see now how fully your grief is justified, and how completely your husband, in a moment of weakness, forgot what he owed to you and — "

"In a moment — ? " cried Tony. She sprang up. She made two steps backward and feverishly dried her eyes. "A moment, Mamma! He *forgot* what he owed to me and to our name? He never *knew* it, from the very beginning! A man that quietly sits down with his wife's dowry — a man without ambition or energy or will-power! A man that has some kind of thick soup made out of hops in his veins instead of blood — and I verily believe he has! And to let himself down to such common doings as this with Babette — and when I reproached him with his good-for-nothingness, to answer with a word that — a word — "

And, arrived once more at the word, the word she would not repeat, quite suddenly she took a step forward and said, in a completely altered, a quieter, milder, interested tone: "How perfectly sweet! Where did you get that, Mamma? " She motioned with her chin toward a little receptacle, a charming basket-work stand woven out of reeds and decorated with ribbon bows, in which the Frau Consul kept her fancy-work.

"I bought it, some time ago," answered the old lady. "I needed it."

"Very smart," Tony said, looking at it with her head on one side. The Frau Consul looked at it too, but without seeing it, for she was in deep thought.

"Now, my dear daughter," she said at last, putting out her hand again, "however things are, you are here, and welcome a hundred times to your old home. We can talk everything over when we are calmer. Take your things off in your room and make yourself comfortable. Ida! " she called into the dining-room, lifting her voice, "lay a place for Madame Permaneder, and one for Erica, my dear."

CHAPTER X

TONY returned to her bed-chamber after dinner. During the meal her Mother had told her that Thomas was aware of her expected arrival; and she did not seem particularly anxious to meet him.

The Consul came at six o'clock. He went into the landscape-room and had a long talk with his Mother.

"How is she?" he asked. "How does she seem?"

"Oh, Tom, I am afraid she is very determined. She is terribly wrought up. And this word — if I only knew what it was he said — "

"I will go up and see her."

"Yes, do, Tom. But knock softly, so as not to startle her, and be very calm, will you? Her nerves are upset. That is the trouble she has with her digestion — she has eaten nothing. Do talk quietly with her."

He went up quickly, skipping a step in his usual way. He was thinking, and twisting the ends of his moustache, but as he knocked, his face cleared — he was resolved to handle the situation as long as possible with humour.

A suffering voice said "Come in," and he opened the door, to find Frau Permaneder lying on the bed fully dressed. The bed curtains were flung back, the down quilt was underneath her back, and a medicine bottle stood on the night-table. She turned round a little and propped her head on her hand, looking at him with her pouting smile. He made a deep bow and spread out his hands in a solemn gesture.

"Well, dear lady! To what are we indebted for the honour of a visit from this personage from the royal city of — ? "

"Oh, give me a kiss, Tom," she said, sat up to offer him her cheek, and then sank back again. "Well, how are you, my dear boy? Quite unchanged, I see, since I saw you in Munich."

"You can't tell much about it with the blinds down, my dear. And you ought not to steal my thunder like that, either. It is more suitable for me to say — " he held her hand in his, and at the same time drew up a chair beside the bed — "as I so often have, that you and Tilda — "

" Oh, for shame, Tom! — How is Tilda? "

" Well, of course. Madame Krauseminz sees she doesn't starve. Which doesn't prevent her eating for the week ahead when she comes here on Thursday."

She laughed very heartily — as she had not for a long time back, in fact. Then she broke off with a sigh, and asked: " And how is business? "

" Oh, we get on. Mustn't complain."

" Thank goodness, here everything is as it should be. Oh, Tom, I don't feel much like chatting pleasantly about trifles! "

" Pity. One should preserve one's sense of humour, *quand même.*"

" All that is at an end, Tom. — You know all? "

" ' You know all '! " he repeated. He dropped her hand and pushed back his chair. " Goodness gracious, how that sounds! ' All '! What-all lies in that ' all '? ' My love and grief I gave thee,' eh? No, listen! "

She was silent. She swept him with an astonished and deeply offended glance.

" Yes, I expected that look," he said, " for without that look you would not be here. But, dear Tony, let me take the thing as much too lightly as you take it too seriously. You will see we shall complement each other very nicely — "

" Too seriously, Thomas? *I* take it too seriously? "

" Yes. — For heaven's sake, don't let's make a tragedy of it! Let us take it in a lower key, not with ' all is at an end ' and ' your unhappy Antonie.' Don't misunderstand me, Tony. You well know that no one can be gladder than I that you have come. I have long wished you would come to us on a visit by yourself, without your husband, so that we could be *en famille* together once more. But to come now, like this — my dear child, I beg your pardon, but it was — foolish. Yes — let me finish! Permaneder has certainly behaved very badly, as I will give him to understand pretty clearly — don't be afraid of that — "

" As to how he has behaved himself, Thomas," she interrupted him, raising herself up to lay a hand upon her breast, " as far as that goes, I have already given him to understand that — and not only ' given him to understand,' I can tell you! I am convinced that further discussion with that man is entirely out of place." And she let herself fall back again and looked sternly and fixedly at the ceiling.

He bowed, as if under the weight of her words, and kept on looking down at his knee and smiling.

"Well, then, I won't send him a stiff letter. It is just as you say. In the end it is after all your affair, and it is quite enough if you put him in his place — it is your duty as his wife. After all, there are some extenuating circumstances. There was a birthday celebration, and he came home a little bit exalted, so to speak, and was guilty of a false step, an unseemly blunder — "

"Thomas," said she, "I do not understand you. I do not understand your tone. You — a man with your principles! But you did not see him. You did not see how drunk he looked — "

"He looked ridiculous enough, I'm sure. But that is it, Tony. You will not see how comic it was — but probably that is the fault of your bad digestion. You caught your husband in a moment of weakness, and you have seen him make himself look ridiculous. But that ought not to outrage you to such an extent. It ought to amuse you a little, perhaps, but bring you closer together as human beings. I will say that I don't mean you could have just let it pass with a laugh and said nothing about it — not at all. You left home; that was a demonstration of a rather extreme kind, perhaps — a bit too severe — but, after all, he deserved it. I imagine he is feeling pretty down in the mouth. I only mean that you must get to take the thing differently — not so insulted — a little more politic point of view. We are just between ourselves. Let me tell you something, Tony. In any marriage, the important thing is, on which side the moral ascendency lies. Understand? Your husband has laid himself open, there is no doubt of that. He compromised himself and made a laughable spectacle — laughable, precisely because what he did was actually so harmless, so impossible to take seriously. But, after all, his dignity is impaired — and the moral advantage has passed over to you. If you know how to use it wisely, your happiness is assured. If you go back, say in a couple of weeks — certainly I must insist on keeping you for ourselves as long as that — if you go back to Munich in a couple of weeks, you will see — "

"I will not go back to Munich, Thomas."

"I beg your pardon?" he asked, putting his hand to his ear and screwing up his face as he bent forward.

She was lying on her back with her head sunk in the pillow, so that her chin stood out with an effect of severity. "Never," she said. And she gave a long, audible outward breath and cleared her throat, also at length and deliberately. It was like a dry cough, which had of late become almost a habit with her, and had probably to do with her digestive trouble. There followed a pause.

"Tony," he said suddenly, getting up and slapping his hand

on the arm of his chair, " you aren't going to make a scandal! "

She gave a side glance and saw him all pale, with the muscles standing out on his temples. Her position was no longer tenable. She bestirred herself and, to hide the fear she really felt of him, grew angry in her turn. She sat up quickly and put her feet to the floor. With glowing cheeks and a frowning brow, making hasty motions of the head and hands, she began: "Scandal, Thomas! You want to tell me not to make a scandal, when I have been insulted, and people spit in my face? Is that worthy of a brother, you will permit me to ask? Circumspection, tact — they are very well in their place. But there are limits, Tom — I know just as much of life as you do, and I tell you there is a point where the care for appearances leaves off, and cowardice begins! I am astonished that such a stupid goose as I am have to tell you this — yes, I am a stupid goose, and I should not be surprised if Permaneder never loved me at all, for I am an ugly old woman, very likely, and Babette is certainly prettier than I am! But did that give him a right to forget the respect he owed to my family, and my up-bringing, and all my feelings? You did not see the way he forgot himself, Tom; and since you did not see it, you cannot under-stand, for I can never tell you how disgusting he was. You did not hear the word that he called after me, your sister, when I took my things and went out of the room, to sleep on the sofa in the living-room. But *I* heard it, and it was a word that — a word — Oh, it was that word, let me tell you, Thomas, that caused me to spend the whole night packing my trunk, to wake Erica early in the morning, and to leave the place, rather than to remain in the neighbourhood of a man who could utter such words. And to such a man, as I said before, I will never, never return, not so long as I have any self-respect, or care in the least what becomes of me in my life on this earth."

" And will you now have the goodness, to tell me what this cursed word was? Yes or no? "

" Never, Thomas! Never would I permit that word to cross my lips. I know too well what I owe to you and to myself within these walls."

" Then it's no use talking with you! "

" That may easily be. I am sure I do not want to discuss it any further."

" What do you expect to do? Get a divorce? "

" Yes, Tom; such is my firm determination. I feel that I owe it to myself, my child, and my family."

" That is all nonsense, of course," he said in a dispassionate tone.

He turned on his heel and moved away, as if his words had settled the matter. " It takes two to make a divorce, my child. Do you think Permaneder will just say yes and thank you kindly? The idea is absurd."

" Oh, you can leave that to me," she said, quite undismayed. " You mean he will refuse on account of the seventeen thousand marks current. But Grünlich wasn't willing, either, and they made him. There are ways and means, I'm sure. I'll go to Dr. Gieseke. He is Christian's friend, and he will help me. Oh, yes, of course, I know it was not the same thing then. It was ' incapacity of the husband to provide for his family.' You see, I know my way about in these affairs. Dear me, you act as if this were the first time in my life that I got a divorce! But even so, Tom. Perhaps there is nothing that applies to this case. Perhaps it is impossible — you may be right. But it is all the same; my resolve is fixed. Let him keep the money. There are higher things in life. He will never see me again, either way."

She coughed again. She had left the bed and seated herself in an easy-chair, resting one elbow on its arm. Her chin was so deeply buried in her hand that her four bent fingers clutched her under lip. She sat with her body turned to the right, staring with red, excited eyes out of the window.

The Consul walked up and down, sighed, shook his head, shrugged his shoulders. He paused in front of her, fairly wringing his hands.

" You are a child, Tony, a child," said he in a discouraged, almost pleading tone. " Every word you have spoken is the most utter childish nonsense. Will you make an effort, now, if I beg you, to think about the thing for just one minute like a grown woman? Don't you see that you are acting as if something very serious and dreadful had happened to you — as if your husband had cruelly betrayed you and heaped insults on you before all the world? Do try to realize that nothing of the sort has happened! Not a single soul in the world knows anything about that silly affair that happened at the top of your staircase in Kaufinger Street. Your dignity, and ours, will suffer no slightest diminution if you go calmly and composedly back to Permaneder — of course, with your nose in the air! But, on the other hand, if you don't go back, if you give this nonsense so much importance as to make a scandal out of it, then you will be wounding our dignity indeed."

She jerked her chin out of her hand and stared him in the face.

" That's enough, Thomas Buddenbrook. Be quiet now; it's my turn. Listen. So you think there is no shame and no scandal so

long as people don't get to hear it? Ah, no! The shame that gnaws
at us secretly and eats away our self-respect — that is far, far
worse. Are we Buddenbrooks the sort of people to be satisfied if
everything looks ' tip-top,' as you say here, on the outside, no matter how much mortification we have to choke down, inside our
four walls? I cannot help feeling astonished at you, Tom. Think
of our Father and how he would act to-day — and then judge as
he would! No, no! Clean and open dealings must be the rule.
Why, you can open your books any day, for all the world to see,
and say, ' Here they are, look at them.' We should all of us be just
the same. I know how God has made me. I am not afraid. Let
Julchen Möllendorpf pass me in the street and not speak, if she
wants to. Let Pfiffi Buddenbrook sit here on Thursday afternoons
and shake all over with spite, and say, ' Well, that is the second
time! But, *of course*, both times the men were to blame! ' I feel
so far above all that now, Thomas — farther than I can tell you!
I know I have done what I thought was right. But if I am to be
so afraid of Julchen Möllendorpf and Pfiffi Buddenbrook as to
swallow down all sorts of insults and let myself be cursed out in a
drunken dialect that isn't even grammar — to stop with a man in
a town where I have to get used to that kind of language and the
kind of scenes I saw that night at the top of the stairs — where I
have to forget my origin and my upbringing and everything that
I am, and learn to disown it altogether in order to act as if I were
satisfied and happy — *that* is what *I* call undignified — *that* is what
I call scandalous, I tell you! "

She broke off, buried her chin once more in her hand, and
stared out of the window. He stood before her, his weight on one
leg, his hands in his trousers pockets. His eyes rested on her unseeing, for he was in deep thought, and slowly moving his head
from side to side.

"Tony," he said. " You're telling the truth. I knew it all along;
but you betrayed yourself just now. It is not the man at all. It is
the place. It isn't this other idiotic business — it is the whole thing
all together. You couldn't get used to it. Tell the truth."

"Thomas," she cried, " it is the truth! " She sprang up as she
spoke, and pointed straight into his face with her outstretched
hand. Her own face was red. She stood there in a warlike pose,
one hand grasping the chair, gesticulating with the other, and
made a long, agitated, passionate speech that welled up in a resist-
less tide. The Consul stared at her amazed. Scarcely would she
pause to draw breath, when new words would come gushing and
bubbling forth. Yes, she found words for everything; she gave

full expression to all the accumulated disgust of her Munich years.
Unassorted, confused, she poured it all out, one thing after another; she kept nothing back. It was like the bursting of a dam —
an assertion of desperate integrity; something elemental, a force
of nature, that brooked no restraint.

"It is the truth!" she cried. "Say it again, Thomas! Oh, I can
tell you plainly, I am no stupid goose any longer; I know what I
have to expect. I don't faint away at my time of life, to hear that
dirty work goes on now and then. I've known people like Teary
Trieschke, and I was married to Bendix Grünlich, and I know the
dissipated creatures there are here in this town. I am no country
innocent, I tell you; and the affair with Babette wouldn't have
made me go off the handle like that, just by itself. No, Thomas,
the thing was that it filled the cup to overflowing — and that didn't
take much, for it was full already, and had been for a long time
— a long time. It would have taken very little to make it run over.
And then this happened! The knowledge that I could not depend
on Permaneder even in that way — that put the top on everything.
It knocked the bottom out of the cask. It brought to a head all at
once my intention to get away from Munich, that had been slowly
growing in my mind a long time before that, Tom; for I cannot
live down there — I swear it before God and all His heavenly
hosts! How wretched I have been, Thomas, you can never know.
When you were there on a visit, I concealed everything, for I am
a tactful woman and do not burden others with my complainings,
nor wear my heart on my sleeve on a week-day. I have always
been rather reserved. But I have suffered, Tom, suffered with my
entire being — with my whole personality, so to speak. Like a
plant, a flower that has been transplanted into a foreign soil — if
I may make such a comparison. You will probably find it a most
unsuitable one, for I am really an ugly old woman — but I could
not be planted in a more foreign soil than that, and I would just
as lief go and live in Turkey! Oh, we should never be transplanted, we northern folk! We should stick to the shore of our
own bay; we can only really thrive upon our native soil! You all
used to laugh at my taste for the nobility. Yes, in these years I
have often thought of what somebody said to me once, in times
gone by. A very clever man. 'Your sympathies are with the
nobility,' he said. 'Shall I tell you why? Because you yourself
belong to the nobility. Your father is a great gentleman, and you
are a princess. A gulf lies between you and the rest of us who do
not belong to the governing classes.' Yes, Tom. We feel like the
nobility, and we realize the difference; we should never try to

live where we are not known, where no one understands our
worth, for we shall have nothing but chagrin, and be laughed at
for our arrogance. Yes, they all found me ridiculously arrogant.
They did not say so, but I felt it every minute, and that made me
suffer, too. Do you think I feel arrogant, Tom — in a place where
they eat cake with a knife, and the very princes speak bad grammar, and if a gentleman picks up a lady's fan it is supposed to be
a love-affair. Get used to it? To people without dignity, morals,
energy, ambition, self-respect, or good manners, lazy and frivolous, stupid and shallow at the same time? — no, never, never, as
long as I am a Buddenbrook and your sister! Eva Ewers managed it — but Eva is not a Buddenbrook, and she has a husband
that amounts to something. It was different with me. You think
back, Tom, from the very beginning: I come from a home where
people work and get things accomplished and have a purpose in
life, and I go down there to Permaneder — and he sits himself
down with my dowry — Oh, that was genuine enough, that was
characteristic — but it was the only good thing there was about it!
And then? I was going to have a baby; that would have made
everything up to me. And what happens? It dies. I don't blame
Permaneder for that, of course; I don't mean that. God forbid.
He did everything he could — and he didn't go to the café for several days. But, after all, it belonged to the same thing. It made me
no happier, as you can well believe. But I didn't give in, and I
didn't grumble. I was alone, and misunderstood, and pointed at
for being arrogant; but I said to myself: 'You yielded him your
consent for life. He is lumpy and lazy, and he caused you a cruel
disappointment. But his heart is pure, and he means well.' And
then I had to bear the sight of him in that last unspeakable minute.
And I said to myself: 'He understands you no better and respects
you no more and no less than the others do, and he calls you names
that one of our workmen up here wouldn't throw at a dog!' I
knew then that nothing bound me to him any more, and that it was
an indignity for me to stay. When I was driving from the station
this afternoon, I passed Nielsen the porter, and he took off his hat
and made me a deep bow, and I bowed back to him — not arro-
gantly, not a bit — I waved my hand, just the way Father used to.
And here I am. You can do what you like: you can harness up all
your work-horses — but you can never drag me back to Munich
again. And to-morrow I go to Gieseke! "

Thus she spoke; and, finishing, sank back exhausted in her chair
and stared again out of the window.

Tom was alarmed, shaken, stupefied. He stood before her and

found no words. He raised his arms up shoulder-high, drawing a long breath. Then he let them fall against his thighs.

"Well, that's an end of it," he said. His voice was calm, and he turned and went toward the door.

Her face wore now the same expression, the same half-pouting, half-injured smile, as when he entered.

"Tom?" she said, with a rising inflection. "Are you vexed with me?"

He held the oval doorknob in one hand and made a gesture of weary protest with the other. "Oh, no. Not at all."

She put out her hand and tipped her head on one side. "Come here, Tom. Your poor sister has had a hard time. Life is hard on her. She has much to bear. And at this minute she has nobody, in all the world — "

He came back; he took her hand; but wearily, indifferently, not looking at her face. Suddenly her lip began to quiver.

"You must go on alone now," she said. "There's nothing good to be looked for from Christian, and I am finished. Failed. Gone to pieces. I can do no more. I am a poor, useless woman, dependent on you all for my living. I could never have dreamed, Tom, that I should be no help to you at all. Now you stand quite alone, and upon you it depends to keep up the honour and dignity of the family. May God help you in the task."

Two large, clear, childish tears rolled down over her cheeks, which were beginning to show, very faintly, the first signs of age.

CHAPTER XI

TONY lost no time. She went resolutely about her affair. In the hope of quieting her, of bringing her slowly to a different frame of mind, the Consul said but little. He asked only one thing: that she should be very quiet and stop entirely in the house — and Erica as well. Perhaps it would blow over. The town did not need to know. The family Thursday afternoon was put off on some pretext.

But on the very next day she wrote to Dr. Gieseke and summoned him to Meng Street. She received him alone, in the middle corridor room on the first floor, where a fire was laid, and she had arranged a heavy table with ink and writing materials and a quantity of foolscap paper from the office. They sat down in two easy-chairs.

"Doctor Gieseke," said Tony. She folded her arms, flung back her head, and looked at the ceiling while she spoke. "You are a man of experience, both professionally and personally. I can speak openly with you." And thereupon she revealed to him the whole story about Babette and what had happened in her sleeping-chamber. Dr. Gieseke regretted being obliged to explain to her that neither the affair on the stairs nor the insult she had undoubtedly received, the precise nature of which she hesitated to divulge, was sufficient ground for a divorce.

"Very good," she said. "Thank you."

And then, at her request, he gave an exposition of the existing legal grounds for divorce, and an even longer discourse after it, which had for its subject-matter the law touching dowry rights. She listened with open mind and strained attention; and then, with cordial thanks, dismissed Dr. Gieseke for the time being.

She went downstairs and demanded audience of her brother in his private office.

"Thomas," she said, "please write to the man at once — I do not like to mention his name. As far as the money goes, I am perfectly informed on that subject. Let him speak. Me he shall never see again, whatever he decides. If he agrees to a divorce, we

will ask him to give an accounting and restore my *dos*. If he refuses, we need not be discouraged. For, as you probably know,
Permaneder's right to my *dos* is, legally speaking, a property right.
We grant that. But on the other hand, thank goodness, I have certain material rights on my side — "

The Consul walked up and down with his hands behind his
back, his shoulders twitching nervously. Tony's face, as she uttered the word *dos* was too unutterably self-satisfied!

He had no time. Heaven knew he had no time. Let her have
patience, and wait, and bethink herself a hundred times. His nearest duty was a journey to Hamburg — indeed, he must go the very
next day, for the purpose of a personal interview with Christian.
Christian had written for help, for money which would have to
come out of the Frau Consul's inheritance. His business was in
frightful condition; he was in constant difficulties. Yet he seemed
to amuse himself royally and went everywhere, to theatres, restau-
rants, and concert halls. To judge from the debts now coming to
light, which he had been able to pile up on the credit of his family
name, he had been living far, far beyond his means. And they
knew in Meng Street, and at the club — yes, the whole town knew
— who was responsible. It was a certain female, a certain Aline
Puvogel, who lived alone with her two pretty children. Christian
was not the only Hamburg business man who possessed her
favours and spent money on her.

In short, Tony's intentions in the matter of her divorce were
not the only dark spot in the Consul's sky; and the journey to
Hamburg was pressing. Besides, it was altogether likely that they
would hear from Herr Permaneder.

The Consul went to Hamburg, and came back angry and depressed. No word had come from Munich, and he felt obliged to
take the first step. He wrote; wrote rather coldly, with curt condescension, to this effect: Antonie, during her life with Permaneder, had been subjected to great disappointments — that would
not be denied. Without going into detail, it was evident that she
could never find happiness in this marriage. Her wish that it
should be dissolved must be justified, to the mind of any reasonable person; and her determination not to return to Munich was
entirely unshakable. And he put the question as to what were
Herr Permaneder's feelings in view of the facts which he had just
stated.

There were more days of suspense. And then came Herr Permaneder's reply.

He answered as no one had expected him to answer — not Dr.

Gieseke, nor the Frau Consul, not Thomas, nor Antonie herself.
He agreed, quite simply, to a divorce.

He wrote that he deeply regretted what had happened, but
that he respected Antonie's wishes, as he saw that he and she had
"never hit it off." If it were true that she had suffered during
those years through him, he begged her to forget and forgive. As
he would probably never see her and Erica again, he sent them
both his hearty good wishes for all happiness on this earth. And
he signed himself, Alois Permaneder. In a postscript he offered to
make immediate restitution of the dowry. He had enough without it to lead a life free from care. He did not require to have
notice given, for business there was none to wind up, the house
belonged to him, and the money was ready any time.

Tony felt a slight twinge of shame, and was almost inclined,
for the first time, to admit that Herr Permaneder's indifference
to money matters might have something good about it.

Now it was Dr. Gieseke's turn again. He communicated with
the husband, and a plea of "mutual incompatibility" was set up
as ground for the divorce. The hearing began — Tony's second
divorce case. She talked about it night and day, and the Consul
lost his temper several times. Tony was in no state to share his
feelings. She was entirely taken up with words like "tangibilities,"
"improvabilities," "accessions," "productivity," "dowry rights,"
and the like, which she used in season and out of season, with
marvellous fluency, her shoulders slightly raised. One point in Dr.
Gieseke's long disquisitions had made a great impression on her:
it had to do with "treasure" found in any piece of property that
has constituted part of a dowry, which was to be regarded as a
component part of the dowry, to be liquidated if the marriage
came to an end. About this "treasure" — which was, of course,
non-existent — she talked to every soul she knew: Ida Jungmann,
Uncle Justus, poor Clothilde, the Broad Street Buddenbrooks —
and they, when they heard how matters stood, just folded their
hands in their laps and looked at each other in speechless joy that
this satisfaction, too, had been vouchsafed them. Therese Weichbrodt was told of it — Erica had gone to stay at the pension again
— and Madame Kethelson too, though this last, for more than one
reason, understood not a single word.

Then came the day when the divorce was pronounced; when
the last formalities were gone through, and Tony asked Thomas
for the family papers and set down this last event with her own
hand. Yes, it was done. All that remained was to get used to it.

She did it gallantly. She bore, with unscathed dignity, the tiny dagger-thrusts of the ladies from Broad Street; she met the Hagen-ströms and Möllendorpfs on the street and looked with chilling indifference straight over their heads; and she quite gave up going into society — the more easily that it had for some years past for-saken her Mother's house for her brother's. She had her own im-mediate family, the Frau Consul, Tom, and Gerda; she had Ida Jungmann and her motherly friend Sesemi Weichbrodt; and she had Erica, upon whose future she probably built her own last secret hopes, and upon whose aristocratic upbringing she ex-pended much care and thought.

Thus she lived, and thus time went on.

Later, in some way that was never quite clear, there came to certain members of the family knowledge of that "word," the desperate word which had escaped from Herr Permaneder on that never-to-be-forgotten night.

What was it, then, that he had said?

"Go to the devil, you filthy sprat-eating slut!"

And thus Tony Buddenbrook's second marriage came to an end.

PART SEVEN

CHAPTER I

A CHRISTENING — a christening in Broad Street!

All, everything is there that was dreamed of by Madame Permaneder in the days of her expectancy. In the dining-room, the maid-servant, moving noiselessly so as not to disturb the services in the next room, is filling the cups with steaming hot chocolate and whipped cream. There are quantities of cups, crowded together on the great round tray with the gilded shell-shaped handles. And Anton the butler is cutting a towering layer-cake into slices, and Mamsell Jungmann is arranging flowers and sweets in silver dessert-dishes, with her head on one side, and both little fingers stuck out.

Soon the company will have seated themselves in the salon and sitting-room, and all these delicacies will be handed round. It is to be hoped they will hold out, since it is the whole family which has gathered here, in the broader, if not quite in the broadest sense of the word. For it is, through the Överdiecks, connected distantly with the Kistenmakers, and through them with the Möllendorpfs — and so on. One simply must draw the line somewhere! But the Överdiecks are represented, and, indeed, by no less a personage than the head of the family, the venerable Doctor Kaspar Överdieck, reigning Burgomaster, more than eighty years old.

He came in a carriage, and mounted the steps leaning on his staff and Thomas Buddenbrook's arm. His presence enhances the dignity of the occasion — and, beyond a question, this occasion is worthy of every dignity!

For within, in the salon, there is a flower-decked small table, serving as an altar, with a young priest in black vestments and a stiff snowy ruff like a millstone round his neck, reciting the service; and there is a great, strapping, particularly well-nourished person, richly arrayed in red and gold, bearing upon her billowing arms a small something, half smothered in laces and satin bows: an heir — a first-born son! A Buddenbrook! Do we really grasp the meaning of the fact?

Can we realize the thrill of that first whisper, that first little hint that travelled from Broad Street to Mengstrasse? Or Frau Permaneder's speechless ecstasy, as she embraced her mother, her brother, and — very gently — her sister-in-law? And now, with the spring — the spring of the year 1861 — he has come: he, the heir of so many hopes, whom they have expected for so many years, talked of him, longed for him, prayed to God and tormented Dr. Grabow for him; at length he has come — and looks most unimposing.

His tiny hands play among the gilt trimmings of his nurse's bodice; his head, in a lace cap trimmed with pale blue ribbons, lies sidewise on the pillow, turned heedlessly away from the preacher; he stares out into the room, at all his relatives, with an old, knowing look. Those eyes, under their long-lashed lids, blend the light blue of the Father's and the brown of the Mother's iris into a pale, indefinite, changeful golden-brown; but bluish shadows lie in the deep corners on both sides of the nose, and these give the little face, which is hardly yet a face at all, an aged look not suited to its four weeks of existence. But, please God, they mean nothing — for has not his Mother the same? And she is in perfectly good health. And anyhow, he lives — he lives, and is a son; which was the cause, four weeks ago, for great rejoicing.

He lives — and it might have been otherwise. The Consul will never forget the grip of good Dr. Grabow's hand, as he said to him, four weeks ago, when he could leave the mother and child: "Give thanks to God, my dear friend — there wasn't much to spare." The Consul has not dared to ask his meaning. He put from him in horror the thought that his son — this tiny creature, yearned for in vain so many years — had slipped into the world without breath to cry out, almost — *almost* — like Antonie's second daughter. But he knows that that hour, four weeks ago, was a desperate one for mother and child; and he bends tenderly over Gerda, who reclines in an easy-chair in front of him, next his Mother, her feet, in patent-leather shoes, crossed before her on a velvet cushion.

How pale she still is! And how strangely lovely in her pallor, with that heavy dark-red hair and those mysterious eyes that rest upon the preacher in half-veiled mockery! Herr Andreas Pringsheim, *pastor marianus*, succeeded thus young to the headship of St. Mary's after old Kölling's sudden death. He holds his chin in the air and his hands prayerfully folded beneath it. He has short, curly blond hair and a smooth-shaven, bony face, with a somewhat theatrical range of expression, from fanatical zeal to an exalted serenity. He comes from Franconia, where he has been for some

years, serving a small Lutheran community among Catholics; and
his effort after a clear and moving delivery has resulted in exaggerated mannerisms; an *r* rolled upon his front teeth and long,
obscure, or crudely accented vowel-sounds.

He gives thanks to God, in a voice now low and soft, now
loud and swelling — and the family listen: Frau Permaneder,
clothed in a dignity that hides her pride and her delight; Erica
Grünlich, now almost fifteen years old, a blooming young girl
with a long braid and her father's rosy skin; and Christian, who
has arrived that morning, and sits letting his deep-set eyes rove
from side to side all over the room. Pastor Tiburtius and his wife
have not shrunk from the long journey, but have come from Riga
to be present at the ceremony. The ends of Sievert Tiburtius'
long, thin whiskers are parted over his shoulders, and his small
grey eyes now and then open wider and wider, most unexpectedly,
and grow larger and more prominent till they almost jump out of
his head. Clara's gaze is dark and solemn and severe, and she sometimes lifts her hand to a head that always seems to ache. But they
have brought a splendid present to the Buddenbrooks: a huge
brown bear stuffed in a standing position. A relative of the Pastor's shot him somewhere in the heart of Russia, and now he stands
below in the vestibule with a card-tray between his paws.

The Krögers have their son Jürgen visiting them; he is a post-
office official in Rostock, a quiet, simply-dressed man. Where
Jacob is, nobody knows but his mother, who was an Överdieck.
She, poor, weak woman, secretly sells the household silver to send
money to the disinherited son. And the ladies Buddenbrook are
there, deeply rejoiced over the happy family event — which does
not prevent Pfiffi from remarking that the child looks rather un-
healthy: a view which the Frau Consul, born Stüwing, and likewise Friederike and Henriette, feel bound to endorse. But poor
Clothilde, lean, grey, resigned, and hungry, is moved by the words
of Pastor Pringsheim and the prospect of layer-cake and chocolate. The guests not belonging to the family are Herr Friedrich
Wilhelm Marcus and Sesemi Weichbrodt.

Now the Pastor turns to the god-parents and instructs them in
their duty. Justus Kröger is one. Consul Buddenbrook refused at
first to ask him. "Why invite the old man to commit a piece of
folly?" he says. "He has frightful scenes with his wife every day
over Jacob; their little property is slowly melting away — out of
pure worry he is even beginning to be careless in his dress! But
you know what will happen: if we ask him, he will send the child
a heavy gold service and refuse to be thanked for it!" But when

Uncle Justus heard who was to be asked in his place — Stephan Kistenmaker had been mentioned — he was so enormously piqued that they had to ask him after all. The gold mug he presented was, to Thomas's great relief, not exaggeratedly heavy.

And the second god-father? It is this dignified old gentleman with the snow-white hair, high neck-band, and soft black broadcloth coat with the red handkerchief sticking out of the back pocket, sitting here bent over his stick, in the most comfortable arm-chair in the house. It is, of course, Burgomaster Dr. Överdieck. It is a great event — a triumph! Good heavens, how could it have come about? he is hardly even a relative! The Buddenbrooks must have dragged the old man in by the hair! In fact, it *is* rather a feat: a little intrigue planned by the Consul and Madame Permaneder. At first it was merely a joke, born of the great relief of knowing that mother and child were safe. " A boy, Tony," cried the Consul. " He ought to have the Burgomaster for godfather! " But she took it up in earnest, whereupon he considered the matter seriously and agreed to make a trial. They hid behind Uncle Justus, and got him to send his wife to her sister-in-law, the wife of Överdieck the lumber dealer. She accepted the task of preparing the old father-in-law; then Thomas Buddenbrook made a visit to the head of the state and paid his respects — and the thing was done.

Now the nurse lifts up the child's cap, and the Pastor cautiously sprinkles two or three drops out of the gilt-lined silver basin in front of him, upon the few hairs of little Buddenbrook, as he slowly and impressively names the names with which he is baptizing him: Justus, Johann, Kaspar. Follows a short prayer, and then the relatives file by to bestow a kiss upon the brow of the unconcerned little creature. Therese Weichbrodt comes last, to whom the nurse has to stoop with her burden; in return for which Sesemi gives him two kisses, that go off with small explosions, and says, between them: " You good che-ild! "

Three minutes later, the guests have disposed themselves in salon and living-room, and the sweets are passed. Even Pastor Pringsheim, the toes of his broad, shiny boots showing under his black vestments, sits and sips the cool whipped cream off his hot chocolate, chatting easily the while, and wearing his serene expression, which is most effective by way of contrast with his sermon. His manner says, as plainly as words: " See how I can lay aside the priest and become the jolly ordinary guest! " He is a versatile, an accommodating sort of man. To the Frau Consul he speaks rather unctuously, to Thomas and Gerda like a man of

the world, and with Frau Permaneder he is downright jocose,
making jokes and gesturing fluently. Now and then, whenever
he thinks of it, he folds his hands in his lap, tips back his head,
glooms his brows, and makes a long face. When he laughs he
draws the air in through his teeth in little jerks.

Suddenly there is a stir in the corridor, the servants are heard
laughing, and in the doorway appears a singular figure, come to
offer congratulations. It is Grobleben: Grobleben, from whose
thin nose, no matter what the time of year, there ever hangs a
drop, which never falls. Grobleben is a workman in one of the
Consul's granaries, and he has an extra job, too, at the house, as
boots. Every morning early he appears in Broad Street, takes the
boots from before the door, and cleans them below in the court.
At family feasts he always appears in holiday attire, presents flowers, and makes a speech, in a whining, unctuous voice, with the
drop pendent from his nose. For this, he always gets a piece of
money — but that is *not* why he does it!

He wears a black coat — an old one of the Consul's — greased
leather top-boots, and a blue woollen scarf round his neck. In his
wizened red hand he holds a bunch of pale-coloured roses, which
are a little past their best, and slowly shed their petals on the carpet. He blinks with his small red eyes, but apparently sees nothing. He stands still in the doorway, with his flowers held out in
front of him, and begins straightway to speak. The old Frau Consul nods to him encouragingly and makes soothing little noises,
the Consul regards him with one eyebrow lifted, and some of the
family — Frau Permaneder, for instance — put their handkerchiefs
to their mouths.

"I be a poor man, yer honour 'n' ladies 'n' gentlemen, but I've
a feelin' hairt; 'n' the happiness of my master comes home to me,
it do, seein's he's allus been so good t' me; 'n' so I've come, yer
honour 'n' ladies 'n' gentlemen, to congratulate the Herr Consul
'n' the Frau Consul, 'n' the whole respected family, from a full
hairt, 'n' that the child may prosper, for that they desarve fr'm
God 'n' man, for such a master as Consul Buddenbrook there aren't
so many, he's a noble gentleman, 'n' our Lord will reward him for
all. . . ."

"Splendid, Grobleben! That was a beautiful speech. Thank
you very much, Grobleben. What are the roses for?"

But Grobleben has not nearly done. He strains his whining
voice and drowns the Consul out.

". . . 'n' I say th' Lord will reward him, him and the whole
respected family; 'n' when his time has come to stan' before His

throne, for stan' we all must, rich *and* poor, 'n' one'll have a fine polished hard-wood coffin 'n' 'tother 'n' old box, yet all on us must come to mother earth at th' last, yes, we must all come to her at th' last — to mother earth — to mother — "

" Oh, come, come, Grobleben! This isn't a funeral, it's a christening. Get along with your mother earth! "

". . . 'n' these be a few flowers," concludes Grobleben.

" Thank you, Grobleben, thank you. This is too much — what did you pay for them, man? But I haven't heard such a speech as that for a long time! Wait a minute — here, go out and give yourself a treat, in honour of the day! " And the Consul puts his hand on the old man's shoulder and gives him a thaler.

" Here, my good man," says the Frau Consul. " And I hope you love our blessed Lord? "

" I be lovin' him from my hairt, Frau Consul, thet's the holy truth! " And Grobleben gets another thaler from her, and a third from Frau Permaneder, and retires with a bow and a scrape, taking the roses with him by mistake, except for those already fallen on the carpet.

The Burgomaster takes his leave now, and the Consul accompanies him down to his carriage. This is the signal for the party to break up — for Gerda Buddenbrook must rest. The old Frau Consul, Tony, Erica, and Mamsell Jungmann are the last to go.

" Well, Ida," says the Consul, " I have been thinking it over: you took care of us all, and when little Johann gets a bit older — He still has the monthly nurse now, and after that he will still need a day-nurse, I suppose — but will you be willing to move over to us when the time comes? "

" Yes, indeed, Herr Consul, if your wife is satisfied."

Gerda is content to have it so, and thus it is settled.

In the act of leaving, however, and already at the door, Frau Permaneder turns. She comes back to her brother and kisses him on both cheeks, and says: " It has been a lovely day, Tom. I am happier than I have been for years. We Buddenbrooks aren't quite at the last gasp yet, thank God, and whoever thinks we are is mightily mistaken. Now that we have little Johann — it is so beautiful that he is christened Johann — it looks to me as if quite a new day will dawn for us all! "

CHAPTER II

CHRISTIAN BUDDENBROOK, proprietor of the firm of H. C. F. Burmeester and Company of Hamburg, came into his brother's living-room, holding in his hand his modish grey hat and his walking-
stick with the nun's bust. Tom and Gerda sat reading together.
It was half past nine on the evening of the christening day.

" Good evening," said Christian. " Oh, Thomas, I must speak
with you at once. — Please excuse me, Gerda. — It is urgent,
Thomas."

They went into the dark dining-room, where the Consul lighted
a gas-jet on the wall, and looked at his brother. He expected
nothing good. Except for the first greeting, he had had no opportunity to speak with Christian, but he had looked at him, during
the service, and noted that he seemed unusually serious, and even
more restless than common: in the course of Pastor Pringsheim's
discourse he had left the room for several minutes. Thomas had
not written him since the day in Hamburg when he had paid over
into his brother's hands an advance of 10,000 marks current on his
inheritance, to settle his indebtedness. " Just go on as you are going," he had said, " and you'll soon run through all your money.
As far as I am concerned, I hope you will cross my path very
little in future. You have put my friendship to too hard a test in
these three years." Why was he here now? Something must be
driving him.

" Well? " asked the Consul.

" I'm done," Christian said. He let himself down sidewise on
one of the high-backed chairs around the dining-table, and held
his hat and stick between his thin knees.

" May I ask what it is you are done with, and what brings you
to me? " said the Consul. He remained standing.

" I'm done," repeated Christian, shaking his head from side to
side with frightful earnestness and letting his little round eyes
stray restlessly back and forth. He was now thirty-three years
old, but he looked much older. His reddish-blond hair was grown
so thin that nearly all the cranium was bare. His cheeks were
sunken, the cheek-bones protruded sharply, and between them,

naked, fleshless, and gaunt, stood the huge hooked nose.

" If it were only this — ! " he went on, and ran his hand down the whole of his left side, very close, but not touching it. " It isn't a pain, you know — it is a misery, a continuous, indefinite ache. Dr. Drögemuller in Hamburg tells me that my nerves on this side are all too short. Imagine, on my whole left side, my nerves aren't long enough! Sometimes I think I shall surely have a stroke here, on this side, a permanent paralysis. You have no idea. I never go to sleep properly. My heart doesn't beat, and I start up suddenly, in a perfectly terrible fright. That happens not once but ten times before I get to sleep. I don't know if you know what it is. I'll tell you about it more precisely. It is — "

" Not now," the Consul said coldly. " Am I to understand that you have come here to tell me this? I suppose not."

" No, Thomas. If it were only that — but it is not that — alone. It is the business. I can't go on with it."

" Your affairs are in confusion again? " The Consul did not start, he did not raise his voice. He asked the question quite calmly, and looked sidewise at his brother, with a cold, weary glance.

" No, Thomas. For to tell you the truth — it is all the same now — I never really was in order, even with the ten thousand, as you know yourself. They only saved me from putting up the shutters at once. The thing is — I had more losses at once, in coffee — and with the failure in Antwerp — That's the truth. So then I didn't do any more business; I just sat still. But one has to live — so now there are notes and other debts — five thousand thaler. You don't know the hole I'm in. And on top of everything else, this agony — "

" Oh, so you just sat still, did you? " cried the Consul, beside himself. His self-control was gone now. " You let the wagon stick in the mud and went off to enjoy yourself! You think I don't know the kind of life you've been living — theatres and circus and clubs — and women — "

" You mean Aline. Yes, Thomas, you have very little understanding for that sort of thing, and it's my misfortune, perhaps, that I have so much. You are right when you say it has cost me too much; and it will cost me a goodish bit more, for — I'll tell you something, just here between two brothers — the third child, the little girl, six months old, she is my child."

" You fool, you! "

" Don't say that, Thomas. You should be just, even if you are angry, to her and to — why shouldn't it be my child? And as for

Aline, she isn't in the least worthless, and you ought not to say she is. She is not at all promiscuous; she broke with Consul Holm on my account, and he has much more money than I have. That's how decent she is. No, Thomas, you simply can't understand what a splendid creature she is — and *healthy* — she is as *healthy* — ! " He repeated the word, and held up one hand before his face with the fingers crooked, in the same gesture as when he used to tell about " Maria " and the depravity of London. " You should see her teeth when she laughs. I've never found any other teeth to compare with them, not in Valparaiso, or London, or anywhere else in the world. I'll never forget the evening I first met her, in the oyster-room, at Uhlich's. She was living with Consul Holm then. Well, I told her a story or so, and was a bit friendly; and when I went home with her afterwards — well, Thomas, that's a different sort of feeling from the one you have when you do a good stroke of business! But you don't like to hear about such things — I can see that already — and anyhow, it's over with. I'm saying good-bye to her, though I shall keep in touch with her on account of the child. I'll pay up everything I owe in Hamburg, and shut up shop. I can't go on. I've talked with Mother, and she is willing to give me the five thousand thaler to start with, so I can put things in order; and I hope you will agree to it, for it is much better to say quite simply that Christian Buddenbrook is winding up his business and going abroad, than for me to make a failure. You think so too, don't you? I intend to go to London again, Thomas, and take a position. It isn't good for me to be independent — I can see that more and more. The responsibility — whereas in a situation one just goes home quite care-free, at the end of the day. And I liked living in London. Do you object? "

During this exposition, the Consul had turned his back on his brother, and stood with his hands in his pockets, describing figures on the floor with his foot.

" Very good, go to London," he said, shortly, and without turning more than half-way toward his brother, he passed into the living-room.

But Christian followed him. He went up to Gerda, who sat there alone, reading, and put out his hand.

" Good night, Gerda. Well, Gerda, I'm off for London. Yes, it's remarkable how one gets tossed about hither and yon. Now it's again into the unknown, into a great city, you know, where one meets an adventure at every third step, and sees so much of life. Strange — do you know the feeling? One gets it here — sort of in the pit of the stomach — it's very odd."

CHAPTER III

JAMES MÖLLENDORPF, the oldest of the merchant senators, died in a grotesque and horrible way. The instinct of self-preservation became very weak in this diabetic old man; and in the last years of his life he fell a victim to a passion for cakes and pastries. Dr. Grabow, as the Möllendorpf family physician, had protested energetically, and the distressed relatives employed gentle constraint to keep the head of the family from committing suicide with sweet bake-stuffs. But the old Senator, mental wreck as he was, rented a room somewhere, in some convenient street, like Little Groping Alley, or Angelswick, or Behind-the-Wall — a little hole of a room, whither he would secretly betake himself to consume sweets. And there they found his lifeless body, the mouth still full of half-masticated cake, the crumbs upon his coat and upon the wretched table. A mortal stroke had supervened, and put a stop to slow dissolution.

The horrid details of the death were kept as much as possible from the family, but they flew about the town, and were discussed at length on the Bourse, in the club, and at the Harmony, in all the business offices, in the Assembly of Burgesses — likewise at all the balls, dinners, and evening parties, for the death occurred in February of the year '62, and the season was in full swing. Even the Frau Consul's friends talked about it, on the Jerusalem evenings, in the pauses of Lea Gerhardt's reading aloud; the little Sunday-school children discussed it in awesome whispers as they crossed the Buddenbrook entry; and Herr Stuht, in Bell-Founders' Street, went into ample detail over it with his wife, who moved in the highest circles.

But interest could not long remain concentrated upon the past. And even with the first rumour of the old man's death, the great question had at once sprung up: who was to succeed him?

What suspense, what subterranean activity! A stranger, intent on the sights of the mediaeval town, would have noticed nothing; but beneath the surface there was unimaginable bustle and commotion, as one firm and unassailable honest conviction after another was exploded; and slowly, slowly the while, divergent views approached each other! Passions are stirred, Ambition and Vanity wrestle together in silence. Dead and buried hopes spring once more to life — and again are blasted. Old Kurz, the merchant, in Bakers' Alley, who gets three or four votes at every election, will sit quaking at home on the fatal day, and listen to the shouting, but he will not be elected this time either. He will continue to take his walks abroad, displaying outwardly his usual mingling of civic pride and self-satisfaction: but he will bear down with him into the grave the secret chagrin of never having been elected Senator.

James Möllendorpf's death was discussed at the Buddenbrook Thursday dinner-table; and Frau Permaneder, after the proper expressions of sympathy, began to let her tongue play upon her upper lip and look across artfully at her brother. The Buddenbrook ladies marked the look. They exchanged piercing glances, and with one accord shut their eyes and their lips tightly together. The Consul had, for a second, responded to the sly smile his sister gave him, and then given the talk another turn. He knew that the thought which Tony hugged to her breast in secret was being spoken in the street.

Names were suggested and rejected, others came up and were sifted out. Henning Kurz in Bakers' Alley was too old. They needed new blood. Consul Huneus, the lumber dealer, whose millions would have weighted the scale heavily in his favour, was constitutionally ineligible, as his brother already sat in the Senate. Consul Eduard Kistenmaker, the wine dealer, and Consul Hermann Hagenström were names that kept their places on the list. But from the very first was heard the name of Thomas Buddenbrook; and as election day approached, it grew constantly plainer that he and Hermann Hagenström were the favoured candidates.

Hermann Hagenström had his admirers and hangers-on — there was no doubt of that. His zeal in public affairs, the spectacular rise of the firm of Strunck and Hagenström, the showy house the Consul kept, the luxurious life he led, the pâtés-de-foie-gras he ate for breakfast — all these could not fail to make an impression. This large, rather over-stout man with the short, full, reddish beard and the snub nose coming down flat on his upper lip, this man whose grandfather nobody knew, not even himself, and whose father had made himself socially impossible by a rich but doubtful marriage; this man had become a brother-in-law of the Huneus' and the Möllendorpfs, had ranged his name alongside those of the five or six reigning families in the town, and was undeniably a remarkable and a respected figure. The novel and therewith the attrac-

tive element in his personality — that which singled him out for a
leading position in the eyes of many — was its liberal and tolerant
strain. His light, large way of making money and spending it
again differed fundamentally from the patient, persistent toil and
the inherited principles of his fellow merchants. This man stood
on his own feet, free from the fetters of tradition and ancestral
piety; and all the old ways were foreign to him. His house was
not one of the ancient patrician mansions, built with senseless
waste of space, in tall white galleries mounting above a stone-paved
ground floor. His home on Sand Street, the southern extension of
Broad Street, was a modern dwelling, not conforming to any set
style of architecture, with a simple painted façade, but furnished
inside with every luxury and planned with the cleverest economy
of space. Recently, on the occasion of one of his large evening
parties, he had invited a prima donna from the government theatre,
to sing after dinner to his guests — among them his witty, art-
loving brother — and had paid her an enormous fee for her services. Hermann Hagenström was not the man to vote in the Assembly for the application of large sums of money to preserve and
restore the town's mediaeval monuments. But it was a fact that he
was the first, absolutely the first man in town to light his house and
his offices with gas. Yes, if Consul Hagenström could be said to
represent any tradition whatever, it was the free, progressive, tolerant, unprejudiced habit of thought which he had inherited from
his father, old Hinrich — and on this was based all the admiration
people undoubtedly felt for him.

Thomas Buddenbrook's prestige was of a different kind. People
honoured in him not only his own personality, but the personalities
of his father, grandfather, and great-grandfather as well: quite
apart from his own business and public achievement, he was the
representative of a hundred years of honourable tradition. And
the easy, charming way, indeed, with which he carried the family
standard made no small part of his success. What distinguished
him, even among his professional fellow citizens, was an unusual
degree of formal culture, which, wherever he went, aroused both
wonder and respect in about equal degrees.

On Thursdays at the Buddenbrooks', the coming election received only brief and passing comment in the presence of the
Consul. Whenever it was mentioned, the old Frau Consul discreetly averted her light eyes. But Frau Permaneder, now and
then, could not refrain from displaying her astonishing knowledge
of the Constitution. She had gone very thoroughly into the decrees touching the election of a member of the Senate, precisely

as once she thoroughly informed herself on the laws governing
divorce. She talked about voting chambers, ballots, and electors,
she weighed all the possible eventualities, she could recite ver-
batim and glibly the oath taken by the voters. She spoke of the
" free and frank discussion " which the Constitution ordains must
be held over each name upon the list of candidates, and vivaciously
wished she might be present when Hermann Hagenström's character was being pulled to pieces! A moment later she leaned over
and began to count the prune-pits on her brother's dessert-plate:
tinker, tailor, soldier, sailor — finishing triumphantly with " senator " when she came to the last pit. But after dinner she could
not hold in any longer. She took her brother's arm and drew him
into the bow-window.

"Oh, Tom! *Tom!* Suppose you are really elected — if our coat-
of-arms is put up in the Senate-chamber at the Town Hall I shall
just die of joy, I know I shall. I shall fall dead at the news — you'll
see! "

"Now, Tony dear! Have a little self-control, a little dignity, I
beg of you. You are not usually lacking in dignity. Am I going
around like Henning Kurz? We amount to something even without the 'Senator.' And I hope you won't die, whichever way it
turns out! "

And the agitations, the consultations, the struggles of opinion
took their course. Consul Peter Döhlman, the rake with a business
now entirely ruined, which existed only in name, and the twenty-
seven-year-old daughter whose inheritance he was eating up,
played his part by attending two dinners, one given by Thomas
Buddenbrook and the other by Hermann Hagenström, and both
times addressing his host, in his loud, resounding voice, as "Senator." But Siegismund Gosch, old Gosch the broker, went about
like a raging lion, and engaged to throttle anybody, out of hand,
who wasn't minded to vote for Consul Buddenbrook.

"Consul Buddenbrook, gentlemen — ah, there's a man for you!
I stood at his father's side in the '48, when, with a word, he tamed
the unleashed fury of the mob. His father, and his father's father
before him, would have been Senator were there any justice on
this earth! "

But at bottom it was not so much Consul Buddenbrook himself
whose personality fired Gosch's soul to its innermost depths. It
was rather the young Frau Consul, Gerda Arnoldsen. Not that
the broker had ever exchanged a word with her. He did not belong to her circle of wealthy merchant families, nor sit at their
tables, nor pay visits to them. But, as we have seen, Gerda Bud-

denbrook had but to arrive in the town to be singled out by the
roving fancy of the sinister broker, ever on the look-out for the
unusual. With unerring instinct he divined that this figure was
calculated to add content to his unsatisfied existence, and he made
himself the slave of one who had scarcely ever heard his name.
Since then he encompassed in his reveries this nervous, exceedingly
reserved lady, to whom he had not even been presented: he lifted
his Jesuit hat to her, on the street, to her great surprise, and treated
her to a pantomime of cringing treachery, gloating over her the
while in his thoughts as a tiger might over his trainer. This dull
existence would afford him no chance of committing atrocities
for this woman's sake — ah, if it only would, with what devilish
indifference would he answer for them! Its stupid conventions
prevented him from raising her, by deeds of blood and horror, to
an imperial throne! — And thus, nothing was left but for him to
go to the Town Hall and cast his vote in favour of her furiously
respected husband — and, perhaps, one day, to dedicate to her his
forthcoming transition of Lope de Vega.

CHAPTER IV

EVERY vacant seat in the Senate must, according to the Constitution, be filled within four weeks. Three of them have passed, and
this is election-day — a day of thaw, at the end of February.

It is about one o'clock, and people are thronging into Broad
Street. They are thronging before the Town Hall, with its ornamental glazed-brick façade, its pointed towers and turrets mounting toward a whitish grey sky, its covered steps supported on outstanding columns, its pointed arcades, through which there is a
glimpse of the market place and the fountain. The crowd stands
steadfastly in the dirty slush that melts beneath their feet; they
look into each other's faces and then straight ahead again, and
crane their necks. For beyond that portal, in the Council Room,
in fourteen armchairs arranged in a semicircle sit the electors, who
have been chosen from the Senate and the Assembly and await the
proposals of the voting chambers.

The affair has spun itself out. It appears that the debate in the
chambers will not die down; the struggle is so bitter that up to
now not one single unanimous choice has been put before the
Council — otherwise the Burgomaster would at once announce
an election. Extraordinary! Rumours — nobody knows whence,
nobody knows how — come from within the building and circu-
late in the street. Perhaps Herr Kaspersen, the elder of the two
beadles, who always refers to himself as a " servant of the State,"
is standing inside there and telling what he hears, out of the corner
of his mouth, through his shut teeth, with his eyes turned the
other way! The story goes that proposals have been laid before
the sitting, but that each of the three chambers has turned in a
different name: namely Hagenström, Kistenmaker, and Buddenbrook. A secret ballot must now be taken, with ballot-papers —
it is to be hoped that it will show a clear plurality! For people
without overshoes are suffering, and stamping their feet to warm
them.

The waiting crowd is made up of all sorts and conditions. There
are sea-faring characters, with bare tattooed necks and their hands
in the pockets of their sailor trousers; grain porters with their in-

comparably respectable countenances, and their blouses and knee-breeches of black glazed calico; drivers who have clambered down from their wagons of piled-up sacks, and stand whip in hand to wait for the decision; servant-maids in neckerchiefs, aprons and thick striped petticoats with little white caps perched on the backs of their heads and market-baskets hanging on their bare arms; fish and vegetable women with their flat straw baskets — even a couple of pretty farm girls with Dutch caps, short skirts, and long flowing sleeves coming out from their gaily-embroidered stay-bodies. Mingled among these, burghers, shop-keepers who have come out hatless from neighbouring shops to exchange their views, sprucely-dressed young men who are apprentices in the business of their fathers or their fathers' friends — and schoolboys with satchels and bundles of books.

Two labourers with bristling sailor beards, stand chewing their tobacco; behind them is an excited lady, craning her neck this way and that to get a glimpse of the Town Hall between their powerful shoulders. She wears a long evening cloak trimmed with brown fur, which she holds together from the inside with both hands. Her face is well covered with a thick brown veil. She shifts her feet about in the melting snow.

" Gawd! Kurz bain't gettin' it this time, nuther, be he? " says the one labourer to the other.

" Naw, ye mutton-head, 'tis certain he bain't. There's no more talk o' him. Th' votin's between Hagenström, Buddenbrook, 'n' Kistenmaker. 'Tis all about they, — now."

" 'Tis whether which one o' th' three be ahead o' the others, eh? "

" So 'tis; yes, they do say so."

" Then I'm minded they'll be choosin' Hagenström."

" Eh, smarty — so they'll be choosin' Hagenström? Ye can tell that to yer grandmother! " And therewith. he spits his tobacco-juice on the ground close to his own feet, the crowd being too dense to admit of a trajectory. He takes hold of his trousers in both hands and pulls them up higher under his belt, and goes on: " Hagenström, he's a great pig — he be so fat he can't breathe through his own nose! If so be it's all o'er wi' Kurz then I'm fer Buddenbrook. 'Tis a very shrewd chap."

" So 'tis, so 'tis. But Hagenström, he's got the money."

" That bain't the question — 'tis no matter o' riches."

" 'n' then this Buddenbrook — he be so devilish fine wi' his cuffs 'n' his silk tie 'n' his stickin'-out moustaches; hast seen him walk? He hops along like a bird."

" Ye ninny, that bain't the question, no more'n th' other."

" They say his sister've put away two men a'ready." The lady in the fur cloak trembles visibly.

" Eh, that soart o' thing — what do we know about it? Likely the Consul he couldn't help it hisself."

The lady in the veil thinks to herself, " He couldn't, indeed! Thank God for that," and presses her hands together, inside her cloak.

" 'n' then," adds the Buddenbrook partisan, " didn't the Burgomaster his own self stan' godfeyther to his son? Can't ye tell somethin' by that? "

" Yes, can't you indeed? " thinks the lady. " Thank heaven, that did do some good." She starts. A fresh rumour from the Town Hall, running zig-zag through the crowd, has reached her ears. The balloting, it seems, has not been decisive. Eduard Kistenmaker, indeed, has received fewer votes than the other two candidates, and his name has been dropped. But the struggle goes on between Buddenbrook and Hagenström. A sapient citizen remarks that if the voting continues to be even, it will be necessary to appoint five arbitrators.

A voice, down in front at the entrance steps, shouts suddenly: " Heine Seehas is 'lected — 'rah for Heine Seehas! " Heine Seehas, be it known, is an habitual drunkard, who peddles hot bread on a little wagon through the streets. Everybody roars with laughter, and stands on tip-toe to see the wag who is responsible for the joke. The lady in the veil is seized with a nervous giggle; her shoulders shake for a moment, and then give a shrug which expresses as plainly as words: " Is this the time for tom-foolery like that? " She collects herself again, and stares with intensity between the two labourers at the Town Hall. But almost at the same moment her hands slip from her cloak, so that it opens in front, her figure relaxes, her shoulders droop, she stands there entirely crushed.

Hagenström! — The word seems to have come from nobody knows where — down from the sky, or up from the earth. It is everywhere at once. There is no contradiction. So it is decided. Hagenström! Hagenström it is, then. One may as well go home. The lady in the veil might have known. It was ever thus. She will go home — she feels the tears rising in her throat.

This state of things has lasted a second or so, when there occurs a shouting and a backward jostling of the throng. It runs through the whole assemblage, as those in front press back those behind, and at the same time something red appears in the doorway. It is the coats of the beadles Kaspersen and Uhlefeldt. They are in full-dress uniform, with white riding breeches, three-cornered hats, yellow gauntlet gloves, and short dress swords. They appear side by side, and make their way through the crowd, which falls back before them.

They move like fate: silent, resolved, inexorable, not looking to right or left, with gaze directed toward the ground. They take, according to instructions, the route marked out by the election. And it is *not* in the direction of Sand Street! They have turned to the right — they are going down Broad Street!

The lady in the veil cannot believe her eyes. However, all about her, people are seeing just what she sees; they are pushing on after the beadles, and saying to each other: "It isn't Hagenström, it's Buddenbrook!" And a group of gentlemen emerge from the portal, in excited conversation, and hurry with rapid steps down Broad Street, to be the first to offer congratulations.

Then the lady holds her cloak together and runs for it. She runs, indeed, as seldom lady runs. Her veil blows up, revealing her flushed face — no matter for that; and one of her furred goloshes keeps flapping open in the sloppy snow and hindering her frightfully: yet she outruns them all! She gains the house at the corner of Bakers' Street, she rings the alarm-bell at the vestibule-door — fire, murder, thieves! — she shouts at the maid who opens: "They're coming, Kathrin, they're coming," takes the stairs, and storms into the living-room. Her brother himself sits there, certainly a little pale. He puts down his paper and makes a gesture, almost as if to ward her off. But she puts her arms about him, and repeats: "They're coming, Tom, they're coming! You are the man — and Hermann Hagenström is out!"

That was Friday. On the following day, Senator Buddenbrook stood in the Council Hall, in the seat of the deceased James Möllendorpf, and in the presence of the City Fathers there assembled, and the Delegation of Burgesses, he took the oath: "I will conscientiously perform the duties of my office, strive with all my power for the good of the State, faithfully obey the Constitution, honourably pursue the public weal, and in the discharge of my office, regard neither my own advantage nor that of my relatives and friends. I will support the laws of the State and do justice on all alike, whether rich or poor. In all things where secrecy is needful, I will not speak, and especially will I not reveal what is given me to keep silent. So help me God!"

CHAPTER V

OUR desires and our performance are conditioned by certain needs of our nervous systems which are very hard to define in words. What people called Thomas Buddenbrook's " vanity " — his care for his personal appearance, his extravagant dressing — was at bottom not vanity but something else entirely. It was, originally, no more than the effort of a man of action to be certain, from head to toe, of the adequacy and correctness of his bearing. But the demands made by himself and by others upon his talents and his capacities were constantly increased. He was overwhelmed by public and private affairs. When the Senate sat to appoint its committees, one of the main departments, the administration of the taxes, fell to his lot. But tolls, railways, and other administrative business claimed his time as well; and he presided at hundreds of committees that called into play all the capacities he possessed: he had to summon every ounce of his flexibility, his foresight, his power to charm, in order not to wound the sensibilities of his elders, to defer constantly to them, and yet to keep the reins in his own hands. If his so-called vanity notably increased at the same time, if he felt a greater and greater need to refresh himself bodily, to renew himself, to change his clothing several times a day, all this meant simply that Thomas Buddenbrook, though he was barely thirty-seven years old, was losing his elasticity, was wearing himself out fast.

When good Dr. Grabow begged him to relax a little, he answered, " Oh, my dear Doctor, I haven't reached that point yet! " By which he meant that he still had an interminable deal of work to do before he arrived at the goal and could settle back to enjoy himself. The truth was, he hardly believed himself in such a condition. Yet it drove him on, it left him no peace. Even when he seemed to rest, as he sat with the paper after dinner, a thousand ideas whirled about in his brain, while the veins stood out on his temples, and he twisted the ends of his moustaches with a certain still intensity of passion. He concentrated with equal violence whether the subject of his thought was a business manœuvre, a public speech, or a decision to renew his entire stock of body linen, in order to be sure that he had enough, for a while, at least.

If such wholesale buying afforded him passing relief and satisfaction, he could indulge himself in it without scruple, for his
business at this time was as brilliant as ever it had been in his grandfather's day. The repute of the firm grew, not only in the town
but round about, and throughout the whole community he continued to be held in ever greater regard. His talents were admitted
on all hands, with admiration or envy as the case might be; while
he himself wrestled ceaselessly, at times despairingly, to evolve
an order and method of work which should enable him to over-
take the flights of his own restless imagination.

Thus, when, in the summer of 1863, Senator Buddenbrook
went about with his mind full of plans for the building of a great
new house, it was not arrogance which impelled him. He was
driven by his own inability to be quiet — which his fellow-
burghers would have been right in ascribing to his " vanity " —
for it was another manifestation of the same thing. To make a
new home, and a radical change in his outward life; to pack up,
to re-install himself afresh, to weed out all the accumulations of
bygone years and set aside everything old or superfluous: all this,
even in imagination, gave him feelings of freshness, newness,
spotlessness, stimulation. All of which he must have craved indeed, for he attacked the plan with great enthusiasm, and already
had his eye on a suitable location.

There was a property of considerable extent at the lower end
of Fishers' Lane. The house, grey with age, in bad repair, was
offered for sale on the death of its owner, an ancient spinster, the
relic of a forgotten family, who had dwelt there alone. On this
piece of land the Senator thought to build his house; and he
surveyed it with a speculative eye when he passed the spot on his
way to the harbour. The neighbourhood was pleasant enough —
good burgher-houses, the most modest among them being the
narrow little façade opposite, with a small flower-shop on the
ground floor.

He threw himself into the affair. He made a rough estimate of
the expense involved, and though the sum he fixed provisionally
was by no means a small one, he felt he could compass it without
undue effort. But then he would suddenly have the thought that
the whole thing was a senseless folly, and confess to himself that
his present house had plenty of room for himself, his wife, their
child, and their servants. But the half-conscious cravings were
stronger; and in the desire to have them strengthened and justified
from outside, he first revealed his plan to his sister.

" Well, Tony, what do you say to it? The whole house is a sort of band-box, isn't it — and the winding stair is really a joke. It isn't quite the thing, is it? and now that you've had me made Senator — in a word, don't you think I owe it to myself? "

Ah, in the eyes of Madame Permaneder, what was there he did not owe to himself? She was full of practical enthusiasm. She crossed her arms on her breast and walked up and down with her shoulders raised and her head in the air.

" Of course you do, Tom; goodness gracious, yes! What possible objection could there be? And when you have married an Arnoldsen, with a hundred thousand thaler to boot — I'm very proud to be the first you've told it to. It was lovely of you. And if you do do it, Tom, why, you must do it well, that's what I say. It must be grand."

" H'm, well, yes, I agree with you. I'm willing to spend something on it. I'll have Voigt, and we'll go over the plans together. Voigt has a great deal of taste."

The second opinion which Thomas called in was Gerda's. She praised the idea unreservedly. The confusion of moving would not be pleasant, but the prospect of a large music-room with good acoustic properties impressed her most happily. As for the old Frau Consul, she was quite prepared to think of the new house as a logical consequence of all the other blessings which had fallen to her lot, and to give thanks to God therefor, accordingly. Since the birth of the heir, and the recent election, she gave freer expression to her motherly pride, and had a way of saying " my son, the Senator," which the Broad Street Buddenbrooks found most offensive.

These aging spinsters felt that all too little shadow set off the sunshine through which Thomas's outward life ran its brilliant course. It was no great consolation — at the Thursday family gatherings — to pour contempt on poor, good-natured Clothilde. As for Christian — Christian, through the good offices of Mr. Richardson, his former chief, had found a situation in London, whence he had lately telegraphed a fantastic desire to marry Fräulein Puvogel, an idea upon which his mother had firmly set her foot — Christian now belonged, quite simply, to Jacob Kröger's class, and was, as it were, a dead issue. They consoled themselves, to some extent, with the little weaknesses of the old Frau Consul and Frau Permaneder. They would bring the conversation round to the subject of coiffures: the Frau Consul was capable of saying, in the blandest way, that she always wore " her " hair very simply, whereas it was plain to any one gifted

by God with intelligence, and certainly to the Misses Buddenbrook, that the immutable red-blonde hair under the old lady's
cap could no longer by any stretch be called "her" hair. Still
more gratifying was it to get Cousin Tony started on the subject
of those nefarious persons who had formerly had an influence
on her life. Teary Trietschke! Grünlich! Permaneder! Hagenström! — Tony, when she was egged on to it, would utter these
names into the air like so many little trumpetings of disgust, with
her shoulders well up. They had a sweet sound in the ears of the
daughters of Uncle Gotthold.

They could not dissimulate, and they would accept no responsibility for omitting to say that little Johann was frightfully
slow about learning to walk and talk. They were really quite
right: it was an admitted fact that Hanno — this was the nickname
adopted by the Frau Senator for her son — at a time when he was
able to call all the members of his family by name with fair correctness, was incapable of pronouncing the names Friederike,
Henriette, and Pfiffi so that any one could understand what he
said. And at fifteen months he had not taken a single step alone.
The Misses Buddenbrook, shaking their heads pessimistically, declared that the child would be halt and tongue-tied to the end of
his days.

They later admitted the error of their gloomy prophecy; but
nobody, in fact, denied that Hanno was a little backward. His
early infancy was a struggle for life, and his family was in constant anxiety. At birth he had been too feeble to cry out; and soon
after the christening a three-day attack of cholera-infantum was
almost enough to still for ever the little heart set pumping, in
the first place, with such difficulty. But he survived; and good
Dr. Grabow did his best, by the most painstaking care and nourishment, to strengthen him for the difficult period of teething.
The first tiny white point had barely pricked through the gum,
when the child was attacked by convulsions, which repeated
themselves with greater and greater violence, until again the
worst was to be feared. Once more the old doctor speechlessly
pressed the parents' hands. The child lay in profound exhaustion,
and the vacant look in the shadowy eyes indicated an affection
of the brain. The end seemed almost to be wished for.

But Hanno regained some little strength, consciousness returned; and though the crisis which he had survived greatly
hindered his progress in walking and talking, there was no longer
any immediate danger to be feared.

The child was slender of limb, and rather tall for his age. His hair, pale brown and very soft, began to grow rapidly, and fell waving over the shoulders of his full, pinafore-like frocks. The family likenesses were abundantly clear, even now. From the first he possessed the Buddenbrook hand, broad, a little too short, but finely articulated, and his nose was precisely the nose of his father and great-grandfather, though the nostrils would probably remain more delicate. But the whole lower part of his face, longish and narrow, was neither Buddenbrook nor Kröger, but from the mother's side of the house. This was true of the mouth in particular, which, when closed, began very early to wear an anxious, woebegone expression that later matched the look of his strange, gold-brown, blue-shadowed eyes.

So he began to live: brooded over by his father's reserved tenderness, clothed and nurtured under his mother's watchful eye; prayed over by Aunt Antonie, presented with tops and hobbyhorses by the Frau Consul and Uncle Justus; and when his charming little perambulator appeared on the streets, it was looked after with interest and expectation. Madame Decho, the stately nurse, had attended the child up to now; but it had been settled that when they moved into the new house, not she, but Ida Jungmann, should move in with them, and the latter's place with the old Frau Consul be filled by somebody else.

Senator Buddenbrook carried out his plan. He had no difficulty in obtaining title to the property in Fishers' Lane. The Broad Street house was turned over to Gosch the broker, who dramatically declared himself prepared to assume the task of disposing of it. Stephan Kistenmaker, who had a growing family, and, with his brother Eduard, made good money in the wine business, bought it at once. Herr Voigt undertook the new building, and soon there was a clean plan to unroll before the eyes of the family on Thursday afternoons, when they could, in fancy, see the façade already before them: an imposing brick façade with sandstone caryatides supporting the bow-window, and a flat roof, of which Clothilde remarked, in her pleasant drawl, that one might drink afternoon coffee there. The Senator planned to transfer the business offices to his new building, which would, of course, leave empty the ground floor of the house in Meng Street. But here also things turned out well: for it appeared that the City Fire Insurance Company wanted to rent the rooms by the month for their offices — which was quickly arranged.

Autumn came, and the grey walls crumbled to heaps of rubbish, and Thomas Buddenbrook's new house rose above its roomy cellars, while winter set in and slowly waned again. In all the town there was no pleasanter topic of conversation. It was "tip-top" — it was the finest dwelling-house far and wide. But it must cost like the deuce — the old Consul would never have spent money so recklessly. Thus the neighbours, the middle-class dwellers in the gabled houses, looking out at the workmen on the scaffoldings, enjoying the sight of the rising walls, and speculating on the date of the carpenters' feast.

It came at length, and was celebrated with due circumstance. Up on the flat-topped roof an old master mason made the festal speech and flung the champagne bottle over his shoulder, while the tremendous wreath, woven of roses, green garlands, and gay-coloured leaves, swayed between standards, heavily in the breeze. The workmen's feast was held at a neighbouring inn, at long tables, with beer, sandwiches, and cigars; and Senator Budden-brook and his wife and his little son on Madame Decho's arm, walked the narrow space between the tables and bowed his thanks at the cheers they gave him.

When they got outside, they put little Hanno back into his carriage, and Thomas and Gerda crossed the road to have another look at the red facade with the white caryatides. They stood before the flower-shop with the narrow door and the poor little show-window, in which only a few pots of bulbs stood on a green glass slab. Iwersen, the proprietor, a blond giant of a man, in woollen jacket, was in the doorway with his wife. She was of a quite different build, slender and delicate, with a dark, southern-looking face. She held a four- or five-year-old boy by one hand, while with the other she was pushing a little carriage back and forth, in which a younger child lay asleep; and she was plainly expecting a third blessing.

Iwersen made a low, awkward bow; his wife, continuing to push the little carriage back and forth, looked calmly and observ-antly at the Frau Senator with her narrow black eyes, as the lady approached them on her husband's arm.

Thomas paused and pointed with his walking-stick at the great garland far above them.

"You did a good job, Iwersen," said he.

"No, Herr Sen'tor. That's the wife's work. She's the one fer these affairs."

"Oh," said the Senator, raised his head with a little jerk, and gave, for a second, a clear friendly look straight into Frau Iwer-sen's face. Then, without adding a word, he courteously waved his hand, and they moved on their way.

CHAPTER VI

ONE Sunday at the beginning of July — Senator Buddenbrook
had moved some four weeks before — Frau Permaneder appeared
at her brother's house toward evening. She crossed the cool
ground floor, paved with flags and decorated with reliefs by
Thorwaldsen, whence there was a door leading into the bureau;
she rang at the vestibule door — it could be opened from the
kitchen by pressing on a rubber bulb — and entered the spacious
lobby, where, at the foot of the steps, stood the bear presented by
Tiburtius and Clara. Here she learned from Anton that the Senator was still at work.

"Very good, Anton," she said. "I will go to him."

Yet she did not go at once into the office, but passed the door
that led into it and stood at the bottom of the splendid staircase,
which as far as the first storey had a cast-iron balustrade, but at
the distance of the second storey became a wide pillared balcony in
white and gold, with a great gilt chandelier hanging down from
the skylight's dizzy height.

"Very elegant," said Frau Permaneder, softly, in a tone of
great satisfaction, gazing up into this spacious magnificence. To
her it meant, quite simply, the power, the brilliance, and the
triumph of the Buddenbrook family. But now it occurred to her
that she was not, in fact, come upon a very cheerful errand, and
she slowly turned away and passed through the door into the
office.

Thomas sat there quite alone, in his place by the window, writing a letter. He glanced up, raised an eyebrow, and put out his
hand to his sister.

"'Evening, Tony. What's the good word?"

"Oh, nothing very good, Tom. Oh, your staircase — it's just
too splendid! Why are you sitting here writing in the dark?"

"It was a pressing letter. Well — nothing very good, eh?
Come into the garden, a little. It is pleasanter out there."

As they crossed the entry, a violin adagio came trillingly down
from the storey above.

"Listen," said Tony, and paused a moment. "Gerda is playing. How heavenly! What a woman! She isn't a woman, she's a fairy. How is Hanno, Tom?"

"Just having his supper, with Jungmann. Too bad he is so slow about walking—"

"Oh, that will come, Tom, that will come. Are you pleased with Ida?"

"Why not?"

They crossed the flags at the back, leaving the kitchen on the right, went through a glass door and up two steps into the lovely, scented flower-garden.

"Well?" the Senator asked.

It was warm and still. The fragrance from the neat beds and borders hung in the evening air, and the fountain, surrounded by tall pale purple iris, sent its stream gently plashing heavenward, where the first stars began to gleam. In the background, an open flight of steps flanked by low obelisks, led up to a gravelled terrace, with an open wooden pavilion, a closed marquee, and some garden chairs. On the left hand was the property wall between them and the next garden; on the right the side wall of the next house was covered with a wooden trellis intended for climbing plants. There were a few currant and gooseberry bushes at the sides of the terrace steps, but there was only one tree, a large, gnarled walnut by the left-hand wall.

"The thing is this," answered Frau Permaneder, with some hesitation, as the brother and sister began to pace the gravel path of the fore part of the garden. "Tiburtius has written—"

"Clara?" questioned Thomas. "Please don't make a long story of it."

"Yes. Tom. She is in bed; she is very bad—the doctor is afraid of tuberculosis—of the brain.—I can hardly speak the words. Here is the letter Tiburtius wrote me, and enclosed another for Mother, which we are to give her when we have prepared her a little. It tells the same story. And there is this second enclosure, to Mother, from Clara herself—written in pencil, in a shaky hand. And Tiburtius wrote that she herself said they were the last she should write, for it seems the sad thing is she makes no effort to live. She was always longing for Heaven—" finished Frau Permaneder, and wiped her eyes.

The Senator walked at her side, his hands behind his back, his head bowed.

"You are so quiet, Tom. But you are right—what is there to say? Just now, too, when Christian lies ill in Hamburg—"

For this was, in fact, the state of things. Christian's "misery" in the left side had increased so much of late that it had become actual pain, severe enough to make him forget all smaller woes. He was quite helpless, and had written to his mother from London that he was coming home, for her to take care of him. He quit his situation in London and started off, but at Hamburg had been obliged to take to his bed; the doctor diagnosed his ailment as rheumatism of the joints, and he had been removed from his hotel to a hospital. Any further journey was for the time impossible. There he lay, and dictated to his attendant letters that betrayed extreme depression.

"Yes," said the Senator, quietly. "It seems as if one thing just followed on another.

She put her arm for an instant across his shoulders.

"But *you* mustn't give way, Tom. This is no time for you to be down-hearted. You need all your courage — "

"Yes, God knows I need it."

"What do you mean, Tom? Tell me, why were you so quiet Thursday afternoon at dinner, if I may ask? "

"Oh — business, my child. I had to sell no very small quantity of grain not very advantageously — or, rather, I had to sell a large quantity very much at a loss."

"Well, that happens, Tom. You sell at a loss to-day, and to-morrow you make it good again. To get discouraged over a thing of that kind — "

"Wrong, Tony," he said, and shook his head. "My courage does not go down to zero because I have a piece of bad luck. It's the other way on. I believe in that, and events show it."

"But what is the matter with it, then? " she asked, surprised and alarmed. "One would think you have enough to make you happy, Tom. Clara is alive, and with God's help she will get better. And as for everything else — here we are, walking about, in your own garden, and it all smells so sweet — and yonder is your house, a dream of a house — Hermann Hagenström's is a dog-kennel beside it! And you have done all that — "

"Yes, it is almost too beautiful, Tony. I'll tell you — it is too new. It jars on me a little — perhaps that is what is the matter with me. It may be responsible for the bad mood that comes over me and spoils everything. I looked forward immensely to all this; but the anticipation was the best part of it — it always is. Everything gets done too slowly — so when it is finished the pleasure is already gone."

"The pleasure is gone, Tom? At your age? "

" A man is as young, or as old, as he feels. And when one gets one's wish too late, or works too hard for it, it comes already weighted with all sorts of small vexatious drawbacks — with all the dust of reality upon it, that one did not reckon with in fancy. It is so irritating — so *irritating* — "

" Oh yes. — But what do you mean by ' as old as you feel '? "

" Why, Tony — it is a mood, certainly. It may pass. But just now I feel older than I am. I have business cares. And at the Directors' meeting of the Buchen Railway yesterday, Consul Hagenström simply talked me down, refuted my contentions, nearly made me appear ridiculous. I feel that could not have happened to me before. It is as though something had begun to slip — as though I haven't the firm grip I had on events. — What is success? It is an inner, and indescribable force, resourceful-ness, power of vision; a consciousness that I am, by my mere ex-istence, exerting pressure on the movement of life about me. It is my belief in the adaptability of life to my own ends. Fortune and success lie with ourselves. We must hold them firmly — deep within us. For as soon as something begins to slip, to relax, to get tired, *within us*, then everything without us will rebel and struggle to withdraw from our influence. One thing follows another, blow after blow — and the man is finished. Often and often, in these days, I have thought of a Turkish proverb; it says, ' When the house is finished, death comes.' It doesn't need to be death. But the decline, the falling-off, the beginning of the end. You know, Tony," he went on, in a still lower voice, putting his arm underneath his sister's, " when Hanno was christened, you said: ' It looks as if quite a new life would dawn for us all! ' I can still hear you say it, and I thought then that you were right, for I was elected Senator, and was fortunate in my business, and this house seemed to spring up out of the ground. But the ' Senator ' and this house are superficial after all. I know, from life and from history, something you have not thought of: often, the outward and visible material signs and symbols of happiness and success only show themselves when the process of decline has already set in. The outer manifestations take time — like the light of that star up there, which may in reality be already quenched, when it looks to us to be shining its brightest."

He ceased to speak, and they walked for a while in silence, while the fountain gently murmured, and a whispering sounded from the top of the walnut tree. Then Frau Permaneder breathed such a heavy sigh that it sounded like a sob.

" How sadly you talk, Tom. You never spoke so sadly before.

But it is good to speak out, and it will help you to put all that kind of thoughts out of your mind."

"Yes, Tony, I must try to do that, I know, as well as I can. And now give me the enclosures from Clara and the Pastor. It will be best, won't it, for me to take over the matter, and speak to-morrow morning with Mother? Poor Mother! If it is really tuberculosis, one may as well give up hope."

CHAPTER VII

" You don't even ask me? You go right over my head? "

" I have done as I had to do."

" You have acted like a distracted person, in a perfectly unreasonable way.

" Reason is not the highest thing on earth."

" Please don't make phrases. The question is one of the most ordinary justice, which you have most astonishingly ignored."

" Let me suggest to you, my son, that you yourself are ignoring the duty and respect which you owe to your mother."

" And I answer you, my dear Mother, by telling you that I have never for a moment forgotten the respect I owe you; but that my attributes as a son became void when I took my father's place as head of the family and of the firm."

" I desire you to be silent, Thomas! "

" No, I will not be silent, so long as you fail to realize the extent of your own weakness and folly."

" I have a right to dispose of my own property as I choose! "

" Within the limits of justice and reason."

" I could never have believed you would have the heart to wound me like this! "

" And I could never have believed that my own Mother would slap me in the face! "

" Tom! Why, Tom! " Frau Permaneder's anguished voice got itself a hearing at last. She sat at the window of the landscape-room, wringing her hands, while her brother paced up and down in a state of high excitement, and the Frau Consul, beside herself with angry grief, sat on the sofa, leaning with one hand on its upholstered arm, while the other struck the table to emphasize her words. All three wore mourning for Clara, who was now no longer of this earth; and all three were pale and excited.

What was going on? Something amazing, something dreadful, something at which the very actors in the scene themselves stood aghast and incredulous. A quarrel, an embittered disagreement between mother and son!

It was a sultry August afternoon. Only ten days after the Senator had gently prepared his mother and given her the letters from Clara and Tiburtius, the blow fell, and he had the harder task of breaking to the old lady the news of death itself. He travelled to Riga for the funeral, and returned with his brother-in-law, who spent a few days with the family of his deceased wife, and also visited Christian in the hospital at Hamburg. And now, two days after the Pastor had departed for home, the Frau Consul, with obvious hesitation, made a certain revelation to her son.

" One hundred and twenty-seven thousand, five hundred marks current," cried he, and shook his clasped hands in front of him. " If it were the dowry, even! If he wanted to keep the eighty thousand marks! Though, considering there's no heir, even that — ! But to promise him Clara's whole inheritance, right over my head! Without saying aye, yes, or no! "

" Thomas, for our blessed Lord's sake, do me some sort of justice, at least. Could I act otherwise? Tell me, could I? She who has been taken from us, and is now with God, she wrote me from her death-bed, with faltering hand, a pencilled letter. 'Mother,' she wrote, ' we shall see each other no more on this earth, and these are, I know, my dying words to you. With my last conscious thoughts, I appeal to you for my husband. God gave us no children; but when you follow me, let what would have been mine if I had lived go to him to enjoy during his lifetime. Mother, it is my last request — my dying prayer. You will not refuse it.' — No, Thomas, I did not refuse it — I could not. I sent a despatch to her, and she died in peace." The Frau Consul wept violently.

" And you never told me a syllable. Everybody conceals things from me, and acts without my authority," repeated the Senator.

" Yes, Thomas, I have kept silent. For I felt I *must* fulfil the last wish of my dying child, and I knew you would have tried to prevent me! "

" Yes! By God, I would have! "

" You would have had no right to, for three of my children would have been on my side."

" I think my opinion has enough weight to balance that of two women and a degenerate fool."

" You speak of your brother and sisters as heartlessly as you do to me."

" Clara was a pious, ignorant woman, Mother. And Tony is a child — and, anyhow, she knew nothing about the affair at all until now — or she might have talked at the wrong time, eh? And Christian? Oh, he got Christian's consent, did Tiburtius! Who would have thought it of him? Do you know now, or don't you grasp it yet — what he is, this ingenious pastor? He is a rogue, and a fortune-hunter! "

" Sons-in-law are always rogues," said Frau Permaneder, in a hollow voice.

" He is a fortune-hunter! What does he do? He travels to Hamburg, and sits down by Christian's bed. He talks to him — ' Yes,' says Christian, ' yes, Tiburtius, God bless you! Have you any idea of the pain I suffer in my left side? ' — Oh, the idiots, the scoundrels! They joined hands against me! " And the Senator, perfectly beside himself, leaned against the wrought-iron fire-screen and pressed his clenched hands to his temples.

This paroxysm of anger was out of proportion to the circumstances. No, it was not the hundred and twenty-seven thousand marks that had brought him to this unprecedented state of rage. It was rather that his irritated senses connected this case with the series of rebuffs and misfortunes which had lately attended him in both public and private business. Nothing went well any more. Nothing turned out as he intended it should. And now, had it come to this, that in the house of his fathers they " went over his head " in matters of the highest importance? That a pastor from Riga could thus bamboozle him behind his back? He could have prevented it if he had only been told! But events had taken their course without him. It was this which he felt could not have happened earlier — would not have dared to happen earlier! Again his faith tottered — his faith in himself, his luck, his power, his future. And it was nothing but his own inward weakness and despair that broke out in this scene before mother and sister.

Frau Permaneder stood up and embraced her brother. " Tom," she said, " do control yourself. Try to be calm. You will make yourself ill. Are things so very bad? Tiburtius doesn't need to live so very long, perhaps, and the money would come back after he dies. And if you want it to, it can be altered — can it not be altered, Mamma? "

The Frau Consul answered only with sobs.

" Oh, no, no," said the Consul, pulling himself together, and making a weak gesture of dissent. " Let it be as it is. Do you think I would carry it into court and sue my own mother, and add a public scandal to the family one? It may go as it is," he concluded, and walked lifelessly to the glass door, where he paused and stood.

" But you need not imagine," he said in a suppressed voice, " that things are going so brilliantly with us. Tony lost eighty thousand marks, and Christian, beside the setting up of fifty thousand that he has run through with, has already had thirty thousand in advance, and will need more, as he is not earning anything, and will have to take a cure at Öynhausen. And now Clara's dowry is permanently lost, and her whole inheritance besides for an indefinite period. And business is poor; it seems to have gone to the devil precisely since the time when I spent more than a hundred thousand marks on my house. No, things are not going well in a family where there are such scenes as this to-day. Let me tell you one thing; if Father were alive, if he were here in this room, he would fold his hands and commend us to the mercy of God."

CHAPTER VIII

Wars and rumours of war, billeting and bustle! Prussian officers tread the parquetry floors of Senator Buddenbrook's bel-étage, kiss the hand of the lady of the house, and frequent the club with Christian, who is back from Öynhausen. In Meng Street Mamsell Severin, Riekchen Severin, the Frau Consul's new companion, helps the maids to drag piles of mattresses into the old garden-house, which is full of soldiers.

Confusion, disorder, and suspense reign. Troops march off through the gate, new ones come in. They overrun the town; they eat, sleep, fill the ears of the citizens with the noise of rolling drums, commands, and trumpet calls — and march off again. Royal princes are fêted, entry follows entry. Then quiet again — and suspense.

In the late autumn and winter the victorious troops return. Again they are billeted in the town for a time, are mustered out and go home — to the great relief of the cheering citizens. Peace comes — the brief peace, heavy with destiny, of the year 1865.

And between two wars, little Johann played. Unconscious and tranquil, with his soft curling hair and voluminous pinafore frocks, he played in the garden by the fountain, or in the little gallery partitioned off for his use by a pillared railing from the vestibule of the second storey — played the plays of his four and a half years — those plays whose meaning and charm no grown person can possibly grasp: which need no more than a few pebbles, or a stick of wood with a dandelion for a helmet, since they command the pure, powerful, glowing, untaught and unintimidated fancy of those blissful years before life touches us, when neither duty nor remorse dares to lay upon us a finger's weight, when we may see, hear, laugh, dream, and feel amazement, when the world yet makes upon us not one single demand; when the impatience of those whom we should like so much to love does not yet torment us for evidence of our ability to succeed in the impending struggle. Ah, only a little while, and that struggle will be upon us — and they will do their best to bend us to their will and cut us to their pattern, to exercise us, to lengthen us, to shorten us, to corrupt us. . . .

Great things happened while little Hanno played. The war flamed up, and its fortunes swayed this way and that, then inclined to the side of the victors; and Hanno Buddenbrook's native city, which had shrewdly stuck with Prussia, looked on not without satisfaction at wealthy Frankfort, which had to pay with her independence for her faith in Austria.

But with the failure in July of a large firm of Frankfort wholesale dealers, immediately before the armistice, the firm of Johann Buddenbrook lost at one fell swoop the round sum of twenty thousand thaler.

PART EIGHT

CHAPTER I

WHEN Herr Hugo Weinschenk — in his buttoned-up frock-coat, with his drooping lower lip and his narrow black moustaches, which grew, in the most masculine way imaginable, right into the corners of his mouth; with both his fists held out in front of him, and making little motions with his elbows at about the height of his waist — when Herr Hugo Weinschenk, now for some time Director of the City Fire Insurance Company, crossed the great entry in Meng Street and passed, with a swinging, pompous stride, from his front to his back office, he gave an impressive impersonation of an energetic and prosperous man.

And Erica Grünlich, on the other hand, was now twenty years old: a tall, blooming girl, fresh-coloured and pretty, full of health and strength. If chance took her up or down the stairs just as Herr Weinschenk passed that way — and chance did this not seldom — the Director took off his top-hat, displaying his short black hair, which was already greying at the temples, minced rather more than ever at the waist of his frockcoat, and greeted the young girl with an admiring glance from his bold and roving brown eye. Whereat Erica ran away, sat down somewhere in a window, and wept for hours out of sheer helpless confusion.

Fräulein Grünlich had grown up under Therese Weichbrodt's care and correction: her thoughts did not fly far afield. She wept over Herr Weinschenk's top-hat, the way he raised his eyebrows at sight of her and let them fall; over his regal bearing and his balancing fists. Her mother, Frau Permaneder, saw further.

Her daughter's future had troubled her for years; for Erica was at a disadvantage compared with other young girls of her age. Frau Permaneder not only did not go into society, she was actually at war with it. The conviction that the " best people " thought slightingly of her because of her two divorces, had become almost a fixed idea; and she read contempt and aversion where probably there was only indifference. Consul Hermann Hagenström, for instance, simple and liberal-minded man that he was, would very likely have been perfectly glad to greet her on the street; his money had only increased his joviality and good nature. But she stared, with her head flung back, past his "goose-liver-paté" face, which, to use her own strong language, she "hated like the plague" — and her look, of course, distinctly forbade him. So Erica grew up outside her uncle's social circle; she frequented no balls, and had small chance of meeting eligible young gentlemen.

Yet it was Frau Antonie's most ardent hope, especially after she herself had "failed in business," as she said, that her daughter might realize her own unfulfilled dream of a happy and advantageous marriage, which should redound to the glory of the family and sink the mother's failure in final oblivion. Tony longed for this beyond everything, and chiefly now for her brother's sake, who had latterly shown so little optimism, as a sign to him that the luck of the family was not yet lost, that they were by no means "at the end of their rope." Her second dowry, the eighteen thousand thaler so magnanimously returned by Herr Permaneder, lay waiting for Erica; and directly Frau Antonie's practiced glance marked the budding tenderness between her daughter and the Director, she began to trouble Heaven with a prayer that Herr Weinschenk might be led to visit them.

He was. He appeared in the first storey, where he was received by the three ladies, mother, daughter, and granddaughter, talked for ten minutes, and promised to return another day for coffee and more leisurely conversation.

This too came to pass, and the acquaintance progressed. The Director was a Silesian by birth. His old father, in fact, still lived in Silesia; but the family seemed not to come into consideration, Hugo being, evidently, a "self-made man." He had the self-consciousness of such men: a not quite native, rather insecure, mistrustful, exaggerated air. His grammar was not perfect, and his conversation was distinctly clumsy. And his countrified frock coat had shiny spots; his cuffs, with large jet cuff-buttons, were not quite fresh; and the nail on the middle finger of his left hand had been crushed in some accident, and was shrivelled and blackened. The impression, on the whole, was rather unpleasing; yet it did not prevent Hugo Weinschenk from being a highly worthy young man, industrious and energetic, with a yearly salary of twelve thousand marks current; nor from being, in Erica Grünlich's eyes, handsome to boot.

Frau Permaneder quickly looked him over and summed him up. She talked freely with her mother and the Senator. It was clear to her that here was a case of two interests meeting and complementing each other. Director Weinschenk was, like Erica, devoid of every social connection: the two were thus, in a manner, marked out for each other — it was plainly the hand of God himself. If the Director, who was nearing the forties, his hair already sprinkled with grey, desired to found a family appropriate to his station and connections, here was an opening for him into one of the best circles in town, calculated to advance him in his calling and consolidate his position. As for Erica's welfare, Frau Permaneder could feel confident that at least her own lot would be out of the question. Herr Weinschenk had not the faintest resemblance to Herr Permaneder; and he was differentiated from Bendix Grünlich by his position as an old-established official with a fixed salary — which, of course, did not preclude a further career.

In a word, much good will was shown on both sides. Herr Weinschenk's visits followed each other in quick succession, and by January — January of the year 1867 — he permitted himself to make a brief and manly offer for Erica Grünlich's hand.

From now on he belonged to the family. He came on children's day, and was received civilly by the relatives of his betrothed. He must soon have seen that he did not fit very well; but he concealed the fact under an increased assurance of manner, while the Frau Consul, Uncle Justus, and the Senator — though hardly the Broad Street Buddenbrooks — practised a tactful complaisance toward the socially awkward, hard-working official.

And tact was needed. For pauses would come at the family table, when Director Weinschenk tried to make conversation by asking if " orange marmalade " was a " pudden "; when he gave out the opinion that Romeo and Juliet was a piece by Schiller; when his manner with Erica's cheek or arm became too roguish. He uttered his views frankly and cheerfully, rubbing his hands like a man whose mind is free from care, and leaning back sidewise against the arm of his chair. Some one always needed to fill in the pause by a sprightly or diverting remark.

He got on best with the Senator, who knew how to steer a safe course between politics and business. His relations with Gerda Buddenbrook were hopeless. This lady's personality put him off to such a degree that he was incapable of finding anything to talk about with her for two minutes on end. The fact that she played the violin made a strong impression upon him; and he finally confined himself, on each Thursday afternoon encounter, to the jovial enquiry, " Well, how's the fiddle? " After the third time, however, the Frau Senator refrained from reply.

Christian, on the other hand, used to look at his new relative down his nose, and the next day imitate him and his conversation

with full details. The second son of the deceased Consul Buddenbrook had been relieved of his rheumatism in Öynhausen; but a
certain stiffness of the joints was left, as well as the periodic misery in the left side, where all the nerves were too short, and sundry
other ills to which he was heir, as difficulty in breathing and swallowing, irregularity of the heart action, and a tendency to paralysis — or at least to a fear of it. He did not look like a man at the
end of the thirties. His head was entirely bald except for vestiges
of reddish hair at the back of the neck and on the temples; and
his small round roving eyes lay deeper than ever in their sockets.
And his great bony nose and his lean, sallow cheeks were startlingly
prominent above his heavy drooping red moustaches. His trousers,
of beautiful and lasting English stuff, flapped about his crooked
emaciated legs.

He had come back once more to his mother's house, and had
a room on the corridor of the first storey. But he spent more of
his time at the club than in Meng Street, for life there was not made
any too pleasant for him. Riekchen Severin, Ida Jungmann's successor, who now reigned over the Frau Consul's household and
managed the servants, had a peasant's instinct for hard facts. She
was a thick-set country-bred creature, with coarse lips and fat red
cheeks. She perceived directly that it was not worth while to put
herself out for this idle story-teller, who was silly and ill by turns,
whom his brother, the Senator — the real head of the family — ignored with lifted eyebrows. So she quite calmly neglected Christian's wants. " Gracious, Herr Buddenbrook," she would say,
" you needn't think as I've got time for the likes of you! " Christian would look at her with his nose all wrinkled up, as if to say
" Aren't you ashamed of yourself? " and go his stiff-kneed way.

" Do you think," he said to Tony, " that I have a candle to go
to bed by? Very seldom. I generally take a match." The sum his
mother could allow him was small. " Hard times," he would say.
" Yes, things were different once. Why, what do you suppose?
Sometimes I've had to borrow money for tooth-powder! "

" Christian! " cried Frau Permaneder. " How undignified!
And going to bed with a match! " She was shocked and outraged
in her deepest sensibilities — but that did not mend matters.

The tooth-powder money Christian borrowed from his old
friend Andreas Gieseke, Doctor of Civil and Criminal Jurisprudence. He was fortunate in this friendship, and it did him credit;
for Dr. Gieseke, though as much of a rake as Christian, knew how
to keep his dignity. He had been elected Senator the preceding
winter, for Dr. Överdieck had sunk gently to his long rest, and Dr.

Langhals sat in his place. His elevation did not affect Andreas Gieseke's mode of life. Since his marriage with Fräulein Huneus, he had acquired a spacious house in the centre of the town; but as everybody knew, he also owned a certain comfortable little vine-clad villa in the suburb of St. Gertrude, which was charmingly furnished, and occupied quite alone by a still young and uncommonly pretty person of unknown origin. Above the house-door, in ornamental gilt lettering, was the word "Quisisana," by which name the retired little dwelling was known throughout the town, where they pronounced it with a very soft *s* and a very broad *a*. Christian Buddenbrook, as Senator Gieseke's best friend, had obtained entry into Quisisana, and been successful there, as formerly with Aline Puvogel in Hamburg, and on other occasions in London, Valparaiso, and sundry other parts of the world. He "told a few stories," and was "a little friendly"; and now he visited the little vine-clad house on the same footing as Senator Gieseke himself. Whether this happened with the latter's knowledge and consent, is of course doubtful. What is certain is, that Christian found there, without money and without price, the same friendly relaxation as Dr. Gieseke, who, however, had to pay for the same with his wife's money.

A short time after the betrothal of Hugo Weinschenk and Erica Grünlich, the Director proposed to his relative that he should enter the Insurance office; and Christian actually worked for two weeks in the service of the Company. But the misery in his side began to get worse, and his other, indefinable ills as well; and the Director proved to be a domineering superior, who did not hesitate, on the occasion of a little misunderstanding, to call his relative a booby. So Christian felt constrained to leave this post too.

Madame Permaneder, at this period of the family's history, was in such a joyful mood that her happiness found vent in shrewd observations about life: how, when all was said and done, it had its good side. Truly, she bloomed anew in these weeks; and their invigorating activity, the manifold plans, the search for suitable quarters, and the feverish preoccupation with furnishings brought back with such force the memories of her first betrothal that she could not but feel young again — young and boundlessly hopeful. Much of the graceful high spirits of girlhood returned to her ways, and movements; indeed, she profaned the mood of one entire Jerusalem evening by such uncontrollable hilarity that even Lea Gerhardt let the book of her ancestor fall in her lap and stared about the room with the great, innocent, startled eyes of the deaf.

Erica was not to be parted from her mother. The Director

agreed — nay, it was even his wish, — that Frau Antonie should live
with the Weinschenks, at least at first, and help the inexperienced
Erica with her housekeeping. And it was precisely this which
called up in her the most priceless feeling, as though no Bendix
Grünlich or Alois Permaneder had ever existed, and all the trials,
disappointments, and sufferings of her life were as nothing, and she
might begin anew and with fresh hopes. She bade Erica be grateful to God, who bestowed upon her the one man of her desire,
whereas the mother had been obliged to offer up her first and
dearest choice on the altar of duty and reason. It was Erica's name
which, with a hand trembling with joy, she inscribed in the family
book next the Director's. But she, Tony Buddenbrook, was the
real bride. It was she who might once more ransack furniture and
upholstery shops and test hangings and carpets with a practised
hand; she who once more found and rented a truly "elegant"
apartment. It was she who was once more to leave the pious and
roomy parental mansion and cease to be a divorced wife; she who
might once more lift her head and begin a new life, calculated to
arouse general remark and enhance the prestige of the family.
Even — was it a dream? — dressing-gowns appeared upon the horizon: two dressing-gowns, for Erica and herself, of soft, woven
stuff, with close rows of velvet trimming from neck to hem!

The weeks fled by — the last weeks of Erica Grünlich's maiden-
hood. The young pair had made calls in only a few houses; for the
Director, a serious and preoccupied man, with no social experience,
intended to devote what leisure he had to intimate domesticity.
There was a betrothal dinner in the great salon of the house in
Fishers' Lane, at which, besides Thomas and Gerda, there were
present the bridal pair and Henriette, Friederike and Pfiffi Buddenbrook, and some close friends of the Senator; and the Director
continually pinched the bare shoulders of his fiancée, rather to the
disgust of the other guests. And the wedding day drew near.

The marriage was solemnized in the columned hall, as on that
other occasion when it was Frau Grünlich who wore the myrtle.
Frau Stuht from Bell-Founders' Street, the same who moved in
the best circles, helped to arrange the folds of the bride's white
satin gown and pin on the decorations. The Senator gave away
the bride, supported by Christian's friend Senator Gieseke, and
two school friends of Erica's acted as bridesmaids. Director Hugo
Weinschenk looked imposing and manly, and only trod once on
Erica's flowing veil on the way to the improvised altar. Pastor
Pringsheim held his hands clasped beneath his chin, and performed

the service with his accustomed air of sweet exaltation; and everything went off with dignity and according to rule. When the rings
were exchanged, and the deep and the treble " yes " sounded in the
hush (both a trifle husky), Frau Permaneder, overpowered by
the past, the present, and the future, burst into audible sobs: just
the unthinking, unembarrassed tears of her childhood. And the
sisters Buddenbrook — Pfiffi, in honour of the day, was wearing a
gold chain to her pince-nez — smiled a little sourly, as always on
such occasions. But Mademoiselle Weichbrodt, who had grown
shorter with the lengthening years, and had the oval brooch with
the miniature of her mother around her thin neck — Sesemi said,
with the disproportionate solemnity which hides deep emotion:
" Be happy, you good che-ild! "

Followed a banquet, as solemn as solid, beneath the eyes of the
white Olympians, looking down composedly from their blue background. As it drew toward its end, the newly wedded pair disappeared, to begin their wedding journey, which was to include visits to several large cities. All this was at the middle of April; and
in the next two weeks, Frau Permaneder, assisted by the upholsterer Jacobs, accomplished one of her masterpieces: she moved
into and settled the spacious first storey which she had rented in a
house halfway down Baker Alley. There, in a bower of flowers,
she welcomed the married pair on their return.

And thus began Tony Buddenbrook's third marriage.

Yes, this was really the right way to put it. The Senator himself, one Thursday afternoon when the Weinschenks were not
present, had called it that, and Frau Permaneder quite relished the
joke. All the cares of the new household fell upon her, but she
reaped her reward in pride and pleasure. One day she happened
to meet on the street Frau Consul Julchen Möllendorpf, born
Hagenström, into whose face she looked with a challenging, triumphant glance; it actually dawned upon Frau Möllendorpf that
she had better speak first, and she did. Tony waxed so important
in her pride and joy, when she showed off the new house to visiting
relatives, that little Erica, beside her, seemed but a guest herself.

Frau Antonie displayed the house to their guests, the train of
her morning gown dragging behind her, her shoulders up and
her head thrown back, carrying on her arm the key-basket with
its bow of satin ribbon. She displayed the furniture, the hangings,
the translucent porcelain, the gleaming silver, the large oil paintings. These last had been purchased by the Director, and were
nearly all still-lifes of edibles or nude figures of women, for such

was Hugo Weinschenk's taste. Tony's every movement seemed to say: "See, I have managed all this for the third time in my life! It is almost as fine as Grünlich's, and much finer than Permaneder's!"

The old Frau Consul came, in a black and grey striped silk, giving out a discreet odour of patchouli. She surveyed everything with her pale, calm eyes and, without any loud expressions of admiration, professed herself pleased with the effect. The Senator came, with his wife and child; he and Gerda hugely enjoyed Tony's blissful self-satisfaction, and with difficulty prevented her from killing her adored little Johann with currant bread and port wine. The Misses Buddenbrook came, and were unanimously of opinion that it was all very fine — of course, being modest people themselves, they would not care to live in it. Poor, lean, grey, patient, hungry Clothilde came, submitted to the usual teasing, and drank four cups of coffee, praising everything the while, in her usual friendly drawl. Even Christian appeared now and then, when there was nobody at the club, drank a little glass of Benedictine, and talked about a project he had of opening an agency for champagne and brandy. He knew the business, and it was a light, agreeable job, in which a man could be his own master, write now and then in a note-book, and make thirty thaler by turning over his hand. Then he borrowed a little money from Frau Permaneder to buy a bouquet for the leading lady at the theatre; came, by God knows what train of thought, to Maria and the depravity in London; and then lighted upon the story of the mangy dog that travelled all the way from Valparaiso to San Francisco in a handsatchel. By this time he was in full swing, and narrated with such gusto, verve, and irresistible drollery that he would have held a large audience spell-bound.

He narrated like one inspired; he possessed the gift of tongues. He narrated in English, Spanish, low German, and Hamburgese; he depicted stabbing affrays in Chile and pickpocketings in Whitechapel. He drew upon his repertory of comic songs, and half sung, half recited, with incomparable pantomime and highly suggestive gesture:

> "I sauntered out one day,
> In an idle sort o' way,
> And chanced to see a maid, ahead o' me.
> She'd such a charmin' air,
> Her — behind — was French, I'd swear,
> And she wore her 'at as rakish as could be.
> I says, 'My pretty dear,
> Since you an' I are 'ere,

Perhaps you'd take me arm and walk along? '
   She turned her pretty 'ead,
   And looked — at me — and said,
'You just get on, my lad, and hold your tongue! ' "

From this he went off on an account of a performance at the
Renz Circus, in Hamburg, and reproduced a turn by a troupe of
English vaudeville artists, in such a way that you felt you were
actually present. There was the usual hubbub behind the curtain,
shouts of " Open the door, will you! " quarrels with the ring-
master; and then, in a broad, lugubrious English-German, a whole
string of stories: the one about the man who swallowed a mouse in
his sleep, and went to the vet., who advised him to swallow a cat;
and the one about " my grandmother — lively old girl, she was " —
who, on her way to the railway station, encounters all sorts of adventures, ending with the train pulling out of the station in front
of the nose of the " lively old girl." And then Christian broke off
with a triumphant " Orchestra! " and made as if he had just waked
up and was very surprised that no music was forthcoming.

But, quite suddenly, he stopped. His face changed, his motions
relaxed. His little deep round eyes began to stray moodily about;
he rubbed his left side with his hand, and seemed to be listening to
uncanny sounds within himself. He drank another glass of liqueur,
which relieved him a little. Then he tried to tell another story, but
broke down in a fit of depression.

Frau Permaneder, who in these days was uncommonly prone
to laugh and had enjoyed the performance hugely, accompanied
her brother to the door, in rather a prankish mood. " Adieu,
Herr Agent," said she. " Minnesinger — Ninnysinger! Old goose!
Come again soon! " She laughed full-throatedly behind him and
went back into her house.

But Christian did not mind. He did not even hear her, so deep
was he in thought. " Well," he said to himself, " I'll go over to
Quisisana for a bit." His hat a little awry, leaning on his stick with
the nun's bust for a handle, he went slowly and stiffly down the
steps.

CHAPTER II

In the spring of 1868, one evening towards ten o'clock, Frau Permaneder entered the first story of her brother's house. Senator Buddenbrook sat alone in the living-room, which was done in olive-green rep, with a large round centre-table and a great gas-lamp hanging down over it from the ceiling. He had the *Berlin Financial Gazette* spread out in front of him on the table, and was reading it, with a cigarette held between the first and second fingers of his left hand, and a gold pince-nez on his nose — he had now for some time been obliged to use glasses for reading. He heard his sister's footsteps as she passed through the dining-room, took off his glasses, and peered into the darkness until Tony appeared between the portières and in the circle of light from the lamp.

"Oh, it is you? How are you? Back from Pöppenrade? How are your friends? "

"Evening, Tom. Thanks, Armgard is very well. Are you here alone? "

"Yes; I'm glad you have come. I ate my dinner all alone to-night like the Pope. I don't count Mamsell Jungmann, because she is always popping up to look after Hanno. Gerda is at the Casino. Christian fetched her, to hear Tamayo play the violin."

"Bless and save us — as Mother says. — Yes, I've noticed lately that Gerda and Christian get on quite well together."

"Yes, I have too. Since he came back for good, she seems to have taken to him. She sits and listens to him when he tells about his troubles — dear me, I suppose he entertains her. She said to me lately: 'There is nothing of the burgher about Christian, Thomas — he is even less of a burgher than you are, yourself! "

"Burgher, Tom? What did she mean? Why, it seems to me there is no better burgher on top of the earth than you are! "

"Oh, well — she didn't mean it just in that sense. Take off your things and sit down a while, my child. How splendid you look! The country air did you good."

"I'm in very good form," she said, as she took off her mantle and the hood with lilac silk ribbons and sat down with dignity in an easy-chair by the table. "My sleep and my digestion both improved very much in this short time. The fresh milk, and the farm sausages and hams — one thrives like the cattle and the crops. And the honey, Tom, I have always considered honey one of the very best of foods. A pure nature product — one knows just what one's eating. Yes, it was really very sweet of Armgard to remember an old boarding-school friendship and send me the invitation. Herr von Maiboom was very polite, too. They urged me to stay a couple of weeks longer, but I know Erica is rather helpless without me, especially now, with little Elisabeth — "

"How is the child?"

"Doing nicely, Tom. She is really not bad at all, for four months, even if Henriette and Friederike and Pfiffi did say she wouldn't live."

"And Weinschenk? How does he like being a father? I never see him except on Thursdays — "

"Oh, he is just the same. You know he is a very good, hardworking man, and in a way a model husband; he never stops in anywhere, but comes straight home from the office and spends all his free time with us. But — you see, Tom — we can speak quite openly, just between ourselves — he requires Erica to be always lively, always laughing and talking, because when he comes home tired and worried from the office, he needs cheering up, and his wife must amuse him and divert him."

"Idiot!" murmured the Senator.

"What? Well, the bad thing about it is, that Erica is a little bit inclined to be melancholy. She must get it from me, Tom. Sometimes she is very serious and quiet and thoughtful; and then he scolds and grumbles and complains, and really, to tell the truth, is not at all sympathetic. You can't help seeing that he is a man of no family, and never enjoyed what one would call a refined bringing-up. To be quite frank — a few days before I went to Pöppenrade, he threw the lid of the soup-tureen on the floor and broke it, because the soup was too salt."

"How charming!"

"Oh, no, it wasn't, not at all! But we must not judge. God knows, we are all weak creatures — and a good, capable, industrious man like that — Heaven forbid! No, Tom, a rough shell with a sound kernel inside is not the worst thing in this life. I've just come from something far sadder than that, I can tell you! Armgard wept bitterly, when she was alone with me — "

"You don't say! Is Herr von Maiboom — ?"

"Yes, Tom — that is what I wanted to tell you. We sit here

visiting, but I really came to-night on a serious and important errand."

" Well, what is the trouble with Herr von Maiboom? "

" He is a very charming man, Ralf von Maiboom, Thomas; but he is very wild — a hail-fellow-well-met with everybody. He gambles in Rostock, and he gambles in Warnemünde, and his debts are like the sands of the sea. Nobody could believe it, just living a couple of weeks at Pöppenrade. The house is lovely, everything looks flourishing, there is milk and sausage and ham and all that, in great abundance. So it is hard to measure the actual situation. But their affairs are in frightful disorder — Armgard confessed it to me, with heart-breaking sobs."

" Very sad."

" You may well say so. But, as I had already suspected, it turned out that I was not invited over there just for the sake of my *beaux yeux*."

" How so? "

" I will tell you, Tom. Herr von Maiboom needs a large sum of money immediately. He knew the old friendship between his wife and me, and he knew that I am your sister. So, in his extremity, he put his wife up to it, and she put me up to it. — You understand? "

The Senator passed his finger-tips across his hair and screwed up his face a little.

" I think so," he said. " Your serious and important business evidently concerns an advance on the Pöppenrade harvest — if I am not mistaken. But you have come to the wrong man, I think, you and your friends. In the first place, I have never done any business with Herr von Maiboom, and this would be a rather strange way to begin. In the second place — though, in the past, Grandfather, Father, and I myself have made advances on occasion to the landed gentry, it was always when they offered a certain security, either personally or through their connections. But to judge from the way you have just characterized Herr von Maiboom and his prospects, I should say there can be no security in his case."

" You are mistaken, Tom. I have let you have your say, but you are mistaken. It is not a question of an advance, at all. Maiboom has to have thirty-five thousand marks current — "

" Heavens and earth! "

" — five-and-thirty thousand marks current, to be paid within two weeks. The knife is at his throat — to be plain, he has to sell at once, immediately."

" In the blade — oh, the poor chap! " The Senator shook his

head as he stood, playing with his pince-nez on the tablecloth.
" That is a rather unheard-of thing for our sort of business," he
went on. " I have heard of such things, mostly in Hesse, where a
few of the landed gentry are in the hands of the Jews. Who knows
what sort of cut-throat it is that has poor Herr von Maiboom in
his clutches? "

" Jews? Cut-throats? " cried Frau Permaneder, astonished beyond measure. " But it's *you* we are talking about, Tom! "

Thomas Buddenbrook suddenly threw down his pince-nez on
the table so that it slid along on top of the newspaper, and turned
toward his sister with a jerk.

" Me? " he said, but only with his lips, for he made no sound.
Then he added aloud: " Go to bed, Tony. You are tired out."

" Why, Tom, that is what Ida Jungmann used to say to us, when
we were just beginning to have a good time. But I assure you I was
never wider awake in my life than now, coming over here in the
dead of night to make Ármgard's offer to you — or rather, indi-
rectly, Ralf von Maiboom's — "

" And I will forgive you for making a proposal which is the
product of your naïveté and the Maibooms' helplessness."

" Helplessness? Naïveté, Thomas? I don't understand you — I
am very far from understanding you. You are offered an opportunity to do a good deed, and at the same time the best stroke of
business you ever did in your life — "

" Oh, my darling child, you are talking the sheerest nonsense,"
cried the Senator, throwing himself back impatiently in his chair.
" I beg your pardon, but you make me angry with your ridiculous
innocence. Can't you understand that you are asking me to do
something discreditable, to engage in underhand manœuvres?
Why should I go fishing in troubled waters? Why should I fleece
this poor land-owner? Why should I take advantage of his necessity to do him out of a year's harvest at a usurious profit to myself? "

" Oh, is that the way you look at it! " said Frau Permaneder,
quite taken aback and thoughtful. But she recovered in a moment
and went on: " But it is not at all necessary to look at it like that,
Tom. How are you forcing him, when it is he who comes to you?
He needs the money, and would like the matter arranged in a
friendly way, and under the rose. That is why he traced out the
connection between us, and invited me to visit."

" In short, he has made a mistake in his calculations about me
and the character of my firm. I have my own traditions. We have
been in business a hundred years without touching that sort of

transaction, and I have no idea of beginning at this late day."

"Certainly, Tom, you have your traditions, and nobody respects them more than I do. And I know Father would not have done it — God forbid! Who says he would? But, silly as I am, I know enough to know that you are quite a different sort of man from Father, and since you took over the business it has been different from what it was before. That is because you were young and had enterprise and brains. But lately I am afraid you have let yourself get discouraged by this or that piece of bad luck. And if you are no longer having the same success you once did, it is because you have been too cautious and conscientious, and let slip your chances for good *coups* when you had them — "

"Oh, my dear child, stop, please; you irritate me! " said the Senator sharply, and turned away. "Let us change the subject."

"Yes, you are vexed, Tom, I can see it. You were from the beginning, and I have kept on, on purpose, to show you you are wrong to feel yourself insulted. But I know the real reason why you are vexed: it is because you are not so firmly decided not to touch the business. I know I am silly; but I have noticed about myself — and about other people too — that we are most likely to get angry and excited in our opposition to some idea when we ourselves are not quite certain of our own position, and are inwardly tempted to take the other side."

"Very fine," said the Senator, bit his cigarette-holder, and was silent.

"Fine? No, it's very simple — one of the simplest things life has taught me. But let it go, Tom. I won't urge you. Don't imagine that I think I could persuade you — I know I don't know enough. I'm only a silly female. It's a pity. Well, never mind. — It interested me very much. On the one hand I was shocked and upset about the Maibooms, but on the other I was pleased for you. I said to myself: 'Tom has been going about lately feeling very down in the mouth. He used to complain, but now he does not even complain any more. He has been losing money, and times are poor — and all that just now, when God has been good to me, and I am feeling happier than I have for a long time.' So I thought, 'This would be something for him: a stroke of luck, a good *coup*. It would offset a good deal of misfortune, and show people that luck is still on the side of the firm of Johann Buddenbrook.' And if you had undertaken it, I should have been so proud to have been the means — for you know it has always been my dream and my one desire, to be of some good to the family name. — Well, never mind. It is settled now. What I feel vexed about is that Maibo

has to sell, in any case, and if he looks around in the town here, he will find a purchaser — and it will be that rascal Hermann Hagen-ström! "

" Oh, yes — he probably would not refuse it," the Senator said bitterly; and Frau Permaneder answered, three times, one after the other: " You see, you see, you see! "

Thomas Buddenbrook suddenly began to shake his head and laugh angrily.

" We are silly. We sit here and work ourselves up — at least, you do — over something that is neither here nor there. So far as I know, I have not even asked what the thing is about — what Herr von Maiboom actually has to sell. I do not know Pöppenrade."

" Oh, you would have had to go there," she said eagerly. " It's not far from here to Rostock — and from there it is no distance at all. And as for what he has to sell — Pöppenrade is a large estate, I know for a fact that it grows more than a thousand sacks of wheat. But I don't know details. About rye, oats, or barley, there might be five hundred sacks of them, more or less. Everything is of the best, I can say that. But I can't give you any figures, I am such a goose, Tom. You would have to go over."

A pause ensued.

" No, it is not worth wasting words over," the Senator said decidedly. He folded his pince-nez and put it into his pocket, buttoned up his coat, and began to walk up and down the room with firm and rapid strides, which studiously betrayed no sign that he was giving the subject any further consideration.

He paused by the table and turned toward his sister, drumming lightly on the surface with his bent forefinger as he said: " I'll tell you a little story, my dear Tony, which will illustrate my attitude toward this affair. I know your weakness for the nobility, and the Mecklenburg nobility in particular — please don't mind if one of these gentry gets rapped a bit. You know, there is now and then one among them who doesn't treat the merchant classes with any great respect, though perfectly aware that he can't do without them. Such a man is too much inclined to lay stress on the superiority — to a certain extent undeniable — of the producer over the middleman. In short, he sometimes acts as if the merchant were like a peddling Jew to whom one sells old clothes, quite conscious that one is being overreached. I flatter myself that in my dealings with these gentry I have not usually made the impression of a morally inferior exploiter; to tell the truth, the boot has sometimes been on the other foot — I've run across men who were far less scrupulous than I am! But in one case, it only needed a single bold stroke to bring me into social relations. The man was the lord of Gross-Poggendorf, of whom you have surely heard. I had considerable dealings with him some while back: Count Strelitz, a very smart-appearing man, with a square eye-glass (I could never make out why he did not cut himself), patent-leather top-boots, and a riding-whip with a gold handle. He had a way of looking down at me from a great height, with his eyes half shut and his mouth half open. My first visit to him was very telling. We had had some correspondence. I drove over, and was ushered by a servant into the study, where Count Strelitz was sitting at his writing-table. He returns my bow, half gets up, finishes the last lines of a letter; then he turns to me and begins to talk business, looking over the top of my head. I lean on the sofa-table, cross my arms and my legs, and enjoy myself. I stand five minutes talking. After another five minutes, I sit down on the table and swing my leg. We get on with our business, and at the end of fifteen minutes he says to me, very graciously, 'won't you sit down?' 'Beg pardon?' I say. 'Oh, don't mention it — I've been sitting for some time!'"

"Did you say that? Really?" cried Frau Permaneder, enchanted. She had straightway forgotten all that had gone before, and lived for the moment entirely in the anecdote.

"'I've been sitting for some time' — oh, that is too good!"

"Well, and I assure you that the Count altered his tune at once. He shook hands when I came, and asked me to sit down — in the course of time we became very friendly. But I have told you this in order to ask you if you think I should have the right, or the courage, or the inner self-confidence to behave in the same way to Herr von Maiboom if, when we met to discuss the bargain, he were to forget to offer me a chair?"

Frau Permaneder was silent. "Good," she said then, and got up. "You may be right; and, as I said, I'm not going to press you. You know what you must do and what leave undone, and that's an end of it. If you only feel that I spoke in good part — you do, don't you? All right. Good night, Tom. Or — no, wait — I must go and say 'How do you do' to the good Ida and give Hanno a little kiss. I'll look in again on my way out." With that she went.

CHAPTER III

She mounted the stairs to the second storey, left the little balcony on her right, went along the white-and-gold balustrade and through an ante-chamber, the door of which stood open on the corridor, and from which a second exit to the left led into the Senator's dressing-room. Here she softly turned the handle of the door opposite and went in.

It was an unusually large chamber, the windows of which were draped with flowered curtains. The walls were rather bare: aside from a large black-framed engraving above Ida's bed, representing Giacomo Meyerbeer surrounded by the characters in his operas, there was nothing but a few English coloured prints of children with yellow hair and little red frocks, pinned to the window hangings. Ida Jungmann sat at the large extension-table in the middle of the room, darning Hanno's stockings. The faithful Prussian was now at the beginning of the fifties. She had begun early to grow grey, but her hair had never become quite white, having remained a mixture of black and grey; her erect bony figure was as sturdy, and her brown eyes as bright, clear, and unwearied as twenty years ago.

"Well, Ida, you good soul," said Frau Permaneder, in a low but lively voice, for her brother's little story had put her in good spirits, " and how are you, you old stand-by, you? "

"What's that, Tony — stand-by, is it? And how do you come to be here so late? "

" I've been with my brother — on pressing business. Unfortunately, it didn't turn out. — Is he asleep? " she asked, and gestured with her chin toward the little bed on the left wall, its head close to the door that led into the parents' sleeping chamber.

"Sh-h! " said Ida. "Yes, he is asleep." Frau Permaneder went on her tip-toes toward the little bed, cautiously raised the curtain, and bent to look down at her sleeping nephew's face.

The small Johann Buddenbrook lay on his back, his little face, in its frame of long light-brown hair, turned toward the room. He was breathing softly but audibly into the pillow. Only the fingers

showed beneath the too long, too wide sleeves of his nightgown:
one of his hands lay on his breast, the other on the coverlet, with
the bent fingers jerking slightly now and then. The half-parted
lips moved a little too, as if forming words. From time to time a
pained expression mounted over the little face, beginning with a
trembling of the chin, making the lips and the delicate nostrils
quiver and the muscles of the narrow forehead contract. The long
dark eyelashes did not hide the blue shadows that lay in the corners
of the eyes.

" He is dreaming," said Frau Permaneder, moved.

She bent over the child and gently kissed his slumbering cheek;
then she composed the curtains and went back to the table, where
Ida, in the golden light from the lamp, drew a fresh stocking over
her darning-ball, looked at the hole, and began to fill it in.

" You are darning, Ida — funny, I can't imagine you doing anything else."

" Yes, yes, Tony. The boy tears everything, now he has begun
to go to school."

" But he is such a quiet, gentle child."

" Ye-s, he is. But even so — "

" Does he like going to school? "

" Oh, no-o, Tony. He would far rather have gone on here with
me. And I should have liked it better too. The masters haven't
known him since he was a baby, the way I have — they don't know
how to take him, when they are teaching him. It is often hard for
him to pay attention, and he gets tired so easily — "

" Poor darling! Have they whipped him yet? "

" No, indeed. Sakes alive, how could they have the heart, if the
boy once looked at them — ? "

" How was it the first time he went? Did he cry? "

" Yes, indeed, he did. He cries so easily — not loud, but sort of
to himself. And he held your brother by the coat and begged to
be allowed to stop at home — "

" Oh, my brother took him, did he? — Yes, that is a hard moment, Ida. I remember it like yesterday. I *howled*. I do assure
you. I howled like a chained-up dog; I felt dreadfully. And why?
Because I had had such a good time at home. I noticed at once that
all the children from the nice houses wept, and the others not at all
— they just stared and grinned at us. — Goodness, what is the matter with him, Ida? "

She turned in alarm toward the little bed, where a cry had interrupted her chatter. It was a frightened cry, and it repeated itself
in an even more anguished tone the next minute; and then three,

four, five times more, one after another. "Oh, oh, *oh!*" It became a loud, desperate protest against something which he saw or
which was happening to him. The next moment little Johann sat
upright in bed, stammering incomprehensibly, and staring with
wide-open, strange golden-brown eyes into a world which he, and
he alone, could see.

"That's nothing," said Ida. "It is the *pavor*. It is sometimes
much worse than that." She put her work down calmly and
crossed the room, with her long heavy stride, to Hanno's bed.
She spoke to him in a low, quieting voice, laid him down, and
covered him again.

"Oh, I see — the *pavor*," repeated Frau Permaneder. "What
will he do now? Will he wake up?"

But Hanno did not waken at all, though his eyes were wide and
staring, and his lips still moved.

> "'In my — little — garden — go —,'"

said Hanno, mumblingly,

> "'All — my — onions — water —'"

"He is saying his piece," explained Ida Jungmann, shaking her
head. "There, there, little darling — go to sleep now."

> "'Little man stands — stands there —
> He begins — to — sneeze —'"

He sighed. Suddenly his face changed, his eyes half closed; he
moved his head back and forth on the pillow and said in a low,
plaintive sing-song:

> "'The moon it shines,
> The baby cries,
> The clock strikes twelve,
> God help all suff'ring folk to close their eyes.'"

But with the words came so deep a sob that tears rolled out from
under his lashes and down his cheeks and wakened him. He put
his arms around Ida, looked about him with tear-wet eyes, murmured something in a satisfied tone about "Aunt Tony," turned
himself a little in his bed, and then went quietly off to sleep.

"How very strange," said Frau Permaneder, as Ida sat down at
the table once more. "What was all that?"

"They are in his reader," answered Fraulein Jungmann. "It
says underneath 'The Boys' Magic Horn.' They are all rather
queer. He has been having to learn them, and he talks a great deal

about that one with the little man. Do you know it? It is really
rather frightening. It is a little dwarf that gets into everything:
eats up the broth and breaks the pot, steals the wood, stops the
spinning-wheel, teases everybody — and then, at the end, he asks
to be prayed for! It touched the child very much. He has thought
about it day in and day out; and two or three times he said: 'You
know, Ida, he doesn't do that to be wicked, but only because he is
unhappy, and it only makes him more unhappy still. . . . But if
one prays for him, then he does not need to do it any more!' Even
to-night, when his Mama kissed him good night before she went
to the concert, he asked her to 'pray for the little man.'"

"And did he pray too?"

"Not aloud, but probably to himself. — He hasn't said much
about the other poem — it is called 'The Nursery Clock' — he has
only wept. He weeps so easy, poor little lad, and it is so hard for
him to stop."

"But what is there so sad about it?"

"How do I know? He has never been able to say any more
than the beginning of it, the part that makes him cry in his sleep.
And that about the waggoner, who gets up at three from his bed
of straw — that always made him weep too."

Frau Permaneder laughed emotionally, and then looked serious.

"I'll tell you, Ida, it's no good. It isn't good for him to feel
everything so much. 'The waggoner gets up at three from his
bed of straw' — why, of course he does! That's why he is a waggoner. I can see already that the child takes everything too much
to heart — it consumes him, I feel sure. We must speak seriously
with Grabow. But there, that is just what it is," she went on, folding her arms, putting her head on one side, and tapping the floor
nervously with her foot. "Grabow is getting old; and aside from
that, good as he is — and he really is a very good man, a perfect
angel — so far as his skill is concerned, I have no such great opinion
of it, Ida, and may God forgive me if I am wrong. Take this
nervousness of Hanno's, his starting up at night and having such
frights in his sleep. Grabow knows what it is, and all he does is to
tell us the Latin name of it — *pavor nocturnus*. Dear knows, that
is very enlightening, of course! No, he is a dear good man, and a
great friend of the family and all that — but he is no great light.
An important man looks different — he shows when he is young
that there is something in him. Grabow lived through the '48. He
was a young man then. Do you imagine he was the least bit thrilled
over it — over freedom and justice, and the downfall of privilege
and arbitrary power? He is a cultivated man; but I am convinced

that the unheard-of laws concerning the press and the universities did not interest him in the least. He has never behaved even the least little bit wild, never jumped over the traces. He has always had just the same long, mild face, and always prescribed pigeon and French bread, and when anything is serious, a teaspoon of tincture of althaea. — Good night, Ida. No, I think there are other doctors in the world! Too bad I have missed Gerda. Yes, thanks, there is a light in the corridor. Good night."

When Frau Permaneder opened the dining-room door in passing, to call a good night to her brother in the living-room, she saw that the whole storey was lighted up, and that Thomas was walking up and down with his hands behind his back.

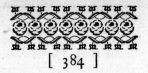

CHAPTER IV

THE SENATOR, when he was alone again, sat down at the table, took out his glasses, and tried to resume his reading. But in a few minutes his eyes had roved from the printed page, and he sat for a long time without changing his position, gazing straight ahead of him between the portières into the darkness of the salon.

His face, when he was alone, changed so that it was hardly recognizable. The muscles of his mouth and cheeks, otherwise obedient to his will, relaxed and became flabby. Like a mask the look of vigour, alertness, and amiability, which now for a long time had been preserved only by constant effort, fell from his face, and betrayed an anguished weariness instead. The tired, worried eyes gazed at objects without seeing them; they became red and watery. He made no effort to deceive even himself; and of all the dull, confused, rambling thoughts that filled his mind he clung to only one: the single, despairing thought that Thomas Buddenbrook, at forty-three years, was an old, worn-out man.

He rubbed his hand over his eyes and forehead, drawing a long, deep breath, mechanically lighted another cigarette, though he knew they were bad for him, and continued to gaze through the smoke-haze into the darkness. What a contrast between that relaxed and suffering face and the elegant, almost military style of his hair and beard! the stiffened and perfumed moustaches, the meticulously shaven cheeks and chin, and the careful hair-dressing which sedulously hid a beginning thinness. The hair ran back in two longish bays from the delicate temples, with a narrow parting on top; over the ears it was not long and waving, but kept short-cut now, in order not to betray how grey it had grown. He himself felt the change and knew it could not have escaped the eyes of others: the contrast between his active, elastic movements and the dull pallor of his face.

Not that he was in reality less of an important and indispensable personage than he always had been. His friends said, and his enemies could not deny, that Senator Buddenbrook was the Burgomaster's right hand: Burgomaster Langhals was even more emphatic on that point than his predecessor Överdieck had been. But the firm of Johann Buddenbrook was no longer what it had been — this seemed to be common property, so much so that Herr Stuht discussed it with his wife over their bacon broth — and Thomas Buddenbrook groaned over the fact.

At the same time, it was true that he himself was mainly responsible. He was still a rich man, and none of the losses he had suffered, even the severe one of the year '66, had seriously undermined the existence of the firm. But the notion that his luck and his consequence had fled, based though it was more upon inward feelings than upon outward facts, brought him to a state of lowness and suspicion. He entertained, of course, as before, and set before his guests the normal and expected number of courses. But, as never before, he began to cling to money and, in his private life, to save in small and petty ways. He had a hundred times regretted the building of his new house, which he felt had brought him nothing but bad luck. The summer holidays were given up, and the little city garden had to take the place of mountains or seashore. The family meals were, by his express and emphatic command, of such simplicity as to seem absurd by contrast with the lofty, splendid dining-room, with its extent of parquetry floors and its imposing oak furniture. For a long time now, there had been dessert only on Sundays. His own appearance was as elegant as ever; but the old servant, Anton, carried to the kitchen the news that the master only changed his shirt now every *other* day, as the washing was too hard on the fine linen. He knew more than that. He knew that he was to be dismissed. Gerda protested: three servants were few enough to do the work of so large a house as it should be done. But it was no use: old Anton, who had so long sat on the box when Thomas Buddenbrook drove down to the Senate, was sent away with a suitable present.

Such decrees as these were in harmony with the joyless state of affairs in the firm. That fresh enterprising spirit with which young Thomas Buddenbrook had taken up the reins — that was all gone, now; and his partner, Herr Friedrich Wilhelm Marcus — who, with his small capital, could not have had a prepondering influence in any case — was by nature lacking in initiative.

Herr Marcus' pedantry had so increased in the course of years that it had become a distinct eccentricity. It took him a quarter of an hour of stroking his moustaches, casting side-glances, and giving little coughs, just to cut his cigar and put the tip in his pocket-book. Evenings, when the gas-light made every corner of the office as bright as day, he still used a tallow candle on his own desk. Every half-hour he would get up and go to the tap and put water on his head. One morning there had been an empty sack untidily left under his desk. He took it for a cat and began to shoo it out with loud imprecations, to the joy of the office staff. No, he was not the man to give any quickening impulse to the business in the face of his partner's present lassitude. Mortification and a sort of desperate irritation often seized upon the Senator: as now, when he sat and stared wearily into the darkness, bringing home to himself the petty retail transactions and the pennywise policies to which the firm of Johann Buddenbrook had lately sunk.

But, after all, was it not best thus? Misfortune too has its time, he thought. Is it not better, while it holds sway, to keep oneself still, to wait in quiet and assemble one's inner powers? Why must this proposition come up just now, to shake him untimely out of his canny resignation and make him a prey to doubts and suspicions? Was the time come? Was this a sign? Should he feel encouraged to stand up and strike a blow? He had refused with all the decisiveness he could put into his voice, to think of the proposition; but had that settled it? It seemed not, since here he sat and brooded over it. "We are most likely to get angry in our opposition to some idea when we ourselves are not quite certain of our own position." A deucedly sly little person, Tony was!

What had he answered her? He had spoken very impressively, he recollected, about "underhand manœuvres," "fishing in troubled waters," "fleecing the poor land-owner," "usury," and so on. Very fine! But really one might ask if this were just the right time for so many large words. Consul Hermann Hagenström would not have thought of them, and would not have used them. Was he, Thomas Buddenbrook, a man of action, a business man — or was he a finicking dreamer?

Yes, that was the question. It had always been, as far back as he could remember, the question. Life was harsh: and business, with its ruthless unsentimentality, was an epitome of life. Did Thomas Buddenbrook, like his father, stand firmly on his two feet, in face of this hard practicality of life? Often enough, even far back in the past, he had seen reason to doubt it. Often enough, from his youth onwards, he had sternly brought his feelings into line. To inflict punishment, to take punishment, and not to think of it as punishment, but as something to be taken for granted — should he never completely learn that lesson?

He recalled the catastrophe of the year 1866, and the inexpress-

ibly painful emotions which had then overpowered him. He had
lost a large sum of money in the affair — but that had not been the
unbearable thing about it. For the first time in his career he had
fully and personally experienced the ruthless brutality of business
life and seen how all better, gentler, and kindlier sentiments creep
away and hid themselves before the one raw, naked, dominating
instinct of self-preservation. He had seen that when one suffers
a misfortune in business, one is met by one's friends — and one's
best friends — not with sympathy, not with compassion, but with
suspicion — cold, cruel, hostile suspicion. But he had known all
this before; why should he be surprised at it? And in stronger
and hardier hours he had blushed for his own weakness, for his
own distress and sleepless nights, for his revulsion and disgust at
the hateful and shameless harshness of life!

How foolish all that was! How ridiculous such feelings had
been! How could he entertain them? — unless, indeed, he were
a feeble visionary and not a practical business man at all! Ah, how
many times had he asked himself that question? And how many
times had he answered it: in strong and purposeful hours with one
answer, in weak and discouraged ones with another! But he was
too shrewd and too honest not to admit, after all, that he was a
mixture of both.

All his life, he had made the impression on others of a practical
man of action. But in so far as he legitimately passed for one —
he, with his fondness for quotations from Goethe — was it not
because he deliberately set out to do so? He had been successful
in the past, but was that not because of the enthusiasm and impetus
drawn from reflection? And if he were now discouraged, if his
powers were lamed — God grant it was only for a time — was not
his depression the natural consequence of the conflict that went
on within himself? Whether his father, grandfather, and great-
grandfather would have bought the Pöppenrade harvest in the
blade was not the point after all. The thing was that they were
practical men, more naturally, more vigorously, more impeccably
practical than he was himself.

He was seized by a great unrest, by a need for movement, space,
and light. He shoved back his chair, went into the salon, and
lighted several burners of the chandelier over the centre-table.
He stood there, pulling slowly and spasmodically at the long ends
of his moustaches and vacantly gazing about the luxurious room.
Together with the living-room it occupied the whole front of the
house; it had light, ornate furniture and looked like a music-room,
with the great grand piano, Gerda's violin-case, the étagère with

music books, the carved music-stand, and the bas-reliefs of singing cupids over the doors. The bow-window was filled with
palms.

Senator Buddenbrook stood for two or three minutes motionless. Then he went back through the living-room into the dining-
room and made light there also. He stopped at the sideboard and
poured a glass of water, either to be doing something or to quiet
his heart. Then he moved quickly on through the house, lighting
up as he went. The smoking-room was furnished in dark colours
and wainscoted. He absently opened the door of the cigar cabinet
and shut it again, and at the table lifted the lid of a little oak box
which had playing-cards, score-cards, and other such things in it.
He let some of the bone counters glide through his fingers with a
rattling sound, clapped the lid shut, and began again to walk up
and down.

A little room with a small stained-glass window opened into the
smoking-room. It was empty except for some small light serving-
tables of the kind which fit one within another. On one of them
a liqueur cabinet stood. From here one entered the dining-room,
with its great extent of parquetry flooring and its four high windows, hung with wine-coloured curtains, looking out into the
garden. It also occupied the whole breadth of the house. It was
furnished by two low, heavy sofas, covered with the same wine-
coloured material as the curtains, and by a number of high-
backed chairs standing stiffly along the walls. Behind the
fire-screen was a chimney-place, its artificial coals covered with
shining red paper to make them look glowing. On the marble
mantel-shelf in front of the mirror stood two towering Chinese
vases.

The whole storey was now lighted by the flame of single gas-
jets, and looked like a party the moment after the last guest is
gone. The Senator measured the room throughout its length,
and then stood at one of the windows and looked down into the
garden.

The moon stood high and small between fleecy clouds, and the
little fountain splashed in the stillness on the overhanging boughs
of the walnut tree. Thomas looked down on the pavilion which
enclosed his view, on the little glistening white terrace with the
two obelisks, the regular gravel paths, and the freshly turned
earth of the neat borders and beds. But this whole minute and
punctilious symmetry, far from soothing him, only made him
feel the more exasperated. He held the catch of the window,

leaned his forehead on it, and gave rein to his tormenting thoughts again.

What was he coming to? He thought of a remark he had let fall to his sister — something he had felt vexed with himself the next minute for saying, it seemed so unnecessary. He was speaking of Count Strelitz and the landed aristocracy, and he had expressed the view that the producer had a social advantage over the middleman. What was the point of that? It might be true and it might not; but was he, Thomas Buddenbrook, called upon to express such ideas — was he called upon to even think them? Should he have been able to explain to the satisfaction of his father, his grandfather — or any of his fellow townsmen — how he came to be expressing, or indulging in, such thoughts? A man who stands firm and confident in his own calling, whatever it may be, recognizes only it, understands only it, values only it.

Then he suddenly felt the blood rushing to his face as he recalled another memory, from farther back in the past. He saw himself and his brother Christian, walking around the garden of the Meng Street house, involved in a quarrel — one of those painful, regrettable, heated discussions. Christian, with artless indiscretion, had made a highly undesirable, a compromising remark, which a number of people had heard; and Thomas, furiously angry, irritated to the last degree, had called him to account. At bottom, Christian had said, at bottom every business man was a rascal. Well! was that foolish and trifling remark, in point of fact, so different from what he himself had just said to his sister? He had been furiously angry then, had protested violently — but what was it that sly little Tony said? "When we ourselves are not quite certain of our own position . . ."

"No," said the Senator, suddenly, aloud, lifted his head with a jerk, and let go the window fastening. He fairly pushed himself away from it. "That settles it," he said. He coughed, for the sound of his own voice in the emptiness made him feel unpleasant. He turned and began to walk quickly through all the rooms, his hands behind his back and his head bowed.

"That settles it," he repeated. "It will have to settle it. I am wasting time, I am sinking into a morass, I'm getting worse than Christian." It was something to be glad of, at least, that he was in no doubt where he stood. It lay, then, in his own hands to apply the corrective. Relentlessly. Let us see, now — let us see — what sort of offer was it they had made? The Pöppenrade harvest, in the blade? "I will do it!" he said in a passionate whisper, even stretching out one hand and shaking the forefinger. "I will do it!"

It would be, he supposed, what one would call a *coup:* an opportunity to double a capital of, say, forty thousand marks current — though that was probably an exaggeration. — Yes, it was a sign — a signal to him that he should rouse himself! It was the first step, the beginning, that counted; and the risk connected with it was a sort of offset to his moral scruples. If it succeeded, then he was himself again, then he would venture once more, then he would know how to hold fortune and influence fast within his grip.

No, Messrs. Strunck and Hagenström would not be able to profit by this occasion, unfortunately for them. There was another firm in the place, which, thanks to personal connections, had the upper hand. In fact, the personal was here the decisive factor. It was no ordinary business, to be carried out in the ordinary way. Coming through Tony, as it had, it bore more the character of a private transaction, and would need to be carried out with discretion and tact. Hermann Hagenström would hardly have been the man for the job. He, Thomas Buddenbrook, as a business man, was taking advantage of the market — and he would, by God, when he sold, know how to do the same. On the other hand, he was doing the hard-pressed land-owner a favour which he was called upon to do, by reason of Tony's connection with the Maibooms. The thing to do was to write, to write this evening — not on the business paper with the firm name, but on his own personal letter-paper with "Senator Buddenbrook" stamped across it. He would write in a courteous tone and ask if a visit in the next few days would be agreeable. But it was a difficult business, none the less — slippery ground, upon which one needed to move with care. — Well, so much the better for him.

His step grew quicker, his breathing deeper. He sat down a moment, sprang up again, and began roaming about through all the rooms. He thought it all out again; he thought about Herr Marcus, Hermann Hagenström, Christian, and Tony; he saw the golden harvests of Pöppenrade wave in the breeze, and dreamed of the upward bound the old firm would take after this coup; scornfully repulsed all his scruples and hesitations, put out his hand and said "I'll do it!"

Frau Permaneder opened the door and called out "Good-bye!" He answered her without knowing it. Gerda said good-night to Christian at the house door and came upstairs, her strange deepset eyes wearing the expression that music always gave them. The

Senator stopped mechanically in his walk, asked mechanically about the concert and the Spanish virtuoso, and said he was ready to go to bed.

But he did not go. He took up his wanderings again. He thought about the sacks of wheat and rye and oats and barley which should fill the lofts of the Lion, the Walrus, the Oak, and the Linden; he thought about the price he intended to ask — of course it should not be an extravagant price. He went softly at midnight down into the counting-house and, by the light of Herr Marcus' tallow candle, wrote a letter to Herr von Maiboom of Pöppenrade — a letter which, as he read it through, his head feeling feverish and heavy, he thought was the best and most tactful he had ever written.

That was the night of May 27. The next day he indicated to his sister, treating the affair in a light, semi-humorous way, that he had thought it all over and decided that he could not just refuse Herr von Maiboom out of hand and leave him at the mercy of the nearest swindler. On the thirtieth of May he went to Rostock, whence he drove in a hired wagon out to the country.

His mood for the next few days was of the best, his step elastic and free, his manners easy. He teased Clothilde, laughed heartily at Christian, joked with Tony, and played with Hanno in the little gallery for a whole hour on Sunday, helping him to hoist up miniature sacks of grain into a little brick-red granary, and imitating the hollow, drawling shouts of the workmen. And at the Burgesses' meeting of the third of June he made a speech on the most tiresome subject in the world, something connected with taxation, which was so brilliant and witty that everybody agreed with it unanimously, and Consul Hagenström, who had opposed him, became almost a laughing-stock.

CHAPTER V

Was it forgetfulness, or was it intention, which would have made Senator Buddenbrook pass over in silence a certain fact, had not his sister Tony, the devotee of the family papers, announced it to all the world: the fact, namely, that in those documents the founding of the firm of Johann Buddenbrook was ascribed to the date of the 7th of July, 1768, the hundredth anniversary of which was now at hand?

Thomas seemed almost disturbed when Tony, in a moving voice, called his attention to the fact. His good mood had not lasted. All too soon he had fallen silent again, more silent than before. He would leave the office in the midst of work, seized with unrest, and roam about the garden, sometimes pausing as if he felt confined in his movements, sighing, and covering his eyes with his hand. He said nothing, gave his feelings no vent — to whom should he speak, then? When he told his partner of the Pöppenrade matter, Herr Marcus had for the first time in his life been angry with him, and had washed his hands of the whole affair. But Thomas betrayed himself to his sister Tony, when they said good-bye on the street one Thursday evening, and she alluded to the Pöppenrade harvest. He gave her hand a single quick squeeze, and added passionately " Oh, Tony, if I had only sold it already! " He broke off abruptly, and they parted, leaving Frau Permaneder dismayed and anxious. The sudden hand-pressure had something despairing, the low words betrayed pent-up feeling. But when Tony, as chance offered, tried to come back to the subject, he wrapped himself in silence, the more forbidding because of his inward mortification over having given way — his inward bitterness at being, as he felt, feeble and inadequate to the situation in hand.

He said now, slowly and fretfully: " Oh, my dear child, I wish we might ignore the whole affair! "

" Ignore it, Tom? Impossible! Unthinkable! Do you think you could suppress the fact? Do you imagine the whole town would forget the meaning of the day? "

"I don't say it is possible — I only say I wish it were. It is pleasant to celebrate the past, when one is gratified with the present and the future. It is agreeable to think of one's forefathers when one feels at one with them and conscious of having acted as they would have done. If the jubilee came at a better time — but just now, I feel small inclination to celebrate it."

"You must not talk like that, Tom. You don't mean it; you know perfectly that it would be a shame to let the hundredth anniversary of the firm of Johann Buddenbrook go by without a sign or a sound of rejoicing. You are a little nervous now, and I know why, though there is really no reason for it. But when the day comes, you will be as moved as all the rest of us."

She was right; the day could not be passed over in silence. It was not long before a notice appeared in the papers, calling attention to the coming anniversary and giving a detailed history of the old and estimable firm — but it was really hardly necessary. In the family, Justus Kröger was the first to mention the approaching event, on the Thursday afternoon; and Frau Permaneder saw to it that the venerable leather portfolio was solemnly brought out after dessert was cleared away, and the whole family, by way of foretaste, perused the dates and events in the life of the first Johann Buddenbrook, Hanno's great-great-grandfather: when he had varioloid and when genuine smallpox, when he fell out of the third-storey window on to the floor of the drying-house, and when he had fever and delirium — she read all that aloud with pious fervour. Not content with that, she must go back into the 16th century, to the oldest Buddenbrook of whom there was knowledge, to the one who was Councillor in Grabau, and the Rostock tailor who had been "very well off" and had so many children, living and dead. "What a splendid man!" she cried; and began to rummage through yellow papers and read letters and poems aloud.

On the morning of the seventh of July, Herr Wenzel was naturally the first with his congratulations.

"Well, Herr Sen'ter, many happy returns!" he said, gesturing freely with razor and strop in his red hands. "A hundred years! And nearly half of it, I may say, I have been shaving in the respected family — oh, yes, one goes through a deal with the family, when one sees the head of it the first thing in the morning! The deceased Herr Consul was always the most talkative in the morning, too: 'Wenzel,' he would ask me, 'Wenzel, what do you think about the rye? Should I sell or do you think it will go up again?'"

"Yes, Wenzel, and I cannot think of these years without you, either. Your calling, as I've often said to you, has a certain charm about it. When you have made your rounds, you are wiser than anybody: you have had the heads of nearly all the great houses under your hand, and know the mood of each one. All the others can envy you that, for it is really valuable information."

" 's a good bit of truth in that, Herr Sen'ter. But what about the Herr Sen'ter's own mood, if I may be so bold to ask? Herr Sen'ter's looking a trifle pale again this morning."

" Am I? Well, I have a headache — and so far as I can see, it will get worse before it gets better, for I suspect they'll put a good deal of strain on it to-day."

" I'm afraid so, Herr Sen'ter. The interest is great — the interest is very great. Just look out o' window when I've done with you. Hosts of flags! And down at the bottom of the Street the ' Wullenwewer ' and the ' Friederike Överdieck ' with all their pennons flying."

" Well, let's be quick, then, Wenzel; there's no time to lose, evidently."

The Senator did not don his office jacket, as he usually did of a morning, but put on at once a black cutaway coat with a white waistcoat and light-coloured trousers. There would certainly be visits. He gave a last glance in the mirror, a last pressure of the tongs to his moustache, and turned with a little sigh to go. The dance was beginning. If only the day were all over! Would he have a single minute to himself, a single minute to relax the muscles of his face? All day long he should certainly have to receive, with tact and dignity, the congratulations of a host of people, find just the right word and just the right tone for everybody, be serious, hearty, ironic, jocose, and respectful by turns; and from afternoon late into the night there would be the dinner at the Ratskeller.

It was not true that his head ached. He was only tired. Already, though he had just risen, with his nerves refreshed by sleep, he felt his old, indefinable burden upon him. Why had he said his head ached — as though he always had a bad conscience where his own health was concerned? Why? Why? However, there was no time now to brood over the question.

He went into the dining-room, where Gerda met him gaily. She too was already arrayed to meet their guests, in a plaid skirt, a white blouse, and a thin silk zouave jacket over it, the colour of her heavy hair. She smiled and showed her white teeth, so large and regular, whiter than her white face; her eyes, those close-set, enigmatic brown eyes, were smiling too, to-day.

" I've been up for hours — you can tell from that how excited I am," she said, " and how hearty my congratulations are."

" Well, well! So the hundred years make an impression on you too? "

" Tremendous. But perhaps it is only the excitement of the celebration. What a day! Look at that, for instance." She pointed to the breakfast-table, all garlanded with garden flowers. " That is Fräulein Jungmann's work. But you are mistaken if you think you can drink tea now. The family is in the drawing-room already, waiting to make a presentation — something in which I too have had a share. Listen, Thomas. This is, of course, only the beginning of a stream of callers. At first I can stand it, but at about midday I shall have to withdraw, I am sure. The barometer has fallen a little, but the sky is still the most staring blue. It makes the flags look lovely, of course, and the whole town is flagged — but it will be frightfully hot. Come into the salon. Breakfast must wait. You should have been up before. Now the first excitement will have to come on an empty stomach."

The Frau Consul, Christian, Clothilde, Ida Jungmann, Frau Permaneder, and Hanno were assembled in the salon, the last two supporting, not without difficulty, the family present, a great commemorative tablet. The Frau Consul, deeply moved, embraced her eldest-born.

" This is a wonderful day, my dear son — a wonderful day," she repeated. " We must thank God unceasingly, with all our hearts, for His mercies — for all His mercies." She wept.

The Senator was attacked by weakness in her embrace. He felt as though something within him freed itself and flew away. His lips trembled. An overwhelming need possessed him to lay his head upon his mother's breast, to close his eyes in her arms, to breathe in the delicate perfume that rose from the soft silk of her gown, to lie there at rest, seeing nothing more, saying nothing more. He kissed her and stood erect, putting out his hand to his brother, who greeted him with the absent-minded embarrassment which was his usual bearing on such occasions. Clothilde drawled out something kindly. Ida Jungmann confined herself to making a deep bow, while she played with the silver watch-chain on her flat bosom.

" Come here, Tom," said Frau Permaneder uncertainly. " We can't hold it any longer, can we, Hanno? " She was holding it almost alone, for Hanno's little arms were not much help; and she looked, what with her enthusiasm and her effort, like an enraptured martyr. Her eyes were moist, her cheeks burned, and her tongue played, with a mixture of mischief and nervousness, on her upper lip.

"Here I am," said the Senator. "What in the world is this? Come, let me have it; we'll lean it against the wall." He propped it up next to the piano and stood looking at it, surrounded by the family.

In a large, heavy frame of carved nut-wood were the portraits of the four owners of the firm, under glass. There was the founder, Johann Buddenbrook, taken from an old oil painting — a tall, grave old gentleman, with his lips firmly closed, looking severe and determined above his lace jabot. There was the broad and jovial countenance of Johann Buddenbrook, the friend of Jean Jacques Hoffstede. There was Consul Johann Buddenbrook, in a stiff choker collar, with his wide, wrinkled mouth and large aquiline nose, his eyes full of religious fervour. And finally there was Thomas Buddenbrook himself, as a somewhat younger man. The four portraits were divided by conventionalized blades of wheat, heavily gilded, and beneath, likewise in figures of brilliant gilt, the dates 1768–1868. Above the whole, in the tall, Gothic hand of him who had left it to his descendants, was the quotation: "My son, attend with zeal, to thy business by day; but do none that hinders thee from thy sleep at night."

The Senator, his hands behind his back gazed for a long time at the tablet.

"Yes, yes," he said abruptly, and his tone was rather mocking, "an undisturbed night's rest is a very good thing." Then, seriously, if perhaps a little perfunctorily, "Thank you very much, my dear family. It is indeed a most thoughtful and beautiful gift. What do you think — where shall we put it? Shall we hang it in my private office?"

"Yes, Tom, over the desk in your office," answered Frau Permaneder, and embraced her brother. Then she drew him into the bow-window and pointed.

Under a deep blue sky, the two-coloured flag floated above all the houses, right down Fishers' Lane, from Broad Street to the wharf, where the "Wullenwewer" and the "Friederike Överdieck" lay under full flag, in their owner's honour.

"The whole town is the same," said Frau Permaneder, and her voice trembled. "I've been out and about already. Even the Hagenströms have a flag. They couldn't do otherwise. — I'd smash in their window!" He smiled, and they went back to the table together. "And here are the telegrams, Tom, the first ones to come — the personal ones, of course; the others have been sent to the office." They opened a few of the dispatches: from the family in Hamburg, from the Frankfort Buddenbrooks, from Herr Arnoldsen in Amsterdam, from Jürgen Kröger in Wismar. Suddenly Frau Permaneder flushed deeply.

" He is a good man, in his way," she said, and pushed across to her brother the telegram she had just opened: it was signed Permaneder.

" But time is passing," said the Senator, and looked at his watch. " I'd like my tea. Will you come in with me? The house will be like a bee-hive after a while."

His wife, who had given a sign to Ida Jungmann, held him back.

" Just a moment, Thomas. You know Hanno has to go to his lessons. He wants to say a poem to you first. Come here, Hanno. And now, just as if no one else were here — you remember? Don't be excited."

It was the summer holidays, of course, but little Hanno had private lessons in arithmetic, in order to keep up with his class. Somewhere out in the suburb of St. Gertrude, in a little ill-smelling room, a man in a red beard, with dirty fingernails, was waiting to discipline him in the detested " tables." But first he was to recite to Papa a poem painfully learned by heart, with Ida Jungmann's help, in the little balcony on the second floor.

He leaned against the piano, in his blue sailor suit with the white V front and the wide linen collar with a big sailor's knot coming out beneath. His thin legs were crossed, his body and head a little inclined in an attitude of shy, unconscious grace. Two or three weeks before, his hair had been cut, as not only his fellow pupils, but the master as well, had laughed at it; but his head was still covered with soft abundant ringlets, growing down over the forehead and temples. His eyelids drooped, so that the long brown lashes lay over the deep blue shadows; and his closed lips were a little wry.

He knew well what would happen. He would begin to cry, would not be able to finish for crying; and his heart would contract, as it did on Sundays in St. Mary's, when Herr Pfühl played on the organ in a certain piercingly solemn way. It always turned out that he wept when they wanted him to do something — when they examined him and tried to find out what he knew, as Papa so loved to do. If only Mamma had not spoken of getting excited! She meant to be encouraging, but he felt it was a mistake. There they stood, and looked at him. They expected, and feared, that he would break down — so how was it possible *not* to? He lifted his lashes and sought Ida's eyes. She was playing with her watch-chain, and nodded to him in her usual honest, crabbed way. He would have liked to cling to her and have her take him away; to hear nothing but her low, soothing voice, saying "There, little Hanno, be quiet, you need not say it."

"Well, my son, let us hear it," said the Senator, shortly. He had sat down in an easy-chair by the table and was waiting. He did not smile — he seldom did on such occasions. Very serious, with one eyebrow lifted, he measured little Hanno with cold and scrutinizing glance.

Hanno straightened up. He rubbed one hand over the piano's polished surface, gave a shy look at the company, and, somewhat emboldened by the gentle looks of Grandmamma and Aunt Tony, brought out, in a low, almost a hard voice: "'The Shepherd's Sunday Hymn,' by Uhland."

"Oh, my dear child, not like that," called out the Senator. "Don't stick there by the piano and cross your hands on your tummy like that! Stand up! Speak out! That's the first thing. Here, stand here between the curtains. Now, hold your head up — let your arms hang down quietly at your sides."

Hanno took up his position on the threshold of the living-room and let his arms hang down. Obediently he raised his head, but his eyes — the lashes drooped so low that they were invisible. They were probably already swimming in tears.

"'This is the day of our —'"

he began, very low. His father's voice sounded loud by contrast when he interrupted: "One begins with a bow, my son. And then, much louder. Begin again, please: 'Shepherd's Sunday Hymn' —"

It was cruel. The Senator was probably aware that he was robbing the child of the last remnant of his self-control. But the boy should not let himself be robbed. He should have more manliness by now. "'Shepherd's Sunday Hymn,'" he repeated encouragingly, remorselessly.

But it was all up with Hanno. His head sank on his breast, and the small, blue-veined right hand tugged spasmodically at the brocaded portière.

"'I stand alone on the vacant plain,'"

he said, but could get no further. The mood of the verse possessed him. An overmastering self-pity took away his voice, and the tears could not be kept back: they rolled out from beneath his lashes. Suddenly the thought came into his mind: if he were only ill, a little ill, as on those nights when he lay in bed with a slight fever and sore throat, and Ida came and gave him a drink, and put a compress on his head, and was kind — He put his head down on the arm with which he clung to the portière, and sobbed.

"Well," said the Senator, harshly, "there is no pleasure in that." He stood up, irritated. "What are you crying about? Though it is certainly a good enough reason for tears, that you haven't the courage to do anything, even for the sake of giving me a little pleasure! Are you a little girl? What will become of you if you go on like that? Will you always be drowning yourself in tears, every time you have to speak to people?"

"I never *will* speak to people, never!" thought Hanno in despair.

"Think it over till this afternoon," finished the Senator, and went into the dining-room. Ida Jungmann knelt by her fledgling and dried his eyes, and spoke to him, half consoling, half reproachful.

The Senator breakfasted hurriedly, and the Frau Consul, Tony, Clothilde, and Christian meanwhile took their leave. They were to dine with Gerda, as likewise were the Krögers, the Weinschenks, and the three Misses Buddenbrook from Broad Street, while the Senator, willy-nilly, must be present at the dinner in the Ratskeller. He hoped to leave in time to see his family again at his own house.

Sitting at the be-garlanded table, he drank his hot tea out of a saucer, hurriedly ate an egg, and on the steps took two or three puffs of a cigarette. Grobleben, wearing his woollen scarf in defiance of the July heat, with a boot over his left forearm and the polish-brush in his right, a long drop pendent from his nose, came from the garden into the front entry and accosted his master at the foot of the stairs, where the brown bear stood with his tray.

"Many happy returns, Herr Sen'ter, many happy — 'n' one is rich 'n' great, 'n' t'other's pore — "

"Yes, yes, Grobleben, you're right, that's just how it is!" And the Senator slipped a piece of money into the hand with the brush, and crossed the entry into the anteroom of the office. In the office the cashier came up to him, a tall man with honest, faithful eyes, to convey, in carefully selected phrases, the good wishes of the staff. The Senator thanked him in a few words, and went on to his place by the window. He had hardly opened his letters and glanced into the morning paper lying there ready for him, when a knock came on the door leading into the front entry, and the first visitors appeared with their congratulations.

It was a delegation of granary labourers, who came straddling in like bears, the corners of their mouths drawn down with befitting solemnity and their caps in their hands. Their spokesman spat tobacco-juice on the floor, pulled up his trousers, and talked in great excitement about "a hun'erd year" and "many more hun'erd year." The Senator proposed to them a considerable increase in their pay for the week, and dismissed them. The office staff of the revenue department came in a body to congratulate their chief. As they left, they met in the doorway a number of sailors, with two pilots at the head, from the "Wullenwewer" and the "Friederike Överdieck," the two ships belonging to the firm which happened at the time to be in port. Then there was a deputation of grain-porters, in black blouses, knee-breeches, and top-hats. And single citizens, too, were announced from time to time: Herr Stuht from Bell-Founders' Street came, with a black coat over his flannel shirt, and Iwersen the florist, and sundry other neighbours. There was an old postman, with watery eyes, earrings, and a white beard — an ancient oddity whom the Senator used to salute on the street and call him Herr Postmaster: he came, stood in the doorway, and cried out "Ah bain't come fer *that*, Herr Sen'ter! Ah knows as iverybody gits summat as comes here to-day, but ah bain't come fer that, an' so ah tells ye!" He received his piece of money with gratitude, none the less. There was simply no end to it. At half past ten the servant came from the house to announce that the Frau Senator was receiving guests in the salon.

Thomas Buddenbrook left his office and hurried upstairs. At the door of the salon he paused a moment for a glance into the mirror to order his cravat, and to refresh himself with a whiff of the eau-de-cologne on his handkerchief. His body was wet with perspiration, but his face was pale, his hands and feet cold. The reception in the office had nearly used him up already. He drew a long breath and entered the sunlit room, to be greeted at once by Consul Huneus, the lumber dealer and multi-millionaire, his wife, their daughter, and the latter's husband, Senator Dr. Gieseke. These had all driven in from Travemünde, like many others of the first families of the town, who were spending July in a cure which they interrupted only for the Buddenbrook jubilee.

They had not been sitting for three minutes in the elegant armchairs of the salon when Consul Överdieck, son of the deceased Burgomaster, and his wife, who was a Kistenmaker, were announced. When Consul Huneus made his adieux, his place was taken by his brother, who had a million less money than he, but made up for it by being a senator.

Now the ball was open. The tall white door, with the relief of the singing cupids above it, was scarcely closed for a moment; there was a constant view from within of the great staircase, upon which the light streamed down from the skylight far above, and of the stairs themselves, full of guests either entering or taking their leave. But the salon was spacious, the guests lingered in groups to talk, and the number of those who came was for some time far greater than the number of those who went away. Soon the maid-servant gave up opening and shutting the door that led into the salon and left it wide open, so that the guests stood in the corridor as well. There was the drone and buzz of conversation in masculine and feminine voices, there were handshakings, bows, jests, and loud, jolly laughter, which reverberated among the columns of the staircase and echoed from the great glass panes of the skylight. Senator Buddenbrook stood by turns at the top of the stairs and in the bow-window, receiving the congratulations, which were sometimes mere formal murmurs and sometimes loud and hearty expressions of good will. Burgomaster Dr. Langhals, a heavily built man of elegant appearance, with a shaven chin nestling in a white neck-cloth, short grey mutton-chops, and a languid diplomatic air, was received with general marks of respect. Consul Eduard Kistenmaker the wine-merchant, his wife, who was a Möllendorpf, and his brother and partner Stephan, Senator Buddenbrook's loyal friend and supporter, with his wife, the rudely healthy daughter of a landed proprietor, arrive and pay their respects. The widowed Frau Senator Möllendorpf sits throned in the centre of the sofa in the salon, while her children, Consul August Möllendorpf and his wife Julchen, born Hagenström, mingle with the crowd. Consul Hermann Hagenström supports his considerable weight on the balustrade, breathes heavily into his red beard, and talks with Senator Dr. Cremer, the Chief of Police, whose brown beard, mixed with grey, frames a smiling face expressive of a sort of gentle slyness. State Attorney Moritz Hagenström, smiling and showing his defective teeth, is there with his beautiful wife, the former Fräulein Puttfarken of Hamburg. Good old Dr. Grabow may be seen pressing Senator Buddenbrook's hand for a moment in both of his, to be displaced next moment by Contractor Voigt. Pastor Pringsheim, in secular garb, only betraying his dignity by the length of his frock coat, comes up the steps with outstretched arms and a beaming face. And Herr Friedrich Wilhelm Marcus is present, of course. Those gentle-

men who come as delegates from any body such as the Senate, the Board of Trade, or the Assembly of Burgesses, appear in
frock coats. It is half-past eleven. The heat is intense. The lady
of the house withdrew a quarter of an hour ago.

Suddenly there is a hubbub below the vestibule door, a stamping and shuffling of feet, as of many people entering together; and
a ringing, noisy voice echoes through the whole house. Everybody
rushes to the landing, blocks up the doors to the salon, the dining-
room, and the smoking-room, and peers down. Below is a group of
fifteen or twenty men with musical instruments, headed by a
gentleman in a brown wig, with a grey nautical beard and yellow
artificial teeth, which he shows when he talks. What is happening?
It is Consul Peter Döhlmann, of course: he is bringing the band
from the theatre, and mounts the stairs in triumph, swinging a
packet of programmes in his hand!

The serenade in honour of the hundredth anniversary of the
firm of Johann Buddenbrook begins: in these impossible conditions, with the notes all running together, the chords drowning
each other, the loud grunting and snarling of the big bass trumpet
heard above everything else. It begins with " Now let us all thank
God," goes over into the adaptation of Offenbach's " La Belle
Hélène," and winds up with a *pot-pourri* of folk-songs — quite an
extensive programme! And a pretty idea of Döhlmann's! They
congratulate him on it; and nobody feels inclined to break up until
the concert is finished. They stand or sit in the salon and the corridor; they listen and talk.

Thomas Buddenbrook stood with Stephan Kistenmaker, Senator
Dr. Gieseke, and Contractor Voigt, beyond the staircase, near the
open door of the smoking-room and the flight of stairs up to the
second storey. He leaned against the wall, now and then contribut-
ing a word to the conversation, and for the rest looking out into
space across the balustrade. It was hotter than ever, and more
oppressive; but it would probably rain. To judge from the shadows that drove across the skylight there must be clouds in the
sky. They were so many and moved so rapidly that the changeful, flickering light on the staircase came in time to hurt the eyes.
Every other minute the brilliance of the gilt chandelier and the
brass instruments below was quenched, to blaze out the next minute as before. Once the shadows lasted a little longer, and six or
seven times something fell with a slight crackling sound upon the
panes of the skylight — hail-stones, no doubt. Then the sunlight
streamed down again.

There is a mood of depression in which everything that would ordinarily irritate us and call up a healthy reaction, merely weighs us down with a nameless, heavy burden of dull chagrin. Thus Thomas brooded over the break-down of little Johann, over the feelings which the whole celebration aroused in him, and still more over those which he would have liked to feel but could not. He sought again and again to pull himself together, to clear his countenance, to tell himself that this was a great day which was bound to heighten and exhilarate his mood. And indeed the noise which the band was making, the buzz of voices, the sight of all these people gathered in his honour, did shake his nerves; did, together with his memories of the past and of his father, give rise in him to a sort of weak emotionalism. But a sense of the ridiculous, of the disagreeable, hung over it all — the trumpery music, spoiled by the bad acoustics, the banal company chattering about dinners and the stock market — and this very mingling of emotion and disgust heightened his inward sense of exhaustion and despair.

At a quarter after twelve, when the musical program was drawing to a close, an incident occurred which in no wise interfered with the prevailing good feeling, but which obliged the master of the house to leave his guests for a short time. It was of a business nature. At a pause in the music the youngest apprentice in the firm appeared, coming up the great staircase, overcome with embarrassment at sight of so many people. He was a little, stunted fellow; and he drew his red face down as far as possible between his shoulders and swung one long, thin arm violently back and forth to show that he was perfectly at his ease. In the other hand he had a telegram. He mounted the steps, looking everywhere for his master, and when he had discovered him he passed with blushes and murmured excuses through the crowds that blocked his way.

His blushes were superfluous — nobody saw him. Without looking at him or breaking off their talk, they slightly made way, and they hardly noticed when he gave his telegram to the Senator, with a scrape, and the latter turned a little away from Kistenmaker, Voigt, and Gieseke to read it. Nearly all the telegrams that came to-day were messages of congratulation; still, during business hours, they had to be delivered at once.

The corridor made a bend at the point where the stairs mounted to the second storey, and then went on to the back stairs, where there was another, a side entrance into the dining-room. Opposite the stairs was the shaft of the dumb-waiter, and at this point there was a sizable table, where the maids usually polished the silver. The Senator paused here, turned his back to the apprentice, and opened the despatch.

Suddenly his eyes opened so wide that any one seeing him would have started in astonishment, and he gave a deep, gasping intake of breath which dried his throat and made him cough.

He tried to say " Very well," but his voice was inaudible in the clamour behind him. " Very well," he repeated; but the second word was only a whisper.

As his master did not move or turn round or make any sign, the hump-backed apprentice shifted from one foot to the other, then made his outlandish scrape again and went down the back stairs.

Senator Buddenbrook still stood at the table. His hands, holding the despatch, hung weakly down in front of him; he breathed in difficult, short breaths through his mouth; his body swayed back and forth, and he shook his head meaninglessly, as if stunned. " That little bit of hail," he said, " that little bit of hail." He repeated it stupidly. But gradually his breathing grew longer and quieter, the movement of his body less; his half-shut eyes clouded over with a weary, broken expression, and he turned around, slowly nodding his head, opened the door into the dining-room, and went in. With bent head he crossed the wide polished floor and sat down on one of the dark red sofas by the window. Here it was quiet and cool. The sound of the fountain came up from the garden, and a fly buzzed on the pane. There was only a dull murmur from the front of the house.

He laid his weary head on the cushion and closed his eyes. " That's good, that's good," he muttered, half aloud, drawing a deep breath of relief and satisfaction, " Oh, that *is* good! "

He lay five minutes thus, with limbs relaxed and a look of peace upon his face. Then he sat up, folded the telegram, put it in his breast pocket, and rose to rejoin his guests.

But in the same minute he sank back with a disgusted groan upon the sofa. The music — it was beginning again; an idiotic racket, meant to be a galop, with the drum and cymbals marking a rhythm in which the other instruments all joined either ahead of or behind time; a naïve, insistent, intolerable hullabaloo of snarling, crashing, and feebly piping noises, punctuated by the silly tootling of the piccolo.

CHAPTER VI

"Oh, Bach, Sebastian Bach, dear lady!" cried Edmund Pfühl, Herr Edmund Pfühl, the organist of St. Mary's, as he strode up and down the salon with great activity, while Gerda, smiling, her head on her hand, sat at the piano; and Hanno listened from a big chair, his hands clasped round his knees. "Certainly, as you say, it was he through whom the victory was achieved by harmony over counterpoint. He invented modern harmony, assuredly. But how? Need I tell you how? By progressive development of the contrapuntal style — you know it as well as I do. Harmony? Ah, no! By no means. Counterpoint, my dear lady, counterpoint! Whither, I ask you, would experiments in harmony have led? While I have breath to speak, I will warn you against mere experiments in harmony!"

His zeal as he spoke was great, and he gave it free rein, for he felt at home in the house. Every Wednesday afternoon there appeared on the threshold his bulky, square, high-shouldered figure, in a coffee-coloured coat, whereof the skirts hung down over his knees. While awaiting his partner, he would open lovingly the Bechstein grand piano, arrange the violin parts on the stand, and then prelude a little, softly and artistically, with his head sunk, in high contentment, on one shoulder.

An astonishing growth of hair, a wilderness of tight little curls, red-brown mixed with grey, made his head look big and heavy, though it was poised easily upon a long neck with an extremely large Adam's apple that showed above his low collar. The straight, bunchy moustaches, of the same colour as the hair, were more prominent than the small snub nose. His eyes were brown and bright, with puffs of flesh beneath them; when he played they looked as though their gaze passed through whatever was in their way and rested on the other side. His face was not striking, but it had at least the stamp of a strong and lively intelligence. His eyelids were usually half drooped, and he had a way of relaxing his lower jaw without opening his mouth, which gave him a flabby, resigned expression like that sometimes seen on the face of a sleeping person.

The softness of his outward seeming, however, contrasted strongly with the actual strength and self-respect of his character. Edmund Pfühl was an organist of no small repute, whose reputation for contrapuntal learning was not confined within the walls of his native town. His little book on Church Music was recommended for private study in several conservatories, and his fugues and chorals were played now and then where an organ sounded to the glory of God. These compositions, as well as the voluntaries he played on Sundays at Saint Mary's, were flawless, impeccable, full of the relentless, severe logicality of the *Strenge Satz.* Such beauty as they had was not of this earth, and made no appeal to the ordinary layman's human feeling. What spoke in them, what gloriously triumphed in them, was a technique amounting to an ascetic religion, a technique elevated to a lofty sacrament, to an absolute end in itself. Edmund Pfühl had small use for the pleasant and the agreeable, and spoke of melody, it must be confessed, in slighting terms. But he was no dry pedant, notwithstanding. He would utter the name of Palestrina in the most dogmatic, awe-inspiring tone. But even while he made his instrument give out a succession of archaistic virtuosities, his face would be all aglow with feeling, with rapt enthusiasm, and his gaze would rest upon the distance as though he saw there the ultimate logicality of all events, issuing in reality. This was the musician's look; vague and vacant precisely because it abode in the kingdom of a purer, profounder, more absolute logic than that which shapes our verbal conceptions and thoughts.

His hands were large and soft, apparently boneless, and covered with freckles. His voice, when he greeted Gerda Buddenbrook, was low and hollow, as though a bite were stuck in his throat: "Good morning, honoured lady!"

He rose a little from his seat, bowed, and respectfully took the hand she offered, while with his own left he struck the fifths on the piano, so firmly and clear that she seized her Stradivarius and began to tune the strings with practised ear.

"The G minor concerto of Bach, Herr Pfühl. The whole adagio still goes badly, I think."

And the organist began to play. But hardly were the first chords struck, when it invariably happened that the corridor door would open gently, and without a sound little Johann would steal across the carpet to an easy-chair, where he would sit, his hands clasped round his knees, motionless, and listen to the music and the conversation.

"Well, Hanno, so you want a little taste of music, do you?"

said Gerda in a pause, and looked at her son with her shadowy eyes, in which the music had kindled a soft radiance.

Then he would stand up and put out his hand to Herr Pfühl with a silent bow, and Herr Pfühl would stroke with gentle affection the soft light-brown hair that hung gracefully about brow and temples.

" Listen, now my child," he would say, with mild impressiveness; and the boy would look at the Adam's apple that went up and down as the organist spoke, and then go back to his place with his quick, light steps, as though he could hardly wait for the music to begin again.

They played a movement of Haydn, some pages of Mozart, a sonata of Beethoven. Then, while Gerda was picking out some music, with her violin under her arm, a surprising thing happened: Herr Pfühl, Edmund Pfühl, organist at St. Mary's, glided over from his easy interlude into music of an extraordinary style; while a sort of shame-faced enjoyment showed upon his absent coun- tenance. A burgeoning and blooming, a weaving and singing rose beneath his fingers; then, softly and dreamily at first, but ever clearer and clearer, there emerged in artistic counterpoint the ancestral, grandiose, magnificent march motif — a mounting to a climax, a complication, a transition; and at the resolution of the dominant the violin chimed in, fortissimo. It was the overture to *Die Meistersinger*.

Gerda Buddenbrook was an impassioned Wagnerite. But Herr Pfühl was an equally impassioned opponent — so much so that in the beginning she had despaired of winning him over.

On the day when she first laid some piano arrangements from *Tristan* on the music-rack, he played some twenty-five beats and then sprung up from the music-stool to stride up and down the room with disgust painted upon his face.

" I cannot play that, my dear lady! I am your most devoted servant — but I cannot. That is not music — believe me! I have always flattered myself I knew something about music — but this is chaos! This is demagogy, blasphemy, insanity, madness! It is a perfumed fog, shot through with lightning! It is the end of all honesty in art. I will not play it! " And with the words he had thrown himself again on the stool, and with his Adam's apple working furiously up and down, with coughs and sighs, had ac- complished another twenty-five beats. But then he shut the piano and cried out:

" Oh, fie, fie! No, this is going too far. Forgive me, dear lady, if I speak frankly what I feel. You have honoured me for years,

and paid me for my services; and I am a man of modest means. But
I must lay down my office, I assure you, if you drive me to it by
asking me to play these atrocities! Look, the child sits there listening — would you then utterly corrupt his soul? "

But let him gesture as furiously as he would, she brought him
over — slowly, by easy stages, by persistent playing and persuasion.
" Pfühl," she would say, " be reasonable, take the thing calmly.
You are put off by his original use of harmony. Beethoven seems
to you so pure, clear, and natural, by contrast. But remember how
Beethoven himself affronted his contemporaries, who were
brought up in the old way. And Bach — why, good Heavens, you
know how he was reproached for his want of melody and clearness! You talk about honesty — but what do you mean by honesty
in art? Is it not the antithesis of hedonism? And, if so, then that is
what you have here. Just as much as in Bach. I tell you, Pfühl,
this music is less foreign to your inner self than you think! "

" It is all juggling and sophistry — begging your pardon," he
grumbled. But she was right, after all: the music was not so impossible as he thought at first. He never, it is true, quite reconciled
himself to *Tristan*, though he eventually carried out Gerda's wish
and made a very clever arrangement of the Liebestod for violin
and piano. He was first won over by certain parts of *Die Meistersinger;* and slowly a love for this new art began to stir within him.
He would not confess it — he was himself aghast at the fact, and
would pettishly deny it when the subject was mentioned. But after
the old masters had had their due, Gerda no longer needed to urge
him to respond to a more complex demand upon his virtuosity;
with an expression of shame-faced pleasure, he would glide into
the weaving harmonies of the *Leit-motiv*. After the music, however, there would be a long explanation of the relation of this style
of music to that of the *Strenge Satz;* and one day Herr Pfühl
admitted that, while not personally interested in the theme, he
saw himself obliged to add a chapter to his book on Church Music,
the subject of which would be the application of the old key-
system to the church- and folk-music of Richard Wagner.

Hanno sat quite still, his small hands clasped round his knees, his
mouth, as usual, a little twisted as his tongue felt out the hole in a
back tooth. He watched his mother and Herr Pfühl with large
quiet eyes; and thus, so early, he became aware of music as an
extraordinarily serious, important, and profound thing in life. He
understood only now and then what they were saying, and the
music itself was mostly far above his childish understanding. Yet

he came again, and sat absorbed for hours — a feat which surely faith, love, and reverence alone enabled him to perform.

When only seven, he began to repeat with one hand on the piano certain combinations of sound that made an impression on him. His mother watched him smiling, improved his chords, and showed him how certain tones would be necessary to carry one chord over into another. And his ear confirmed what she told him.

After Gerda Buddenbrook had watched her son a little, she decided that he must have piano lessons.

"I hardly think," she told Herr Pfühl, "that he is suited for solo work; and on the whole I am glad, for it has its bad side apart from the dependence of the soloist upon his accompanist, which can be very serious too; — if I did not have you, for instance! — there is always the danger of yielding to more or less complete virtuosity. You see, I know whereof I speak. I tell you frankly that, for the soloist, a high degree of ability is only the first step. The concentration on the tone and phrasing of the treble, which reduces the whole polyphony to something vague and indefinite in the consciousness, must surely spoil the feeling for harmony — unless the person is more than usually gifted — and the memory as well, which is most difficult to correct later on. I love my violin, and I have accomplished a good deal with it; but to tell the truth, I place the piano higher. What I mean is this: familiarity with the piano, as a means of summarizing the richest and most varied structures, as an incomparable instrument for musical reproduction, means for me a clearer, more intimate and comprehensive intercourse with music. Listen, Pfühl. I would like to have you take him, if you will be so good. I know there are two or three people here in the town who give lessons — women, I think. But they are simply piano-teachers. You know what I mean. I feel that it matters so little whether one is trained upon an instrument, and so much whether one knows something about music. I depend upon you. And you will see, you will succeed with him. He has the Buddenbrook hand. The Buddenbrooks can all strike the ninths and tenths — only they have never set any store by it," she concluded, laughing. And Herr Pfühl declared himself ready to undertake the lessons.

From now on, he came on Mondays as well as Wednesdays, and gave little Hanno lessons, while Gerda sat beside them. He went at it in an unusual way, for he felt that he owed more to his pupil's dumb and passionate zeal than merely to employ it in playing the piano a little. The first elementary difficulties were hardly got

over when he began to theorize, in a simple way, with graphic
illustrations, and to give his pupil the foundations of the theory of
harmony. And Hanno understood. For it was all only a confirmation of what he had always known.

As far as possible, Herr Pfühl took into consideration the eager
ambition of the child. He spent much thought upon the problem,
how best to lighten the material load that weighed down the
wings of his fancy. He did not demand too much finger dexterity
or practice of scales. What he had in mind, and soon achieved,
was a clear and lively grasp of the key system on Hanno's part,
an inward, comprehensive understanding of its relationships, out
of which would come, at no distant day, the quick eye for possible
combinations, the intuitive mastery over the piano, which would
lead to improvisation and composition. He appreciated with a
touching delicacy of feeling the spiritual needs of this young
pupil, who had already heard so much, and directed it toward the
acquisition of a serious style. He would not disillusionize the deep
solemnity of his mood by making him practise commonplaces.
He gave him chorals to play, and pointed out the laws controlling
the development of one chord into another.

Gerda, sitting with her embroidery or her book, just beyond
the portières, followed the course of the lessons.

"You outstrip all my expectations," she told Herr Pfühl, later
on. "But are you not going too fast? Aren't you getting too
far ahead? Your method seems to me eminently creative — he
has already begun to try to improvise a little. But if the method
is beyond him, if he hasn't enough gift, he will learn absolutely
nothing."

"He has enough gift," Herr Pfühl said, and nodded. "Sometimes I look into his eyes, and see so much lying there — but he
holds his mouth tight shut. In later life, when his mouth will
probably be shut even tighter, he must have some kind of outlet
— a way of speaking — "

She looked at him — at this square-built musician with the red-
brown hair, the pouches under the eyes, the bushy moustaches,
and the inordinate Adam's apple — and then she put out her hand
and said: "Thank you, Pfühl. You mean well by him. And who
knows, yet, how much you are doing for him?"

Hanno's feeling for his teacher was one of boundless gratitude
and devotion. At school he sat heavy and hopeless, unable, despite
strenuous coaching, to understand his tables. But he grasped
without effort all that Herr Pfühl told him, and made it his own
— if he could make more his own that which he had already owned

before. Edmund Pfühl, like a stout angel in a tail-coat, took him
in his arms every Monday afternoon and transported him above
all his daily misery, into the mild, sweet, grave, consoling kingdom of sound.

The lessons sometimes took place at Herr Pfühl's own house,
a roomy old gabled dwelling full of cool passages and crannies,
in which the organist lived alone with an elderly housekeeper.
Sometimes, too, little Buddenbrook was allowed to sit up with the
organist at the Sunday service in St. Mary's — which was quite
a different matter from stopping below with the other people, in
the nave. High above the congregation, high above Pastor Pringsheim in his pulpit, the two sat alone, in the midst of a mighty
tempest of rolling sound, which at once set them free from the
earth and dominated them by its own power; and Hanno was
sometimes blissfully permitted to help his master control the stops.

When the choral was finished, Herr Pfühl would slowly lift
his fingers from the keyboard, so that only the bass and the funda-
mental would still be heard, in lingering solemnity; and after a
meaningful pause, the well-modulated voice of Pastor Pringsheim
would rise up from under the sounding-board in the pulpit. Then
it happened not infrequently that Herr Pfühl would, quite simply,
begin to make fun of the preacher: his artificial enunciation, his
long, exaggerated vowels, his sighs, his crude transitions from
sanctity to gloom. Hanno would laugh too, softly but with heart-
felt glee; for those two up there were both of the opinion — which
neither of them expressed — that the sermon was silly twaddle,
and that the real service consisted in that which the Pastor and
his congregation regarded merely as a devotional accessory:
namely, the music.

Herr Pfühl, in fact, had a constant grievance in the small understanding there was for his accomplishments down there among
the Senators, Consuls, citizens, and their families. And thus, he
liked to have his small pupil by him, to whom he could point out
the extraordinary difficulties of the passages he had just played.
He performed marvels of technique. He had composed a melody
which was just the same read forward or backward, and based
upon it a fugue which was to be played "crab-fashion." But
after performing this wonder: "Nobody knows the difference,"
he said, and folded his hands in his lap with a dreary look, shaking
his head hopelessly. While Pastor Pringsheim was delivering his
sermon, he whispered to Hanno: "That was a crab-fashion imitation, Johann. You don't know what that is yet. It is the imitation of a theme composed backward instead of forward — a

very, very difficult thing. Later on, I will show you what an imitation in the *Strenge Satz* involves. As for the ' crab,' I would never ask you to try that. It isn't necessary. But do not believe those who tell you that such things are trifles, without any musical value. You will find the crab in musicians of all ages. But exercises like that are the scorn of the mediocre and the superficial musician. Humility, Hanno, *humility* — is the feeling one should have. Don't forget it."

On his eighth birthday, April 15th, 1869, Hanno played before the assembled family a fantasy of his own composition. It was a simple affair, a motif entirely of his own invention, which he had slightly developed. When he showed it to Herr Pfühl, the organist, of course, had some criticism to make.

"What sort of theatrical ending is that, Johann? It doesn't go with the rest of it. In the beginning it is all pretty good; but why do you suddenly fall from B major into the six-four chord on the fourth note with a minor third? These are tricks; and you tremolo here, too — where did you pick that up? I know, of course: you have been listening when I played certain things for your mother. Change the end, child: then it will be quite a clean little piece of work."

But it appeared that Hanno laid the greatest stress precisely on this minor chord and this finale; and his mother was so very pleased with it that it remained as it was. She took her violin and played the upper part, and varied it with runs in demi-semi-quavers. That sounded gorgeous: Hanno kissed her out of sheer happiness, and they played it together to the family on the 15th of April.

The Frau Consul, Frau Permaneder, Christian, Clothilde, Herr and Frau Consul Kröger, Herr and Frau Director Weinschenk, the Broad Street Buddenbrooks, and Therese Weichbrodt were all bidden to dinner at four o'clock, with the Senator and his wife, in honour of Hanno's birthday; and now they sat in the salon and looked at the child, perched on the music-stool in his sailor suit, and at the elegant, foreign appearance his mother made as she played a wonderful cantilena on the G string, and then, with profound virtuosity, developed a stream of purling, foaming cadences. The silver on the end of her bow gleamed in the gas-light.

Hanno was pale with excitement, and had hardly eaten any dinner. But now he forgot all else in his absorbed devotion to his task, which would, alas, be all over in ten minutes! The little melody he had invented was more harmonic than rhythmic in its

structure; there was an extraordinary contrast between the simple
primitive material which the child had at his command, and the
impressive, impassioned, almost over-refined method with which
that material was employed. He brought out each leading note
with a forward inclination of the little head; he sat far forward on
the music-stool, and strove by the use of both pedals to give each
new harmony an emotional value. In truth, when Hanno concentrated upon an effect, the result was likely to be emotional
rather than merely sentimental. He gave every simple harmonic
device a special and mysterious significance by means of retar-
dation and accentuation; his surprising skill in effects was displayed
in each chord, each new harmony, by a suddenly introduced
pianissimo. And he sat with lifted eyebrows, swaying back and
forth with the whole upper part of his body. Then came the
finale, Hanno's beloved finale, which crowned the elevated simplicity of the whole piece. Soft and clear as a bell sounded the E
minor chord, tremolo pianissimo, amid the purling, flowing notes
of the violin. It swelled, it broadened, it slowly, slowly rose:
suddenly, in the forte, he introduced the discord C sharp, which
led back to the original key, and the Stradivarius ornamented it
with its welling and singing. He dwelt on the dissonance until
it became fortissimo. But he denied himself and his audience the
resolution; he kept it back. What would it be, this resolution,
this enchanting, satisfying absorption into the B major chord? A
joy beyond compare, a gratification of overpowering sweetness! Peace! Bliss! The kingdom of Heaven: only not yet —
not yet! A moment more of striving, hesitation, suspense, that
must become well-nigh intolerable in order to heighten the ultimate moment of joy. — Once more — a last, a final tasting of
this striving and yearning, this craving of the entire being, this
last forcing of the will to deny oneself the fulfilment and the
conclusion, in the knowledge that joy, when it comes, lasts only
for the moment. The whole upper part of Hanno's little body
straightened, his eyes grew larger, his closed lips trembled, he
breathed short, spasmodic breaths through his nose. At last, at
last, joy would no longer be denied. It came, it poured over him;
he resisted no more. His muscles relaxed, his head sank weakly
on his shoulder, his eyes closed, and a pathetic, almost an anguished
smile of speechless rapture hovered about his mouth; while his
tremolo, among the rippling and rustling runs from the violin, to
which he now added runs in the bass, glided over into B major,
swelled up suddenly into forte, and after one brief, resounding
burst, broke off.

It was impossible that all the effect which this had upon Hanno should pass over into his audience. Frau Permaneder, for instance, had not the slightest idea what it was all about. But she had seen the child's smile, the rhythm of his body, the beloved little head swaying enraptured from side to side — and the sight had penetrated to the depths of her easily moved nature.

"How the child can play! Oh, how he can play!" she cried, hurrying to him half-weeping and folding him in her arms. "Gerda, Tom, he will be a Meyerbeer, a Mozart, a —" As no third name of equal significance occurred to her, she confined herself to showering kisses on her nephew, who sat there, still quite exhausted, with an absent look in his eyes.

"That's enough, Tony," the Senator said softly. "Please don't put such ideas into the child's head."

CHAPTER VII

THOMAS BUDDENBROOK was, in his heart, far from pleased with the development of little Johann.

Long ago he had led Gerda Arnoldsen to the altar, and all the Philistines had shaken their heads. He had felt strong and bold enough then to display a distinguished taste without harming his position as a citizen. But now, the long-awaited heir, who showed so many physical traits of the paternal inheritance — did he, after all, belong entirely to the mother's side? He had hoped that one day his son would take up the work of the father's lifetime in his stronger, more fortunate hands, and carry it forward. But now it almost seemed that the son was hostile, not only to the surroundings and the life in which his lot was cast, but even to his father as well.

Gerda's violin-playing had always added to her strange eyes, which he loved, to her heavy, dark-red hair and her whole exotic appearance, one charm the more. But now that he saw how her passion for music, strange to his own nature, utterly, even at this early age, possessed the child, he felt in it a hostile force that came between him and his son, of whom his hopes would make a Buddenbrook — a strong and practical-minded man, with definite impulses after power and conquest. In his present irritable state it seemed to him that this hostile force was making him a stranger in his own house.

He could not, himself, approach any nearer to the music practised by Gerda and her friend Herr Pfühl; Gerda herself, exclusive and impatient where her art was concerned, made it cruelly hard for him.

Never had he dreamed that music was so essentially foreign to his family as now it seemed. His grandfather had enjoyed playing the flute, and he himself always listened with pleasure to melodies that possessed a graceful charm, a lively swing, or a tender melancholy. But if he happened to express his liking for any such composition, Gerda would be sure to shrug her shoulders and say with a pitying smile, "How can you, my friend? A thing like that, without any musical value whatever!"

He hated this "musical value." It was a phrase which had no meaning for him save a certain chilling arrogance. It drove him on, in Hanno's presence, to self-assertion. More than once he remonstrated angrily, "This constant harping on musical values, my dear, strikes me as rather tasteless and opinionated." To which she rejoined: "Thomas, once for all, you will never understand anything about music as an art, and, intelligent as you are, you will never see that it is more than an after-dinner pleasure and a feast for the ears. In every other field you have a perception of the banal — in music not. But it is the test of musical comprehension. What pleases you in music? A sort of insipid optimism, which, if you met with it in literature, would make you throw down the book with an angry or sarcastic comment. Easy gratification of each unformed wish, prompt satisfaction before the will is even roused — that is what pretty music is like — and it is like nothing else in the world. It is mere flabby idealism."

He understood her; that is, he understood what she said. But he could not follow her: could not comprehend why melodies which touched or stirred him were cheap and worthless, while compositions which left him cold and bewildered possessed the highest musical value. He stood before a temple from whose threshold Gerda sternly waved him back — and he watched while she and the child vanished within.

He betrayed none of his grief over this estrangement, though the gulf seemed to widen between him and his little son. The idea of suing for his child's favour seemed frightful to him. During the day he had small time to spare; at meals he treated him with a friendly cordiality that had at times a tonic severity. "Well, comrade," he would say, giving him a tap or two on the back of the head and seating himself opposite his wife, "well, and how are you? Studying? And playing the piano, eh? Good! But not too much piano, else you won't want to do your task, and then you won't go up at Easter." Not a muscle betrayed the anxious suspense with which he waited to see how Hanno took his greeting and what his reply would be. Nothing revealed his painful inward shrinking when the child merely gave him a shy glance of the gold-brown, shadowy eyes — a glance that did not even reach his father's face — and bent again over his plate.

It was monstrous for him to brood over this childish awkwardness. It was his fatherly duty to occupy himself a little with the child: so, while the plates were changed, he would examine him and try to stimulate his sense for facts. How many inhabitants were there in the town? What streets led from the Trave to the upper town? What were the names of the granaries that belonged to the firm? Out with it, now; speak up! But Hanno was silent. Not with any idea of wounding or annoying his father! But these inhabitants, these streets and granaries, which were normally a matter of complete indifference to him, became positively hateful when they were made the subject of an examination. However lively he was beforehand, however gaily he had laughed and talked with his father, his mood would go down to zero at the first symptom of an examination, and his resistance would collapse entirely. His eyes would cloud over, his mouth take on a despondent droop, and he would be possessed by a feeling of profound regret at the thoughtlessness of Papa, who surely knew that such tests came to nothing and only spoiled the whole meal for everybody! With eyes swimming in tears he looked down at his plate. Ida would nudge him and whisper to him: the streets, the granaries. Oh, that was all useless, perfectly useless. She did not understand. He did know the names — at least some of them. It would have been easy to do what Papa asked — if only he were not possessed and prevented by an overpowering sadness! A severe word from his father and a tap with the fork against the knife rest brought him to himself with a start. He cast a glance at his mother and Ida and tried to speak. But the first syllables were already drowned in sobs. "That's enough," shouted the Senator, angrily. "Keep still — you needn't tell me! You can sit there dumb and silly all the rest of your life!" And the meal would be finished in uncomfortable silence.

When the Senator felt troubled about Hanno's passionate preoccupation with his music, it was this dreaminess, this weeping, this total lack of freshness and energy, that he fixed upon.

All his life the boy had been delicate. His teeth had been particularly bad, and had been the cause of many painful illnesses and difficulties. It had nearly cost him his life to cut his first set; the gums showed a constant tendency to inflammation, and there were abscesses, which Mamsell Jungmann used to open with a needle at the proper time. Now his second teeth were beginning to come in, and the suffering was even greater. He had almost more pain than he could bear, and he spent many sleepless, feverish nights. His teeth, when they came, were as white and beautiful as his mother's; but they were soft and brittle, and crowded each other out of shape when they came in; so that little Hanno was obliged, for the correction of all these evils, to make the acquaintance early in life of a very dreadful man — no less than Herr Brecht, the dentist, in Mill Street.

Even this man's name was significant: it suggested the frightful sensation in Hanno's jaw when the roots of a tooth were pulled, lifted, and wrenched out; the sound of it made Hanno's heart contract, just as it did when he cowered in an easy-chair in Herr Brecht's waiting-room, with the faithful Jungmann sitting opposite, and looked at the pictures in a magazine, while he breathed in the sharp-smelling air of the room and waited for the dentist to open the door of the operating-room, with his polite and horrible " Won't you come in, please? "

This operating-room possessed one strange attraction, a gorgeous parrot with venomous little eyes, which sat in a brass cage in the corner and was called, for unknown reasons, Josephus. He used to say " Sit down; one moment, please," in a voice like an old fish-wife's; and though the hideous circumstances made this sound like mockery, yet Hanno felt for the bird a curious mixture of fear and affection. Imagine — a parrot, a big, bright-coloured bird, that could talk and was called Josephus! He was like something out of an enchanted forest; like Grimm's fairy tales, which Ida read aloud to him. And when Herr Brecht opened the door, his invitation was repeated by Josephus in such a way that somehow Hanno was laughing when he went into the operating-room and sat down in the queer big chair by the window, next the treadle machine.

Herr Brecht looked a good deal like Josephus. His nose was of the same shape, above his grizzled moustaches. The bad thing about him was that he was nervous, and dreaded the tortures he was obliged to inflict. " We must proceed to extraction, Fräulein," he would say, growing pale. Hanno himself was in a pale cold sweat, with staring eyes, incapable of protesting or running away; in short, in much the same condition as a condemned criminal. He saw Herr Brecht, with the forceps in his sleeve, bend over him, and noticed that little beads were standing out on his bald brow, and that his mouth was twisted. When it was all over, and Hanno, pale and trembling, spat blood into the blue basin at his side, Herr Brecht too had to sit down, and wipe his forehead and take a drink of water.

They assured little Johann that this man would do him good and save him suffering in the end. But when Hanno weighed his present pains against the positive good that had accrued from them, he felt that the former far outweighed the latter; and he regarded these visits to Mill Street as so much unnecessary torture. They removed four beautiful white molars which had just come in, to make room for the wisdom teeth expected later: this required four weeks of visits, in order not to subject the boy to too great a strain. It was a fearful time! — a long drawn-out martyrdom, in which dread of the next visit began before the last one, with its attendant exhaustion, was fairly over. When the last tooth was drawn, Hanno was quite worn out, and was ill in bed for a week.

This trouble with his teeth affected not only his spirits but also the functioning of all his other organs. What he could not chew he did not digest, and there came attacks of gastric fever, accompanied by fitful heart action, according as the heart was either weakened or too strongly stimulated. And there were spells of giddiness, while the *pavor nocturnus*, that strange affliction beloved of Dr. Grabow, continued unabated. Hardly a night passed that little Johann did not start up in bed, wringing his hands with every mark of unbearable anguish, and crying out piteously for help, as though some one were trying to choke him or some other awful thing were happening. In the morning he had forgotten it all. Dr. Grabow's treatment consisted of giving fruit-juice before the child went to bed; which had absolutely no effect.

The physical arrests and the pains which Hanno suffered made him old for his age; he was what is called precocious; and though this was not very obvious, being restrained in him, as it were, by his own unconscious good taste, still it expressed itself at times in the form of a melancholy superiority. "How are you, Hanno?" somebody would ask: his grandmother or one of the Broad Street Buddenbrooks. A little resigned curl of the lip, or a shrug of the shoulders in their blue sailor suit, would be the only answer.

"Do you like to go to school?"

"No," answered Hanno, with quiet candour — he did not consider it worth while to try to tell a lie in such cases.

"No? But one has to learn writing, reading, arithmetic — "

"And so on," said little Johann.

No, he did not like going to school — the old monastic school with its cloisters and vaulted classrooms. He was hampered by his illnesses, and often absent-minded, for his thoughts would linger among his harmonic combinations, or upon the still unravelled marvel of some piece which he had heard his mother and Herr Pfühl playing; and all this did not help him on in the sciences. These lower classes were taught by assistant masters and seminarists, for whom he entertained mingled feelings: a dread of possible future punishments and a secret contempt for their social inferiority, their spiritual limitations, and their physical unkemptness. Herr Tietge, a little grey man in a greasy black coat, who had

taught in the school even in the time of the deceased Marcellus
Stengel; who squinted abominably and sought to remedy this defect by wearing glasses as thick and round as a ship's port-holes —
Herr Tietge told little Johann how quick and industrious his
father had been at figures. Herr Tietge had severe fits of coughing, and spat all over the floor of his platform.

Hanno had, among his schoolmates, no intimates save one. But
this single bond was very close, even from his earliest school days.
His friend was a child of aristocratic birth but neglected appearance, a certain Count Mölln, whose first name was Kai.

Kai was a lad of about Hanno's height, dressed not in a sailor
suit, but in shabby clothes of uncertain colour, with here and
there a button missing, and a great patch in the seat. His arms
were too long for the sleeves of his coat, and his hands seemed
impregnated with dust and earth to a permanent grey colour;
but they were unusually narrow and elegant, with long fingers
and tapering nails. His head was to match: neglected, uncombed,
and none too clean, but endowed by nature with all the marks of
pure and noble birth. The carelessly parted hair, reddish-blond in
colour, waved back from a white brow, and a pair of light blue
eyes gleamed bright and keen from beneath. The cheek bones
were slightly prominent: while the nose, with its delicate nostrils
and slightly aquiline curve, and the mouth, with its short upper
lip, were already quite unmistakable and characteristic.

Hanno Buddenbrook had seen the little count once or twice,
even before they met at school, when he took his walks with Ida
northward from the Castle Gate. Some distance outside the town,
nearly as far as the first outlying village, lay a small farm, a tiny,
almost valueless property without even a name. The passer-by
got the impression of a dunghill, a quantity of chickens, a dog-hut,
and a wretched, kennel-like building with a sloping red roof. This
was the manor-house, and therein dwelt Kai's father, Count Eberhard Mölln.

He was an eccentric, hardly ever seen by anybody, busy on his
dunghill with his dogs, his chickens, and his vegetable-patch: a
large man in top-boots, with a green frieze jacket. He had a bald
head and a huge grey beard like the tail of a turnip; he carried
a riding-whip in his hand, though he had no horse to his name,
and wore a monocle stuck into his eye under the bushy eyebrow.
Except him and his son, there was no Count Mölln in all the
length and breadth of the land any more: the various branches of a
once rich, proud, and powerful family had gradually withered
off, until now there was only an aunt, with whom Kai's father

was not on terms. She wrote romances for the family story-papers, under a dashing pseudonym. The story was told of Count Eberhard that when he first withdrew to his little farm, he devised a means of protecting himself from the importunities of peddlers, beggars, and busy-bodies. He put up a sign which read: "Here lives Count Mölln. He wants nothing, buys nothing, and gives nothing away." When the sign had served its purpose, he removed it.

Motherless — for the Countess had died when her child was born, and the housework was done by an elderly female — little Kai grew up like a wild animal, among the dogs and chickens; and here Hanno Buddenbrook had looked at him shyly from a distance, as he leaped like a rabbit among the cabbages, romped with the dogs, and frightened the fowls by turning somersaults.

They met again in the schoolroom, where Hanno probably felt again his first alarm at the little Count's unkempt exterior. But not for long. A sure instinct had led him to pay no heed to the outward negligence; had shown him instead the white brow, the delicate mouth, the finely shaped blue eyes, which looked with a sort of resentful hostility into his own; and Hanno felt sympathy for this one alone among all his fellows. But he would never, by himself, have taken the first steps; he was too timid for that. Without the ruthless impetuosity of little Kai they might have remained strangers, after all. The passionate rapidity of his approach even frightened Hanno, at first. The neglected little count sued for the favour of the quiet, elegantly dressed Hanno with a fiery, aggressive masculinity impossible to resist. Kai could not, it is true, help Hanno with his lessons. His untamed spirits were as hostile to the " tables " as was little Buddenbrook's dreamy abstractedness. But he gave him everything he had: glass bullets, wooden tops, even a broken lead pistol which was his dearest treasure. During the recess he told him about his home and the puppies and chickens, and walked with him at midday as far as he dared, though Ida Jungmann, with a packet of sandwiches, was always waiting for her fledgling at the school gate. It was from Ida that Kai heard little Buddenbrook's nickname; he took it up, and never called him henceforth by anything else.

One day he demanded that Hanno, instead of going to the Mill-wall, should take a walk with him to his father's house to see the baby guinea-pigs. Fräulein Jungmann finally yielded to the teasing of the two children. They strolled out to the noble domain, viewed the dunghill, the vegetables, the fowls, dogs, and guinea-pigs, and even went into the house, where in a long low room on the ground floor, Count Eberhard sat in defiant isolation, reading at a clumsy table. He asked crossly what they wanted.

Ida Jungmann could not be brought to repeat the visit. She insisted that, if the two children wished to be together, Kai could visit Hanno instead. So for the first time, with honest admiration, but no trace of shyness, Kai entered Hanno's beautiful home. After that he went often. Soon nothing but the deep winter snows prevented him from making the long way back again for the sake of a few hours with his friend.

They sat in the large play-room in the second storey and did their lessons together. There were long sums that covered both sides of the slate with additions, subtractions, multiplications, and divisions, and had to come out to zero in the end; otherwise there was a mistake, and they must hunt and hunt till they had found the little beast and exterminated him. Then they had to study grammar, and learn the rules of comparison, and write down very neat, tidy examples underneath. Thus: " Horn is transparent, glass is more transparent, light is most transparent." They took their exercise-books and conned sentences like the following: " I received a letter, saying that he felt aggrieved because he believed that you had deceived him." The fell intent of this sentence, so full of pitfalls, was that you should write *ei* where you ought to write *ie*, and contrariwise. They had, in fact, done that very thing, and now it must be corrected. But when all was finished they might put their books aside and sit on the window-ledge while Ida read to them.

The good soul read about Cinderella, about the prince who could not shiver and shake, about Rumpelstiltskin, about Rapunzel and the Frog Prince — in her deep, patient voice, her eyes half-shut, for she knew the stories by heart, she had read them so often. She wet her finger and turned the page automatically.

But after a while Kai, who possessed the constant craving to do something himself, to have some effect on his surroundings, would close the book and begin to tell stories himself. It was a good idea, for they knew all the printed ones, and Ida needed a rest sometimes, too. Kai's stories were short and simple at first, but they expanded and grew bolder and more complicated with time. The interesting thing about them was that they never stood quite in the air, but were based upon a reality which he presented in a new and mysterious light. Hanno particularly liked the one about the wicked enchanter who tortured all human beings by his malignant art; who had captured a beautiful prince named Josephus and turned him into a green-and-red parrot, which he kept in a gilded cage. But in a far distant land the chosen hero was growing up, who should one day fearlessly advance at the head of an invincible army of dogs, chickens, and guinea-pigs and slay the base enchanter with a single sword-thrust, and deliver all the world — in particular, Hanno Buddenbrook — from his clutches. Then Josephus would be restored to his proper form and return to his kingdom, in which Kai and Hanno would be appointed to high offices.

Senator Buddenbrook saw the two friends together now and then, as he passed the door of the play-room. He had nothing against the intimacy, for it was clear that the two lads did each other good. Hanno gentled, tamed, and ennobled Kai, who loved him tenderly, admired his white hands, and, for his sake, let Ida Jungmann wash his own with soap and a nail-brush. And if Hanno could absorb some of his friend's wild energy and spirits, it would be welcome, for the Senator realized keenly the constant feminine influence that surrounded the boy, and knew that it was not the best means for developing his manly qualities.

The faithful devotion of the good Ida could not be repaid with gold. She had been in the family now for more than thirty years. She had cared for the previous generations with self-abnegation; but Hanno she carried in her arms, lapped him in tender care, and loved him to idolatry. She had a naïve, unshakable belief in his privileged station in life, which sometimes went to the length of absurdity. In whatever touched him she showed a surprising, even an unpleasant effrontery. Suppose, for instance, she took him with her to buy cakes at the pastry-shop: she would poke among the sweets on the counter and select a piece for Hanno, which she would coolly hand him without paying for it — the man should feel himself honoured, indeed! And before a crowded show-window she would ask the people in front, in her west-Prussian dialect, pleasantly enough, but with decision, to make a place for her charge. He was so uncommon in her eyes that she felt there was hardly another child in the world worthy to touch him. In little Kai's case, the mutual preference of the two children had been too strong for her. Possibly she was a little taken by his name, too. But if other children came up to them on the Mill-wall, as she sat with Hanno on a bench, Fräulein Jungmann would get up almost at once, make some excuse or other — it was late, or there was a draught — and take her charge away. The pretexts she gave to little Johann would have led him to believe that all his contemporaries were either scrofulous or full of " evil humours," and that he himself was a solitary exception; which did not tend to increase his already deficient confidence and ease of manner.

Senator Buddenbrook did not know all the details; but he saw enough to convince him that his son's development was not taking the desired course. If he could only take his upbringing in his own hands, and mould his spirit by daily and hourly contact! But he had not the time. He perceived the lamentable failure of his occasional efforts: he knew they only strained the relations between father and son. In his mind was a picture which he longed to reproduce: it was a picture of Hanno's great-grandfather, whom he himself had known as a boy: a clear-sighted man, jovial, simple, sturdy, humorous — why could not little Johann grow up like that? If only he could suppress or forbid the music, which was surely not good for the lad's physical development, absorbed his powers, and took his mind from the practical affairs of life! That dreamy nature — did it not almost, at times, border on irresponsibility?

One day, some three quarters of an hour before dinner, Hanno had gone down alone to the first storey. He had practised for a long time on the piano, and now was idling about in the living-room. He half lay, half sat, on the chaise-longue, tying and untying his sailor's knot, and his eyes, roving aimlessly about, caught sight of an open portfolio on his mother's nut-wood writing-table. It was the leather case with the family papers. He rested his elbow on the sofa-cushion, and his chin in his hand, and looked at the things for a while from a distance. Papa must have had them out after second breakfast, and left them there because he was not finished with them. Some of the papers were sticking in the portfolio, some loose sheets lying outside were weighted with a metal ruler, and the large gilt-edged notebook with the motley paper lay there open.

Hanno slipped idly down from the sofa and went to the writing-table. The book was open at the Buddenbrook family tree, set forth in the hand of his various forbears, including his father; complete, with rubrics, parentheses, and plainly marked dates. Kneeling with one knee on the desk-chair, leaning his head with its soft waves of brown hair on the palm of his hand, Hanno looked at the manuscript sidewise, carelessly critical, a little contemptuous, and supremely indifferent, letting his free hand toy with Mamma's gold-and-ebony pen. His eyes roved all over these names, masculine and feminine, some of them in queer old-fashioned writing with great flourishes, written in faded yellow or thick black ink, to which little grains of sand were sticking. At the very bottom, in Papa's small, neat handwriting that ran so fast over the page, he read his own name, under that of his parents: Justus, Johann, Kasper, born April 15, 1861. He liked looking at it. He straightened up a little, and took the ruler and pen, still rather idly; let his eye travel once more over the whole genealogical host; then, with absent care, mechanically and dreamily, he made with the gold pen a beautiful, clean double line diagonally across the entire page, the upper one heavier than the lower, just as he had been taught to embellish the page of his arithmetic book. He looked at his work with his head on one side, and then moved away.

After dinner the Senator called him up and surveyed him with his eyebrows drawn together.

" What is this? Where did it come from? Did you do it? "

Hanno had to think a minute, whether he really had done it; and then he answered " Yes."

" What for? What is the matter with you? Answer me! What possessed you, to do such a mischievous thing? " cried the Senator, and struck Hanno's cheek lightly with the rolled-up notebook.

And little Johann stammered, retreating, with his hand to his cheek, " I thought — I thought — there was nothing else coming."

CHAPTER VIII

NOWADAYS, when the family gathered at table on Thursdays, under the calmly smiling gaze of the immortals on the walls, they had a new and serious theme. It called out on the faces of the female Buddenbrooks, at least the Broad Street ones, an expression of cold restraint. But it highly excited Frau Permaneder, as her manner and gestures betrayed. She tossed back her head, stretched out her arms before her, or flung them above her head as she talked; and her voice showed by turns anger and dismay, passionate opposition and deep feeling. She would pass over from the particular to the general, and talk in her throaty voice about wicked people, interrupting herself with the little cough that was due to poor digestion. Or she would utter little trumpetings of disgust: Teary Trietschke, Grünlich, Permaneder! A new name had now been added to these, and she pronounced it in a tone of indescribable scorn and hatred: "The District Attorney!"

But when Director Hugo Weinschenk entered — late, as usual, for he was overwhelmed with work; balancing his two fists and weaving about more than ever at the waist of his frock-coat — and sat down at table, his lower lip hanging down with its impudent expression under his moustaches, then the conversation would come to a full stop, and heavy silence would brood over the table until the Senator came to the rescue by asking the Director how his affair was going on — as if it were an ordinary business dealing.

Hugo Weinschenk would answer that things were going very well, very well indeed, they could not go otherwise; and then he would blithely change the subject. He was much more sprightly than he used to be; there was a certain lack of restraint in his roving eye, and he would ask ever so many times about Gerda Buddenbrook's fiddle without getting any reply. He talked freely and gaily — only it was a pity his flow of spirits prevented him from guarding his tongue; for he now and then told anecdotes which were not at all suited to the company. One, in particular, was about a wet-nurse who prejudiced the health of her charge by the fact that she suffered from flatulence. Too late, or not at all, he remarked that his wife was flushing rosy red, that Thomas, the Frau Consul and Gerda were sitting like statues, and the Misses Buddenbrook exchanging glances that were fairly boring holes in each other. Even Riekchen Severin was looking insulted at the bottom of the table, and old Consul Kröger was the single one of the company who gave even a subdued snort.

What was the trouble with Director Weinschenk? This industrious, solid citizen with the rough exterior and no social graces, who devoted himself with an obstinate sense of duty to his work alone — this man was supposed to have been guilty, not once but repeatedly, of a serious fault: he was accused of, he had been indicted for, performing a business manœuvre which was not only questionable, but directly dishonest and criminal. There would be a trial, the outcome of which was not easy to guess. What was he accused of? It was this: certain fires of considerable extent had taken place in different localities, which would have cost his company large sums of money. Director Weinschenk was accused of having received private information of such accidents through his agents, and then, in wrongful possession of this information, of having transferred the back insurance to another firm, thus saving his own the loss. The matter was now in the hands of the State Attorney, Dr. Moritz Hagenström.

"Thomas," said the Frau Consul in private to her son, "please explain it to me. I do not understand. What do you make of the affair?"

"Why, my dear Mother," he answered, "what is there to say? It does not look as though things were quite as they should be — unfortunately. It seems unlikely to me that Weinschenk is as guilty as people think. In the modern style of doing business, there is a thing they call usance. And usance — well, imagine a sort of manœuvre, not exactly open and above-board, something that looks dishonest to the man in the street, yet perhaps quite customary and taken for granted in the business world: that is usance. The boundary line between usance and actual dishonesty is extremely hard to draw. Well — if Weinschenk has done anything he shouldn't, he has probably done no more than a good many of his colleagues who will not get caught. But — I don't see much chance of his being cleared. Perhaps in a larger city he might be, but here everything depends on cliques and personal motives. He should have borne that in mind in selecting his lawyer. It is true that we have no really eminent lawyer in the whole town, nobody with superior oratorical talent, who knows all the ropes and is versed in dubious transactions. All our jurists hang together; they have family connections, in many cases; they eat together; they work together, and they are accustomed to considering each other. In my opinion, it would have been clever to take a town lawyer. But what did Weinschenk do? He thought it necessary — and this in itself makes his innocence look doubtful — to get a lawyer from Berlin, a Dr. Breslauer, who is a regular rake, an accomplished orator and up to all the tricks of the trade. He has the reputation of having got so-and-so many dishonest bank-rupts off scot-free. He will conduct this affair with the same cleverness — for a consideration. But will it do any good? I can see already that our town lawyers will band together to fight him tooth and nail, and that Dr. Hagenström's hearers will already be prepossessed in his favour. As for the witnesses: well, Wein-schenk's own staff won't be any too friendly to him, I'm afraid. What we indulgently call his rough exterior — he would call it that, himself, too — has not made him many friends. In short, Mother, I am looking forward to trouble. It will be a pity for Erica, if it turns out badly; but I feel most for Tony. You see, she is quite right in saying that Hagenström is glad of the chance. The thing concerns all of us, and the disgrace will fall on us too; for Weinschenk belongs to the family and eats at our table. As far as I am concerned, I can manage. I know what I have to do: in public, I shall act as if I had nothing whatever to do with the affair. I will not go to the trial — although I am sorry not to, for Breslauer is sure to be interesting. And in general I must behave with complete indifference, to protect myself from the imputation of wanting to use my influence. But Tony? I don't like to think what a sad business a conviction will be for her. She protests ve-hemently against envious intrigues and calumniators and all that; but what really moves her is her anxiety lest, after all her other troubles, she may see her daughter's honourable position lost as well. It is the last blow. She will protest her belief in Wein-schenk's innocence the more loudly the more she is forced to doubt it. Well, he may be innocent, after all. We can only wait and see, Mother, and be very tactful with him and Tony and Erica. But I'm afraid — "

It was under these circumstances that the Christmas feast drew near, to which little Hanno was counting the days, with a beating heart and the help of a calendar manufactured by Ida Jungmann, with a Christmas tree on the last leaf.

The signs of festivity increased. Ever since the first Sunday in Advent a great gaily coloured picture of a certain Ruprecht had been hanging on the wall in grandmama's dining-room. And one morning Hanno found his covers and the rug beside his bed sprinkled with gold tinsel. A few days later, as papa was lying with his newspaper on the living-room sofa, and Hanno was reading " The Witch of Endor " out of Gerock's " Palm Leaves," an " old man " was announced. This had happened every year since Hanno was a baby — and yet was always a surprise. They asked him in, this " old man," and he came shuffling along in a big coat with the fur side out, sprinkled with bits of cotton-wool and tinsel. He wore a fur cap, and his face had black smudges on it, and his beard was long and white. The beard and the big, bushy eye-brows were also sprinkled with tinsel. He explained — as he did every year — in a harsh voice, that *this* sack (on his left shoulder) was for good children, who said their prayers (it contained apples and gilded nuts); but that *this* sack (on his right shoulder) was for naughty children. The " old man " was, of course, Ru-precht; perhaps not actually the real Ruprecht — it might even be Wenzel the barber, dressed up in Papa's coat turned fur side out — but it was as much Ruprecht as possible. Hanno, greatly im-pressed, said Our Father for him, as he had last year — both times interrupting himself now and again with a little nervous sob — and was permitted to put his hand into the sack for good chil-dren, which the " old man " forgot to take away.

The holidays came, and there was not much trouble over the report, which had to be presented for Papa to read, even at Christmas-time. The great dining-room was closed and mysteri-ous, and there were marzipan and ginger-bread to eat — and in the streets, Christmas had already come. Snow fell, the weather was frosty, and on the sharp clear air were borne the notes of the barrel-organ, for the Italians, with their velvet jackets and their black moustaches, had arrived for the Christmas feast. The shop-windows were gay with toys and goodies; the booths for the Christmas fair had been erected in the market-place; and wherever you went you breathed in the fresh, spicy odour of the Christmas trees set out for sale.

The evening of the twenty-third came at last, and with it the present-giving in the house in Fishers' Lane. This was attended by the family only — it was a sort of dress rehearsal for the Christ-mas Eve party given by the Frau Consul in Meng Street. She clung to the old customs, and reserved the twenty-fourth for a celebration to which the whole family group was bidden; which, accordingly, in the late afternoon, assembled in the landscape-room.

The old lady, flushed of cheek, and with feverish eyes, arrayed in a heavy black-and-grey striped silk that gave out a faint scent of patchouli, received her guests as they entered, and embraced them silently, her gold bracelets tinkling. She was strangely excited this evening — " Why, Mother, you're fairly trembling," the Senator said when he came in with Gerda and Hanno. " Everything will go off very easily." But she only whispered, kissing all three of them, " For Jesus Christ's sake — and my blessed Jean's."

Indeed, the whole consecrated programme instituted by the deceased Consul had to be carried out to the smallest detail; and the poor lady fluttered about, driven by her sense of responsibility for the fitting accomplishment of the evening's performance, which must be pervaded with a deep and fervent joy. She went restlessly back and forth, from the pillared hall where the choir-boys from St. Mary's were already assembled, to the dining-room, where Riekchen Severin was putting the finishing touches to the tree and the tableful of presents, to the corridor full of shrinking old people — the " poor " who were to share in the presents — and back into the landscape-room, where she rebuked every unnecessary word or sound with one of her mild sidelong glances. It was so still that the sound of a distant hand-organ, faint and clear like a toy music-box, came across to them through the snowy streets. Some twenty persons or more were sitting or standing about in the room; yet it was stiller than a church — so still that, as the Senator cautiously whispered to Uncle Justus, it reminded one more of a funeral!

There was really no danger that the solemnity of the feast would be rudely broken in upon by youthful high spirits. A glance showed that almost all the persons in the room were arrived at an age when the forms of expression are already long ago fixed. Senator Thomas Buddenbrook, whose pallor gave the lie to his alert, energetic, humorous expression; Gerda, his wife, leaning back in her chair, the gleaming, blue-ringed eyes in her pale face gazing fixedly at the crystal prisms in the chandelier; his sister, Frau Permaneder; his cousin, Jürgen Kröger, a quiet, neatly-dressed official; Friederike, Henriette, and Pfiffi, the first two more long and lean, the third smaller and plumper than ever, but all three wearing their stereotyped expression, their sharp, spiteful smile at everything and everybody, as though they were perpetually saying " Really — it seems incredible! " Lastly, there was poor, ashen-grey Clothilde, whose thoughts were probably fixed upon the coming meal. — Every one of these persons was past forty. The hostess herself, her brother Justus and his wife, and little Therese Weichbrodt were all well past sixty; while old Frau Consul Buddenbrook, Uncle Gotthold's widow, born Stüwing, as well as Madame Kethelsen, now, alas almost entirely deaf, were already in the seventies.

Erica Weinschenk was the only person present in the bloom of youth; she was much younger than her husband, whose cropped, greying head stood out against the idyllic landscape behind him. When her eyes — the light blue eyes of Herr Grünlich — rested upon him, you could see how her full bosom rose and fell without a sound, and how she was beset with anxious, bewildered thoughts about usance and book-keeping, witnesses, prosecuting attorneys, defence, and judges. Thoughts like these, un-Christmaslike though they were, troubled everybody in the room. They all felt uncanny at the presence in their midst of a member of the family who was actually accused of an offence against the law, the civic weal, and business probity, and who would probably be visited by shame and imprisonment. Here was a Christmas family party at the Buddenbrooks' — with an accused man in the circle! Frau Permaneder's dignity became majestic, and the smile of the Misses Buddenbrook more and more pointed.

And what of the children, the scant posterity upon whom rested the family hopes? Were they conscious too of the slightly uncanny atmosphere? The state of mind of the little Elisabeth could not be fathomed. She sat on her bonne's lap in a frock trimmed by Frau Permaneder with satin bows, folded her small hands into fists, sucked her tongue, and stared straight ahead of her. Now and then she would utter a brief sound, like a grunt, and the nurse would rock her a little on her arm. But Hanno sat still on his footstool at his mother's knee and stared up, like her, into the chandelier.

Christian was missing — where was he? At the last minute they noticed his absence. The Frau Consul's characteristic gesture, from the corner of her mouth up to her temple, as though putting back a refractory hair, became frequent and feverish. She gave an order to Mamsell Severin, and the spinster went out through the hall, past the choir-boys and the " poor " and down the corridor to Christian's room, where she knocked on the door.

Christian appeared straightway; he limped casually into the landscape-room, rubbing his bald brow. " Good gracious, children," he said, " I nearly forgot the party! "

" You nearly forgot — " his mother repeated, and stiffened.

" Yes, I really forgot it was Christmas. I was reading a book of travel, about South America. — Dear me, I've seen such a lot of

Christmases! " he added, and was about to launch out upon a description of a Christmas in a fifth-rate variety theatre in London — when all at once the church-like hush of the room began to work upon him, and he moved on tip-toe to his place, wrinkling up his nose.

"Rejoice, O Daughter of Zion! " sang the choir-boys. They had previously been indulging in such audible practical jokes that the Senator had to get up and stand in the doorway to inspire respect. But now they sang beautifully. The clear treble, sustained by the deeper voices, soared up in pure, exultant, glorifying tones, bearing all hearts along with them: softening the smiles of the spinsters, making the old folk look in upon themselves and back upon the past; easing the hearts of those still in the midst of life's tribulations, and helping them to forget for a little while.

Hanno unclasped his hands from about his knees. He looked very pale, and cold, played with the fringe of his stool, and twisted his tongue about among his teeth. He had to draw a deep breath every little while, for his heart contracted with a joy almost painful at the exquisite bell-like purity of the chorale. The white folding doors were still tightly closed, but the spicy poignant odour drifted through the cracks and whetted one's appetite for the wonder within. Each year with throbbing pulses he awaited this vision of ineffable, unearthly splendour. What would there be for him, in there? What he had wished for, of course; there was always that — unless he had been persuaded out of it beforehand. The theatre, then, the long-desired toy theatre, would spring at him as the door opened, and show him the way to his place. This was the suggestion which had stood heavily underlined at the top of his list, ever since he had seen *Fidelio;* indeed, since then, it had been almost his single thought.

He had been taken to the opera as compensation for a particularly painful visit to Herr Brecht; sitting beside his mother, in the dress circle, he had followed breathless a performance of *Fidelio,* and since that time he had heard nothing, seen nothing, thought of nothing but opera, and a passion for the theatre filled him and almost kept him sleepless. He looked enviously at people like Uncle Christian, who was known as a regular frequenter and might go every night if he liked: Consul Döhlmann, Gosch the broker — how could they endure the joy of seeing it every night? He himself would ask no more than to look once a week into the hall, before the performance: hear the voices of the instruments being tuned, and gaze for a while at the curtain! For he loved it

all, the seats, the musicians, the drop-curtain — even the smell of
gas.

Would his theatre be large? What sort of curtain would it
have? A tiny hole must be cut in it at once — there was a peep-
hole in the curtain at the theatre. Had Grandmamma, or rather
had Mamsell Severin — for Grandmamma could not see to everything herself — been able to find all the necessary scenery for
Fidelio? He determined to shut himself up to-morrow and give a
performance all by himself, and already in fancy he heard his
little figures singing: for he was approaching the theatre by way
of his music.

"Exult, Jerusalem!" finished the choir; and their voices, following one another in fugue form, united joyously in the last
syllable. The clear accord died away; deep silence reigned in the
pillared hall and the landscape-room. The elders looked down, oppressed by the pause; only Director Weinschenk's eyes roved
boldly about, and Frau Permaneder coughed her dry cough, which
she could not suppress. Now the Frau Consul moved slowly to
the table and sat among her family. She turned up the lamp and
took in her hands the great Bible with its edges of faded gold-leaf.
She stuck her glasses on her nose, unfastened the two great leather
hasps of the book, opened it to the place where there was a book-
mark, took a sip of *eau sucrée*, and began to read, from the yel-
lowed page with the large print, the Christmas chapter.

She read the old familiar words with a simple, heart-felt accent
that sounded clear and moving in the pious hush. " 'And to men
good-will,' " she finished, and from the pillared hall came a trio of
voices: "Holy night, peaceful night!" The family in the landscape-room joined in. They did so cautiously, for most of them
were unmusical, as a tone now and then betrayed. But that in no
wise impaired the effect of the old hymn. Frau Permaneder sang
with trembling lips; it sounded sweetest and most touching to the
heart of her who had a troubled life behind her, and looked back
upon it in the brief peace of this holy hour. Madame Kethelsen
wept softly, but comprehended nothing.

Now the Frau Consul rose. She grasped the hands of her grandson Johann and her granddaughter Elisabeth, and proceeded
through the room. The elders of the family fell in behind, and
the younger brought up the rear; the servants and poor joined in
from the hall; and so they marched, singing with one accord "Oh,
Evergreen" — Uncle Christian sang "Oh, Everblue," and made
the children laugh by lifting up his legs like a jumping-jack —

through the wide-open, lofty folding doors, and straight into Paradise.

The whole great room was filled with the fragrance of slightly singed evergreen twigs and glowing with light from countless tiny flames. The sky-blue hangings with the white figures on them added to the brilliance. There stood the mighty tree, between the dark red window-curtains, towering nearly to the ceiling, decorated with silver tinsel and large white lilies, with a shining angel at the top and the manger at the foot. Its candles twinkled in the general flood of light like far-off stars. And a row of tiny trees, also full of stars and hung with comfits, stood on the long white table, laden with presents, that stretched from the window to the door. All the gas-brackets on the wall were lighted too, and thick candles burned in all four of the gilded candelabra in the corners of the room. Large objects, too large to stand upon the table, were arranged upon the floor, and two smaller tables, likewise adorned with tiny trees and covered with gifts for the servants and the poor, stood on either side of the door.

Dazzled by the light and the unfamiliar look of the room, they marched once around it, singing, filed past the manger where lay the little wax figure of the Christ-child, and then moved to their places and stood silent.

Hanno was quite dazed. His fevered glance had soon sought out the theatre, which, as it stood there upon the table, seemed larger and grander than anything he had dared to dream of. But his place had been changed — it was now opposite to where he had stood last year, and this made him doubtful whether the theatre was really his. And on the floor beneath it was something else, a large, mysterious something, which had surely not been on his list; a piece of furniture, that looked like a commode — could it be meant for him?

"Come here, my dear child," said the Frau Consul, "and look at this." She lifted the lid. "I know you like to play chorals. Herr Pfühl will show you how. You must tread all the time, sometimes more and sometimes less; and then, not lift up the hands, but change the fingers so, *peu à peu*."

It was a harmonium — a pretty little thing of polished brown wood, with metal handles at the sides, gay bellows worked with a treadle, and a neat revolving stool. Hanno struck a chord. A soft organ tone released itself and made the others look up from their presents. He hugged his grandmother, who pressed him tenderly to her, and then left him to receive the thanks of her other guests.

He turned to his theatre. The harmonium was an overpowering dream — which just now he had no time to indulge. There was a superfluity of joy; and he lost sight of single gifts in trying to see and notice everything at once. Ah, here was the prompter's box, a shell-shaped one, and a beautiful red and gold curtain rolled up and down behind it. The stage was set for the last act of *Fidelio*. The poor prisoners stood with folded hands. Don Pizarro, in enormous puffed sleeves, was striking a permanent and awesome attitude, and the minister, in black velvet, approached from behind with hasty strides, to turn all to happiness. It was just as in the theatre, only almost more beautiful. The Jubilee chorus, the finale, echoed in Hanno's ears, and he sat down at the harmonium to play a fragment which stuck in his memory. But he got up again, almost at once, to take up the book he had wished for, a mythology, in a red binding with a gold Pallas Athene on the cover. He ate some of the sweetmeats from his plate full of marzipan, gingerbread, and other goodies, looked through various small articles like writing utensils and school-bag — and for the moment forgot everything else, to examine a penholder with a tiny glass bulb on it: when you held this up to your eye, you saw, like magic, a broad Swiss landscape.

Mamsell Severin and the maid passed tea and biscuits; and while Hanno dipped and ate, he had time to look about. Every one stood talking and laughing; they all showed each other their presents and admired the presents of others. Objects of porcelain, silver, gold, nickel, wood, silk, cloth, and every other conceivable material lay on the table. Huge loaves of decorated gingerbread, alternating with loaves of marzipan, stood in long rows, still moist and fresh. All the presents made by Frau Permaneder were decorated with huge satin bows.

Now and then some one came up to little Johann, put an arm across his shoulders, and looked at his presents with the overdone, cynical admiration which people manufacture for the treasures of children. Uncle Christian was the only person who did not display this grown-up arrogance. He sauntered over to his nephew's place, with a diamond ring on his finger, a present from his mother; and his pleasure in the toy theatre was as unaffected as Hanno's own.

"By George, that's fine," he said, letting the curtain up and down, and stepping back for a view of the scenery. "Did you ask for it? Oh, so you did ask for it!" he suddenly said after a pause, during which his eyes had roved about the room as though he were full of unquiet thoughts. "Why did you ask for it?

What made you think of it? Have you been in the theatre?
Fidelio, eh? Yes, they give that well. And you want to imitate it,
do you? Do opera yourself, eh? Did it make such an impression
on you? Listen, son — take my advice: don't think too much
about such things — theatre, and that sort of thing. It's no good.
Believe your old uncle. I've always spent too much time on them,
and that is why I haven't come to much good. I've made great
mistakes, you know."

Thus he held forth to his nephew, while Hanno looked up at
him curiously. He paused, and his bony, emaciated face cleared up
as he regarded the little theatre. Then he suddenly moved forward
one of the figures on the stage, and sang, in a cracked and hollow
tremolo, "Ha, what terrible transgression!" He sat down on the
piano-stool, which he shoved up in front of the theatre, and began
to give a performance, singing all the rôles and the accompaniment
as well, and gesticulating furiously. The family gathered at his
back, laughed, nodded their heads, and enjoyed it immensely. As
for Hanno, his pleasure was profound. Christian broke off, after
a while, very abruptly. His face clouded, he rubbed his hand over
his skull and down his left side, and turned to his audience with his
nose wrinkled and his face quite drawn.

"There it is again," he said. "I never have a little fun without
having to pay for it. It is not an ordinary pain, you know, it is a
misery, down all this left side, because the nerves are too short."

But his relatives took his complaints as little seriously as they had
his entertainment. They hardly answered him, but indifferently
dispersed, leaving Christian sitting before the little theatre in silence. He blinked rapidly for a bit and then got up.

"No, child," said he, stroking Hanno's head: "amuse yourself
with it, but not too much, you know: don't neglect your work for
it, do you hear? I have made a great many mistakes. — I think I'll
go over to the club for a while," he said to the elders. "They are
celebrating there to-day, too. Good-bye for the present." And
he went off across the hall, on his stiff, crooked legs.

They had all eaten the midday meal earlier than usual to-day,
and been hungry for the tea and biscuits. But they had scarcely
finished when great crystal bowls were handed round full of a
yellow, grainy substance which turned out to be almond cream.
It was a mixture of eggs, ground almonds, and rose-water, tasting
perfectly delicious; but if you ate even a tiny spoonful too much,
the result was an attack of indigestion. However, the company
was not restrained by fear of consequences — even though Frau
Consul begged them to "leave a little corner for supper." Clo-

thilde, in particular, performed miracles with the almond cream, and lapped it up like so much porridge, with heart-felt gratitude. There was also wine jelly in glasses, and English plum-cake. Gradually they all moved over to the landscape-room, where they sat with their plates round the table.

Hanno remained alone in the dining-room. Little Elisabeth Weinschenk had already been taken home; but he was to stop up for supper, for the first time in his life. The servants and the poor folk had had their presents and gone; Ida Jungmann was chattering with Riekchen Severin in the hall — although generally, as a governess, she preserved a proper distance between herself and the Frau Consul's maid. — The lights of the great tree were burnt down and extinguished, the manger was in darkness. But a few candles still burned on the small trees, and now and then a twig came within reach of the flame and crackled up, increasing the pungent smell in the room. Every breath of air that stirred the trees stirred the pieces of tinsel too, and made them give out a delicate metallic whisper. It was still enough to hear the hand-organ again, sounding through the frosty air from a distant street.

Hanno abandoned himself to the enjoyment of the Christmas sounds and smells. He propped his head on his hand and read in his mythology book, munching mechanically the while, because that was proper to the day: marzipan, sweet-meats, almond cream, and plum-cake; until the chest-oppression caused by an over-loaded stomach mingled with the sweet excitation of the evening and gave him a feeling of pensive felicity. He read about the struggles of Zeus before he arrived at the headship of the gods; and every now and then he listened into the other room, where they were going at length into the future of poor Aunt Clothilde.

Clothilde, on this evening, was far and away the happiest of them all. A smile lighted up her colourless face as she received congratulations and teasing from all sides; her voice even broke now and then out of joyful emotion. She had at last been made a member of the Order of St. John. The Senator had succeeded by subterranean methods in getting her admitted, not without some private grumblings about nepotism, on the part of certain gentlemen. Now the family all discussed the excellent institution, which was similar to the homes in Mecklenburg, Dobberthien, and Ribnitz, for ladies from noble families. The object of these establishments was the suitable care of portionless women from old and worthy families. Poor Clothilde was now assured of a small but certain income, which would increase with the years, and finally, when she had succeeded to the highest class, would secure her a decent home in the cloister itself.

Little Hanno stopped awhile with the grown-ups, but soon strayed back to the dining-room, which displayed a new charm now that the brilliant light did not fairly dazzle one with its splendours. It was an extraordinary pleasure to roam about there, as if on a half-darkened stage after the performance, and see a little behind the scenes. He touched the lilies on the big fir-tree, with their golden stamens; handled the tiny figures of people and animals in the manger, found the candles that lighted the transparency for the star of Bethlehem over the stable; lifted up the long cloth that covered the present-table, and saw quantities of wrapping-paper and pasteboard boxes stacked beneath.

The conversation in the landscape-room was growing less and less agreeable. Inevitably, irresistibly, it had arrived at the one dismal theme which had been in everybody's mind, but which they had thus far avoided, as a tribute to the festal evening. Hugo Weinschenk himself dilated upon it, with a wild levity of manner and gesture. He explained certain details of the procedure — the examination of witnesses had now been interrupted by the Christmas recess — condemned the very obvious bias of the President, Dr. Philander, and poured scorn on the attitude which the Public Prosecutor, Dr. Hagenström, thought it proper to assume toward himself and the witnesses for the defence. Breslauer had succeeded in drawing the sting of several of his most slanderous remarks; and he had assured the Director that, for the present, there need be no fear of a conviction. The Senator threw in a question now and then, out of courtesy; and Frau Permaneder, sitting on the sofa with elevated shoulders, would utter fearful imprecations against Dr. Moritz Hagenström. But the others were silent: so profoundly silent that the Director at length fell silent too. For little Hanno, over in the dining-room, the time sped by on angels' wings; but in the landscape-room there reigned an oppressive silence, which dragged on till Christian came back from the club, where he had celebrated Christmas with the bachelors and good fellows.

The cold stump of a cigar hung between his lips, and his haggard cheeks were flushed. He came through the dining-room and said, as he entered the landscape-room, "Well, children, the tree was simply gorgeous. Weinschenk, we ought to have had Breslauer come to see it. He has never seen anything like it, I am sure."

He encountered one of his mother's quiet, reproachful sideglances, and returned it with an easy, unembarrassed questioning look. At nine o'clock the party sat down to supper.

It was laid, as always on these occasions, in the pillared hall. The Frau Consul recited the ancient grace with sincere conviction:

"Come, Lord Jesus, be our guest,
And bless the bread thou gavest us"

— to which, as usual on the holy evening, she added a brief prayer, the substance of which was an admonition to remember those who, on this blessed night, did not fare so well as the Buddenbrook family. This accomplished, they all sat down with good consciences to a lengthy repast, beginning with carp and butter sauce and old Rhine wine.

The Senator put two fish-scales into his pocket, to help him save money during the coming year. Christian, however, ruefully remarked that he hadn't much faith in the prescription; and Consul Kröger had no need of it. His pittance had long since been invested securely, beyond the reach of fluctuations in the exchange. The old man sat as far away as possible from his wife, to whom he hardly ever spoke nowadays. She persisted in sending money to Jacob, who was still roaming about, nobody knew where, unless his mother did. Uncle Justus scowled forbiddingly when the conversation, with the advent of the second course, turned upon the absent members of the family, and he saw the foolish mother wipe her eyes. They spoke of the Frankfort Buddenbrooks and the Duchamps in Hamburg, and of Pastor Tiburtius in Riga, too, without any ill-will. And the Senator and his sister touched glasses in silence to the health of Messrs. Grünlich and Permaneder — for, after all, did they not in a sense belong to the family too?

The turkey, stuffed with chestnuts, raisins, and apples, was universally praised. They compared it with other years, and decided that this one was the largest for a long time. With the turkey came roast potatoes and two kinds of compote, and each dish held enough to satisfy the appetite of a family all by itself. The old red wine came from the firm of Möllendorpf.

Little Johann sat between his parents and choked down with difficulty a small piece of white meat with stuffing. He could not begin to compete with Aunt Tilda, and he felt tired and out of sorts. But it was a great thing none the less to be dining with the grown-ups, and to have one of the beautiful little rolls with poppy-seed in his elaborately folded serviette, and three wine-glasses in front of his place. He usually drank out of the little gold mug which Uncle Justus gave him. But when the red, white, and brown meringues appeared, and Uncle Justus poured some oily, yellow

Greek wine into the smallest of the three glasses, his appetite re-
vived. He ate a whole red ice, then half a white one, then a little
piece of the chocolate, his teeth hurting horribly all the while.
Then he sipped his sweet wine gingerly and listened to Uncle
Christian, who had begun to talk.

He told about the Christmas celebration at the club, which had
been very jolly, it seemed. " Good God! " he said, just as if he
were about to relate the story of Johnny Thunderstorm, " those
fellows drank Swedish punch just like water."

" Ugh! " said the Frau Consul shortly, and cast down her eyes.

But he paid no heed. His eyes began to wander — and thought
and memory became so vivid that they flickered like shadows
across his haggard face.

" Do any of you know," he asked, " how it feels to drink too
much Swedish punch? I don't mean getting drunk: I mean the
feeling you have the next day — the after-effects. They are very
queer and unpleasant; yes, queer and unpleasant at the same time."

" Reason enough for describing them," said the Senator.

" *Assez*, Christian. That does not interest us in the least," said
the Frau Consul. But he paid no attention. It was his peculiarity
that at such times nothing made any impression on him. He was
silent awhile, and then it seemed that the thing which moved him
was ripe for speech.

" You go about feeling ghastly," he said, turning to his brother
and wrinkling up his nose. " Headache, and upset stomach — oh,
well, you have that with other things, too. But you feel *filthy* " —
here he rubbed his hands together, his face entirely distorted.
" You wash your hands, but it does no good; they feel dirty and
clammy, and there is grease under the nails. You take a bath: no
good, your whole body is sticky and unclean. You itch all over,
and you feel disgusted with yourself. Do you know the feeling,
Thomas? you do know it, don't you? "

" Yes, yes," said the Senator, making a gesture of repulsion with
his hand. But Christian's extraordinary tactlessness had so increased with the years that he never perceived how unpleasant he
was making himself to the company, nor how out of place his
conversation was in these surroundings and on this evening. He
continued to describe the evil effects of too much Swedish punch;
and when he felt that he had exhausted the subject, he gradually
subsided.

Before they arrived at the butter and cheese, the Frau Consul
found occasion for another little speech to her family. If, she
said, not quite everything in the course of the years had gone as

we, in our short-sightedness, desired, there remained such manifold blessings as should fill our hearts with gratitude and love. For it was precisely this mingling of trials with blessings which showed that God never lifted his hand from the family, but ever guided its destinies according to His wise design, which we might not seek to question. And now, with hopeful hearts, we might drink together to the family health and to its future — that future when all the old and elderly of the present company would be laid to rest; and to the children, to whom the Christmas feast most properly belonged.

As Director Weinschenk's small daughter was no longer present, little Johann had to make the round of the table alone and drink severally with all the company, from Grandmamma to Mamsell Severin. When he came to his father, the Senator touched the child's glass with his and gently lifted Hanno's chin to look into his eyes. But his son did not meet his glance: the long, gold-brown lashes lay deep, deep upon the delicate bluish shadows beneath his eyes.

Therese Weichbrodt took his head in both her hands, kissed him explosively on both cheeks, and said with such a hearty emphasis that surely God must have heeded it, "Be happy, you good che-ild!"

An hour later Hanno lay in his little bed, which now stood in the ante-chamber next to the Senator's dressing-room. He lay on his back, out of regard for his stomach, which was feeling far from pleasant over all the things he had put into it that evening. Ida came out of her room in her dressing-gown, waving a glass about in circles in the air in order to dissolve its contents. He drank the carbonate of soda down quickly, made a wry face, and fell back again.

"I think I'll just have to give it all up, Ida," he said.

"Oh, nonsense, Hanno. Just lie still on your back. You see, now: who was it kept making signs to you to stop eating, and who was it that wouldn't do it?"

"Well, perhaps I'll be all right. When will the things come, Ida?"

"To-morrow morning, first thing, my dearie."

"I wish they were here — I wish I had them now."

"Yes, yes, my dearie — but just have a good sleep now." She kissed him, put out the light, and went away.

He lay quietly, giving himself up to the operation of the soda he had taken. But before his eyes gleamed the dazzling brilliance of the Christmas tree. He saw his theatre and his harmonium, and

his book of mythology; he heard the choir-boys singing in the
distance: "Rejoice, Jerusalem!" Everything sparkled and glit-
tered. His head felt dull and feverish; his heart, affected by the
rebellious stomach, beat strong and irregularly. He lay for long,
in a condition of mingled discomfort, excitement, and reminiscent
bliss, and could not fall asleep.

Next day there would be a third Christmas party, at Fräulein
Weichbrodt's. He looked forward to it as to a comic performance
in the theatre. Therese Weichbrodt had given up her *pensionnat*
in the past year. Madame Kethelsen now occupied the first storey
of the house on the Mill Brink, and she herself the ground floor,
and there they lived alone. The burden of her deformed little
body grew heavier with the years, and she concluded, with Christian humility and submission, that the end was not far off. For
some years now she had believed that each Christmas was her last;
and she strove with all the powers at her command to give a departing brilliance to the feast that was held in her small overheated
rooms. Her means were very narrow, and she gave away each year
a part of her possessions to swell the heap of gifts under the tree:
knick-knacks, paper-weights, emery-bags, needle-cushions, glass
vases, and fragments of her library, miscellaneous books of every
shape and size. Books like "The Secret Journal of a Student of
Himself," Hebel's "Alemannian Poems," Krummacher's "Para-
bles" — Hanno had once received an edition of the "Pensées de
Blaise Pascal," in such tiny print that it had to be read with a glass.

Bishop flowed in streams, and Sesemi's ginger-bread was very
spicy. But Fräulein Weichbrodt abandoned herself with such
trembling emotion to the joys of each Christmas party that none
of them ever went off without a mishap. There was always some
small catastrophe or other to make the guests laugh and enhance
the silent fervour of the hostess' mien. A jug of bishop would be
upset and overwhelm everything in a spicy, sticky red flood. Or
the decorated tree would topple off its wooden support just as
they solemnly entered the room. Hanno fell asleep with the mishap of the previous year before his eyes. It had happened just
before the gifts were given out. Therese Weichbrodt had read
the Christmas chapter, in such impressive accents that all the vowels got inextricably commingled, and then retreated before her
guests to the door, where she made a little speech. She stood upon
the threshold, humped and tiny, her old hands clasped before her
childish bosom, the green silk cap-ribbons falling over her fragile
shoulders. Above her head, over the door, was a transparency,
garlanded with evergreen, that said "Glory to God in the High-

est." And Sesemi spoke of God's mercy; she mentioned that this was her last Christmas, and ended by reminding them that the words of the apostle commended them all to joy — wherewith she trembled from head to foot, so much did her whole poor little body share in her emotions. " Rejoice! " said she, laying her head on one side and nodding violently: " and again I say unto you, rejoice! " But at this moment the whole transparency, with a puffing, crackling, spitting noise, went up in flames, and Mademoiselle Weichbrodt gave a little shriek and a side-spring of unexpected picturesqueness and agility, and got herself out of the way of the rain of flying sparks.

As Hanno recalled the leap which the old spinster performed, he giggled nervously for several minutes into his pillow.

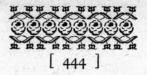

CHAPTER IX

FRAU PERMANEDER was going along Broad Street in a great hurry. There was something abandoned about her air: she showed almost none of the impressive bearing usual to her on the street. Hunted and harassed, in almost violent haste, she had as it were been able to save only a remnant of her dignity — like a beaten king who gathers what is left of his army about him to seek safety in the arms of flight.

She looked pitiable indeed. Her upper lip, that arched upper lip that had always done its share to give charm to her face, was quivering now, and the eyes were large with apprehension. They were very bright and stared fixedly ahead of her, as though they too were hurrying onward. Her hair came in disorder from under her close hat, and her face showed the pale yellow tint which it always had when her digestion took a turn for the worse.

Her digestion was obviously worse in these days. The family noticed that on Thursdays. And no matter how hard every one tried to keep off the rocks, the conversation always made straight for them and stuck there: on the subject of Hugo Weinschenk's trial. Frau Permaneder herself led up to it. She would call on God and her fellow men to tell her how Public Prosecutor Moritz Hagenström could sleep of nights. For her part, she could not understand it — she never would! Her agitation increased with every word. "Thank you, I can't eat," she would say, and push away her plate. She would elevate her shoulders, toss her head, and in the height of her passion fall back upon the practice, acquired in her Munich years, of taking nothing but beer, cold Bavarian beer, poured into an empty stomach, the nerves of which were in rebellion and would revenge themselves bitterly. Toward the end of the meal she always had to get up and go down to the garden or the court, where she suffered the most dreadful fits of nausea, leaning upon Ida Jungmann or Riekchen Severin. Her stomach would finally relieve itself of its contents, and contract with spasms of pain, which sometimes lasted for minutes and would continue at intervals for a long time.

It was about three in the afternoon, a windy, rainy January day. Frau Permaneder turned the corner at Fishers' Lane and hurried down the steep declivity to her brother's house. After a hasty knock she went from the court straight into the bureau, her eye flying across the desks to where the Senator sat in his seat by the window. She made such an imploring motion with her head that he put down his pen without more ado and went to her.

" Well? " he said, one eyebrow lifted.

" A moment, Thomas — it's very pressing; there's no time to waste."

He opened the baize door of his private office, closed it behind him when they were both inside, and looked at his sister inquiringly.

" Tom," she said, her voice quavering, wringing her hands inside her muff, " you must give it to us — lay it out for us — you will, won't you? — the money for the bond, I mean. We haven't it — where should we get twenty-five thousand marks from, I should like to know? You will get them back — you'll get them back all too soon, I'm afraid. You understand — the thing is this: in short, they have reached a point where Hagenström demands immediate arrest or else a bond of twenty-five thousand marks. And Weinschenk will give you his word not to stir from the spot — "

" Has it really come to that? " the Senator said, shaking his head.

" Yes, they have succeeded in getting that far, the villains! " Frau Permaneder sank upon the sofa with an impotent sob. " And they will go on; they will go on to the end, Tom."

" Tony," he said, and sat down sidewise by his mahogany desk, crossing one leg over the other and leaning his head on his hand, " tell me straight out, do you still have faith in his innocence? "

She sobbed once or twice before she answered, hopelessly: " Oh, no, Tom. How could I? I've seen so much evil in the world. I haven't believed in it from the beginning, even, though I tried my very best. Life makes it so very hard, you know, to believe in any one's innocence. Oh, no — I've had doubts of his good conscience for a long time, and Erica has not known what to make of him — she confessed it to me, with tears — on account of his behaviour at home. We haven't talked about it, of course. He got ruder and ruder, and kept demanding all the time that Erica should be lively and divert his mind and make him forget his troubles. And he broke the dishes when she wasn't. You can't imagine what it was like, when he shut himself up evenings with his papers: when anybody knocked, you could hear him jump up and shout ' Who's there? ' "

They were silent.

" But suppose he *is* guilty, Tom. Suppose he did do it," began Frau Permaneder afresh, and her voice gathered strength. " He wasn't working for his own pocket, but for the company — and then — good Heavens, in this life, people have to realize — there are other things to be taken into consideration. He married into our family — he is one of us, now. They can't just go and stick him into prison like that! "

He shrugged his shoulders.

" What are you shrugging your shoulders for, Tom? Do you mean that you are willing to sit down under the last and crowning insult these adventurers think they can offer us? We must do something! He mustn't be convicted! Aren't you the Burgo- master's right hand? My God, can't the Senate just pardon him if it likes? You know, before I came to you, I nearly went to Cremer, to get him — to implore him to intervene and take a stand in the matter — he is Chief of Police — "

" Oh, child, that is all just nonsense."

" Nonsense, Tom? And Erica? And the child? " said she, lift- ing up her muff, with her two imploring hands inside. She was still a moment, she let her arms fall, her chin began to quiver, and two great tears ran down from under her drooping lids. She added softly, " And me? "

" Oh, Tony, be brave," said the Senator. Her helplessness went through him. He pushed his chair up to hers and stroked her hair, in an effort to console her. " Everything isn't over, yet. Perhaps it will come out all right. Of course I will give you the money — that goes without saying — and Breslauer's very clever."

She shook her head, weeping.

" No, Tom, it will not come out all right. I've no hope that it will. They will convict him, and put him in prison — and then the hard time will come for Erica and me. Her dowry is gone: it all went to the setting-out, the furniture and pictures; we sha'n't get a quarter of it back by selling. And the salary was always spent. We never put a penny by. We will go back to Mother, if she will take us, until he is free. And then where can we go? We'll just have to sit on the rocks." She sobbed.

" On the rocks? "

" Oh, that's just an expression — a figure. What I mean is, it won't turn out all right. I've had too much to bear — I don't know how I came to deserve it all — but I can't hope any more. Erica will be like me — with Grünlich and Permaneder. But now you can see just how it is — and how it all comes over you! Could I help it? Could any one help it, I ask you, Tom? " she repeated drearily, and looked at him with her tear-swimming eyes. "Everything I've ever undertaken has gone wrong and turned to misfortune — and I've meant everything so well. God knows I have! And now this too — This is the last straw — the very last."

She wept, leaning on the arm which he gently put about her: wept over her ruined life and the quenching of this last hope.

A week later, Herr Director Hugo Weinschenk was sentenced to three and a half years' imprisonment, and arrested at once.

There was a very large crowd at the final session. Lawyer Breslauer of Berlin made a speech for the defence the like of which had never been heard before. Gosch the broker went about for weeks afterwards bursting with enthusiasm for the masterly pathos and irony it displayed. Christian Buddenbrook heard it too, and afterward got behind a table at the club, with a pile of newspapers in front of him, and reproduced the whole speech. At home he declared that jurisprudence was the finest profession there was, and he thought it would just have suited him. The Public Prosecutor himself, Dr. Moritz Hagenström, who was a great connoisseur, said in private that the speech had been a genuine treat to him. But the famous advocate's talents did not prevent his colleagues from thumping him on the back and telling him he had not pulled the wool over their eyes.

The necessary sale followed upon the disappearance of the Director; and when it was over, people in town began gradually to forget about Hugo Weinschenk. But the Misses Buddenbrook, sitting on Thursday at the family table, declared that they had known the first moment, from the man's eyes, that he was not straight, that his conscience was bad, and that there would be trouble in the end. Certain considerations, which they wished now they had not regarded, had led them to suppress these painful observations.

PART NINE

CHAPTER I

SENATOR BUDDENBROOK followed the two gentlemen, old Dr. Grabow and young Dr. Langhals, out of the Frau Consul's bed-chamber into the breakfast-room and closed the door.

"May I ask you to give me a moment, gentlemen?" he said, and led them up the steps, through the corridor, and into the landscape-room, where, on account of the raw, damp weather, the stove was already burning. "You will understand my anxiety," he said. "Sit down and tell me something reassuring, if possible."

"Zounds, my dear Senator," answered Dr. Grabow, leaning back comfortably, his chin in his neck-cloth, his hat-brim propped in both hands against his stomach. Dr. Langhals put his top-hat down on the carpet beside him and regarded his hands, which were exceptionally small and covered with hair. He was a heavy dark man with a pointed beard, a pompadour hair-cut, beautiful eyes, and a vain expression.

"There is positively no reason for serious disquiet at present," Dr. Grabow went on. "When we take into consideration our honoured patient's powers of resistance — my word, I think, as an old and tried councillor, I ought to know what that resistance is — it is simply astonishing, for her years, I must say."

"Yes, precisely: for her years," said the Senator, uneasily, twisting his moustaches.

"I don't say," went on Dr. Grabow, in his gentle voice, "that your dear Mother will be walking out to-morrow. You can tell that by looking at her, of course. There is no denying that the inflammation has taken a disappointing turn in the last twenty-four hours. The chill yesterday afternoon did not please me at all, and to-day there is actually pain in the side. And some fever — oh, nothing to speak of, but still — In short, my dear Senator, we shall probably have to reckon with the troublesome fact that the lung is slightly affected."

"Inflammation of the lungs then?" asked the Senator, and looked from one physician to the other.

"Yes — pneumonia," said Dr. Langhals, with a solemn and correct bow.

"A slight inflammation, however, and confined to the right side," answered the family physician. "We will do our best to localize it."

"Then there is ground for serious concern, after all?" The Senator sat quite still and looked the speaker full in the face.

"Concern — oh, we must be concerned to limit the affection. We must ease the cough, and go at the fever energetically. The quinine will see to that. And by the by, my dear Senator, let me warn you against feeling alarm over single symptoms, you know. If the difficulty in breathing increases, or there should be a little delirium in the night, or a good deal of discharge to-morrow — a sort of rusty-looking mucous, with a little blood in it — well, all that is to be expected, entirely regular and normal. Do reassure dear Madame Permaneder on this point too — she is nursing the patient with such devotion. — How is she feeling? I quite forgot to ask how she has been, in the last few days."

"She is about as usual," the Senator said. "I have not heard of anything new. She is not taking much thought for her own condition, these days — "

"Of course, of course. And, apropos: your sister needs rest, especially at night, and Mamsell Severin has not time to give her all the rest she needs. What about a nurse, my dear Senator? Why not have one of our good Grey Sisters, in whom you feel such an interest? The Mother Superior would be glad to send you one."

"You consider it necessary?"

"I am only suggesting it. The sisters are invaluable — their experience and calmness are always so soothing to the patient, especially in an illness like this, where there is a succession of disquieting symptoms. Well — let me repeat, no anxiety, my dear Senator. And we shall see, we shall see. We will have another talk this evening."

"Positively," said Dr. Langhals, took his hat and got up, with his colleague. But the Senator had not finished: he had another question, another test to make.

"Gentlemen," he said, "one word more. My brother Christian is a nervous man. He cannot stand much. Do you advise me to send him word? Should I suggest to him to come home?"

"Your brother Christian is not in town?"

"No, he is in Hamburg — for a short time, on business, I understand."

Dr. Grabow gave his colleague a glance. Then he laughingly shook the Senator's hand and said, "Well, we'll let him attend to his business in peace. No use upsetting him unnecessarily. If any

change comes which seems to make it advisable, to quiet the patient, or to raise her spirits — well, there is plenty of time still,
plenty of time."

The gentlemen traversed the pillared hall and stood on the steps
awhile, talking about other matters: politics, and the agitations and
changes due to the war just then ended.

"Well, good times will be coming now, eh, Herr Senator?
Money in the country, and fresh confidence everywhere."

And the Senator partially agreed with him. He said that the
grain trade with Russia had been greatly stimulated since the out-
break of war, and mentioned the dimensions to which the import
trade in oats had attained — though the profit, it was true, had
been very unevenly divided.

The physicians took their leave, and Senator Buddenbrook
turned to go back to the sick-room. He revolved what Dr.
Grabow had said. He had spoken with reserve — he gave the impression of avoiding anything definite. The single plain word was
"inflammation of the lungs"; which became no more reassuring
after Dr. Langhals added the scientific terminology. Pneumonia —
at the Frau Consul's age. The fact that there were two physicians
coming and going was in itself disquieting. Grabow had arranged
that very unobtrusively. He intended to retire before long, and
as young Dr. Langhals would then be taking over the practice, he,
Dr. Grabow, would be pleased if he might bring him in now and
again.

When the Senator entered the darkened room, his mien appeared alert and his bearing energetic. He was used to hiding his
cares and weariness under an air of calmness and poise; and the
mask glided over his features as he opened the door, almost as
though by a single act of will.

Frau Permaneder sat by the high bed, the hangings of which
were thrust back, and held her mother's hand. The old lady was
propped up on pillows. She turned her head as her son came in,
and looked searchingly with her pale blue eyes into his face — a
look of calm self-control, yet of deliberate insistence. Coming as
it did, slightly sidewise, there was almost something sinister about
it, too. Two red spots stood out upon the pallor of her cheeks,
but there were no signs of weakness or exhaustion. The old lady
was very wide awake, more so in fact than those around her — for,
after all, she was the person most concerned. And she mistrusted
this illness; she was not at all disposed to lie down and let it have
its own way.

"What did they say, Thomas?" she asked in a brisk, decided

voice which made her cough directly. She tried to keep the cough behind her closed lips, but it burst out and made her put her hand to her side.

" They said," answered the Senator, when the spasm was over, stroking her hand, " they said that our dear, good mother will be up again in a few days. The wretched cough is responsible for your lying here. The lung is of course slightly affected — it is not exactly inflammation," he hastened to say, as he saw her narrowing gaze, " but even if it were, that needn't necessarily be so bad. It might be much worse," he finished. " In short, the lung is somewhat irritated, and they may be right — where is Mamsell Severin? "

" Gone to the chemist's," said Frau Permaneder.

" Yes, you see. She has gone to the chemist's again, and you look as though you might go to sleep any minute, Tony. No, it isn't good enough. If only for a day or so, we should have a nurse in, don't you think so? I will find out if my Mother Superior up at the Grey Sisters has any one free."

" Thomas," said the Frau Consul, this time in a more cautious voice, so as not to let loose another cough, " believe me, you cause a good deal of feeling by your protection of the Catholic order against the black Protestant Sisters. You have shown the Catholics a distinct preference. Pastor Pringsheim complained to me about it very strenuously a little time ago."

" Well, he needn't. I am convinced that the Grey Sisters are more faithful, devoted, and self-sacrificing than the Black ones are. The Protestants aren't the real thing. They all marry the first chance they get, They are worldly, egotistical, and ordinary, while the Grey Sisters are perfectly disinterested. I am sure they are much nearer Heaven. And they are better for us for the very reason that they owe me some gratitude. What should we have done without Sister Leandra when Hanno had convulsions? I only hope she is free! "

And Sister Leandra came. She put down her cloak and little handbag, took off the grey veil which she wore on the street over her white one, and went softly about her work, in her gentle, friendly way, the rosary at her waist clicking as she moved. She remained a day and a night with the querulous, not always patient sufferer, and then withdrew, almost apologetic over the human weakness that enforced a little repose. She was replaced by another sister, but came back again after she had slept.

The Frau Consul required constant attendance at her bedside. The worse her condition grew, the more she bent all her thoughts and all her energies upon her illness, for which she felt a naïve hatred. Nearly all her life she had been a woman of the world, with a quiet, native, and permanent love of life and good living. Yet she had filled her latter years with piety and charitable deeds: largely out of loyalty toward her dead husband, but also, perhaps, by reason of an unconscious impulse which bade her make her peace with Heaven for her own strong vitality, and induce it to grant her a gentle death despite the tenacious clutch she had always had on life. But the gentle death was not to be hers. Despite many a sore trial, her form was quite unbowed, her eyes still clear. She still loved to set a good table, to dress well and richly, to ignore events that were unpleasant, and to share with complacency in the high regard that was everywhere felt for her son. And now this illness, this inflammation of the lungs, had attacked her erect form without any previous warning, without any preparation to soften the blow. There had been no spiritual anticipation, none of that mining and sapping of the forces which slowly, painfully estranges us from life and rouses in us the sweet longing for a better world, for the end, for peace. No, the old Frau Consul, despite the spiritual courses of her latter years, felt scarce prepared to die; and she was filled with agony of spirit at the thought that if this were indeed the end, then this illness, of itself, in awful haste, in the last hour, must, with bodily torments, break down her spirit and bring her to surrender.

She prayed much; but almost more she watched, as often as she was conscious, over her own condition: felt her pulse, took her temperature, and fought her cough. But the pulse was poor, the temperature mounted after falling a little, and she passed from chills to fever and delirium; her cough increased, bringing up a blood-impregnated mucous, and she was alarmed by the difficulty she had in breathing. It was accounted for by the fact that now not only a lobe of the right lung, but the whole right lung, was affected, with even distinct traces of a process in the left, which Dr. Langhals, looking at his nails, called hepatization, and about which Dr. Grabow said nothing at all. The fever wasted the patient relentlessly. The digestion failed. Slowly, inexorably, the decline of strength went on.

She followed it. She took eagerly, whenever she could, the concentrated nourishment which they gave her. She knew the hours for her medicines better than the nurse; and she was so absorbed in watching the progress of her case that she hardly spoke to any one but the physicians, and displayed actual interest only when talking with them. Callers had been admitted in the beginning, and the old ladies of her social circle, pastors' wives and members of the Jerusalem evenings, came to see her; but she received them with apathy and soon dismissed them. Her relatives felt the difference in the old lady's greeting: it was almost disdainful, as though she were saying to them: "You can't do anything for me." Even when little Hanno came, in a good hour, she only stroked his cheek and turned away. Her manner said more plainly than words: "Children, you are all very good — but — perhaps — I may be dying!" She received the two physicians, on the other hand, with very lively interest, and went into the details of her condition.

One day the Gerhardt ladies appeared, the descendants of Paul Gerhardt. They came in their mantles, with their flat shepherdess hats and their provision-baskets, from visiting the poor, and could not be prevented from seeing their sick friend. They were left alone with her, and God only knows what they said as they sat at her bedside. But when they departed, their eyes and their faces were more gentle, more radiant, more blissfully remote than ever; while the Frau Consul lay within, with just such eyes and just such an expression, quite still, quite peaceful, more peaceful than ever before; her breath came very softly and at long intervals, and she was visibly declining from weakness to weakness. Frau Permaneder murmured a strong word in the wake of the Gerhardt ladies, and sent at once for the physicians. The two gentlemen had barely entered the sick-chamber when a surprising alteration took place in the patient. She stirred, she moved, she almost sat up. The sight of her trusted and faithful professional advisers brought her back to earth at a bound. She put out her hands to them and began: "Welcome, gentlemen. To-day, in the course of the day — "

The illness had attacked both lungs — of that there was no more room for doubt.

"Yes, my dear Senator," Dr. Grabow said, and took Thomas Buddenbrook by the hand, "it is now both lungs — we have not been able to prevent it. That is always serious, you know as well as I do. I should not attempt to deceive you. No matter what the age of the patient, the condition is serious; and if you ask me again to-day whether in my opinion your brother should be written to — or perhaps a telegram would be better — I should hesitate to deter you from it. How is he, by the way? A good fellow, Christian; I've always liked him immensely. — But for Heaven's sake, my dear Senator, don't draw any exaggerated conclusions from what I say. There is no immediate danger — I am foolish to take the word in my mouth! But still — under the circumstances, you know, one must reckon with the unexpected. We are very well satisfied with your mother as a patient. She helps all she can, she doesn't leave us in the lurch; no, on my word, she is an incomparable patient! So there is still great hope, my dear sir. And we must hope for the best."

But there is a moment when hope becomes something artificial and insincere. There is a change in the patient. He alters — there is something strange about him — he is not as he was in life. He speaks, but we do not know how to reply: what he says is strange, it seems to cut off his retreat back to life, it condemns him to death. And when that moment comes, even if he is our dearest upon this earth, we do not know how to wish him back. If we could bid him arise and walk, he would be as frightful as one risen from his coffin.

Dreadful symptoms of the coming dissolution showed themselves, even though the organs, still in command of a tenacious will, continued to function. It had now been weeks since Frau Consul first took to her bed with a cold; and she began to have bed sores. They would not heal, and grew worse and worse. She could not sleep, because of pain, coughing and shortness of breath, and also because she herself clung to consciousness with all her might. Only for minutes at a time did she lose herself in fever; but now she began, even when she was conscious, to talk to people who had long been dead. One afternoon, in the twilight, she said suddenly, in a loud, fervent, anxious voice, " Yes, my dear Jean, I am coming! " And the immediacy of the reply was such that one almost thought to hear the voice of the deceased Consul calling her.

Christian arrived. He came from Hamburg, where he had been, he said, on business. He only stopped a short time in the sick-room, and left it, his eyes roving wildly, rubbing his forehead, and saying " It's frightful — it's frightful — I can't stand it any longer."

Pastor Pringsheim came, measured Sister Leandra with a chilling glance, and prayed with a beautifully modulated voice at the bed-side.

Then came the brief " lightening ": the flickering up of the dying flame. The fever slackened; there was a deceptive return of strength, and a few plain, hopeful words, that brought tears of joy to the eyes of the watchers at the bedside.

" Children, we shall keep her; you'll see, we shall keep her after all! " cried Thomas Buddenbrook. " She will be with us next Christmas! "

But even in the next night, shortly after Gerda and her husband had gone to bed, they were summoned back to Meng Street by Frau Permaneder, for the mother was struggling with death. A cold rain was falling, and a high wind drove it against the window-panes.

The bed-chamber, as the Senator and his wife entered it, was lighted by two sconces burning on the table; and both physicians were present. Christian too had been summoned from his room, and sat with his back to the bed and his forehead bowed in his hands. They had sent for the dying woman's brother, Justus Kröger, and he would shortly be here. Frau Permaneder and Erica were sobbing softly at the foot of the bed. Sister Leandra and Mamsell Severin had nothing more to do, and stood gazing in sad-ness on the face of the dying.

The Frau Consul lay on her back, supported by a quantity of pillows. With both her blue-veined hands, once so beautiful, now so emaciated, she ceaselessly stroked the coverlet in trembling haste. Her head in the white nightcap moved from side to side with dreadful regularity. Her lips were drawn inward, and opened and closed with a snap at every tortured effort to breathe, while the sunken eyes roved back and forth or rested with an envious look on those who stood about her bed, up and dressed and able to breathe. They were alive, they belonged to life; but they could help her no more than this, to make the sacrifice that consisted in watching her die. . . . And the night wore on, without any change.

"How long can it go on, like this?" asked Thomas Budden-brook, in a low tone, drawing Dr. Grabow away to the bottom of the room, while Dr. Langhals was undertaking some sort of in-jection to give relief to the patient. Frau Permaneder, her hand-kerchief in her hand, followed her brother.

"I can't tell, my dear Senator," answered Dr. Grabow. "Your dear mother may be released in the next few minutes, or she may live for hours. It is a process of strangulation: an oedema — "

"I know," said Frau Permaneder, and nodded while the tears ran down her cheeks. "It often happens in cases of inflammation of the lungs — a sort of watery fluid forms, and when it gets very bad the patient cannot breathe any more. Yes, I know."

The Senator, his hands folded, looked over at the bed.

"How frightfully she must suffer," he whispered.

"No," Dr. Grabow said, just as softly, but in a tone of authority, while his long, mild countenance wrinkled more than ever. "That is a mistake, my dear friend, believe me. The consciousness is very clouded. These are largely reflex motions which you see; depend

upon it." And Thomas answered: " God grant it " — but a child
could have seen from the Frau Consul's eyes that she was entirely
conscious and realized everything.

They took their places again. Consul Kröger came and sat
bowed over his cane at the bedside, with reddened eyelids.

The movements of the patient increased. This body, delivered
over to death, was possessed by a terrible unrest, an unspeakable
craving, an abandonment of helplessness, from head to foot. The
pathetic, imploring eyes now closed with the rustling movement
of the head from side to side, now opened with a heart-breaking
expression, so wide that the little veins of the eyeballs stood out
blood-red. And she was still conscious!

A little after three, Christian got up. " I can't stand it any more,"
he said, and went out, limping, and supporting himself on the
furniture on his way to the door. Erica Weinschenk and Mamsell
Severin had fallen asleep to the monotonous sound of the raucous
breathing, and sat rosy with slumber on their chairs.

About four it grew much worse. They lifted the patient and
wiped the perspiration from her brow. Her breathing threatened
to stop altogether. " Let me sleep," she managed to say. " Give
me a sleeping-draught." Alas, they could give her nothing to
make her sleep.

Suddenly she began again to reply to voices which the others
could not hear. " Yes, Jean, not much longer now." And then,
" Yes, dear Clara, I am coming."

The struggle began afresh. Was this a wrestling with death?
Ah, no, for it had become a wrestling with life for death, on the
part of the dying woman. " I want — ," she panted, " I want — I
cannot — let me sleep! Have mercy, gentlemen — let me sleep! "

Frau Permaneder sobbed aloud as she listened, and Thomas
groaned softly, clutching his head a moment with both hands.
But the physicians knew their duty: they were obliged, under all
circumstances, to preserve life just as long as possible; and a narcotic would have effected an unresisting and immediate giving-up
of the ghost. Doctors were not made to bring death into the
world, but to preserve life at any cost. There was a religious and
moral basis for this law, which they had known once, though they
did not have it in mind at the moment. So they strengthened the
heart action by various devices, and even improved the breathing
by causing the patient to retch.

By five the struggle was at its height. The Frau Consul, erect
in convulsions, with staring eyes, thrust wildly about her with her
arms as though trying to clutch after some support or to reach

the hands which she felt stretching toward her. She was answering constantly in every direction to voices which she alone heard, and which evidently became more numerous and urgent. Not only her dead husband and daughter, but her parents, parents-in-law, and other relatives who had passed before her into death, seemed to summon her; and she called them all by name — though the names were some of them not familiar to her children. "Yes," she cried, " yes, I am coming now — at once — a moment — I cannot — oh, let me sleep! "

At half-past five there was a moment of quiet. And then over her aged and distorted features there passed a look of ineffable joy, a profound and quivering tenderness; like lightning she stretched up her arms and cried out, with an immediate suddenness swift as a blow, so that one felt there was not a second's space between what she heard and what she answered, with an expression of absolute submission and a boundless and fervid devotion: " Here I am! " and parted.

They were all amazed. What was it? Who had called her? To whose summons had she responded thus instantly?

Some one drew back the curtains and put out the candles, and Dr. Grabow gently closed the eyes of the dead.

They all shivered in the autumn dawn that filled the room with its sallow light. Sister Leandra covered the mirror of the toilet table with a cloth.

CHAPTER II

THROUGH the open door Frau Permaneder could be seen praying in the chamber of death. She knelt there alone, at a chair near the bed, with her mourning garments flowing about her on the floor. While she prayed, her hands folded before her on the seat of the chair, she could hear her brother and sister-in-law in the breakfast-room, where they stood and waited for the prayer to come to an end. But she did not hurry on that account. She finished, coughed her usual little dry cough, gathered her gown about her, and rose from the chair, then moved toward her relatives with a perfectly dignified bearing in which there was no trace of confusion.

" Thomas," she said, with a note of asperity in her voice, " it strikes me, that as far as Severin is concerned, our blessed mother was cherishing a viper in her bosom."

" What makes you think that? "

" I am perfectly furious with her. I shall try to behave with dignity, but — has the woman any right to disturb us at this solemn moment by her common ways? "

" What has she been doing? "

" Well in the first place, she is outrageously greedy. She goes to the wardrobe and takes out Mother's silk gowns, folds them over her arm, and starts to retire. ' Why, Riekchen,' I say, ' what are you doing with those? ' ' Frau Consul promised me.' ' My dear Severin! ' I say, and show her, in a perfectly ladylike way, what I think of her unseemly haste. Do you think it did any good? She took not only the silk gowns, but a bundle of underwear as well, and went out. I can't come to blows with her, can I? And it isn't Severin alone. There are wash-baskets full of stuff going out of the house. The servants divide up things before my face — Severin has the keys to the cupboards. I said to her: ' Fräulein Severin, I shall be much obliged for the keys.' And she told me, in good set terms, that I've nothing to say to her, she's not in my service, I didn't engage her, and she will keep the keys until she leaves! "

" Have you the keys to the silver-chest? Good. Let the rest go. That sort of thing is inevitable when a household breaks up, espe-

cially when the rule has been rather lax already. I don't want to
make any scenes. The linen is old and worn. We can see what
there is there. Have you the lists? Good. We'll have a look at
them."

They went into the bed-chamber and stood a while in silence
by the bed; Frau Antonie removed the white cloth from the face
of the dead. The Frau Consul was arrayed in the silk garment in
which she would that afternoon lie upon her bier in the hall.
Twenty-eight hours had passed since she drew her last breath.
The mouth and chin, without the false teeth, looked sunken and
senile, and the pointed chin projected sharply. All three tried their
best to recognize their mother's face in this sunken countenance
before them, with its eyelids inexorably closed. But under the old
lady's Sunday cap there showed, as in life, the smooth, reddish-
brown wig over which the Misses Buddenbrook had so often made
merry. Flowers were strewn on the coverlet.

"The most beautiful wreaths have come," said Frau Permaneder. "From all the families in town, simply from everybody. I
had everything carried up to the corridor. You must look at them
afterwards, Gerda and Tom. They are heart-breakingly lovely."

"How are they progressing down in the hall?" asked the Senator.

"They will soon be done. Tom. Jacobs has taken the greatest
pains. And the —" she choked down a sob —" the coffin has come.
But you must take off your things, my dears," she went on, carefully replacing the white cloth over the face of the dead. "It is
cold in here, but there is a little fire in the breakfast-room. Let me
help you, Gerda. Such an elegant mantle, one must be careful
with it. Let me give you a kiss — you know I love you, even if
you have always despised me. No, I won't make your hair untidy when I take off your hat — Your lovely hair! Such hair
Mother had too, when she was young. She was never so splendid
as you are, but there was a time, and since I was born, too, when
she was really beautiful. How true it is, isn't it, what your old
Grobleben always says: we must all return to earth at last: such
a simple man, too. Here, Tom. These are the most important
lists."

They returned to the next room and sat down at the round table,
while the Senator took up the paper, on which was a list of objects to be divided among the nearest heirs. Frau Permaneder's
eyes never left her brother's face, and her own wore a strained, excited look. There was something in her mind, a question hard to
put, upon which, nevertheless, all her thoughts were bent, and

which must, in the next few hours, come up for discussion.

"I think," said the Senator, "we may as well keep to the usual rule, that presents go back; so —"

His wife interrupted him.

"Pardon me, Thomas. It seems to me — where is Christian?"

"Oh, goodness, yes, Christian!" cried Frau Permaneder. "We've forgotten him!"

She went to ring the bell. But at the same moment Christian opened the door. He entered rather quickly, closed it behind him with a slight bang, and stood there frowning, his little deep round eyes not resting on anybody, but rolling from side to side. His mouth opened and shut under the bushy red moustaches. His mood seemed irritated and defiant.

"I heard you were here," he said. "If the things are to be talked about, it is proper that I should be told."

"We were just about to call you," the Senator said indifferently. "Sit down."

His eyes rested, as he spoke, on the white studs in Christian's shirt. He himself was in irreproachable mourning: a black cloth coat, blinding white shirt set off at the collar with a black tie, and black studs instead of the gold ones he usually wore. Christian saw his glance. He drew up a chair to the table and sat down, saying as he did so, with a gesture toward his shirt, "I know I have on white studs. I haven't got round to buying black — or rather, I haven't bothered. In the last few years I've seen times when I had to borrow money for tooth-powder, and go to bed by the light of a match. I don't know that I am altogether and entirely to blame. Anyhow, there are other things in the world more important than black studs. I don't set much store by appearances — I never have."

Gerda looked at him as he spoke, and now she gave a little laugh. The Senator remarked: "I doubt if you could bear out the truth of the last statement."

"No? Perhaps you know better than I do, Thomas. I say I don't set much store by them. I've seen too much of the world, and lived with too many different sorts of men, with too many different ways, to care what — and anyhow, I am a grown man" — his voice grew suddenly loud — "I am forty-three years old, and my own master and in a position to warn everybody not to mix in my affairs."

The Senator was quite astonished. "It seems to me you have something on your mind, my friend," he said. "As far as the studs go, I haven't so much as mentioned them, if my memory serves me. Wear whatever mourning you choose, or none at all if that pleases you; but don't imagine you make any impression on me with your cheap broadmindedness — "

"I am not trying to make an impression on you."

"Tom — Christian! " said Frau Permaneder. " Don't let us have any hard words — not to-day — when in the next room — Just go on, Thomas. Presents are to be returned? That is only right."

And Thomas went on. He began with the large things, and wrote down for himself the articles he could use in his own house: the candelabra in the dining-room, the great carved chest that stood in the downstairs entry. Frau Permaneder paid extraordinarily close attention. No matter what the article was, the future possession of which was at the moment in question, she would say with an incomparable air, " Oh, well, I'm willing to take it " — as if the whole world owed her thanks for her act of self-sacrifice. She accepted for herself, her daughter, and her granddaughter far and away the largest share of the furnishings.

Christian had some pieces of furniture, an Empire table-clock and the harmonium. He seemed satisfied enough. But when they came to dividing the table-linen and silver and the sets of dishes, he displayed, to the great astonishment of the others, an eagerness that was almost avidity.

"What about me? " he would say. " I must ask you not to forget me, please."

"Who is forgetting you? Look: I've put a whole tea-service and a silver tray down to you. I've taken the gilt Sunday service, as we are probably the only ones who would have a use for it."

"I'm willing to take the every-day onion pattern," said Frau Permaneder.

"And what about me? " cried Christian. He was possessed now by that excitement which sometimes seized him and sat so extraordinarily on his haggard cheek. " I certainly want a share in the dishes. And how many forks and spoons do I get? Almost none at all, it seems to me."

"But, my dear man, what do you want of them? You have no use for them at all. I don't understand. It is better the things should continue in the family — "

"But suppose I say I want them — if only in remembrance of Mother," Christian cried defiantly.

To which the Senator impatiently replied, " I don't feel much like making jokes; but am I to judge from your words that you would like to put a soup-tureen on your chest of drawers and keep it there in memory of Mother? Please don't get the idea that we want to cheat you out of your share. If you get less of the effects, you will get more elsewhere. The same is true of the linen."

" I don't want the money. I want the linen and dishes."

" Whatever for? "

Christian's reply to this was one that made Gerda Buddenbrook turn and gaze at him with an enigmatic expression in her eyes. The Senator hastily donned his pince-nez to look the better, and Frau Permaneder simply folded her hands. He said: " Well, I am thinking of getting married, sooner or later."

He said this rather low and quickly, with a short gesture, as though he were tossing something to his brother across the table. Then he leaned back, avoiding their eyes, looking surly, defiant, and yet extremely embarrassed. There was a long pause. At last the Senator broke it by saying:

" I must say, Christian, your ideas come rather late. That is, of course, if this really is anything serious, and not the same kind of thing you proposed to Mother a while ago."

" My intentions have remained what they were," Christian said. He did not look at anybody or change his expression.

" That is impossible, I should think. Were you waiting for Mother's death — ? "

" I had that amount of consideration, yes. You seem to think, Thomas, that you have a monopoly of all the tact and feeling in the world — "

" I don't know what justifies you in making remarks like that. And, moreover, I must admire the extent of your consideration. On the day after Mother's death, you propose to display your lack of filial feeling by — "

" Only because the subject came up. But the point is that now Mother cannot be affected by any step I may take — no more to-day than she would be a year from now. Good Lord, Thomas, Mother couldn't have any actual *right* — but I saw it from her point of view, and had consideration for that, as long as she lived. She was an old woman, a woman of a past generation, with different views about life — "

" I can only say that I concur with her absolutely in this particular view."

" I cannot be bothered about that."

" But you will be bothered about it, my dear sir."

Christian looked at him.

" No," he shouted. " I won't! I can't do it. Suppose I tell you I can't? I must know what I have to do, mustn't I? I am a grown man — "

" You don't in the least know what you have to do. Your being
what you call a grown man is only very external."

" I know very well what I have to do. In the first place, I have
to act like a man of honour! You don't know how the thing
stands. With Tony and Gerda here we can't really talk — but I
have already told you I have responsibilities — The last child, little
Gisela — "

" I know nothing about any little Gisela — and I don't care to.
I am perfectly convinced they are making a fool of you. In any
case, what sort of responsibility can you have toward a person like
the one you have in mind — other than the legal one, which you
can perform as before — ? "

" Person, Thomas, *person?* You are making a mistake about her.
Aline — "

" Silence! " roared Senator Buddenbrook in a voice like thunder. The two brothers glared across the table into each other's
faces. Thomas was pale and trembling with scorn; the rims of
Christian's deep little eyes had got suddenly red, his mouth and
eyes spread wide open, his lean cheeks seemed nothing but hol-
lows, and a pair of red patches showed just under the cheek-bones.
Gerda looked rather disdainfully from one to the other, and Tony
wrung her hands, imploring — " Tom, Christian! And Mother
lying there in the next room! "

" You have no sense of shame," went on the Senator. " How can
you bring yourself — what must it cost you — to mention that
name, on this spot, under these circumstances? You have a lack
of feeling that amounts to a disease! "

" Will you tell me why I should not mention Aline's name? "
Christian was so beside himself that Gerda looked at him with increasing intentness. " I do mention it, as you hear, Thomas; I intend to marry her — for I have a longing for a home, and for peace
and quiet — and I insist — you hear the word I use — I insist that
you keep out of my affairs. I am free. I am my own master! "

" Oh, you fool, you! When you hear the will read, you will see
just how much you are your own master! You won't get the
chance to squander Mother's inheritance as you have run through
with the thirty thousand marks already! I have been made the
guardian of your affairs, and I will see to it that you never get your
hands on more than a monthly sum at a time — that I swear! "

" Well, you know better than I who it was that instigated
Mother to make such a will! But I am surprised, very much so,
that Mother did not give the office to somebody that had a little
more brotherly feeling for me than you have." Christian no longer

knew what he was saying; he leaned over the table, knocking on it all the while with his knuckle, glaring up, red-eyed, his moustaches bristling, at his brother, who, on his side, stood looking down at him, pale, and with half-closed lids.

Christian went on, and his voice was hollow and rasping. " Your heart is full of coldness and ill-will toward me, all the while. As far back as I can remember I have felt cold in your presence — you freeze me with a perfect stream of icy contempt. You may think that is a strange expression, but what I feel is just like that. You repulse me, just by looking at me — and you hardly ever even so much as look at me. How have you got a right to treat me like that? You are a man too, you have your own weaknesses. You have always been a better son to our parents; but if you really stood so much closer to them than I do, you might have absorbed a little of their Christian charity. If you have no brotherly love to spare for me, you might have had some Christlike love. But you are entirely without affection. You never came near me in the hospital, when I lay there and suffered with rheumatism — "

" I have more serious things to think about than your illnesses. And my own health — "

" Oh, come, Thomas, your health is magnificent. You wouldn't be sitting here for what you are, if your health weren't far and away better than mine."

" I may be perhaps worse off than you are! "

" Worse than I am — come, that's too much! Gerda, Tony! He says he is worse off than I am. Perhaps it was you that came near dying, in Hamburg, of rheumatism. Perhaps you have had to endure torments in your left side, perfectly indescribable torments, for every little trifling irregularity! Perhaps all your nerves are short on the left side! All the authorities say that is what is the matter with me. Perhaps it happens to you that you come into your room when it is getting dark and see a man sitting on the sofa, nodding at you, when there is no man there? "

" Christian! " Frau Permaneder burst out in horror. " What are you saying? And, my God! what are you quarrelling about? Is it an honour for one to be worse off than the other? If it were, Gerda and I might have something to say, too. — And with Mother lying in there! How can you? "

" Don't you realize, you fool," cried Thomas Buddenbrook, in a passion, " that all these horrors are the consequence and effect of your vices, your idleness, and your self-tormenting? Go to work! Stop petting your condition and talking about it! If you do go crazy — and I tell you plainly I don't think it at all unlikely

— I shan't be able to shed a tear; for it will be entirely your own fault."

" No, and when I die you won't shed any tears either."

" You won't die," said the Senator bitingly.

" I shan't die? Very good, I shan't die, then. We'll see who dies first. Work! Suppose I can't work? My God! I can't do the same thing long at a time! It kills me. If you have been able to, and are able to, thank God for it, but don't sit in judgment on others, for it isn't a virtue. God gives strength to one, and not to another. But that is the way you are made, Thomas. You are self-righteous. Oh, wait, that is not what I am going to say, nor what I accuse you of. I don't know where to begin, and however much I can say is only a millionth part of the feeling I have in my heart against you. You have made a position for yourself in life; and there you stand, and push everything away which might possibly disturb your equilibrium for a moment — for your equilibrium is the most precious thing in the world to you. But it isn't the most precious thing in life, Thomas — no, before God, it is not. You are an egotist, that is what you are. I am still fond of you, even when you are angry, and tread on me, and thunder me down. But when you get silent: when somebody says something and you are suddenly dumb, and withdraw yourself, quite elegant and remote, and repulse people like a wall and leave the other fellow to his shame, without any chance of justifying himself —! Yes, you are without pity, without love, without humility. — Oh," he cried, and stretched both arms in front of him, palms outward, as though pushing everything away from him, " Oh, how sick I am of all this tact and propriety, this poise and refinement — sick to death of it! "

The outburst was so genuine, so heart-felt, it sounded so full of loathing and satiety, that it was actually crushing. Thomas shrank a little and looked down in front of him, weary and without a word.

At last he said, and his voice had a ring of feeling, " I have become what I am because I did not want to become what you are. If I have inwardly shrunk from you, it has been because I needed to guard myself — your being, and your existence, are a danger to me — that is the truth."

There was another pause, and then he went on, in a crisper tone: " Well, we have wandered far away from the subject. You have read me a lecture on my character — a somewhat muddled lecture, with a grain of truth in it. But we are not talking about me, but about you. You are thinking of marrying; and I should like to convince you that it is impossible for you to carry out your plan. In

bitterly as well. "Dear me, Tom, you know you will do whatever you think best — the rest of us are not likely to withhold our consent for long. But if we might put in a word — to beg you," she went on, almost dully, but her lip was trembling too — "the house — Mother's house — the family home, in which we have all been so happy! We must sell it — ?"

The Senator shrugged his shoulders again. "Child, you will believe me when I tell you that I feel everything you can say, as much as you do yourself. But those are only our feelings; they aren't actual objections. What has to be done, remains the problem. Here we have this great piece of property — what shall we do with it? For years back, ever since Father's death, the whole back part has been going to pieces. A family of cats is living rent-free in the billiard-room, and you can't walk there for fear of going through the floor. Of course, if I did not have my house in Fishers' Lane — But I have, and what should I do with it? Do you think I might sell that instead? Tell me yourself, to whom? I should lose half the money I put into it. We have property enough, Tony; we have far too much, in fact. The granary buildings, and two great houses. The invested capital is out of all proportion to the value of the property. No, no, we must sell."

But Frau Permaneder was not listening. She was sitting bent over on the sofa, withdrawn into herself with her own thoughts.

"Our house," she murmured. "I remember the house-warming. We were no bigger than that. The whole family was there. And Uncle Hoffstede read a poem. It is in the family papers. I know it by heart. Venus Anadyomene. The landscape-room. The dining-hall! And strange people —!"

"Yes, Tony. They must have felt the same — the family of whom Grandfather bought the house. They had lost their money and had to give up their home, and they are all dead and gone now. Everything has its time. We ought to be grateful to God that we are better off than the Ratenkamps, and are not saying good-bye to the house under such sorry circumstances as theirs."

Sobs, long, painful sobs, interrupted him. Frau Permaneder so abandoned herself to her grief that she did not even dry the tears that ran down her cheeks. She sat bent over, and the warm drops fell unheeded upon the hands lying limp in her lap.

"Tom," said she, and there was a gentle, touching decision in her voice, which, a moment before her sobs had threatened to choke, "you can't understand how I feel at this hour — you cannot understand your sister's feelings! Things have not gone well with her in this life. — I have had everything to bear that fate could think of to inflict upon me. But I have borne it all without flinching, Tom: all my troubles with Grünlich and Permaneder and Weinschenk. For, however my life seemed to go awry, I was never quite lost. I had always a safe haven to fly to. Even this last time, when everything came to an end, when they took away Weinschenck to prison, ' Mother,' I said, ' may we come to you? ' And she said, ' Yes, my children, come! ' Do you remember, Tom, when we were little, and played war, there was always a little spot marked off for us to run to, where we could be safe and not be touched until we were rested again? Mother's house, this house, was my little spot, my refuge in life, Tom. And now — it must be sold —"

She leaned back, buried her face in her handkerchief, and wept unrestrainedly.

He drew down one of her hands and held it in his own.

"I know, dear Tony, I know it all. But we must be sensible. Our dear good Mother is gone. We cannot bring her back. And so — It is madness to keep the house as dead capital. Shall we turn it into a tenement-house? I know it is painful to think of strangers living here; but after all it is better you should *not* see it. You must take a nice, pretty little house or flat somewhere for yourself and your family — outside the Castle Gate, for example. Or would you rather stop on here and let out floors to different families? And you still have the family: Gerda and me, and the Buddenbrooks in Broad Street, and the Krögers, and Therese Weichbrodt, and Clothilde — that is, if Clothilde will condescend to associate with us, now that she's become a lady of the Order of St. John — it's so very exclusive, you know! "

She gave a sigh that was already partly a laugh, and mopped her eyes with her handkerchief, looking like a hurt child whom somebody is helping, with a jest, to forget its pain. Then she resolutely cleared her face and put herself to rights, tossing her head with the characteristic gesture and bringing her chin down on her breast.

"Yes, Tom," she said, and blinked with her tear-reddened eyes, "I'll be good now; I am already. You must forgive me — and you too, Gerda — for breaking down like that. But it may happen to any one, you know. It is a weakness. But, believe me, it is only outward. I am a woman steeled by misfortunes. And that about the dead capital is very convincing to me, Tom — I've enough intelligence to understand that much, anyhow. I can only repeat that you must do what you think best. You must think and act for us all; for Gerda and I are only women, and Christian — well, God help him, poor soul! We cannot oppose you, for whatever we could say would be only sentiment, not real objections, it is very plain. To whom will you sell it, Tom? Do you think it will go off right away? "

" Ah, child — how do I know? But I talked a little this morning with old Gosch the broker; he did not seem disinclined to under-take the business."

" That is a good idea, Tom. Siegismund Gosch has his weak-nesses, of course. That thing about his translation from the Spanish — I can't remember the man's name, but it is very odd, one must admit. However, he was Father's friend, and he is an honest man through and through. — What shall you ask? A hundred thousand marks would be the least, I should think."

And " A hundred thousand marks would be the least, wouldn't it, Tom? " she was still asking, the door-knob in her hand, as the Senator and his wife went down the steps. Then she was alone, and stood there in the middle of the room with her hands clasped palms down in front of her, looking all around with large, helpless eyes. Her head, heavy with the weight of her thoughts, adorned with the little black lace cap, sank slowly, shaking all the while, deeper and deeper on one shoulder.

CHAPTER III

LITTLE Johann was to go to take his farewell of his grandmother's mortal remains. His father so arranged it, and, though Hanno was afraid, he made not a syllable of objection. At table, the day after the Frau Consul's dying struggle, the Senator, in his son's presence and apparently with design, had commented harshly upon the conduct of Uncle Christian, who had slipped away and gone to bed when the patient's suffering was at its height. "That was his nerves, Thomas," Gerda had answered. But with a glance at Hanno, which had not escaped the child, the Senator had severely retorted that an excuse was not in place. The agony of their departed mother had been so sore that one had felt ashamed even to be sitting there free from pain — not to mention entertaining the cowardly thought of trying to escape any suffering of mind called up by the sight. From which, Hanno had gathered that it would not be safe to object to the visit to the open coffin.

The room looked as strange to him as it had at Christmas, when, on the day before the funeral, between his father and his mother, he entered it from the hall. There was a half-circle of potted plants, arranged alternately with high silver candelabra; and against the dark green leaves gleamed from a black pedestal the marble copy of Thorwaldsen's Christ, which belonged in the corridor outside. Black crape hangings fluttered everywhere in the draught, hiding the sky-blue tapestries and the smiling immortals who had looked down from these walls upon so many festive dinner-tables. Little Johann stood beside the bier among his black-clad relatives. He had a broad mourning band on his own sailor suit, and his senses felt misty with the scent from countless bouquets and wreaths — and with another odour that came wafted now and then on a current of air, and smelled strange, yet somehow familiar.

He stood beside the bier and looked at the motionless white figure stretched out there severe and solemn, amid white satin. This was not Grandmamma. There was her Sunday cap with the white silk ribbons, and her red-brown hair beneath it. But the pinched nose was not hers, nor the drawn lips, nor the sharp chin, nor the yellow, translucent hands, whose coldness and stiffness one could see. This was a wax-doll — to dress it up and lay it out like that seemed rather horrible. He looked across to the land-scape-room, as though the real Grandmamma might appear there the next minute. But she did not come: she was dead. Death had turned her for ever into this wax figure that kept its lids and lips so forbiddingly closed.

He stood resting on his left leg, the right knee bent, balancing lightly on the toe, and clutched his sailor knot with one hand, the other hanging down. He held his head on one side, the curly light-brown locks swaying over the temples, and looked with his gold-brown, blue-encircled eyes in brooding repugnance upon the face of the dead. His breath came long and shuddering, for he kept expecting that strange, puzzling odour which all the scent of the flowers sometimes failed to disguise. When the odour came, and he perceived it, he drew his brows still more together, his lip trembled, and the long sigh which he gave was so like a tear-less sob that Frau Permaneder bent over and kissed him and took him away.

And after the Senator and his wife, and Frau Permaneder and Erica, had received for long hours the condolences of the entire town, Elisabeth Buddenbrook, born Kröger, was consigned to earth. The out-of-town families, from Hamburg and Frankfort, came to the funeral and, for the last time, received hospitality in Meng Street. And the hosts of the sympathizers filled the hall and the landscape-room, the corridor and the pillared hall; and Pastor Pringsheim of St. Mary's, erect among burning tapers at the head of the coffin, turning his face up to heaven, his hands folded be-neath his chin, preached the funeral sermon.

He praised in resounding tones the qualities of the departed: he praised her refinement and humility, her piety and cheer, her mildness and her charity. He spoke of the Jerusalem evenings and the Sunday-school; he gilded with matchless oratory the whole long rich and happy earthly course of her who had left them; and when he came to the end, since the word " end " needed some sort of qualifying adjective, he spoke of her " peaceful end."

Frau Permaneder was quite aware of the dignity, the representa-tive bearing, which she owed to herself and the community in this hour. She, her daughter Erica, and her granddaughter Elisabeth occupied the most conspicuous places of honour, close to the pas-tor at the head of the coffin; while Thomas, Gerda, Clothilde, and little Johann, as likewise old Consul Kröger, who had a chair to sit

in, were content, as were the relatives of the second class, to occupy less prominent places. Frau Permaneder stood there, very
erect, her shoulders elevated, her black-bordered handkerchief
between her folded hands; and her pride in the chief rôle which it
fell to her lot to perform was so great as sometimes entirely to obscure her grief. Conscious of being the focus of all eyes, she kept
her own discreetly cast down; yet now and again she could not
resist letting them stray over the assembly, in which she noted the
presence of Julchen Möllendorpf, born Hagenström, and her husband. Yes, they had all had to come: Möllendorpfs, Kistenmakers,
Langhals, Överdiecks — before Tony Buddenbrook left her parental roof for ever, they had all gathered here, to offer her, despite
Grünlich, despite Permaneder, despite Hugo Weinschenk, their
sympathy and condolences.

Pastor Pringsheim's sermon went on, turning the knife in the
wound that death had made: he caused each person present to remember his own dead, he knew how to make tears flow where
none would have flowed of themselves — and for this the weeping
ones were grateful to him. When he mentioned the Jerusalem
evenings, all the old friends of the dead began to sob — excepting
Madame Kethelsen, who did not hear a word he said, but stared
straight before her with the remote air of the deaf, and the Gerhardt sisters, the descendants of Paul, who stood hand in hand in a
corner, their eyes glowing. They were glad for the death of their
friend, and could have envied her but that envy and unkindness
were foreign to their natures.

Poor Mademoiselle Weichbrodt blew her nose all the time, with
a short, emphatic sound. The Misses Buddenbrook did not weep.
It was not their habit. Their bearing, less angular than usual, expressed a mild satisfaction with the impartial justice of death.

Pastor Pringsheim's last "amen" resounded, and the four
bearers, in their black three-cornered hats, their black cloaks billowing out behind them with the swiftness of their advance, came
softly in and put their hands upon the coffin. They were four
lackeys, known to everybody, who were engaged to hand the
heavy dishes at every large dinner in the best circles, and who
drank Möllendorpf's claret out of the carafes, between the courses.
But, also, they were indispensable at every funeral of the first or
second class, being of large experience in this kind of work. They
knew that the harshness of this moment, when the coffin was laid
hold upon by strange hands and borne away from the survivors,
must be ameliorated by tact and swiftness. Their movements were
quick, agile, and noiseless; hardly had any one time to be sensible

of the pain of the situation, before they had lifted the burden from the bier to their shoulders, and the flower-covered casket swayed away smoothly and with decorum through the pillared hall.

The ladies pressed tenderly about Frau Permaneder and her daughter to offer their sympathy. They took her hand and murmured, with drooping eyes, precisely no more and no less than what on such occasions must be murmured; while the gentlemen made ready to go down to the carriages.

Then came, in a long, black procession, the slow drive through the grey, misty streets out through the Burg Thor, along the leafless avenue in a cold driving rain, to the cemetery, where the funeral march sounded behind half-bare shrubbery on the edge of the little grove, and the great sandstone cross marked the Buddenbrook family lot. The stone lid of the grave, carven with the family arms, lay close to the black hole framed in dripping greens.

A place had been prepared down below for the new-comer. In the last few days, the Senator had supervised the work of pushing aside the remains of a few early Buddenbrooks. The music sounded, the coffin swayed on the ropes above the open depth of masonry; with a gentle commotion it glided down. Pastor Pringsheim, who had put on pulse-warmers, began to speak afresh, his voice ringing fervid and emotional above the open grave. He bent over the grave and spoke to the dead, calling her by her full name, and blessed her with the sign of the cross. His voice ceased; all the gentlemen held their top-hats in front of their faces with their black-gloved hands; and the sun came out a little. It had stopped raining, and into the sound of the single drops that fell from the trees and bushes there broke now and then the short, fine, questioning twitter of a bird.

All the gentlemen turned a moment to press the hands of the sons and brother of the dead once more.

Thomas Buddenbrook, as the others filed by, stood between his brother Christian and his uncle Justus. His thick dark woollen overcoat was dewed with fine silver drops. He had begun of late to grow a little stout, the single sign of age in his carefully preserved exterior, and his cheeks, behind the pointed protruding ends of his moustaches, looked rounder than they used; but it was a pale and sallow roundness, without blood or life. He held each man's hand a moment in his own, and his slightly reddened eyes looked them all, with weary politeness, in the face.

CHAPTER IV

A WEEK later there sat in Senator Buddenbrook's private office, in the leather chair beside the writing-desk, a little smooth-shaven old man with snow-white hair falling over his brow and temples. He sat in a crouching position, supporting both hands on the white top of his crutch-cane, and his pointed chin on his hands; while he directed at the Senator a look of such malevolence, such a crafty, penetrating glance, that one wondered why the latter did not avoid contact with such a man as this. But the Senator sat apparently at ease, leaning back in his chair, talking to this baleful apparition as to a harmless ordinary citizen. Broker Siegismund Gosch and the head of the firm of Johann Buddenbrook were discussing the price of the Meng Street house.

It took a long time. The offer of twenty-eight thousand thaler made by Herr Gosch seemed too low to the Senator, and the broker called heaven to witness that it would be an act of madness to add a single groschen to the sum. Thomas Buddenbrook spoke of the central position and unusual extent of the property; but Herr Gosch, with picturesque gestures, in low and sibilant tones, expatiated upon the criminal risk he would be running. He waxed almost poetic. Ha! Could his honoured friend tell him when, to whom, for how much, he would be able to get rid of the house again? How often, in the course of the century, would there be a demand for such a house? Perhaps his friend and patron could assure him that to-morrow, on the train from Buchen, there was arriving an Indian nabob who wished to establish himself in the Buddenbrook mansion? He, Siegismund Gosch, would have it on his hands, simply on his hands, and it would be the ruin of him. He would be a beaten man, his race would be run, his grave dug — yes, it would be dug — and, as the phrase enchanted him, he repeated it, and added something more about chattering apes and clods of earth falling upon the lid of his coffin.

But the Senator was not satisfied. He spoke of the ease with which the property could be divided, emphasized his responsibility toward his sister, and remained by the sum of thirty thousand

thaler. After which he had to listen, with a mixture of enjoyment
and impatience, to a rejoinder from Herr Gosch, which lasted
some two hours, during which the broker sounded, as it were, all
the registers of his character. He played two rôles at once: first,
the hypocritical villain, with a sweet voice, his head on one side,
and a smile of open-hearted simplicity. Stretching out his large,
white hand, with the long, trembling fingers, he said " Agree, my
dear young patron: eighty-four thousand marks — it is the offer of
an honest old man." But a child could have seen that this was all
lies and treachery — a deceiving mask, behind which the man's
deep villainy peeped forth.

Thomas Buddenbrook finally declared that he must take time
to think, and that in any case he must consult his sister, before he
accepted the twenty-eight thousand thaler — which was unlikely.
Then he turned the conversation to indifferent topics and asked
Herr Gosch about business and his health.

Things were going badly with Herr Gosch. He made a fine,
sweeping gesture to wave away the imputation that he was a prosperous man. The burdens of old age approached, they were at
hand even now; as aforesaid, his grave was dug. He could not
even carry his glass of grog to his lips without spilling half of it,
his arm trembled so like the devil. It did no good to curse. The
will no longer availed. And yet — ! He had his life behind him —
not such a poor life, after all. He had looked at the world with his
eyes open. Revolutions had thundered by, their waves had beat
upon his heart — so to speak. Ha! Those were other times, when
he had stood at the side of Consul Johann Buddenbrook, the Senator's father, at that historic sitting, and defied the fury of the
raging mob. A frightful experience! No, his life had not been
poor, either outwardly or inwardly. Hang it — he had been conscious of powers — and as the power is, so is the ideal — as Feuer-
bach says. And even now — even now, his soul was not impoverished, his heart was still young: it had never ceased, and would
never cease, to be capable of great emotions, to live fervently in
and for his ideals. They would go with him to his grave. — But
were ideals, after all, meant to be realized? No, a thousand times
no! We might long for the stars, but should we ever reach them?
No, hope, not realization, was the most beautiful thing in life:
" L'esperance, tout trompeuse qu'elle est, sert au moins à nous
mener à la fin de la vie par un chemin agréable." La Rochefou-
cauld said that, and it was fine, wasn't it? Oh, yes, his honoured
friend and patron, of course, did not need to console himself with
that sort of thing. The waves of life had lifted him high on their

shoulders, and fortune played about his brow. But for the lonely and submerged, who dreamed alone in the darkness —

Suddenly — "*You* are happy," he said, laying his hand on the Senator's knee, and looking up at him with swimming eyes. "Don't deny it — it would be sacrilege. You are happy. You hold fortune in your arms. You have reached out your strong arms and conquered her — your strong hands," he corrected himself, not liking the sound of "arms" twice so close together. He was silent, and the Senator's deprecating, patient reply went unheard. He seemed to be darkly dreaming for a moment; then he got up.

"We have been chatting," he said, "but we came together on business. Time is money. Let us not waste it in hesitation. Listen to me. Since it is you: since it is you, you understand — " here it almost looked as though Herr Gosch was about to give way again to another rhapsody; but he restrained himself. He made a wide, sweeping gesture, and cried: "Twenty-nine thousand thaler, eighty-seven thousand marks current, for your mother's house! Is it a bargain?" And Senator Buddenbrook agreed.

Frau Permaneder, of course, found the sum ridiculously small. Considering the memories that clung about it, she would have thought a million down no more than an honest price for their old home. But she rapidly adjusted herself — the more readily that her thoughts and efforts were soon taken up by plans for the future.

She rejoiced from the bottom of her heart over all the good furniture that had fallen to her share. And though there was no idea of bustling her away from under the parental roof, she plunged at once, with the greatest zest, into the business of finding and renting a new home. The leave-taking would be hard — the very thought of it brought tears to her eyes. But the prospect of a change was not without its own charm too. It was almost like another setting-out — the fourth one! And so again she looked at houses and visited Jacob's; again she bargained for portières and stair-carpets. And while she did all that, her heart beat faster — yes, even the heart of this old woman who was steeled by the misfortunes of life!

Weeks passed like this: four, five, six weeks. The first snow fell, the stoves crackled. Winter was here again; and the Buddenbrooks began to consider sadly what sort of Christmas feast they should have this year. But now something happened: something surprising and dramatic beyond all words, something that simply knocked you off your feet. Frau Permaneder paused in the midst of her business, like one paralyzed.

"Thomas," she said, "am I crazy? Is Gosch dreaming? It is too absurd, too outlandish — " She held her temples with both her hands. The Senator shrugged his shoulders.

"My dear child, nothing at all is decided yet. But there is the possibility — and if you think it over quietly, you will see that there is nothing so extraordinary about it, after all. It is a little startling, I admit. It gave me a start when Gosch first told me. But absurd? What makes it absurd? "

"I should die," said she. She sat down in a chair and stopped there without moving.

What was going on? Simply that a buyer had appeared for the house; or, rather, a possible purchaser showed a desire to go over it, with a view to negotiations. And this possible purchaser was — Hermann Hagenström, wholesale dealer and Consul for the Kingdom of Portugal.

When the first rumour reached Frau Permaneder, she was stunned, incredulous, incapable of grasping the idea. But when the rumour became concrete, when it actually took shape in the person of Consul Hermann Hagenström, standing, as it were, before the door, then she pulled herself together, and animation came back to her.

"This must not happen, Thomas. As long as I live, it must not happen. When one sells one's house, one is bound to look out for the sort of master it gets. Our Mother's house! Our house! The landscape-room! "

"But what stands in the way? "

"What stands in the way? Heavens, Thomas! Mountains stand in the way — or they ought to! But he doesn't see them, this fat man with the snub nose! He doesn't care about them. He has no delicacy and no feeling — he is like the beasts that perish. From time immemorial the Hagenströms and we have been rivals. Old Hinrich played Father and Grandfather some dirty tricks; and if Hermann hasn't tripped you up yet, it is only because he hasn't had a chance. When we were children, I boxed his ears in the open street, for very good reasons; and his precious little sister Julchen nearly scratched me to pieces for it. That was all child-ishness, then. But they have always looked on and enjoyed it whenever we had a piece of bad luck — and it was mostly I myself who gave them the pleasure. God willed it so. Whatever the Consul did to injure you or overreach you in a business way, that I can't speak of, Tom. You must know better than I. But the last straw was when Erica made a good marriage and he wormed around and wormed around until he managed to spoil it and get her husband shut up, through his brother, who is a cat! And now they have the nerve — "

"Listen, Tony. In the first place, we have nothing more to say in the matter. We made our bargain with Gosch, and he has the right to deal with whomever he likes. But there is a sort of irony about it, after all — "

"Irony? Well, if you like to call it that — but what I call it is a disgrace, a slap in the face; because that is just what it would be. You don't realize what it would be like, in the least. But it would mean to everybody that the Buddenbrook family are finished and done for: they clear out, and the Hagenströms squeeze into their place, rattlety-bang! No, Thomas, never will I consent to sit by while this goes on. I will never stir a finger in such baseness. Let him come here if he dares. I won't receive him, you may be sure of that. I will sit in my room with my daughter and my grand-daughter, and turn the key in the door, and forbid him to enter. — That is just what I will do."

"I know, Tony, you will do what you think best; and you will probably consider well beforehand if it will be wise not to preserve the ordinary social forms. For of course you don't imagine that Consul Hagenström would feel wounded by your conduct? Not in the least, my child. It would neither please nor displease him — he would simply be mildly surprised, that is all. The trouble is, you imagine he has the same feelings toward you that you have toward him. That is a mistake, Tony. He does not hate us in the least. He doesn't hate anybody. He is highly successful and ex-tremely good-natured. As I've told you more than ten times al-ready, he would speak to you on the street with the utmost cor-diality if you didn't put on such a belligerent air. I'm sure he is surprised at it — for two minutes; of course not enough to upset the equilibrium of a man to whom nobody can do any harm. What is it you reproach him with? Suppose he has outstripped me in business, and even now and then got ahead of me in some public affair? That only means he is a better business man and a cleverer politician than I am. — There's no reason at all for you to laugh in that scornful way. — But to come back to the house. The truth is, it has lost most of its old significance for us — that has gradually passed over to mine. I say this to console you in ad-vance; on the other hand, it is plain why Consul Hagenström is thinking of buying. These people have come up in the world, their family is growing, they have married into the Möllendorpf family, and become equal to the best in money and position. But so far, there has been something lacking, the outward sign of their position, which they were evidently willing to do without: the historic consecration — the legitimization, so to speak. But now they seem to have made up their minds to have that too; and some of it they will get by moving into a house like this one. You wait and see: mark my words, the Consul will preserve everything as much as possible as it is, he will even keep the ' Dominus providebit ' over the door — though, to do him justice, it hasn't been the Lord at all, but Hermann Hagenström himself, single-handed, that has put the family and the firm where they are! "

" Bravo, Tom! Oh, it does me good to hear you say something spiteful about them once in a while! That's really all I want! Oh, if I only had your head! Wouldn't I just give it to him! But there you stand — "

" You see, my head doesn't really do me much good."

" There you stand, I say, with that awful calmness, which I simply don't understand at all, and tell me how Hermann Hagenström does things. Ah, you may talk as you like, but you have a heart in your body, the same as I have myself, and I simply don't believe you feel as calm inside as you make out. All the things you say are nothing but your own efforts to console yourself."

" Now, Tony, you are getting pert. What I *do* is all you have anything to do with — what I think is my own affair."

" Tell me one thing, Tom: wouldn't it be like a nightmare to you? "

" Exactly."

" Like something you dreamed in a fever? "

" Why not? "

" Like the most ridiculous kind of farce? "

" There, there, now, that's enough! "

And Consul Hagenström appeared in Meng Street, accompanied by Herr Gosch, who held his Jesuit hat in his hand, crouched over like a conspirator, and peered past the maid into the landscape-room even while he handed her his card.

Hermann Hagenström looked the City man to the life: an imposing Stock Exchange figure, in a coat the fur of which seemed a foot long, standing open over an English winter suit of good fuzzy yellow-green tweed. He was so uncommonly fat that not only his chin, but the whole lower part of his face, was double — a fact which his full short-trimmed blond beard could not disguise. When he moved his forehead or eyebrows, deep folds came even in the smoothly shorn skin of his skull. His nose lay flatter upon his upper lip than ever, and breathed down into his moustaches.

Now and then his mouth had to come to the rescue and fly open for a deep breath. When it did this it always made a little smacking noise, as the tongue came away from the roof of his mouth.

Frau Permaneder coloured when she heard this once well-known sound. A vision of lemon buns with truffled sausage on top, almost threatened, for a moment, the stony dignity of her bearing. She sat on the sofa, her arms crossed and her shoulders lifted, in an exquisitely fitting black gown with flounces up to the waist, and a dainty mourning cap on her smooth hair. As the two gentlemen entered, she made a remark to her brother the Senator, in a calm, indifferent tone. He had not had the heart to leave her in the lurch at this hour; and he now walked to the middle of the room to meet their guests, while Tony remained on the sofa. He exchanged a hearty greeting with Herr Gosch and a correct and courteous one with the Consul; then Tony rose of her own accord, performed a measured bow to both of them at once, and, without any excess of zeal, associated herself with her brother's invitation to the two gentlemen to be seated.

They all sat down, and the Consul and the broker talked by turns for the next few minutes. Herr Gosch's voice was offensively obsequious as he begged them to pardon the intrusion on their privacy — you could hear a malign undercurrent in it none the less — but Herr Consul Hagenström was anxious to go through the house with a view to possible purchase. And the Consul, in a voice that again called up visions of lemon-bun and goose-liver, said the same thing in different words. Yes, in fact, this was the idea he had in mind and hoped to be able to carry out — provided the broker did not try to drive too hard a bargain with him, ha, ha! He did not doubt but the matter could be settled to the satisfaction of everybody concerned.

His manner was free and easy and like a man of the world's, which did not fail to make a certain impression on Madame Permaneder; the more so that he nearly always turned to her as he spoke. His tone was almost apologetic when he went into detail upon the grounds for his desire to purchase. "Room!" he said. "We need more room. My house in Sand Street — you wouldn't believe it, my dear madam, nor you, Herr Senator, but in fact, it is getting so small we can't turn round in it. I'm not speaking of company. It only takes the family, and the Huneus, and the Möllendorpfs and my brother Moritz's family, and there we are — in fact, packed in like sardines. So, then — well, why should we, you know!"

He spoke in an almost fretful tone, while manner and gestures expressed: "You see for yourselves, there's no reason why I should put up with that sort of thing, when there is plenty of money to do what we like!"

"I thought of waiting," he went on, "till Zerline and Bob should want a house. Then they could take mine, and I could find something larger for myself. But in fact — you know," he interrupted himself, "my daughter Zerline has been engaged to Bob, my brother the attorney's eldest, for years. The wedding won't be put off much longer — two years at most. They are young — so much the better. Well — in fact — why should I wait for them and let slip a good chance when it offers? There would be no sense in that."

Everybody agreed. The conversation paused for a while on the subject of the approaching wedding. Marriages — advantageous marriages — between first cousins were not uncommon in the town, and this one excited no disapproval. The plans of the young pair were inquired into — with reference to the wedding journey. They thought of going to the Riviera, to Nice and so on. That was what they seemed to want to do — and why shouldn't they, you know? The younger children were mentioned, and the Consul spoke of them with easy satisfaction, shrugging his shoulders. He himself had five children, and his brother Moritz had four sons and daughters. Yes, they were all flourishing, thanks. Why shouldn't they be, — you know? In fact, they were all very well. And he came back to the growing up of the family, and to their narrow quarters. "Yes, this is something else entirely," he said. "I've seen that already, on the way upstairs. This house is a pearl, certainly a pearl — if you can compare anything so large with anything so small, ha, ha! Why, even the hangings here — I own up to having had my eye on the hangings all the time I've been talking. A most charming room — in fact. When I think that you have passed all your life in these surroundings — in fact — "

"With some interruptions," said Frau Permaneder, in that extraordinarily throaty voice of which she sometimes availed herself.

"Oh, yes, interruptions," repeated the Consul, with a civil smile. Then he glanced at Senator Buddenbrook and the broker; and, as those gentlemen were in conversation together, he drew up his chair to Frau Permaneder's sofa and leaned toward her, so that she felt his heavy breathing close under her nose. Being too polite to turn away, she sat as stiff and erect as possible and looked down at him under her drooping lids. But he was quite unconscious of her discomfort.

"Let me see, my dear Madame Permaneder," he said. "Seems

to me we've done business together before now. In fact — what was it we were dickering over then? Sweetmeats, wasn't it, or tit-bits of some sort — and now a whole house! "

" I don't remember," said Frau Permaneder. She held her neck as stiff as she could, for his face was really disgustingly, indecently near.

" You don't remember? "

" No, really, I don't remember anything at all about sweetmeats. I have a sort of hazy recollection of lemon-buns, with sausage on top — some disgusting sort of school luncheon — I don't know whether it was yours or mine. We were all children then. — But this matter of the house is entirely Herr Gosch's affair. I have nothing to do with it."

She gave her brother a quick, grateful look, for he had seen her need and come to her rescue by asking if the gentlemen were ready to make the round of the house. They were quite ready, and took temporary leave of Frau Permaneder, expressing the hope of seeing her again when they had finished. The Senator led the two gentlemen out through the dining-room.

He took them upstairs and down, and showed them the rooms in the second storey as well as those on the corridor of the first, and the ground floor, including the kitchen and cellars. As the visit fell in business hours, they refrained from visiting the offices of the Insurance Company. But the new Director was mentioned, and Consul Hagenström declared him to be a very honest chap — a remark which was received by the Senator in silence.

They went through the garden, lying bare and wretched under half-melting snow, looked at the Portal, and returned to the laundry, in the front courtyard; and thence by the narrow paved walk that led between walls to the back courtyard with the oak-tree, and the " back building." Here there was nothing but old age, neglect, and dilapidation. Grass and moss grew between the paving-stones, the steps were in a state of advanced decay, and they could only look into the billiard-room without entering, — the floor was so bad — so the family of cats that lived there rent-free was not disturbed.

Consul Hagenström said very little — he was obviously planning. " Well, yes," he kept saying, as he looked and turned away, suggesting by his manner that in case he bought the house all this would of course be different. He stood, with the same air, on the ground-floor of the back building and looked up at the empty attic. " Yes, well," he repeated, and set in motion the thick, rotting

cable with a rusty iron hook on the end that had been hanging
there for years. Then he turned on his heel.

"Best thanks for your trouble, Herr Senator," he said. "We're
at the end, I suppose." He scarcely uttered a word on the rapid
return to the front building, or later when the two gentlemen paid
their respects to Frau Permaneder in the landscape-room and the
Senator accompanied them down the steps and across the entry.
But hardly had they said good-bye and Consul Hagenström turned
with his companion to walk down the street, when it was seen
that a very lively conversation began at once between the two.

The Senator returned to the room where Frau Permaneder,
with her severest manner, sat bolt upright in the window, knitting
with two huge wooden needles a black worsted frock for her
granddaughter Elisabeth, and now and then casting a glance into
the gossip's glass. Thomas walked up and down a while in silence,
with his hands in his trousers pockets.

"Yes, we have put it in the broker's hands," he said at
length. "We must wait and see what comes of it. My opinion is
that he will buy the whole property, live here in the front, and
utilize the back part in some other way."

She did not look at him, or change her position, or cease to knit.
On the contrary, the needles flew back and forth faster than ever.

"Oh, certainly — of course he'll buy it. He'll buy the whole
thing," she said, and it was her throaty voice she used. "Why
shouldn't he buy it — you know? In fact, there would be no sense
in that at all! "

She raised her eyebrows and looked severely through her pince-
nez — which she now used for sewing, but never managed to put
on straight — at her knitting-needles. They flew like lightning
round and round each other, clacking all the while.

Christmas came: the first Christmas without the Frau Consul.
They spent the evening of the twenty-fourth at the Senator's
house, without the old Krögers and without the Misses Buddenbrook; for the old children's day had now ceased to exist, and
Thomas Buddenbrook did not feel like making presents to everybody who used to attend the Frau Consul's celebration. Only
Frau Permaneder and Erica, with little Elisabeth, Christian, Clothilde, and Mademoiselle Weichbrodt, were invited. The latter
insisted on holding the customary present-giving on the twenty-
fifth, in her own stuffy little rooms, where it was attended with the
usual mishap.

There was no troop of poor retainers to receive shoes and woollen underwear, and there were no choir-boys, when they assembled in Fishers' Lane on the twenty-fourth. They joined quite simply together in " Holy Night," and Therese Weichbrodt read the Christmas chapter instead of the Frau Senator, who did not particularly care for such things. Then they went through the suite of rooms into the hall, singing in a subdued way the first stanza of " O Evergreen."

There was no special ground for rejoicing. Nobody's face was beaming with joy, there was no lively conversation. What was there to talk about? They thought of the departed mother, discussed the sale of the house and the well-lighted apartment which Frau Permaneder had rented in a pleasant house outside Holsten Gate, with a view on the green square of Linden Place, and what would happen when Hugo Weinschenk came out of prison. At intervals little Johann played on the piano something which he had been learning with Herr Pfühl, or accompanied his mother, not faultlessly, but with a lovely singing tone, in a Mozart sonata. He was praised and kissed, but had to be taken off to bed by Ida Jungmann, for he was pale and tired on account of a recent stomach upset.

Even Christian was disinclined to talk or joke. After the violent altercation in the breakfast-room he had not let fall another syllable about getting married. He lived on in the old way, on terms with his brother which were not very honourable to himself. He made a brief effort, rolling his eyes about, to awaken sympathy in the company for the misery in his side; went early to the club; and came back to supper, which was held after the prescribed traditions. And then the Buddenbrooks had this Christmas too behind them, and were glad of it.

In the beginning of the year 1872, the household of the deceased Frau Consul was broken up. The servants went, and Frau Permaneder thanked God to see the last of Mamsell Severin, who had continued to question her authority in the most unpleasant manner, and now departed with the silk gowns and linen which she had accumulated. Furniture wagons stood before the door, and the old house was emptied of its contents. The great carved chest, the gilt candelabra, and the other things that had fallen to his share, the Senator took to his house in Fishers' Lane; Christian moved with his into a three-room bachelor apartment near the club; and the little Permaneder-Weinschenk family took possession with theirs of the well-lighted flat in Linden Place, which was after all not without some claims to elegance. It was a pretty little apartment, and the front door of it had a bright copper plate with the name A. Permaneder-Buddenbrook, Widow, in ornamental lettering.

The house in Meng Street was hardly emptied when a host of workmen appeared and began to tear down the back-building; the dust from the old mortar darkened the air. The property had passed into the hands of Consul Hermann Hagenström. He had set his heart upon it, and had outbid an offer which Siegismund Gosch received for it from Bremen. He immediately began to turn it to the best advantage, in the ingenious way for which he had been so long admired. In the spring he moved with his family into the front house, where he left everything almost untouched, save for the necessary renovations and certain very modern improvements. For instance, he had the old bell-pulls taken out and the house fitted throughout with electric bells. And hardly had the back-building been demolished when a new, neat, and airy structure rose in its place, which fronted on Bakers' Alley and was intended for shops and warehouses.

Frau Permaneder had frequently sworn to her brother that no power on earth could bring her ever to look at the parental home again. But it was hardly possible to carry out this threat. Her way sometimes led her of necessity past the shops which had been quickly and advantageously rented, and past the show-windows of the back-building, or the dignified gable front on the other side, where now, beneath the "Dominus Providebit," was to be read the name of Consul Hermann Hagenström. When she saw that, Frau Permaneder, on the open street, before ever so many people, simply began to weep aloud. She put back her head like a bird beginning to sing, pressed her handkerchief to her eyes, uttered a wail of mingled protest and lament, and, giving no heed to the passers-by or to the remonstrances of her daughter, gave her tears free vent.

They were the unashamed, refreshing tears of her childhood, which she still retained despite all the storms and shipwrecks of her life.

PART TEN

CHAPTER I

OFTEN, in an hour of depression, Thomas Buddenbrook asked himself what he was, or what there was about him to make him think even a little better of himself than he did of his honest, limited, provincial fellow-burghers. The imaginative grasp, the brave idealism of his youth was gone. To work at his play, to play at his work, to bend an ambition that was half-earnest, half-whimsical, toward the accomplishment of aims that even to himself possessed but a symbolic value — for such blithe scepticism and such an enlightened spirit of compromise, a great deal of vitality is necessary, as well as a sense of humour. And Thomas Buddenbrook felt inexpressibly weary and disgusted.

What there was in life for him to reach, he had reached. He was well aware that the high-water mark of his life — if that were a possible way to speak of such a commonplace, humdrum sort of existence — had long since passed.

As for money matters, his estate was much reduced and the business, in general, on the decline. Counting his mother's inheritance and his share of the Meng Street property, he was still worth more than six hundred thousand marks. But the working capital of the firm had lain fallow for years, under the penny wise policies of which the Senator had complained at the time of the affair of the Pöppenrade harvest. Since the blow he had then received, they had grown worse instead of better; until now, at a time when prospects were brighter than ever — when everybody was flushed with victory, the city had at last joined the Customs Union, and small retail firms all over the country were growing within a few years into large wholesale ones — the firm of Johann Buddenbrook rested on its oars and reaped no advantage from the favourable time. If the head of the firm were asked after his business, he would answer, with a deprecating wave of the hand, " Oh, it's not much good, these days." As a lively rival, a close friend of the Hagenströms, once put it, Thomas Buddenbrook's function on 'Change was now largely decorative! The jest had for its point a jeer at the Senator's carefully preserved and faultless exterior —

and it was received as a masterpiece of wit by his fellow-citizens.

Thus the Senator's services to the old firm were no longer what they had been in the time of his strength and enthusiasm; while his labours for the good of the community had at the same time reached a point where they were circumscribed by limitations from without. When he was elected to the Senate, in fact, he had reached those limitations. There were thereafter only places to keep, offices to hold, but nothing further that he could achieve: nothing but the present, the narrow reality; never any grandiose plans to be carried out in the future. He had, indeed, known how to make his position and his power mean more than others had made them mean in his place: even his enemies did not deny that he was "the Burgomaster's right hand." But Burgomaster himself Thomas Buddenbrook could never become. He was a merchant, not a professional man; he had not taken the classical course at the gymnasium, he was not a lawyer. He had always done a great deal of historical and literary reading in his spare time, and he was conscious of being superior to his circle in mind and understanding, in inward as well as outward culture; so he did not waste much time in lamenting the lack of external qualifications which made it impossible for him to succeed to the first place in his little community. "How foolish we were," he said to Stephan Kistenmaker — but he really only meant himself by "we" — "that we went into the office so young, and did not finish our schooling instead." And Stephan Kistenmaker answered: "You're right there. But how do you mean?"

The Senator now chiefly worked alone at the great mahogany writing-desk in his private office. No one could see him there when he leaned his head on his hand and brooded, with his eyes closed. But he preferred it, also, because the hair-splitting pedantries of Herr Marcus had become unendurable to him. The way the man for ever straightened his writing-materials and stroked his beard would in itself have driven Thomas Buddenbrook from his seat in the counting-room. The fussiness of the old man had increased with the years to a positive mania; but what made it intolerable to the Senator was the fact that of late he had begun to notice something of the same sort in himself. He, who had once so hated all smallness and pettiness, was developing a pedantry which seemed to him the outgrowth of anybody else's character rather than his own.

He was empty within. There was no stimulus, no absorbing task into which he could throw himself. But his nervous activity, his inability to be quiet, which was something entirely different from his father's natural and permanent fondness for work, had not lessened, but increased — it had indeed taken the upper hand and become his master. It was something artificial, a pressure on the nerves, a depressant, in fact, like the pungent little Russian cigarettes which he was perpetually smoking. This craving for activity had become a martyrdom; but it was dissipated in a host of trivialities. He was harassed by a thousand trifles, most of which had actually to do with the upkeep of his house and his wardrobe; small matters which he could not keep in his head, over which he procrastinated out of disgust, and upon which he spent an utterly disproportionate amount of time and thought.

What outsiders called his vanity had lately increased in a way of which he was himself ashamed, though he was without the power to shake off the habits he had formed. Nowadays it was nine o'clock before he appeared to Herr Wenzel, in his nightshirt, after hours of heavy, unrefreshing sleep; and quite an hour and a half later before he felt himself ready and panoplied to begin the day, and could descend to drink his tea in the first storey. His toilette was a ritual consisting of a succession of countless details which drove him half mad: from the cold douche in the bathroom to the last brushing of the last speck of dust off his coat, and the last pressure of the tongs on his moustache. But it would have been impossible for him to leave his dressing-room with the consciousness of having neglected a single one of these details, for fear he might lose thereby his sense of immaculate integrity — which, however, would be dissipated in the course of the next hour and have to be renewed again.

He saved in everything, so far as he could — without subjecting himself to gossip. But he did not save where his clothes were concerned — he still had them made by the best Hamburg tailor, and spared no expense in the care and replenishing of his wardrobe. A spacious cabinet, like another room, was built into the wall of his dressing-room; and here, on long rows of hooks, on wooden hangers, were coats, smoking jackets, frock-coats, evening clothes, clothes for all occasions, all seasons, and all grades of formality; the carefully creased trousers were arranged on chairs beneath. The top of his chest of drawers was covered with combs, brushes, and toilet preparations for hair and beard; while within it was the supply of body linen of all possible kinds, which was constantly changed, washed, worn out, and renewed.

He spent in this dressing-room not only the early hours of each morning, but also a long time before every dinner, every sitting of the Senate, every public appearance — in short, before every

occasion on which he had to show himself among his fellow men
— even before the daily dinner with his wife, little Johann, and
Ida Jungmann. And when he left it, the fresh underwear on his
body, the faultless elegance of his clothing, the smell of the bril-
liantine on his moustache, and the cool, astringent taste of the
mouth-wash he used — all this gave him a feeling of satisfaction
and adequacy, like that of an actor who has adjusted every detail
of his costume and make-up and now steps out upon the stage.
And, in truth, Thomas Buddenbrook's existence was no different
from that of an actor — an actor whose life has become one long
production, which, but for a few brief hours for relaxation, consumes him unceasingly. In the absence of any ardent objective
interest, his inward impoverishment oppressed him almost without
any relief, with a constant, dull chagrin; while he stubbornly clung
to the determination to be worthily representative, to conceal his
inward decline, and to preserve "the *dehors*" whatever it cost
him. All this made of his life, his every word, his every motion, a
constant irritating pretence.

And this state of things showed itself by peculiar symptoms
and strange whims, which he observed with surprise and disgust.
People who have no rôle to perform before the public, who do not
conceive themselves as acting a part, but as standing unobserved
to watch the performance of others, like to stand with the light at
their backs. But Thomas Buddenbrook could not endure the feeling of standing in the shadow while the light streamed full upon
the faces of those whom he wished to impress. He wanted his
audience, before whom he was to act the rôle of a social light, a
public orator, or a representative business man, to stand before him
in a confused and shadowy mass while a blinding light played
upon his own face. Only this gave him a feeling of separation and
safety, an intoxicating sense of self-production, which was the atmosphere in which he achieved success. It had come to be the case
that precisely this intoxication was the most bearable condition
he knew. When he stood up at table, wine-glass in hand, to reply
to a toast, with his charming manner, easy gestures, and witty
turns of phrase, which struck unerringly home and released waves
of merriment down the length of the table, then he might feel, as
well as seem, the Thomas Buddenbrook of former days. It was
much harder to keep the mastery over himself when he was sitting
idle. For then his weariness and disgust rose up within him,
clouded his eyes, relaxed his bearing and his facial muscles. At
such times, he was possessed by one desire: to steal away, to be
alone, to lie in silence, with his head resting on a cool pillow.

Frau Permaneder had dined that evening in Fishers' Lane. She was the only guest, for her daughter, who was to have gone, had visited her husband that afternoon in the prison, and felt, as she usually did, exhausted and incapable of further effort. So she had stayed at home.

Frau Antonie had spoken at table of the mental condition of her son-in-law, which, it appeared, was very bad; and the question arose whether one might not, with some hope of success, petition the Senate for a pardon. After dinner the three relatives sat in the living-room, at the round table beneath the great gas-lamp. The Frau Senator bent her lovely face over some embroidery, and the gas-light lit up gleams in her dark hair; Frau Permaneder, with careful fingers, fastened an enormous red satin bow on to a tiny yellow basket, intended as a birthday present for a friend. Her glasses were stuck absolutely awry and useless on her nose. The Senator sat with his legs crossed, partly turned away from the table, in a large upholstered easy-chair, reading the paper; he drew in the smoke of his Russian cigarette and let it out again in a light grey stream between his moustaches.

It was a warm summer Sunday evening. The lofty window was open, and the lifeless, rather damp air flowed into the room. From where they sat at the table they could look between the grey gables of intervening houses at the stars and the slowly moving clouds. There was still light in Iwersen's little flower-shop across the way. Further on in the quiet street a concertina was being played with a good many false notes, probably by the son of Dankwart the driver. But sometimes the street was noisy with a troop of sailors, singing, smoking, arm in arm, going, no doubt, from one doubtful waterside public-house to another still more doubtful one, and obviously in a jovial mood. Their rough voices and swinging tread would die off down a cross-street.

The Senator laid down his newspaper, put his glasses in his waistcoat pocket, and rubbed his hand over his eyes and forehead.

"Feeble — very feeble indeed, this paper," he said. "I always think when I read it of what Grandfather used to say about a dish that had no particular taste or consistency: it tastes as if you were hanging your tongue out of the window. One, two, three, and you've finished with the whole stupid thing."

"You are certainly right about that, Tom," said Frau Permaneder, letting fall her work and looking at her brother sidewise, past her glasses but not through them. "What is there in it? I've always said, ever since I was a mere slip of a girl, that this town paper is a wretched sheet! I read it too, of course, for want of a

better one; but it isn't so very thrilling to hear that wholesale dealer
Consul So-and-so is going to celebrate his silver wedding! We
ought to read other papers: the *Königsberg Gazette*, or the *Rhenish Gazette;* then we'd — "

She interrupted herself. She had taken up the paper as she
spoke, and let her eye run contemptuously down the columns.
But her glance was arrested by a short notice of four or five lines,
which she read through, clutching her eye-glasses, her mouth
slowly opening. Then she uttered two shrieks, with the palms of
her hands pressed against her cheeks, and her elbows held out
straight.

" Oh, impossible — impossible! Imagine your not seeing that at
all. It is frightful! Oh, *poor* Armgard! It had to come to her like
that! "

Gerda had lifted her head from her work, and Thomas, startled,
looked at his sister. Much upset, Frau Permaneder read the notice
aloud, in a guttural, portentous tone. It came from Rostock, and
it said that, the night before, Herr Ralf von Maiboom, owner of
the Pöppenrade estate, had committed suicide by shooting himself with a revolver, in the study of the manor-house. " Pecuniary
difficulties seem to have been the cause of the act. Herr von Maiboom leaves a wife and three children." She finished and let the
paper fall in her lap, then leaned back and looked at her brother and
sister with wide, piteous eyes.

Thomas Buddenbrook had turned away while he listened, and
looked past his sister between the portières, into the dark salon.

" With a revolver? " he asked, after silence had reigned some
two minutes. And then, after another pause, he said in a low voice,
slowly and mockingly: " That is the nobility for you! "

Then he fell again to musing, and the rapidity with which he
drew the ends of his moustaches through his fingers was in remarkable contrast to the vacant fixity of his gaze. He did not listen to the lamentations of his sister, or to her speculations on what
poor Armgard would do now. Nor did he notice that Gerda,
without turning her head in his direction, was fixing him with a
searching and steady gaze from her close-set, blue-shadowed eyes.

CHAPTER II

THOMAS BUDDENBROOK did not contemplate the future of little Johann with the weary dejection which was now his settled mood when he thought about his own life and his own end. The family feeling which led him to cherish the past history of his house extended itself even more strongly into its future; and he was influenced, too, by the loving and expectant curiosity concentrated upon his son by his family and his friends and acquaintances, even by the Buddenbrook ladies in Broad Street. He said to himself that, however hopeless and thwarted he himself felt, he was still, wherever his son was concerned, capable of inexhaustible streams of energy, endurance, achievement, success — yes, that at this one spot his chilled and artificial life could still be warmed into a genuine and glowing warmth of hopes and fears and affections.

Perhaps, some day, it would be granted to him to look back upon his past from a quiet corner and watch the renascence of the old time, the time of Hanno's great-grandfather! Was such a hope, after all, entirely vain? He had felt that the music was his enemy; but it had almost begun to look as if it had no such important bearing upon the situation. Granted that the child's fondness for improvising, without notes, was evidence of a not quite common gift; in the systematic lessons with Herr Pfühl he had not showed by any means extraordinary progress. The preoccupation with music was no doubt due to his mother's influence; and it was not surprising that during his early years this influence had been preponderant. But the time was close at hand when it would be the father's turn to influence his son, to draw him over to his side, to neutralize the feminine influence by introducing a masculine one in its place. And the Senator determined not to let any such opportunities pass without improving them.

Hanno was now eleven years old. The preceding Easter, he had, by the skin of his teeth and by dint of two extra examinations in mathematics and geography, been passed into the fourth form — as had likewise his young friend Count Mölln. It had been settled that he should attend the mercantile side of the school —

for it went without saying that he would be a merchant and take over the family business. When his father asked him if he felt any inclination toward his future career, he answered yes — a simple, unadorned, embarrassed "yes," which the Senator tried to make a little more convincing by asking leading questions, but mostly without success.

If the Senator had had two sons, he would assuredly have allowed the second to go through the gymnasium and study. But the firm demanded a successor. And, besides, he was convinced he was doing the boy a kindness in relieving him of the unnecessary Greek. He was of opinion that the mercantile course was the easier to master, and that Hanno would therefore come through with greater credit and less strain if he took it, considering his defects — his slowness of comprehension, his absent, dreaming ways, and his physical delicacy, which often obliged him to be absent from school. If little Johann Buddenbrook were to achieve the position in life to which he was called, they must be mindful before everything else, by care and cherishing on the one hand, by sensible toughening on the other, to strengthen his far from robust constitution.

Hanno had grown sturdier in the past year; but, despite his blue sailor suit, he still looked a little strange in the playground of the school, by contrast with the blond Scandinavian type that predominated there. He now wore his brown hair parted on the side and brushed away from his white forehead. But it still inclined to fall in soft ringlets over the temples; and his eyes were as golden-brown as ever, and as veiled with their brown lashes. His legs, in long black stockings, and his arms, in the loose quilted blue sleeves of his suit, were small and soft like a girl's, and he had, like his mother, the blue shadows under his eyes. And still, in those eyes, especially when they gave a side glance, as they often did, there was that timid and defensive look; while the mouth closed with the old, woebegone expression which he had had even as a baby, or went slightly crooked when he explored the recesses of his mouth for a defective tooth. And there would come upon his face when he did this a look as if he were cold.

Dr. Langhals had now entirely taken over Dr. Grabow's practice and had become the Buddenbrook family physician. From him they learned the reason why the child's skin was so pale and his strength so inadequate. It seemed that Hanno's organism did not produce red corpuscles in sufficient number. But there was a remedy for this defect: cod-liver oil, which, accordingly, Dr. Langhals prescribed in great quantities: good, thick, greasy, yellow cod-liver oil, to be taken from a porcelain spoon twice a day. The Senator gave the order, and Ida Jungmann, with stern affection, saw it carried out. In the beginning, to be sure, Hanno threw up after each spoonful. His stomach seemed to have a prejudice against the good cod-liver oil. But he got used to it in the end — and if you held your breath and chewed a piece of rye bread immediately after, the nausea was not so severe.

His other troubles were all consequent upon this lack of red corpuscles, it appeared: secondary phenomena, Dr. Langhals called them, looking at his fingernails. But it was necessary to attack these other enemies ruthlessly. As for the teeth, for these Herr Brecht and his Josephus lived in Mill Street: to take care of them, to fill them; when necessary, to extract them. And for the digestion there was castor-oil, thick, clear castor-oil that slipped down your throat like a lizard, after which you smelled and tasted it for three days, sleeping and waking. Oh, why were all these remedies of such surpassing nastiness? One single time — Hanno had been rather ill, and his heart action had shown unusual irregularity — Dr. Langhals had with some misgiving prescribed a remedy which little Hanno had actually enjoyed, and which had done him a world of good. These were arsenic pills. But however much he asked to have the dose repeated — for he felt almost a yearning for these sweet, soothing little pills — Dr. Langhals never prescribed them again.

Castor-oil and cod-liver oil were excellent things. But Dr. Langhals was quite at one with the Senator in the view that they could not of themselves make a sound and sturdy citizen of little Johann if he did not do his part. There was gymnasium drill once a week in the summer, out on the Castle Field, where the youth of the city were given the opportunity to develop their strength and courage, their skill and presence of mind, under the guidance of Herr Fritsche, the drill-master. But to his father's annoyance, Hanno showed a distinct distaste for the manly sports — a silent, pronounced, almost haughty opposition. Why was it that he cared so little for playmates of his own class and age, with whom he would have to live, and was for ever sticking about with this little unwashed Kai, who was a good child, of course, but not precisely a proper friend for the future? Somehow or other a boy must know from the beginning how to gain the confidence and respect of his comrades, upon whose good opinion of him he will be dependent for the rest of his life! There were, on the other hand, the two sons of Consul Hagenström, two fine strapping boys, twelve and fourteen years old, strong and full of spirits, who insti-

tuted prizefights in the neighbouring woods, were the best gym-
nasts in the school, swam like otters, smoked cigars, and were
ready for any deviltry. They were popular, feared, and respected.
Their cousins, the two sons of Dr. Moritz Hagenström, the State
Attorney, were of a more delicate build, and gentler ways. They
distinguished themselves in scholarship, and were model pupils:
zealous, industrious, quiet, attentive, devoured by the ambition to
bring home a report card marked "Number 1." They achieved
their ambition, and were respected by their stupider and lazier
colleagues. But — not to speak of his masters — what must his
fellow-pupils think of Hanno, who was not only a very mediocre
scholar, but a weakling into the bargain; who tried to get out of
everything for which a scrap of courage, strength, skill, and energy
were needed? When Senator Buddenbrook passed the little balcony on his way to his dressing-room, he would hear from Hanno's
room, which was the middle one of the three on that floor since
he had grown too large to sleep with Ida Jungmann, the notes of
the harmonium, or the hushed and mysterious voice of Kai, Count
Mölln telling a story.

Kai avoided the drill classes, because he detested the discipline
which had to be observed there. "No, Hanno," he said, "I'm not
going. Are you? Deuce take it! Anything that would be any fun
is forbidden." Expressions like "deuce take it" he got from his
father. Hanno answered: "If Herr Fritsche ever one single day
smelled of anything but beer and sweat, I might consider it. Don't
talk about it, Kai. Go on. Tell that one about the ring you got out
of the bog — you didn't finish it." "Very good," said Kai. "But
when I nod, then you must play." And he went on with his story.

If he was to be believed, he had once, on a warm evening, in a
strange, unrecognizable region, slid down a slippery, immeasurable
cliff, at the foot of which, by the flickering, livid light from will-
o'-the-wisps, he saw a black marsh, from which silvery bubbles
mounted with a hollow gurgling sound. One of these bubbles,
which kept coming up near the bank, took the form of a ring
when it burst; and he had succeeded in seizing it, after long and
dangerous efforts — after which it burst no more, but remained in
his grasp, a firm and solid ring, which he put on his finger. He
rightly ascribed unusual powers to this ring; for by its help he
climbed up the slippery cliff and saw, a little way off in the rosy
mist, a black castle. It was guarded to the teeth, but he had forced
an entrance, always by the help of the ring, and performed
miracles of rescue and deliverance. All this Hanno accompanied
with sweet chords on his harmonium. Sometimes, if the difficulties

were not too great, these stories were acted in the marionette theatre, to musical accompaniment. But Hanno attended the drill class only on his father's express command — and then Kai went too.

It was the same with the skating in the wintertime, and with the bathing in summer at the wooden bathing establishment of Herr Asmussen, down on the river. "Bathing and swimming — let the boy have bathing and swimming — he must bathe and swim," Dr. Langhals had said. And the Senator was entirely of the same opinion. But Hanno had a reason for absenting himself from the bathing, as well as from the skating and the drill class. The two sons of Consul Hagenström, who took part in all such exercises with great skill and credit, singled Hanno out at once. And though they lived in his own grandmother's house, that fact did not prevent them from making his life miserable. They lost no opportunity of tormenting him. At drill they pinched him and derided him. They rolled him in the dirty snow at the ice-rink; and in the water they came up to him with horrid noises. Hanno did not try to escape. It would have been useless anyhow. He stood, with his girlish arms, up to his middle in the turbid water of the pool, which had large patches of duck-weed growing on it, and awaited his tormentors with a scowl — a dark look and twisted lips. They, sure of their prey, came on with long splashing strides. They had muscular arms, these two young Hagenströms, and they clutched him round his body and ducked him — ducked him a good long time, so that he swallowed rather a lot of the dirty water and gasped for breath a long time after. One single time he was a little avenged. One afternoon the two Hagenströms were holding him down under the water, when one of them suddenly gave a shriek of pain and fury and lifted his plump leg, from which drops of blood were oozing. Beside him rose the head of Kai, Count Mölln, who had somehow got hold of the price of admission, swum up invisible in the water, and bitten young Hagenström — bitten with all his teeth into his leg, like a furious little dog. His blue eyes flashed through the red-blond hair that hung down wet all over his face. He paid richly for the deed, did the little Count, and left the swimming-pool much the worse for the encounter. But Consul Hagenström's son limped perceptibly when he went home.

Nourishing remedies and physical exercise were the basis of the treatment calculated to turn Senator Buddenbrook's son into a strong and healthy lad. But no less painstakingly did the Senator strive to influence his mind and give him lively impressions of the practical world in which he was to live.

He began gradually to introduce him into the sphere of his future activities. He took him on business expeditions down to the
harbour and let him stand by on the quay while he spoke to the
dockers in a mixture of Danish and dialect or gave orders to the men
who with hollow, long-drawn cries were hauling up the sacks
to the granary floor. He took him into dark little warehouse offices to confer with superintendents. All this life of the harbours,
ships, sheds, and granaries, where it smelled of butter, fish, sea-
water, tar, and greasy iron, had been to Thomas Buddenbrook
from childhood up the most fascinating thing on earth. But his
son gave no spontaneous expression of his own enchantment with
the sight; and so the father was fain to arouse it in him. "What are
the names of the boats that ply to Copenhagen? The *Naiad*, the
Halmstadt, the *Friederike Overdieck* — why, if you know those,
my son, at least that's something! You'll soon learn the others.
Some of those people over there hauling up the grain have the
same name as you — they were named after your grandfather, as
you were. And their children are often named after me — or
Mamma. We give them little presents every year. — Now this next
granary — we don't stop at it; we go past and don't talk to the
men; it is a rival business."

"Should you like to come, Hanno?" he said another time.
"There is a ship of our line being launched to-day, and I shall
christen it. Do you want to go?" And Hanno signified that he
wanted to go. He went with his father, listened to his speech, and
saw him break a bottle of champagne on the prow of the ship;
saw how she glided down the ways, which had been smeared with
green soap, and into the water.

On certain days of the year, as New Year's and Palm Sunday,
when there were confirmations, Senator Buddenbrook drove out
on a round of visits to particular houses in which he had social relations. His wife did not like these visits, and excused herself on
the ground of headache and nervousness, so Hanno would be asked
to go along in her place; and here, too, he signified his desire to go.
He climbed into the carriage beside his father, and sat silent by his
side in the reception-rooms, watching his easy, tactful, assured, and
carefully graduated manner toward their hosts. He heard District
Commander Colonel Herr von Rinnlingen tell his father how
greatly he appreciated the honour of his visit, and saw how his
father, in reply, put on an air of amiable depreciation and laid his
arm an instant across the Colonel's shoulders. In another place the
same remark was made, and he received it with quiet seriousness,
and in a third with an ironically exaggerated compliment in return.

All this with a floridity of speech and gesture which he obviously liked to produce for the admiration of his son, and from which he promised himself the most edifying results.

But the little boy saw more than he should have seen; the shy, gold-brown, blue-shadowy eyes observed too well. He saw not only the unerring charm which his father exercised upon everybody: he saw as well, with strange and anguished penetration, how cruelly hard it was upon him. He saw how his father, paler and more silent after each visit, would lean back in his corner of the carriage with closed eyes and reddened eyelids; he realized with a sort of horror that on the threshold of the next house a mask would glide over his face, a galvanized activity take hold of the weary frame. Thus the visits, the social intercourse with one's kind, instead of giving little Johann, quite simply, the idea that one has practical interests in common with one's fellow men, which one looks after oneself, expecting others to do the same, appeared to him like an end in themselves; instead of straightforward and single-minded participation in the common business, he saw his father perform an artificial and complicated part, by dint of a fearful effort and an exaggerated, consuming virtuosity. And when he thought that some day he should be expected to perform the same part, under the gaze of the whole community, Hanno shut his eyes and shivered with rebellion and disgust.

Ah, that was not the effect Thomas Buddenbrook looked for from the influence of his own personality upon his son's! What he had hoped to do was to stimulate self-confidence in the boy, and a sense of the practical side of life. This was what he had in mind — and nothing else.

"You seem to enjoy good living, my boy," said he, when Hanno asked for a second portion of the sweet or a half-cup of coffee after dinner. "Well, then, you must become a merchant and earn a lot of money. Should you like to do that?" Little Johann said he would.

Sometimes when the family were invited to dinner, Aunt Antonie or Uncle Christian would begin to tease Aunt Clothilde and imitate her meek, drawling accents. Then little Johann, stimulated by the heavy red wine which they gave him, would ape his elders and make some remarks to Aunt Clothilde in the same vein. And then how Thomas Buddenbrook would laugh! He would give a loud, hearty, jovial roar, like a man put in high spirits by some unexpected piece of good luck, and join in on his son's side against poor Aunt Clothilde, though for his own part he had long since given up these witticisms at the expense of his poor rela-

tive. It was so easy, so safe, to tease poor, limited, modest, lean
and hungry Clothilde, that, harmless though it was, he felt it rather
beneath him. But he wished he did not, for it was the same story
over again: too many considerations, too many scruples. Why
must he be for ever opposing these scruples against the hard, practical affairs of life? Why could he never learn that it was possible
to grasp a situation, to see around it, as it were, and still to turn it
to one's own advantage without any feeling of shame? For precisely this, he said to himself, is the essence of a capacity for practical life!

And thus, how happy, how delighted, how hopeful he felt
whenever he saw even the least small sign in little Johann of a capacity for practical life!

CHAPTER III

THE EXTENDED summer trip which had once been customary with
the Buddenbrooks had now been given up for some years. Indeed,
when the Frau Senator, in the previous spring, had wished to make
her old father in Amsterdam a visit and play a few duets with him,
the Senator had given his consent rather curtly. But it had become the rule for Gerda, little Johann, and Fräulein Jungmann to
spend the holidays at the Kurhouse, in Travemünde, for the sake of
Hanno's health.

Summer holidays at the seashore! Did anybody really understand the joy of that? After the dragging monotony and worry
of the endless school terms came four weeks of peaceful, care-free
seclusion, full of the good smell of sea-weed and the whispering of
the gentle surf. Four weeks! At the beginning it seemed endless;
you could not believe that it would end; it was almost indelicate
to suggest such a thing! Little Johann could not comprehend the
crudity of a master who could say: " After the holidays we shall
take up our work at — " this or that point! After the holidays! He
appeared to be already rejoicing in the thought, this strange man
in the shiny worsted suit! After the holidays! What a thought!
And how far, far off in the grey distance lay everything that was
on the other side of the holidays, on the other side of those four
weeks!

The inspection of the school report, with its record of examinations well or badly got through, would be at last over, and the
journey in the overcrowded carriage. Hanno would wake the first
morning in his room at the Kurhouse, in one of the Swiss cottages
that were united by a small gallery to the main building and the
pastry-shop. He would have a vague feeling of happiness that
mounted in his brain and made his heart contract. He would open
his eyes and look with eager pleasure at the old-fashioned furniture of the cleanly little room. A moment of dazed and sleepy
bliss: then he would be conscious that he was in Travemünde —
for four immeasurable weeks in Travemünde. He did not stir. He
lay on his back in the narrow yellow wooden bed, the linen of

which was extremely thin and soft with age. He even shut his eyes again and felt his chest rising in deep, slow breaths of happy anticipation.

The room lay in yellow daylight that came in through the striped blind. Everything was still — Mamma and Ida Jungmann were asleep. Nothing was to be heard but a measured, peaceful sound which meant that the man was raking the gravelled paths of the Kurgarten below, and the buzzing of a fly that had got between the blind and the window and was storming the pane — you could see his shadow shooting about in long zigzag lines. Peace! Only the sound of the rake and the dull buzzing noise. This gently animated quiet filled little Johann with a priceless sensation: the feeling of quiet, well-cared-for, elegant repose which was the atmosphere of the resort, and which he loved better than anything else. Thank God, none of the shiny worsted coats who were the chosen representatives of grammar and the rule of three on this earth was in the least likely to come here — for here it was rather exclusive and expensive.

An access of joy made him spring up and run barefoot to the window. He put up the blind and unfastened the white-painted hook of the window; and as he opened it the fly escaped and flew away over the flower-beds and the gravelled paths. The music pavilion, standing in a half-circle of beech-trees opposite the main building, was still empty and quiet. The Leuchtenfield, which took its name from the lighthouse that stood on it, somewhere off to the right, stretched its extent of short sparse grass under the pale sky, to a point where the grass passed into a growth of tall, coarse water-plants; and then came the sand, with its rows of little wooden huts and tall wicker beach-chairs looking out to the sea. It lay there, the sea, in peaceful morning light, striped blue and green; and a steamer came in from Copenhagen, between the two red buoys that marked its course, and one did not need to know whether it was the *Naiad* or the *Friederike Överdieck*. Hanno Buddenbrook drew in a deep, quiet, blissful breath of the spicy air from the sea and greeted her tenderly, with a loving, speechless, grateful look.

Then the day began, the first of those paltry twenty-eight days, which seemed in the beginning like an eternity of bliss, and which flew by with such desperate haste after the first two or three. They breakfasted on the balcony or under the great chestnut tree near the children's playground, where the swing hung. Everything — the smell of the freshly washed table-cloth when the waiter shook it out, the tissue paper serviettes, the unaccustomed bread, the eggs they ate out of little metal cups, with ordinary spoons instead of bone ones like those at home — all this, and everything, enchanted little Johann.

And all that followed was so easy and care-free — such a wonderfully idle and protected life. There was the forenoon on the beach, while the Kurhouse band gave its morning programme; the lying and resting at the foot of the beach-chair, the delicious, dreamy play with the soft sand that did not make you dirty, while you let your eyes rove idly and lose themselves in the green and blue infinity beyond. There was the air that swept in from that infinity — strong, free, wild, gently sighing and deliciously scented; it seemed to enfold you round, to veil your hearing and make you pleasantly giddy, and blessedly submerge all consciousness of time and space. And the bathing here was a different affair altogether from that in Herr Asmussen's establishment. There was no duck-weed here, and the light green water foamed away in crystalline clearness when you stirred it up. Instead of a slimy wooden floor there was soft sand to caress the foot — and Consul Hagenström's sons were far away, in Norway or the Tyrol. The Consul loved to make an extended journey in the holidays, and — why shouldn't he?

A walk followed, to warm oneself up, along the beach to Seagull Rock or Ocean Temple, a little lunch by the beach-chair; then the time came to go up to one's room for an hour's rest, before making a toilette for the table-d'hôte. The table-d'hôte was very gay, for this was a good season at the baths, and the great dining-room was filled with acquaintances of the Buddenbrooks, Hamburg families, and even some Russians and English people. A black-clad gentleman sat at a tiny table and served the soup out of a silver tureen. There were four courses, and the food tasted nicer and more seasoned than that at home, and many people drank champagne. These were the single gentlemen who did not allow their business to keep them chained in town all the week, and who got up some little games of roulette after dinner: Consul Peter Döhlmann, who had left his daughter at home, and told such extremely funny stories that the ladies from Hamburg laughed till their sides ached and they begged him for mercy; Senator Dr. Cremer, the old Superintendent of Police; Uncle Christian, and his friend Dr. Gieseke, who was also without his family, and paid everything for Uncle Christian. After dinner, the grown-ups drank coffee under the awnings of the pastry-shop, and the band played, and Hanno sat on a chair close to the steps of the pavilion and listened unwearied. He was settled for the afternoon. There was a shooting-gallery in the Kurgarten, and at the right of the Swiss cottage were the stables, with horses and donkeys, and the cows whose foaming, fragrant milk one drank warm every evening. One could go walking in the little town or along the front; one could go out to the Prival in a boat and look for amber on the beach, or play croquet in the children's playground, or listen to Ida Jungmann reading aloud, sitting on a bench on the wooded hillside where hung the great bell for the table-d'hôte. But best of all was it to go back to the beach and sit in the twilight on the end of the breakwater, with your face turned to the open horizon. Great ships passed by, and you signalled them with your handkerchief; and you listened to the little waves slapping softly against the stones; and the whole space about you was filled with a soft and mighty sighing. It spoke so benignly to little Johann! it bade him close his eyes, it told him that all was well. But just then Ida would say, " Come, little Hanno. It's supper-time. We must go. If you were to sit here and go to sleep, you'd die." How calm his heart felt, how evenly it beat, after a visit to the sea! Then he had his supper in his room — for his mother ate later, down in the glass verandah — and drank milk or malt extract, and lay down in his little bed, between the soft old linen sheets, and almost at once sleep overcame him, and he slept, to the subdued rhythm of the evening concert and the regular pulsations of his quiet heart.

On Sunday the Senator appeared, with the other gentlemen who had stopped in town during the week, and remained until Monday morning. Ices and champagne were served at the table-d'hôte, and there were donkey-rides and sailing-parties out to the open sea. Still, little Johann did not care much for these Sundays. The peaceful isolation of the bathing-place was broken in upon. A crowd of townsfolk — good middle-class trippers, Ida Jungmann called them — populated the Kurgarten and crowded the beach, drank coffee and listened to the music. Hanno would have liked to stay in his room until these kill-joys in their Sunday clothes went away again. No, he was glad when everything returned to its regular course on Monday — and he felt relieved to feel his father's eyes no more upon him.

Two weeks had passed; and Hanno said to himself, and to every one who would listen to him, that there was still as much time left as the whole of the Michaelmas holidays amounted to. It consoled him to say this, but after all it was a specious consolation, for the crest of the holidays had been reached, and from now on they were going downhill — so quickly, so frightfully quickly, that he would have liked to cling to every moment, not to let it escape; to lengthen every breath he drew of the sea-air; to taste every second of his joy.

But the time went on, relentless: in rain and sun, sea-wind and land-wind, long spells of brooding warmth and endless noisy storms that could not get away out to sea and went on for ever so long. There were days on which the north-east wind filled the bay with dark green floods, covered the beach with seaweed, mussels, and jelly-fish, and threatened the bathing-huts. The turbid, heavy sea was covered far and wide with foam. The mighty waves came on in awful, awe-inspiring calm, and the under side of each was a sharp metallic green; then they crashed with an ear-splitting roar, hissing and thundering along the sand. There were other days when the west wind drove back the sea for a long distance, exposing a gently rolling beach and naked sand-banks everywhere, while the rain came down in torrents. Heaven, earth, and sea flowed into each other, and the driving wind carried the rain against the panes so that not drops but rivers flowed down, and made them impossible to see through. Then Hanno stayed in the salon of the Kurhouse and played on the little piano that was used to play waltzes and schottisches for the balls and was not so good for improvising on as the piano at home: still one could sometimes get amusing effects out of its muffled and clacking keys. And there were still other days, dreamy, blue, windless, broodingly warm, when the blue flies buzzed in the sun above the Leuchtenfield, and the sea lay silent and like a mirror, without stir or breath. When there were only three days left Hanno said to himself, and to everybody else, that the time remaining was just as long as Whitsuntide holiday; but, incontestable as this reckoning was, it did not convince even himself. He knew now that the man in the worsted coat was right, and that they would, in very truth, begin again where they had left off, and go on to this and that.

The laden carriage stood before the door. The day had come. Early in the morning Hanno had said good-bye to sea and strand. Now he said it to the waiters as they received their fees, to the music pavilion, the rose-beds, and the whole long summer as well. And amid the bows of the hotel servants the carriage drove off.

They passed the avenue that led to the little town, and rolled along the front. Ida Jungmann sat, white-haired, bright-eyed, and angular, opposite Hanno on the back seat, and he squeezed his head into the corner and looked past her out of the window. The morning sky was overcast; the Trave was full of little waves that hurried before the wind. Now and then rain-drops spattered the pane. At the farther end of the front, people sat before their house

doors and mended nets; barefoot children ran past, and stared in-
quisitively at the occupants of the carriage. *They* did not need to
go away!

As they left the last houses behind, Hanno bent forward once
more to look after the lighthouse; then he leaned back and closed
his eyes. "We'll come back again next year, darling," Ida Jungmann said in her grave, soothing voice. It needed only that to make
Hanno's chin tremble and the tears run down beneath his long
dark lashes.

His face and hands were brown from the sea air. But if his stay
at the baths had been intended to harden him, to give him more
resistance, more energy, more endurance, then it had failed of its
purpose; and Hanno himself was aware of this lamentable fact.
These four weeks of sheltered peace and adoration of the sea had
not hardened him: they had made him softer than ever, more
dreamy and more sensitive. He would be no better able to endure
the rigours of Herr Tietge's class. The thought of the rules and
history dates which he had to get by heart had not lost its power to
make him shudder; he knew the feeling too well, and how he
would fling them away in desperation and go to bed, and suffer
next day the torments of the unprepared. And he would be exactly as much afraid of catastrophes at the recitation hour, of his
enemies the Hagenströms, and of his father's injunctions not to be
faint-hearted whatever else he was.

But he felt cheered a little by the fresh morning drive through
flooded country roads, amid the twitterings of birds. He thought
of seeing Kai again, and Herr Pfühl; of his music lessons, the
piano and his harmonium. And as the morrow was Sunday, a
whole day still intervened between him and the first lesson-hour.
He could feel a few grains of sand from the beach, still inside his
buttoned boot—how lovely! He would ask old Grobleben to
leave them there. Let it all begin again—the worsted-coats, the
Hagenströms, and the rest. He had what he had. When the waves
of tribulation went over him once more he would think of the sea
and of the Kurgarten, and of the sound made by the little waves,
coming hither out of the mysterious slumbering distance. One
single memory of the sound they made as they splashed against the
breakwater could make him oppose an invincible front to all the
pains and penalties of his life.

Then came the ferry, and Israelsdorfer Avenue, Jerusalem Hill,
and the Castle Field, on the right side of which rose the walls of
the prison where Uncle Weinschenk was. Then the carriage rolled
along Castle Street and over the Koberg, crossed Broad Street,

and braked down the steep decline of Fishers' Lane. There was the
red house-front with the bow-window and the white caryatides;
and as they went from the midday warmth of the street into the
coolness of the stone-flagged entry the Senator, with his pen in his
hand, came out of the office to greet them.

Slowly, slowly, with secret tears, little Johann learned to live
without the sea; to lead an existence that was frightened and bored
by turns; to keep out of the way of the Hagenströms; to console
himself with Kai and Herr Pfühl and his music.

The Broad Street Buddenbrooks and Aunt Clothilde, directly
they saw him again, asked him how he liked school after the holidays. They asked it teasingly, with that curiously superior and
slighting air which grown people assume toward children, as if
none of their affairs could possibly be worthy of serious consideration; but Hanno was proof against their questions.

Three or four days after the home-coming, Dr. Langhals, the
family physician, appeared in Fishers' Lane to observe the results
of the cure. He had a long consultation with the Frau Senator,
and then Hanno was summoned and put, half undressed, through
a long examination of his " status praesens," as Dr. Langhals called
it, looking at his fingernails. He tested Hanno's heart action and
measured his chest and his lamentable muscular development. He
inquired particularly after all his functions, and lastly, with a hypo-
dermic syringe, took a drop of blood from Hanno's slender arm to
be tested at home. He seemed, in general, not very well satisfied.

" We've got rather brown," he said, putting his arm around
Hanno as he stood before him. He arranged his small black-
felled hand upon the boy's shoulder, and looked up at the Frau
Senator and Ida Jungmann. " But we still look very down in the
mouth."

" He is homesick for the sea," said Gerda Buddenbrook.

" Oh, so you like being there? " asked Dr. Langhals, looking with
his shallow eyes into Hanno's face. Hanno coloured. What did
Dr. Langhals mean by his question, to which he plainly expected
an answer? A fantastic hope rose up in him, inspired by the belief
that nothing was impossible to God — despite all the worsted-
coated men there were in the world.

" Yes," he brought out, with his wide eyes full upon Dr. Langhals' face. But after all, it seemed, the physician had nothing particular in mind when he asked the question.

" Well, the effect of the bathing and the good air is bound to
show itself in time," Dr. Langhals said. He tapped little Johann
on the shoulder and then put him away, with a nod toward the

Frau Senator and Ida Jungmann — a superior, benevolent nod, the
nod of the omniscient physician, used to have people hanging on
his lips. He got up, and the consultation was at an end.

It was Aunt Antonie who best understood his yearning for the
sea, and the wound in his heart that healed so slowly and was so
likely to bleed afresh under the strain of everyday life. Aunt
Antonie loved to hear him talk about Travemünde, and entered
freely into his longings and enthusiasm.

" Yes, Hanno," she said, " the truth is the truth, and Travemünde
is and always will be a beautiful spot. Till I go down to my grave
I shall remember the weeks I spent there when I was a slip of a
girl — and such a silly young girl! I lived with people I was fond
of, and who seemed to care for me; I was a pretty young thing in
those days, — though I'm an old woman now — and full of life and
high spirits. They were splendid people, I can tell you, respectable
and kind-hearted and straight-thinking; and they were cleverer
and better educated, too, than any I've known since, and they had
more enthusiasm. Yes, my life seemed very full when I lived with
them, and I learned a great deal which I've never forgotten — information, beliefs, opinions, ways of looking at things. If other
things hadn't interfered — as all sorts of things did, the way life
does, you know — I might have learned a great deal more from
them. Shall I tell you how silly I was in those days? I thought
I could get the pretty star out of the jelly-fish, and I carried a
quantity home with me and spread them in the sun on the balcony
to dry. But when I looked at them again, of course there was nothing but a big wet spot, and a smell of rotten sea-weed."

CHAPTER IV

In the beginning of the year 1873 the Senate pardoned Hugo Weinschenk, and the former Director left prison, six months before his time was up.

Frau Permaneder, if she had told the truth, would have admitted that she was not so very glad. She had been living peacefully with her daughter and granddaughter in Linden Place, and had for society the house in Fishers' Lane and her friend Armgard von Maiboom, who had lived in the town since her husband's death. Frau Antonie had long been aware that there was no place for her outside the walls of her native city. She had her Munich memories, her weak digestion, and an increasing need of quiet and repose; and she felt not the least inclination to move to a large city of the united Fatherland, still less to migrate to another country.

"My dear child," she said to her daughter, "I must ask you something very serious. Do you still love your husband with your whole heart? Would you follow him with your child wherever he went in the wide world — as, unfortunately, it is not possible for him to remain here?"

And Frau Erica Weinschenk, amid tears that might have meant anything at all, replied just as dutifully as Tony herself, in similar circumstances, had once replied to the same question, in the villa outside Hamburg. So it was necessary to contemplate a parting in the near future.

On a day almost as dreadful as the day when he had been arrested, Frau Permaneder brought her son-in-law from the prison, in a closed carriage, to her house in Linden Place. And there he stayed, after he had greeted his wife and child in a dazed, helpless way, in the room that had been prepared for him, smoking from early to late, without going out, without even taking his meals with his family — a broken grey-haired man.

He had always had a very strong constitution, and the prison life could hardly have impaired his physical health. But his condition was, none the less, pitiable in the extreme. This man had in all probability done no more than his business colleagues did every day and thought nothing of; if he had not been caught, he would have gone on his way with head erect and conscience clear. Yet it was dreadful to see how his ruin as a citizen, the judicial correction, and the three years' imprisonment, had operated to break down his morale. His testimony before the court had been given with the most sincere conviction; and people who understood the technicalities of the case supported his contention that he had merely executed a bold manœuvre for the credit of his firm and himself — a manœuvre known in the business world as usance. The lawyers who had convicted him knew, in his opinion, nothing whatever about such things and lived in quite a different world. But their conviction, endorsed by the governing power of the state, had shattered his self-esteem to such a degree that he could not look anybody in the face. Gone was his elastic tread, the way he had of wriggling at the waist of his frock-coat and balancing with his fists and rolling his eyes about. Gone was the ignorant self-assurance with which he had delivered his uninformed opinions and put his questions. The change was such that his family shuddered at it — and indeed it was frightful to see such cowardice, dejection, and lack of self-respect.

Herr Hugo Weinschenk spent eight or ten days doing nothing but smoking: then he began to read the papers and write letters. The consequence of the letters was that after another eight or ten days he explained vaguely that there seemed to be a position for him in London, whither he wished to travel alone to arrange matters personally, and then to send for wife and child.

Accompanied by Erica, he drove to the station in a closed carriage and departed without having once seen any other members of the family.

Some days later a letter addressed to his wife arrived from Hamburg. It said that he had made up his mind not to send for his wife and child, or even to communicate with them, until such time as he could offer them a life fitting for them to live. And this letter was the very last sign of life from Hugo Weinschenk. No one from then henceforward heard anything from him. The experienced Frau Permaneder made several energetic attempts to get into touch with him, in order, as she importantly explained, to get evidence upon which to sue him for divorce on the ground of wilful desertion. But he was, and remained, missing. And thus it came about that Erica Weinschenk and her small daughter Elisabeth remained now, as before, with Erica's mother, in the light and airy apartment in Linden Place.

CHAPTER V

THE MARRIAGE of which little Johann had been the issue had never lost charm in the town as a subject for conversation. Since both of the parties to it were still felt to have something queer about them, the union itself must partake of that character of the strange and uncanny which they each possessed. To get behind it even a little, to look beneath the scanty outward facts to the bottom of this relation, seemed a difficult, but certainly a stimulating task. And in bedrooms and sitting-rooms, in clubs and casinos, yes, even on 'Change itself, people still talked about Gerda and Thomas Buddenbrook.

How had these two come to marry, and what sort of relationship was theirs? Everybody remembered the sudden resolve of Thomas Buddenbrook eighteen years ago, when he was thirty years old. "This one or no one," he had said. It must have been something of the same sort with Gerda, for it was well known that she had refused everybody up to her twenty-seventh year, and then forthwith lent an ear to this particular wooer. It must have been a love match, people said: they granted that the three hundred thousand thaler had probably not played much of a rôle. But of that which any ordinary person would call love, there was very little to be seen between the pair. They had displayed from the very beginning a correct, respectful politeness, quite extraordinary between husband and wife. And what was still more odd it seemed not to proceed out of any inner estrangement, but out of a peculiar, silent, deep mutual knowledge. This had not at all altered with the years. The one change due to the passage of time was an outward one. It was only this: that the difference in years began to make itself plainly visible.

When you saw them together you felt that here was a rapidly aging man, already a little heavy, with his young wife at his side. Thomas Buddenbrook was going off very much, and this despite the now almost laughable vanity by which he kept himself up. On the other hand, Gerda had scarcely altered in these eighteen years. She seemed to be, as it were, conserved in the nervous coldness which was the essence of her being. Her lovely dark red hair had kept its colour, the white skin its smooth texture, the figure its lofty aristocratic slimness. In the corners of her rather too small and close-set brown eyes were the same blue shadows. You could not trust those eyes. Their look was strange, and what was written in it impossible to decipher. This woman's personality was so cool, so reserved, so repressed, so distant, she showed so little human warmth for anything but her music — how could one help feeling a vague mistrust? People unearthed wise old saws on the subject of human nature and applied them to Senator Buddenbrook's wife. Still waters were known to run deep. Some people were slyer than foxes. And as they searched for an explanation, their limited imaginations soon led them to the theory that the lovely Gerda was deceiving her aging husband.

They watched, and before long they felt sure that Gerda's conduct, to put it mildly, passed the bounds of propriety in her relations with Herr Lieutenant von Throta.

Renée Maria von Throta came from the Rhineland. He was second lieutenant of one of the infantry battalions quartered in the town. The red collar of his uniform went well with his black hair, which he wore parted on the side and combed back in a high, thick curling crest from his white forehead. He looked big and strong enough, but was most unmilitary in speech and manner. He had a way of running one hand in between the buttons of his half-open undress coat and of sitting with his head supported on the back of his hand. His bows were devoid of military stiffness, and you could not hear his heels click together as he made them. And he had no more respect for his uniform than for ordinary clothes. Even the slim youthful moustaches that ran slantwise down to the corners of his mouth had neither point nor consistency; they only confirmed the unmartial impression he gave. The most remarkable thing about him was his eyes, so large, black, and extraordinarily brilliant that they seemed like glowing bottomless depths when he visited anything or anybody with his glance which was sparkling, ardent, or languishing by turns.

He had probably gone into the army against his will, or at least without any inclination for it; and despite his physique he was no good in the service. He was unregarded by his comrades, and shared but little in their interests — the interests and pleasures of young officers lately back from a victorious campaign. And they found him a disagreeable oddity, who did not care for horses or hunting or play or women. All his thoughts were bent on music. He was to be seen at all the concerts, with his languishing eyes and his lax, unmilitary, theatrical attitudes; on the other hand he despised the club and the casino and never went near them.

He made the duty calls which his position demanded; but the Buddenbrook house was the only one at which he visited — too much, people thought, and the Senator himself thought so too.

No one dreamed what went on in Thomas Buddenbrook. No one must guess. But it was just this keeping everybody in ignorance of his mortification, his hatred, his powerlessness, that was so cruelly hard! People were beginning to find him a little ludicrous; but perhaps their laugh would have turned to pity if they had even dimly suspected how much he was on his guard against their laughter! He had seen it coming long before, he had felt it beforehand, before any one else had such an idea in his head. His much-carped-at vanity had its source largely in this fear. He had been first to see, with dismay, the growing disparity between himself and his lovely wife, on whom the years had not laid a finger. And now, since the advent of Herr von Throta, he had to fight with the last remnant of his strength to dissimulate his own misgivings, in order that they might not make him a laughing-stock in the eyes of the community.

Gerda Buddenbrook and the eccentric young officer met each other, naturally, in the world of music. Herr von Throta played the piano, violin, viola, cello, and flute, and played them all unusually well. Often the Senator became aware of an impending visit when Herr von Throta's man passed the office-door with his master's cello-case on his back. Thomas Buddenbrook would sit at his desk and watch until he saw his wife's friend enter the house. Then, overhead in the salon, the harmonies would rise and surge like waves, with singing, lamenting, unearthly jubilation; would lift like clasped hands outstretched toward Heaven; would float in vague ecstasies; would sink and die away into sobbing, into night and silence. But they might roll and seethe, weep and exult, foam up and enfold each other, as unnaturally as they liked! They were not the worst. The worst, the actually torturing thing, was the silence. It would sometimes reign so long, so long, and so profoundly, above there in the salon, that it was impossible not to feel afraid of it. There would be no tread upon the ceiling, not even a chair would move — simply a soundless, speechless, deceiving, *secret* silence. Thomas Buddenbrook would sit there, and the torture was such that he sometimes softly groaned.

What was it that he feared? Once more people had seen Herr von Throta enter his house. And with their eyes he beheld the picture just as they saw it: Below, an aging man, worn out and crotchety, sat at his window in the office; above, his beautiful wife made music with her lover. *And not that alone.* Yes, that was the way the thing looked to them. He knew it. He was aware, too, that the word "lover" was not really descriptive of Herr von Throta. It would have been almost a relief if it were. If he could have understood and despised him as an empty-headed, ordinary youth who worked off his average endowment of high spirits in a little music, and thus beguiled the feminine heart! He tried to think of him like that. He tried to summon up the instincts of his father to meet the case: the instincts of the thrifty merchant against the frivolous, adventurous, unreliable military caste. He called Herr von Throta "the lieutenant," and tried to think of him as that; but in his heart he was conscious that the name was inappropriate.

What was it that Thomas Buddenbrook feared? Nothing — nothing to put a name to. If there had only been something tangible, some simple, brutal fact, something to defend himself against! He envied people the simplicity of their conceptions. For while he sat there in torments, with his head in his hands, he knew all too well that "betrayal," "adultery," were not words to describe the singing things, the abysmally silent things, that were happening up there.

He looked up sometimes at the grey gables, at the people passing by, at the jubilee present hanging above his desk with the portraits of his forefathers: he thought of the history of his house, and said to himself that this was all that was wanting: that his person should become a byword, his name and family life a scandal among the people. This was all that was lacking to set the crown upon the whole. And the thought, again, almost did him good, because it was a simple, comprehensible, normal thought, that one could think and express — quite another matter from this brooding over a mysterious disgrace, a blot upon his family 'scutcheon.

He could bear it no more. He shoved back his chair, left the office, and went upstairs. Whither should he go? Into the salon, to be greeted with unembarrassed slight condescension by Herr von Throta, to ask him to supper and be refused? For one of the worst features of the case was that the lieutenant avoided him, refused all official invitations from the head of the house, and confined himself to the free and private intercourse with its mistress.

Should he wait? Sit down somewhere, perhaps in the smoking-room, until the lieutenant went, and then go to Gerda and speak out, and call her to account? Ah, one did not speak out with Gerda, one did not call her to account. Why should one? Their alliance was based on mutual consideration, tact, and silence. To become a laughing-stock before her, too — no, surely he was not called upon to do that. To play the jealous hsuband would be to grant that outsiders were right, to proclaim a scandal, to cry it aloud. Was he jealous? Of whom? Of what? Alas, no! Jealousy — the word meant action: mistaken, crazy, wrong action, perhaps, but at least action, energetic, fearless, and conclusive. No, he only felt a slight anxiety, a harassing worry, over the whole thing.

He went into his dressing-room and bathed his face with eau-de-cologne. Then he descended to the music-room, determined to break the silence there, cost what it would. He laid his hand on the door-knob — but now the music struck up again with a stormy outburst of sound, and he shrank back.

One day in such an hour, he was leaning over the balcony of the second floor, looking down the well of the staircase. Everything was quite still. Little Johann came out of his room, down the gallery steps, and across the corridor, on his way to Ida Jungmann's room. He slipped along the wall with his book, and would have passed his father with lowered eyes, and a murmured greeting; but the Senator spoke to him.

" Well, Hanno, and what are you doing? "

" Studying my lessons, Papa. I am going to Ida, to have her hear my translation — "

" Well, and what do you have to-morrow? "

Hanno, still looking down, made an obvious effort to give a prompt, alert, and correct answer to the question. He swallowed once and said, " We have Cornelius Nepos, some accounts to copy, French grammar, the rivers of North America, German theme-correcting — "

He stopped and felt provoked with himself; he could not remember any more, and wished he had said *and* and let his voice fall, it sounded so abrupt and unfinished. " Nothing else," he said as decidedly as he could, without looking up. But his father did not seem to be listening. He held Hanno's free hand and played with it absently, unconsciously fingering the slim fingers.

And then Hanno heard something that had nothing to do with the lessons at all: his father's voice, in a tone he had never heard before, low, distressed, almost imploring: " Hanno — the lieutenant has been more than two hours with Mamma — "

Little Hanno opened wide his gold-brown eyes at the sound; and they looked, as never before, clear, large, and loving, straight into his father's face, with its reddened eyelids under the light brows, its white puffy cheeks and long stiff moustaches. God knows how

much he understood. But one thing they both felt: in the long
second when their eyes met, all constraint, coldness, and misunderstanding melted away. Hanno might fail his father in all that demanded vitality, energy and strength. But where fear and suffering were in question, there Thomas Buddenbrook could count on
the devotion of his son. On that common ground they met as one.

He did not realize this — he tried not to realize it. In the days
that followed, he urged Hanno on more sternly than ever to practical preparations for his future career. He tested his mental powers, pressed him to commit himself upon the subject of his calling,
and grew irritated at every sign of rebellion or fatigue. For the
truth was that Thomas Buddenbrook, at the age of forty-eight,
began to feel that his days were numbered, and to reckon with his
own approaching death.

His health had failed. Loss of appetite, sleeplessness, dizziness,
and the chills to which he had always been subject forced him
several times to call in Dr. Langhals. But he did not follow the doctor's orders. His will-power had grown flabby in these years of
idleness or petty activity. He slept late in the morning, though
every evening he made an angry resolve to rise early and take the
prescribed walk before breakfast. Only two or three times did
he actually carry out the resolve; and it was the same with everything else. And the constant effort to spur on his will, with the
constant failure to do so, consumed his self-respect and made him
a prey to despair. He never even tried to give up his cigarettes; he
could not do without the pleasant narcotic effect; he had smoked
them from his youth up. He told Dr. Langhals to his vapid face:
"You see, Doctor, it is your duty to forbid me cigarettes — a
very easy and agreeable duty. But I have to obey the order —
that is my share, and you can look on at it. No, we will work together over my health; but I find the work unevenly divided —
too much of yours falls to me. Don't laugh; it is no joke. One is
so frightfully alone — well, I smoke. Will you have one?" He
offered his case.

All his powers were on the decline. What strengthened in him
was the conviction that it could not last long, that the end was close
at hand. He suffered from strange apprehensive fancies. Sometimes at table it seemed to him that he was no longer sitting with
his family, but hovering above them somewhere and looking down
upon them from a great distance. "I am going to die," he said to
himself. And he would call Hanno to him repeatedly and say:
"My son, I may be taken away from you sooner than you think.
And then you will be called upon to take my place. I was called

upon very young myself. Can you understand that I am troubled by your indifference? Are you now resolved in your mind? Yes? Oh, 'yes' is no answer! Again you won't answer me! What I ask you is, have you resolved, bravely and joyfully, to take up your burden? Do you imagine that you won't have to work, that you will have enough money without? You will have nothing, or very, very little; you will be thrown upon your own resources. If you want to live, and live well, you will have to work hard, harder even than I did."

But this was not all. It was not only the burden of his son's future, the future of his house, that weighed him down. There was another thought that took command, that mastered him and spurred on his weary thoughts. And it was this: As soon as he began to think of his mortal end not as an indefinite remote event, almost a contingency, but as something near and tangible for which it behoved him to prepare, he began to investigate himself, to examine his relations to death and questions of another world. And his earliest researches in this kind discovered in himself an irremediable unpreparedness.

His father had united with his hard practical sense a literal faith, a fanatic Bible-Christianity which his mother, in her latter years, had adhered to as well; but to himself it had always been rather repellent. The worldly scepticism of his grandfather had been more nearly his own attitude. But the comfortable superficiality of old Johann could not satisfy his metaphysical and spiritual needs, and he ended by finding in evolution the answer to all his questions about eternity and immortality. He said to himself that he had lived in his forbears and would live on in his descendants. And this line which he had taken coincided not only with his sense of family, his patrician self-consciousness, his ancestor-worship, as it were; it had also strengthened his ambitions and through them the whole course of his existence. But now, before the near and penetrating eye of death, it fell away; it was nothing, it gave him not one single hour of calm, of readiness for the end.

Thomas Buddenbrook had played now and then throughout his life with an inclination to Catholicism. But he was at bottom, none the less, the born Protestant: full of the true Protestant's passionate, relentless sense of personal responsibility. No, in the ultimate things there was, there could be, no help from outside, no mediation, no absolution, no soothing-syrup, no panacea. Each one of us, alone, unaided, of his own powers, must unravel the riddle before it was too late, must wring for himself a pious readiness before the hour of death, or else part in despair. Thomas Buddenbrook turned away, desperate and hopeless, from his only son, in whom he had once hoped to live on, renewed and strong, and began in fear and haste to seek for the truth which must somewhere exist for him.

It was high summer of the year 1874. Silvery, high-piled clouds drifted across the deep blue sky above the garden's dainty symmetry. The birds twittered in the boughs of the walnut tree, the fountain splashed among the irises, and the scent of the lilacs floated on the breeze, mingled, alas, with the smell of hot syrup from a sugar-factory nearby. To the astonishment of the staff, the Senator now often left his work during office hours, to pace up and down in the garden with his hands behind his back, or to work about, raking the gravel paths, tying up the rose-bushes, or dredging mud out of the fountain. His face, with its light eyebrows, seemed serious and attentive as he worked; but his thoughts travelled far away in the dark on their lonely, painful path.

Sometimes he seated himself on the little terrace, in the pavilion now entirely overgrown with green, and stared across the garden at the red brick rear wall of the house. The air was warm and sweet; it seemed as though the peaceful sounds about him strove to lull him to sleep. Weary of loneliness and silence and staring into space, he would close his eyes now and then, only to snatch them open and harshly frighten peace away. "I must think," he said, almost aloud. "I must arrange everything before it is too late."

He sat here one day, in the pavilion, in the little reed rocking-chair, and read for four hours, with growing absorption, in a book which had, partly by chance, come into his hands. After second breakfast, cigarette in mouth, he had unearthed it in the smoking-room, from behind some stately volumes in the corner of a bookcase, and recalled that he had bought it at a bargain one day years ago. It was a large volume, poorly printed on cheap paper and poorly sewed; the second part, only, of a famous philosophical system. He had brought it out with him into the garden, and now he turned the pages, profoundly interested.

He was filled with a great, surpassing satisfaction. It soothed him to see how a master-mind could lay hold on this strong, cruel, mocking thing called life and enforce it and condemn it. His was the gratification of the sufferer who has always had a bad conscience about his sufferings and concealed them from the gaze of a harsh, unsympathetic world, until suddenly, from the hand of an authority, he receives, as it were, justification and license for his suffering — justification before the world, this best of all possible worlds which the master-mind scornfully demonstrates to be the worst of all possible ones!

He did not understand it all. Principles and premises remained unclear, and his mind, unpractised in such reading, was not able to follow certain trains of thought. But this very alternation of vagueness and clarity, of dull incomprehension with sudden bursts of light, kept him enthralled and breathless, and the hours vanished without his looking up from his book or changing his position in his chair.

He had left some pages unread in the beginning of the book, and hurried on, clutching rapidly after the main thesis, reading only this or that section which held his attention. Then he struck on a comprehensive chapter and read it from beginning to end, his lips tightly closed and his brows drawn together with a concentration which had long been strange to him, completely withdrawn from the life about him. The chapter was called " On Death, and its Relation to our Personal Immortality."

Only a few lines remained when the servant came through the garden at four o'clock to call him to dinner. He nodded, read the remaining sentences, closed the book, and looked about him. He felt that his whole being had unaccountably expanded, and at the same time there clung about his senses a profound intoxication, a strange, sweet, vague allurement which somehow resembled the feelings of early love and longing. He put away the book in the drawer of the garden table. His hands were cold and unsteady, his head was burning, and he felt in it a strange pressure and strain, as though something were about to snap. He was not capable of consecutive thought.

What was this? He asked himself the question as he mounted the stairs and sat down to table with his family. What is it? Have I had a revelation? What has happened to me, Thomas Buddenbrook, Councillor of this government, head of the grain firm of Johann Buddenbrook? Was this message meant for me? Can I bear it? I don't know what it was: I only know it is too much for my poor brain.

He remained the rest of the day in this condition, this heavy lethargy and intoxication, overpowered by the heady draught he had drunk, incapable of thought. Evening came. His head was heavy, and since he could hold it up no longer, he went early to bed. He slept for three hours, more profoundly than ever before in his life. And, then, suddenly, abruptly, with a start, he awoke and felt as one feels on realizing, suddenly, a budding love in the heart.

He was alone in the large sleeping chamber; for Gerda slept

now in Ida Jungmann's room, and the latter had moved into one of the three balcony rooms to be nearer little Johann. It was dark, for the curtains of both high windows were tightly closed. He lay on his back, feeling the oppression of the stillness and of the heavy, warm air, and looked up into the darkness.

And behold, it was as though the darkness were rent from before his eyes, as if the whole wall of the night parted wide and disclosed an immeasurable, boundless prospect of light. "I shall live!" said Thomas Buddenbrook, almost aloud, and felt his breast shaken with inward sobs. "This is the revelation: that I shall live! For *it* will live — and that this *it* is not I is only an illusion, an error which death will make plain. This is it, this is it! Why?" But at this question the night closed in again upon him. He saw, he knew, he understood, no least particle more; he let himself sink deep in the pillows, quite blinded and exhausted by the morsel of truth which had been vouchsafed.

He lay still and waited fervently, feeling himself tempted to pray that it would come again and irradiate his darkness. And it came. With folded hands, not daring to move, he lay and looked.

What *was* Death? The answer came, not in poor, large-sounding words: he felt it within him, he possessed it. Death was a joy, so great, so deep that it could be dreamed of only in moments of revelation like the present. It was the return from an unspeakably painful wandering, the correction of a grave mistake, the loosening of chains, the opening of doors — it put right again a lamentable mischance.

End, dissolution! These were pitiable words, and thrice pitiable he who used them! What would end, what would dissolve? Why, this his body, this heavy, faulty, hateful incumbrance, which *prevented him from being something other and better.*

Was not every human being a mistake and a blunder? Was he not in painful arrest from the hour of his birth? Prison, prison, bonds and limitations everywhere! The human being stares hopelessly through the barred window of his personality at the high walls of outward circumstance, till Death comes and calls him home to freedom!

Individuality? — All, all that one is, can, and has, seems poor, grey, inadequate, wearisome; what one is not, can not, has not, that is what one looks at with a longing desire that becomes love because it fears to become hate.

I bear in myself the seed, the tendency, the possibility of all capacity and all achievement. Where should I be were I not here? Who, what, how could I be, if I were not I — if this my external self, my consciousness, did not cut me off from those who are not I? Organism! Blind, thoughtless, pitiful eruption of the urging will! Better, indeed, for the will to float free in spaceless, timeless night than for it to languish in prison, illumined by the feeble, flickering light of the intellect!

Have I hoped to live on in my son? In a personality yet more feeble, flickering, and timorous than my own? Blind, childish folly! What can my son do for me — what need have I of a son? Where shall I be when I am dead? Ah, it is so brilliantly clear, so overwhelmingly simple! I shall be in all those who have ever, do ever, or ever shall say " I " — *especially, however, in all those who say it most fully, potently, and gladly!*

Somewhere in the world a child is growing up, strong, well-grown, adequate, able to develop its powers, gifted, untroubled, pure, joyous, relentless, one of those beings whose glance heightens the joy of the joyous and drives the unhappy to despair. *He* is my son. He is I, myself, soon, soon; as soon as Death frees me from the wretched delusion that I am not he as well as myself.

Have I ever hated life — pure, strong, relentless life? Folly and misconception! I have but hated myself, because I could not bear it. I love you, I love you all, you blessed, and soon, soon, I shall cease to be cut off from you all by the narrow bonds of myself; soon will that in me which loves you be free and be in and with you — in and with you all.

He wept, he pressed his face into the pillows and wept, shaken through and through, lifted up in transports by a joy without compare for its exquisite sweetness. This it was which since yesterday had filled him as if with a heady, intoxicating draught, had worked in his heart in the darkness of the night and roused him like a budding love! And in so far as he could now understand and recognize — not in words and consecutive thoughts, but in sudden rapturous illuminations of his inmost being — he was already free, already actually released and free of all natural as well as artificial limitations. The walls of his native town, in which he had wilfully and consciously shut himself up, opened out; they opened and disclosed to his view the entire world, of which he had in his youth seen this or that small portion, and of which Death now promised him the whole. The deceptive perceptions of space, time and history, the preoccupation with a glorious historical continuity of life in the person of his own descendants, the dread of some future final dissolution and decomposition — all this his spirit now put aside. He was no longer prevented from grasping eternity. Nothing began, nothing left off. There was only an endless pres-

ent; and that power in him which loved life with a love so exquisitely sweet and yearning — the power of which his person was
only the unsuccessful expression — that power would always know
how to find access to this present.

"I shall live," he whispered into his pillow. He wept, and in
the next moment knew not why. His brain stood still, the vision
was quenched. Suddenly there was nothing more — he lay in
dumb darkness. "It will come back," he assured himself. And before sleep inexorably wrapped him round, he swore to himself
never to let go this precious treasure, but to read and study, to
learn its powers, and to make inalienably his own the whole conception of the universe out of which his vision sprang.

But that could not be. Even the next day, as he woke with a
faint feeling of shame at the emotional extravagances of the night,
he suspected that it would be hard to put these beautiful designs
into practice.

He rose late and had to go at once to take part in the debate at
an assembly of burgesses. Public business, the civic life that went
on in the gabled narrow streets of this middle-sized trading city,
consumed his energies once more. He still planned to take up the
wonderful reading again where he had left it off. But he questioned of himself whether the events of that night had been anything firm and permanent; whether, when Death approached, they
would be found to hold their ground.

His middle-class instincts rose against them — and his vanity,
too: the fear of being eccentric, of playing a laughable rôle. Had
he really seen these things? And did they really become him —
him, Thomas Buddenbrook, head of the firm of Johann Buddenbrook?

He never succeeded in looking again into the precious volume
— to say nothing of buying its other parts. His days were consumed by nervous pedantry: harassed by a thousand details, all
of them unimportant, he was too weak-willed to arrive at a reasonable and fruitful arrangement of his time. Nearly two weeks after
that memorable afternoon he gave it up — and ordered the maid-
servant to fetch the book from the drawer in the garden table and
replace it in the bookcase.

And thus Thomas Buddenbrook, who had held his hands
stretched imploringly upward toward the high ultimate truth,
sank now weakly back to the images and conceptions of his childhood. He strove to call back that personal God, the Father of all
human beings, who had sent a part of Himself upon earth to suffer
and bleed for our sins, and who, on the final day, would come to

judge the quick and the dead; at whose feet the justified, in the course of the eternity then beginning, would be recompensed for the sorrows they had borne in this vale of tears. Yes, he strove to subscribe to the whole confused unconvincing story, which required no intelligence, only obedient credulity; and which, when the last anguish came, would sustain one in a firm and childlike faith. — But would it, really?

Ah, even here there was no peace. This poor, well-nigh exhausted man, consumed with gnawing fears for the honour of his house, his wife, his child, his name, his family, this man who spent painful effort even to keep his body artificially erect and well-preserved — this poor man tortured himself for days with thoughts upon the moment and manner of death. How would it really be? Did the soul go to Heaven immediately after death, or did bliss first begin with the resurrection of the flesh? And, if so, where did the soul stay until that time? He did not remember ever having been taught this. Why had he not been told this important fact in school or in church? How was it justifiable for them to leave people in such uncertainty? He considered visiting Pastor Pringsheim and seeking advice and counsel; but he gave it up in the end for fear of being ridiculous.

And finally he gave it all up — he left it all to God. But having come to such an unsatisfactory ending of his attempts to set his spiritual affairs in order, he determined at least to spare no pains over his earthly ones, and to carry out a plan which he had long entertained.

One day little Johann heard his father tell his mother, as they drank their coffee in the living-room after the midday meal, that he expected Lawyer So-and-So to make his will. He really ought not to keep on putting it off. Later, in the afternoon, Hanno practised his music for an hour. When he went down the corridor after that, he met, coming up the stairs, his father and a gentleman in a long black overcoat.

" Hanno," said the Senator, curtly. And little Johann stopped, swallowed, and said quickly and softly: " Yes, Papa."

" I have some important business with this gentleman," his father went on. " Will you stand before the door into the smoking-room and take care that nobody — absolutely nobody, you understand — disturbs us? "

" Yes, Papa," said little Johann, and took up his post before the door, which closed after the two gentlemen.

He stood there, clutching his sailor's knot with one hand, felt with his tongue for a doubtful tooth, and listened to the earnest

subdued voices which could be heard from inside. His head, with
the curling light-brown hair, he held on one side, and his face with
the frowning brows and blue-shadowed, gold-brown eyes, wore
that same displeased and brooding look with which he had inhaled
the odour of the flowers, and that other strange, yet half-familiar
odour, by his grandmother's bier.

Ida Jungmann passed and said, "Well, little Hanno, why are
you hanging about here? "

And the hump-backed apprentice came out of the office with
a telegram, and asked for the Senator.

But, both times, little Johann put his arm in its blue sailor sleeve
with the anchor on it horizontally across the door; both times he
shook his head and said softly, after a pause, " No one may go in.
Papa is making his will."

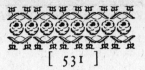

CHAPTER VI

IN the autumn Dr. Langhals said, making play like a woman with
his beautiful eyes: "It is the nerves, Senator; the nerves are to
blame for everything. And once in a while the circulation is not
what it should be. May I venture to make a suggestion? You need
another little rest. These few Sundays by the sea, during the summer, haven't amounted to much, of course. It's the end of September, Travemünde is still open, there are still a few people there.
Drive over, Senator, and sit on the beach a little. Two or three
weeks will do you a great deal of good."

And Thomas Buddenbrook said "yes" and "amen." But when
he told his family of the arrangement, Christian suggested going
with him.

"I'll go with you, Thomas," he said, quite simply. "You don't
mind, I suppose." And the Senator, though he did mind very
much, said "yes" and "amen" to this arrangement as well.

Christian was now more than ever master of his own time. His
fluctuating health had constrained him to give up his last undertaking, the champagne and spirit agency. The man who used to
come and sit on his sofa and nod at him in the twilight had happily
not recurred of late. But the misery in the side had, if anything,
grown worse, and added to this was a whole list of other infirmities
of which Christian kept the closest watch, and which he described
in all companies, with his nose wrinkled up. He often suffered
from that long-standing dread of paralysis of the tongue, throat,
and œsophagus, even of the extremities and of the brain — of
which there were no actual symptoms, but the fear in itself was
almost worse. He told in detail how, one day when he was making
tea, he had held the lighted match not over the spirit-lamp, but
over the open bottle of methylated spirit instead; so that not only
himself, but the people in his own and the adjacent buildings,
nearly went up in flames. And he dwelt in particular detail, straining every resource he had at his command to make himself perfectly clear, upon a certain ghastly anomaly which he had of late
observed in himself. It was this: that on certain days, i.e., under

certain weather conditions, and in certain states of mind, he could not see an open window without having a horrible and inexplicable impulse to jump out. It was a mad and almost uncontrollable desire, a sort of desperate foolhardiness. The family were dining on Sunday in Fishers' Lane, and he described how he had to summon all his powers, and crawl on hands and knees to the window to shut it. At this point everybody shrieked; his audience rebelled, and would listen no more.

He told these and similar things with a certain horrible satisfaction. But the thing about himself which he did not know, which he never studied and described, but which none the less grew worse and worse, was his singular lack of tact. He told in the family circle anecdotes of such a nature that the club was the only possible place for them. And even his sense of personal modesty seemed to be breaking down. He was on friendly terms with his sister-in-law, Gerda. But when he displayed to her the beautiful weave and texture of his English socks, he did not stop at that, but rolled up his wide, checkered trouser-leg to far above the knee: " Look," he said, wrinkling his nose in distress: " Look how thin I'm getting. Isn't it striking and unusual? " And there he sat, sadly gazing at his crooked, bony leg and the gaunt knee visible through his white woollen drawers.

His mercantile activity then, was a thing of the past. But such hours as he did not spend at the club he liked to fill in with one sort of occupation or another; and he would proudly point out that he had never actually ceased to work. He extended his knowledge of languages and embarked upon a study of Chinese — though this was for the sake of acquiring knowledge, simply, with no practical purpose in view. He worked at it industriously for two weeks. He was also, just at this time, occupied with a project of enlarging an English-German dictionary which he had found inadequate. But he really needed a little change, and it would be better too for the Senator to have somebody with him; so he did not allow his business to keep him in town.

The two brothers drove out together to the sea along the turnpike, which was nothing but a puddle. The rain drummed on the carriage-top, and they hardly spoke. Christian's eyes roved hither and yon; he was as if listening to uncanny noises. Thomas sat muffled in his cloak, shivering, gazing with bloodshot eyes, his moustaches stiffly sticking out beyond his white cheeks. They drove up to the Kurhouse in the afternoon, their wheels grating in the wet gravel. Old Broker Gosch sat in the glass verandah, drinking rum punch. He stood up, whistling through his teeth, and they all sat down together to have a little something warm while the trunks were being carried up.

Herr Gosch was a late guest at the cure, and there were a few other people as well: an English family, a Dutch maiden lady, and a Hamburg bachelor, all of them presumably taking their rest before table-d'hôte, for it was like the grave everywhere but for the sound of the rain. Let them sleep! As for Herr Gosch, he was not in the habit of sleeping in the daytime. He was glad enough to get a few hours' sleep at night. He was far from well; he was taking a late cure for the benefit of this trembling which he suffered from in all his limbs. Hang it, he could hardly hold his glass of grog; and more often than not he could not write at all — so that the translation of Lope de Vega got on but slowly. He was in a very low mood indeed, and even his curses lacked relish. " Let it go hang! " was his constant phrase, which he repeated on every occasion and often on none at all.

And the Senator? How was he feeling? How long were the gentlemen thinking of stopping?

Oh, Dr. Langhals had sent him out on account of his nerves. He had obeyed orders, of course, despite the frightful weather — what doesn't one do out of fear of one's physician? He was really feeling more or less miserable, and they would probably remain till there was a little improvement.

" Yes, I'm pretty wretched too," said Christian, irritated at Thomas's speaking only of himself. He was about to fetch out his repertoire — the nodding man, the spirit-bottle, the open window — when the Senator interrupted him by going to engage the rooms.

The rain did not stop. It washed away the earth, it danced upon the sea, which was driven back by the southwest wind and left the beaches bare. Everything was shrouded in grey. The steamers went by like wraiths and vanished on the dim horizon.

They met the strange guests only at table. The Senator, in mackintosh and goloshes, went walking with Gosch; Christian drank Swedish punch with the barmaid in the pastry-shop.

Two or three times in the afternoon it looked as though the sun were coming out; and a few acquaintances from town appeared — people who enjoyed a holiday away from their families: Senator Dr. Gieseke, Christian's friend, and Consul Peter Döhlmann, who looked very ill indeed, and was killing himself with Hunyadi-Janos water. The gentlemen sat together in their overcoats, under the awnings of the pastry-shop, opposite the empty bandstand, drinking their coffee, digesting their five courses, and talking desultorily as they gazed over the empty garden.

The news of the town — the last high water, which had gone into the cellars and been so deep that in the lower part of the town people had to go about in boats; a fire in the dockyard sheds; a senatorial election — these were the topics of conversation. Alfred Lauritzen, of the firm of Stürmann & Lauritzen, tea, coffee, and spice merchants, had been elected, and Senator Buddenbrook had not approved of the choice. He sat smoking cigarettes, wrapped in his cloak, almost silent except for a few remarks on this particular subject. One thing was certain, he said, and that was that *he* had not voted for Herr Lauritzen. Lauritzen was an honest fellow and a good man of business. There was no doubt of that; but he was middle-class, respectable middle-class. His father had fished herrings out of the barrel and handed them across the counter to servant-maids with his own hands — and now they had in the Senate the proprietor of a retail business. His, Thomas Buddenbrook's grandfather had disowned his eldest son for " marrying a shop "; but that was in the good old days. " The standard is being lowered," he said. " The social level is not so high as it was; the Senate is being democratized, my dear Gieseke, and that is no good. Business ability is one thing — but it is not everything. In my view we should demand something more. Alfred Lauritzen, with his big feet and his boatswain's face — it is offensive to me to think of him in the Senate-house. It offends something in me, I don't know what. It goes against my sense of form — it is a piece of bad taste, in short."

Senator Gieseke demurred. He was rather piqued by this expression of opinion. After all, he himself was only the son of a Fire Commissioner. No, the labourer was worthy of his hire. That was what being a republican meant. " You ought not to smoke so much, Buddenbrook," he ended. " You won't get any sea air."

" I'll stop now," said Thomas Buddenbrook, flung away the end of his cigarette, and closed his eyes.

The conversation dragged on; the rain set in again and veiled the prospect. They began to talk about the latest town scandal — about P. Philipp Kassbaum, who had been falsifying bills of exchange and now sat behind locks and bars. No one felt outraged over the dishonesty: they spoke of it as an act of folly, laughed a bit, and shrugged their shoulders. Senator Dr. Gieseke said that the convicted man had not lost his spirits. He had asked for a mirror, it seemed, there being none in his cell. " I'll need a looking-glass," he was reported to have said: "I shall be here for some time." He had been, like Christian and Dr. Gieseke, a pupil of the lamented Marcellus Stengel.

They all laughed again at this, through their noses, without a sign of feeling. Siegismund Gosch ordered another grog in a tone of voice that was as good as saying, "What's the use of living?" Consul Döhlmann sent for a bottle of brandy. Christian felt inclined to more Swedish punch, so Dr. Gieseke ordered some for both of them. Before long Thomas Buddenbrook began to smoke again.

And the idle, cynical, indifferent talk went on, heavy with the food they had eaten, the wine they drank, and the damp that depressed their spirits. They talked about business, the business of each one of those present; but even this subject roused no great enthusiasm.

"Oh, there's nothing very good about mine," said Thomas Buddenbrook heavily, and leaned his head against the back of his chair with an air of disgust.

"Well, and you, Döhlmann," asked Senator Gieseke, and yawned. "You've been devoting yourself entirely to brandy, eh?"

"The chimney can't smoke, unless there's a fire," the Consul retorted. "I look into the office every few days. Short hairs are soon combed."

"And Strunck and Hagenström have all the business in their hands anyhow," the broker said morosely, with his elbows sprawled out on the table and his wicked old grey head in his hands.

"Oh, nothing can compete with a dung-heap, for smell," Döhlmann said, with a deliberately coarse pronunciation, which must have depressed everybody's spirits the more by its hopeless cynicism. "Well, and you, Buddenbrook — what are you doing now? Nothing, eh?"

"No," answered Christian, "I can't, any more." And without more ado, having perceived the mood of the hour, he proceeded to accentuate it. He began, his hat on one side, to talk about his Valparaiso office and Johnny Thunderstorm. "Well, in that heat — 'Good God! Work, Sir? No, Sir. As you see, Sir.' And they puffed their cigarette-smoke right in his face. Good God!" It was, as always, an incomparable expression of dissolute, impudent, lazy good-nature. His brother sat motionless.

Herr Gosch tried to lift his glass to his thin lips, put it back on the table again, cursing through his shut teeth, and struck the offending arm with his fist. Then he lifted the glass once more, and spilled half its contents, draining the remainder furiously at a gulp.

"Oh, you and your shaking, Gosch!" Peter Döhlmann exclaimed. "Why don't you just let yourself go, like me? I'll croak if I don't drink my bottle every day — I've got as far as that; and I'll croak if I do. How would you feel if you couldn't get rid of your dinner, not a single day — I mean, after you've got it in your stomach?" And he favoured them with some repulsive details of his condition, to which Christian listened with dreadful interest, wrinkling his nose as far as it could go and countering with a brief and forcible account of his "misery."

It rained harder than ever. It came straight down in sheets and filled the silence of the Kurgarten with its ceaseless, forlorn, and desolate murmur.

"Yes, life's pretty rotten," said Senator Gieseke. He had been drinking heavily.

"I'd just as lief quit," said Christian.

"Let it go hang," said Herr Gosch.

"There comes Fike Dahlbeck," said Senator Gieseke. The proprietress of the cow-stalls, a heavy, bold-faced woman in the forties, came by with a pail of milk and smiled at the gentlemen. Senator Gieseke let his eyes rove after her.

"What a bosom," he said. Consul Döhlmann added a lewd witticism, with the result that all the gentlemen laughed once more, through their noses.

The waiter was summoned.

"I've finished the bottle, Schröder," said Consul Döhlmann. "May as well pay — we have to some time or other. You, Christian? Gieseke pays for you, eh?"

Senator Buddenbrook roused himself at this. He had been sitting there, hardly speaking, wrapped in his cloak, his hands in his lap and his cigarette in the corner of his mouth. Now he suddenly started up and said sharply, "Have you no money with you, Christian? Then I'll lend it to you."

They put up their umbrellas and emerged from their shelter to take a little stroll.

Frau Permaneder came out once in a while to see her brother. They would walk as far as Sea-Gull Rock or the little Ocean Temple; and here Tony Buddenbrook, for some reason or other, was always seized by a mood of vague excitement and rebellion. She would repeatedly emphasize the independence and equality of all human beings, summarily repudiate all distinctions of rank or class, use some very strong language on the subject or privilege and arbitrary power, and demand in set terms that merit should receive its just reward. And then she talked about her own life. She talked well, she entertained her brother capitally. This child of fortune, so long as she walked upon this earth, had never once needed to suppress an emotion, to choke down or swallow anything she felt. She had never received in silence either the blows or the caresses of fate. And whatever she had received, of joy or sorrow, she had straightway given forth again, in a flow of childish, self-important trivialities. Her digestion was not perfect, it is true. But her heart — ah, her heart was light, her spirit was free; freer than she herself comprehended. She was not consumed by the inexpressible. No sorrow weighed her down, or strove to speak but could not. And thus it was that her past left no mark upon her. She knew that she had led a troubled life — she knew it, that is, but at bottom she never believed in it herself. She recognized it as a fact, since everybody else believed it — and she utilized it to her own advantage, talking of it and making herself great with it in her own eyes and those of others. With outraged virtue and dignity she would call by name all those persons who had played havoc with her life and, in consequence, with the prestige of the Buddenbrook family; the list had grown long with time: Teary Trietschke! Grünlich! Permaneder! Tiburtius! Weinschenk! the Hagenströms! the State Attorney! Severin! — "What *filoux*, all of them, Thomas! God will punish them — that is my firm belief."

Twilight was falling as they came up to the Ocean Temple, for the autumn was far advanced. They stood on one of the little chambers facing the bay — it smelled of wood, like the bathing cabins at the Kur, and its walls were scribbled over with mottoes, initials, hearts and rhymes. They stood and looked out over the dripping slope across the narrow, stony strip of beach, out to the turbid, restless sea.

"Great waves," said Thomas Buddenbrook. "How they come on and break, come on and break, one after another, endlessly, idly, empty and vast! And yet, like all the simple, inevitable things, they soothe, they console, after all. I have learned to love the sea more and more. Once, I think, I cared more for the mountains — because they lay farther off. Now I do not long for them. They would only frighten and abash me. They are too capricious, too manifold, too anomalous — I know I should feel myself vanquished in their presence. What sort of men prefer the monotony of the sea? Those, I think, who have looked so long and deeply into the

complexities of the spirit, that they ask of outward things merely
that they should possess one quality above all: simplicity. It is
true that in the mountains one clambers briskly about, while beside
the sea one sits quietly on the shore. This is a difference, but a
superficial one. The real difference is in the look with which one
pays homage to the one and to the other. It is a strong, challenging
gaze, full of enterprise, that can soar from peak to peak; but the
eyes that rest on the wide ocean and are soothed by the sight of its
waves rolling on forever, mystically, relentlessly, are those that
are already wearied by looking too deep into the solemn perplexi-
ties of life. — Health and illness, that is the difference. The man
whose strength is unexhausted climbs boldly up into the lofty mul-
tiplicity of the mountain heights. But it is when one is worn out
with turning one's eyes inward upon the bewildering complexity
of the human heart, that one finds peace in resting them on the
wideness of the sea."

Frau Permaneder was silent and uncomfortable, — as simple people are when a profound truth is suddenly expressed in the middle
of a conventional conversation. People don't say such things, she
thought to herself; and looked out to sea so as not to show her
feeling by meeting his eyes. Then, in the silence, to make amends
for an embarrassment which she could not help, she drew his arm
through hers.

CHAPTER VII

Winter had come, Christmas had passed. It was January, 1875. The snow, which covered the foot-walks in a firm-trodden mass, mingled with sand and ashes, was piled on either side of the road in high mounds that were growing greyer and more porous all the time, for the temperature was rising. The pavements were wet and dirty, the grey gables dripped. But above all stretched the heavens, a cloudless tender blue, while millions of light atoms seemed to dance like crystal motes in the air.

It was a lively sight in the centre of the town, for this was Saturday, and market-day as well. Under the pointed arches of the Town Hall arcades the butchers had their stalls and weighed out their wares red-handed. The fish-market, however, was held around the fountain in the market-square itself. Here fat old women, with their hands in muffs from which most of the fur was worn off, warming their feet at little coal-braziers, guarded their slippery wares and tried to cajole the servants and housewives into making purchases. There was no fear of being cheated. The fish would certainly be fresh, for the most of them were still alive. The luckiest ones were even swimming about in pails of water, rather cramped for space, but perfectly lively. Others lay with dreadfully goggling eyes and labouring gills, clinging to life and slapping the marble slab desperately with their tails — until such time as their fate was at hand, when somebody would seize them and cut their throats with a crunching sound. Great fat eels writhed and wreathed about in extraordinary shapes. There were deep vats full of black masses of crabs from the Baltic. Once in a while a big flounder gave such a desperate leap that he sprang right off his slab and fell down upon the slippery pavement, among all the refuse, and had to picked up and severely admonished by his possessor.

Broad Street, at midday, was full of life. Schoolchildren with knapsacks on their backs came along the street, filling it with laughter and chatter, snowballing each other with the half-melting snow. Smart young apprentices passed, with Danish sailor caps or suits cut after the English model, carrying their portfolios and obviously pleased with themselves for having escaped from school. Among the crowd were settled, grey-bearded, highly respectable citizens, wearing the most irreproachable national-liberal expression on their faces, and tapping their sticks along the pavement. These looked across with interest to the glazed-brick front of the Town Hall, where the double guard was stationed; for the Senate was in session. The sentries trod their beat, wearing their cloaks, their guns on their shoulders, phlegmatically stamping their feet in the dirty half-melted snow. They met in the centre of their beat, looked at each other, exchanged a word, turned, and moved away each to his own side. Sometimes a lieutenant would pass, his coat-collar turned up, his hands in his pockets, on the track of some grisette, yet at the same time permitting himself to be admired by young ladies of good family; and then each sentry would stand at attention in front of his box, look at himself from head to foot, and present arms. It would be a little time yet before they would perform the same salute before the members of the Senate, the sitting lasted some three quarters of an hour; it would probably adjourn before that.

But one of the sentries suddenly heard a short, discreet whistle from within the building. At the same moment the entrance was illumined by the red uniform of Uhlefeld the beadle, with his dress sword and cocked hat. His air of preoccupation was simply enormous as he uttered a stealthy " Look out " and hastily withdrew. At the same moment approaching steps were heard on the echoing flags within.

The sentries front-faced, inflated their chests, stiffened their necks, grounded their arms, and then, with a couple of rapid motions, presented arms. Between them there had appeared, lifting his top hat, a gentleman of scarcely medium height, with one light eyebrow higher than the other and the pointed ends of his moustaches extending beyond his pallid cheeks. Senator Thomas Buddenbrook was leaving the Town Hall to-day long before the end of the sitting. He did not take the street to his own house, but turned to the right instead. He looked correct, spotless, and elegant as, with the rather hopping step peculiar to him, he walked along Broad Street, constantly saluting people whom he met. He wore white kid gloves, and he had his stick with the silver handle under his left arm. A white dress tie peeped forth from between the lapels of his fur coat. But his head and face, despite their careful grooming, looked rather seedy. People who passed him noticed that his eyes were watering and that he held his mouth shut in a peculiar cautious way; it was twisted a little to one side, and one could see by the muscles of his cheeks and temples that he was clenching his jaw. Sometimes he swallowed, as if a liquid kept rising in his mouth.

"Well, Buddenbrook, so you are cutting the session? That is something new," somebody said unexpectedly to him at the beginning of Mill Street. It was his friend and admirer Stephan Kistenmaker, whose opinion on all subjects was the echo of his own. Stephan Kistenmaker had a full greying beard, bushy eyebrows, and a long nose full of large pores. He had retired from the wine business a few years back with a comfortable sum, and his brother Edouard carried it on by himself. He lived now the life of a private gentleman; but, being rather ashamed of the fact, he always pretended to be overwhelmed with work. "I'm wearing myself out," he would say, stroking his grey hair, which he curled with the tongs. "But what's a man good for, but to wear himself out?" He stood hours on 'Change, gesturing imposingly, but doing no business. He held a number of unimportant offices, the latest one being Director of the city bathing establishments; but he also functioned as juror, broker, and executor, and laboured with such zeal that the perspiration dripped from his brow.

"There's a session, isn't there, Buddenbrook — and you are taking a walk?"

"Oh, it's you," said the Senator in a low voice, moving his lips cautiously. "I'm suffering frightfully — I'm nearly blind with pain."

"Pain? Where?"

"Toothache. Since yesterday. I did not close my eyes last night. I have not been to the dentist yet, because I had business in the office this morning, and then I did not like to miss the sitting. But I couldn't stand it any longer. I'm on my way to Brecht."

"Where is it?"

"Here on the left side, the lower jaw. A back tooth. It is decayed, of course. The pain is simply unbearable. Good-bye, Kistenmaker. You can understand that I am in a good deal of a hurry."

"Yes, of course — don't you think I am, too? Awful lot to do. Good-bye. Good luck! Have it out — get it over with at once — always the best way."

Thomas Buddenbrook went on, biting his jaws together, though it made the pain worse to do so. It was a furious burning, boring pain, starting from the infected back tooth and affecting the whole side of the jaw. The inflammation throbbed like red-hot hammers;

it made his face burn and his eyes water. His nerves were terribly affected by the sleepless night he had spent. He had had to control himself just now, lest his voice break as he spoke.

He entered a yellow-brown house in Mill Street and went up to the first storey, where a brass plate on the door said, "Brecht, Dentist." He did not see the servant who opened the door. The corridor was warm and smelled of beefsteak and cauliflower. Then he suddenly inhaled the sharp odour of the waiting-room into which he was ushered. "Sit down! One moment!" shrieked the voice of an old woman. It was Josephus, who sat in his shining cage at the end of the room and regarded him sidewise out of his venomous little eyes.

The Senator sat down at the round table and tried to read the jokes in a volume of *Fliegende Blätter*, flung down the book, and pressed the cool silver handle of his walking-stick against his cheek. He closed his burning eyes and groaned. There was not a sound, except for the noise made by Josephus as he bit and clawed at the bars of his cage. Herr Brecht might not be busy; but he owed it to himself to make his patient wait a little.

Thomas Buddenbrook stood up precipitately and drank a glass of water from the bottle on the table. It tasted and smelled of chloroform. Then he opened the door into the corridor and called out in an irritated voice: if there were nothing very important to prevent it, would Herr Brecht kindly make haste — he was suffering.

And immediately the bald forehead, hooked nose, and grizzled moustaches of the dentist appeared in the door of the operating-room. "If you please," he said. "If you please," shrieked Josephus. The Senator followed on the invitation. He was not smiling. "A bad case," thought Herr Brecht, and turned pale.

They passed through the large light room to the operating-chair in front of one of the two largest windows. It was an adjustable chair with an upholstered head-rest and green plush arms. As he sat down, Thomas Buddenbrook briefly explained what the trouble was. Then he leaned back his head and closed his eyes.

Herr Brecht screwed up the chair a bit and got to work on the tooth with a tiny mirror and a pointed steel instrument. His hands smelled of almond soap, his breath of cauliflower and beefsteak.

"We must proceed to extraction," he said, after a while, and turned still paler.

"Very well, proceed, then," said the Senator, and shut his eyes more tightly.

There was a pause. Herr Brecht prepared something at his

chest of drawers and got out his instruments. Then he approached the chair again.

"I'll paint it a little," he said; and began at once to apply a strong-smelling liquid in generous quantities. Then he gently implored the patient to sit very still and open his mouth very wide — and then he began.

Thomas Buddenbrook clutched the plush arm-rests with both his hands. He scarcely felt the forceps close around his tooth; but from the grinding sensation in his mouth, and the increasingly painful, really agonizing pressure on his whole head, he was made amply aware that the thing was under way. Thank God, he thought, now it can't last long. The pain grew and grew, to limitless, incredible heights; it grew to an insane, shrieking, inhuman torture, tearing his entire brain. It approached the catastrophe. 'Here we are, he thought. Now I must just bear it.'

It lasted three or four seconds. Herr Brecht's nervous exertions communicated themselves to Thomas Buddenbrook's whole body, he was even lifted up a little on his chair, and he heard a soft, squeaking noise coming from the dentist's throat. Suddenly there was a fearful blow, a violent shaking as if his neck were broken, accompanied by a quick cracking, crackling noise. The pressure was gone, but his head buzzed, the pain throbbed madly in the inflamed and ill-used jaw; and he had the clearest impression that the thing had not been successful: that the extraction of the tooth was not the solution of the difficulty, but merely a premature catastrophe which only made matters worse.

Herr Brecht had retreated. He was leaning against his instrument-cupboard, and he looked like death. He said: "The crown — I thought so."

Thomas Buddenbrook spat a little blood into the blue basin at his side, for the gum was lacerated. He asked, half-dazed: "What did you think? What about the crown?"

"The crown broke off, Herr Senator. I was afraid of it. — The tooth was in very bad condition. But it was my duty to make the experiment."

"What next?"

"Leave it to me, Herr Senator."

"What will you have to do now?"

"Take out the roots. With a lever. There are four of them."

"Four. Then you must take hold and lift four times."

"Yes — unfortunately."

"Well, this is enough for to-day," said the Senator. He started to rise, but remained seated and put his head back instead.

" My dear Sir, you mustn't demand the impossible of me," he said. " I'm not very strong on my legs, just now. I have had enough for to-day. Will you be so kind as to open the window a little? "

Herr Brecht did so. " It will be perfectly agreeable to me, Herr Senator, if you come in to-morrow or next day, at whatever hour you like, and we can go on with the operation. If you will permit me, I will just do a little more rinsing and pencilling, to reduce the pain somewhat."

He did the rinsing and pencilling, and then the Senator went. Herr Brecht accompanied him to the door, pale as death, expending his last remnant of strength in sympathetic shoulder-shruggings.

" One moment, please! " shrieked Josephus as they passed through the waiting-room. He still shrieked as Thomas Buddenbrook went down the steps.

With a lever — yes, yes, that was to-morrow. What should he do now? Go home and rest, sleep, if he could. The actual pain in the nerve seemed deadened; in his mouth was only a dull, heavy burning sensation. Home, then. He went slowly through the streets, mechanically exchanging greetings with those whom he met; his look was absent and wandering, as though he were absorbed in thinking how he felt.

He got as far as Fishers' Lane and began to descend the left-hand sidewalk. After twenty paces he felt nauseated. " I'll go over to the public house and take a drink of brandy," he thought, and began to cross the road. But just as he reached the middle, something happened to him. It was precisely as if his brain was seized and swung around, faster and faster, in circles that grew smaller and smaller, until it crashed with enormous, brutal, pitiless force against a stony centre. He performed a half-turn, fell, and struck the wet pavement, his arms outstretched.

As the street ran steeply down hill, his body lay much lower than his feet. He fell upon his face, beneath which, presently, a little pool of blood began to form. His hat rolled a little way off down the road; his fur coat was wet with mud and slush; his hands, in their white kid gloves, lay outstretched in a puddle.

Thus he lay, and thus he remained, until some people came down the street and turned him over.

CHAPTER VIII

Frau Permaneder mounted the main staircase, holding up her gown in front of her with one hand and with the other pressing her muff to her cheek. She tripped and stumbled more than she walked; her cheeks were flushed, her capote sat crooked on her head, and little beads stood on her upper lip. . . . Though she met no one, she talked continually as she hurried up, in whispers out of which now and then a word rose clear and audible and emphasized her fear. "It's nothing," she said. "It doesn't mean anything. God wouldn't let anything happen. He knows what he's doing, I'm very sure of that. . . . Oh, my God, I'll pray every day — " She prattled senselessly in her fear, as she rushed up to the second storey and down the corridor.

The door of the ante-chamber opened, and her sister-in-law came toward her. Gerda Buddenbrook's lovely white face was quite distorted with horror and disgust; and her close-set, blue-shadowed brown eyes opened and shut with a look of anger, distraction, and shrinking. As she recognized Frau Permaneder, she beckoned quickly with outstretched arms and embraced her, putting her head on her sister-in-law's shoulder.

"Gerda! Gerda! What is it?" Frau Permaneder cried. "What has happened? What does it mean? They said he fell — unconscious? How is he? — God won't let the worst happen, I know. Tell me, for pity's sake!"

But the reply did not come at once. She only felt how Gerda's whole form was shaken. Then she heard a whisper at her shoulder.

"How he looked," she heard, "when they brought him! His whole life long, he never let any one see even a speck of dust on him. — Oh, it is insulting, it is vile, for the end to have come like that!"

Subdued voices came out to them. The dressing-room door opened, and Ida Jungmann stood in the doorway in a white apron, a basin in her hands. Her eyes were red. She looked at Frau Permaneder and made way, her head bent. Her chin was trembling.

The high flowered curtains stirred in the draught as Tony, fol-

lowed by her sister-in-law, entered the chamber. The smell of
carbolic, ether, and other drugs met them. In the wide mahogany
bed, under the red down coverlet, lay Thomas Buddenbrook, on
his back, undressed and clad in an embroidered nightshirt. His
half-open eyes were rolled up; his lips were moving under the dis-
ordered moustaches, and babbling, gurgling sounds came out.
Young Dr. Langhals was bending over him, changing a bloody
bandage for a fresh one, which he dipped into a basin at the bedside. Then he listened at the patient's chest and felt his pulse.

On the bed-clothes at the foot of the bed sat little Johann,
clutching his sailor's knot and listening broodingly to the sounds
behind him, which his father was making. The Senator's bemired
clothing hung over a chair.

Frau Permaneder cowered down at the bedside, seized one of
her brother's hands — it was cold and heavy — and stared wildly
into his face. She began to understand that, whether God knew
what he was doing or not, he was at all events bent on "the
worst"!

"Tom!" she clamoured, "do you know me? How are you?
You aren't going to leave us? You won't go away from us? Oh,
it *can't* be!"

Nothing answered her, that could be called an answer. She
looked imploringly up at Dr. Langhals. He stood there with his
beautiful eyes cast down; and his manner, not without a certain
self-satisfaction, expressed the will of God.

Ida Jungmann came back into the room, to make herself useful
if she could. Old Dr. Grabow appeared in person, looked at the
patient with his long, mild face, shook his head, pressed all their
hands, and then stood as Dr. Langhals stood. The news had gone
like the wind through the whole town. The vestibule door rang
constantly, and inquiries after the Senator's condition came up into
the sick-chamber. It was unchanged — unchanged. Every one received the same answer.

The two physicians were in favour of sending for a sister of
charity — at least for the night. They sent for Sister Leandra, and
she came. There was no trace of surprise or alarm in her face as
she entered. Again she laid aside her leather bag, her outer hood
and cloak, and again she set to work in her gentle way.

Little Johann sat hour after hour on the bed-clothes, watching
everything and listening to the gurgling noises. He was to have
gone to an arithmetic lesson; but he understood perfectly that
what was happening here was something over which the worsted-
coats had no jurisdiction. He thought of his lessons only for a

moment, and with scorn. He wept, sometimes, when Frau Permaneder came up and pressed him to her; but mostly he sat dry-eyed, with a shrinking, brooding gaze, and his breath came irregularly and cautiously, as if he expected any moment to smell that strange and yet familiar smell.

Toward four o'clock Frau Permaneder took a sudden resolve. She asked Dr. Langhals to come with her into the next room; and there she folded her arms and laid back her head, with the chin dropped.

"Herr Doctor," she said, "there is one thing you can do, and I beg you to do it. Tell me the truth. I am a woman steeled by adversity; I have learned to bear the truth. You may depend upon me. Please tell me plainly: Will my brother be alive to-morrow?"

Dr. Langhals turned his beautiful eyes aside, looked at his finger-nails, and spoke of our human powerlessness, and the impossibility of knowing whether Frau Permaneder's brother would outlive the night, or whether he would be called away the next minute.

"Then I know what I have to do," said she; went out of the room; and sent for Pastor Pringsheim.

Pastor Pringsheim appeared, without his vestments or neckruff, in a long black gown. He swept Sister Leandra with an icy stare, and seated himelf in the chair which they placed for him by the bedside. He asked the patient to recognize and hear him. Then, as this appeal was unsuccessful, he addressed himself at once to God and prayed in carefully modulated tones, with his Frankish pronunciation, with emphasis now solemn and now abrupt, while waves of fanaticism and sanctimony followed each other across his face. He pronounced his *r* in a sleek and oily way peculiar to himself alone, and little Johann received an irresistible impression that he had just been eating rolls and coffee.

He said that he and the family there present no longer importuned God for the life of this dear and beloved sufferer, for they saw plainly that it was God's will to take him to Himself. They only begged Him for the mercy of a gentle death. And then he recited, appropriately and with effect, two of the prayers customary on such occasions. Then he got up. He pressed Gerda Buddenbrook's hand, and Frau Permaneder's, and held little Johann's head for a moment between both his hands, regarding the drooping eyelashes with an expression of the most fervent pity. He saluted Ida Jungmann, stared again at Sister Leandra, and took his leave.

Dr. Langhals had gone home for a little. When he came back there had been no change. He spoke with the nurse, and went again. Dr. Grabow came once more, to see that everything was being done. Thomas Buddenbrook went on babbling and gurgling, with his eyes rolled up. Twilight was falling. There was a pale winter glow at sunset, and it shone through the window upon the soiled clothing lying across the chair.

At five o'clock Frau Permaneder let herself be carried away by her feelings, and committed an indiscretion. She suddenly began to sing, in her throaty voice, her hands folded before her.

"Come, Lord,"

she sang, quite loud, and they all listened without stirring.

"Come, Lord, receive his failing breath;
Strengthen his hands and feet, and lead him unto death."

But in the devoutness of her prayer, she thought only of the words as they welled up from her heart, and forgot that she did not know the whole stanza; after the third line she was left hanging in the air, and had to make up for her abrupt end by the increased dignity of her manner. Everybody shivered with embarrassment. Little Johann coughed so hard that the coughs sounded like sobs. And then, in the sudden pause, there was no sound but the agonizing gurgles of Thomas Buddenbrook.

It was a relief when the servant announced that there was something to eat in the next room. But they had only begun, sitting in Gerda's bedroom, to take a little soup, when Sister Leandra appeared in the doorway and quietly beckoned.

The Senator was dying. He hiccoughed gently two or three times, was silent, and ceased to move his lips. That was the only change. His eyes had been quite dead before.

Dr. Langhals, who was on the spot a few minutes later, put the black stethoscope to the heart, listened, and, after this scientific test, said " Yes, it is over."

And Sister Leandra, with the forefinger of her gentle white hand, softly closed the eyes of the dead.

Then Frau Permaneder flung herself down on her knees by the bed, pressed her face into the coverlet, and wept aloud, surrendering herself utterly and without restraint to one of those refreshing bursts of feeling which her happy nature had always at its command. Her face still streamed with tears, but she was soothed and comforted and entirely herself as she rose to her feet and began straightway to occupy her mind with the announcements of the death — an enormous number of elegant cards, which must be ordered at once.

Christian appeared. He had heard the news of the Senator's stroke in the club, which he had left at once. But he was so afraid of seeing some awful sight that he went instead for a long walk outside the walls, and was not to be found. Now, however, he came in, and on the threshold heard of his brother's death.

" It isn't possible," he said, and limped up the stairs, his eyes rolling wildly.

He stood at the bedside between his sister and his sister-in-law; with his bald head, his sunken cheeks, his drooping moustaches, and his huge beaked nose, he stood there on his bent legs, looking a little like an interrogation-point, and gazed with his little round deep eyes into his brother's face, as it lay so silent, so cold, so detached and inaccessible. The corners of Thomas's mouth were drawn down in an expression almost scornful. Here he lay, at whom once Christian had flung the reproach that he was too heartless to weep at a brother's death. He was dead now himself: he had simply withdrawn, silent, elegant, and irreproachable, into the hereafter. He had, as so often in his life, left it to others to feel put in the wrong. No matter now, whether he had been right or wrong in his cold and scornful indifference toward his brother's afflictions, the " misery," the nodding man, the spirit bottle, the open window. None of that mattered now; for death, with arbitrary and incomprehensible partiality, had singled him out, and taken him up, and given him an awesome dignity and importance. And yet Death had rejected Christian, had held him off, and would not have him at any price — would only keep on making game of him and mocking him with all these tricks and antics which nobody took seriously. Never in his life had Thomas Buddenbrook so impressed his brother as at this hour. Success is so definite, so conclusive! Death alone can make others respect our sufferings; and through death the most pitiable sufferings acquire dignity. " You have won — I give in," Christian thought. He knelt on one knee, with a sudden awkward gesture, and kissed the cold hand on the coverlet. Then he stepped back and moved about the room, his eyes darting back and forth.

Other visitors came — the old Krögers, the Misses Buddenbrook, old Herr Marcus. Poor Clothilde, lean and ashen, stood by the bed; her face was apathetic, and she folded her hands in their worsted gloves. " You must not think, Tony and Gerda," said she, and her voice dragged very much, " that I've no feeling because I don't weep. The truth is, I have no more tears." And as she stood there, incredibly dry and withered, it was evident that she spoke the truth.

Then they all left the room to make way for an elderly female, an unpleasant old creature with a toothless, mumbling jaw, who had come to help Sister Leandra wash and dress the corpse.

Gerda Buddenbrook, Frau Permaneder, Christian, and little Johann sat under the big gas-lamp around the centre-table in the living-room, and worked industriously until far on into the evening. They were addressing envelopes and making a list of people who ought to receive announcements. Now and then somebody thought of another name. Hanno had to help, too; his handwriting was plain, and there was need of haste.

It was still in the house and in the street. The gas-lamp made a soft hissing noise; somebody murmured a name; the papers rustled. Sometimes they looked at each other and remembered what had happened.

Frau Permaneder scratched busily. But regularly once every five minutes she would put down her pen, lift her clasped hands up to her mouth, and break out in lamentations. "I can't realize it!" she would cry — meaning that she was gradually beginning to realize. "It is the end of everything," she burst out another time, in sheer despair, and flung her arms around her sister-in-law's neck with loud weeping. After each outburst she was strengthened, and took up her work again.

With Christian it was as with poor Clothilde. He had not shed a tear — which fact rather mortified him. It was true, too, that his constant preoccupation with his own condition had used him up emotionally and made him insensitive. Now and then he would start up, rub his hand over his bald brow, and murmur, "Yes, it's frightfully sad." He said it to himself, with strong self-reproach, and did his best to make his eyes water.

Suddenly something happened to startle them all: little Johann began to laugh. He was copying a list of names, and had found one with such a funny sound that he could not resist it. He said it aloud and snorted through his nose, bent over, sobbed, and could not control himself. The grown people looked at him in bewildered incredulity; and his mother sent him up to bed.

CHAPTER IX

SENATOR BUDDENBROOK had died of a bad tooth. So it was said in the town. But goodness, people don't die of a bad tooth! He had had a toothache; Herr Brecht had broken off the crown; and thereupon the Senator had simply fallen in the street. Was ever the like heard?

But however it had happened, that was no longer the point. What had next to be done was to send wreaths — large, expensive wreaths which would do the givers credit and be mentioned in the paper: wreaths which showed that they came from people with sympathetic hearts and long purses. They were sent. They poured in from all sides, from organizations, from families and individuals: laurel wreaths, wreaths of heavily-scented flowers, silver wreaths, wreaths with black bows or bows with the colours of the City on them, or dedications printed in heavy black type or gilt lettering. And palms — simply quantities of palms.

The flower-shops did an enormous business, not least among them being Iwersen's, opposite the Buddenbrook mansion. Frau Iwersen rang many times in the day at the vestibule door, and handed in arrangements in all shapes and styles, from Senator This or That, or Consul So-and-So, from office staffs and civil servants. On one of these visits she asked if she might go up and see the Senator a minute. Yes, of course, she was told; and she followed Frau Permaneder up the main staircase, gazing silently at its magnificence.

She went up heavily, for she was, as usual, expecting. Her looks had grown a little common with the years; but the narrow black eyes and the Malay cheek-bones had not lost their charm. One could still see that she must once have been exceedingly pretty. She was admitted into the salon, where Thomas Buddenbrook lay upon his bier.

He lay in the centre of the large, light room, the furniture of which had been removed, amid the white silk linings of his coffin, dressed in white silk, shrouded in white silk, in a thick and stupefying mingling of odours from the tuberoses, violets, roses, and other flowers with which he was surrounded. At his head, in a half-circle of silver candelabra, stood the pedestal draped in mourning, supporting the marble copy of Thorwaldsen's Christ. The wreaths, garlands, baskets, and bunches stood or lay along the walls, on the floor, and on the coverlet. Palms stood around the bier and drooped over the feet of the dead. The skin of his face was abraded in spots, and the nose was bruised. But his hair was dressed with the tongs, as in life, and his moustache, too, had been drawn through the tongs for the last time by old Herr Wenzel, and stuck out stiff and straight beyond his white cheeks. His head was turned a little to one side, and an ivory cross was stuck between the folded hands.

Frau Iwersen remained near the door, and looked thence, blinking, over to the bier. Only when Frau Permaneder, in deep black, with a cold in her head from much weeping, came from the living-room through the portières and invited Frau Iwersen to come nearer, did she dare to venture a little farther forward on the parquetry floor. She stood with her hands folded across her prominent abdomen, and looked about her with her narrow black eyes: at the plants, the candelabra, the bows and the wreaths, the white silk, and Thomas Buddenbrook's face. It would be hard to describe the expression on the pale, blurred features of the pregnant woman. Finally she said " Yes — " sobbed just once, a brief inarticulate sound, and turned away.

Frau Permaneder loved these visits. She never stirred from the house, but superintended with tireless zeal the homage that pressed about the earthly husk of her departed brother. She read the newspaper articles aloud many times in her throaty voice: those same newspapers which at the time of the jubilee had paid tribute to her brother's merits, now mourned the irreparable loss of his personality. She stood at Gerda's side to receive the visits of condolence in the living-room and there was no end of these; their name was legion. She held conferences with various people about the funeral, which must of course be conducted in the most refined manner. She arranged farewells: she had the office staff come in a body to bid their chief good-bye. The workmen from the granaries came too. They shuffled their huge feet along the parquetry floor, drew down the corners of their mouths to show their respect, and emanated an odour of chewing tobacco, spirits, and physical exertion. They looked at the dead lying in his splendid state, twirled their caps, first admired and then grew restive, until at length one of them found courage to go, and the whole troop followed shuffling on his heels. Frau Permaneder was enchanted.

She asserted that some of them had tears running down into their beards. This simply was not the fact; but she saw it, and it made her happy.

The day of the funeral dawned. The metal casket was hermetically sealed and covered with flowers, the candles burned in their silver holders, the house filled with people, and, surrounded by mourners from near and far, Pastor Pringsheim stood at the head of the coffin in upright majesty, his impressive head resting upon his ruff as on a dish.

A high-shouldered functionary, a brisk intermediate something between a waiter and a major-domo, had in charge the outward ordering of the solemnity. He ran with the softest speed down the staircase and called in a penetrating whisper across the entry, which was filled to overflowing with tax-commissioners in uniform and grain-porters in blouses, knee-breeches, and tall hats: " The rooms are full, but there is a little room left in the corridor."

Then everything was hushed. Pastor Pringsheim began to speak. He filled the whole house with the rolling periods of his exquisitely modulated, sonorous voice. He stood there near the figure of Thorwaldsen's Christ and wrung his hands before his face or spread them out in blessing; while below in the street, before the house door, beneath a white wintry sky, stood the hearse drawn by four black horses, with the other carriages in a long row behind it. A company of soldiers with grounded arms stood in two rows opposite the house door, with Lieutenant von Throta at their head. He held his drawn sword on his arm and looked up at the bow-window with his brilliant eyes. Many people were craning their necks from windows nearby or standing on the pavements to look.

At length there was a stir in the vestibule, the lieutenant's muffled word of command sounded, the soldiers presented arms with a rattle of weapons, Herr von Throta let his sword sink, and the coffin appeared. It swayed cautiously forth of the house door, borne by the four men in black cloaks and cocked hats, and a gust of perfume came with it, wafted over the heads of bystanders. The breeze ruffled the black plumes on top of the hearse, tossed the manes of the horses standing in line down to the river, and dishevelled the mourning hat-scarves of the coachman and grooms. Enormous single flakes of snow drifted down from the sky in long slanting curves.

The horses attached to the hearse, all in black trappings so that only their restless rolling eyeballs could be seen, now slowly got in motion. The hearse moved off, led by the four black servants.

The company of soldiers fell in behind, and one after another the coaches followed on. Christian Buddenbrook and the pastor got into the first; little Johann sat in the second, with a well-fed Hamburg relative. And slowly, slowly, with mournful long-drawn pomp, Thomas Buddenbrook's funeral train wound away, while the flags at half-mast on all the houses flapped before the wind. The office staff and the grain-porters followed on foot.

The casket, with the mourners behind, followed the well-known cemetery paths, past crosses and statues and chapels and bare weeping-willows, to the Buddenbrook family lot, where the military guard of honour already stood, and presented arms again. A funeral march sounded in subdued and solemn strains from behind the shrubbery.

Once more the heavy gravestone, with the family arms in relief, had been moved to one side; and once more the gentlemen of the town stood there, on the edge of the little grove, beside the abyss walled in with masonry into which Thomas Buddenbrook was now lowered to join his fathers. They stood there with bent heads, these worthy and well-to-do citizens: prominent among them were the Senators, in white gloves and cravats. Beyond them was the throng of officials, clerks, grain-porters, and warehouse labourers.

The music stopped. Pastor Pringsheim spoke. While his voice, raised in blessing, still lingered on the air, everybody pressed round to shake hands with the brother and son of the deceased.

The ceremony was long and tedious. Christian Buddenbrook received all the condolences with his usual absent, embarrassed air. Little Johann stood by his side, in his heavy reefer jacket with the gilt buttons, and looked at the ground with his blue-shadowed eyes. He never looked up, but bent his head against the wind with a sensitive twist of all his features.

PART ELEVEN

CHAPTER I

IT sometimes happens that we may recall this or that person whom we have lately seen and wonder how he is. And then, with a start, we remember that he has disappeared from the stage, that his voice no longer swells the general concert — that he is, in short, departed from among us, and lies somewhere outside the walls, beneath the sod.

Frau Consul Buddenbrook, she that was a Stüwing, Uncle Gotthold's widow, passed away. Death set his reconciling and atoning seal upon the brow of her who in her life had been the cause of such violent discord; and her three daughters, Friederike, Henriette, and Pfiffi, received the condolences of their relatives with an affronted air which seemed to say: "You see, your persecutions have at last brought her down to her grave!" As if the Frau Consul were not as old as the hills already!

And Madame Kethelsen had gone to her long rest. In her later years she had suffered much from gout; but she died gently and simply, resting upon a childlike faith which was much envied by her educated sister, who had always had her periodic attacks of rationalistic doubt, and who, though she grew constantly smaller and more bent, was relentlessly bound by an iron constitution to this sinful earth.

Consul Peter Döhlmann was called away. He had eaten up all his money, and finally fell a prey to Hunyadi-Janos, leaving his daughter an income of two hundred marks a year. He depended upon the respect felt in the community for the name of Döhlmann to insure her being admitted into the Order of St. John.

Justus Kröger also departed this life, which was a loss, for now nobody was left to prevent his wife selling everything she owned to send money to the wretched Jacob, who was still leading a dissolute existence somewhere in the world.

Christian Buddenbrook had likewise disappeared from the streets of his native city. He would have been sought in vain within her walls. He had moved to Hamburg, less than a year after his brother's death, and there he united himself, before God

and men, with Fräulein Aline Puvogel, a lady with whom he had
long stood in a close relationship. No one could now stop him.
His inheritance from his mother, indeed, half the interest of which
had always found its way to Hamburg, was managed by Herr
Stephan Kistenmaker — in so far as it was not already spent in
advance. Herr Kistenmaker, in fact, had been appointed administrator by the terms of his deceased friend's will. But in all other
respects Christian was his own master. Directly the marriage became known, Frau Permaneder addressed to Frau Aline Buddenbrook in Hamburg a long and extraordinarily violent letter, beginning "Madame!" and declaring in carefully poisoned words that
she had absolutely no intention of recognizing as a relative either
the person addressed or any of her children.

Herr Kistenmaker was executor and administrator of the Buddenbrook estate and guardian of little Johann. He held these
offices in high regard. They were an important activity which
justified him in rubbing his head on the Bourse with every indi-
cation of overwork and telling everybody that he was simply
wearing himself out. Besides, he received two per cent. of the
revenues, very punctually. But he was not too successful in the
performance of his duties, and Gerda Buddenbrook soon had
reason to feel dissatisfied.

The business was to close, the firm to go into liquidation, and
the estate to be settled within a year. This was Thomas Buddenbrook's wish, as expressed in his will. Frau Permaneder felt much
upset. "And Hanno? And little Johann — what about Hanno?"
She was disappointed and grieved that her brother had passed over
his son and heir and had not wished to keep the firm alive for him
to step into. She wept for hours to think that one should dispose
thus summarily of that honourable shield, that jewel cherished by
four generations of Buddenbrooks: that the history of the firm
was now to close, while yet there existed a direct heir to carry it
on. But she finally consoled herself by thinking that the end of
the firm was not, after all, the end of the family, and that her
nephew might as easily, in a new and different career, perform
the high task allotted to him — that task being to carry on the
family name and add fresh lustre to the family reputation. It could
not be in vain that he possessed so much likeness to his great-
grandfather.

The liquidation of the business began, under the auspices of
Herr Kistenmaker and old Herr Marcus; and it took a most de-
plorable course. The time was short, and it must be punctiliously
kept to. The pending business was disposed of on hurried and

unfavourable terms. One precipitate and disadvantageous sale followed another. The granaries and warehouses were turned into money at a great loss; and what was not lost by Herr Kistenmaker's over-zealousness was wasted by the procrastination of old Herr Marcus. In town they said that the old man, before he left his house in winter warmed not only his coat and hat, but his walking-stick as well. If ever a favourable opportunity arose, he invariably let it slip through his fingers. And so the losses piled up. Thomas Buddenbrook had left, on paper, an estate of six hundred and fifty thousand marks. A year after the will was opened it had become abundantly clear that there was no question of such a sum.

Indefinite, exaggerated rumours of the unfavourable liquidation got about, and were fed by the news that Gerda Buddenbrook meant to sell the great house. Wonderful stories flew about, of the reasons which obliged her to take such a step; of the collapse of the Buddenbrook fortune. Things were thought to look very badly: and a feeling began to grow up in the town, of which the widowed Frau Senator became aware, at first with surprise and astonishment, and then with growing anger. When she told her sister-in-law, one day, that she had been pressed in an unpleasant way for the payment of some considerable accounts, Frau Permaneder had at first been speechless, and then had burst out into frightful laughter. Gerda Buddenbrook was so outraged that she expressed a half-determination to leave the city for ever with little Johann and go back to Amsterdam to play duets with her old father. But this called forth such a storm of protest from Frau Permaneder that she was obliged to give up the plan for the time being.

As was to be expected, Frau Permaneder protested against the sale of the house which her brother had built. She bewailed the bad impression it would make and complained of the blow it would deal the family prestige. But she had to grant it would be folly to continue to keep up the spacious and splendid dwelling that had been Thomas Buddenbrook's costly hobby, and that Gerda's idea of a comfortable little villa outside the wall, in the country, had, after all, much to commend it.

A great day dawned for Siegismund Gosch the broker. His old age was illumined by an event so stupendous that for many hours it held his knees from trembling. It came about that he sat in Gerda Buddenbrook's salon, in an easy-chair, opposite her and discussed tête-à-tête the price of her house. His snow-white locks streamed over his face, his chin protruded grimly, he succeeded for once in looking thoroughly hump-backed. He hissed when he talked, but his manners were cold and businesslike, and nothing betrayed the emotions of his soul. He bound himself to take over the house, stretched out his hand, smiled cunningly, and bid eighty-five thousand marks — which was a possible offer, for some loss would certainly have to be taken in this sale. But Herr Kistenmaker's opinion must be heard; and Gerda Buddenbrook had to let Herr Gosch go without making the bargain. Then it appeared that Herr Kistenmaker was not minded to allow any interference in what he considered his prerogative. He mistrusted Herr Gosch's offer; he laughed at it, and swore that he could easily get much more. He continued to swear this, until at length he was forced to dispose of the property for seventy-five thousand marks to an elderly spinster who had returned from extended travel and decided to settle in the town.

Herr Kistenmaker also arranged for the purchase of the new house, a pleasant little villa for which he paid rather too high a price, but which was about what Gerda Buddenbrook wanted. It lay outside the Castle Gate, on a chestnut-bordered avenue; and thither, in the autumn of the year 1876, the Frau Senator moved with her son, her servants, and a part of her household goods — the remainder, to Frau Permaneder's great distress, being left behind to pass into the possession of the elderly gentlewoman.

As if these were not changes enough, Mamsell Jungmann, after forty years in the service of the Buddenbrook family, left it to return to her native West Prussia to live out the evening of her life. To tell the truth, she was dismissed by the Frau Senator. This good soul had taken up with little Johann when the previous generation had outgrown her. She had cherished him fondly, read him fairy stories, and told him about the uncle who died of hiccoughs. But now little Johann was no longer small. He was a lad of fifteen years, to whom, despite his lack of strength, she could no longer be of much service; and with his mother her relations had not for a long time been on a very comfortable footing. She had never been able to think of this lady, who had entered the family so much later than herself, as a proper Buddenbrook; and of late she had begun, with the freedom of an old servant, to arrogate to herself exaggerated authority. She stirred up dissension in the household by this or that encroachment; the position became untenable; there were disagreements — and though Frau Permaneder made an impassioned plea in her behalf, as for the old house and the furniture, old Ida had to go.

She wept bitterly when the hour came to bid little Johann farewell. He put his arms about her and embraced her. Then, with his hands behind his back, resting his weight on one leg while the other poised on the tips of the toes, he watched her out of sight; his face wore the same brooding, introspective look with which he had stood at his father's death-bed, and his grandmother's bier, witnessed the breaking-up of the great household, and shared in so many events of the same kind, though of lesser outward significance. The departure of old Ida belonged to the same category as other events with which he was already familiar: breakings-up, closings, endings, disintegrations — he had seen them all. Such events did not disturb him — they had never disturbed him. But he would lift his head, with the curling light-brown hair, inflate one delicate nostril, and it was as if he cautiously sniffed the air about him, expecting to perceive that odour, that strange and yet familiar odour which, at his grandmother's bier, not all the scent of the flowers had been able to disguise.

When Frau Permaneder visited her sister-in-law, she would draw her nephew to her and tell him of the Buddenbrook family past, and of that future for which, next to the mercy of God, they would have to thank little Johann. The more depressing the present appeared, the more she strove to depict the elegance of the life that went on in the houses of her parents and grand-parents; and she would tell Hanno how his great-grandfather had driven all over the country with his carriage and four horses. One day she had a severe attack of cramps in the stomach because Friederike, Henriette, and Pfiffi had asserted that the Hagenströms were the crême de la crême of town society.

Bad news came of Christian. His marriage seemed not to have improved his health. He had become more and more subject to uncanny delusions and morbid hallucinations, until finally his wife had acted upon the advice of a physician and had him put into an institution. He was unhappy there, and wrote pathetic letters to his relatives, expressive of a fervent desire to leave the establish-ment, where, it seemed, he was none too well treated. But they kept him shut up, and it was probably the best thing for him. It also put his wife in a position to continue her former inde-pendent existence without prejudice to her status as a married woman or to the practical advantages accruing from her marriage.

CHAPTER II

THE ALARM-CLOCK went off with cruel alacrity. It was a hoarse
rattling and clattering that it made, rather than a ringing, for it
was old and worn out; but it kept on for a painfully long time,
for it had been thoroughly wound up.

Hanno Buddenbrook was startled to his inmost depths. It was
like this every morning. His very entrails rebelled, in rage, protest,
and despair, at the onslaught of this at once cruel and faithful
monitor standing on the bedside table close to his ear. However,
he did not get up, or even change his position in the bed; he only
wrenched himself away from some blurred dream of the early
morning and opened his eyes.

It was perfectly dark in the wintry room. He could distinguish
nothing, not even the hands on the clock. But he knew it was six
o'clock, because last night he had set his alarm for six. Last night
— And as he lay on his back, with his nerves rasped by the shock
of waking, struggling for sufficient resolution to make a light and
jump out of bed, everything that had filled his mind yesterday
came gradually back into his consciousness.

It was Sunday evening; and after having been maltreated by
Herr Brecht for several days on end, he had been taken as a reward
to a performance of *Lohengrin*. He had looked forward for a
whole week to this evening with a joy which absorbed his entire
existence. Only, it was a pity that on such occasions the full
pleasure of the anticipation had to be marred by disagreeable
commonplaces that went on up to the very last minute. But at
length Saturday came, school was over for the week, and Herr
Brecht's little drill had bored and buzzed away in the mouth for
the last time. Now everything was out of the way and done with
— for he had obstinately put off his preparation for Monday until
after the opera. What was Monday to him? Was it likely it would
ever dawn? Who believes in Monday, when he is to hear *Lohengrin* on Sunday evening? He would get up early on Monday and
get the wretched stuff done — and that was all there was to it.
Thus he went about free from care, fondled the coming joy in his
heart, dreamed at his piano, and forgot all unpleasantness to come.

And then the dream became reality. It came over him with all its enchantment and consecration, all its secret revelations and tremors, its sudden inner emotion, its extravagant, unquenchable intoxication. It was true that the music of the overture was rather too much for the cheap violins in the orchestra; and the fat conceited-looking Lohengrin with straw-coloured hair came in rather hind side foremost in his little boat. And his guardian, Herr Stephan Kistenmaker, had sat in the next box and grumbled about the boy's being taken away from his lessons and having his mind distracted like that. But the sweet, exalted splendour of the music had borne him away upon its wings.

The end had come at length. The singing, shimmering joy was quenched and silent. He had found himself back home in his room, with a burning head and the consciousness that only a few hours of sleep, there in his bed, separated him from dull everyday existence. And he had been overpowered by an attack of the complete despondency which was all too familiar an experience. Again he had learned that beauty can pierce one like a pain, and that it can sing profoundly into shame and a longing despair that utterly consume the courage and energy necessary to the life of every day. His despondency weighed him down like mountains, and once more he told himself, as he had done before, that this was more than his own individual burden of weaknesses that rested upon him: that his burden was one which he had borne upon his soul from the beginning of time, and must one day sink under at last.

He had wound the alarm-clock and gone to sleep — and slept that dead and heavy sleep that comes when one wishes never to awake again. And now Monday was here, and he had not prepared a single lesson.

He sat up and lighted the bedside candle. But his arms and shoulders felt so cold that he lay down again and pulled up the covers.

The hand pointed to ten minutes after six. Oh, it was absurd to get up now! He should hardly have time to make a beginning, for there was preparation in nearly every lesson. And the time he had fixed was already past. Was it as certain, then, as it had seemed to him yesterday that he would be called up in Latin and Chemistry? It was certainly to be expected — in all human probability it would happen. The names at the end of the alphabet had lately been called in the Ovid class, and presumably they would begin again at the beginning. But, after all, it wasn't so absolutely certain, beyond a peradventure — there were exceptions to every rule.

Chance sometimes worked wonders, he knew. He sank deeper and deeper into these false and plausible speculations; his thoughts began to run in together — he was asleep.

The little schoolboy bedchamber, cold and bare, with the copper-plate of the Sistine Madonna over the bed, the extension-table in the middle, the untidy book-shelf, a stiff-legged mahogany desk, the harmonium, and the small wash-hand stand, lay silent in the flickering light of the candle. The window was covered with icy-crystals, and the blind was up in order that the light might come earlier. And Hanno slept, his cheek pressed into the pillow, his lips closed, the eyelashes lying close upon his cheek; he slept with an expression of the most utter abandonment to slumber, the soft, light-brown hair clustering about his temples. And slowly the candle-flame lost its reddish-yellow glow, as the pale, dun-coloured dawn stole into the room through the icy coating on the window-pane.

At seven he woke once more, with a start of fear. He must get up and take upon himself the burden of the day. There was no way out of it. Only a short hour now remained before school would begin. Time pressed; there was no thought of preparation now. And yet he continued to lie, full of exasperation and rebellion against this brutal compulsion that was upon him to forsake his warm bed in the frosty dawning and go out into the world, into contact with harsh and unfriendly people. " Oh, only two little tiny minutes more," he begged of his pillow, in overwhelming tenderness. And then he gave himself a full five minutes more, out of sheer bravado, and closed his eyes, opening one from time to time to stare despairingly at the clock, which went stupidly on in its insensate, accurate way.

Ten minutes after seven o'clock, he tore himself out of bed and began to move about the room with frantic haste. He let the candle burn, for the daylight was not enough by itself. He breathed upon a crystal and, looking out, saw a thick mist abroad.

He was unutterably cold, and a shiver sometimes shook his entire body. The ends of his fingers burned; they were so swollen that he could do nothing with the nail-brush. As he washed the upper parts of his body, his almost lifeless hand let fall the sponge, and he stood a moment stiff and helpless, steaming like a sweating horse.

At last he was dressed. Dull-eyed and breathless, he stood at the table, collected his despairing senses with a jerk, and began to put together the books he was likely to need to-day, murmuring in an

anguished voice: "Religion, Latin, chemistry," and shuffling together the wretched ink-spotted paper volumes.

Yes, he was already quite tall, was little Johann. He was more
than fifteen years old, and no longer wore a sailor costume, but a
light-brown jacket suit with a blue-and-white spotted cravat.
Over his waistcoat he wore a long, thin gold chain that had belonged to his grandfather, and on the fourth finger of his broad
but delicately articulated right hand was the old seal ring with the
green stone. It was his now. He pulled on his heavy winter
jacket, put on his hat, snatched his school-bag, extinguished the
candle, and dashed down the stair to the ground floor, past the
stuffed bear, and into the dining-room on the right.

Fräulein Clementine, his mother's new factotum, a thin girl with
curls on her forehead, a pointed nose, and short-sighted eyes,
already sat at the breakfast-table.

"How late is it, really?" he asked between his teeth, though he
already knew with great precision.

"A quarter before eight," she answered, pointing with a thin,
red, rheumatic-looking hand at the clock on the wall. "You must
get along, Hanno." She set a steaming cup of cocoa before him,
and pushed the bread and butter, salt, and an egg-cup toward his
place.

He said no more, clutched a roll, and began, standing, with his
hat on and his bag under his arm, to swallow his cocoa. The hot
drink hurt the back tooth which Herr Brecht had just been working at. He let half of it stand, pushed away the egg, and with a
sound intended for an adieu ran out of the house.

It was ten minutes to eight when he left the garden and the
little brick villa behind him and dashed along the wintry avenue.
Ten, nine, eight minutes more. And it was a long way. He could
scarcely see for the fog. He drew it in with his breath and breathed
it out again, this thick, icy cold fog, with all the power of his
narrow chest; he stopped his still throbbing tooth with his tongue,
and did fearful violence to his leg muscles. He was bathed in
perspiration; yet he felt frozen in every limb. He began to have
a stitch in his side. The morsel of breakfast revolted in his stomach
against this morning jaunt which it was taking; he felt nauseated,
and his heart fluttered and trembled so that it took away his breath.

The Castle Gate — only the Castle Gate — and it was four minutes to eight! As he panted on through the streets, in an extremity
of mingled pain, perspiration, and nausea, he looked on all sides for
his fellow pupils. No, there was no one else; they were all on the

spot — and now it was beginning to strike eight. Bells were ringing all over the town, and the chimes of St. Mary's were playing,
in celebration of this moment, "now let us all thank God." They
played half the notes falsely; they had no idea of rhythm, and they
were badly in want of tuning. Thus Hanno, in the madness of despair. But what was that to him? He was late; there was no longer
any room for doubt. The school clock was usually a little behind,
but not enough to help him this time. He stared hopelessly into
people's faces as they passed him. They were going to their offices
or about their business; they were in no particular hurry; nothing
was threatening them. Some of them looked at him and smiled at
his distracted appearance and sulky looks. He was beside himself
at these smiles. What were they smiling at, these comfortable, un-
hurried people? He wanted to shout after them and tell them their
smiling was very uncivil. Perhaps *they* would just enjoy falling
down dead in front of the closed entrance gate of the school!

The prolonged shrill ringing which was the signal for morning
prayers struck on his ear while he was still twenty paces from the
long red wall with the two cast-iron gates, which separated the
court of the school-building from the street. He felt that his legs
had no more power to advance: he simply let his body fall forward, the legs moved willy-nilly to prevent his stumbling, and thus
he staggered on and arrived at the gate just as the bell had ceased
ringing.

Herr Schlemiel, the porter, a heavy man with the face and rough
beard of a labourer, was just about to close the gate. "Well!" he
said, and let Buddenbrook slip through. Perhaps, perhaps, he
might still be saved! What he had to do now was to slip unobserved into his classroom and wait there until the end of prayers,
which were held in the drill-hall, and to act as if everything were
in order. Panting, exhausted, in a cold perspiration, he slunk across
the courtyard and through the folding doors with glass panes that
divided it from the interior.

Everything in the establishment was now new, clean, and adequate. The time had been ripe; and the grey, crumbling walls of
the ancient monastic school had been levelled to the ground to
make room for the spacious, airy, and imposing new building. The
style of the whole had been preserved, and corridors and cloisters
were still spanned by the fine old Gothic vaulting. But the lighting and heating arrangements, the ventilation of the classrooms,
the comfort of the masters' rooms, the equipment of the halls for
the teaching of chemistry, physics and design, all this had been

carried out on the most modern lines with respect to comfort and sanitation.

The exhausted Hanno stuck close to the wall and kept his eyes open as he stole along. Heaven be praised, the corridors were empty. He heard distantly the hubbub made by the hosts of masters and pupils going into the drill-hall, to receive there a little spiritual strengthening for the labours of the week. But here everything was empty and still, and his road up the broad linoleum-covered stairs lay free. He stole up cautiously on his tip-toes, holding his breath, straining his ears for sounds from above. His classroom, the lower second of the *Realschule*, was in the first storey, opposite the stairs, and the door was open. Crouched on the top step, he peered down the long corridor, on both sides of which were the entrances to the various classrooms, with porcelain signs above them. Three rapid, noiseless steps forward — and he was in his own room.

It was empty. The curtains of the three large windows were still drawn, and the gas was burning in the chandelier with a soft hissing noise. Green shades diffused the light over the three rows of desks. These desks each had room for two pupils; they were made of light-coloured wood, and opposite them, in remote and edifying austerity, stood the master's platform with a blackboard behind it. A yellow wainscoting ran round the lower part of the wall, and above it the bare white-washed surface was decorated with a few maps. A second blackboard stood on an easel by the master's chair.

Hanno went to his place, which was nearly in the centre of the room. He stuffed his bag into the desk, sank upon the hard seat, laid his arms on the sloping lid, and rested his head upon them. He had a sensation of unspeakable relief. The room was bare, hard, hateful, and ugly; and the burden of the whole threatening forenoon, with its numerous perils, lay before him. But for the moment he was safe; he had saved his skin, and could take things as they came. The first lesson, Herr Ballerstedt's class in religious instruction, was comparatively harmless. He could see, by the vibration of the little strips of paper over the ventilator next the ceiling, that warm air was streaming in, and the gas, too, did its share to heat the room. He could actually stretch out here and feel his stiffened limbs slowly thawing. The heat mounted to his head: it was very pleasant, but not quite healthful; it made his ears buzz and his eyes heavy.

A sudden noise behind him made him start and turn around.

And behold, from behind the last bench rose the head and shoulders of Kai, Count Mölln. He crawled out, did this young man, got up, shook himself, slapped his hands together to get the dust off, and came up to Hanno with a beaming face.

"Oh, it's you, Hanno," he said. "And I crawled back there because I took you for a piece of the faculty when you came in."

His voice cracked as he spoke, because it was changing, which Hanno's had not yet begun to do. He had kept pace with Hanno in his growth, but his looks had not altered, and he still wore a dingy suit of no particular colour, with a button or so missing and a big patch in the seat. His hands, too, were not quite clean; narrow and aristocratic-looking though they were, with long, slender fingers and tapering nails. But his brow was still pure as alabaster beneath the carelessly parted reddish-yellow hair that fell over it, and the glance of the sparkling blue eyes was as keen and as profound as ever. In fact, the contrast was even more striking between his neglected toilette and the racial purity of his face, with its delicate bony structure, slightly aquiline nose, and short upper lip, upon which the down was beginning to show.

"Oh, Kai," said Hanno, with a wry face, putting his hand to his heart. "How can you frighten me like that? What are you doing up here? Why are you hiding? Did you come late too?"

"Dear me, no," Kai said. "I've been here a long time. Though one doesn't much look forward to getting back to the old place, when Monday morning comes around. *You* must know that yourself, old fellow. No, I only stopped up here to have a little game. The deep one seems to be able to reconcile it with his religion to hunt people down to prayers. Well, I get behind him, and I manage to keep close behind his back whichever way he turns, the old mystic! So in the end he goes off, and I can stop up here. But what about you?" he said sympathetically, sitting down beside Hanno on the bench. "You had to run, didn't you? Poor old chap! You look perfectly worn out. Your hair is sticking to your forehead." He took a ruler from the table and carefully combed little Johann's hair with it. "You overslept, didn't you? Look," he interrupted himself, "here I am sitting in the sacred seat of number one — Adolf Todtenhaupt's place! Well, it won't hurt me for once, I suppose. You overslept, didn't you?"

Hanno had put his head down on his arms again. "I was at the opera last night," he said, heaving a long sigh.

"Right — I'd forgot that. Well, was it beautiful?"

He got no answer.

"You are a lucky fellow, after all," went on Kai perseveringly. "I've never been in the theatre, not a single time in my whole life, and there isn't the smallest prospect of my going — at least, not for years."

"If only one did not have to pay for it afterwards," said Hanno gloomily.

"The headache next morning — well, I know how that feels, anyhow." Kai stooped and picked up his friend's coat and hat, which lay on the floor beside the bench, and carried them quietly out into the corridor.

"Then I take for granted you haven't done the verses from the *Metamorphoses?*" he asked as he came back.

"No," said Hanno.

"Have you prepared for the geography test?"

"I haven't done anything, and I don't know anything," said Hanno.

"Not the chemistry nor the English, either? *Benissimo!* Then there's a pair of us — brothers-in-arms," said Kai, with obvious gratification. "I'm in exactly the same boat," he announced jauntily. "I did no work Saturday, because the next day was Sunday; and I did no work on Sunday, because it was Sunday! No, nonsense, it was mostly because I'd something better to do." He spoke with sudden earnestness, and a slight flush spread over his face. "Yes, perhaps it may be rather lively to-day, Hanno."

"If I get only one more bad mark, I shan't go up," said Johann; "and I'm sure to get it when I'm called up for Latin. The letter B comes next, Kai, so there's not much help for it."

"We shall see: What does Caesar say? 'Dangers may threaten me in the rear; but when they see the front of Caesar — '" But Kai did not finish. He was feeling rather out of sorts himself; he went to the platform and sat down in the master's chair, where he began to rock back and forth, scowling. Hanno still sat with his forehead resting on his arms. So they remained for a while in silence.

Then, somewhere in the distance, a dull humming was heard, which quickly swelled to a tumult of voices, approaching, imminent.

"The mob," said Kai, in an exasperated tone. "Goodness, how fast they got through. They haven't taken up ten minutes of the period!"

He got down from the platform and went to the door to mingle with the incoming stream. Hanno, for his part, lifted up his head for a minute, screwed up his mouth, and remained seated.

Stamping, shuffling, with a confusion of masculine voices, treble
and falsetto, they flooded up the steps and over the corridor. The
classroom suddenly became full of noise and movement. This
was the lower second form of the *Realschule*, some twenty-five
strong, comrades of Hanno and Kai. They loitered to their places
with their hands in their pockets or dangling their arms, sat down,
and opened their Bibles. Some of the faces were pleasant, strong,
and healthy; others were doubtful or suspicious-looking. Here
were tall, stout, lusty rascals who would soon go to sea or else begin
a mercantile career, and who had no further interest in their school
life; and small, ambitious lads, far ahead of their age, who were
brilliant in subjects that could be got by heart. Adolf Todtenhaupt was the head boy. He knew everything. In all his school
career he had never failed to answer a question. Part of his reputation was due to his silent, impassioned industry; but part was also
due to the fact that the masters were careful not to ask him anything he might not know. It would have pained and mortified them
and shaken their faith in human perfectibility to have Adolf Todtenhaupt fail to answer. He had a head full of remarkable bumps,
to which his blond hair clung as smooth as glass; grey eyes with
black rings beneath them, and long brown hands that stuck out beneath the too short sleeves of his neatly brushed jacket. He sat
down next Hanno Buddenbrook with a mild, rather sly smile, and
bade his neighbour good morning in the customary jargon, which
reduced the greeting to a single careless monosyllable. Then he began to employ himself silently with the class register, holding his
pen in a way that was incomparably correct, with the slender fingers outstretched; while about him people yawned, laughed,
conned their lessons, and chattered half aloud.

After two minutes there were steps outside. The front rows of
pupils rose, and some of those seated farther back followed their
example. The rest scarcely interrupted what they were doing as
Herr Ballerstedt came into the room, hung his hat on the door, and
betook himself to the platform.

He was a man in the forties, with a pleasant *embonpoint*, a large
bald spot, a short beard, a rosy complexion, and a mingled expression of unctuousness and sensuality on his humid lips. He took out
his notebook and turned over the leaves in silence; but as the order
in the classroom left much to be desired, he lifted his head,
stretched out his arm over the desk, and waved his flabby white
fist a few times powerlessly in the air. His face grew slowly red
— such a dark red that his beard looked pale-yellow by contrast.
He moved his lips and struggled spasmodically and fruitlessly for

half a minute to speak, and finally brought out a single syllable, a short, suppressed grunt that sounded like "Well!" He still struggled after further expression, but in the end gave it up, returned to his notebook, calmed down, and became quite composed once more. This was Herr Ballerstedt's way.

He had intended to be a priest; but on account of his tendency to stutter and his leaning toward the good things of life he had become a pedagogue instead. He was a bachelor of some means, wore a small diamond on his finger, and was much given to eating and drinking. He was the head master who associated with his fellow masters only in working hours; and outside them he spent his time chiefly with the bachelor society of the town — yes, even with the officers of the garrison. He ate twice a day in the best hotel and was a member of the club. If he met any of his elder pupils in the streets, late at night or at two or three o'clock in the morning, he would puff up the way he did in the classroom, fetch out a " Good morning," and let the matter rest there, on both sides. From this master Hanno Buddenbrook had nothing to fear and was almost never called up by him. Herr Ballerstedt had been too often associated with Hanno's Uncle Christian in all too purely human affairs, to make him inclined to conflict with Johann in an official capacity.

" Well," he said, looked about him once more, waved his flabby fist with the diamond upon it, and glanced into his notebook. " Perlemann, the synopsis."

Somewhere in the class, up rose Perlemann. One could hardly see that he had risen; he was one of the small and forward ones. " The synopsis," he said, softly and politely, craning his neck forward with a nervous smile. " The Book of Job falls into three sections. First, the condition of Job before he fell under the chastening of the Lord: Chapter One, Verses one to six: second, the chastening itself, and its consequences, Chapter — "

" Right, Perlemann," interrupted Herr Ballerstedt, touched by so much modesty and obligingness. He put down a good mark in his book. " Continue, Heinricy."

Heinricy was one of the tall rascals who gave themselves no trouble over anything. He shoved the knife he had been playing with into his pocket, and got up noisily, with his lower lip hanging, and coughing in a gruff voice. Nobody was pleased to have him called up after the gentle Perlemann. The pupils sat drowsing in the warm room, some of them half asleep, soothed by the purring sound of the gas. They were all tired after the holiday; they had all crawled out of warm beds that morning with their teeth

chattering, groaning in spirit. And they would have preferred to
have the gentle Perlemann drone on for the remainder of the
period. Heinricy was almost sure to make trouble.

" I wasn't here when we had this," he said, none too respectfully.

Herr Ballerstedt puffed himself up, waved his fist, struggled
to speak, and stared young Heinricy in the face with his eyebrows
raised. His head shook with the effort he made; but he finally
managed to bring out a " Well! " and the spell was broken. He
went on with perfect fluency. " There is never any work to be got
out of you, and you always have an excuse ready, Heinricy. If
you were ill the last time, you could have had help in that part; besides, if the first part dealt with the condition before the tribulation, and the second part with the tribulation itself, you could
have told by counting on your fingers that the third part must
deal with the condition after the tribulation! But you have no
application or interest whatever; you are not only a poor creature,
but you are always ready to excuse and defend your mistakes. But
so long as this is the case, Heinricy, you cannot expect to make any
improvement, and so I warn you. Sit down, Heinricy. Go on,
Wasservogel."

Heinricy, thick-skinned and defiant, sat down with much shuffling and scraping, whispered some sort of saucy comment in his
neighbour's ear, and took out his jack-knife again. Wasservogel
stood up: a boy with inflamed eyes, a snub nose, prominent ears,
and bitten finger-nails. He finished the summary in a rather whining voice, and began to relate the story of Job, the man from the
land of Uz, and what happened to him. He had simply opened his
Bible, behind the back of the pupil ahead of him; and he read
from it with an air of utter innocence and concentration, staring
then at a point on the wall and translated what he read, coughing
the while, into awkward and hesitating modern German. There
was something positively repulsive about Wasservogel; but Herr
Ballerstedt gave him a large meed of praise. Wasservogel had the
knack of making the masters like him; and they praised him in
order to show that they were incapable of being led away by his
ugliness to blame him unjustly.

The lesson continued. Various pupils were called up to display
their knowledge touching Job, the man from the land of Uz.
Gottlob Kassbaum, son of the unfortunate merchant P. Phillipp
Kassbaum, got an excellent mark, despite the late distressing circumstances of his family, because he knew that Job had seven

thousand sheep, three thousand camels, five hundred yoke of oxen, five hundred asses, and a large number of servants.

Then the Bibles, which were already open, were permitted to be opened, and they went on reading. Wherever Herr Ballerstedt thought explanation necessary, he puffed himself up, said " Well! " and after these customary preliminaries made a little speech upon the point in question, interspersed with abstract moral observations. Not a soul listened. A slumberous peace reigned in the room. The heat, with the continuous influx of warm air and the still lighted gas burners, had become oppressive, and the air was well-nigh exhausted by these twenty-five breathing and steaming organisms. The warmth, the purring of the gas, and the drone of the reader's voice lulled them all to a point where they were more asleep than awake. Kai, Count Mölln, however, had a volume of Edgar Allan Poe's *Tales* inside his Bible, and read in it, supporting his head on his hand. Hanno Buddenbrook leaned back, sank down in his seat, and looked with relaxed mouth and hot, swimming eyes at the Book of Job, in which all the lines ran together into a black haze. Now and then, as the Grail *motif* or the Wedding March came into his mind, his lids drooped and he felt an inward soothing; and then he would wish that this safe and peaceful morning hour might go on for ever.

Yet it ended, as all things must end. The shrill sound of the bell, clanging and echoing through the corridor, shook the twenty-five brains out of their slumberous calm.

" That is all," said Herr Ballerstedt. The register was handed up to him and he signed his name in it, as evidence that he had performed his office.

Hanno Buddenbrook closed his Bible and stretched himself, yawning. It was a nervous yawn; and as he dropped his arms and relaxed his limbs he had to take a long, deep breath to bring his heart back to a steady pulsation, for it weakly refused its office for a second. Latin came next. He cast a beseeching glance at Kai, who still sat there reading and seemed not to have remarked the end of the lesson. Then he drew out his Ovid, in stitched covers of marbled paper, and opened it at the lines that were to have been learned by heart for to-day. No, it was no use now trying to memorize any of it: the regular lines, full of pencil marks, numbered by fives all the way down the page, looked hopelessly unfamiliar. He barely understood the sense of them, let alone trying to say a single one of them by heart. And of those in to-day's preparation he had not puzzled out even the first sentence.

"What does that mean—'*deciderant, patula Jovis arbore glandes*'?" he asked in a despairing voice, turning to Adolf Todtenhaupt, who sat beside him working on the register.

"What?" asked Todtenhaupt, continuing to write. "The acorns from the tree of Jupiter—that is the oak; no, I don't quite know myself—"

"Tell me a bit, Todtenhaupt, when it comes my turn, will you?" begged Hanno, and pushed the book away. He scowled at the cool and careless nod Todtenhaupt gave by way of reply; then he slid sidewise off the bench and stood up.

The scene had changed. Herr Ballerstedt had left the room, and his place was taken by a weak enervated little man who stood straight and severe on the platform. He had a sparse white beard and a thin red neck that rose out of a narrow turned-down collar. He held his top hat upside down in front of him, clasped in two small hands covered with white hair. His real name was Professor Hückopp, but he was called "Spider" by the pupils. He was in charge of classrooms and corridors during the recess. "Out with the gas! Up with the blinds! Up with the windows!" he said, and gave his voice as commanding a tone as possible, moving his little arm in the air with an awkward, energetic gesture, as if he were turning a crank. "Everybody downstairs, into the fresh air, as quick as possible!"

The gas went out, the blinds flew up, the sallow daylight filled the room. The cold mist rushed in through the wide-open windows, and the lower second crowded past Professor Hückopp to the exit. Only the head boy might remain upstairs.

Hanno and Kai met at the door and went down the stairs together, and across the architecturally correct vestibule. They were silent. Hanno looked pathetically unwell, and Kai was deep in thought. They reached the courtyard and began to stroll up and down across the wet red tiles, among school companions of all ages and sizes.

A youthful looking man with a blond pointed beard kept order down here: Dr. Goldener, the "dressy one." He kept a *pensionnat* for the sons of the rich landowners from Mecklenburg and Holstein, and dressed, on account of these aristocratic youths, with an elegance not apparent in the other masters. He wore silk cravats, a dandified coat, and pale-coloured trousers fastened down with straps under the soles of his boots, and used perfumed handkerchiefs with coloured borders. He came of rather simple people, and all this elegance was not very becoming—his huge feet, for example, looked absurd in the pointed buttoned boots he wore.

He was vain of his plump red hands, too, and kept rubbing them together, clasping them before him, and regarding them with every mark of admiration. He carried his head laid far back on one side, and constantly made faces by blinking, screwing up his nose, and half-opening his mouth, as though he were about to say: "What's the matter now?" But his refinement led him to overlook all sorts of small infractions of the rules. He overlooked this or that pupil who had brought a book with him into the court-yard to prepare a little at the eleventh hour; he overlooked the fact that one of his boarding-pupils handed money to the porter, Herr Schlemiel, and asked him to get some pastry; he overlooked a small trial of strength between two third-form pupils, which re-sulted in a beating of one by the other, and around which a ring of connoisseurs was quickly formed; and he overlooked certain sounds behind him which indicated that a pupil who had made himself unpopular by cheating, cowardice, or other weakness was being forcibly escorted to the pump.

It was a lusty, not too gentle race, that of these comrades of Hanno and Kai among whom they walked up and down. The ideals of the victorious, united fatherland were those of a some-what rude masculinity; its youth talked in a jargon at once brisk and slovenly; the most despised vices were softness and dandyism, the most admired virtues those displayed by prowess in drinking and smoking, bodily strength and skill in athletics. Whoever went out with his coat-collar turned up incurred a visit to the pump; while he who let himself be seen in the streets with a walking-stick must expect a public and ignominious correction adminis-tered in the drill-hall.

Hanno's and Kai's conversation was in striking contrast to that which went on around them among their fellows. This friendship had been recognized in the school for a long time. The masters suffered it grudgingly, suspecting that it meant disaffection and future trouble. The pupils could not understand it, but had settled down to regarding it with a sort of embarrassed dislike, and to thinking of the two friends as outlaws and eccentrics who must be left to their own devices. They recognized, it is true, the wild-ness and insubordination of Kai, Count Mölln, and respected him accordingly. As for Hanno Buddenbrook, big Heinricy, who thrashed everybody, could not make up his mind to lay a finger on him by way of chastisement for dandyism or cowardice. He refrained out of an indefinite respect and awe for the softness of Hanno's hair, the delicacy of his limbs, and his sad, shy, cold glance.

" I'm scared," Hanno said to Kai. He leaned against the wall of the school, drawing his jacket closer about him, yawning and shivering, " I'm so scared, Kai, that it hurts me all over my body. Now just tell me this: is Herr Mantelsack the sort of person one ought to be afraid of? Tell me yourself! If this beastly Ovid lesson were only over! If I just had my bad mark, in peace, and stopped where I am, and everything was in order! I'm not afraid of that. It is the row that goes beforehand that I hate! "

Kai was still deep in thought. " This Roderick Usher is the most remarkable character ever conceived," he said suddenly and abruptly. " I have read the whole lesson-hour. If ever I could write a tale like that! "

Kai was absorbed in his writing. It was to this he had referred when he said that he had something better to do than his preparation, and Hanno had understood him. Attempts at composition had developed out of his old propensity for inventing tales; and he had lately completed a composition in the form of a fantastic fairy tale, a narrative of symbolic adventure, which went forward in the depths of the earth among glowing metals and mysterious fires, and at the same time in the souls of men: a tale in which the primeval forces of nature and of the soul were interchanged and mingled, transformed and refined — the whole conceived and written in a vein of extravagant and even sentimental symbolism, fervid with passion and longing.

Hanno knew the tale well, and loved it; but he was not now in a frame of mind to think of Kai's work or of Edgar Allan Poe. He yawned again, and then sighed, humming to himself a *motif* he had lately composed on the piano. This was a habit with him. He would often give a long sigh, a deep indrawn breath, from the instinct to calm the fluctuating and irregular action of his heart; and he had accustomed himself to set the deep breathing to a musical theme of his own or some one else's invention.

" Look, there comes the Lord God," said Kai. " He is walking in his garden."

" Fine garden," said Hanno. He began to laugh nervously, and could not stop; putting his handkerchief to his mouth the while and looking across the courtyard at him whom Kai called the Lord God.

This was Director Wulicke, the head of the school, who had appeared in the courtyard: an extremely tall man with a slouch hat, a short heavy beard, a prominent abdomen, trousers that were far too short, and very dirty funnel-shaped cuffs. He strode across the flagstones with a face so angry in its expression that he seemed to be actually suffering, and pointed at the pump with outstretched arm. The water was running! A train of pupils ran before him and stumbled in their zeal to repair the damage. Then they stood about, looking first at the pump and then at the Director, their faces pictures of distress; and the Director, meanwhile, had turned to Dr. Goldener, who hurried up with a very red face and spoke to him in a deep hollow voice, fairly babbling with excitement between the words.

This Director Wulicke was a most formidable man. He had succeeded to the headship of the school after the death, soon after 1871, of the genial and benevolent old gentleman under whose guidance Hanno's father and uncle had pursued their studies. Dr. Wulicke was summoned from a professorship in a Prussian high school; and with his advent an entirely new spirit entered the school. In the old days the classical course had been thought of as an end in itself, to be pursued at one's ease, with a sense of joyous idealism. But now the leading conceptions were authority, duty, power, service, the career; "the categorical imperative of our philosopher Kant" was inscribed upon the banner which Dr. Wulicke in every official speech unfurled to the breeze. The school became a state within a state, in which not only the masters but the pupils regarded themselves as officials, whose main concern was the advancement they could make, and who must therefore take care to stand well with the authorities. Soon after the new Director was installed in his office the tearing down of the old school began, and the new one was built up on the most approved hygienic and aesthetic principles, and everything went swimmingly. But it remained an open question whether the old school, as an institution, with its smaller endowment of modern comfort and its larger share of gay good nature, courage, charm, and good feeling, had not been more blest and blessing than the new.

As for Dr. Wulicke himself personally, he had all the awful mystery, duplicity, obstinacy, and jealousy of the Old Testament God. He was as frightful in his smiles as in his anger. The result of the enormous authority that lay in his hands was that he grew more and more arbitrary and moody — he was even capable of making a joke and then visiting with his wrath anybody who dared to laugh. Not one of his trembling creatures knew how to act before him. They found it safest to honour him in the dust, and to protect themselves by a frantic abasement from the fate of being whirled up in the cloud of his wrath and crushed for ever under the weight of his righteous displeasure.

The name Kai had given Dr. Wulicke was known only to himself and Hanno, and they took the greatest pains not to let any of the others overhear it, for they could not possibly understand. No, there was not one single point on which those two stood on common ground with their schoolfellows. Even the methods of revenge, of "getting even," which obtained in the school were foreign to Hanno and Kai; and they utterly distained the current nicknames, which did not in the least appeal to their more subtle sense of humour. It was so poor, it showed such a paucity of invention, to call thin Professor Hückopp "Spider" and Herr Ballerstedt "Cocky." It was such scant compensation for their compulsory service to the state! No, Kai, Count Mölln, flattered himself that he was not so feeble as that! He invented, for his own and Hanno's use, a method of alluding to all their masters by their actual names, with the simple prefix, thus: Herr Ballerstedt, Herr Hückopp. The irony of this, its chilly remoteness and mockery, pleased him very much. He liked to speak of the "teaching body"; and would amuse himself for whole recesses with imagining it as an actual creature, a sort of monster, with a repulsively fantastic form. And they spoke in general of the "Institution" as if it were similar to that which harboured Hanno's Uncle Christian.

Kai's mood improved at sight of the Lord God, who still pervaded the playground and put everybody in a pallid fright by pointing, with fearful rumblings, to the wrapping papers from the luncheons which strewed the courtyard. The two lads went off to one of the gates, through which the masters in charge of the second period were now entering. Kai began to make bows of exaggerated respect before the red-eyed, pale, shabby-looking seminarists, who crossed over to go to their sixth and seventh form pupils in the back court. And when the grey-haired mathematics master, Herr Tietge, appeared, holding a bundle of books on his back with a shaking hand, bent, yellow, cross-eyed, spitting as he walked along, Kai said, "Good-morning, old dead man." He said this, in a loud voice and gazed straight up into the air with his bright, sharp gaze.

Then the bell clanged loudly, and the pupils began to stream through the entrances into the building. Hanno could not stop laughing. He was still laughing so hard on the stairs that his classmates looked at him and Kai with wonder and cold hostility, and even with a slight disgust at such frivolity.

There was a sudden hush in the classroom, and everybody stood up, as Herr Professor Mantelsack entered. He was the Professor *ordinarius,* for whom it was usual to show respect. He pulled the door to after him, bowed, craned his neck to see if all the class were standing up, hung his hat on its nail, and went quickly to the platform, moving his head rapidly up and down as he went. He took his place and stood for a while looking out the window and running his forefinger, with a large seal ring on it, around inside his collar. He was a man of medium size, with thin grey hair, a curled Olympian beard, and short-sighted prominent sapphire-blue eyes gleaming behind his spectacles. He was dressed in an open frock-coat of soft grey material, which he habitually settled at the waist with his short-fingered, wrinkled hand. His trousers were, like all the other masters', even the elegant Dr. Goldener's, far too short, and showed the legs of a pair of very broad and shiny boots.

He turned sharply away from the window and gave vent to a little good-natured sigh, smiling familiarly at several pupils. His mood was obviously good, and a wave of relief ran through the classroom. So much — everything, in fact — depended on whether Dr. Mantelsack was in a good mood! For the whole form was aware that he gave way to the feeling of the moment, whatever that might happen to be, without the slightest restraint. He was most extraordinarily, boundlessly, naïvely unjust, and his favour was as inconstant as that of fortune herself. He had always a few favourites — two or three — whom he called by their given names, and these lived in paradise. They might say almost anything they liked; and after the lesson Dr. Mantelsack would talk with them just like a human being. But a day would come — perhaps after the holidays — when for no apparent reason they were dethroned, cast out, rejected, and others elevated to their place. The mistakes of these favourites would be passed over with neat, careful corrections, so that their work retained a respectable appearance, no matter how bad it was; whereas he would attack the other copybooks with heavy, ruthless pen, and fairly flood them with red ink, so that their appearance was shocking indeed. And as he never troubled to count the mistakes, but distributed bad marks in proportion to the red ink he had expended, his favourites always emerged with great credit from these exercises. He was not even aware of the rank injustice of this conduct. And if anybody had ever had the temerity to call his attention to it, that person would have been for ever deprived of even the chance of becoming a favourite and being called by his first name. There was nobody who was willing to let slip the chance.

Now Dr. Mantelsack crossed his legs, still standing, and began to turn over the leaves of his notebook. Hanno Buddenbrook wrung his hands under the desk. B, the letter B, came next. Now he would hear his name, he would get up, he would not know a line, and there would be a row, a loud, frightful catastrophe — no matter how good a mood Dr. Mantelsack might be in. The seconds dragged out, each a martyrdom. "Buddenbrook" — Now he would say "Buddenbrook." "Edgar," said Dr. Mantelsack, closing his notebook with his finger in it. He sat down, as if all were in the best of order.

What? Who? Edgar? That was Lüders, the fat Lüders boy over there by the window. Letter L, which was not next at all! No! Was it possible? Dr. Mantelsack's mood was so good that he simply selected one of his favourites, without troubling in the least about whose turn it was.

Lüders stood up. He had a face like a pug dog, and dull brown eyes. He had an advantageous seat, and could easily have read it off, but he was too lazy. He felt too secure in his paradise, and answered simply, "I had a headache yesterday, and couldn't study."

"Oh, so you are leaving me in the lurch, Edgar," said Dr. Mantelsack with tender reproach. "You cannot say the lines on the Golden Age? What a shocking pity, my friend! You had a headache? It seems to me you should have told me before the lesson began, instead of waiting till I called you up. Didn't you have a headache just lately, Edgar? You should do something for them, for otherwise there is danger of your not passing. Timm, will you take his place?"

Lüders sat down. At this moment he was the object of universal hatred. It was plain that the master's mood had altered for the worse, and that Lüders, perhaps in the very next lesson, would be called by his last name. Timm stood up in one of the back seats. He was a blond country-looking lad with a light-brown jacket and short, broad fingers. He held his mouth open in a funnel shape, and hastily found the place, looking straight ahead the while with the most idiotic expression. Then he put down his head and began to read, in long-drawn-out, monotonous, hesitating accents, like a child with a first lesson-book: "Aurea prima sata est ætas!"

It was plain that Dr. Mantelsack was calling up quite at random, without reference to the alphabet. And thus it was no longer so imminently likely that Hanno would be called on, though this might happen through unlucky chance. He exchanged a joyful glance with Kai and began to relax somewhat.

But now Timm's reading was interrupted. Whether Dr.

Mantelsack could not hear him, or whether he stood in need of exercise, is not to be known. But he left his platform and walked slowly down through the room. He paused near Timm, with his book in his hand; Timm meanwhile had succeeded in getting his own book out of sight, but was now entirely helpless. His funnel-shaped mouth emitted a gasp, he looked at the *Ordinarius* with honest, troubled blue eyes, and could not fetch out another syllable.

" Well, Timm," said Dr. Mantelsack. " Can't you get on? "

Timm clutched his brow, rolled up his eyes, sighed windily, and said with a dazed smile: " I get all mixed up, Herr Doctor, when you stand so close to me."

Dr. Mantelsack smiled too. He smiled in a very flattered way and said "Well, pull yourself together and get on." And he strolled back to his place.

And Timm pulled himself together. He drew out and opened his book again, all the time apparently wrestling to recover his self-control and staring about the room. Then he dropped his head and was himself again.

" Very good," said the master, when he had finished. " It is clear that you have studied to some purpose. But you sacrifice the rhythm too much, Timm. You seem to understand the elisions; yet you have not been really reading hexameters at all. I have an impression as if you had learned the whole thing by heart, like prose. But, as I say, you have been diligent, you have done your best — and whoever does his best —; you may sit down."

Timm sat down, proud and beaming, and Dr. Mantelsack gave him a good mark in his book. And the extraordinary thing was that at this moment not only the master, but also Timm himself and all his classmates, sincerely felt that Timm was a good industrious pupil who had fully deserved the mark he got. Hanno Buddenbrook, even, thought the same, though something within him revolted against the thought. He listened with strained attention to the next name.

" Mumme," said Dr. Mantelsack. " Again: *aurea prima —* "

Mumme! Well! Thank Heaven! Hanno was now in probable safety. The lines would hardly be asked for a third time, and in the sight-reading the letter B had just been called up.

Mumme got up. He was tall and pale, with trembling hands and extraordinary large round glasses. He had trouble with his eyes, and was so short-sighted that he could not possibly read standing up from a book on the desk before him. He had to learn, and he had learned. But to-day he had not expected to be called up; he was, besides, painfully ungifted; and he stuck after the first few words. Dr. Mantelsack helped him, he helped him again in a sharper tone, and for the third time with intense irritation. But when Mumme came to a final stop, the *Ordinarius* was mastered by indignation.

"This is entirely insufficient, Mumme. Sit down. You cut a disgraceful figure, let me tell you, sir. A *cretin!* Stupid and lazy both —it is really too much."

Mumme was overwhelmed. He looked the child of calamity, and at this moment everybody in the room despised him. A sort of disgust, almost like nausea, mounted again in Hanno Buddenbrook's throat; but at the same time he observed with horrid clarity all that was going forward. Dr. Mantelsack made a mark of sinister meaning after Mumme's name, and then looked through his notebook with frowning brows. He went over, in his disgust, to the order of the day, and looked to see whose turn it really was. There was no doubt that this was the case: and just as Hanno was overpowered by this knowledge, he heard his name — as if in a bad dream.

"Buddenbrook!" Dr. Mantelsack had said "Buddenbrook." The scale was in the air again. Hanno could not believe his senses. There was a buzzing in his ears. He sat still.

"Herr Buddenbrook!" said Dr. Mantelsack, and stared at him sharply through his glasses with his prominent sapphire-blue eyes. "Will you have the goodness?"

Very well, then. It was to be. It had to come. It had come differently from his expectations, but still, here it was, and he was none the less lost. But he was calm. Would it be a very big row? He rose in his place and was about to utter some forlorn and absurd excuse to the effect that he had "forgotten" to study the lines, when he became aware that the boy ahead of him was offering him his open book.

This boy, Hans Hermann Kilian, was a small brown lad with oily hair and broad shoulders. He had set his heart on becoming an officer, and was so possessed by an ideal of comradeship that he would not leave in the lurch even little Buddenbrook, whom he did not like. He pointed with his finger to the place.

Hanno gazed down upon it and began to read. With trembling voice, his face working, he read of the Golden Age, when truth and justice flourished of their own free will, without laws or compulsions. "Punishment and fear did not exist," he said, in Latin. "No threats were graven upon the bronze tablets, nor did those who came to petition fear the countenance of the judges. . . ."

He read in fear and trembling, read with design badly and dis-
jointedly, purposely omitted some of the elisions that were marked
with pencil in Kilian's book, made mistakes in the lines, progressed
with apparent difficulty, and constantly expected the master to
discover the fraud and pounce upon him. The guilty satisfaction
of seeing the open book in front of him gave him a pricking sensation in his skin; but at the same time he had such a feeling of disgust
that he intentionally deceived as badly as possible, simply to make
the deceit seem less vulgar to himself. He came to the end, and a
pause ensued, during which he did not dare look up. He felt convinced that Dr. Mantelsack had seen all, and his lips were perfectly
white. But at length the master sighed and said:

" Oh, Buddenbrook! *Si tacuisses!* You will permit me the
classical thou, for this once. Do you know what you have done?
You have conducted yourself like a vandal, a barbarian. You are a
humourist, Buddenbrook; I can see that by your face. If I ask
myself whether you have been coughing or whether you have
been reciting this noble verse, I should incline to the former.
Timm showed small feeling for rhythm, but compared to you he
is a genius, a rhapsodist! Sit down, unhappy wretch! You have
studied the lines, I cannot deny it, and I am constrained to give you
a good mark. You have probably done your best. But tell me —
have I not been told that you are musical, that you play the piano?
How is it possible? Well, very well, sit down. You have worked
hard — that must suffice."

He put a good mark down in his book, and Hanno Buddenbrook
took his seat. He felt as Timm, the rhapsodist had felt before him
— that he really deserved the praise which Dr. Mantelsack gave
him. Yes, at the moment he was of the opinion that he was, if
rather a dull, yet an industrious pupil, who had come off with
honour, comparatively speaking. He was conscious that all his
schoolmates, not excepting Hans Hermann Kilian, had the same
view. Yet he felt at the same time somewhat nauseated. Pale,
trembling, too exhausted to think about what had happened, he
closed his eyes and sank back in lethargy.

Dr. Mantelsack, however, went on with the lesson. He came to
the verses that were to have been prepared for to-day, and called
up Petersen. Petersen rose, fresh, lively, sanguine, in a stout attitude, ready for the fray. Yet to-day, even to-day, was destined to
see his fall. Yes, the lesson hour was not to pass without a catastrophe far worse than that which had befallen the hapless, short-
sighted Mumme.

Petersen translated, glancing now and then at the other page of his book, which should have had nothing on it. He did it quite cleverly: he acted as though something there distracted him — a speck of dust, perhaps, which he brushed with his hand or tried to blow away. And yet — there followed the catastrophe.

Dr. Mantelsack made a sudden violent movement, which was responded to on Petersen's part by a similar movement. And in the same moment the master left his seat, dashed headlong down from his platform, and approached Petersen with long, impetuous strides.

" You have a crib in your book," he said as he came up.

" A crib — I — no," stammered Petersen. He was a charming lad, with a great wave of blond hair on his forehead and lovely blue eyes which now flickered in a frightened way.

" You have no crib in your book? "

" A crib, Herr Doctor? No, really, I haven't. You are mistaken. You are accusing me falsely." Petersen betrayed himself by the unnatural correctness of his language, which he used in order to intimidate the master. " I am not deceiving you," he repeated, in the greatness of his need. " I have always been honourable, my whole life long."

But Dr. Mantelsack was all too certain of the painful fact.

" Give me your book," he said coldly.

Petersen clung to his book; he raised it up in both hands and went on protesting. He stammered, his tongue grew thick. " Believe me, Herr Doctor. There is nothing in the book — I have no crib — I have not deceived you — I have always been honourable — "

" Give me your book," repeated the master, stamping his foot.

Then Petersen collapsed, and his face grew grey.

" Very well," said he, and delivered up his book. " Here it is. Yes, there is a crib in it. You can see for yourself; there it is. But I haven't used it," he suddenly shrieked, quite at random.

Dr. Mantelsack ignored this idiotic lie, which was rooted in despair. He drew out the crib, looked at it with an expression of extreme disgust, as if it were a piece of decaying offal, thrust it into his pocket, and threw the volume of Ovid contemptuously back on Petersen's desk.

" Give me the class register," he said in a hollow voice.

Adolf Todtenhaupt dutifully fetched it, and Petersen received a mark for dishonesty which effectually demolished his chances of being sent up at Easter. " You are the shame of the class," said Dr. Mantelsack.

Petersen sat down. He was condemned. His neighbour avoided

contact with him. Every one looked at him with a mixture of pity, aversion, and disgust. He had fallen, utterly and completely, because he had been found out. There was but one opinion as to Petersen, and that was that he was, in very truth, the shame of the class. They recognized and accepted his fall, as they had the rise of Timm and Buddenbrook and the unhappy Mumme's mischance. And Petersen did too.

Thus most of this class of twenty-five young folk, being of sound and strong constitution, armed and prepared to wage the battle of life as it is, took things just as they found them, and did not at this moment feel any offence or uneasiness. Everything seemed to them to be quite in order. But one pair of eyes, little Johann's, which stared gloomily at a point on Hans Hermann Kilian's broad back, were filled, in their blue-shadowed depths, with abhorrence, fear, and revulsion. The lesson went on. Dr. Mantelsack called on somebody, anybody — he had lost all desire to test any one. And after Adolf Todtenhaupt, another pupil, who was but moderately prepared, and did not even know what "*patula Jovis arbore*" meant, had been called on, Buddenbrook had to say it. He said it in a low voice, without looking up, because Dr. Mantelsack asked him, and he received a nod of the head for the answer.

And now that the performance of the pupils was over, the lesson had lost all interest. Dr. Mantelsack had one of the best scholars read at his own sweet will, and listened just as little as the twenty-four others, who began to get ready for the next class. This one was finished, in effect. No one could be marked on it, nor his interest or industry judged. And the bell would soon ring. It did ring. It rang for Hanno, and he had received a nod of approbation. Thus it was.

"Well!" said Kai to Hanno, as they walked down the Gothic corridor with their classmates, to go to the chemistry class, "what do you say now about the brow of Caesar? You had wonderful luck!"

"I feel sick, Kai," said little Johann, "I don't like that kind of luck. It makes me sick." Kai knew he would have felt the same in Hanno's place.

The chemistry hall was a vaulted chamber like an amphitheatre with benches rising in tiers, a long table for the experiments, and two glass cases of phials. The air in the classroom had grown very hot and heavy again; but here it was saturated with an odour of sulphuretted hydrogen from a just-completed experiment, and smelled abominable. Kai flung up the window and then stole

Adolf Todtenhaupt's copy-book and began in great haste to copy down the lesson for the day. Hanno and several others did the same. This occupied the entire pause till the bell rang, and Dr. Marotzke came in.

This was the "deep one," as Kai and Hanno called him. He was a medium-sized dark man with a very yellow skin, two large lumps on his brow, a stiff smeary beard, and hair of the same kind. He always looked unwashed and unkempt, but his appearance probably belied him. He taught the natural sciences, but his own field was mathematics, in which subject he had the reputation of being an original thinker. He liked to hold forth on the subject of metaphysical passages from the Bible; and when in a good-natured or discursive mood, he would entertain the boys of the first and second forms with marvellous interpretations of mysterious passages. He was, besides all this, a reserve officer, and very enthusiastic over the service. As an official who was also in the army, he stood very well with Director Wulicke. He set more store by discipline than any of the other masters: he would review the ranks of sturdy youngsters with a professional eye, and he insisted on short, brisk answers to questions. This mixture of mysticism and severity was not, on the whole, attractive.

The copy-books were shown, and Dr. Marotzke went around and touched each one with his finger. Some of the pupils who had not done theirs at all, put down other books or turned this one back to an old lesson; but he never noticed.

Then the lesson began, and the twenty-five boys had to display their industry and interest with respect to boric acid, and chlorine, and strontium, as in the previous period they had displayed it with respect to Ovid. Hans Hermann Kilian was commended because he knew that $BaSO_4$, or barytes, was the metal most commonly used in counterfeiting. He was the best in the class, anyhow, because of his desire to be an officer. Kai and Hanno knew nothing at all, and fared very badly in Dr. Marotzke's notebook.

And when the tests, recitation, and marking were over, the interest in chemistry was about exhausted too. Dr. Marotzke began to make a few experiments; there were a few pops, a few coloured gases; but that was only to fill out the hour. He dictated the next lesson; and then the third period, too, was a thing of the past.

Everybody was in good spirits now — even Petersen, despite the blow he had received. For the next hour was likely to be a jolly one. Not a soul felt any qualms before it, and it even promised occasion for entertainment and mischief. This was English, with Candidate Modersohn, a young philologian who had been for a few weeks on trial in the faculty — or, as Kai, Count Mölln, put it, he was filling a limited engagement with the company. There was little prospect, however, of his being re-engaged. His classes were much too entertaining.

Some of the form remained in the chemistry hall, others went up to the classroom; nobody needed to go down and freeze in the courtyard, because Herr Modersohn was in charge up in the corridors, and he never dared send any one down. Moreover, there were preparations to be made for his reception.

The room did not become in the least quieter when it rang for the fourth hour. Everybody chattered and laughed and prepared to see some fun. Count Mölln, his head in his hands, went on reading Roderick Usher. Hanno was audience. Some of the boys imitated the voices of animals; there was the shrill crowing of a cock; and Wasservogel, in the back row, grunted like a pig without anybody's being able to see that the noise came from his inside. On the blackboard was a huge chalk drawing, a caricature, with squinting eyes, drawn by Timm the rhapsodist. And when Herr Modersohn entered he could not shut the door, even with the most violent efforts, because there was a thick fir-cone in the crack; Adolf Todtenhaupt had to take it away.

Candidate Modersohn was an undersized, insignificant looking man. His face was always contorted with a sour, peevish expression, and he walked with one shoulder thrust forward. He was frightfully self-conscious, blinked, drew in his breath, and kept opening his mouth as if he wanted to say something if he could only think of it. Three steps from the door he trod on a cracker of such exceptional quality that it made a noise like dynamite. He jumped violently; then, in these straits, he smiled exactly as though nothing had happened and took his place before the middle row of benches, stooping sideways, in his customary attitude, and resting one palm on the desk in front of him. But this posture of his was familiar to everybody; somebody had put some ink on the right spot, and Herr Modersohn's small clumsy hand got all inky. He acted as though he had not noticed, laid his wet black hand on his back, blinked, and said in a soft, weak voice: " The order in the classroom leaves something to be desired."

Hanno Buddenbrook loved him in that moment, sat quite still, and looked up into his worried, helpless face. But Wasservogel grunted louder than ever, and a handful of peas went rattling against the window and bounced back into the room.

" It's hailing," somebody said, quite loudly. Herr Modersohn appeared to believe this, for he went without more ado to the platform and asked for the register. He needed it to call the names from, for, though he had been teaching the class for five or six weeks, he hardly knew any of them by name.

"Feddermann," he said, "will you please recite the poem?"

"Absent," shouted a chorus of voices. And there sat Feddermann, large as life, in his place, shooting peas with great skill and accuracy.

Herr Modersohn blinked again and selected a new name. "Wasservogel," he said.

"Dead," shouted Petersen, attacked by a grim humour. And the chorus, grunting, crowing, and with shouts of derision, asseverated that Wasservogel was dead.

Herr Modersohn blinked afresh. He looked about him, drew down his mouth, and put his finger on another name in the register. "Perlemann," he said, without much confidence.

"Unfortunately, gone mad," uttered Kai, Count Mölln, with great clarity and precision. And this also was confirmed by the chorus amid an ever-increasing tumult.

Then Herr Modersohn stood up and shouted in to the hubbub: "Buddenbrook, you will do me a hundred lines imposition. If you laugh again, I shall be obliged to mark you."

Then he sat down again. It was true that Hanno had laughed. He had been seized by a quiet but violent spasm of laughter, and went on because he could not stop. He had found Kai's joke so good — the "unfortunately" had especially appealed to him. But he became quiet when Herr Modersohn attacked him, and sat looking solemnly into the Candidate's face. He observed at that moment every detail of the man's appearance: saw every pathetic little hair in his scanty beard, which showed the skin through it; saw his brown, empty, disconsolate eyes; saw that he had on what appeared to be two pairs of cuffs, because the sleeves of his shirt came down so long; saw the whole pathetic, inadequate figure he made. He saw more: he saw into the man's inner self. Hanno Buddenbrook was almost the only pupil whom Herr Modersohn knew by name, and he availed himself of the knowledge to call him constantly to order, give him impositions, and tyrannize over him. He had distinguished Buddenbrook from the others simply because of his quieter behaviour — and of this he took advantage to make him feel his authority, an authority he did not dare exert upon the real offenders. Hanno looked at him and reflected that Herr Modersohn's lack of fine feeling made it almost impossible even to pity him! "I don't bully you," he addressed the Candidate, in his thoughts: "I don't share in the general tormenting like

the others — and how do you repay me? But so it is, and so will it
be, always and everywhere," he thought; and fear, and that sensation almost amounting to physical nausea, rose again in him. " And
the most dreadful thing is that I can't help seeing through you
with such disgusting clearness! "

At last Herr Modersohn found some one who was neither dead
nor crazy, and who would take it upon himself to repeat the English verse. This was a poem called " The Monkey," a poor childish
composition, required to be committed to memory by these growing lads whose thoughts were already mostly bent on business, on
the sea, on the coming conflicts of actual life.

> " Monkey, little, merry fellow,
>   Thou art nature's punchinello . . ."

There were endless verses — Kassbaum read them, quite simply,
out of his book. Nobody needed to trouble himself about what
Herr Modersohn thought. The noise grew worse and worse, the
feet shuffled and scraped on the dusty floor, the cock crowed, the
pig grunted, peas filled the air. The five-and-twenty were drunk
with disorder. And the unregulated instincts of their years awoke.
They drew obscene pictures on pieces of paper, passed them
about, and laughed at them greedily.

All at once everything was still. The pupil who was then reciting interrupted himself; even Herr Modersohn got up and listened.
They heard something charming: a pure, bell-like sound, coming
from the bottom of the room and flowing sweetly, sensuously,
with indescribably tender effect, on the sudden silence. It was a
music-box which somebody had brought, playing " *Du, du, liegst
mir am Herzen* " in the middle of the English lesson. But precisely
at that moment when the little melody died away, something
frightful ensued. It broke like a sudden storm over the heads of
the class, unexpected, cruel, overwhelming, paralyzing.

Without anybody's having knocked, the door opened wide with
a great shove, and a presence came in, high and huge, growled, and
stood with a single stride in front of the benches. It was the Lord
God.

Herr Modersohn grew ashy pale and dragged down the chair
from the platform, dusting it with his handkerchief. The pupils
had sprung up like one man. They pressed their arms to their
sides, stood on their tip-toes, bent their heads, and bit their tongues
in the fervour of their devotion. The deepest silence reigned.
Somebody gasped with the effort he made — then all was still
again.

Director Wulicke measured the saluting columns for a while with his eye. He lifted his arm with its dirty funnel-shaped cuff, and let it fall with the fingers spread out, as if he were attacking a keyboard. " Sit down," he said in his double-bass voice.

The pupils sank back into their seats. Herr Modersohn pulled up the chair with trembling hands, and the Director sat down beside the dais. "Please proceed," he said. That was all, but it sounded as frightful as if the words he uttered had been " Now we shall see, and woe to him who — "

The reason for his coming was clear. Herr Modersohn was to give evidence of his ability to teach, to show what the lower second had learned in the six or seven hours he had been with them. It was a question of Herr Modersohn's existence and future. The Candidate was a sorry figure as he stood on the platform and called again on somebody to recite " The Monkey." Up to now it had been only the pupils who were examined, but now it was the master as well. Alas, it went badly on both sides! Herr Director Wulicke's appearance was entirely unexpected, and only two or three of the pupils were prepared. It was impossible for Herr Modersohn to call up Adolf Todtenhaupt for the whole hour on end; after " The Monkey " had been recited once, it could not be asked for again, and so things were in a bad way. When the reading from Ivanhoe began, young Count Mölln was the only person who could translate it at all, he having a personal interest in the novel. The others hemmed and hawed, stuttered, and got hopelessly stuck. Hanno Buddenbrook was called up and could not do a line. Director Wulicke gave utterance to a sound that was as though the lowest string of his double-bass had been violently plucked, and Herr Modersohn wrung his small, clumsy, inky hands repeating plaintively over and over. " And it went so well — it always went so well! "

He was still saying it, half to the pupils and half to the Director, when the bell rang. But the Lord God stood erect with folded arms before his chair and stared in front of him over the heads of the class. Then he commanded that the register be brought, and slowly marked down for laziness all those pupils whose performances of the morning had been deficient — or entirely lacking — six or seven marks at one fell swoop. He could not put down a mark for Herr Modersohn, but he was much worse than the others. He stood there with a face like chalk, broken, done for. Hanno Buddenbrook was among those marked down. And Director Wulicke said besides, " I will spoil all your careers for you." Then he went.

The bell rang; class was over. It was always like that. When you expected trouble it did not come. When you thought all was well — then, the catastrophe. It was now impossible for Hanno to go up at Easter. He rose from his seat and went drearily out of the room, seeking the aching back tooth with his tongue.

Kai came up to him and put his arm across his shoulders. Together they walked down to the courtyard, among the crowd of excited comrades, all of whom were discussing the extraordinary event. He looked with loving anxiety into Hanno's face and said, " Please forgive, Hanno, for translating. It would have been better to keep still and get a mark. It's so cheap — "

" Didn't I say what ' *patula Jovis arbore* ' meant? " answered Hanno. " Don't mind, Kai. That doesn't matter. One just mustn't mind."

" I suppose that's true. Well, the Lord God is going to ruin your career. You may as well resign yourself, Hanno, because if it is His inscrutable will — . Career — what a lovely word ' career ' is! Herr Modersohn's career is spoilt too. He will never get to be a master, poor chap! There are assistant masters, you may know, and there are head masters; but never by any chance a plain master. This is a mystery not to be revealed to youthful minds; it is only intended for grown-ups and persons of mature experience. An ordinary intelligence might say that either one is a master or one is not. I might go up to the Lord God or Herr Marotzke and explain this to him. But what would be the result? They would consider it an insult, and I should be punished for insubordination — all for having discovered for them a much higher significance in their calling than they themselves were aware of! No, let's not talk about them — they're all thick-skinned brutes! "

They walked about the court; Kai made jokes to help Hanno forget his bad mark, and Hanno listened and enjoyed.

" Look, here is a door, an outer door. It is open, and outside there is the street. How would it be if we were to go out and take a little walk? It is recess, and we have still six minutes. We could easily be back in time. But it is perfectly impossible. You see what I mean? Here is the door. It is open, there is no grating, there is nothing, nothing whatever to prevent us. And yet it is impossible for us to step outside for even a second — it is even impossible for us to think of doing so. Well, let's not think of it, then. Let's take another example: we don't say, for instance, that it is nearly half-past twelve. No, we say, ' It's nearly time for the geography period '! You see? Now, I ask, is this any sort of a life to lead?

Everything is wrong. Oh, Lord, if the institution would just once let us out of her loving embrace! "

"Well, and what then? No, Kai, we should just have to do something then; here, at least we are taken care of. Since my Father died Herr Stephan Kistenmaker and Pastor Pringsheim have taken over the business of asking me every day what I want to be. I don't know. I can't answer. I can't be anything. I'm afraid of everything — "

"How can anybody talk so dismally? What about your music? "

"What about my music, Kai? There is nothing to it. Shall I travel round and give concerts? In the first place, they wouldn't let me; and in the second place, I should never really know enough. I can play very little. I can only improvise a little when I am alone. And then, the traveling about must be dreadful, I imagine. It is different with you. You have more courage. You go about laughing at it all — you have something to set against it. You want to write, to tell wonderful stories. Well, that *is* something. You will surely become famous, you are so clever. The thing is, you are so much livelier. Sometimes in class we look at each other, the way we did when Petersen got marked because he read out of a crib, when all the rest of us did the same. The same thought is in both our minds — but you know how to make a face and let it pass. I can't. I get so tired of things. I'd like to sleep and never wake up. I'd like to die, Kai! No, I am no good. I can't want anything. I don't even want to be famous. I'm afraid of it, just as much as if it were a wrong thing to do. Nothing can come of me, that is perfectly sure. One day, after confirmation-class, I heard Pastor Pringsheim tell somebody that one must just give me up, because I come of a decayed family."

"Did he say that? " Kai asked with deep interest.

"Yes; he meant my Uncle Christian, in the institution in Hamburg. One must just give me up — oh, I'd be so happy if they would! I have so many worries; everything is so hard for me. If I give myself a little cut or bruise anywhere, and make a wound that would heal in a week with anybody else, it takes a month with me. It gets inflamed and infected and makes me all sorts of trouble. Herr Brecht told me lately that all my teeth are in a dreadful condition — not to mention the ones that have been pulled already. If they are like that now, what will they be when I am thirty or forty years old? I am completely discouraged."

"Oh, come," Kai said, and struck into a livelier gait. "Now you must tell me something about your playing. I want to write something marvellous — perhaps I'll begin it to-day, in drawing period. Will you play this afternoon? "

Hanno was silent a moment. A flush came upon his face, and a painful, confused look.

" Yes, I'll play — I suppose — though I ought not. I ought to practise my sonatas and études and then stop. But I suppose I'll play; I cannot help it, though it only makes everything worse."

" Worse? "

Hanno was silent.

" I know what you mean," said Kai after a bit, and then neither of the lads spoke again.

They were both at the same difficult age. Kai's face burned, and he cast down his eyes. Hanno looked pale and serious; his eyes had clouded over, and he kept giving sideways glances.

Then the bell rang, and they went up.

The geography period came next, and an important test on the kingdom of Hesse-Nassau. A man with a red beard and brown tail-coat came in. His face was pale, and his hands were very full of pores, but without a single hair. This was " the clever one," Dr. Mühsam. He suffered from occasional haemorrhages, and always spoke in an ironic tone, because it was his pose to be considered as witty as he was ailing. He possessed a Heine collection, a quantity of papers and objects connected with that cynical and sickly poet. He proceeded to mark the boundaries of Hesse-Nassau on the map that hung on the wall, and then asked, with a melancholy, mocking smile, if the gentlemen would indicate in their books the important features of the country. It was as though he meant to make game of the class and of Hesse-Nassau as well; yet this was an important test, and much dreaded by the entire form.

Hanno Buddenbrook knew next to nothing about Hesse-Nassau. He tried to look on Adolf Todtenhaupt's book; but Heinrich Heine, who had a penetrating observation despite his suffering, melancholy air, pounced on him at once and said: " Herr Buddenbrook, I am tempted to ask you to close your book, but that I suspect you would be glad to have me do so. Go on with your work."

The remark contained two witticisms. First, that Dr. Mühsam addressed Hanno as Herr Buddenbrook, and, second, that about the copy-book. Hanno continued to brood over his book, and handed it in almost empty when he went out with Kai.

The difficulties were now over with for the day. The fortunate ones who had come through without marks, had light and easy

consciences, and life seemed like play to them as they betook
themselves to the large well-lighted room where they might sit
and draw under the supervision of Herr Drägemüller. Plaster casts
from the antique stood about the room, and there was a great cupboard containing divers pieces of wood and doll-furniture which
served as models. Herr Drägemüller was a thick-set man with a
full round beard and a smooth, cheap brown wig which stood out
in the back of the neck and betrayed itself. He possessed two wigs,
one with longer hair, the other with shorter; if he had had his
beard cut he would don the shorter wig as well. He was a man
with some droll peculiarities of speech. For instance, he called a
lead pencil a "lead." He gave out an oily-alcoholic odour; and it
was said of him that he drank petroleum. It always delighted him
to have an opportunity to take a class in something besides drawing. On such occasions he would lecture on the policy of Bis-
marck, accompanying himself with impressive spiral gestures from
his nose to his shoulder. Social democracy was his bugbear — he
spoke of it with fear and loathing. "We must keep together," he
used to say to refractory pupils, pinching them on the arm. "Social democracy is at the door!" He was possessed by a sort of spasmodic activity: would sit down next a pupil, exhaling a strong
spirituous odour, tap him on the forehead with his seal ring, shoot
out certain isolated words and phrases like "Perspective! Light
and shade! The lead! Social democracy! Stick together!" — and
then dash off again.

Kai worked at his new literary project during this period, and
Hanno occupied himself with conducting, in fancy, an overture
with full orchestra. Then school was over, they fetched down
their things, the gate was opened, they were free to pass, and they
went home.

Hanno and Kai went the same road together as far as the little
red villa, their books under their arms. Young Count Mölln had
a good distance farther to go alone before he reached the paternal
dwelling. He never wore an overcoat.

The morning's fog had turned to snow, which came down in
great white flocks and rapidly became slush. They parted at the
Buddenbrook gate; but when Hanno was half-way up the garden
Kai came back to put his arm about his neck. "Don't give up —
better not play!" he said gently. Then his slender, jaunty figure
disappeared in the whirling snow.

Hanno put down his books on the bear's tray in the corridor and
went into the living room to see his mother. She sat on the sofa
reading a book with a yellow paper cover, and looked up as he

crossed the room. She gazed at him with her brown, close-set, blue-shadowed eyes; as he stood before her, she took his head in both her hands and kissed him on the brow.

He went upstairs, where Fräulein Clementine had some luncheon ready for him, washed, and ate. When he was done he took out of his desk a packet of little biting Russian cigarettes and began to smoke. He was no stranger to their use by now. Then he sat down at the harmonium and played something from Bach: something very severe and difficult, in fugue form. At length he clasped his hands behind his head and looked out the window at the snow noiselessly tumbling down. Nothing else was to be seen; for there was no longer a charming little garden with a plashing fountain beneath his window. The view was cut off by the grey side-wall of the neighbouring villa.

Dinner was at four o'clock, and Hanno, his mother, and Fräulein Clementine sat down to it. Afterward Hanno saw that there were preparations for music in the salon, and awaited his mother at the piano. They played the Sonata Opus 24 of Beethoven. In the adagio the violin sang like an angel; but Gerda took the instrument from her chin with a dissatisfied air, looked at it in irritation, and said it was not in tune. She played no more, but went up to rest.

Hanno remained in the salon. He went to the glass door that led out on the small verandah and looked into the drenched garden. But suddenly he took a step back and jerked the cream-coloured curtains across the door, so that the room lay in a soft yellow twilight. Then he went to the piano. He stood for a while, and his gaze, directed fixed and unseeing upon a distant point, altered slowly, grew blurred and vague and shadowy. He sat down at the instrument and began to improvise.

It was a simple *motif* which he employed — a mere trifle, an unfinished fragment of melody in one bar and a half. He brought it out first, with unsuspected power, in the bass, as a single voice: indicating it as the source and fount of all that was to come, and announcing it, with a commanding entry, by a burst of trumpets. It was not quite easy to grasp his intention; but when he repeated and harmonized it in the treble, with a timbre like dull silver, it proved to consist essentially of a single resolution, a yearning and painful melting of one tone into another — a short-winded, pitiful invention, which nevertheless gained a strange, mysterious, and significant value precisely by means of the meticulous and solemn precision with which it was defined and produced. And now there began more lively passages, a restless coming and going of syncopated sound, seeking, wandering, torn by shrieks like a soul in unrest and tormented by some knowledge it possesses and cannot conceal, but must repeat in ever different harmonies, questioning, complaining, protesting, demanding, dying away. The syncopation increased, grew more pronounced, driven hither and thither by scampering triplets; the shrieks of fear recurred, they took form and became melody. There was a moment when they dominated, in a mounting, imploring chorus of wind-instruments that conquered the endlessly thronging, welling, wandering, vanishing harmonies, and swelled out in unmistakable simple rhythms — a crushed, childlike, imposing, imploring chorale. This concluded with a sort of ecclesiastical cadence. A *fermate* followed, a silence. And then, quite softly, in a timbre of dull silver, there came the first *motif* again, the paltry invention, a figure either tiresome or obscure, a sweet, sentimental dying-away of one tone into another. This was followed by a tremendous uproar, a wild activity, punctuated by notes like fanfares, expressive of violent resolve. What was coming? Then came horns again, sounding the march; there was an assembling, a concentrating, firm, consolidated rhythms; and a new figure began, a bold improvisation, a sort of lively, stormy hunting song. There was no joy in this hunting song; its note was one of defiant despair. Signals sounded through it; yet they were not only signals but cries of fear; while throughout, winding through it all, through all the writhen, bizarre harmonies, came again that mysterious first *motif*, wandering in despair, torturingly sweet. And now began a ceaseless hurry of events whose sense and meaning could not be guessed, a restless flood of sound-adventures, rhythms, harmonies, welling up uncontrolled from the keyboard, as they shaped themselves under Hanno's labouring fingers. He experienced them, as it were; he did not know them beforehand. He sat a little bent over the keys, with parted lips and deep, far gaze, his brown hair covering his forehead with its soft curls. What was the meaning of what he played? Were these images of fearful difficulties surmounted, flames passed through and torrents swum, castles stormed and dragons slain? But always — now like a yelling laugh, now like an ineffably sweet promise — the original *motif* wound through it all, the pitiful phrase with its notes melting into one another! Now the music seemed to rouse itself to new and gigantic efforts: wild runs in octaves followed, sounding like shrieks; an irresistible mounting, a chromatic upward struggle, a wild relentless longing, abruptly broken by startling, arresting pianissimi which gave a sensation as if the ground were disappearing from beneath one's feet, or like a sudden abandonment and sinking into a gulf of desire.

Once, far off and softly warning, sounded the first chords of the imploring prayer; but the flood of rising cacophonies overwhelmed them with their rolling, streaming, clinging, sinking, and struggling up again, as they fought on toward the end that must come, must come this very moment, at the height of this fearful climax — for the pressure of longing had become intolerable. And it came; it could no longer be kept back — those spasms of yearning could not be prolonged. And it came as though curtains were rent apart, doors sprang open, thorn-hedges parted of themselves, walls of flame sank down. The resolution, the redemption, the complete fulfilment — a chorus of jubilation burst forth, and everything resolved itself in a harmony — and the harmony, in sweet *ritardando*, at once sank into another. It was the *motif*, the *first motif!* And now began a festival, a triumph, an unbounded orgy of this very figure, which now displayed a wealth of dynamic colour which passed through every octave, wept and shivered in tremolo, sang, rejoiced, and sobbed in exultation, triumphantly adorned with all the bursting, tinkling, foaming, purling resources of orchestral pomp. The fanatical worship of this worthless trifle, this scrap of melody, this brief, childish harmonic invention only a bar and a half in length, had about it something stupid and gross, and at the same time something ascetic and religious — something that contained the essence of faith and renunciation. There was a quality of the perverse in the insatiability with which it was produced and revelled in: there was a sort of cynical despair; there was a longing for joy, a yielding to desire, in the way the last drop of sweetness was, as it were, extracted from the melody, till exhaustion, disgust, and satiety supervened. Then, at last; at last, in the weariness after excess, a long, soft arpeggio in the minor trickled through, mounted a tone, resolved itself in the major, and died in mournful lingering away.

Hanno sat still a moment, his chin on his breast, his hands in his lap. Then he got up and closed the instrument. He was very pale, there was no strength in his knees, and his eyes were burning. He went into the next room, stretched himself on the chaise-lounge, and remained for a long time motionless.

Later there was supper, and he played a game of chess with his mother, at which neither side won. But until after midnight he still sat in his room, before his harmonium, and played — played in thought only, for he must make no noise. He did this despite his firm intention to get up the next morning at half-past five, to do some most necessary preparation.

This was one day in the life of little Johann.

CHAPTER III

Cases of typhoid fever take the following course.

The patient feels depressed and moody — a condition which grows rapidly worse until it amounts to acute despondency. At the same time he is overpowered by physical weariness, not only of the muscles and sinews, but also of the organic functions, in particular of the digestion — so that the stomach refuses food. There is a great desire for sleep, but even in conditions of extreme fatigue the sleep is restless and superficial and not refreshing. There is pain in the head, the brain feels dull and confused, and there are spells of giddiness. An indefinite ache is felt in all the bones. There is blood from the nose now and then, without apparent cause. — This is the onset.

Then comes a violent chill which seizes the whole body and makes the teeth chatter; the fever sets in, and is immediately at its height. Little red spots appear on the breast and abdomen, about the size of a lentil. They go away when pressed by the finger, but return at once. The pulse is unsteady; there are about a hundred pulsations to the minute. The temperature goes up to 104°. Thus passes the first week.

In the second week the patient is free from pain in the head and limbs; but the giddiness is distinctly worse, and there is so much humming in the ears that he is practically deaf. The facial expression becomes dull, the mouth stands open, the eyes are without life. The consciousness is blurred, desire for sleep takes entire possession of the patient, and he often sinks, not into actual sleep, but into a leaden lethargy. At other intervals there are the loud and excited ravings of delirium. The patient's helplessness is complete, and his uncleanliness becomes repulsive. His gums, teeth, and tongue are covered with a blackish deposit which makes his breath foul. He lies motionless on his back, with distended abdomen. He has sunk down in the bed, with his knees wide apart. Pulse and breathing are rapid, jerky, superficial and laboured; the pulse is fluttering, and gallops one hundred and twenty to the minute. The eyelids are half closed, the cheeks are no longer glowing,

but have assumed a bluish colour. The red spots on breast and abdomen are more numerous. The temperature reaches 105.8°.

In the third week the weakness is at its height. The patient raves no longer: who can say whether his spirit is sunk in empty night or whether it lingers, remote from the flesh, in far, deep, quiet dreams, of which he gives no sound and no sign? He lies in total insensibility. This is the crisis of the disease.

In individual cases the diagnosis is sometimes rendered more difficult; as, for example, when the early symptoms — depression, weariness, lack of appetite, headache and unquiet sleep — are nearly all present while the patient is still going about in his usual health; when they are scarcely noticeable as anything out of the common, even if they are suddenly and definitely increased. But a clever doctor, of real scientific acumen — like, for example, Dr. Langhals, the good-looking Dr. Langhals with the small, hairy hands — will still be in a position to call the case by its right name; and the appearance of the red spots on the chest and abdomen will be conclusive evidence that his diagnosis was correct. He will know what measures to take and what remedies to apply. He will arrange for a large, well-aired room, the temperature of which must not be higher than 70°. He will insist on absolute cleanliness, and by means of frequent shifting and changes of linen will keep the patient free from bedsores — if possible; in some cases it is not possible. He will have the mouth frequently cleansed with moist linen rags. As for treatment, preparations of iodine, potash, qui nine, and antipyrin are indicated — with a diet as light and nourish ing as possible, for the patient's stomach and bowels are pr foundly attacked by the disease. He will treat the consuming fe by means of frequent baths, into which the patient will ofte put every three hours, day and night, cooling them gradually the foot end of the tub, and always, after each bath, administ something stimulating, like brandy or champagne.

But all these remedies he uses entirely at random, in th that they may be of some use in the case; ignorant whet one of them will have the slightest effect. For there is o which he does not know at all; with respect to one fact, h in complete darkness. Up to the third week, up to the of the disease, he cannot possibly tell whether this illr he calls typhoid, is an unfortunate accident, the disagre quence of an infection which might perhaps have b and which can be combated with the resources of me or whether it is, quite simply, a form of dissolution as it were, of death. And then, whether death ch

this form or another is all the same — against him there is no remedy.

Cases of typhoid take the following course:

When the fever is at its height, life calls to the patient: calls out to him as he wanders in his distant dream, and summons him in no uncertain voice. The harsh, imperious call reaches the spirit on that remote path that leads into the shadows, the coolness and peace. He hears the call of life, the clear, fresh, mocking summons to return to that distant scene which he had already left so far behind him, and already forgotten. And there may well up in him something like a feeling of shame for a neglected duty; a sense of renewed energy, courage, and hope; he may recognize a bond existing still between him and that stirring, colourful, callous existence which he thought he had left so far behind him. Then, however far he may have wandered on his distant path, he will turn back — and live. But if he shudders when he hears life's voice, if the memory of that vanished scene and the sound of that lusty summons make him shake his head, make him put out his hand to ward off as he flies forward in the way of escape that has opened to him — then it is clear that the patient will die.

CHAPTER IV

" It is not right, it is not right, Gerda," said old Fräulein Weichbrodt, perhaps for the hundredth time. Her voice was full of
reproach and distress. She had a sofa place to-day in the circle
that sat round the centre-table in the drawing-room of her former
pupil. Gerda Buddenbrook, Frau Permaneder, her daughter Erica,
poor Clothilde, and the three Misses Buddenbrook made up the
group. The green capstrings still fell down upon the old lady's
childish shoulders; but she had grown so tiny, with her seventy-
five years of life, that she could scarcely raise her elbow high
enough to gesticulate above the surface of the table.

" No, it is not right, and so I tell you, Gerda," she repeated. She
spoke with such warmth that her voice trembled. " I have one
foot in the grave, my time is short — and you can think of leaving
me — of leaving us all — for ever! If it were just a visit to Amsterdam that you were thinking of — but to leave us for ever — ! "
She shook her bird-like old head vigorously, and her brown eyes
were clouded with her distress. " It is true, you have lost a great
deal — "

" No, she has not lost a great deal, she has lost everything," said
Frau Permaneder. " We must not be selfish, Therese. Gerda
wishes to go, and she is going — that is all. She came with Thomas,
one-and-twenty years ago; and we all loved her, though she very
likely didn't like any of us. — No, you didn't, Gerda; don't deny
it! — But Thomas is no more — and nothing is any more. What
are we to her? Nothing. We feel it very much, we cannot help
feeling it; but yet I say, go, with God's blessing, Gerda, and thanks
for not going before, when Thomas died."

It was an autumn evening, after supper. Little Johann (Justus,
Johann, Kaspar) had been lying for nearly six months, equipped
with the blessing of Pastor Pringsheim, out there at the edge of the
little grove, beneath the sandstone cross, beneath the family arms.
The rain rustled the half-leafless trees in the avenue, and sometimes gusts of wind drove it against the window-panes. All eight
ladies were dressed in black.

The little family had gathered to take leave of Gerda Buddenbrook, who was about to leave the town and return to Amsterdam,
to play duets once more with her old father. No duties now restrained her. Frau Permaneder could no longer oppose her decision. She said it was right, she knew it must be so; but in her
heart she mourned over her sister-in-law's departure. If the Senator's widow had remained in the town, and kept her station and
her place in society, and left her property where it was, there
would still have remained a little prestige to the family name. But
let that be as it must, Frau Antoine was determined to hold her
head high while she lived and there were people to look at her.
Had not her grandfather driven with four horses all over the
country?

Despite the stormy life that lay behind her, and despite her weak
digestion, she did not look her fifty years. Her skin was a little
faded and downy, and a few hairs grew on her upper lip — the
pretty upper lip of Tony Buddenbrook. But there was not a white
hair in the smooth coiffure beneath the mourning cap.

Poor Clothilde bore up under the departure of her relative, as
one must bear up under the afflictions of this life. She took it with
patience and tranquillity. She had done wonders at the supper
table, and now she sat among the others, lean and grey as of yore,
and her words were drawling and friendly.

Erica Weinschenk, now thirty-one years old, was likewise not
one to excite herself unduly over her aunt's departure. She had
lived through worse things, and had early learned resignation.
Submission was her strongest characteristic: one read it in her
weary light-blue eyes — the eyes of Bendix Grünlich — and heard
it in the tones of her patient, sometimes plaintive voice.

The three Misses Buddenbrook, Uncle Gotthold's daughters,
wore their old affronted and critical air; Friederike and Henriette,
the eldest, had grown leaner and more angular with the years;
while Pfiffi, the youngest, now fifty-three years old, was much
too little and fat.

Old Frau Consul Kröger, Uncle Justus' widow, had been asked
too, but she was rather ailing — or perhaps she had no suitable
gown to put on: one couldn't tell which.

They talked about Gerda's journey and the train she was to
take; about the sale of the villa and its furnishings, which Herr
Gosch had undertaken. For Gerda was taking nothing with her —
she was going away as she had come.

Then Frau Permaneder began to talk about life. She was very
serious and made observations upon the past and the future —

though of the future there was in truth almost nothing to be said.

"When I am dead," she declared, "Erica may move away if she likes. But as for me, I cannot live anywhere else; and so long as I am on earth, we will come together here, we who are left. Once a week you will come to dinner with me — and we will read the family papers." She put her hand on the portfolio that lay before her on the table. "Yes, Gerda, I will take them over, and be glad to have them. Well, that is settled. Do you hear, Tilda? Though it might exactly as well be you who should invite us, for you are just as well off as we are now. Yes — so it goes. I've struggled against fate, and done my best, and you have just sat there and waited for everything to come round. But you are a goose, you know, all the same — please don't mind if I say so — "

"Oh, Tony," Clothilde said, smiling.

"I am sorry I cannot say good-bye to Christian," said Gerda, and the talk turned aside to that subject. There was small prospect of his ever coming out of the institution in which he was confined, although he was probably not too bad to go about in freedom. But the present state of things was very agreeable for his wife. She was, Frau Permaneder asserted, in league with the doctor; and Christian would, in all probability, end his days where he was.

There was a pause. They touched delicately and with hesitation upon recent events, and when one of them let fall little Johann's name, it was still in the room, except for the sound of the rain, which fell faster than before.

This silence lay like a heavy secret over the events of Hanno's last illness. It must have been a frightful onslaught. They did not look in each other's eyes as they talked; their voices were hushed, and their words were broken. But they spoke of one last episode — the visit of the little ragged count who had almost forced his way to Hanno's bedside. Hanno had smiled when he heard his voice, though he hardly knew any one; and Kai had kissed his hands again and again.

"He kissed his hands?" asked the Buddenbrook ladies.

"Yes, over and over."

They all thought for a while of this strange thing, and then suddenly Frau Permaneder burst into tears.

"I loved him so much," she sobbed. "You don't any of you know how much — more than any of you — yes, forgive me, Gerda — you are his mother. — Oh, he was an angel."

"He is an angel, now," corrected Sesemi.

"Hanno, little Hanno," went on Frau Permander, the tears flowing down over her soft faded cheeks. "Tom, Father, Grandfather, and all the rest! Where are they? We shall see them no more. Oh, it is so sad, so hard! "

" There will be a reunion," said Friederike Buddenbrook. She folded her hands in her lap, cast down her eyes, and put her nose in the air.

" Yes — they say so. — Oh, there are times, Friederike, when that is no consolation, God forgive me! When one begins to doubt — doubt justice and goodness — and everything. Life crushes so much in us, it destroys so many of our beliefs — ! A reunion — if that were so — "

But now Sesemi Weichbrodt stood up, as tall as ever she could. She stood on tip-toe, rapped on the table; the cap shook on her old head.

" It *is so!* " she said, with her whole strength; and looked at them all with a challenge in her eyes.

She stood there, a victor in the good fight which all her life she had waged against the assaults of Reason: hump-backed, tiny, quivering with the strength of her convictions, a little prophetess, admonishing and inspired.

The Principal Works of Thomas Mann

First Editions in German

DER KLEINE HERR FRIEDEMANN
[Little Herr Friedemann]. Tales   *Berlin, S. Fischer Verlag.*   1898

BUDDENBROOKS
Novel   *Berlin, S. Fischer Verlag.*   1901

TRISTAN
Contains *Tonio Kröger*. Tales   *Berlin, S. Fischer Verlag.*   1903

FIORENZA
Drama   *Berlin, S. Fischer Verlag.*   1905

KÖNIGLICHE HOHEIT
[Royal Highness]. Novel   *Berlin, S. Fischer Verlag.*   1909

DER TOD IN VENEDIG
[Death in Venice]. Short novel   *Berlin, S. Fischer Verlag.*   1913

DAS WUNDERKIND
[The Infant Prodigy]. Tales   *Berlin, S. Fischer Verlag.*   1914

BETRACHTUNGEN EINES UNPOLITISCHEN
Autobiographical reflections   *Berlin, S. Fischer Verlag.*   1918

HERR UND HUND
[A Man and His Dog]. Idyll
Contains also *Gesang vom Kindchen,* an idyll in verse
    Berlin, S. Fischer Verlag.   1919

WÄLSUNGENBLUT
Tale   *München, Phantasus Verlag.*   1921

BEMÜHUNGEN
Essays   *Berlin, S. Fischer Verlag.*   1922

REDE UND ANTWORT
Essays   *Berlin, S. Fischer Verlag.*   1922

BEKENNTNISSE DES HOCHSTAPLERS FELIX KRULL: BUCH DER KINDHEIT
Fragment of a novel   *Stuttgart, Deutsche Verlags-Anstalt.*   1923

DER ZAUBERBERG
[The Magic Mountain]. Novel   *Berlin, S. Fischer Verlag.*   1924

UNORDNUNG UND FRÜHES LEID
[Disorder and Early Sorrow]. Short novel
    Berlin, S. Fischer Verlag.   1926

KINO
Fragment of a novel   *Berlin, S. Fischer Verlag.* 1926

PARISER RECHENSCHAFT
Travelogue   *Berlin, S. Fischer Verlag.* 1926

DEUTSCHE ANSPRACHE: EIN APPELL AN DIE VERNUNFT
Lecture   *Berlin, S. Fischer Verlag.* 1930

DIE FORDERUNG DES TAGES
Essays   *Berlin, S. Fischer Verlag.* 1930

MARIO UND DER ZAUBERER
[Mario and the Magician]. Short novel
    Berlin, S. Fischer Verlag. 1930

GOETHE ALS REPRÄSENTANT DES BÜRGERLICHEN ZEITALTERS
Lecture   *Berlin, S. Fischer Verlag.* 1932

JOSEPH UND SEINE BRÜDER
[Joseph and His Brothers]. Novel
 I. Die Geschichten Jaakobs *Berlin, S. Fischer Verlag.* 1933
 II. Der junge Joseph *Berlin, S. Fischer Verlag.* 1934
 III. Joseph in Ägypten *Vienna, Bermann-Fischer Verlag.* 1936
 IV. Joseph, der Ernährer *Stockholm, Bermann-Fischer Verlag.* 1943

LEIDEN UND GRÖSSE DER MEISTER
Essays   *Berlin, S. Fischer Verlag.* 1935

FREUD UND DIE ZUKUNFT
Lecture   *Vienna, Bermann-Fischer Verlag.* 1936

EIN BRIEFWECHSEL
[An Exchange of Letters]
    Zurich, Dr. Oprecht & Helbling AG. 1937

SCHOPENHAUER
Essay   *Stockholm, Bermann-Fischer Verlag.* 1938

ACHTUNG, EUROPA!
Manifesto   *Stockholm, Bermann-Fischer Verlag.* 1938

DIE SCHÖNSTEN ERZÄHLUNGEN
Contains *Tonio Kröger, Der Tod in Venedig, Unordnung und
frühes Leid, Mario und der Zauberer*
    Stockholm, Bermann-Fischer Verlag. 1938

DAS PROBLEM DER FREIHEIT
Essay   *Stockholm, Bermann-Fischer Verlag.* 1939

LOTTE IN WEIMAR
[The Beloved Returns]. Novel
    Stockholm, Bermann-Fischer Verlag. 1939

DIE VERTAUSCHTEN KÖPFE: EINE INDISCHE LEGENDE
[The Transposed Heads: A Legend of India]
    Stockholm, Bermann-Fischer Verlag. 1940

Deutsche Hörer
[Listen, Germany!] Broadcasts
Stockholm, Bermann-Fischer Verlag.   1942

Das Gesetz
[The Tables of the Law]
Stockholm, Bermann-Fischer Verlag.   1944

Doktor Faustus: Das Leben des deutschen Tonsetzers Adrian
Leverkühn, erzählt von einem Freunde
Novel   Stockholm, Bermann-Fischer Verlag.   1947

Die Entstehung des Doktor Faustus
[The Story of a Novel]
Amsterdam, Bermann-Fischer Verlag.   1949

Der Erwählte
[The Holy Sinner]. Novel
Frankfurt am Main, S. Fischer Verlag.   1951

Die Betrogene
[The Black Swan]. Short Novel
Frankfurt am Main, S. Fischer Verlag.   1953

Altes und Neues: Kleine Prosa aus fünf Jahrzehnten.
[Small prose pieces of five decades]
Frankfurt am Main, S. Fischer Verlag.   1953

Bekenntnisse des Hochstaplers Felix Krull: Der Memoiren
erster Teil
[Confessions of Felix Krull]. Novel
Frankfurt am Main, S. Fischer Verlag.   1954

Nachlese: Prosa 1951–1955
Frankfurt am Main, S. Fischer Verlag.   1956

American Editions in Translation

published by Alfred A. Knopf, New York

Royal Highness: A Novel of German Court Life
Translated by A. Cecil Curtis   1916

Buddenbrooks
Translated by H. T. Lowe-Porter   1924

Death in Venice and Other Stories
Translated by Kenneth Burke. Contains Der Tod in Venedig,
Tristan, and Tonio Kröger (out of print)*   1925

The Magic Mountain
Translated by H. T. Lowe-Porter. Two volumes   1927

---

* Included in Stories of Three Decades, translated by H. T. Lowe-Porter.

THE PRINCIPAL WORKS OF THOMAS MANN

* Included in *Stories of Three Decades*, translated by H. T. Lowe-Porter.

THE PRINCIPAL WORKS OF THOMAS MANN

THIS PEACE
Translated by H. T. Lowe-Porter (out of print)   1938

THIS WAR
Translated by Eric Sutton (out of print)   1940

THE BELOVED RETURNS
[Lotte in Weimar]
Translated by H. T. Lowe-Porter   1940

THE TRANSPOSED HEADS: A LEGEND OF INDIA
Translated by H. T. Lowe-Porter   1941

ORDER OF THE DAY
Political Essays and Speeches of Two Decades
*Translated by H. T. Lowe-Porter, Agnes E. Meyer, and Eric
Sutton (out of print)*   1942

LISTEN, GERMANY!
Twenty-five Radio Messages to the German People over BBC
(out of print)   1943

THE TABLES OF THE LAW
Translated by H. T. Lowe-Porter   1945

ESSAYS OF THREE DECADES
Translated by H. T. Lowe-Porter   1947

DOCTOR FAUSTUS: THE LIFE OF THE GERMAN COMPOSER ADRIAN
LEVERKÜHN AS TOLD BY A FRIEND
Translated by H. T. Lowe-Porter   1948

THE HOLY SINNER
Translated by H. T. Lowe-Porter   1951

THE BLACK SWAN
Translated by Willard R. Trask   1954

CONFESSIONS OF FELIX KRULL, CONFIDENCE MAN: THE EARLY YEARS
Translated by Denver Lindley   1955

LAST ESSAYS
*Translated by Richard and Clara Winston and Tania and
James Stern*   1959

A SKETCH OF MY LIFE
Translated by H. T. Lowe-Porter   1960

THE STORY OF A NOVEL: THE GENESIS OF DOCTOR FAUSTUS
Translated by Richard and Clara Winston   1961

THE PRINCIPAL WORKS OF THOMAS MANN